DOWN THE LONG WIND

'I, Gwalchmai, son of Lot of Orcade, do now swear to follow the lord Arthur, emperor of the Britains, dragon of the island; to fight at his will against all his enemies, to hold with him and obey him at all times and places. My sword is his sword until death. This I swear in the name of Father, Son and Spirit, and if I fail of my oath may the earth open and swallow me, the sky break and fall on me, the sea rise and drown me. So be it.'

Arthur reached out his hand for the sword, and I suddenly remembered.

'My lord,' I began, 'the sword cannot . . .'

He ignored me and caught the hilt from my hand, lifting the weapon. The lightning did not spring from it against him as it had against Cei. Instead the radiance lit it, growing greater and whiter until it seemed that Arthur held a star. And he said, 'And I, Arthur, emperor of the Britains, do now swear to support Gwalchmai son of Lot, in arms and in goods, faithfully in honour, in all times and places until death. This I swear in the name of Father, Son and Spirit, and if I fail of my oath, may the earth open and swallow me, the sky break and fall on me, the sea rise and drown me. And I swear to use this sword, of Light, in Light to work Light upon this realm, so help me God.'

GILLIAN BRADSHAW

Down The Long Wind

A Methuen Paperback

A Methuen Paperback

DOWN THE LONG WIND

British Library Cataloguing in Publication Data

Bradshaw, Gillian
  Down the long wind—(A Methuen paperback).
  I. Title   II. Bradshaw, Gillian. Hawk of May
  III. Bradshaw, Gillian. Kingdom of summer
  IV. Bradshaw, Gillian. In winter's shadow
  813'.54[F]   PS3552.R235

  ISBN 0-413-17610-X

First published in Great Britain
in three separate volumes
Hawk of May 1981
Kingdom of Summer 1981
In Winter's Shadow 1982
by Eyre Methuen Ltd
Copyright © 1980, 1981, 1982 by Gillian Bradshaw
First published in Great Britain in a single volume 1988
and reprinted 1988
by Methuen London Ltd
81 Fulham Road, London SW3 6RB

Printed and bound in Great Britain
by Richard Clay Ltd, Bungay, Suffolk

Contents

Hawk of May

Parentibus Optimis
'Siquid adhuc ego sum, muneris omne tui est.'

One

When my father received the news of the Pendragon's death, I was playing boats by the sea.

I was then eleven years old, and as poor a warrior as any boy in my father's realm of the Innsi Erc, the Orcades Islands. Since I also was a very poor hunter, I had little in common with the other boys, the sons of the noble clans of our island, with whom I lived and trained in the Boys' House; and I had still less in common with my elder brother, Agravain, who led the others in making my life difficult, almost as difficult as my father's plans for me did. To escape from the insistent world of warriors and warriors-to-be, I went sometimes to my younger brother, but more often to a secret place I had by the sea.

It is about an hour's ride south of my father's fortress of Dun Fionn. A small stream falls down the cliff that edges our island on the west, carving a gully into the rock. At the bottom, trapped by a ledge of harder stone, the stream forms a deep pool behind a gravelly beach before it escapes into the ocean. Overhanging cliff walls make it invisible from the cliff-top, so no one but myself ever discovered its existence. As it was also very beautiful, this made it mine. I gave the place a name – Llyn Gwalch, 'Hawk's Stream' in British— and considered it to be a world apart from and better than the Orcades and Dun Fionn. Sometimes I took my harp there, and sang to the waves that came pounding at the beach, flowing into the pool at high tide and hissing in the gravel at low tide. Sometimes I would build fortresses of gravel and mud, and plan battles by the stream as though it were a great river, the boundary between mighty kingdoms. I would picture myself as a great warrior, good at every art of war and sung of in every king's hall in the western world, admired by Agravain and my father. But my favourite game was to build boats and to set them sailing out of the dark pool into the wild grey sea that pounded at every shore of the world at once. I sent my boats west: to Erin, from which my father had sailed years before; and beyond Erin, to that strange island or islands which druids and poets say lie west of the sunset, invisible to all but a few mortals, where the Sidhe live in eternal happiness.

I loved my Llyn Gwalch dearly, and jealously guarded it against any intruders from the outside world. I told only my younger brother Medraut of its existence, and then only after swearing him to secrecy. So, when I heard the clatter of a stone from the path above my head, I drew back hurriedly from the curragh I was building and began to clamber up the gully. I had left my pony tethered at the top, and I did not want anyone to come down looking for me.

'Gwalchmai?' The voice from the cliff-top was Agravain's.

'I'm coming!' I called, and scrambled faster.

'You'd better hurry,' said Agravain. He sounded angry. 'Father's waiting for us. He sent me to find you.'

I reached the top of the cliff, shook my hair out of my eyes, stared at Agravain. 'What does he want?' I didn't like the sound of it. My father hated to wait, and he would certainly be angry by the time I got back to Dun Fionn.

'It's no business of yours what he wants.' Agravain was, indeed, angry, tired of looking for me, and probably afraid that some of our father's anger would spill over on to him. 'By the sun and the wind, can't you hurry?'

'I am hurrying.' I was untying my pony as I spoke.

'Don't answer back to me! You're going to be in trouble enough as it is. We're late, and Father won't like you appearing in front of the guest like that. You're a mess.'

'Guest?' About to mount, I paused. 'Is he a bard or a warrior? Where's he from?'

'Britain. I don't know what kingdom. Father sent me out to look for you as soon as he'd spoken with the man, and it's a good thing Diuran saw you riding south, or I'd still be looking.' Agravain kicked his horse and set off across the cliff-top at a gallop. 'Come on, you little coward!'

I swung on to my pony and followed him, ignoring the over-familiar insult. I must be a coward, anyway. If I wasn't, I wouldn't ignore the insult. I'd fight with Agravain, even if I did always lose, and we'd be friends afterwards. He was always friendly after a fight.

A guest, from Britain, and an urgent summons. The Briton must have brought some important message. My father had many spies in Britain who reported to him

10

regularly—but they sent their messages by indirect means, never coming to Dun Fionn themselves. A messenger from Britain meant some important event, a major victory over or defeat by the Saxons, the death of some important king, anything which my father could use to further his influence in the south. The Saxons had suffered a major defeat at the hands of the Pendragon's young war-leader only a year before, so it couldn't be that. Some king dead, then, and my father about to make a bargain with his successor? A bargain which had some part in it which Agravain and I could fulfil? I urged my pony faster and passed Agravain at a gallop, anxious and miserable now. My father always made plans for me, but I fulfilled very few of them. The sea-wind and the wind of my speed dried the salt in my hair, and my pony's hooves echoed the beat of the surf; better to think about these than about my father. It would be good to get the confrontation over quickly, as quickly as possible. At least, I thought, looking for some good, Agravain hasn't asked me what I was doing at Llyn Gwalch.

The thought of my brother made me look back in alarm. He was a good hundred paces behind me, struggling with his horse on the rough path and scowling furiously. There were two things I could do better than he: riding and harp-playing. He liked to forget this and, as he was infinitely the better at fighting, I tried not to remind him. Now I had done so. I cringed, knowing that he would pick a quarrel with me on a pretext later in the day, and slowed my pony to a trot.

He passed me without saying anything and rode in front of me, also at a trot. That was Agravain. He wanted to be first, and nearly always was. First-born, first choice to succeed my father as king, first among the boys of the island who trained to be warriors. My father was immensely proud of him, and never stayed angry at him for long. I stared at my brother's back and wished that I could be like him.

We rode on to Dun Fionn in silence.

The fortress is built from a very light stone, from which it takes its name, 'White Fortress'. It is a new stronghold, completed in the year of Agravain's birth, three years before my own, but already it was as famous and powerful as any of the other, older forts, Temair or Emhain Macha in Erin, or Camlann and Din Eidyn in Britain. It stands at the highest point of the cliff, overlooking the sea, ringed by a bank and

11

ditch and its thick, high walls. Two gate-towers, copied from old Roman forts, flank the single westward-facing gate. The fortress was designed by my father, and the power and fame were the result of a myriad of schemes and man-oeuvres, political and military, carried out with unvaried success. If it was my mother who was the ultimate source of the schemes, it was my father, King Lot mac Cormac of the Innsi Erc, who had carried them out in such a way as to make himself one of the most powerful kings in either Britain or Erin. As Agravain and I rode in the gates, I wondered ner-vously what he wanted me to do.

We left our horses in the stable and hurried to our father's room behind the feast Hall. The room was small and plain, and the dusty sunlight filtered in through the space left between wall and roof for the smoke. My father had evident-ly been waiting for some time: the messenger must have left the room long before, and the air had the tense, still feeling of a conversation interrupted. My mother sat on the bed, study-ing a map, a goblet of imported wine on the lamp table beside her. Another goblet on its side – Lot's – lay near it, aban-doned. When we entered, my father turned from pacing the floor to face us. My mother glanced up, then fell to studying the map again. The air tingled with expectation: my father was angry.

He was not a tall man, yet unmistakably he was king, radiating arrogance and command. His thick yellow hair and beard seemed almost to stand out from his head, unable to contain the energy of his lean body, and his hot blue eyes could scorch anyone who crossed him. My ancestors come from Ulster, and they say that Lugh of the Long Hand, the sun god, had many sons in my father's line. All who spoke with Lot for any length of time came away at least half con-vinced of it.

He ignored Agravain and glared at me. 'Where have you been, these two hours?'

When I fumbled for words, Agravain answered. 'He was down by the sea, collecting oysters or some such thing. I found him a good hour's ride from here.'

Lot glared harder. 'Why didn't you stay here and practise your spear-throwing? You need the practice badly enough.'

As always happened in my father's presence, all my words were dried in my throat, and I stared unhappily at the floor.

12

Lot snorted. 'You'll never make a warrior. But you could try, at least, to learn enough not to disgrace your clan.'

When I still found nothing to say and would not meet his eyes, he clenched his fists angrily; then, giving a liquid shrug, turned and began to pace again. 'Enough of that. Can either of you reason out why I called you?'

'You got a message from Britain,' Agravain answered quickly, eagerly. 'What's happened there? Did the Saxons defeat someone and do the kings want your aid now?'

My mother Morgawse looked up from her map and smiled, and her eyes rested for a moment on me. My heart leapt. 'Have you nothing to say, Gwalchmai?' Her voice was low, soft and beautiful. She was herself beautiful: very tall, dark where Lot was fair; her eyes were darker than the sea at midnight. She left breathless anyone who only looked at her, and drew eyes as a whirlpool draws water. The legitimate daughter of the High King Uther, she had been given in marriage to Lot when she was thirteen, the seal of an alliance she had since worked constantly against. She hated her father Uther with all her soul. I worshipped her.

Lot paused, glanced towards her, realizing that she had decided something about the map. He nodded to himself, then glanced back to me.

'There . . . there's an important king dead, isn't there?' I asked, taking my courage in both hands. 'Is it Vortipor?'

My father gave me a surprised look, then smiled fiercely. 'Indeed. There is a king dead. But not Vortipor of Dyfed.' He walked over to the bed and stood, looking at the map, tracing Dyfed with his finger, then following the line of the Saefern river up through Powys, then tracing the sea coast of Elmet and Ebrauc up to Rheged, down again along the east border of Britain. Morgawse's eyes were glowing with a deep, dark fire, with triumph and silent joy. I knew then who was dead, and what my parents were planning. There was only one king whose death would bring such joy to my mother.

'Uther, Pendragon of Britain, lies dead at Camlann,' said Morgawse, very softly. 'The High King is dead, and of sickness.' Her smile was softer than snow-flakes falling from a black winter night.

Agravain stood in silence a moment, then gasped, 'Uther!' in wonder.

Lot laughed, throwing back his head and clapping his

13

hands together. 'Uther, dead! I had thought the old mare's son had more years left in him than that!'

I looked at Morgawse. She was rumoured a sorceress through all of Britain. I wondered if Uther had suffered, how long the sickness had lasted. If she had done the thing . . . no, how could anyone in the Orcades kill a man in Dumnonia . . . and I was glad that the man she hated was dead.

'. . . that is not all,' my father was saying. 'There is a debate over who is to succeed him.'

Of course there was a debate. I had heard it debated often enough even in the Orcades. Uther had no heir, only many bastards. There would be civil war in Britain, as there had been thirty years before at the death of Vortigern. My father, who had made three of the kings then reigning in Britain, would have a chance to try his hand at making a High King.

Lot went on, talking out his own plans now, back and forth across the floor, the dust swirling in the sun-beam. '. . . Docmail of Gwynedd claimed the High Kingship at the council, saying that the kings of Gwyned ought to be High Kings because they are descended from the Roman High King Maximus, but Gwlgawd of Gododdin opposed him . . . Docmail made alliances with Dyfed and Powys, and he has sent messages to Gwlgawd telling him to renounce his claim to the Pendragonship. Gwlgawd is afraid and seeks to form an alliance of his own. He has sent messengers to Caradoc of Ebrauc . . . and to me.' Lot smiled again, triumphantly, and stopped short by the bed, looking at the map. 'Caradoc may join or not, as he pleases. I will come. With my warband and supplies from Gwlgawd, we can sweep Docmail into the sea! And Gwlgawd . . . he will be easy to control.' He snapped away from the map and again began pacing, his eyes blazing, fists clenched as he reckoned kings and kingdoms, loyalties and enmities. 'If we arrive in the North in force to join Gwlgawd, Strathclyde will probably join Docmail, and Urien of Rheged may claim the Pendragonship for himself – a force to be feared, Urien – still, he is my brother-in-law, and must try negotiations before he declares war; we can spin out negotiations . . .'

'Be careful,' snapped Morgawse. 'The alliances will be unsettled, and one can never rely on any alliance in Britain. There will be other claimants to the title before this war is ended, and too many kingdoms have not yet declared themselves.'

Lot nodded, without breaking his step. 'Of course. And we must separate the kings as much as possible; and see that we divide the spoils evenly with our allies—Diuran can help with that, and Aidan. And then there must be time and a blind eye to blood feuds, at intervals, but we cannot let the Ui Niaill begin fighting or there'll be no stopping it.' He fell silent, considering how to control blood feuds. In the end, he would ask Morgawse, and she would tell him what she had long before thought out, and it would work.

Feeling very nervous, I managed to stammer, 'W-what about Arthur?'

Lot scarcely glanced at me, though Morgawse gave me a sharp look. Arthur had been Uther's war-leader and, if half the stories told were true, the High King's warband would follow him, Uther or no Uther. Because of this Arthur had power, although he was only one of Uther's bastards and a clanless man. He could have no claim to the Pendragonship himself, but he was certainly in a position to make a High King.

'Arthur?' Lot shrugged, still thinking of blood feuds. 'He will support no one. He will continue to fight the Saxons, with the royal warband – or as much of it as he can support.'

'Be careful,' Morgawse warned again, even more sharply. 'The lord Arthur is dangerous. He is the finest war-leader in Britain, and he will not remain neutral if he is provoked.'

'Oh, have no fear.' Lot was still casual. 'I will be very careful of your precious half-brother. I've seen him command.'

'So have I.' Her voice was soft, but Lot stopped, meeting her eyes for a moment. He was silent, looking at her. It seemed for a moment as though the sunlight paled, and the dust hung frozen in the air, and some chasm opened behind the world. I shivered. I recognized that dark light in her eyes. Hate, the black tide that had drowned Uther, turning his friends to enemies, stirring up foreign invasion and civil dis-sension, until at last that chasm had swallowed him, perhaps . . . and now Morgawse's hatred turned towards Arthur. I wondered again how Uther had died.

Agravain shifted slightly. He had stood silently during the talk, his eyes glowing with excitement. He knew that, with his fifteenth birthday in another month, he was old enough to be taken along on the campaign. Now, in the stillness, he burst in with 'Am I coming?'

My father remembered us, spun about, grinning again. He crossed the room to my brother and slapped him on the shoulder. 'Of course. Why do you think I called you? We leave next month, in March. I am giving Diuran charge of half the warband and the auxiliaries from the Hebrides, and I will give him charge of you as well. Pay attention, and he will show you how a warband is run.'

Agravain ignored the question of how to run warbands and plunged into what excited him. 'Can I fight in the battles?'

Lot grinned even more, resting his hand on Agravain's shoulder. 'So eager? You are not to fight until I am certain you know how – but no one learns to fight by casting spears at targets. You will go into the battles.'

Agravain seized Lot's hand, kissed it, ablaze with delight. 'Thank you, Father!'

Lot threw his arms about his first-born son, gave him a rough hug, shook him, laughing. 'It is well. You will receive arms tomorrow, early, you and the others who are of age. Go and tell Orlamh that he is to prepare you for the ceremony.'

Agravain left the room to tell Orlamh, my father's chief druid, and was nearly jumping with delight at each step. I turned to follow him, but my father said, 'Gwalchmai. Wait.'

The room seemed to shrink into a trap. I turned back and waited.

When Agravain was gone, Lot went to the lamp table and picked up his goblet, poured some wine into it. The sunlight struck it, bringing out a deep red fire as he poured it. He sat down on the bed and stared at me, weighing me up. I had felt that stare often enough before, but still I shifted uneasily and avoided his eyes. My father sighed.

'Well?' he asked.

'What?' I looked at the bedspread.

My father's voice went on: 'Your brother is very excited about this war, and eager to prove himself and win honour for himself and for our clan. What of you?'

'I'm not old enough for the war,' I said nervously. 'I still have at least two more years in the Boys' House. And everyone knows that I'm a poor warrior.' I glanced up at Lot.

16

The corners of his mouth drew down. 'Yes, everyone knows that.' He drank some more of the wine. The sunlight caught on his gold collar and brooch, glittered on his hair, making him look more like Lugh the sun god than ever. He looked over to my mother. 'I don't understand it.'

I became angry. Another thing that everyone knew was that my younger brother Medraut was not Lot's son, though no one knew whose he was, and Lot suspected something similar of me. I certainly do not look like my father, as Agravain does. I resemble my mother enough to disguise any other inheritance. Though I sometimes doubted myself whether I was Lot's son, I didn't like Lot to do it.

He caught my anger. 'Oh? What is it now?'

Afraid again, I forced myself to relax. 'Nothing.'

Lot sighed deeply and rubbed his forehead. 'I am going away next month. It is to a war, which means I may not come back. I do not think that I shall die this time, but one must be prepared. So, since I will have other things to think of until I leave, I want to know, now . . .' he dropped his hand and stared at me fiercely, his hot eyes full of energy and arrogance and harsh brightness. 'I wish to know, Gwalchmai, what you are going to become.'

Paralysed, I fumbled for an answer, finally replied, 'I don't know,' simply, and met his eyes. I held them for an instant.

He slammed his fist against the lamp table and swore softly. 'By the wind, by the Hounds of Hell, you don't know! I will tell you: I don't know either. But I wonder. You are a member of a kingly clan, son of a king and a High King's daughter. I am a war-leader, your mother a planner of wars. And what can you do but ride horses and play songs on the harp? Oh, to be sure, to be a bard is an honourable profession – but not for the sons of kings. And now we go off to war, Agravain and the clan and I. If Agravain is killed, or should our ally Gwlgawd prove a traitor, do you know what will become of you?'

'I could not be king!' I said, shocked. 'You can choose anyone in our clan as your successor, Diuran or Aidan or anyone, and all of them better suited than me.'

'But they are not my sons. I want one of my sons to be king after me.' Lot stared a little while longer. 'But I would not choose you.'

'You could not,' I said.

'And it does not even make you angry?' asked my father, bitterly.

'Why should it? I don't want to be king.'

'Then what do you want to be?'

I dropped my eyes again. 'I don't know.'

Lot stood, violently. 'You must! I want to know what you will become while I am away at war!'

I shook my head. Desperation loosened my tongue. 'I'm sorry, Father. I don't know. Only . . . not a king, or a bard, or . . . I don't know. I want something, something else. I don't know what it is. I can't be be a proper warrior, I've no talent for it. But one day . . . nothing is important enough now, but sometimes I have dreams and . . . and there is something in songs. And once I dreamt about a sword, burning, with a lot of red around it, and the sun and the sea . . .' I lost myself in my thoughts, trying to name what it was that moved within me. 'I can't understand it yet. But it is important that I wait for it, because it is more important to fight for this than for anything – only I don't understand what it is . . .' I trailed off weakly, met my father's eyes again, and again looked away.

Lot waited for more, realized there was none, and shook his head. 'I do not understand you. You speak like a druid, pretending to prophesy. Do you want to be a druid? I thought not. What, then?'

'I don't know,' I said wretchedly, and stared at the floor. I could feel his eyes still on me, but I did not look up again. After a bit the rushes sounded as he walked back to the bed.

'Well, I expected as much.' His voice was cold and brisk. 'You don't even know what you are speaking of, and you can't fight. When a quarrel begins, instead of standing up you run off. Agravain and your teachers say that you are afraid. Afraid. A coward. That's what they call you in the Boys' House, I hear. One without honour.'

I bit my lip to hold back the angry shout. I cared something for my honour, but I didn't look on it as others looked on theirs. Perhaps, I thought, it is not the same thing.

'Stay here at Dun Fionn, then,' said Lot. 'Go and play your harp and ride your horses. Now get out of here.'

I turned to leave, but just as I reached the door I felt my mother's eyes on me and looked back. I realized suddenly that she had been watching me ever since I had spoken of my dreams. Her eyes were darker than night and more beautiful than stars. When they met mine she smiled, a slow, secret, wonderful smile that was mine alone.

As I left the room, my misery lightened by her notice, I felt her eyes following me into the open air. And, even though I worshipped her, even though I could set her smile in the balance with my father's anger and be contented, still I wondered again how her father Uther had died, and was uneasy.

Two

My father sent out the call to the kings of the Orcades, telling them to gather their warbands, the rest of their men and their ships and supplies and come to Dun Fionn. Slowly they began arriving, tall men in brightly coloured cloaks, warriors glittering with jewellery, their sharp long-bladed thrusting spears glinting, short throwing spears in quivers and swords on baldrics flashing by their sides. Their white-washed shields were flung over their shoulders, and often painted or enamelled with bright colours. The kings and finest warriors wore chain mail, imported from northern Britain ôr from Gaul, shining like fish scales. Lesser men had leather jerkins sewn with metal. The warriors brought their war-hounds, great grey beasts whose collars shone with silver, and hawks sat on the shoulders of the kings, ruffling sharp-edged feathers and glaring with brilliant eyes. They came and encamped about Dun Fionn, a camp from each island that was subject to my father, and more from the Picts and Dalriada to the south as well as the men from our own tribe. All told, there were more than a thousand professional warriors, and some three thousand other men. Going south-east of Dun Fionn one could see their ships, row upon row of great twenty-oared curraghs, sails furled against their masts. There was a constant coming and going of these ships: going to fetch more supplies or to send messages from Dun Fionn to our allies in Gododdin; coming in with the supplies and messages and more men. About and within Dun Fionn itself was a great hustle and bustle as my father organized and planned and prepared, my mother always beside him. Not only did he have to feed his great host, but to mediate the quarrels between his various under-kings, prevent blood feuds between rival clans, and arrange details of the alliance with Gwlgawd king of Goddodin. I saw little of either him or Morgawse.

I hung about the fringe of things, staring and wondering. It was the first time I saw my father marshal his power, and I was astounded at the strength displayed before me. I understood, even then, that it could not be supported long in one place without a war. The cost was tremendous. But the bright colours, the splendour, the glitter of arms, the loud, laughing confidence of the warriors and their ready fellowship – these all impressed me immensely and filled me with vague yearnings I did my best to smother. I was no warrior whom any great lord would wish to have in his warband. And yet, and yet, and yet . . .

It was glorious. I sometimes wished fiercely, like any other boy on the island, that I was going too, to win honour and fame for myself, my clan and my lord.

Agravain had no doubts that he would do well in the war. He received his weapons with the other fourteen- and fifteen-year-olds, and strutted and boasted more and louder than any of them. He picked fights with me even more frequently than usual, being so stiff with tension and eagerness that his temper snapped, as they say, at a footfall.

In mid-March the army sailed for Gododdin. They would make their way about the coast of southern Pictland by sail or oar, as the wind held, then follow the estuary which halves Manau Gododdin, and beach their ships near Gododdin's royal fortress, Din Eidyn, and fortify a camp there. My father had been sending letters to various of the kings, including those in alliance with Docmail of Gwynedd, the rival of our ally Gwlgawd in the contest for the High Kingship. As a result, one member of that alliance, Vortipor of Dyfed, was now wavering in his allegiance and likely to desert Docmail at any moment. But it was uncertain whether Vortipor would join my father or claim the Pendragonship for himself. Vortipor was more crafty than a fox, and could not be trusted any more than a viper. He was almost more trouble as an ally than as an enemy. Almost: Dyfed is a strong, rich land, and the men there learned their way of fighting from the Romans. Vortipor himself kept the title of 'Protector', to remind Britain of the days when his province had sheltered the whole island from Irish raiders. Vortipor was himself of Irish descent, but his ways were as Roman as his fighting, and he had support, too much to be ignored. My father and mother had debated for hours over what course he would take and what to do when he took it. From the Boys' House I could see the light in my father's room late at night. It was strange to see it dark when the army sailed and Dun Fionn was left with only a token guard. All the lights seemed

21

to have gone with the army, leaving only some torn and yellow patches in the grass, and the black spots where the camp fires had burned.

Still, from my point of view, the time became a pleasant one. Without Agravain or my father about, I had more freedom than at any time in my life. In the Boys' House, the training and competition became less rigorous and intense. There were no older boys to bully us, and no more late feasts for the men who trained us to ache from or quarrel about the next day. Most of the boys used the free time to play hurley. I occasionally joined them, but as I am a bad player, spent more of my time at Llyn Gwalch, or in riding about the island.

The Orcades are very beautiful islands, and gentle ones, despite their British name of Ynysoedd Erch, 'Frightful Islands'. The climate is mild, varying only a little throughout the year: in winter it is warmer at Dun Fionn than at Camlann far to the south. The land rolls in low, stony hills covered with short grass and heather which provide pasture for sheep and cattle and a good living for farmers. The wide grey sea, full of fish, pounds eternally at the shore, which is rocky and steep, especially at the west coast of my home island, and sea-birds of all kinds nest in the cliffs. The sound of the sea is always present at Dun Fionn, so much so that it becomes a sound like the beating of one's heart, too continual to notice. The puffins clamour on the cliff sides, and the gulls wail over the grey-green of the waves, calling to each other across their flashing white wings. The sound of their voices seems almost as beautiful, sometimes, as the voices of the skylarks inland, who on sunny days seem to drip music from the sky like honey from a comb. They say that the land one lives in when young becomes a part of one. I believe this, for even today, the sea and the mourning of the seagulls bring back to me Llyn Gwalch in the mist, with the mist wetness dripping from the heather.

That spring the islands were particularly beautiful.

I sometimes rode out with my younger brother Medraut beside me, sharing with him all my thoughts and telling him stories. He thought me a better story-teller than my father's bard Orlamh and, though this was only because he was unused to the bardic style, it delighted me.

Medraut was seven at the time, a beautiful child. Whoever

his father was, I was sure he must be noble. Medraut had fair hair of a paler shade than Lot's, and wide grey eyes. His complexion was our mother's, his features his unknown father's. But his spirit was closer to Lot's. He wanted to be a warrior, and had no doubts that he would be. His favourite tales were those of CuChulainn, the hero of Ulster. He was very brave, being altogether unafraid of tall horses and weapons and bulls and other such things most children fear. Once, when we were climbing down the cliff to look for gulls' eggs, he slipped and hung by his hands from a narrow ledge until I could come and help him. When I asked him if he had not been afraid (and I was shaking with fear) he stared at me in surprise and answered no, why should he have been? He had known, he said, that I would save him. Not only was he brave (and generous as a High King and fierce as a wildcat: qualities of a great warrior) but he also loved and admired me. I could not understand both of these existing together, but I accepted them joyfully and gave to him all I had, save what would bewilder him. Though precocious, he was only seven, and that is too young to care for dreams properly.

At times, though, instead of playing at Llyn Gwalch or with Medraut or riding about the island, I practised with my weapons on my own. Until that time I had been the despair of my teachers, who were all aging members of the royal clan, men who had fought for my father and for his father before him, and who could not understand why, when they had finished giving their set lessons to me and the other noble boys, I should spend my time playing the harp or disappearing into unknown parts of the island. I needed more practice, they told me; I ought to spend my time with spears, not harps and horses. And in the past I had always said nothing, and vanished as soon as their backs were turned. But now the sight of the great host had moved something in me, and I strove to improve myself in the arts of war. To my surprise, I discovered that I was doing better, and not only because I was practising more. Without Agravain at my elbow with every spear I threw, without his friends and our cousins taunting me when I practised with spear or sword, I could throw or thrust straighter and more strongly.

But the most important thing that happened to me after the army left was unconnected with any of these. Morgawse taught me to read.

23

She came up one afternoon as I was throwing spears at a straw target, in the yard behind the Boys' House. One moment I was staring at the target, spear in hand, and the next I felt her eyes on my back and turned.

She stood by the corner of the House, dark and pale in the gold of the afternoon sun. She wore a dress of dark red wool, caught tightly with a golden belt at the waist, low cut to reveal the line of her white neck. She wore a brooch of gold set with garnets, golden arm rings, and gold in the black hair that seemed to drink the light. I dropped the spear and stared at her. In that instant she did not seem like a mortal woman, but like one of the Sidhe, the people from the hollow hills.

Then she was crossing the yard, smiling, and the spell was broken.

'Gwalchmai!' she said. 'I have seen little of you, my hawk, these past few months, so busy have I been with this planning for your father's war.'

I started when she called me 'hawk', although my name, in her native tongue of British, means 'Hawk of May'. The name is such a warrior-like one – 'hawk' being a common poetic name for a warrior – that I always tried to forget its meaning. But when my mother used the name for me, I loved it and her.

'M–mother,' I stammered. 'I . . .'

'You are sorry for the loss?' she asked. 'So am I, my hawk.'

This could not be true, I knew. My mother had given me to a nursemaid immediately after giving birth to me, and had shown no great interest in me since. But I believed her, because she said it and I wanted to believe her.

'Yes, I am sorry,' I told her.

She smiled again, her deep, secret smile. 'Well, we shall have to talk a bit, shall we not? I see that you are doing as your father wished and practising with your weapons.' She eyed the pile of throwing spears beside me – I had just withdrawn them from the target, or the ground about the target, and there was nothing to show the quality of my aim. 'Will you show me how well you throw them?'

I picked up the spear I had dropped, looking at her, then turned to the target, determined to hit it. Perhaps because of this determination, the spear went in well, slightly to the left of the centre, ploughing completely through the straw. Morgawse raised her eyebrows in surprised pleasure. I picked up another spear and sent it through the target, this time a little raggedly, then threw the other five in succession. Only one missed the target, and one hit the centre. I turned back to my mother, beaming.

She smiled at me again. 'So, it seems that you are not so poor a warrior as Lot thinks, if not so fine a one as Agravain. Well done, my falcon.'

I wanted to sing. I glanced down and murmured, 'You bring me luck. I have to do everything well when you are here, Mother.'

She laughed. 'My! So you have a way with words too, then? I think we should spend more time together, Gwalch-mai.'

I swallowed and nodded. My mother was the wisest and most beautiful woman in all the islands of Britain and Erin. To be allowed to spend time near her was a gift from the gods.

'Listen, then,' she said. 'I have been talking to Orlamh. He says that you are a fine harper, as good as many bardic students, but more interested in the stories and sweet tunes than in the knowledge involved. It seems to me that it would be a fine thing if you could learn the histories and genealogies without having to know the chants by heart. Would you like to learn to read?'

My jaw dropped. Reading was the rarest of all skills in the Orcades. The druids had their ogham script, but they taught it to no one but their initiates, and forbade its use for any purpose but memorial inscriptions, saying that what a man memorizes he has for ever, but what he writes down he may easily lose. To learn to read meant to learn Latin, which was spoken in parts of southern Britain, but used as a written language from Erin to Constantinople. In all the Orcades, I believe only my mother could read. The skill is common enough in Britain and, now, in Erin in the monasteries there, but in the Orcades it was regarded as a kind of magic. And now my mother was offering to share her power with me!

'Well?' asked Morgawse.

'I . . . Yes, yes, very much!' I choked out.

Morgawse gave a smile of satisfaction, almost, I thought for a moment, of triumph, and nodded. 'When you are finished with weapons practice, then, I will give you your first lesson. Come to my room.'

25

'I'll come right n . . .'

She shook her head. 'Come after you have finished with these. Hit the target fifty times for me. The Latin will wait.'

I hurried with the spears until I realized that hasty throwing would not help me hit the target, and finally got my fifty hits. I raced to the Boys' House, dropped the spears in their corner – I would have been whipped for leaving them in the yard where they could rust – and ran to my mother's room.

The first lesson was a simple one, though it seemed hard to me. First my mother drew out the letters of the alphabet on a wax tablet with the sharp end of a stylus, explaining to me meanwhile what an alphabet was. Then she gave me the tablet and told me to copy the letters. I did this, several times, and she told me which sounds they made. Then she took back the tablet, criticized the way I had drawn the letters, and smoothed over the wax with the blunt end of the stylus, afterwards drawing the letters again. She smiled, then, and handed me the tablet and the stylus, telling me to memorize the letters and come back after weapons practice the next day.

I ran to Medraut and told him about it, showed him the letter forms, told him what Morgawse had said about my skill with weapons, and jumped for joy all over the stables.

The rest of the summer was wonderful. I continued my lessons in Latin, rising from the alphabet to groups of syllables to the words they composed, and finally to writing out sentences which my mother set for me. I improved with my weapons to a point where I could hold my own with the other boys and was no longer the butt of every joke. My twelfth birthday came in late May, and I began to dream of when I would be fourteen and able to take up arms, a dream which now I hoped to fulfil. I could become a warrior in my father's warband, and he would be pleased. The war, though, seemed incredibly remote from the slowly passing summer days, with their long green twilights and the short nights when the stars were like silver shield rivets in the soft sky. But my mother listened tensely to the reports from Britain, and sent messages to Lot, advising him.

It was not as easy as my father had planned. At the very beginning, my father and our ally were surprised by a sudden attack from Urien, king of Rheged. Lot had counted on the marriage-tie holding Urien back for another month or so, and, even though the British king was defeated and forced to

26

withdraw, my father and Gwlgawd were forced to cancel their plans for raiding Gwynedd immediately. Urien's defeat confused the situation in other ways as well, for Vortipor of Dyfed was sufficiently impressed by it to declare himself the ally of Gododdin and the Orcades, and commence raiding Powys, his neighbour, while March ap Meirchiawn of Strathclyde managed to win Urien's support for his own claims to the High Kingship. Vortipor then changed his mind, wanted the High Kingship for himself, found allies and attacked Gwynedd. He was defeated; my father and his allies took advantage of the situation to attack Gwynedd themselves, and won a victory and a great deal of plunder, but, returning from this expedition, encountered Urien and March and their allies. There was a great battle.

It was nearly two weeks later before we heard, even with good winds and fast ships. Gwlgawd our ally was dead, though his son Mynyddog had succeeded him and renewed the alliance. But our enemies had prevailed, and the army had fled across Britain to Din Eidyn, leaving its supplies and the plunder from Gwynedd. My father was sending back as many ships as he could find men to man, and he asked for supplies. My mother found them ruthlessly and hurriedly, and sent them south with some advice. I thought at the time that she was troubled for Lot and Agravain and the rest; but I believe she was angry, angry with Lot for losing the battle, and angry even more at the delay in her plans.

But the rest of the summer was passed in fruitless quarrelling and recrimination among the kings of Britain. March of Strathclyde and Urien of Rheged, recently allied, returned to their more usual dislike for one another, and Urien claimed the High Kingship for himself, which led to still more quarrels and scheming. Then it was harvest time, and the large armies which the kings had raised dissolved as the men went home to their farms, leaving only the kings and the royal warbands; and still nothing happened, while every king was afraid to raid, not knowing who his enemies were. In the south and east the Saxons were becoming very restless and beginning to raid their neighbours. Only the old royal warband, still led by my mother's half-brother Arthur, prevented a large-scale invasion.

Towards the end of October Lot finally despaired of the war beginning again in earnest, and the army came home for the winter.

Every king took his own warband home to his own island. They settled like tired hawks in their hill-top fortresses and sighed with relief that it was over for the year and they had time to recover their strength and heal their wounds.

When Lot returned with his warband it was not a shining, stirring sight as before. It had been a bad war, an uncertain, nerve-straining war, and they were tired. Their shields were hacked, the bright colours chipped, their spears notched and dull, colourful cloaks tattered. Many bore wounds. Come spring, though, and they'd be thrusting up those hacked shields as proof of how bravely they had fought, flaunting their scars in each other's faces, polishing their spears and eager to go again. But as they came into Dun Fionn, tramping stolidly through the pouring rain, it did not seem possible that they would ever boast.

Morgawse, Medraut and I stood at the gate, watching the warband come up. Morgawse wore a dark, striped dress, a silver brooch on her dark cloak. She wore the rain in her hair like jewels. Lot, riding at the head of the warband, straightened to see her, and urged his horse to a canter. He dismounted before her in a rush and swept her into his arms, burying his face in her neck, saying her name in a hoarse whisper. I saw her face over his shoulder, the still, cold disgust in her eyes mixed with a strange pride in her power.

'Welcome home, my lord,' she murmured, disengaging herself. 'We are glad to see you home unharmed.'

Lot nodded, muttered, and looked towards the Hall and his chambers there.

'And where is Agravain, my son?' she asked, softly.

Lot recollected himself, took one arm from about her and turned to the warband, which was now pouring through the gate, talking and laughing with the gladness of coming home. 'Agravain!' he shouted.

A blond head jerked up, and Agravain rode across to Lot. He was a little older, a little taller, much dirtier, and looked more like Lot, but I recognized at once that he was not much changed. He slid off his horse, smiling widely, delighted to be back.

'Greetings, Mother,' he said.

'A thousand welcomes,' said Morgawse. 'There is a feast tonight for the both of you . . . but you will want to rest now.

To sleep, my lord.' She smiled at Lot.

My father grinned, took her arm and hurried off.

Agravain watched them go, then turned to Medraut and me. 'Well,' he said, then grinned hugely. 'By the sun and the wind, it's good to see you again!' and he hugged both of us hard. 'What a summer!'

'I can get you some ale if you want to come into the Hall and talk,' I suggested, glad – in spite of everything, very glad – to have him home.

'A marvellous idea!' said Agravain. 'Especially the ale.' He looked at Medraut, rumpled his hair. 'Gwalchmai, I swear our brother's grown inches since last I saw him. Even you've grown.'

'You too.'

'Have I?' he asked delightedly. 'That's wonderful! When I'm tall enough Father will give me a mail-coat. He promised.'

We walked over to the feast Hall, where I got him some ale and asked him about the war. He was near to bursting from eagerness to tell someone and told us for an hour and a half.

He had not, it seemed, actually fought as a warrior, but he had ridden in the middle of the warband, and in the great battle had thrown spears at the enemy.

'I think one of them may have hit someone,' he said hopefully. 'But, of course, we couldn't go back to see whether it had. We barely escaped alive at all!'

His manner was a little different from what it had been when he left. His energy, always overflowing, had found a channel. He enjoyed being a warrior. He had copied the speech and mannerisms of the older warriors so as to fit into their society. But underneath it I could tell he was exactly the same.

He was overjoyed to be back. The last months of the war had been especially unpleasant. A major blood feud had almost begun between two of Lot's under-kings, and at one point there had been a threat of war with Gododdin as the warbands tried to ease their tension by sneering at foreigners. The peace and familiarity of home seemed, after this, marvellously attractive.

After talking himself out, Agravain yawned and decided to go to sleep. He stayed in the Hall to rest since he was officially a warrior, and I didn't see him till late the next day.

Lot, after settling himself and the warband back into Dun Fionn, began to work towards the next season's war. It would plainly be a war lasting several years, and such enterprises are costly. The plunder taken that summer would not pay for even the fighting that had acquired it, let alone buy new weapons, and the harvest had been a bad one. My father increased the amount of tribute he demanded from his subject kings by as much as he dared; the subject kings raised the taxes on their people; and the people grumbled. There had not been a war on this scale for nineteen years, and no one was used to it.

For a little while Agravain tried to help our father at the business of governing. He stayed, listening, while Lot flattered the embassies and cajoled the messengers of dissatisfied kings, and took one party to a blood feud off drinking or hunting while Lot persuaded the other, by threats and promises, to compromise and make peace. He attended while old men made endless complaints to Lot about the increased tribute and proclaimed their masters' nobility and long support as reasons for not paying it, and he tried not to fall asleep while Lot issued warnings and blandishments in return. But presently Agravain found statecraft boring, and complaining that our father paid no attention to any of his ideas, turned once more to his weapons and his own friends. Lot was annoyed at first – Agravain had understood very little of what he had heard, and on the occasions he did suggest some course of action, it was invariably the wrong one – but Agravain was still the chosen heir to the kingship, and Lot was determined that he should know the chief men and clans of the kingdom, and how to deal with them. However, our father concluded that Agravain was still the chosen heir to the kingship, and Lot was determined that he should know the chief men and clans of the kingdom, and how to deal with them. However, our father concluded that Agravain was young, that the hunting was good that year, and it was excusable for a young man in such circumstances to tire of the talk of his elders. So he allowed Agravain to do as he pleased, knowing there would be many more chances for him to learn the art of government. For my part, I was not surprised that Agravain preferred his hunting trips. He needed action, quick and preferably violent, simply to keep himself occupied. Statecraft offers exercise for cunning, organization, eloquence and subtlety, rarely for direct action. My father was more cunning than a fox, and enjoyed the complicated processes by which he kept his subject kings obedient, kept them paying the tribute, prevented their wars and blood feuds while at the same time holding their favour and thus his own position. Agravain did not understand the delicate nature of Lot's 'game', tired quickly, and ran off to seek entertainment. He went a-hunting, but he did not forget me.

A few weeks after the warband returned, towards the end of November, he came to the yard of the Boys' House while I was at weapons practice. I was working with the throwing spears again. It is harder to throw a spear straight while running than it is to master a thrusting spear or a sword, but important to be able to do so. Thus, I spent most of my practice time hurling spears at a straw target, sometimes running towards it, sometimes standing still. I was standing this time.

Agravain walked up behind me and stood watching as I made three casts at the target. All of them hit, one in the centre. Agravin frowned. 'You've been working at these, this summer, haven't you?'

I turned to him, flushing a little with pride. I had not yet shown off my new skill before my father and brother, and I was eager to. I nodded. 'Yes, an hour a day with the throwing spears, and an hour with the thrusting spear or sword and shield, beyond the training time. I'm better than I used to be.'

He nodded, then scowled. 'You're better, and that's good. But if you try to throw like that in a battle you'll be run through . . .'

'Durrough says there's no harm in standing like this, and he's the trainer . . .'

'He doesn't expect much from you. Put your left foot further back and your left arm closer to your body. You have to hold a shield, you know!'

'But . . .'

'Oh, by the sun, why are you arguing? I'm trying to help you.' He grinned.

Was he? The grin faded as I continued to stare at him, and he scowled again, fists clenching and unclenching restlessly. I took the stance he suggested and hurled the spear, nervously. I missed.

He shook his head. 'By the sun and the wind, not like that! Hold the spear straight, may the Morrigan take you—not that a war-goddess would want someone who throws like that!'

I cringed, threw another spear. It, too, missed.

Agravain snorted. 'You can't see what I mean. Here, let me show you.' He stooped over, picked up my other spears and hurled them. All three hit the target squarely and cleanly. 'That's the way. Now you try.'

We went and fetched the spears. I stood, and Agravain corrected my stance. 'Try again now,' he told me.

I looked at the spear in my hand, heavy, shafted with wood from the dark hills of Pictland, headed with dull iron. The weight of it in my hand was suddenly very great.

'Go on, Gwalchmai,' Agravain said impatiently. 'You said that you were better. Show me! Or are you afraid of your own spear again? Not much of a hawk if you are.'

Morgawse still called me 'her falcon'. Hawk of May. It was such a fine, warrior-like name. It was what I wanted for myself.

I threw the spear, and it flew crooked. Agravain snorted and slapped his thigh. 'You may have learned to throw better when you stand like a farmer ploughing, but you had better learn to throw standing like a warrior if you want to be one. Or do you want to be a bard? A druid? A horse tamer?'

'No,' I whispered. 'Agravain . . .'

'I'd wager you still spend most of your day on horseback,' he continued, oblivious. 'But that's no use. Horses are a luxury, and no more than that: the real fighting is always done on foot. Horses are like gold brooches and fine clothes, excellent for a warrior to own to show others that he is rich and important, but dispensable to the real business. For that you have to throw spears properly. Try again.'

'Agravain . . .' I repeated, gathering my courage.

'What's the matter now? Are you afraid to throw? Stop being foolish.'

I felt foolish. I clutched the spear desperately. I would throw it standing my way. It was not the usual stance, but it did not leave me vulnerable, either. I put my left leg forward, dropped my left arm. I really am good, I told myself. I can hit the target this way. I have to now. I must.

I threw and missed.

Agravain nodded reasonably. 'Now will you do it my

way? If you want to be a man and a warrior you must listen to . . .'

'Stop it!' I shouted, furious.

Agravain stopped, astounded.

'You are not helping me. You aren't trying to help, though you may think you are . . .'

'I am trying to help you. Are you calling me a liar?'

'No! But I don't want your help. If I'm no warrior, let me fail in my own way, and don't bother me with right ways and wrong ways. If I'm not a warrior, perhaps I will be a bard or a druid. Mother is teaching me to read so . . .'

'She is doing what?' demanded Agravain, aghast.

'Teaching me to read. She's been doing it all summer, while you were gone . . .'

'Do you want to be a sorcerer?' Agravain's eyes blazed and his bright hair glittered like the sun.

'No . . . I just want to read . . .' I was confused.

He slapped me across the face, so hard that I fell backwards. His face had gone red with anger. 'You want to be better than us! Morgawse is a witch, everyone knows that, and you want to learn from her because you're such a poor warrior. A word in the dark instead of a sword in the sunlight, that's what you want. Power, the sort of power fit only for cowards, for traitors and kin-wrecked men and women and clan-murderers . . .'

'Agravain! I don't! I only . . .'

'Stop lying to me!'

I scrambled to my feet, facing my brother. I felt a blind fury descend on me, cold as ice, cold as Morgawse's eyes. 'I am not a liar,' I said, hearing my voice cold and quiet, like someone else's. 'I do not dishonour my clan.'

He laughed at me. 'You are always dishonouring our clan. Do you call it no dishonour that the king's own son can't throw a spear straight? That he can't kill as much as a sparrow when hunting? That all he *can* do is ride horses and play the harp – play the harp! That you want to learn sorcery and the casting of curses so that you won't have to fight . . .'

'It's not true!' I screamed.

'Now you want to make me a liar!' yelled Agravain, and struck out at me.

It is good that I was not right by the spears: if I had been, I believe I would have used one. I jumped on my brother with a

33

fury which surprised him, and struck as hard as I could. I felt cold, deathly cold, filled with a black sea. My fist hit Agravain's face, contacted again. He grunted with pain, and I felt a thrill of exultation. I wanted to hurt him, to hurt everyone who hurt me, who hurt Morgawse, who hurt Medraut, who belonged to a world I could not enter, and hurt, and hurt, and kept on hurting.

Agravain flung me off and fought back, coolly, calmly, not even very excited any more. I realized that he had not really believed his own accusations, had only been angry at my doing something he could not . . . I tripped and sprawled on the grass. Agravain kicked me, jumped on top of me and told me to yield.

I thought of Morgawse's eyes; of Medraut's, admiring. I thought of my father smiling and imagined praise, of warriors, bright weapons and swift war-hounds. I tried to fight some more. Agravain became angry and hit harder. I scratched him. He cursed.

'Call you a hawk, but you fight like a woman! Like a witch! Yield, you little bastard – you're no true brother of mine . . .'

I tried still, to fight, and was hurt worse. The black wave ebbed a little, taking with it the insane strength it had lent me. I was no warrior, I knew. Not really. I couldn't fight Agravain. I was no true brother of his anyway, and had no real claim to the honour of our clan, so he and Lot, at least, must believe . . . I went limp.

'Yield?' asked Agravain. He was panting.

I felt sick. I had no choice. If I didn't yield, he would only hit me some more, and call me names, and laugh at me.

'I yield.'

Agravain rose, dusted himself off. Two bruises were beginning to blotch his face, but he was otherwise unmarked. I rolled over, got on my hands and knees, stared at the packed earth under the grass of the practice yard, damp from winter rains. I was smeared with it and with blood.

'Remember this, little brother,' said Agravain 'and forget about reading. Try to learn how to throw a spear straight, the right way, and maybe you'll someday make a warrior. I'm willing to forget about this and come and help you some more tomorrow.'

I heard his footsteps going, striding, confident. A warrior, my brother, a sun-bright prince, first-born of a golden warrior king. But I remembered Morgawse, dark and more beautiful than anything on earth, who held Lot's fate in her slim white hands. Morgawse, who hated. Hate. I realized that the black tide had not left me, but was coiled down within my being, waiting. It was hate, strong hate. I was my mother's son.

Morgawse knew when she saw me. I had washed myself somewhat before coming to her, but I had clearly been in a fight and it needed no guessing with whom. She saw when I came into her room that I was ready, and she smiled, a slow, triumphant smile.

She said nothing of it at first. She poured me some of the imported wine from a private store, told me to sit on the bed, and spoke to me gently, compassionately, asking what had happened, and I told her of the quarrel with Agravain.

'He said that you were a witch,' I told her. 'He accused me of wanting to fight my enemies with curses and magic in the dark of the moon, rather than with honest steel.'

'And you wanted no such thing,' she said.

'That is so. I wanted only . . . to be a warrior. To bring honour to our clan, to please Father . . . and even Agravain. Diuran, the warband, everyone. I wanted them not to think that I was worthless. I wanted . . .' I found my throat constricted, and it hurt with a sudden intensity that all my wants were vain. I sipped the wine, rolled it about my mouth, swallowed. The taste was dry and rich. It was red wine. In the shadows of Morgawse's room it was dark as blood, not the ruby fire it had been that day with Lot when I heard that the Pendragon was dead.

'I don't want those things any more,' I said. 'I'm not a warrior.'

'Not of their sort,' said Morgawse. She sat beside me, close. She and the room both smelled of musk, of deep secrets. The pupils of her eyes had expanded, drinking all the light of the room into her sweet darkness.

I sipped the wine again. It was stronger than the ale I was used to. It was good.

'But I want to fight them,' I said. 'With knowledge. With things they don't understand because they are afraid to look at them. I want to show them who I am and make them know I am real.'

'Ah?'

'Is it true that you are a witch?'

'And if it were?' Her voice was soft, softer than an owl's feathers in the darkness.

'If it were, I'd ask you to teach me . . . things.'

She smiled again, a secret smile just between the two of us. 'There are many sorts of power in the world, Gwalchmai,' she said. 'Many powers. They can be used by those who know how to use them, but each sort has its own dangers. Yes, the dangers of some are so great, my hawk, that you could not understand them. Yet the rewards also are great; the greater the power, the greater the reward.' She clutched my hand suddenly. Her grip was cold as winter, strong as hard steel. 'Great rewards, my spring-tide falcon. I have paid certain prices . . .' she laughed. 'There will be more to come. But mine is the greatest sort of power. I will gain . . . immortality. There are none living who can match me in magic now. I have power, my son! I have very great power. I have spoken to the leaders of the wild hunt, to the lord of Yffern, to the kelpies of the deep sea and the demons who dwell in the far keeps of the underworld. I am greater than they. I am a Queen, Gwalchmai, a Queen of a realm which Lot only suspects and is afraid of.

'And I have watched you, my hawk. There is power in you, and strength. Now, at last you have come and asked for teaching. You will recieve it.'

I felt fear, but remembered Agravain's contempt and ignored it. Morgawse spoke of serving Darkness, but what of that? She also spoke of ruling it.

'Then show me,' I said, my voice as low as hers.

'Not so quickly! You forget, I also spoke of dangers. I will teach you, Gwalchmai, but it will be long before you can control the power you seek. But you will learn to. Oh, learn it you will, my hawk, my son . . .'

Taking a knife from a hidden sheath she made a cut at her wrist, then held her arm so that the blood flowed into the cup of wine. She handed the knife to me and, without being told to, I did the same.

Morgawse took the cup and drank from it, lowered it, the red wine and red blood dark about her mouth. She handed it to me.

It was heavy in my hands, fine copper overlaid with gold,

rich, cold, fine and beautiful. I thought of the winter sunlight outside, of Agravain, of the scorn of warriors. For a second the thought returned to me of Llyn Gwalch and the wide purity of the grey sea. No, I thought. That is a lie. I raised the cup slowly and drained it. It was thick, sweet and dark – darker than the deep heart of midnight.

Three

Things were somehow different after that. My mother taught me nothing but more Latin, Agravain 'helped' me in weapons practice and I grimly accepted his help, labouring with the rough wood and heavy metal that was so light and flashing in his hands; I rode about the island, practised my own style of fighting, sometimes on horseback. Agravain quarrelled with me over this, saying that I was ruining myself as a warrior, and that I ought to listen to him – life seemed to have settled into its usual pattern. But there was a difference, a shadow that made all the familiar things seem strange. I had made a pact and was bound to it. A seed had been planted, and I waited sometimes, awake in my bed at night with the soft sleeping breath of the other boys about me in the dark, waited for the plant to grow and blossom with some fantastic black flower.

Agravain noticed nothing. He beat me less hard when we fought, but this was only because I did not fight as hard. I no longer wished to defend an honour I could not understand. Honour belonged to Lot's world, Agravain's world. My world had no room for such things.

Medraut, however, noticed almost immediately. I began to catch him staring at me with confused eyes in the middle of some talk or game. He would ask the question plainly some time, I guessed. I wondered how I would answer.

On Medraut's eighth birthday Lot gave him his choice of any pony in the royal stables. I went with my brother to help him choose one. When Lot named the gift Medraut had been very excited, but on the walk to the stables he calmed down. Together we looked at the ponies – they were all the small shaggy breed common to the northern islands – and discussed the merits of each of them. Medraut listened to my horse-talk in his grave intent way, then, quite suddenly, as I was checking one of the animals' legs, asked, 'Is there something wrong, Gwalchmai?'

I started and looked up from the pony, twisting about on my knees to face him, 'No. Not with his legs, but he has no withers at all . . .'

'No, no, not with the pony. Is there something wrong for you?'

'For me? No. What makes you think so?'

He stood facing me in the cold dusty sunlight of the stable, drably dressed, his grey eyes wide and anxious. The light glinted palely on his hair, the only touch of brightness in the place. He looked vulnerable, and very innocent.

'You've been so strange,' my brother said nervously. 'You go away . . .'

I smiled. 'Well, I've always liked to go riding. Now that you have your own horse you can come with me more often.'

'That's not what I mean.' Medraut's voice was sharp. 'All summer, you've been here. You were here, with everyone. You used to go away with Agravain and Lot, but you were here this summer. But now . . .' Medraut bit his lip and looked away from me. 'Now you're gone. I can't talk to you any more. You even go away with me.'

'I don't understand,' I said, though in truth I had a very good idea of what he meant.

'You had a big fight with Agravain,' said Medraut unhappily.

I looked away, shrugged.

'After that, something happened. You went away from everyone after that.'

I had felt, on some of those days, that I watched the world from a great distance behind the mask that had been my face. Went away . . .

'And you haven't gone to Llyn Gwalch.'

I thought of Llyn Gwalch, the seaweed gleaming on the rocks, the drops of mist and seaspray on the mossy boulders. Such places have no bearing on the world, I told myself. One must live in the world which is real. 'That was a childish game,' I said. 'I'm too old for it now.'

'But what happened?' Medraut crossed the space between us and caught my arm. 'You must tell me!'

'Why?' I glared at him, aloof as the hawk of my name.

He stared at me for a long moment, then put his arms round me and buried his face in my shoulder. It hurt. I had never deserved his love and trust, and now that I had failed in the path he would follow, now that I would never be a warrior and one that a brave man could honour, now I deserved it less than ever. I could not go on lying to him.

Indeed, I suddenly felt that for too long I had been living a pretence. I had told no one of what had happened, and I had been alone, training and eating and sleeping next to other boys, pretending to be one of them, but alone. The feeling grew in me until I could not bear it. I would tell Medraut, who trusted me, who, alone, might understand.

'I went to Morgawse and asked her to teach me sorcery.' I whispered.

He lifted his head from my shoulder, eyes wide, and went still. I put my arm round his shoulder and we were quiet.

'Why?' he asked at last.

'Because I can never be a warrior.'

He thought for a while. 'I wonder . . . do you think I could learn sorcery?' he asked, finally.

I felt the shock as physically as if someone had kicked me in the belly. Not Medraut. Not the young warrior, the child of light, who was everything I wished I could be: proud without being arrogant, fierce without cruelty, sunlight with the searing heat of Lot or Agravain. He could not follow me into failure and darkness. He must not become too close to Morgawse. I thought of her light-drinking eyes.

'No,' I said.

'Why not?'

'It is wrong for you. Very wrong. *mo chroidh*, my heart.'

'But Mother is a sorcerer, and you will be. Why shouldn't I know something about it too?'

'Morgawse is Morgawse. I am only myself. You are Medraut.'

'Why couldn't I learn it? I am clever enough . . .'

'That isn't the point! It is wrong.'

'Is Mother wrong, then? Are you?'

I stopped in the middle of my reply. Medraut had always trusted and admired me. Still . . .

'It is wrong for you. You can be a warrior and fight in the sunlight. I can't, and Mother can't, and that is why we used this path.'

He argued further, but I argued against him, hard and fast. Eventually he abandoned the subject, cheered up, and chose for his pony a grey with a white mane and tail. He called it Liath Macha, 'Grey of Battle', after CuChulainn's horse, and was happy.

Spring came slowly, barely noticeable after the mild

40

winter of the Orcades. But the days grew slowly warmer, the sky was occasionally blue, and the great cold grey sea-fogs rolled less frequently up from the west.

Agravain and I had yet another quarrel over my habit of practising with my weapons on horseback. Lot, however, who happened to be nearby and inquired into the reason for the difference, looked thoughtful.

'Perhaps you are doing ill to punish Gwalchmai for this,' he told Agravain. 'True, we do most of our fighting on foot, and to be able to "jump about a horse's back like a juggler at a fair", as you were pleased to put it, is no great use to a warrior now. But Arthur the war-leader has taught all his men to fight from horseback, and they say that his victories over the Saxons spring from the strength of his cavalry. Let Gwalchmai be.'

Agravain frowned uncomfortably. He had no liking for the idea of the styles of warfare changing, and less for being told that he was wrong. He found a pretext for another quarrel later that day. But he left me more, though not entirely, alone afterwards, and sometimes watched me with a frown. I think that even he was beginning to notice the change in me, and it puzzled him.

By that time Morgawse was beginning to teach me, as she had promised. Not the important things, the summonings and dark spells, but the basic things: the characteristics of that universe that exists alongside of and within our own. I do not know all the law that governs it; neither did Morgawse. But some of it I learned, and many things that before I had not seen became apparent to me.

Once Medraut adjusted to the change in me, we were as close as ever, perhaps closer, though he gave me occasional measuring looks I did not like. But I took him with me on my rides about the island, told him more and more stories, and played the harp for him. I was becoming very good at singing. Any bard, of course, did far better, but I have some small gift for it. I no longer cared that my father considered it shameful for me to spend time harping. I no longer cared what anyone found shameful.

April arrived, a bright month, and my father still had not left for Britain. The war was late in starting. All the laboured-over alliances of the winter fell apart again with the spring, and the British kings scurried to build new ones. Several blood feuds had started, and some old ones reopened, and a war had begun between two of our enemies who had formerly been staunch allies, springing from a quarrel over some plundered cattle. This catastrophe disrupted all the old alliances and added a new faction to the civil war.

All that summer the war wore on without anything becoming clearer, and Lot made ready to invade, fumed, and waited for an invitation. Agravain, sixteen years old and considering himself a man, polished his weapons and hoped.

In early August, Gwynedd's old enemy Dyfed and our one constant ally Gododdin decided to attack Gwynedd. It was a sensible idea, but ill-timed, and our allies finally made the long-awaited step of calling for my father to join them. It was nearing harvest time, and my father knew he could not raise his army, but he summoned his subject kings and their warbands, and sailed by night past Dalriada to attack Strathclyde, and proceed from there to join his allies.

Morgawse rejoiced in her husband's departure. She ruled the Orcades absolutely while he was gone, and she loved the power. She spent very little time with me. There were two reasons for this. The first was simply that, unlike the summer before, there was a great deal for her to do. Most of the men remained in the Orcades to bring in the harvest, and from the harvest she must see that the king's tribute was exacted and collected and stored. But the more forceful reason probably was that she no longer needed to draw me to her. I had come, and been trapped. She did not think that I could escape.

Knowledge of sorcery had not brought me happiness, as I had thought it would. It gave me a secret place, and a secret cause for pride, yes, but I was never entirely certain whether what I felt was pride or whether it was shame. The burdens were heavy. I would see things that no other saw, and they frightened me. Sometimes I heard overhead, the baying of the Hounds of Yffern, which hunt the souls of the damned to Hell, and the clear silver sound of the huntsman's horn. I puzzled at the meaning of this, and it always meant death. I came to realize that I would die, and I feared this. Morgawse also feared it, but she had done something to keep the hunter from her back, something she would not explain, and this gave her security. I envied her. I sought to know more, to cure my fear, to lighten the burden, but I only succeeded in deepening the fear and loading my heart until it sank into the black sea which sometimes possessed me. And I did not think I could escape, either. Nor did I truly want to. There was nowhere else to go.

It was a hard winter. It does not usually snow in the Orcades, but it snowed that winter. In northern Britain, where the war had by then settled, the cold clasped the mountains with a brutal hand, casting great drifts and barriers before the path of any warband hardy enough to plough through them. Usually, most kings allow their warbands to rest in the winter, and most of the warriors scatter to their own households, to gather again when the leaves first begin to bud. That winter was different.

In the east, the Saxons were restless. They had by no means been altogether neutral in the war, but had enthusiastically taken part in the plotting and politicking, and taken what advantage they could from the fighting. They made small border raids which grew into larger ones, driving further and further across the boundaries which had been established in blood in the last major war against them. Arthur, the warleader of the old Pendragon, tried to fight them. But he was a clanless man, and relied on Constantius, the king of Dumnonia, for his support. Constantius had his own warband as well as Arthur's to pay for, and could not spare tribute enough to keep the whole royal warband, for which the whole of Britain had paid taxes when there was a High King. Many warriors followed Arthur by preference, giving up much of the wealth a good warrior expects, but still there were not enough to protect even a part of the border.

The Saxons are a fierce people, young, vigorous, wholly barbarian, overflowing with brutal energy. They seem, however, to have an ability to keep peace among themselves which British kings have never learned. Some of the Saxon kingdoms were officially tributary to the British High King, since they were founded as colonies by the Romans under the last emperors, and sworn to protect the empire. But they are always land hungry, for their numbers increase more and more as other Saxons come over the sea, and the newer kingdoms acknowledged no ancient oaths. Only the strength of the High King, and his warband keeps them from overrunning Britain altogether. Like wolves about a stick stag, they watched the British kings at war.

We did not fear the Saxons in the Orcades, of course, nor

did we have to worry about the other menace to Britain, the Scotti, who came from Erin in their long war-curraghs to plunder all the western shores of Britain. There was no peace between the Scotti and the Orcades – my father had left Erin because of a quarrel with the kings who led them – but the raiders would not brave the long journey to our islands, where they would be met with the cliffs and walls of Dun Fionn.

There were no raiding ships so foolhardy as to brave the Irish Sea in winter, but the Saxons and, most of all, the winter itself, made the British kings cautious, highly unwilling to leave their fortresses. Only my father, faced with no domestic enemies, felt free to travel. Our warband went the length and breadth of Britain, winning rich plunder and supplying themselves from the goods of their enemies.

Medraut was always full of talk of the war, though even more full of talk of how Morgawse was governing. She controlled the realm in a way which made my father's grip seem light. My father required supplies: my mother commanded his subject kings to ship their portion of the yearly tribute they paid directly to Gododdin, using their own ships to do so. They were reluctant, for the journey was long and costly, as well as dangerous, as the North Sea in winter is treacherous and cruel. They asked, at least, for a reduction of the tribute. She refused, and threatened to raise the tribute if they did not comply. One ship making the journey was lost, with all its crew. She told the king concerned that another shipload of tribute must be sent to replace it, saying, 'You must pay for your carelessness.' Justice she administered severely, commanding always the harshest penalties without compromise, and no clan was permitted to conceal a quarrel or offence from her: somehow she discovered their most secret concerns, and summoned them to give her an account of them.

One subject king attempted to stint her on the tribute, and denied any 'mistake' when questioned on the matter. Morgawse seized his emissaries as hostages, and kept one of these hostages even after the king had paid what was due and more. The king of one of the Western Islands, a land only recently won over by my father, was discovered to have been entertaining emissaries from the king of the Dalriada, a great kingdom to the south. She summoned him to Dun Fionn; he refused to come. She took one of the hostages he had given my father, had him killed, and sent his head back to his lord on a spear. The the king did come to Dun Fionn. She pretended to believe his oaths that it was all a mistake, and she paid him the blood-price for his servant, but she took his own son as a hostage to supply the place of the one she had killed.

All that she wished for was done, over all my father's kingdom, and if the subject kings hated her – well, they also feared her, and obeyed, Medraut and I also feared her, and adored.

She worked magic, too, that winter, in her room. Usually she was alone, but sometimes she let me watch. Whatever she was doing, it strengthened her. Every day she seemed more beautiful. She went bare-armed in the cold, her long dark cloak flapping from her shoulder, fastened with a brooch set with stones as red as blood. No blood, though, showed in her white skin, and the gaze of her eyes was softer than darkness. Any room she entered seemed to dim, and others, beside her, seemed faint and unreal.

Medraut still said nothing more about learning sorcery, but I could tell that he often thought of it. There were pauses in our closeness when he watched me, thinking, perhaps envying, or wondering what it was I saw which made me swerve about the empty air. But such times were of short duration, and he would come back near to me, asking me about the day's depression or telling me his thoughts. We often rode out together on our ponies, thundering along at full gallop in the low hills, scattering the sheep and trailing plumes of steam, or stopping to throw snowballs. I was most nearly happy when I was with Medraut.

He had his ninth birthday that winter, and entered the Boys' House to begin learning the proper use of weapons. He excelled among the boys of his age, as I had expected. He was quick, nimble, intelligent, and he learned rapidly. He was so much better than the others at riding that he had nothing to learn from his teachers. He was deficient only in skill in composing on the harp, but he made up for this with his speed in learning a song, and his enthusiasm for the music. Being together in the Boys' House we were with each other most of the day, but we shared everything and never quarrelled.

When Morgawse asked me about Medraut, I found myself evading her questions. She was beautiful, she seemed to me perfect, she ruled the Darkness – but I did not want Medraut to follow her.

In March Lot and the warband returned, but only briefly. I saw Agravain, and was shocked at the change in him. He had now completed his growing spurt – he was nearly eighteen – and seemed entirely a young warrior, and more like Lot than ever. He was tall, and his gold hair, which he wore long, to his shoulders, glowed in the sun. The whole warband was in fine condition. Though the winter fighting had been difficult, the plunder had been rich, and there had been plenty of time to rest – but my brother stood out among them. He had a fine bright cloak, jewellery won from the men of Gwynedd and Strathclyde, Elmet and Rheged, where he had fought; he had mail-coat, and his weapons gleamed. He rode up to the gates of Dun Fionn behind our father on a high-stepping horse, carrying the standard. The people of Dun Fionn, and the clansmen from the surrounding countryside who had come to watch, cheered to see their king and his son together, so splendid they were. Agravain grinned and raised the standard, the warband laughed and shouted the war-cry as one, and the people cheered even louder.

Agravain was once more pleased to be home, to see Medraut and me again. He told us about the war, about the long series of carefully planned and successful raids, about how he had killed his first man in a border clash in Strathclyde, how he had travelled over all Britain, and once even fought with a Saxon raiding party in Gododdin. He had become what he had been destined to be: a warrior prince, a someday king of the Orcades. He no longer resented my few small talents, but accepted my gains in skill with a good-humoured laugh and some praise, glad to see me, eager to be friendly. He was confident, and had no more need of pettiness. Medraut was very impressed, and held Agravain's great spear while Agravain talked, stroking the worn shaft. I listened, but mainly I watched Agravain. Splendid sun-descended hero, knowing nothing of Morgawse's 'greatest power', of the strength that lies in Darkness. I envied him.

He did not stay for long. After checking the state of the islands and collecting more warriors, Lot sailed off again. The war was going well. The young men were as anxious to return to it as to a mistress they found beautiful.

By May, when I had my fourteenth birthday and left the

Boys' House, the situation in Britain seemed to have taken a definite shape at last. My father stood firmly in our old alliance with Gododdin and Dyfed; Powys and Brycheiniog opposed him uncertainly and Ebrauc squarely – the middle kingdoms of Britain, all anxious to have a Romanized, anti-Saxon king – and finally Gwynedd, the first claimant to the High Kingship, in a shaky alliance with Rheged and Strathclyde–the anti-Irish, anti-Roman party. In the balance was the kingdom of the East Angles, a Saxon kingdom which had sent envoys to both Dyfed and Gwynedd during the winter, and Dumnonia, the most Romanized British kingdom, resolutely neutral. It appeared as though a few pitched battles would decide the war.

But, in June, all plans were swept away together.

The Saxons, as I have said, were restless. Those who had been settled longest raided the most widely, killing, looting, carrying off men, women and children as thralls, but chiefly seizing lands. They needed it. Since the borders were last determined more Saxons had come to Britain: relations, fellow clansmen, fellow tribesmen, new families drawn by the promise of better land, families ousted from old lands by new invaders, and single men drawn by the desire for war and adventure. They all wanted land to farm, to own, to build their squat, smoky villages on. They had much of the best already. The old land of the Cantii, the gentle hills and woodland about the old heart and capital of Britain; the fenlands that had belonged to the ancient tribe of the Icenii, and formed another province; the oldest Saxon kingdoms, Deira and Bernicia, given by the Roman High Kings to their Saxon mercenaries – all these were theirs, and it was not enough. They were officially subject to the British High King, successor of the Roman High Kings, and they had sworn him the same oath the British kings swore, but they never thought of keeping it. They resented the British who kept them back, when Rome itself had fallen before their kind. They needed only a small excuse to start them on a full-scale invasion of Britain.

And, in June, a great force of Saxons landed on the south-west coast, the Saxon Shore, taking the Roman fort of Anderida, allying themselves with the South Saxons and sweeping into eastern Dumnonia, crushing all before them. Their leader was a man named Cerdic, and they said that he was a king such as men would follow to the gates of Hell. They certainly followed him into Dumnonia. And what Cerdic and his tribe began was continued by the other Saxon tribes. First the South Saxons, then the East Saxons, then the tribes of the Angles, the Jutes, the Franks, the Frisians and Swabians all swept into their neighbouring British kingdoms, not just to raid but to settle there.

Despite this, the British did not turn their attention to fighting the Saxons. The civil war had gained momentum now. There were blood feuds involved in it, and honour, and many ancient hatreds. A man will not suddenly drop so old an enmity for a new one. The Saxons had been defeated before and could be defeated again. So the civil war continued, and the Saxons were allowed to seize portions of the eastern marches, while Cerdic began forging a kingdom. The western lands, such as Gwynedd, which did not have a border with the Saxons, were pleased that their British enemies were in difficulties; and everyone agreed that Dumnonia had been too large before, nearly the whole of an old province; and that it was well that the principal sufferer from the invasion was the one neutral kingdom. My father was annoyed at the Saxons and with this Cerdic, but he was confident that, when the war was over, he could see that the Saxons got some of the land they wanted and that Cerdic, after acquiring honour and a kingdom, was conveniently assassinated (it is not safe to allow great leaders to live among the enemy). Then a Britain slightly reduced in size would be ruled from Dun Fionn.

So, after some dislocation, the war might have continued, had the invasion not elicited another claim to the High Kingship.

Uther's war-leader had been the lord Arthur, from the time that Arthur was twenty-one, and Uther could have chosen many others for the position than this one of his many illegitimate sons. Arthur was twenty-five when Cerdic invaded, and had been fighting the Saxons throughout the civil war, supported only by Dumnonia, of all the British kingdoms. All acknowledged that he was a brilliant war-leader, the most innovative and successful since Ambrosius Aurelianus, who was the first High King after the legions left. And yet, no one had expected that Arthur would take sides in the struggle, or, indeed, that he would do anything

48

but fight the Saxons. But when he saw the Saxons invading on a large scale and realized that the Britons were not going to drop the civil war to fight their common enemy (he thought half like a Roman, when it came to such matters) he was apparently 'provoked', the circumstance my mother had warned against.

He rode with the royal warband to Camlann, the royal fortress of Britain, abandoning his lonely and massively outnumbered position against the Saxons. There he met Constantius, king of Dumnonia, and there he declared himself High King, Augustus, and Pendragon of Britain.

This produced more effect on the kings of Britain than Cerdic's invasion had. But Arthur ab Uther did not leave them any length of time for their shrieks of protest at usurping bastards. He raised the largest army he could and attacked first Brycheiniog and then Dyfed. He took the royal fortresses of each land after subduing and dispersing the warbands, each time defeating forces larger than his own. The kings of both countries were forced to swear him the Threefold Oath of allegiance, and to provide supplies for Arthur's forces. This accomplished, he proceeded to conquer Gwynedd.

Docmail king of Gwynedd never swore allegiance to Arthur, but proudly took poison in his own fortress of Caer Segeint, cursing Uther's bastard son, three hours before Arthur arrived there on the tail of Docmail's defeated warband. Docmail's son, Maelgwn, who was only a year or so older than myself, had been designated by Docmail as his successor. He swore fealty to Arthur without protest.

It was not yet July, and no other king had even had a chance to prepare to fight the man who claimed the Pendragonship. Arthur moved very fast. By the time Docmail died, however, the new claimant to the title found all the nations in Britain allied against him, foremost among them Urien of Rheged and, with our allies, my father. The simple reason for this sudden concord was this: it looked as though Arthur could win.

Arthur was not caught unprepared by this new alliance. It was discovered that, before claiming the title, he had made an alliance of his own with a king in Less Britain. Less Britain is in Gaul, a rich and powerful land. It was first begun as a colony by the High King Maximus when Rome still stood, and it increased in size as the legions withdrew, and men made landless by the Saxons went there for lack of a better place. When Arthur made his alliance Less Britain was not defending itself against the Saxons or the Goths or the Huns, and there was a civil struggle brewing between the two sons of the old king over who would succeed. The dispute had not reached the point of war, but this was inevitable once the old king died. Bran, the younger brother, had once fought beside Arthur, and had leapt at the chance of an alliance. He sailed from Gaul with his warband and a large army besides, landed at Caer Uisc in Dumnonia, and joined Arthur in Caer Segeint a few days after it fell. From there he was immediately rushed to Dinas Powys, which Arthur wanted to take before the other kings could unite their forces against him. There was a brief, fierce struggle in Powys, and Arthur was again victorious. He rode into the fortress in triumph, accepted the fealty of Rhydderch Hael of Powys, and dispersed Rhydderch's warband.

The other British kings finally managed to unite. They were by no means one army, and by no means ready to fight in unison, but their strength was very great. There were Gwlgawd king of Gododdin, and the king of Elmet, and Caradoc king of Ebrauc, and March Ship-owner of Strathclyde, and Urien of Rheged, called the Lion of Britain – and my father, Lot of Orcade, the strongest king of Caledon, the sun's descendant.

Arthur had the royal warband of Uther, which had followed him faithfully during the preceding two years of civil war, and he had his allies Constantius, King of Dumnoia, and Bran of Less Britain, together with sworn and enforced neutrality from Gwynedd, Dyfed, Brycheiniog and Powys.

The story of the battle between these two forces is one often told, and more often sung, in the halls of all the kings of Britain, Erin and the Saxon lands. In the Orcades we heard of it two weeks before Lot himself returned with the warband.

It was late in July, a hot day, with the air heavy enough to cut with a knife. The messenger came riding up from the harbour on the east coast at a trot, too hot and tired to go faster. Morgawse received the man in her chambers, gave him the obligatory cup of wine and impatiently asked his news. I sat on the bed, watching.

The messenger drank the wine eagerly, mixing it with

about half water. His clothes were stained and dusty and soaked with sweat. He was one of my father's warband, though not a kinsman of mine, as half the warband was, but a Dalriad attracted to us by my father's fame and generosity. His name was Connall.

He began by telling us what the last messenger had said: Arthur, impatient for battle, had ridden north and west with his men, and the armies of the kings of Britain had drifted from various directions to encounter him. Morgawse nodded impatiently, and the messenger hurried to continue. The armies had met east of the upper part of the river Saefern, by one of its tributaries, the Dubhglas. It is hilly country there, and Arthur had had time to place his forces carefully.

Morgawse frowned. From the condition of the messenger it was already obvious that there had been some kind of defeat, and she began to suspect that it had been a severe one. Arthur was famed as a war-leader.

'It was about three weeks ago,' continued Connall. 'We stood about and they stood about, waiting to fight. It was hot – stinking hot. We stood there in our leather jerkins and mail and sweated and waited for Arthur to make up his mind what to do. We could see the standards of Bran and Constantius down the valley from us, but not Arthur's. We cursed the lazy bastard for making us wait, but he was the great enemy, and we had no choice.

'About mid-morning, someone came up carrying the Red Dragon standard, and the enemy all cheered. We became very angry. It seemed a piece of impudence for him to declare himself High King and use the Pendragon standard, and he without a clan. Lot commanded us to charge, and we were ready enough. We raised the war-cry splendidly and ran at them. All the other kings in the valley – for we were all in the valley, the hills being too steep to fight on properly . . . .'

'Fool!' snapped Morgawse. Connall stared at her uncomfortably. 'What idiocy, to allow himself to be trapped by such a . . . continue.'

Realizing that she had been addressing Lot, not himself, Connall went on. 'At all events, we attacked. They put up a good fight. They are strong men in the shield-wall, those men of Less Britain. But there were more of us, and we are no weaklings ourselves. Your son and your husband, Lady, fought gloriously, side by side, thrusting with their spears

51

almost as one, their shields locked together, laughing. They carried everyone before them. And that Urien of Rheged is a fine war-hound, a lion indeed. The men of Rheged . . .'

'I said, continue!' said Morgawse intensely. Her dark eyes narrowed on the messenger. Connall swallowed, looked away from her, and continued.

'Arthur's forces retreated, slowly. We pressed after them down the valley. It was a hard struggle. About noon, though, they began to falter – at least they seemed to – and we redoubled our attack. They broke. Their shield-wall collapsed inward, and they started running as fast as they could.

'We cheered as loudly as we had the breath for – which wasn't very loud, for we were wearied by such fighting in that miserable heat – and ran after them.' Connall's face lit a little as he recalled the elation of the moment, then shadowed suddenly. 'And then Arthur brought out his horsemen.'

Morgawse groaned, threw away her wine-glass. 'From the hills.'

'From the hills. They came down, so fast . . . on horses. One does not ride horses into battle, not against spearmen. They can be spitted so fast that . . . well, no matter. They rode the horses down, hurling their throwing spears, breaking the shield-wall before they reached it – it was breached along the flanks anyway because of our haste after the rest of the army. And then they were among us on those horses, riding us down, stabbing with spears and striking with swords. We had spent all our throwing spears long before, and we did not know how to fight them. We could not re-form our shield-wall, because they were inside it. Arthur was with them – he had only sent someone else to the others with his standard – and he was laughing and shouting the war-cry of the High Kings. The men of Less Britain and Dumnonia, who had been fleeing from us, picked up the cry and rushed back at us. We couldn't hold them, for the horsemen broke our shield-wall and the horses were trampling us underfoot. We broke. Lot kept shouting at us to hold, to regroup about him, but we couldn't. We couldn't. We went running away. Our shield-wall was broken, and we threw away our shields to run faster. Lot stood, Lady, weeping for rage, and your son with him. Some of us remembered our vows to him, and the mead he gave us in this Hall, and we returned to preserve our honour. We tried to retreat slowly, and some others joined us, or came back – but we couldn't hold, even for a little while. Our shields were hacked to pieces, and we were retreating across the bodies of our comrades who were killed while they fled. Lot said – I was by him – "I will die, then, fighting with my warband."'

Morgawse laughed harshly. 'Die! Would that you had. But Arthur had no desire for your death, Lot of Orcade. He wished no more war with the Orcades.'

Connall nodded miserably. 'Constantius came up with his warband and asked us to surrender. I . . . I . . .'

'And you surrendered!' shouted Morgawse. Her face was flushed with anger. 'You surrendered and swore the Threefold Oath never to fight Arthur or any whom Arthur supported, ever again!'

Connall dropped his head. 'It is so. We had no choice. It was surrender or die. And Arthur was not, after all, to be our king.'

Morgawse moved as in pain and covered her face with her hands.

Connall hesitated, then went on. 'The rest of the warband had fled with the armies of the kings of Britain, and was caught with them. They were driven like cattle up the valley into the Dubhglas. There had been rains, and the river was high. It is swift there, too, and there was no crossing it, not in that press. They surrendered, they all surrendered – Arthur had given orders that no one was to kill the kings – and they swore the Threefold Oath of allegiance to Arthur. The next day he gave himself some Roman title and said there would be a council at Camlann. But he told Lot to take us and go home, or he would burn out our ships and have us killed. But he is keeping your son, Lady, for a hostage. He saw that Lot loved Agravain.

'So we went back to Gododdin at great speed. I went ahead, Lady, to bring you this news . . .'

'Arthur Pendragon,' whispered Morgawse, without moving. Her eyes were fixed on something infinitely far away. I shivered, for I knew that the hate she had borne for Uther had been conferred in double measure on Uther's son. 'Artorius, Insularis Draco, Augustus, Imperator Britanniarum. That is his Roman title, man. Arthur, Pendragon, High King of Britain. Arthur . . .' Morgawse dropped her hands, glared at Connall and beyond him. Her face was twisted with a fury and hatred beyond human comprehension. Hate was a black fire in her eyes, deep as the inner black ocean which I knew had swallowed her. 'Arthur!' she screamed. 'Arthur! Oh, this battle is yours, brother, but the war is not over, I swear, I, Morgawse, rightful and legitimate daughter of a High King! Death, death upon you, death upon your seed, that it will rise against you, for all your new gods and empire and sorceries. Death and eternal agony! Be secure now in your new power and glory, you whom Uther loved, but my curse will find you out and give you to damnation for ever, I swear the oath of my people, and may the earth swallow me, may the sky fall on me, may the sea overwhelm me if you do not die by your son's hand!'

Morgawse had risen and lifted her hands. To my eyes, darkness blazed in a corona about her, and she was more beautiful than ever any mortal woman was, and I was blinded by her darkness and beauty and worshipped her in terror with all my heart. Connall, as terrified as I, cringed, unable to mutter a prayer, staring at her with wide eyes. As the final syllables of the binding Threefold Oath fell on the shocked air, she remembered him, and turned on him. She was angry that he had seen her rage, angry as a gooddess. But she laughed, and her control was back, veiling but not hiding the splendour beneath it.

'So, you believe that I am terrible,' she said. 'You do not know how terrible, man, Connall of the Dalriada. Shall I show you?'

He collapsed away from her, cringed towards the door. Morgawse's hands rose and she wove a spell. My eyes saw it as the black strength came together like threads on a loom, into a strange pattern.

'My power makes no great show of warriors, as Lot's does, or Arthur's,' she whispered. 'It is subtle, working in the dark, in the places beyond your sight, hidden in fear in your own mind. No man is free from me. No man, not even Arthur. Certainly not you, Dalriad ... shall I show you, Connall?'

He shook his head, licking his lips. His back was flat against the door, his fingers spread against it. The leather bolt was not fastened, but he was as incapable of opening it as if it had been locked with chains of steel. Morgawse approached him and, beside her, he seemed as pale and unreal as a ghost.

'Do not, *Mor Ríga*, Great Queen,' he muttered.

'You do not wish to know your Queen's power?'

He shook his head, shuddering.

Morgawse stepped back, relaxed her hands. The darkness that had nestled there dissipated into the air. The coldness of the room suddenly vanished. I became aware that it was still July.

'Mention nothing of what I have said to anyone,' said Morgawse, 'and you never will see that power. Leave here.'

Connall fumbled, found the door-bolt, and fled. Just as he left the room, his eyes touched me and widened only a little.

As the door closed and Morgawse sank once more on to the bed and began to laugh, I realized that I, too, was gaining a reputation for witchcraft.

Four

The army came home, each king returning to his own island, and Lot and the warband returned to Dun Fionn.

We rode down to the port when they arrived, and found them still at work beaching the war-curraghs, dragging the long round ships up on to the beach and securing them. We had brought horses and, when he had finished with the ships, Lot rode back with us and the warband to the fortress.

He was very tired, that was plain. His bright energy was dimmed, and his hair had a few early strands of grey to dull its brightness. His eyes were bloodshot and had dark circles beneath them, and lines of bitterness curled about his mouth. He was very quiet.

I was quiet too, riding behind and watching my father. It seemed incredible, unreal, that he had been defeated. It seemed wholly unbelievable that Agravain was a hostage. I wondered how it was for him, all alone in the court of Arthur. Hostages are never badly treated – my father had a hostage from each of his subject kings, and they all fought in the warband and had many of the rights of the other warriors – but the mere fact of being a hostage would be crushing to Agravain. I could see him, striking out at the foreigners who ringed him in and mocked him for his father and his defeat; see him struggling desperately to improve his poor British, miserable, alone in a strange land . . .

I was no compensation for the loss of Agravain, that too was plain. Lot looked at me, at Morgawse, back to his own hands again and again, and always his mouth curled in pain. I wanted, for a while, to help: to try again as I had tried before to be what Lot wanted me to be. But I argued myself out of it, along with my pity for Agravain. I was my mother's son. Though I had left the Boys' House now, I had not taken up arms, to become a warrior and sleep in the Hall with the men. Instead, I stayed in one of the guest houses, or, if they were full, in the house of Orlamh, my father's druid and chief bard. I had little in common with my own clan, a royal clan of warriors, and I was certainly no descendant of Light. And Lot and Agravain had wronged me.

Morgawse, too, was silent, but her silence was that of scorn. She was furious with Lot for being defeated, and she showed him her contempt without words, showed him what she thought of his strength and valour and virility. I watched Lot's hands tighten and loosen on his horse's reins as he stared at her stiff back.

The warband was in poor shape. There were not too many lost or maimed, for their fighting had been largely successful, until they met Arthur. But they had lost all their plunder and fine things to Arthur's men, and returned to Gododdin by forced marches with inadequate supplies. It seemed that the new Pendragon was hungry for wealth and provisions. He would need them to support a large warband, and he would certainly need a large warband if he wished to protect Britain against the Saxons. But now we in the Orcades would pay for Arthur's war, and rely on the next harvest alone for our lives.

When we reached Dun Fionn, we stabled the horses in silence, and in silence the men went to rest. There was a gloomy feast that night, in which the warriors brooded over their mead and Lot sat grim as death at the high table, glaring off to the door that led from the Hall to Morgawse's room. Orlamh, my father's chief bard, sang uncertainly, the songs falling flat on the stale air.

The men were drinking very heavily. I knew, for I was pouring the mead. My father, too, drank heavily. With the drink glinting in his eyes he looked about the hall. He saw me, and his eyes fastened on me. He slammed his goblet down.

'Gwalchmai!' It was the first time he had addressed me directly since his return, and it was a rare occurrence at any time.

I set down the jug of mead. 'Yes, Father?'

'Yes, Father,' Lot repeated bitterly. 'Agravain ... well, Agravain is a hostage. You know that?'

'Yes, Father.'

'You would. You know how to read, write and speak Latin, to play the harp, sing like a bird, make songs, ride horses – damn horses! – and spear men from them, and you know other things. What other things?'

He had never mentioned even the Latin before. I shifted my weight uneasily. All the warriors were watching me, measuring me.

'Nothing else, Father.'

Lot stared at me. The warriors stared at me. I saw that my reputation had indeed reached them. I stared back, determined not to back down.

'You certainly are no warrior,' my father said finally. 'Oh well. Take that harp from Orlamh and play something, something pleasant. I'm tired of his weary plunking.'

Orlamh sighed and gave me the harp. I took it, sat down, and stared at the strings. I was angry, I realized, but not filled with hatred. I felt sorry for Lot. I became more angry, but I still felt sorry for him.

What could I sing? Something to take him away from Dun Fionn and his defeat.

I touched the strings carefully, drew the melody out as gently as if it were a web of glass, and sang the lament of Deirdre on leaving Caledon to go to Erin and her death.

> 'Beloved the land, this eastern land,
> Alba rich in wonders,
> And to depart I had never planned,
> Did I not leave with Noíse.
>
> I have loved Dun Fidhga, loved Dun Finn,
> Beloved is the stronghold above them;
> Inis Draighen, its seas within,
> Dún Suibhne: I loved them.'

The Hall was very still, and the warriors sat quietly, not touching the mead horns by their hands. Was it possible, I wondered in surprise, that I was doing it? Well, the song was very famous and familiar. I sang on, trying to catch the bright irregular rhythms and complex yearning.

> 'Cuan's wood, where Ainnle would go –
> Alas! the time was short,
> Brief the time, as we both knew
> Spent on the shores of Alba . . .
>
> Glen Etive, where first I raised my home,
> Lovely the wood is there,
> The fold for the rays of sun when they roam
> At the dawn of day, Glen Etive.'

And so through the verses. The final stanza came addressed to the beach Deirdre embarked from:

> 'And now beloved is Draighen's beach,
> Beloved now the waves, the sand –
> Never would I go from the east
> Did I not go holding Noíse's hand.'

I swept the notes upward and brought them down slowly to silence, making them weep, thinking of Deirdre, a beautiful woman five hundred years dead, stepping into the boat and going to her doom.

When I finished, the hall was very silent, but with a different kind of silence. Lot looked at me strangely for a moment – then laughed. He was pleased.

I sat and stared at the harp and did not believe it.

'That was good,' said Lot. 'By the sun! Maybe you'll become something after all. Play something else.'

'I . . . I . . .' I said, 'I'm tired. Please. I want to rest.'

His smile vanished again, but he nodded. 'Go and rest, then.'

I set the harp down and left. His eyes followed me, puzzled, all the way out of the Hall.

I did not rest. I lay on my pallet and turned about, and stared at a patch of moonlight crawling across the floor all night. I had pleased my father. To be a bard was a very honourable trade, lower only than that of a king, if one was good enough. I had pleased my father more than Orlamh, who was good. I watched the moonlight and thought: 'I have come too far down the path of Darkness to forsake it.'

And I stared too at the cold black place within me, and wept, within myself, alone in the darkness.

I found the next morning that Lot and Morgawse had not slept that night either. My father had become drunk and made his way to my mother's room to claim his rights. She had tried to throw him out, but he had decided that he was her husband and she must be obedient. For the next few days she wore a high-necked gown to hide the bruises. Lot, though, was the one who looked sick and worn, while Morgawse smiled quietly with complacent satisfaction. I suddenly realized that, if my father used her beauty for his pleasure, she fed upon him like a shadow upon a strong light, and drained his power slowly away. I pushed the thought aside as soon as it occurred to me, for it made me uncomfortable.

August wore away slowly, and September after it. I did all that I had done before – still practised with my weapons, had lessons with Morgawse, went out riding and playing with Medraut – but there was a difference now. Lot ordered that everyone should learn some of the new ways of fighting from horseback, which Arthur had used against the spearmen, and suddenly I was first instead of last, not only among those my age, but even among most of the older men. I was fourteen, beginning to grow, and I knew all the tricks which no one had bothered to study: how to move about on horseback, how to take a spearman on the ground without being thrown from the horse, and make the horse rear and back when the place was too narrow or the press too great to manage – things which called for agility and speed instead of strength and order, and so had been neglected in the usual methods of fighting. The tricks I had practised on my own.

We received news, too, from my father's spies in Britain. My father was hoping that Arthur would be killed in battle, though he was unwilling to arrange such an event himself, for the sake of Agravain and for his oath. But there was no such good fortune. Arthur took tribute from every king in Britain, and even from the Church they have there. This last had cost Arthur almost as much as it gained him. All of Britain – except the Saxon kingdoms – held the faith of this Church, and had done so ever since the last Roman High Kings had decreed that they should, and given the Church many privileges. The Church was very rich, holding much land and goods given it by its followers, and being free from tax or tribute because of the privileges it had been granted. It had been expected that Arthur would honour the rights and privileges of the Church; indeed, it had been expected that he would make generous donations to it. He had been raised in a monastery in the west of Britain, living, with other orphans and bastards, on the charity of the Church; he was supposed to be devout, and to call upon God before his battles. The Church had been eager to recognize him as Pendragon, despite his dubious title to power. When, instead of showering it with gifts, he had demanded supplies, the outrage of the bishops and abbots resounded as far as Dun Fionn.

I did not understand the problem. Though Britain had long been Christian, and Erin had become so, Caledon and the Orcades knew of that faith only by hearsay. I asked my mother about it.

'It is all stupidity and pretence,' she told me sharply. 'The Church claims that there is one god who rules all the world, and that it alone can bring men to this god. It pretends that the nature of this god is all justice and love, yet itself cares nothing for either. But it is rich, and it has a strong hold on men's minds. Arthur,' smiling, 'Arthur will have to beware of it.'

'Will you and Father make an alliance with its leaders?' I asked.

But she frowned. 'No. They will not ally themselves with pagans or heretics – and they say I am a heretic, for that is a word they use freely for all who abandon their teachings, whether they ever believed those teachings or not. Indeed, that was the one thing that made me glad when I left Britain; that I should hear no more of the pious gruntings of priests! No, they would appear ridiculous should they ally themselves with us against a Christian High King. They will have to obey Arthur, since he has power and is willing to use it. But they will look for some other king to support in a rebellion.'

And she and Lot did not send messengers to any of the bishops, even after Arthur had resorted to threats to get the supplies from the Church. But my father listened to all the news and hoped. When Arthur gave some of his new wealth to Bran of Less Britain and sent him home, Lot stayed up all night dictating messages. He also came every day to see how the men were doing at the new methods of fighting, and himself practised them until he was dripping with sweat. He also began scheming for control over the northern Hebrides, renewing an old enmity with Aengus mac Erc of Dalriada. But something of the brightness had gone from these endeavours. My father was not going to control Britain by means of any puppet kings. Arthur controlled Britain.

My mother also laid plans. In September, in the dark of the moon, we killed a black lamb at midnight. I held its head while she cut it open with a stone knife, examining the entrails while it still struggled and bled over us. She was angry with what she saw, but did not explain it to me. Eventually, the next day, I asked her why she could not simply destroy Arthur, as she had destroyed his father.

61

'It is not so simple,' she told me. 'There is some Christian counter-spell he has made against me, and I do not understand the nature of it. Did you not see, in the lamb last night, how the entrails were woven into knots?'

I had not wanted to look. These things still sickened me.

'Do not mind that, though,' she said, beginning to smile. 'I have cursed him, and the curse lives, and has lived. In the end the Darkness will take him, too.'

I watched that Darkness in her eyes as she gloated and was awed by it. I knew that she was planning some other action, though, and that she had killed the lamb to see how it might turn out. She was filled with tension, waiting. But when I asked, she would not tell me what she waited for, only smiling a soft, secret smile.

As October wore slowly away and the great sea-fogs blanketed the islands I began to guess when she would act, if not what she meant to do. At the end of October there is a night called Samhain. It is a festival, one of four great festivals – the others are Midsummer, Lammas and Beltane – which are sacred to the powers of the earth and sky. Samhain is the night when the gates between the worlds lie open. On that night, the dead can come creeping back to the world they left, and places are laid for them at table among the living. Other, yet darker things come across the worlds on Samhain, and they are not usually spoken of, and still other things can be summoned then, by wish or by rite, and these are mentioned least of all. As the end of October approached, I knew what my mother was waiting for.

On the day of Samhain I went to her room for the usual lesson. But most of the day we did nothing but read. Morgawse had bought a Roman poem called the *Aeneid* from a travelling merchant for the value of ten cows in gold. She had seventeen books, which were worth a frightening amount, and I had read all of them. I was enjoying the *Aeneid* more than any of the others, though it was full of strange names and I understood very little of it. I regretted that we had only the first six books, the first half of the poem, and that we had nearly finished these.

> '. . . . *sic orsa loqui vates: "sate sanguine divum,*
> *Tros Anchisiade, facilis descensus Averni:*
> *Noctes atque dies patet atri ianua Ditis;*

> *sed revocare gradum superasque evadere ad auras,*
> *hoc opus, hic labor est.'''*

I smoothed the page and began translating again: 'Thus the . . . prophet?'

'Or poet,' Morgawse murmured. 'Like an ollamh.'

'Thus the prophet began to speak: "You who are sprung from the blood of gods, Trojan, son of Anchises, easy is the descent of Avernus: night and day the gate of black Dis is open; but to recall your step and to come out to the upper air, this is toil, this labour . . ."' I stopped, swallowing suddenly. 'Avernus. That is Yffern, isn't it? The Dark Otherworld?'

She nodded, her eyes cold and amused. 'Does that frighten you, my hawk?'

I put my hand over the page, shaking my head, but the catch was still in my throat. Easy is the descent, but to recall your steps . . . She was still looking at me.

'Very well, enough for today,' she said. 'And what do you think of Aeneas now, my hawk?'

'He still . . . he relies upon his mother, the goddess, for everything. I don't really like him. Not as much as CuChulainn, or Connall Cearnach, or Noíse Mac Usliu. And yet . . .'

'Och, it is an ill thing to rely upon one's mother, then?' she said, laughing, and I looked at her and felt my face grow hot.

'She was less of a goddess than you,' I said.

'Prettily said! Aeneas is weak, and so is his mother Venus. And yet, the Romans consider this their greatest poem. They were not artists. They could not understand the depths of a thing, the passions of the soul. They built a strong empire on the blood of men, and made good roads. Other than that . . . Arthur is half a Roman.'

'He is? But I thought all the Romans left a long time ago.'

'The legions left. "Defend yourselves," Theodosius told the provinces of the Britains, "for we cannot defend you any longer." But they left their memory, men willing to try to set up a fallen empire. In the south, many still think like Romans. Arthur does. That is why he leads the Britons against the Saxons: he wishes to preserve the last stronghold of the empire against the barbarians, one nation defending itself against another. He does not see that Britain is no more one nation than the Saxons are. His is a peculiar way of viewing things, and has many weaknesses. I know them. I have seen and known Arthur.'

She fell silent, thinking, smiling.

'Come here tonight,' she said in a low voice after a long time. 'I have planned that tonight you will have your initiation into real Power. It is a good night for it. I will have you accepted by the Darkness, my son, and you will see why I am strong. After tonight, you will have Power as I do.'

I heard, nodded, bowed and left the room without saying anything. I saddled my horse and went for a long ride out by the sea. I could not stay in Dun Fionn. But with each step my horse made I became more afraid, anticipating something I did not know. I had seen deeply into the Darkness by then, and it frightened me. I desired to be like my mother, to have Power and escape from the fear, but I found the Power still more fearful. I did not know what I wanted, now, but I would go that night.

I realized that the path was familiar, and found that I was going to Llyn Gwalch. Well, why not?

I reached the place where the stream fell over the cliff's edge, combing the gravel with clear fingers. There was a light mist that day, which turned all the low hills so soft a shade of green that it seemed they would dissolve into the gentle sky. The sea beat-beat at the cliff, a sound as constant as my heart. It seemed to me that I had never heard it before.

I dismounted and hobbled my horse, then climbed carefully down the path.

When I reached the beach with its little pond, everything seemed smaller than I remembered it, and I realized how long it had been, and how much I must have grown. But it was still beautiful. My old dreams hung about it yet, glowing faintly in my mind with colours brighter than those of earth. The pond was infinitely deep, still and clear, dark in shade because of the multi-hued gravel lying rounded in its bottom. The sea clutched at the beach, hissed on the stones, and sighed out. Its smell was salt and strong, wild, infinite and sad. A seagull flew over my head, flapping and gliding. It wailed, once, and some more sea-birds hidden in the mist cried back.

I went over to the pool and knelt by it, drank from it, then studied my reflection. A boy, looking fourteen or older, stared back. Thick black hair, held back with a bit of worn leather. Smooth skin still dark from the summer, a face slightly resembling Morgawse's in the shape of the bones. A thoughtful face whose dark eyes met mine openly, trying to look into the confused mind that lurked behind them. It was so very dark in there.

Who is this Gwalchmai? I wondered. A name, but what beyond that? Something beyond my understanding.

I leant back on my heels and looked up at the grey sky. I remembered those dreams I had had of myself as a great warrior, and the dreams that had come at night, the sword burning with light, tattered shreds of glowing colour, and, above them all, the song rising from nowhere. Like the sound of a harp played elsewhere on an empty day, but sweet enough for a man to leave his life behind to hear it better. I remembered playing with boats in that very place, sending them out, so far out, into the open sea, dreaming of the Land of the Ever Young. Lugh's Hall, with its walls woven of gold and white bronze and its roof thatched with the wing-feathers of birds. The sea pounded and sighed on the shore, and the birds keened. I wondered what had happened, and where the Darkness had begun. I felt like a man looking back on his childhood, and I wondered if one could truly be a man at fourteen, and what it was that I had lost. I sat and listened to the gulls, drawing my cloak around me. Tonight it would end. Tonight, truly, it would end.

The night was one of wind and broken moonlight which poured raggedly through the clouds driven over the moon, only to be whipped away again. Crossing the yard from the hall, where I slept most of the time now, to the room of Morgawse the Queen, I looked up at the moon's worn face and thought of the old prayers to it. Gem of the night, breast-jewel of heaven . . . How many, I wondered, had looked up at her face through the years? Warriors planning raids by her light, lovers laughing to her, druids and magicians praying to her, poets making songs to her, all these she must have seen countless times. But surely, it was all chance whether she shone or no, and I could expect no help from her. And perhaps, when I returned this way, I would no longer want any.

The very air seemed to be vibrating when I reached my mother's room, as if with the aftermath of a scream. The door-bolt shivered in my hand like a living thing. There was power in the air, so much dark power that it was hard to breathe.

My mother had already prepared the room. The floor had been laid bare, and the wall-hanging raised so that no light could enter. She had dug a trench across the middle of the floor, and made designs about it with white barley and water, and set candles around it. She stood now in the middle of the room in a gown of a red so dark that it appeared almost black, her bare arms pale and strong and cold-looking in the eerie light. Her hair fell about her, a river of gleaming darkness down to her waist; she was barefoot and ungirded, since it was a time to loosen knots and not to bind them. She was drawing a design in the air about the final candle.

I felt a weakness rise in me, gripping my stomach with icy hands, unstringing my knees. Darkness lay in the air, thick, smothering. I wanted to cry out, beat at it with my hands, run, not looking back to what might follow from the corners of my mind.

I closed the door softly and stood silent, waiting until Morgawse was finished.

She set the final candle down and straightened. She was very tall, and the Darkness hung about her like a cloak, so that all the candle flames bent towards her like seaweed towards a whirlpool. She seemed more than ever to be not of the Earth, but a queen in some other realm. Terrified, I loved her. She smiled when she saw me, a smile blurred by the flickering of the flames and by the darkness she wore around her, but her smile still, secret and triumphant.

'Good,' she said. Her voice seemed to come from a deep void, colder than January ice. 'Go over there. Stand, be still, wait, and watch what I do.'

I obeyed her.

She took a jug of something red, – wine or blood, I was not sure which. If it was not blood, there would be blood before the night was ended. She poured it over the design she had already traced, muttering strange words which I had heard separately before. Then she broke the jug and put half of it at each end of the trench. She turned to me again.

'Could you follow that?'

I nodded, not trusting my voice.

She smiled again and turned to one of the wall-hangings.

Just then, the door opened.

I whirled in guilt and terror, expecting Lot to burst in with angry demands or with armed men. I was ready to fight him, and my hand was at the dagger in my belt.

In the doorway stood Medraut.

'Close the door,' Morgawse ordered calmly. 'Stand there, opposite Gwalchmai.'

'What . . .?' I asked. How could Medraut have stumbled on to this? I had been careful to tell him nothing. 'Medraut, leave. Now. This is not for you.'

He looked at me in surprise, and then his wide innocent eyes fixed themselves on the pattern again with a fierce eagerness. 'But Mother said I should come.'

I suddenly remembered how Medraut had stopped speaking about magic, about unexplained absences of his from training, about a thousand other little things I had never accounted for before, and the realization hit me so that I cried out, 'No!'

He stared at me. 'What do you mean? Morgawse has been teaching me Latin and witchcraft too. We can all learn together now. Oh, I know that you don't want me to, but it will be much better this way, you can't grudge me the Power that much.'

'No!' I repeated. 'You cannot. You will destroy yourself, Medraut. The Darkness will crawl inside your mind and devour your soul until it has eaten all that is you and leaves only a shell. Go, while you can!'

He flushed. Morgawse stood, the rope for the hangings in one hand, watching. Her eyes were on me.

'Why?' asked my brother, growing angry. 'You never gave a true reason. If this is so wrong, why are you here too? It is just that you don't want me to learn. You want to keep me a little boy forever, while you become wise and powerful.'

'Medraut, that is false. It is wrong, but I am all wrong, and you are not, so you must not. Please, for your own sake.'

'So this is wrong, and Mother is wrong, too? That is impossible. Mother is . . . ' His eyes sought and found her, and his anger melted into adoration.

'Medraut, get out of here,' I said again, desperately, though he was not listening now. 'Tonight we will do a very strong and dreadful magic.'

'I came for it,' he said. 'I've been learning too, Gwalch-

67

mai.' And then he spoke in the language of sorcery. The ancient syllables spurted from his mouth like the yammering of some strange animal, incongruous, hideous beyond belief. I could not bear to listen and clapped my hands over my ears, staring at him, feeling the tears start to my eyes.

'It is enough,' said Morgawse. 'Medraut will stay.'

I looked at her, ready to cry out in protest, but could not speak. The room became cold, achingly cold and dark. The candle-flames swam before my eyes, as if from miles away. I sobbed for breath in the black tide that drowned me.

Morgawse jerked back the wall-hanging.

One of my father's warriors lay there, bound hand and foot. I had known there would be blood. The man's eyes above the gag were wild with fear, running about the room without fixing on anything. I recognized Connall of Dalriada.

'Oh,' I said. There was a sick taste in my mouth.

'He went to Lot and told him of my oath,' said Morgawse. 'I fulfil a promise. We will do to him as we did to the lamb last month, but a man is better for these things.' She smiled again, looking at Connall. 'Pull him to the centre.'

Medraut stepped forward. I stood, staring, sick. Connall's eyes met mine. His held the knowledge of horrible death.

I looked at Medraut and thought of what he had said: 'So this is wrong, and Mother is wrong . . .'

Lastly, I looked at Morgawse, and for the first time saw her without illusion: a power wrapped in human flesh, long ago consuming the mind that had invoked it. A dark power, a Queen of Darkness. She had summoned it as a servant for her hate, had welcomed its control when she controlled it, and every day became more it and less herself. A power that drank life and hope and love like wine. Ancient beyond words, evil beyond thought, hideous despite its beauty, the creature stood there and gazed on me with a black, insatiable hunger.

I screamed and my hand rose to ward it off, and I saw that I held my dagger.

Her face changed, became as a women's again, turning to fury. She lifted her arms, and power surrounded her leaping up like fire.

'Gwalchmai!' Medraut was shouting. 'What are you doing?'

'Get out,' I said, finding my voice steady. 'This has not been Morgawse, daughter of Uther for years. You must get out, while there is still time. If you love me, if you love your life, get out of here!'

He looked at me, then at the Queen of Darkness. His face twisted desperately – and then he stepped towards Morgawse, stepped again, past me, to stand beside her. 'You are mad,' he said. 'Mother is perfect. It is Father who is wrong. Put down that knife and come and help us.'

I began to weep. 'She will sacrifice Conall.'

He looked uncomfortable for a moment, but she touched his shoulder and the unease faded from his face. 'She is perfect. He insulted her. He deserves to die.'

'She will kill Father one day.'

Medraut actually laughed. 'Good! Maybe then . . . I will be the successor to the kingship! Mother has promised me. And, after all, Arthur is a bastard too.'

I stared at him where he stood under her upraised hand, his eyes again wild with misery, and with a pain I had only suspected. I had been wrong about him. I should have realized that his ambition was not just to be a fine warrior, but rather to be something beyond his reach. It was too late to help, even if I could have. Too late.

I looked again at the creature who had once been Morgawse, daughter of Uther, and knew that my knife could not harm her. I was only alive because she hoped that I would come. And I could come, could drown in the black tide, forgetting confusion and loneliness and guilt and, yes, gain a kind of immortality. Easy is the descent of Avernus, I thought.

I lowered my hand slowly. Medraut smiled with joy, and my mother smiled again also, at me.

And then I threw the dagger straight into Connall's throat, saw the thanks in his dying eyes, and dragged open the door, fleeing the Darkness that rose up behind me.

I heard Medraut run to the door after me, his shout ringing across the yard; 'Traitor! Traitor, traitor, traitor . . .' There was almost a sob in it.

Then I was in the stables and my horse stood waiting in his stall, ready for me to mount and go flying away from Dun Fionn and from the Darkness which ran behind me, thick with the fury of its Queen and heavy with her desire for my death; and I was mounting and riding off through the moon-light and cloud-shadows, riding away from Dun Fionn, riding . . .

My horse's hooves kicked up stones on the path, and the fortress was limned for a moment against the wracked sky, and then I rounded a hillside and it was gone . . .

Gone.

Five

There was sand and gravel under me, and somewhere very near the sea was pounding.

I lifted my head and looked out over the western sea which beat-hissed on the narrow beach and flooded up towards the deep pool of fresh water by the cliff's base. Llyn Gwalch.

The memory of the night before returned to me, and I lay still for a while and considered it. I felt tired, too tired to feel anything, and the memory was heavy and hard. After a while, though, I realized that I was very thirsty, so I crawled up to the pond and drank from it. The water was very cold, clear and fresh, delicious. I splashed it over my head when I had quenched my thirst, then went over and sat down against the cliff to look out at the sea.

I thought about the wild ride, down along the cliff-path, with the demon of Darkness chasing me, catching at the edges of my mind. I remembered reaching Llyn Gwalch, dismounting and sending my horse on with a slap, then scrambling down the cliff to lie, exhausted, in my only refuge. And apparently it was indeed a refuge, for I was still alive and sane. I wondered how long it would last, then wondered again because it did not seem to matter much. I felt weak and empty but not sick. In fact, I felt better than I had for a long, long time. I was free. Even if I lost my life, I was free.

The sun had risen behind the cliff, and its rays crept closer across the ocean. I smiled at the light and spoke an old poem of greeting to it:

> 'Welcome to you, seasons' sun,
> Travelling the skies from afar
> Winged with glad strides the heights you run
> Joyful mother of evening stars.
>
> With night you sink on the perilous sea
> But arise from the waves' bower
> Leaping from harm and darkness free
> As a young queen in flower.'

And in a moment of dizzy triumph I thought, I have followed

the sun, the young queen. I have recalled my step from Avernus. And then, close behind the triumph came the pain. My mother was trying to kill me. As vividly as if I relived it I saw her fury when I threw the knife at Connall – poor Connall! – and saw the Darkness leaping from the shadows behind her.

I shuddered. I could not return to Dun Fionn. I pressed my hands together until it hurt, trying not to realize what that meant. I would never ride into those light walls again, nor listen to old Orlamh's drily courteous explanations of metre and genealogies, or Diuran's coarse jokes. In one blow I had separated myself from my kinsmen and home for ever. Even if somehow, in some later time, I returned, I would never regain what I had just lost. I had lost the world of warriors before, and now had lost the other world I had desired, and if I were free, it was with the freedom of the outcast; clanless, nameless, placeless. I could not return to Don Fionn – and for that matter, why ever was I safe at Llyn Gwalch?

Perhaps, I thought, distracted from the pain by surprise, perhaps there is some force here that thwarts the Queen.

I remembered Arthur.

Certainly my mother would have destroyed him long before, if she had been able to. She hated him enough. But she was unable to, because of his new gods and his counter-spell that she didn't understand.

I reminded myself sternly that Arthur had defeated my father, and that he kept my brother as his hostage. He ought to be my sworn enemy. And I reminded myself of the constant wars which racked Britain, and the invasions. But the sternness was no use. I began to think of all the places which I had heard of: Camlann with its triple banks, new heart of Britain; Caer Ebrauc, a great city, massively walled, Sorviodunum, Caer Gwent, Caer Legion, splendid fortresses. Monasteries filled with books and learning, great roads from one end of the island to the other, triumphal arches tall as trees, mosaics in the courtyards of rich villas, fountains and statues, theatres and arenas, things I had read of but never seen. Britain, the last remnant of the Empire of the Romans – except for the east; but Constantinople was further away than the Otherworld and more unreachable. Britain, surrounded by men who desired her, unconquered in the midst of defeat. There, in that fabulous land, the High King Arthur

Augustus had raised the dragon standard, and he was protected by a magic Morgawse could not overcome. And I remembered that, although by his acts I might be counted his enemy, by blood he was my uncle, and that might win me a place. I was no warrior to join his warband, but there might be something I could do if I joined him.

Yes. I would try to journey to Camlann, or to the High King Arthur where he was, and I would offer him my service.

This decided, I stared out to sea again and wondered how to go about it.

For some reason, Llyn Gwalch was safe, if only for a little while. But Morgawse had raised the Darkness against me, and I knew that if I climbed back up the cliff I would be destroyed long before I could reach the port in the east of the island. And even if I did reach the port, what would I do for a boat? If I stole a small boat, how could I, a fairly inexperienced sailor, hope to travel the treacherous northern waters to Pictland with the winter coming on? And I had nothing to pay for passage on a larger vessel.

For a moment I thought of going to my father with the story, but dismissed the idea at once. Morgawse would not possibly allow me to tell my father that she had accomplished the death of one of his warriors. I wondered what she would tell him as it was. That I had killed Connall? Probably not. That would require too much explaining. No, she would pretend to know nothing of either Connall's disappearance or mine, and find some way to dispose of Connall's body. My horse would return to the stable riderless, or perhaps be found wandering about the cliff, and my clan would conclude that I had gone mad, and ridden along the cliffs on Samhain. And Medraut – he might weep. I felt sick again. Poor Medraut. If only I could have . . . or have understood. But it was too late. Perhaps it had been too late for a long time. It was best that he thought me dead. If he knew that I was alive, he would hate me.

I stared at the sea and pondered all these things, twisting them about in my mind and running off on tangents. But the answer – or rather, the absence of an answer – remained the same. I was trapped at Llyn Gwalch.

By noon I felt quite hungry, though stronger than I had been when I woke. I looked hopefully in the pool for fish and found none. There were some oysters clinging to the rocks along the cliff-foot, though, and plenty of sea-birds nesting in the face of the cliff, if it came to that. I stripped and swam out, then along the foot of the cliff, collecting oysters in my tunic. I had a good amount when I felt a sudden chill, colder than the water. I looked up. The sun shone on the cliff-face, hazed by a light mist. Half-way down the cliff lay a patch of shadow. I looked upwards, then looked at the shadow again, and realized that there was nothing on the cliff to cast it. Hurriedly, I turned and swam back to the beach, and the cold became merely the usual cold of the north sea in November. So. The creature Morgawse had summoned was waiting for me.

I laid my tunic in the sun, wrapped myself in my cloak, shivering, and ate the oysters. They tasted very good, but I knew that they would not support me for ever. I could not stay at Llyn Gwalch: I could not leave it.

Well, sooner or later I must leave, but I would rest first. I looked up at the sun. It was already dropping towards the horizon, and the mist was thickening imperceptibly. Winter was coming on, and the days were shortening. I dropped my eyes to the beach, the clear stream running out into the ocean over the wave-smoothed stones, the seaweed and driftwood. I smiled, and decided to make a toy boat.

I had not forgotten how. The curragh I made from driftwood and seaweed floated perfectly on the pond. It was a pity I couldn't build one large enough to hold me, but the thing was beautiful enough as it was. I watched it float down the stream, anxious whether it would overturn in the surf. It jerked when it reached the waves, rolled, then caught by the current, began to glide out to sea. I watched it drift away and thought again of the Isles of the Blessed. Suddenly I wondered what they were. The forces of Darkness were real and powerful enough. What about those of Light? Arthur's magic was strong enough to baffle Morgawse: if he could claim the Light's protection, perhaps I could as well.

I had been in a great darkness, near to drowning in it, and the thought of a Light opposed to it was sweet. So, as I watched the curragh bobbing on the waves, I spoke silently within my heart: 'Light, whatever your name is . . . I have broken with the Darkness and it seeks my life. But I would follow you, as a warrior does his lord. I swear the oath of my people, I will serve you before any other for as long as I live. Protect me, as a lord does his warrior, and bring me to Britain. Or let my kinsman, Lugh of the Long Hand, if he exists and is indeed my kinsman, help me from the Islands to which my boat travels I beg you, help.'

The curragh slipped on over the waves as though it bore a message. I watched it until it vanished from sight.

The sun sank slowly down the west, bursting free of the mist at its setting, and splashing red-gold on the face of the sea. There were heavy clouds beneath it, looking like an island. There was one of the great winter fogs coming. It would arrive before morning, and would be cold. I watched until the sun was quite gone, and, after that, watched the twilight deepening its shade from the first soft green into blue, while the sea became first silver, then grey, then silver and black as the moon rose over the cliff, cloaked with pale gold in the mist. I sat drenched with its light and half drunk with it and the earth's beauty. I sang songs to it, and the rise and fall of the sea seemed to answer me. When I lay down at the cliff's base, the driest part of the beach, I had scarcely wrapped my cloak about me when I fell asleep.

I woke around midnight, opened my eyes to stare, rigid with terror, into the blank darkness. Some dream which had swept black wings through my brain departed, leaving a foul memory. There had been a sound. The demon! It had broken into my refuge and must be creeping upon me; best to whimper and dig into the earth.

I sat up and flung back my cloak. I reached for my dagger, remembered that I had left it in Connall's throat. You must go out as a warrior, I told myself.

But there was no shadow on the beach, nor any hint of the Darkness. The moonlight was dim with mist, but I could see clearly enough that I was alone on Llyn Gwalch. There was only a boat, resting, prow first, on the beach.

It was a strange boat, a lovely one. It had a high prow and stern, unlike a curragh, though otherwise it resembled one. But it had neither oars nor mast nor rudder, and the colour was like no wood or hide I had ever seen, but grey-white in the luminous mist. It was no derelict either, I saw. Cushions and coverings were heaped in it. And yet no one sat in it. The prow lay on the stones, and the waves, grown very quiet, lapped and sighed out into the mist. There was no other sound.

I stood slowly, staring. No boat should have landed so at Llyn Gwalch. The current of the stream, combined with an undertow which was often fierce, pushed any floating things on to the rocks at the side. I took a few steps towards the boat. It rested there, half on land, half on water, like a pale flower. I noticed now that it was not a trick of the moonlight in the mist, that the boat really was shimmering softly in the dark. I sensed the magic woven into its fabric, an awareness of it stirring my hair like a faint breeze, and I stopped and watched it.

And yet . . .

It did not feel like a dark magic. It was light and swift and clean, like a seagull swooping over the waves. And though things could be other than they seemed, I had spoken words that afternoon as I watched my curragh sail off, and the silence in my heart had listened.

And even if this were a trick, a trap made by the demon lurking along the cliff, what would it mean except that I would die now instead of later? I decided, and walked forward to place my hand on the boat's prow. It was soft, warm, like a living thing, a trained hawk which rustles its feathers in the eagerness to fly. I took my shoes off, threw them into the boat, and pushed it off the stones, clambering in when it was a few feet from the beach.

While the boat hung there, bobbing in the calm sea, and I searched for an oar, I sensed a stirring above and looked up. The shadow lay on the cliff-top again, like the shadow of a cloud now. My fists clenched, and again I longed for my dagger. Then I started, for the boat began to stir of itself, very slowly, turning from Llyn Gwalch till its prow faced westwards. It began to move forward over the waves which shivered with the moonlight.

The shadow on the cliff grew smaller, darker. It raced down the cliff side, swinging about Llyn Gwalch. A cold darkness seemed to brush past me, like an unseen bird, and the sick, suffocating feeling of the night before touched me again. But the boat was picking up speed, gliding over the waves, and I suddenly remembered what is said of evil and open water, how some spirits may not cross the wide sea. I laughed. The black tendrils fell away from me, over-extended and worn out.

I watched over the stern as Llyn Gwalch shrank behind me,

becoming a pale place in the cliff wall, then a soft spot in the frothing of the light surf in the moonlight, with the waterfall of the stream a chain of silver hung down the cliff – then the mist grew thicker as the boat ran into it, and Llyn Gwalch and the island I had lived on all my life faded from my sight. I could not think to give it any farewell, and looked westward over the boat's prow. We were still increasing in speed. I laughed again, feeling the same exultant triumph and liberty I had felt that morning, and sang a song of triumph in war. The boat leapt forward like a willing horse and glided on, swift as a gull or a falcon, through the fog into the moonlight again, and the foam glittered at its prow as it ran along the path of light cast by the sinking moon.

I yawned, realized that I was still very tired. The cushions I had noticed were soft, the coverlets of silk and ermins much warmer than my worn cloak. It was cold in that rush of speed across the open sea. I lay down and drew the coverings over me, whispering thanks to the boat and to whatever force had sent it.

I do not remember falling asleep, but the next thing I saw was the light of the sunrise pouring on to me, brighter than any dawn I could remember. I lay on my back in the bottom of the boat and stared up at the streamers of colour which covered the sky from the east to the zenith. Such radiance promised a destination of equal loveliness.

I sat up. The boat was still moving, but a little more slowly now. Its prow and sides glowed with reflected fire on the water. Even the sea was like no water I had ever seen before. It was clear, but tinted with emerald and azure, colours brighter than any on Earth, jewel-toned in their brilliance, and they glittered in the dawn light. The sun cast my shadow before the prow of the boat, and we ran down it as down a road. As I watched, birds flew out of the west, white and gold wings flashing. I looked eagerly onward, hoping to see the land they came from.

Soon we approached it. It rose green-gold from the ocean. The sun struck some bright surface, and a pure clear light flashed up like a shout of joy. Truly, this had to be the Plain of Joy which so many songs spoke of. The Light had heard me. I lifted my arms to the morning and sang one of the songs about the islands I was fast approaching:

77

'.... there one sees the Silver Land
Where dragonstones and diamonds rain,
And the sea breaks upon the sand
The crystal tresses from its mane.

Throughout Earth's ages still it sings
To its own hosts its melody;
Its hundred-chorused music rings
Undecaying, deathless, free...'

I hardly had time to finish before the boat swept up to a white dock which jutted from the land into the sea, and there stopped itself, its journey over.

I stood and stepped out on to the dock. I glanced back into the boat, a little afraid to leave it. But then I looked at the land, the green grass, the gold-sanded path leading up from the dock, the tall trees – trees! Things rarely seen in the Orcades – swaying like dancers; and I began to walk up the path, slowly and wondering. I did not feel the stunned disbelief one would expect. Though wonderful, all seemed perfectly natural, as things do in a bright dream. Later, I realized, the astonishment must come. But now it was impossible. This Isle of the Blessed felt more real than the Orcades. It was what I had just left that semed a dream.

I went up the path, savouring the beauty around me. Everywhere there were flowers, no two alike. Their smell blended with the song of the birds, the music of the breeze in the trees. I walked faster, then ran for the sheer joy of motion, until I rounded a bend and stopped, for I had found the Hall that was the centre of the place.

It was much like its descriptions. The walls were of white bronze and gold filaments woven together, polished and brilliant. The roof was of the wing-feathers of every sort of bird that had ever lived, of every colour, and none clashed. It glowed almost as brightly as the sun.

I walked slowly towards it, half afraid, although I knew that I would not be there if it was not intended for me to come. I approached the great silver doors and tapped on them softly. They opened of themselves, revealing their inner hall, which is beyond description. Yet it was enough like any earthly feast hall that I knew where to raise my eyes to the man who sat at the high table, above the others who crowded the place. They were all beautiful enough to bring tears into my eyes, and I felt my humanity and filthy clothing as though they weighed the whole world on me. But the man who sat at the high seat, the lord of the Hall, smiled at me – a bright, fierce smile – and gestured me nearer.

I walked the length of that hall in silence, with the eyes of the company upon me; and I cannot describe or explain what I saw there. Slowly I climbed on to the dais and stopped, facing the lord across the high table, not knowing what to do or say.

He rose and smiled again, and it flashed across my mind that Lot and Agravain really did look much as he would if the blazing radiance of him were dimmed.

'Welcome, kinsman,' said Lugh the sun-lord. 'Be seated. You have travelled far and must be hungry.'

So I sat at the high table in the Hall of the Sidhe, and ate with them and drank the sweet, bright wine that is like an essence of light, and I talked with Lugh of the Long Hand.

He asked me of Lot and I told him of Arthur. He listened to me, then nodded. 'It is fated. One day rises when another is fallen.'

'Does Arthur of Britain, then, serve the Light?' I asked.

'He serves it.' Lugh shrugged. 'This is a greater matter and much is woven into it, and the end is not clear to me. My day, too, is over.'

I stared at him in astonishment. 'You, my lord? But you are ruler here!'

'Yet on Earth, where once I had power, I have little strength. Once all the West turned to me. Now they turn elsewhere. In time what little I have left will cease, and I will become only a memory, and my Hall and my people but a story told to children. In time, not even that.' He spoke calmly, as of certainties, and without regret.

'Is this light to be quenched, then?' I asked, looking about that radiant hall.

Lugh shook his head, smiling at my question. 'This light? Not so. We shall feast here till the Earth's end and beyond. Time does not touch this place, nor death, nor any sorrow. It is better than the Earth where we once dwelt.'

'Then you did live on the Earth, as the songs say?'

'Long ago.' Lugh sipped the wine, and his blue eyes were hot and bright as the sky. 'In what might have been Erin. Men were but a dream in the East, far from my domain. I came into being here in the West, not born as men are born, and here my people lived and made music. My mother was Balor's daughter, my father, Cian, son of Diancecht the Healer. Like yourself, Hawk of May, I am created of both Light and Darkness. And once it was offered to me as well to serve either, and I chose the Light. I reigned in it, for a time, though I knew my reign would be hard and not endure for ever.'

'You know of my mother Morgawse.'

'I know of one who is called the Queen of Air and Darkness, who is become Morgawse. She is an old enemy, once of my people. She seeks the destruction of the world she can no longer possess.'

'But you possessed it once.'

Again he smiled. 'Once I drove my chariot along the wind from Temair of the Kings, though it was not the same Temair where the lord O'Niall now sits. Once my kind ruled over the Earth, commanding fire and water and air as a king commands men. But that time is long past, so that even the land forgets it. Which is as it should be.'

'I have heard a story,' I said, 'which said that the Sons of Mil came to Erin, the first humans to reach its shores, long ago; and they found the Sidhe there, who were then called by another name. And it is said that the Sons of Mil fought with the Sidhe, or that they were judged between by Avairgain the poet of the Sons of Mil, and that Erin was given to Men.'

'The second story is closer to the truth,' said Lugh. 'Though the issue was not decided by Avairgain.'

'Who decided it, then?'

'The High King, the Light who shines for ever. He gave me my kingdom, and he took it away again and bestowed it on the Sons of Mil, and Avairgain the poet told the first Men that this was what had been done. But the Queen of Darkness would not heed me, nor the Light, nor Avairgain, but desired to keep the land for herself.'

'The Light, this Light,' I said. 'I do not know what is meant by it.'

He looked on me gently, amused. 'And how should you? None do, when first they encounter it, and you are newly come from a great darkness. Darkness blinds the eyes. But have you not sworn to follow and serve it?'

'I have.'

80

'Then you will come to know it better soon enough. The Light is a strong lord, a great king, and often a demanding master, though a kind one. The Light is eager for servants and friends, and will show you more things to do than you had thought could be done by any. So, at least, I have found it.'

'You found it . . . but I thought . . .'

'That I was the Light? Not so, indeed. Many have thought that, and once, in Erin, I was worshipped as the Light. But it is sought differently now, better. There have been many changes on Earth. I too am only a servant.'

So we spoke, and drank the wine. I was not aware of time. I do not think one can be aware of time in that place. Perhaps those in the Hall go out, sometimes, into the island – there are songs of the horses of the Sidhe, and chariots of gold racing across fields of flowers, and dancing, and also of wars – but I think all these must happen without time, not at the same time, nor at earlier or later times, but with a sequence set by the spirit and not by the passage of the sun. I cannot make it clear even to myself, but so it was. But when I had spoken to Lugh for a while – I cannot say, 'for some time' – the feasting ended and a man of the Sidhe who had been sitting to my right at the high table rose and went to a great harp in the corner and played upon it. That song was everything all men have dreamed of and sought for, which they only grasp for a few moments before it dissolves into the human world. It was light, fire, the pure ecstasy of immortal joy, totally unmingled with the sorrow which always accompanies it on Earth. I listened and felt as though my spirit would break from my body and go soaring off on that golden wind to the very pinnacle of heaven. I listened, wholly lost in the mazes of the music, feeling nothing by the sequence of each note. I would have sat so for ever, if Lugh had not touched my arm.

At this, I realized that I was weeping. I sat bemused and wondered why, and the harper played on. Lugh rose and gestured for me to come with him. I followed, tearing myself free from the music as painfully as a man might tear his own flesh from a deep wound. We left the Hall, and when the music had grown faint behind the walls it struck me fully, and I sat down on the floor and wept for sorrow. Lugh stood patiently over me in silence.

When my grief had run its course he dropped to one knee

beside me and laid his hand on my shoulder. 'You should not have stayed and listened for so long,' he said gently. 'The songs of the Sidhe are not for Men. For you there is too much pain in ecstasy, and the fire burns too fiercely to be endured. Nonetheless, it is good that you have heard Taliesin sing here. Now you know something of the Light. You must remember it, and when the Darkness surrounds you, think upon it. It will aid you, along with that which I will give you now, if you can accept it'

At this I looked up at him, and he nodded and again gestured for me to follow him. We rose.

He led me through some passageways behind the wall, going down, until I judged that we were underneath the feast hall. It was very quiet there, and the passages were dark but for the faint light that seemed to glow in the walls, and the brighter, quicker fire that surrounded Lugh, Master of All Arts. It was beautiful there, but there was a feeling of great power, like a banked fire. I was not exhausted by the song in the Hall, as I would have been on Earth, and so was sensitive to the strength that beat in the place like the heart's blood.

Lugh stopped before a door of deep-gold-coloured wood latched with red bronze and rested his hand on the latch. He turned to me.

'You have wondered why you were brought here, Hawk of May,' he said. His voice was almost a whisper, but it held the same note as the silent beat of the power burning beyond that door.

'I have, Lord.'

'It is well that you thought to wonder. You were not brought simply to see this island and rejoice, though it was necessary that you see light after so much darkness. Nor were you brought to my hall merely that you might escape the demon which pursued you, though that, too, was necessary. But you were brought for this: to take up arms to fight against the Darkness which you above others now can recognize. You are nearly seventeen now, and this is an age to take up arms.'

'Lord,' I said, 'I still lack half a year before I am fifteen.'

He shook his head. 'While you sat in my Hall, winter passed on Earth, and spring and summer, and another year after them. It is now March in Britain. By the time you return, May will have begun.'

I felt cold then and looked away. I knew the stories of how a man may go to the lands of the Sidhe for what seems a single night, and find on returning that a hundred years have passed, but I had never considered that it might happen to me. Nearly three years. Well, perhaps it was good. I would have grown, and have more strength of arm. But still . . .

Lugh smiled, very gently. 'It will be no longer than that, spring falcon. I give you my word. But, you see, you are past the age to take up arms. And if you return to Earth you will need a weapon to protect yourself from the powers of Darkness which will seek your death. As well as this, you have sworn in your heart to accept the High King of Light for your lord. Do not forget that a warrior must fight for his lord.'

I nodded.

'You must have a weapon,' said Lugh. 'And here I will give you one.'

He opened the door, stood holding it, and I walked slowly into the room.

It was a plain room, altogether dark except for where, at the opposite wall, a sword stood with light glowing deeply in the great ruby set into the pommel. Its shadow fell behind it on the wall in a cross-shape. I sensed the power that burned in it, great and terrible, and I felt a wave of cold fear sweep on to me.

'Lord,' I said to Lugh, who stood behind me in the doorway. 'Lord, this is too great for me. This is not a weapon for Men. I am honoured that you should think of it for me, but I could not bear such a word.'

'But it is a sword for Men,' Lugh said gently. 'True, its power is great enough to destroy many, and the bearing of it often brings the bearer sorrow. But it is a weapon such as only Men need; my kind use other weapons.'

I knew that he was right, but still I stared at the sword where it slumbered against the wall, awaiting the hand that would draw it in fire. And what fire that would be, what consuming Light.

'If you truly do not wish to accept this sword,' said Lugh. 'you may refuse it. I tell you, you can still serve the Light if you reject this.'

For an instant I wanted to accept this offer. But it was impossible. I could not disobey the Light immediately after it had saved me. If my new lord desired that I draw the sword, I must try to draw it. Surely, I comforted myself, the Light would not wish this unless I was able to do so without being destroyed. And whatever else is true, a warrior must obey his rightful lord. So I shook my head. 'I will try to accept this gift.' My mouth was dry and my hands damp.

I did not see but sensed Lugh's smile. 'Go then, and draw it.'

I walked over to it, each step heavy. My death could come here if I had not the strength to lift the sword . . . I was standing before it, and the light, warm, deep red, spilled over me. I dropped to my knees.

'Light,' I said. 'My lord High King, the sea is round me and the sky over me and the earth under me, and if I break faith with you, may the sea rise up and drown me and the sky break and fall on me, and the earth open and swallow me; so be it.' The Threefold Oath was, I knew, unnecessary, but it was always sworn when one's lord gave one arms. I took a deep breath, reached out both hands, closed them on the hilt of the sword, and began to draw it.

It was hot, hot as flame, and my hands were burning. The light in the ruby leapt, rose, fierce and red, red as blood, as the blood which beat in my ears and shook my whole body with its pulse. I pulled at the sword, and light slid along the exposed part of the blade, still red. I was aware of my hands only as centres of pain, was certain that they were being burned off; could almost smell the stink of them . . . . I drew the sword further and suddenly it was clear of the sheath, and I screamed because the light and fire of it suddenly ran along my very soul, and I was burning in it, and saw myself, all of myself, revealed in the light. All the Darkness I had known lay there, and all the Darkness that was a part of me shrieked at me to drop the sword before it slew me. And it was slaying me, for I was impaled by its light, and it was not a sword for mortals at all . . . but the Light wished me to draw it (oh, *Ard Rígh Mor*, Great High King!) so I held on, feeling the air rush white-hot into my lungs, searing every part of me, heart, mind consumed in a light that was no longer red but burning white as the heart of the sun. My strength failed me, and I retreated back into myself, seeking some power that would hold the sword in that agony. For an instant it seemed that I had none, that I would be annihilated, for it was too late to drop the sword . . .

And then I felt a sudden power within me rush into my limbs, clear and white hot, the core of my being, which had long before dreamed of this, and which before this I had barely suspected. I lifted the sword high above my head, the point raised to the sky, dimly aware how it now burned pure and brilliant as a star. I cried out in triumph, not knowing what I said, for I had conquered, and it was mine.

And then, suddenly, the pain was gone, and I was kneeling before the blank wall and the sword was dimming slowly in my hands.

'It is done,' said Lugh, very softly. 'I am glad.'

I looked at the sword, then at my hands. They were not burned at all. I looked at the sword again. Its light had dimmed to a glimmer along the blade. I turned towards Lugh who stood, still, in the doorway, surrounded by a bright clear light, smiling. 'The name of the sword is Caledvwlch, "Hard One",' he said. 'It had a different name before, but now it is yours, and a new name is given it for a new day.'

'It is mine,' I said, still bewildered. A wave of great joy flooded me. 'My lord gave me arms.'

Lugh nodded. 'You are the Light's warrior now. Do not forget that, Hawk of May. Now,' Lugh crossed the room and helped me to my feet, 'our lord is engaged in a war, and you must use that weapon of yours.'

'Where is the battle?' I asked. 'And what warband shall I join?'

'The battle will be about you. And take warning: it is not always to be fought with the sword, even with a sword like yours.'

'I understand, Lord. I have conquered my own Darkness, but cannot destroy it.'

He nodded, smiling. 'And if you remember that, you will be wise. The Darkness can use your own will, and can use others when they are themselves ignorant of it. You have walked in the Darkness and chosen Light, and will be hard to deceive. But it will not be impossible. There is much sorrow on Earth, and the Darkness is very strong . . .' He stopped abruptly, and turned his eyes from the future to the present and me. 'For warband, you will be able to recognize those who serve the Light. Arthur you already know of. Go to him, and accept him as your lord on Earth, if he will have you. But you will need to convince him that you have abandoned the Darkness, first: do not expect that it will be easy Whatever happens, I am certain that great things will be done on the Earth in these days, for there is a great struggle taking place. What the end will be I do not know and cannot see. except that it will be strange and different from what is ex· pected. But I think you will fight honourably. Now, come.'

I followed him from the room, carrying my sword, and he led me through a maze of passageways out, somehow, on to a kind of platform just below the roof of the feast hall, of the kind men use for trimming the thatch. We stood just beneath the roof of feathers and looked out to the west. The sun was going down, covering all the world with light, and it seemed closer and brighter than on Earth. Lugh pointed westward, and I followed the direction he indicated. I could see the whole of his island, right to the sea which circled it, and beyond that still into the sun itself. Just for a moment, it seemed to me that a light like a new star burned behind the sea, beyond the horizon; and in that instant, I felt that I understood the song in the Hall, and to what I had pledged my sword. I fell to my knees and raised the sword before me, whether in homage or in defence I am unsure. Lugh threw his arms up as in acclamation, and the light within him seemed to leap up. Then the sun touched the horizon, covering that other light, and he turned to me again.

'It is time that you go,' he said gently. 'Perhaps you will return one day, when the Earth has passed, and then you can hear the end of that song. But till then, I fear, we will not meet, nor will you ever again come to my realm. So, kinsman, I give you my blessing,' and he rested his hands on my shoulders as I still knelt. 'Carry it well in whatever battles are before you.' He helped me to my feet, then embraced me, more tenderly than my father ever had. 'Go in Light, *mo chroidh*, my heart, and do not wonder at what happens.'

Stepping back, he lifted his hands and spoke a word which the wind caught and repeated about me. The gold and bronze wall of the Hall, the setting sun on the feathers of the roof, dissolved into that sound; and the plains and woods and ocean of the Isles of the Blessed faded slowly with the wind. Last of all, Lugh himself, now standing afire with light, faded into a luminous mist, still smiling, and the last echoes of the magic word carried me back softly, ever so softly, to Earth and sleep.

Six

A hawk was flying in slow circles through the air above me. I watched him tilt his wings, balancing on the wind, then drift up sideways into it. I let my mind drift with him, swinging slowly along the blue sky and not really watching the blur of memories that lay below. I felt light, strong, purposeful: that was enough.

Presently, however, it occurred to me to wonder what had happened, and why I had this strange feeling of confidence, and I looked into my memories.

Llyn Gwalch. I had ridden there, with a demon riding after me through the night. I had stayed there for a day, and afterwards . . . no, a long blaze of colour and light, pain and glory and ecstasy. A song overwhelming everything, and a sorrow too deep for words. And an oath, a commitment. The Isles of the Blessed. Tir Tairngaire, Land of Promise, the Silver Land, the Land of the Living: a crowd of names for it rushed to me. Lugh of the Long Hand – no, it had to be a dream. Indeed, it had the strange enchanted feeling of a dream, in which colours are too bright and time and distance changed, alien and meaningless. Lyn Gwalch, then. I had certainly been there, so presumably I still was, here. Later in the day I would have time to consider the feeling of being changed, but for the moment I had better try to find something to eat.

I sat up, yawning, and looked about me; went rigid.

I was on a hilltop, seated in the low grass and heather that covered it. To one side the hill swept down, up into another range of hills, then clothed in an incredible shadowing of forest bright green with the spring. On the other side, the hill continued into a range of taller hills. The sky was an unimaginably clear blue, and seemed to rise for ever.

'No,' I said out loud. 'It is impossible.' There were no hills this tall in all the Orcades, and no forests. It was not spring, but autumn.

But the earth and sky were indisputably real. I clutched my head, terrified. Where was I? This could not be a dream, but if it were not, then . . . the other couldn't have been a dream either.

'Do not wonder at what happens,' Lugh had said before he sent me back to Earth. I remember the words clearly, and remembered his face as he said them, and the west spread out below the roof of his Hall. I remembered the room beneath the Hall, and the agony of drawing the sword; the joy and power when I had drawn it. The sword . . . my hand fell to my side.

It was there.

I closed my hand about the hilt, and it seemed to flow into and become a part of me. I lifted it, looked at it. It was real. The whole voyage had been real, and the magic of Light was no less real than the power of Darkness. I had sworn fealty to the Light, and it, he, had given me arms. I held in my hand a weapon not forged on Earth.

I laughed, gripping the hilt with both hands, doubt and terror departing without leaving a trace behind them. I sprang to my feet and lifted Caledvwlch to the sun.

'My lord, Great King!' I shouted. 'I thank you for this, and for delivering me from my enemies, and taking my oath!' As I spoke, the sword blazed again with light, but this time it did not burn me; rather, it seemed to radiate my own joy. I lowered it slowly, looking at it. 'And I thank you, too, kinsman, Lord Lugh,' I added, 'for your hospitality.' The light burned a little while longer, then dimmed until it seemed as though I held an ordinary, if very fine, sword in my hands.

I had not really noticed the fashion of it before. It was a two-edged slashing sword, such as a man could use from horseback. It was somewhat longer and thinner than most such swords, and perfectly balanced. The hilt was very beautiful: the cross-piece far longer than usual, each branch coiled with gold which then intertwined up the grip to the pommel, which was set with a ruby. The blade, as the inner light died from it, caught the sunlight with the true 'snake' pattern of well-forged steel. It was sharp, too: I drew the edge along my arm, and it cut every hair without pulling. It would be a fine weapon to use in an ordinary battle, without the addition of unknown powers against the Darkness.

Looking down, I saw that it had a sheath. This was very plain, of simple wood and leather, and fastened to a plain leather baldric. I set the sword down and put this on, then sheathed the sword and adjusted it. It was an easy weight to carry, since I felt lighter with it than without it.

The question now was, which way to walk? I had no idea where I might be. Lugh had said that I should go to Arthur, and Arthur was presumably fighting the Saxons somewhere in Britain, so I was probably in Britain, rather than in Erin or Caledon – or Rome or Constantinople, for that matter. Britain, though, is a large land, and there were few in any of her many kingdoms who would welcome strangers from the Orcades. Well, if Arthur was fighting the Saxons, presumably I had been sent to somewhere near him. That might mean I was near the border of one of the Saxon lands, but, again, it might not. A well-planned raid may strike a region over a hundred miles from the raiders. And most of the British kingdoms bordered Saxon lands on the east. Well then, at least I should not walk east. I checked my directions by the sun. The chain of hills lay directly to my west. These looked to be hard walking, and I was unused to travelling long distances on foot. I looked for easier country.

I looked again at the sky. The hawk I had seen earlier was still visible, circling slowly southward. That seemed as good a direction as any. I started off.

After three steps I had to stop again. My boots pinched dreadfully. Sitting down to check them, I saw that they were far too small. So, for that matter, was everything else I was wearing. I remembered then that Lugh had said that two and a half years had passed during my single day on the Isle of the Blessed.

I stared at the boots. Everyone must think me dead, would even have forgotten me. It was late spring. I must be fully seventeen.

Almost against my will, I recalled tales that are told of those who visit the Sidhe. Sometimes, returning only to look again at their homeland, such travellers crumple into dust when they touch mortal earth and their age returns to them. Or sometimes they themselves were left unchanged, but the world had known centuries since they left, and they wandered about earthly lands for years, asking for persons long and dead and forgotten. I felt sick. Suppose that this had happened to me. Suppose that it was not just two and a half years, but ten, twelve, a hundred years? Suppose I went to the nearest farmstead and asked about Arthur the Pendragon, and the people said 'Who?' and looked at me with strange eyes?

No, I told myself firmly. Lugh said two and a half years, and he would not deceive me. This is spring, and two and a half years from the time I left Llyn Gwalch. And if it is not so, then it is because the Light wills it not to be, and the Light is your sworn lord and you must accept and have faith in his judgements.

I unlaced the boots and took them off. I had been warned, after all, I told myself. And the advantages were great. I had grown somewhat before I left Dun Fionn but now I was fully adult, and could swear service to any lord in Britain – any that would have me, that is. Doubtless I was still a poor fighter.

This thought made me smile, albeit shakily, and I remembered Agravain and Lot and all those who had tried to train me at Dun Fionn, when I had still wanted to be a warrior. It had been hard then, bitterly hard. Now, at least, I knew what my road was and knew that it was good, even if it might be difficult. The ascent from Avernus apparently was not to be made in one step. I remembered suddenly the light I had seen at sunset in the Isles of the Blessed, and struggled to recall what it meant. I could not. But the song in the Hall I could remember, still sharp and brilliantly clear. Too clear: the sorrow flooded over me in a great wave, mingled with homesickness, and I crouched a moment, staring at the heather. Best not to think of that for a while.

I tossed the boots aside – I could easily go barefoot on that grass – and started down the hill.

It was a fine day for walking. It was warm, about as warm as it ever becomes in the Orcades (though it is often much hotter in Britain) and I first loosened, then took off my stained cloak. The sky was very clear and blue, and there was only the slightest of breezes to ripple the grasses. Skylarks dropped music from overhead, rabbits jumped off on all sides, and once, as I walked by the edge of the forest, a herd of deer leapt up and ran off before me in great startled bounds. Flowers abounded, in types I had never seen in the Orcades. The woods were a marvel to me, who had seen none before, and the play of sunlight through the leaves seemed too wonderful for words.

After noon, when I was becoming thirsty, I found a stream running from the hills into the forest. The water was sweet and clear. After drinking, I rested by it for a while, soaking my feet, which were already sore; then set off again, still southward.

As the day wore on, the hills became lower, finally blending into the surrounding countryside. The forest grew thicker, and marvellous as it was, I became uneasy with the trees so tall about me, and began to wish for the open hills of the Orcades and for the sea. My feet were cut and sore, and I was also growing tired and stopping to rest more frequently. I had seen no sign of human habitation all day, and I wondered where in this great land Arthur could be. When it was growing late in the afternoon, however, I found a road.

It astounded me. Never had I seen such a thing. It was paved with great stones, slightly arched in the middle, and the forest had been cleared for some distance about it – although loose scrub had grown since that clearing. It was a road wide enough for the largest cart and firm enough to withstand the fiercest rains and coldest winters. I had heard of the Roman roads, but had always thought their virtues exaggerated. Well, I now knew them to be real.

This road ran east–west, straight as a spear shaft. I walked cautiously from the forest on to it, then began walking west. It was easy walking after the forest, and I made good time.

When twilight was only an hour or so away I saw people coming down the road towards me. The setting sun was behind them, and I could not see them clearly. Nonetheless, I ran forward eagerly to meet them. They were the first humans I had seen since awakening – in fact, the first in two and a half years – and I felt the need of company after the strange forest and stranger things preceding it. Besides that, men meant houses, fire, food. And even more than the hunger, I felt a peculiar turning of my mind towards other men, an eagerness for them, almost as though all humanity was my clan, and I wanted their shared warmth against the vastness and awe of the powers of Light and Darkness. It is a strange feeling, but whenever I have been nearest the Light and, thus, farthest from common humanity, I feel so.

The party emerged as eleven men leading three pack-laden horses and driving a cow. The men were warriors. The sun glinted off the tips of their spears, limned the oval shields slung over their shoulders, and shone warmly on their steel topped helmets. I stopped, frowning. The warriors of the Orcades do not wear helmets, and none of the British warriors who had been attracted to my father's warband had done so either. Most warriors consider it cowardly to wear one, and besides, unless it is very well made a helmet merely blocks one's vision without providing much protection.

As I stood, stupidly staring and thinking this, one of the warriors hailed me, shouting in a language I did not know. Then I realized that I should have fled. I knew Irish, British, Latin and some Pictish, all but one of the languages spoken in Britain. The one I did not know was the Saxon tongue – and Saxons also wore helmets. But I had hesitated too long, and now it was too late to flee. The warriors were almost upon me. I would have to try to bluff, and hope that the Saxon reputation for unthinking violence was mistaken, and that their reputation for lack of imagination and stupidity was correct.

The Saxon who had called before repeated his greeting. I nodded in what I hoped was a half-witted fashion and stood aside to let them pass.

They were all tall men, I saw now, and most had the oddly pale fair hair which is also a part of the Saxons' reputation, though three were dark. They were well armed with swords, throwing and thrusting spears, and the long knives, the *seaxes*, which give them their name. The horses were laden with food: three pigs, grain, and some plain sacks containing either fruit or vegetables. The party walked towards me, more slowly now, and the leader suddenly stopped and frowned. He said something ending on a questioning note. I shook my head.

He took another step towards me, hesitated again, staring intently. He made a gesture with his left hand. One of his comrades made some comment in their odd guttural language, and the leader shook his head dubiously and asked another question. There was a strange note in his voice, of uncertainty, almost of fear, and his comrades had dropped the points of their spears. I shook my head again.

The leader glanced back at his friends, then spoke in British. He had a strange accent, speaking in the back of his throat, and coughing out harsh vowels and swallowing the ends of his words but I understood him well enough. 'I said, greetings to you, whoever you may be.' He hesitated again, watching me, the whites of his eyes showing oddly, then continued belligerently, 'Who are you, and why do you travel this road, so close to nightfall?'

'I . . . am travelling because I must,' I said. 'Come night-fall, I will stop.'

One of the other Saxons stepped forward angrily, levelling his spear. 'That is no answer, Briton! What do you in the domain of the West Saxons? If you be a thrall, where is your master? If you be no thrall, what do you?'

'Eduin!' said the leader in an alarmed tone; and in the abrupt and tense silence that followed he studied me again, as though he did not like what he saw. I stood quietly, thinking hard.

The second Saxon, Eduin, argued something quickly with the leader, gesturing eastward. The leader looked uncertain, chewing his moustache, then became angry, and turned back from his companion to me. 'Where is your master, Briton?' he demanded.

They thought I was a thrall, then, and they had called this the domain of the West Saxons. I struggled to remember what I knew of the Saxon kingdoms. It was so easy to say 'the Saxons' and think of one nation covering all the east of Britain, and ignore the real divisions between them, the different tribes of Saxons, Angles, Jutes, Franks . . . but the West Saxons had attracted attention enough to register on my memory. Cerdic was the king of the West Saxons, and had claimed one of the old Roman provinces, the eastern half of Dumnonia. In such an area, newly conquered or perhaps actively resisting the invaders, any Briton would be either a thrall or an enemy. It was safer to be a thrall, especially when the odds were eleven to one, and that one a poor fighter.

'Well, answer me, Briton!' said the Saxon leader. Again there was a tone in his voice which I could not understand, a note almost of desperation.

'I . . .' What could I say? 'I have none.'

The leader too levelled his spear, the point only a foot from me. 'You are not a thrall, then?' he asked, in a very low voice. 'What, then? Do you fight? I fear no . . .' and he added a word in Saxon. The other warriors drew closer, spears lowered, one or two slinging the shields from their backs, though they plainly did not understand their leader's British.

I realized that my hand had dropped towards Caledvwlch's hilt, and, astonished at myself, stopped it, tried to relax and looked cowed and bewildered. I could not fight them with the sword. I would have to see if I had inherited any of my father's famed cunning.

'But I am a thrall, noble lord!' I said, forcing a note of terror into my voice. It was not difficult to do. 'I – *arglwydd mawr*, great lord, my master's dead, and I don't know . . .'

At my first words the Saxon had relaxed with a shudder. Now he spoke with an arrogant and aggressive self-assurance. 'You try to flee to your British High King, no? Just because Arthur the Bastard is within a hundred miles you run from your master and try to join him.'

'No, my lord!' I cried. 'I only . . . I am running, yes. My master is dead, I told you! And my elder brother with him. I fear, my lord, that they will kill me, too. I need your protection. If I were running to the High King, would I have hailed you, my lord?'

'He would have hid himself, when that we came,' Eduin said to the other. 'He is a thrall brat, Wulf, liken to any.'

Wulf frowned, though. 'How did your master die? Who are "they"? Answer me quickly.'

'There was a duel, my lord,' I replied at once, remembering the stories told by one of my father's spies. 'My master killed a man, about a month back; and the man's kin accepted the blood-price, because of the war, and because the king wished it. But still in their hearts they were angry, and when we were going across the hills to take possession of some lands the king had given him, they sprang on him from an ambush and killed him, and all with him. My brother, another of his thralls, was there, and him they killed as well. I hid beneath a bush until they were gone, and then I ran. I am afraid, my lord, for I know they will kill me too, to stop me from saying that they broke their oaths concerning the blood-price.'

Wulf nodded. My story was apparently plausible. 'What was your master's name, then? And who are these oath-breakers?'

I dropped my eyes and fidgeted. 'My lord,' I whispered. 'I dare not tell you. I am only a thrall. They would kill me.'

He studied me for another moment, then noticed the hilt of my sword for the first time – I had put my cloak back on with the evening cool. He frowned at it unhappily.

'What is that sword? Your master's?'

'Yes.'

He hesitated, began to ask for it, then stopped, shook his head. I looked at my feet.

'And you think we can protect you?' Eduin asked sardonically.

I fidgeted more, praying desperately to the Light that they would ask no more about Caledvwlch.

Eduin laughed harshly. 'It happens we have no need for British brats underfoot, unless they are useful. What can you do?'

I allowed myself to relax a little. Be careful, I warned myself. Fortunately, with my bare feet and outgrown clothing I must look like a thrall, and biddable slaves were rare enough to be potentially valuable. If I made myself appear valuable enough they would let me live, either to keep themselves or to sell, but if I made myself appear too valuable it would be the more difficult to escape, and I might draw questions I could not answer. But if I appeared worthless they would probably kill me out of hand. Light, I thought briefly, why did you let me come here? Well, do not wonder at what happens.

'D-do, my lord? I'm good with horses. I cared for my master's stable. And I can play the harp a little, and serve at table.'

Wulf chewed his lip, said something to Eduin. He still looked anxious. Eduin replied sharply, and Wulf seemed to argue with him. Eduin shrugged and said something which angered Wulf, who turned back to me.

'Very well, Briton, we keep you. If you try to run away, you will be whipped. Care for our horses, and later we will sell you to someone who will use you properly, if we cannot find your master's kinsmen.'

'Thank you, my lord.' I bowed to him, thinking, Later? When? When they reached the army from which they must have set out as a raiding party? They had mentioned that the Pendragon was near. It would seem that I was in the midst of the war. I wondered what had happened in Britain while I was in the Land of Promise.

Wulf explained me to his followers, and the Saxons gave me their horses' leads and commenced walking east without further comment. As I watched them, I became the more certain that they were a foraging party sent to fetch supplies. I cursed my bad luck in finding them. Had I encountered a lone warrior or farmer first I would have had some warning of my location, and could have abandoned the road (assuming that I survived such an encounter) and continued west safely. As it was, I was trapped and in danger. The Saxons would certainly not allow me to keep the sword. I could not understand why they had not asked for it already. And I did not like to think what would happen when they tried to draw it; it would give me away altogether. Moreover, I would have to come up with a name for my imaginary master – if I did not immediately give myself away by some piece of ignorance any thrall would have been free of.

Well, I consoled myself, there must be some way out. Surely the Light would not throw my life away and let my sword fall into the enemies' hands so soon after saving me and giving me arms. The Light had delivered me from Morgawse; surely it could save me from the Saxons. But I was afraid. The Light had saved me from the Darkness, yes, but that was magic working against sorcery, and the Saxons were physical power, flesh, blood and steel. It had happened so quickly that I had had no time to feel anything. But now I wanted to drop the Saxon horses' leads and run. It was as though I had stepped from Morgawse's world into Lot's, where Morgawse could work only indirectly. And the Light?

The Light is High King, I told myself. He has brought you here; he can bring you out.

But the doubt persisted, and the fear. The Saxons had an evil reputation.

At least, I told myself, the High King Arthur is somewhere nearby, making war against these Saxons. Arthur, Arthur, Pendragon of Britain. Arthur who fights the Darkness. When Lugh had told me that, I had not questioned him, but now I began to wonder. Arthur, as far as I knew, fought the Saxons. He had done so, and seemed to be doing it still. But the Saxons could not be the same as the Darkness. I could sense no deep evil in the warriors I walked beside, and, had it been there, I would have known. They acted much like any warriors. They could be atypical, but I doubted it. The Saxons had a reputation for being violent, brutal, slave-drivers and maltreaters of women; for being also dull, gullible, naïve and stupid. There were many jokes about these supposed latter qualities of theirs – though, watching

Eduin's cool wariness, I began to think that this part, at least, of the Saxon reputation might be mistaken. But as to the rest, all warriors are violent and most are brutal, if need be, and all nations are, at times, cruel to slaves and women. Deliberate evil was never ascribed to the Saxons. They seemed, indeed, less given over to torturing, poisoning and black magic than the Romanized Britons, and were certainly better at keeping their oaths to one another. If the Saxons kept more slaves, it was because British and Irish clan holdings couldn't afford or didn't need to keep as many slaves as the Saxon villages could; and the British and Irish women weren't abused as greatly simply because they wouldn't permit it, as the Saxon women apparently did. I could not see that the Saxons were uniquely servants of Darkness. Yet Arthur gave all his strength to the war against the Saxons. If he indeed served the Light, there must be some reason for that.

I remembered, suddenly, how my mother had used my father, and was chilled by it. If some force were using the Saxons that way, and if that force recognized me for what I was when I reached the Saxon camp, this journey could easily mean my death.

Of course, to attempt to escape meant death, and whatever way I came to the Saxon camp would be hazardous. And even if I could survive, and escape from the Saxons, what use would I be to Arthur? He needed warriors, not . . . whatever I was.

Lugh had said, 'Do not wonder at what happens.' Again I fixed upon that. The Light had heard me and delivered me when I spoke to it without words at Llyn Gwalch. It—he—had fashioned the fire of Caledvwlch and given it to me. He had brought me to the kingdom of the West Saxons from a world beyond the Earth. He was unimaginably powerful, and I could not assume that he was ignorant. There had to be some reason for this. I had only to wait, to watch and be strong.

I sighed and turned my attention to leading the horses.

The Saxons did not stop at sunset, but kept on walking stolidly. My feet had gone numb by that time, which was fortunate, for they were blistered and bleeding. My legs ached and felt like stone after the unaccustomed walking. I was ravenously hungry and very thirsty, but I said nothing and struggled to keep up, and the Saxons did not offer to help or wait. I judged that they would not burden themselves with a slave who was useless, so steeled myself so as not to fall behind and perhaps be disposed of. The camp must needs be close if the Saxons continued walking by night without even stopping for a meal. We should not have to go much further.

The stars were out when we reached the camp. It was a large one, for the whole of the army of the West Saxons, and built accordingly. The site was plainly an old hill fort, but had been fortified by the Romans as a military base and a town. The Saxons had moved into some of the old Roman buildings, and added some new Saxon houses of their own, and the wide area of cleared fields about the town had been newly sown with seed. I was impressed by the place, even through my exhaustion. I had never seen a village before, much less an almost-Roman town. The hill was steep, and the bank and ditch about it were clean-cut – the fort was obviously a good one – and nearly all the space enclosed by those banks was filled by the houses of the townsmen, or the tents of the summoned warbands and armies. As it was early summer, and the planting was over, the farming men had been summoned to join the warbands – the *fyrd*, the Saxons call it – and the numbers were very great. But all the camp was orderly and close-guarded. Sentries were posted on the walls, and one of these stopped us before allowing us to enter the fortress, checking carefully that no spy should enter.

My band of Saxons went directly to one area of camp, where they unloaded their supplies. Others crowded around them, asking questions and congratulating and back-slapping in a manner that made it plain that they were the kinsmen of the foraging party. Wulf answered the questions, waved towards me, and I caught the word 'thrall'. Eduin made what sounded like a joke, and laughed. The Saxons glanced at me casually, then gave me a second look, and stared at Caledvwlch. There was another moment of uncomfortable silence before they shrugged and went back to their fire, over which a sheep was roasting. It was nearly done, and filled the air with a scent which made my mouth water. I drifted towards the fire myself, but Wulf stopped me.

'First, care for the horses,' he ordered. 'They are there, tied up. Care for them all, not just these new ones.'

I nodded, though I wanted to either strike him or weep. Only the knowledge that disobedience would mean a beating at the least restrained me. 'Yes, my lord. Where is the food?'

Wulf pointed to a pile of hay of rather poor quality and went over to the fire.

I tended the horses. There were eighteen of them, all in bad condition, and it took me quite a while to finish with them. The poor creatures had obviously had no grain and much hard work for months, and that without the most ordinary care. By the time I was done with them, the sheep had been devoured to the bones and the Saxons were sitting about, drinking mead and boasting. (I knew they were boasting by the tone of their voices. Irish, British, Saxon or Breton, all men boast alike. They even tell the same stories.) I crept up to the fire very quietly and managed to gain one of the sheep bones and a cup of water without being noticed. I was retreating to eat when Wulf noticed me again.

'Here!' he called. 'Are you finished with the horses?'

'Yes, my lord.'

'Horses is sick,' said one of the other Saxons, his accent so heavy I could barely understand him.

'Not sick, my lord,' I replied, trying to sound respectful. 'But they need proper care, or they will become very sick. And they need shoeing.'

'Whu-hut?'

Wulf translated for me. The others nodded wisely, commented on horses and drank some more mead, curiosity satisfied. I guessed that they knew very little about horses, and felt a bit less afraid. I had wondered whether they treated their thralls the same way.

I gnawed my sheep bone, trying to think of a way to slip off into the night while the Saxons drank. The thing seemed impossible. The camp was too well ordered and well guarded, and the sentries would certainly be alert to British thralls trying to leave the camp by night. Besides that, I knew I could not go far before collapsing. Perhaps tomorrow, I thought. They will have to give me some shoes, and when I am rested . . .

'You! Briton!'

I looked up; the voice was Eduin's. 'My lord?'

'You can play the harp?'

'I have said so, my lord.'

'Then take the harp over there by the supplies and play something.'

On the other hand, perhaps they did treat their thralls as they treated their horses. I set the sheep bone down, hobbled over to the harp. The Saxons, pleased to have someone to play for them, leaned back expectantly.

'What kind of song do you wish, my lord?' I asked Wulf.

'A battle song. A good one.'

I let my fingers wander over the harp-strings, tuning a couple of them and considering. A British battle song, full of the deaths of Saxons, would hardly please them. I did not wish to arouse their suspicions by singing in Irish and showing myself to be from so distant a place as the Orcades. I settled for a song from Less Britain about a sword dance (Fire! Steel and fire! Oak-tree, night; Earth and stone and fire-light . . .) They liked it, beating time with their palms against their thighs, eyes gleaming out of the darkness. When I finished they actually gave me a hornful of mead.

'Play another,' said the one with the strong accent.

'Of what kind, my lord?' I asked, savouring the mead.

'A lament for the fallen, harper,' commanded a voice from the dark behind me, in clear and accentless British. The Saxons leapt up as one.

'*Se Cyning!*' exclaimed Eduin. I had heard that title before, affixed to the names of all the important Saxons in Britain. It means 'king'.

'Cerdic!' said Wulf, and added some formal greeting.

The king of the West Saxons returned it, coming forward into the firelight. Another stood behind him, still only a shadow.

Cerdic was not a tall man, and did not even look like a Saxon. He was slight and wiry, with fox-red hair and green eyes. His beard had a tendency to straggle, and he was not remarkably good-looking. But he wore his power with the same casual ease with which he wore his cloak, tossed back over one shoulder and showing the purple as if by accident. He smiled at my Saxons and waved his hand, bidding them to be seated again, then sat himself, managing somehow to be familiar and lordly at once. I could well believe that he was a great leader. But as the firelight caught his eyes, I saw with one of those sudden brief moments of clarity that there was Darkness in him as well, and a ravening hunger which made all his powers, his talents and his followers alike, no more than spears cast at his goal. And from the one who stood behind him I sensed Darkness like a black fire, burning the very shadows about him. This other stepped forward after Cerdic, and brushed off the ground before folding himself down on to it. He was very tall, with the pale blond hair and pale blue eyes one thinks of as natural to the Saxons, and he was very good-looking. He was in his mid-thirties, and dressed like a great nobleman. He felt my eyes on him and glanced in my direction; for an instant our eyes met, and his gaze sharpened suddenly and tore at me, demanding something. I looked away.

Wulf gave the two newcomers some mead, speaking respectfully as he offered it. Cerdic sipped his and raised his eyebrows.

'Fine mead, Wulf Aedmundson,' he said, still in British. 'From your new holding? I told you the Downs were good country for honey. Have you tried growing grapes there yet? – Well, Briton, play as you were bid.'

'Yes, my lord,' I whispered, not looking at him. 'A lament for the fallen.'

His eyes had merely passed over me before; when I spoke he saw me. He glanced at his companion. The other's mouth tightened, and he drummed his fingers on his knee. Cerdic frowned.

I swept the strings with my hand, played a complicated prelude without really thinking. They were important, these two. Cerdic, *Cyning thara West Seaxa*, as his own people would put it, and the other . . . who? He was strong in Darkness. Cerdic, I thought, does not comprehend the Darkness, but, from ambition, wishes to use it; but this other one is like Morgawse.

A lament for the fallen. There are plenty of laments, more than there are battle songs. Laments for those fallen by the hands of the Saxons, men such as I sat among. I sang a famous lament, a slow, fierce, proud thing that was made when the province of south-east Britain was overwhelmed by the Saxons, an old song which called the province by its still older name, the land of the tribe of the Cantii.

> 'Though they made the Saxon hosts to sleep
> By the sea's white cliffs, and made women weep;
> The fullness of glory was not complete,
> The host rides to Yffern in defeat

And in their fields the eagles feast.
Bitter the harvest now to reap:
They fought the Saxons, fought and fell,
We shall gather corpses, make tears our well,
And the host of Cantii will not return . . .'

Cerdic listened intently. When I struck the final note, he nodded. 'A very fine song. And very well sung. You have had more than a little training in harping.'

'Thank you, Great King,' I said in a flattered tone. I could not give him reason to suspect that I was anything more than a common thrall. I drew my cloak closer about my shoulders, as though I found the night cold, and hoped that it would cover my sword.

'Play another,' ordered Cerdic, and I complied.

The king began to talk with Wulf, drinking his mead and paying no more attention to me. But his companion, the other nobleman, watched me still, lids half drawn over those pale but oddly dark eyes.

I played on, realizing that I was better than I had been at any time before. Perhaps it was from hearing the song in Lugh's Hall, perhaps it was simply freedom from the Darkness, but I could tell that I was making the music live upon the strings and in the heart, a thing many professional bards cannot do. I became uneasy, and wished that I had had the sense to play badly at the beginning of the evening.

Cerdic eventually finished whatever business he had come to speak with Wulf about, and rose to leave. I began to relax again.

But when the companion rose, he nodded to me. 'You play well, Briton,' he said. His voice was cool, and he spoke slowly, drawling out his words in a mocking tone. 'Well enough to make yourself valuable. But not so valuable that you should be allowed to bear a sword, which is against all law and custom. Give it here.'

I stared at him for a long moment, horrified, though I should have expected it. Close on the horror followed an un-expected rage, anger at this arrogant Saxon sorcerer treating me as a piece of merchandise, at his demanding my dearest possession; anger at the casual callousness of the other Saxons; and most of all, anger at myself for accepting slavery and abuse instead of laying down my life for my honour as I

102

should have done. I raised my eyes and met the sorcerer's gaze directly, my hand dropping to Caledvwlch. 'I cannot give you the sword.'

'You defy me?' he asked, still drawling and amused. 'A slave defying the King of Bernicia?'

So that was who he was, had to be: Aldwulf of Bernicia, reputed the cruellest of the Saxon kings. I stopped, struggling to control myself. His eyes were again questioning, demanding something. His lips moved, and I recognized the unspoken words, and my grip tightened on the sword as I recalled how Morgawse had taught them to me.

'I am sorry, Great Lord,' I said, my voice sounding, even to myself, too soft. 'The sword is my master's. I cannot give it to any other . . .' I tried desperately to force myself back into the role I had chosen, reminding myself that I was no warrior. 'To no one but my master, or his heir.'

But the Saxon smiled as though he were satisfied at something. I saw that I had made some mistake, that now he knew what he had been demanding of me, and I felt cold.

'So, you are loyal, too,' Aldwulf said, still smiling. 'Keep the sword, then, for your master's heir.' He glanced over to Cerdic and said something in Saxon. Cerdic directed a sharp question to him, and I caught the words, '*ne thrall*', at which some of the other Saxons grunted. Aldwulf replied languidly and shrugged. Cerdic looked thoughtful, turned to Wulf, and asked him some question, to which Wulf replied at some length. When he had finished, Cerdic turned to me.

'Wulf has said that you can take care of horses as well as harp, and that your master, by your report, died today in some blood feud about which you fear to give information. I am considering whether to buy you, Briton. What is your name?'

I stared at my hands on the harp, feeling sick. If the king bought me, how could I escape? And, since Aldwulf was clearly the driving force in this inclination to buy me, what would happen to me if I did not escape?

'Gwalchmai.' I answered Cerdic's question with the truth. 'A warrior's name, not a thrall's.'

'I was born a free man, Chieftain. My master did not care to change my name, seeing that I was used to it.'

'And you are loyal to this murdered master, but not so loyal as to give information about the feud. How long have you been a thrall?'

'Three years, Chieftain.' A good enough length of time.

He looked me up and down carefully, and I cursed my stupidity in singing so well and acting like a free man instead of a thrall. Be no one, I told myself. Make them doubt that you are anything. Here in the seat of his power this man can destroy you with a word.

'He sings well,' Cerdic said to Wulf. 'I will buy him from you, if the price is appropriate.'

Adulf smiled again, looking at me steadily while Cerdic bargained with Wulf and Eduin. After only a little of the bargaining, Cerdic stripped two heavy gold armlets from his right arm, then added a third. A good price. Most slaves, in these days when men were cheap, brought scarcely more than half of that. Cerdic would not pay it because he liked my singing – but that was obvious.

'Well, boy, now I am your master,' Cerdic told me. 'Come.'

'Yes, lord. Did you buy the harp as well?'

'That I give you, *dryhten*, Lord,' said Wulf. 'A token of honour from my clan for their *cyning*.' He sounded sincere. I wondered what he and Cerdic had said to each other.

Cerdic nodded thanks and set off. I stumbled after him, my feet doubly sore after the short rest, carrying the harp.

The king stopped at one or two other camps and a house within the fortress, I guessed to discuss with the leaders of influential clans. He required me to sing something to amuse the various warriors, perhaps so as to show off his new purchase. But Aldwulf abandoned us at the first stop, and I felt much better for his absence.

It was after midnight when the Saxon king finally decided that it was time to rest. We went to a fine Roman government building at the centre of the fortress. I was staggering with exhaustion by then, and didn't even pause to notice the mosaics or the pond in the atrium. Cerdic turned me over to his servants with a brief word of explanation in the courtyard, then went off to his own apartments to sleep.

I stood, facing Cerdic's thralls. They looked back with a strange blend of suspicion and fear – the same look that Wulf had given me when I met his party on the road. I was too tired to puzzle at it, though, and said only, 'I am Gwalchmai. Your master has, I imagine, just told you that he bought me tonight because I harp well and can tend horses. I have been walking or working all day and I am tired. Where can I sleep?'

The thralls hesitated, still unsure of me, then finally showed me through the house to the servants' quarters by the stables, and there I collapsed and fell instantly asleep.

I woke again in less than three hours. I lay still for a little while, dizzy with weariness and stiff, wondering why I had woken. Some dream slid through my mind like a silver fish and vanished. I sighed and sat up, reaching for Caledvwlch.

As my hand closed about the sword-hilt, the ruby began to glow. I sat, staring at it.

'Is there something more I must do tonight, Lord?' I asked, aloud.

There was only silence, and the warm glow which answered a deep, almost buried fire within me.

I stood, adjusted the baldric I had forgotten to take off, and walked from the room.

The black bulk of the house loomed above the stable against the starlit sky. The town was dark, except for the distant watch-fires at the walls. I shivered in the night air, though despite the spring coolness it was not really cold. No, there was a sensation I recognized in the air, a sensation which radiated from the house. I turned back into the house, found my way to the atrium, then, after hesitation, made my way into the mosaiced living quarters of the nobles. All the thralls slept.

It was dark in the house, a deep silence and a black heat, different from but still similar to Morgawse's icy cold. It was difficult to breathe. I stood for a minute, allowing my eyes to adjust, then, with my hand on the hilt of my sword and a prayer to the Light in my mind, I walked forward to the closed door at the end of the corridor, and opened it a bare inch to look beyond it.

The first thing I saw was a shadow that swung backwards and forwards against the wall, and only after that did I see the body that cast it. The man was dead by then, head wrenched grotesquely sideways by the rope he had been hanged from. He looked to be British, but in that light one could not really tell. I recognized the pattern which was drawn on the floor beneath him, drawn in his blood, and the pattern about the single thick candle near the door. Aldwulf of Bernicia knelt before the first pattern, casting a handful of rune-sticks upon it and reading off the words they formed. Cerdic, who stood to one side, his eyes bright from the hunger in them, gave no sign of understanding what the runes meant. I, may the Light protect me, understood.

A shadow seemed to gather about the hanged man's head, and the body swung back and forth more rapidly, sending the shadows spinning across the wall. Aldwulf cast the runes. He had summoned no great power, I saw, but merely a messenger. 'A bargain,' Aldwulf said aloud, speaking in the language of the runes as he cast them, the ancient, cold language of sorcery. His voice was no longer drawling and soft, but harsh and deadly. He arranged the sticks for his message. 'Give a message. To your master. I wish, a bargain.'

The body swung more slowly. Aldwulf cast the runes, read the reply silently, scarcely moving his lips, then arranged the sticks again. 'Death,' he read out. 'For ... Arthur, the High King. For his death, death. An offering. Acceptable.'

The body ceased to swing, but the shadow remained crouched upon it. Again Aldwulf cast the runes, this time reading the reply aloud. 'Not acceptable. Mortal life little. Impossible. Release.' Just below the threshold of hearing a faint keening began, thin as a knife blade, venomous, terrible to hear. Aldwulf placed his hand over the runes and spoke aloud, still in the old language: 'It is no ordinary mortal life. We hold one who must be of the race of the Sidhe, at least in part, a servant of the Light, whose name is Gwalchmai. He carries a sword which is powerful for Light, of use to you.'

I closed my eyes, leaning against the door frame, sickness on me like a great cold hand.

The keening stopped. The body began to swing again, this time in a circle which grew more and more violent. Aldwulf cast the runes. 'Possible,' he read. 'With sword, possible. Kill ... offering first ... No,' he added, covering the runes and looking up again. 'First kill the Pendragon, and you will have your offering.'

The keening began again, and the body jerked on the rope, as though it were trying to come to life again. Aldwulf tossed down the runesticks. 'Impossible. Need sword. For sword, need killing. Kill.'

'Very well,' said Aldwulf. 'But tell your master that, if he does not kill the High King Arthur after I have given him his offering and the sword, I, the Flame-bearer, will seek out as many of his kind as I may and destroy them until he will regret that he cheated me; and I will destroy you first. Do you doubt me, demon?'

The runes themselves jerked into a new pattern. 'The bargain . . . will be fulfilled.'

'In two weeks, then,' said Aldwulf and, rising abruptly, he snuffed out the candle. At once the shadow vanished. The body swung slowly to a halt. Aldwulf walked over to one wall, out of my sight, and I heard him striking a flint. Presently a torch flared up, and Aldwulf walked across the room with it to light another torch on the other wall. He surveyed the body and the pattern on the floor, then looked up at Cerdic and smiled. 'You see, King of the West Saxons?' he asked, his voice again pleasant and drawling.

'Your power is real, Aldwulf,' replied Cerdic. 'But you had proved that to me already. You have arranged with Woden for Arthur to die?'

'Arthur will die when we have made the offering.'

'Woden seems to have a great taste for dead men.' Cerdic commented, eyeing the corpse. 'Will you fetch that self-professed thrall from the stables now, or wait until tomorrow?'

Aldwulf shrugged, and began to scuff out the pattern with his foot. 'Not tonight and not tomorrow. It will be difficult work, and it is important to choose the best time for it, when all things will aid us.' Bending over, he picked up the rune sticks, wiped each one with a cloth before putting it away in a small bag of black leather. 'In two weeks it will be the dark of the moon. It would be best to do it then.'

'Two weeks!' said Cerdic. 'I must keep this youth a prisoner here for two weeks, and only kill him when he begins to think himself safe? No, no, we must do it sooner.'

Aldwulf drew tight the string on his little bag, abruptly so that the rune sticks clicked together sharply. 'If you are afraid, King of the West Saxons, or if you think the price too great, say so.'

'You would do well to think before you say that word, "afraid", to me, Aldwulf of Bernicia. But I do not like this killing of thralls, and like it less if they are to be men of my own household. And I would sooner kill ten men in fair combat than . . .' He left the sentence unfinished, contemplating the hanging body with disgust.

Aldwulf glanced at it, then pulled out his belt knife and began to cut it down. 'You have become very honourable of a sudden. Shall I return to my own kingdom, then, and leave you to kill Arthur – in fair combat?'

Cerdic said nothing. The rope suspending the body parted, and it fell heavily to the floor. Aldwulf stepped back, sheathing his knife, and looked across it at Cerdic.

'I wish Arthur dead,' the king of the West Saxons said slowly. 'And because I cannot kill him by fair means, I will use what means I may. Very well, in two weeks time.'

Aldwulf smiled. 'Brave and ambitious! Good. You must think, as well, that this young fool who is asleep in your stables is not what he pretends to be. He is no thrall, and is probably not even a mortal man such as ourselves. Who knows why he has come here? Certainly he means no good to you and yours. And the gods I worship want his sword, and he must be dead, I think, to get it from him. We were very lucky in finding him.'

Cerdic grunted. 'So you say. When Arthur is dead, then I will believe.'

'What? All that I have done, and still you disbelieve me? What of the flood? What of the horse I gave you? And speaking of that horse . . .'

'He is not yet broken,' Cerdic said harshly. 'Very well, I believe in your powers well enough. I admitted as much. But it is said that Arthur has some Christian or druidical magics to protect him. When he is dead, and only when he is dead, will I believe that your god is stronger.'

'He is strong,' said Aldwulf confidently. 'He is very strong.'

Yes, the Darkness is very strong, I thought as I walked back to my place by the stables. Oh Light, protect me. I am afraid.

Not, I thought, as I lay down in the stable again, that Aldwulf's demon was likely to succeed in killing Arthur where Morgawse had failed. I did not see how they could use the sword for that. Aldwulf might be powerful, but still weaker than the Queen of Darkness. Aldwulf was still mortal, and Morgawse was not.

But knowing that Aldwulf's bargain would not be fulfilled would do me little good if Cerdic and Aldwulf offered me to their demon.

I held my lower lip with my teeth, stifling a desire to jump up and run screaming away from the place. Offer me. Put the rope around my neck and set my body swinging back and forth by the candlelight, possessed by demons. I could almost feel the cord around my neck, see the terrible darkness. Sacrifice me? Why? Because I served the Light, owned a sword and . . .

And was not fully human.

So Aldwulf thought. And suddenly I realized what the expression on Wulf's face and on the faces of his kinsmen had been, the same look with which Cerdic's servants had greeted me. It was the great fear, the fear of the unknown thing from the dark, the unnatural, the supernatural.

I sat up in the darkness, clutching Caledvvlch's hilt.

'I am human,' I said out loud. My blood beat in my ears, I was sick with weariness and fear, my legs ached, feet were sore and blistered, and my clothes itched and were too tight. I was human, I thought, clinging to these things. How could they believe differently?

But they did. They all had, at the first meeting at least. I looked at the ruby in Caledvvlch's hilt, dark in the night as my own fear.

Who am I? I asked myself desperately. Gwalchmai. Gwalchmai ap Lot, a warrior of the Light, yes. But human! What has happened to me?

My king, I said in my heart, My king, I am afraid. The Darkness is very strong, and I who am to fight it do not even know who I am, and fear even myself. How can I escape? Even if I can match Aldwulf, Cerdic has an army, hundreds of warriors, thousands of soldiers, ranks of steel and set minds all afraid of the supernatural: solid, worldly power, unarguable blood and iron. And they do not think that I am human, and my mother is Queen of Darkness and desires my death.

My mother. I thought of her again, and of all that she had taught me. How deeply had it marked me? Deeply enough for Aldwulf to suspect me, deeply enough to unnerve anyone who so much as looked at me. Or perhaps that one day or three years in the Isles of the Blessed had changed me without my noticing it into something completely different, something unalterably alien from my fellow men.

And what land is this, I asked myself. Far, far from home. Far from my kinsmen and my clan, people who knew me and laughed at me and would protect me, and who must all of them think me dead. And I would be better dead than alone as a thrall in a strange kingdom, fated to be hanged as a sacrifice to an alien god, as Connall almost was . . .

Connall of Dalriada, my knife bringing him a quick death. Morgawse's demon, and the escape. Lugh's Hall, the song in it, the fire of Caledvwlch, and the light behind the sunset . . .

I cried, shaking silently in the dark stable. I am sorry, my lord High King, for doubting you. You would not abandon your warriors to die, and I have no right to flee from the battle after you rescued me once.

The light rose slowly into Caledvwlch, glowed, burned, blazed. I held the crosspieces, leaning my forehead against the pommel and feeling the light move within me, rising upward like a flood of music. Have faith. Do not wonder at what happens.

Seven

It was late when I awoke the next day, past mid morning. Cerdic's thralls were pleased when I finally woke, for I was in their way, but strangely they had been unwilling to wake me. When I was up, though, I was told to go to the well to wash and, after I had done so, the chief thrall brought me some clothes. They were worn, but clean, and they fitted well, as did the new pair of boots and the cloak. I felt slightly more human when I had put these on, and I slung Caledvwlch over my shoulder.

At this, the chief thrall frowned. 'What are you doing with that?' he asked. 'You've no right to bear weapons. You must know that.'

I shrugged. 'No one's taken it from me yet, and until they do, I'll keep it.'

He shook his head. 'You can be beaten for that, even killed. Are you new to thraldom?'

I nodded.

'Well then, take my word for it, you had better not keep that sword. Give it to the master.'

'I think that I will keep it, nonetheless,' I said quietly. 'It means something to me.'

The old man looked distressed, then shrugged. 'Well, it is your back risking the whip, not mine. Would you like something to eat?'

'Very much.'

He gave me oatcakes with honey and milk, which I devoured in a very short time. The thrall grinned at me.

'You've had little to eat recently, haven't you? Those warriors the master bought you from must have travelled a fair way. Tell me . . .' A glint came into his eyes. 'Were you with the Pendragon? How goes the war?'

With the coming of daylight and my appetite, he seemed to have forgotten whatever he had felt about me the night before. I smiled, but regretfully shook my head in answer to his question. 'I don't know. I have come from over the sea. I hoped that you could tell me.'

He shook his head. 'They tell us nothing. We have ways of

knowing: we hear from farmers, or overhear – but we're never sure whether what we hear is true or only a rumour. Sometimes we never do know.' He stood and began clearing the dishes. 'My name is Llemyndd ap Llwch, from what used to be eastern Ebrauc. I am the chief thrall here, the steward of Cerdic's house. It was my father who was captured from Ebrauc: I was born Cerdic's thrall. And you? You said that your name is Gwalchmai, but what of your kinsmen and country?'

I was about to answer truthfully, when I felt a sudden uncertainty. This Llemyndd might be other than he seemed. 'How strange,' I said. 'My father's name is Llwch, too.' (which it was, if one put it into British). 'But I am from Gododdin.' I was willing to wager that there would be no thralls from such a distant kingdom in Cerdic's house who could give me the lie, and I had heard something of that country in Dun Fionn.

Llemyndd whistled. 'That is a long way distant.'

I nodded. 'I came south with my elder brother three years ago, by sea. We went to Gaul to buy some of those Gaulish war-horses for breeding. My clan deals in horses, and, as you must know, the Gaulish breed is the best. All the warriors were wanting horses like those the Pendragon has, and my clan thought that there should be a fine profit in it. And there would have been, too, if our ship had not been found by a Saxon longship off the coast of East Anglia.'

'Anglia? That's a long way north. How did you come down here among the Franks and Saxons?'

'Ach, we were not bested by that pirate,' I improvised quickly. 'Mine is a noble clan, and we fought back. But our ship was badly damaged, and we decided to go about to Dumnonia, down the Saxon Shore, and travel to Gododdin by land. But our bad luck turned worse: a storm arose, and we foundered against the cliffs of the Cantii. My brother and I found the keel of the ship and clung to it, praying. The next morning, when the waves stilled, we managed to swim ashore, but we were taken by a Saxon of the land thereabouts.'

Llemyndd nodded wisely and drew the rest of my story from me with great care. I told him what I had told Wulf and Eduin the day before, adding details of how kind my 'master' had been to us, and how I had come to like him, despite resenting the slavery, and how treacherously his enemies had killed him. It was a good story, and a few of the other thralls came in to listen while I was telling it. All were sympathetic, though all looked at me with a searching hesitancy, questioning what they had seen the night before.

My suspicions of Llemyndd proved justified. He tried to trap me, subtly, testing my story with unexpected questions. It is fortunate that he knew less of Gododdin than I did, or I would have been caught at once. But, finally satisfied, he went off, and I suspected that he went to tell Cerdic what I had told him. I doubted, remembering Cerdic's sharp green eyes, that the Saxon would believe the tale.

One of the other household thralls watched Llemyndd leave with a half-concealed bitterness that confirmed what I had suspected. Llemyndd was Cerdic's, mind, spirit and body.

'Now the master will know everything,' said the thrall.

'So that is the way of it, then,' I replied.

'It is indeed.'

The other thralls looked uneasy. 'Hush,' said one. 'You talk too much, Gwawl.'

Gwawl hushed. A few more questions revealed to me that the thralls hated and feared Llemyndd, 'though most of them did not dislike their master Cerdic, to whom Llemyndd reported, and who would punish them for speaking disloyally. 'The master is fair,' I was told. 'Do your job and he will treat you well.' I nodded and settled to trying to discover what my situation actually was.

It took time. The thralls would not talk to me freely the first day, or the second either. They might never have done so but for the music. They were sick for familiar songs. The British are the most civilized people in the West, and they love music as only civilized men can. They sing to themselves constantly, as the men of the Orcades or the Irish do, and any wandering bard is assured of a welcome among them. In Erin or the Orcades it is easy to see why bards and druids are so important, for in those lands it is the trained bards who memorize the laws and recite them to the kings, and who can chant the genealogies and histories and say when it is time for planting corn and such. But the British bards have no other job but to sing songs, while the rest of the work is done by books, and yet they are no less honoured than the Irish *fillidh*. These thralls of Cerdic's could sing as they worked, and a few knew harping, but proper bardic music they had missed for years. The first time I played for them they wept for joy. For a song they would tell me anything I wanted to know of their master's secrets, and not reckon the punishment for telling.

Aldwulf's name was familiar to them. Aldwulf Fflamddwyn, Aldwulf Flame-bearer, they called him. Somehow his private sorcerous name had become the property of all Britain. He was feared by his own men, while Cerdic was loved and admired. Because of this, beyond his own clan he had few warriors in his warband, and when he raised an army from the farmers of his kingdom, more than the ordinary number of men never showed up. Nonetheless, Aldwulf was wealthy and powerful and, allied to Cerdic, he was much to be feared. The alliance between the West Saxons and distant Bernicia, a thing surprising on the face of it, had in fact begun nearly two years before. Cerdic had been bested by Arthur in a series of engagements, and had responded by forming treaties with all the other Saxon kingdoms. It was not a proper military alliance, however, merely an agreement between the Saxon kings to lay aside private differences, and to render aid and sanctuary to any other Saxon who happened to be in difficulties with the British in their territory – 'Saxon territory' being defined as more than half of Britain. A few of the Saxon kings had entered into armed alliance as well, mainly in the south. Aldwulf was not of this number, but had come south, with most of his warband, to give aid and counsel to Cerdic. He wished to prevent the British High King from coming north. He had arrived at the beginning of April and had wormed his way into Cerdic's confidence with gifts and – so the thralls added in whispers – by magic. They were extremely unwilling to speak of the magic to me, but they were sure he was a witch, and one or two of them – including one of Cerdic's few Saxon thralls – told me various tales about his witchcraft, some of which were certainly false. None of the thralls liked Aldwulf, and those that liked Cerdic bewailed the day their master had met the Bernician king.

Cerdic had been fighting the High King Arthur for nearly three years now, and the war had become more difficult for him with each month. He had had great success when first he invaded, but Arthur's first move after establishing himself in power had been to outflank Cerdic's invasion force and plunder his base, the old Saxon Shore fort of Anderida. Cerdic had kept most of his supplies and all his plunder there, and the loss had been great. The Saxon was forced to retreat to Anderida, and Arthur had gone on to win victories against some other Saxon kings, one on a surprise raid as far north as Deira. Cerdic had heard of the last and moved against his British enemies while he thought the High King was staying in the north, only to be caught by Arthur's over-rapid return. It was at this point that Cerdic had arranged his treaties with the other Saxons.

Cerdic's problem was that Arthur had no regular army. He could command the allegiance of any British kingdom, and hence was able to request the king of whatever land he wished to visit to raise the farmers and clansmen of his territory, and most of the kings would comply. Arthur's strength lay in his warband, the largest and finest of any king in Britain. Half of this warband consisted of the infamous cavalry which had caused such grief to my father, but all of the warband owned several horses apiece and could borrow more when Arthur needed to hurry across Britain. This gave the Pendragon a kind of speed and mobility which Cerdic could not hope to equal: Cerdic had no cavalry at all, and, while he could raise a very large army, most of the men in it were clansmen and farmers, who could not fight in the harvest or sowing seasons, and who were ill-trained and ill-equipped, and worst of all, ill-disciplined. Movement of such a force took a long time. Cerdic had also his own warband, of course, those professional warriors who depended upon him alone for their support, but this alone, or even this in alliance with the warbands of several other kings, was no match for the High King Arthur.

Cerdic's thralls had a great deal to say about Arthur. The British thralls, even those who had been born to slavery, admired the High King with great passion and delighted in recounting the ways and occasions on which he had bested the Saxons, in spite of the fact that Cerdic had forbidden anyone to mention Arthur's name within his house without his permission. It seemed to me as I listened that Arthur's warband must be increasing in power, even allowing for the accumulation of legends and the exaggeration of the thralls.

It was reasonable to suppose it: if a king is victorious in battle and generous in his Hall, warriors will flock to him from over all the Western world. Even some notable Saxon warriors had joined the High King's warband. Two and a half years after beginning his war against the Saxons, Arthur must have a band of men unequalled in the West – probably unequalled in the world. They could and regularly did, it seemed, defeat four times their number.

'But the past two years,' one thrall complained to me, 'there's been little to do. The master raises the *fyrd* and gathers his warband, then sits here in Sorviodunum – your pardon, Searisbyrig – sending out raiding parties and spies; and the Emperor just sends raiding parties and spies back.'

It was a sensible move on Cerdic's part, I thought. A large warband, like Arthur's, is expensive to keep. Since he had no kingdom of his own, Arthur relied on tribute from all the kings of Britain. But he had gained the purple by defeating those very kings he exacted the tribute from, and they had not forgotten it. He needed their support and their armies against the Saxons; he could not antagonize them further by demanding vast amounts of tribute. While he fought and defeated the Saxons, he could support himself from plunder and sweeten his subjects' tempers by sharing the booty, but when the Saxons retreated and sat firm in a strong fortified position, content with guarding their borders, Arthur had to rely upon his subjects. They would be the less inclined to support him when they could see no tangible tokens of victory. Cerdic was hoping to provoke the British kingdoms into another civil war, and I learned from one thrall that there were kings in Britain who were willing to overthrow 'the usurping bastard', and that messages had been sent to and from some of these men into this fortress, Sorviodunum or Searisbyrig. Cerdic understood statecraft. Unfortunately, most of his followers did not, and many, to whom he had promised land, felt cheated and muttered angrily that Cerdic was afraid. The war had become a race between Cerdic and Arthur over who would first be forced to raise the full armies and offer a pitched battle. At the moment it seemed that Arthur might win the race, and Cerdic was desperately angry. It was probably because of this that he was willing to employ Aldwulf's sorcery to kill Arthur. Cerdic left to himself was honourable and generous, but ambition was his ruling passion, and honour was sacrificed to the end of obtaining a kingdom. Still, I think, it troubled him. He did not like the thought of killing me after I had served him, and because of it treated me harshly himself, while at the same time commanding his household to allow me great liberties. I think that the idea of killing Arthur by such a means troubled him still more, for he wished frequently to hear songs of the Pendragon's battles, privately, yet grew angry after only a verse or so, and had to be left, brooding over the song and his thoughts. But he remained resolute.

For my part, I came to admire the Pendragon in those weeks. He sounded more than ever to be a lord worth following. At the same time, though, my worries increased. Arthur would have no use for unskilled warriors like myself, who would do nothing but drain his already strained resources.

On the other hand, I told myself whenever I considered this, I might die by Aldwulf's hand at the dark of the moon, and the matter would not concern me at all. And I would throw myself into some other task so as not to think of it.

Cerdic did not set me any tasks in the house, which was fortunate, for I soon realized I did not know how to work as a thrall. I had not noticed how much I took it for granted that I was a king's son, even a younger and despised king's son, and that there were certain things those of a royal clan do not do. I found that I expected others to open doors, fetch things, pick things up. I had no notion of how to go about cleaning a floor or mending the thatch, and was, at first, angry when told to do some menial task. Continually I had to correct myself, and tell myself that these servants were fellow servants. I did not fool them. Coming into the stable one day I heard one of the grooms saying to a house-servant, 'If he's a thrall, I'm the Emperor Theodosius. Do you know . . .' – and he stopped abruptly when he saw me. No; there were few tasks for me as a thrall. But Cerdic expected me to be ready to play the harp at any time of day or night, and I had my own inquiries to make. Besides that, I was attempting to learn the basics of the Saxon tongue . . . and then, there was Ceincaled.

Leaving the stables on my first day as Cerdic's thrall, I saw a crowd of men gathered in a circle on a hillside just beyond the Roman part of the town, and I went to investigate. Aldwulf had mentioned that he gave a horse to Cerdic to prove his power at sorcery, and Cerdic had accepted it as proof, although unable to break the horse. As I came through the circle and saw the stallion that reared in the centre of the ring, I understood why.

No earthly mare had borne that horse. The steeds of the Sidhe, praised in a hundred songs, show their immortality in every line; and that horse was a lord among even such horses as those.

He stood three hands taller at the shoulder than the largest horse I had seen before, and that had been a giant of a plough-horse. He was lovely: pure white, splendid and powerful as a storm on the sea. The white neck curved like the sea's waves before they break, the mane was like foam flung up from the rocks. No seagull skims the water as lightly as those hooves skimmed the earth, and no sea-eagle struck at the ground with such fierceness or such freedom. The horse's nostrils were flared wide and red, defiant in anger, his eyes dark and savage with pride. I held my breath at the sight of him.

The Saxon who had just been thrown scrambled out of the way, and some grooms from Cerdic's stable drove the horse back to the centre of the ring with whips and flapping cloaks, cursing him.

'That beast is a man-killer,' said one of the thralls, who was standing a few feet from me. 'Cerdic cannot believe that he will ever tame it.'

'He is beautiful, that horse,' I said. The man looked at me, surprised and suspicious. He recognized me, shrugged uncomfortably.

'Of course,' he said, 'and strong and swift. He could out-run and out-stay any horse in Britain, that one. But what is the use of all of it, since he can't be ridden? You are new here and wouldn't know, but we have tried for a month now to break him, with kindness and with blows, with riding and with starving, and we are no nearer to taming him than we were when Cerdic first acquired him. I know horses, and I say that this one will die before he obeys a man. And before he dies he will probably take some of us with him . . . Watch out, there! Hey, you! . . . Cerdic won't name him till he's ridden him, but we of his house call the beast Ceincaled, Harsh Beauty, for that, surely, is what he is.'

It took little time for me to see the truth of the man's words. The horse tried to kill every human near him. There was no viciousness in these attempts, no hatred of humanity such as

118

one finds in an animal which has been badly mistreated, but instead a wild, pure, elemental power which could bear no subjection. He was proud, Ceincaled, not with a pride such as men have, but as a falcon or eagle is proud. He was like the music in Lugh's Hall: splendid, but not for men. I wondered what dark spell of Aldwulf's had captured the stallion and brought him from the Plain of Joy to captivity and eventual death in the lands of men.

There were times during the next two weeks when I felt a strong sense of kinship with the stallion. I was not an immortal, but my problem was similar. I was trapped, and all my efforts to escape only wasted my time and brought nearer the time set down for my death.

Cerdic had all of his large warband with him in Sorviodunum (to use the Roman name): three hundred and twelve picked warriors, who guarded the fort. He had also an army of some five thousand – as always, the exact number was uncertain. The camp was continually prepared for war, and raiding parties left or returned nearly every day, if only from short forays. I thought of trying to slip from the camp when one of these arrived, and hung about the gate and a low spot in the walls for a while, until I was warned off the guards, who, besides being exceedingly vigilant, were suspicious. I considered the forest I had walked through, and looked out over it from the hill-top centre of the fortress. I thought it must be easy to disappear into the trees. Unfortunately, though, the forest only extended towards the north-east. There were miles of open plain adjoining the town on the west, where lay the nearest British kingdom. And I was watched, even if there had been some way to cross the walls and the plains. No one forbade me to roam about the town, but some thrall or some warrior always seemed to be about. Cerdic did not wish his semi-human sacrifice to escape. It disturbed me nearly as much as the fear of death and my still unresolved fears about myself. I had always wanted solitude, and to be denied it grated against my nerves.

I prayed to the Light, but he did not respond. I began to want, and want badly, simply to draw Caledvwlch and try to splash my way out of the fort. I knew that it would be certain death to do so, but at least it would be a clean death, and a warrior's death. I was tired of being a thrall. I was trapped, and that word seemed to resound continually through my mind, all of each day. At night I dreamt of it, and I thought of it before anything else each morning when I woke. Trapped, like a hawk that had flown by mistake into a fisherman's net, who, when he beats his wings only discovers how truly entangled he is, and exhausts his strength against the ropes.

I became aware of time with a terrifying intensity, of how the sun rising in the morning splashed the sky with colours whose softness I had never noticed so clearly before; of how the shadows shortened and lengthened as the hours passed during the day. At night I watched the moon, sliding from full down into its fourth quarter, growing thinner with every night that passed. The moon was my friend, my ally. While she still shone I would not die. But she was leaving the sky, and when she had gone, all would be darkness.

Sometimes I felt that the Light had withdrawn in the same way. After alerting me to Cerdic's plan, it became as silent as the moon. Two weeks is not a long time, but those two weeks, full of the tension of waiting and the terror of the trap, seemed endless and, at the same time, seemed to be gone at once. I felt that I had been abandoned by my lord. I was left to myself, and I was afraid of myself as well. I cannot say why it so terrified me to think of myself as not human. Most men would be pleased to consider themselves apart from humanity – or they think they would be. It was not the loneliness, though that may have been a part of it, for I was accustomed to loneliness. Perhaps it was simply fear of the unknown. All fear what they do not understand, the more so when that unknown is a part of themselves.

So I watched the Saxons trying to break Ceincaled, and looked after the horse when he was stabled, to free myself from myself. The purity of the white horse seemed to defy and mock the complexity of the terrors that beset me. His battle was the one I longed for, the simple brilliance of physical struggle.

Two weeks. The moon became a sliver in the sky, a thin hair of light, and the spaces between the stars were very black. The next night there would be no moon. The next night . . . it was my last day, and I had decided nothing. When evening came, if there should still be no escape, I had resolved to draw Caledvwlch and try to see whether I could kill Aldwulf and Cerdic before they killed me.

I stood again in the circle that hemmed in Ceincaled and

watched Cerdic try again to ride the horse, and again be thrown. Across from me, Aldwulf was chewing his beard. He had been trying some new sorcery on the horse to please Cerdic, but his spells had failed and he was shamed and angry.

'By the worm!' said Cerdic, picking himself up. 'I have been cheated.'

He had. I could guess the price that Aldwulf had persuaded him to pay for the horse – a human life, the usual price in bargains with Yffern – and, while the life of some prisoner or thrall might be counted cheap for such a horse, Ceincaled was as useless to Cerdic as if he had been a lame cart-horse. Even though Ceincaled could leave behind every horse in the camp...

By the sun and the wind! Mentally I swore Agravain's favourite oath. I had been blind, looking about in the night of my own shadow, when the sun was behind me. How, I asked myself, beginning to find it very funny, how could I ever been so stupid?

And was my other problem so simple as this? I asked myself as I edged round to Cerdic. All my questioning of my identity, would it too come clear in a burst of light when I looked in the right direction? My High King, lord . . .

'My lord King,' I said to Cerdic, who had noticed my approach and was eyeing me without enthusiasm. 'Could I try to ride the horse?'

Cerdic gave me a furious glare, then hit me hard enough to make me stagger for balance. 'You insolent dog! You slave, do you think to succeed where a king failed? I should have you whipped!' I saw that I had misjudged the degree of his anger about the horse and bowed my head, trying to think and rubbing my jaw.

'Cerdic,' Aldwulf interrupted suddenly. 'You might let him try.'

'What!'

'They may be from the same land. Who knows? The boy has been caring for the horse.' Aldwulf's thought was plain. I would use magic on the horse, tame it, be killed, and the king would have both my sword and the horse. Aldwulf was smiling in a very satisfied fashion. It had been a sore point with him, I think, that his fine horse was unridable.

Cerdic looked at me, remembering what Aldwulf said I

was. 'Very well,' he said at last. 'Try, then.'

'Thank you, Cyning Cerdic,' I said softly. 'I will do my best.'

Cerdic nodded to Aldwulf. I turned back towards Ceincaled.

He had been caught by the grooms again, and waited patiently while they held him, conserving his strength for his rider. I walked over, thanked the man who held him, and took the bridle. As I held it, I suddenly doubted my ability to ride him, which a minute before had seemed so clear. I had always been good with horses, and the stallion knew me now, but that might well be no use at all. He objected not so much to the Darkness in his riders as to being ridden at all. It would take a spirit equal to his own to hold him, and even then he might die rather than accept defeat. But I had to ride him, or die that evening.

I stroked the white neck, whispering to the horse. He jerked away from me, then quieted, waiting, preparing for the battle. He was more intelligent than an ordinary horse. I had watched him fight Cerdic and knew this.

I ran my hand over his back and withers, tightened the girth of the saddle, speaking in a sing-song, in Irish, no longer caring who heard. In my heart I asked the Light to rein in that proud spirit for me, and grant me the victory. Then I placed my left hand on the stallion's shoulder and vaulted to his back.

The only way to describe what happened next is to say that he exploded. The world dissolved into a white cloud of mane, and Ceincaled fought with all his terrible strength and limitless pride. I held his mane and the reins both, gripping hard with my knees and bending down on to his neck, and barely managed to stay on.

He circled the ring, rearing and plunging, and the onlookers were a blur of flesh, bright colours, steel and distorted shouts. I felt that I tried to ride the storm, or hold the north wind with a bridle. It was beyond the power of any human, and now that I tried my strength against an immortal I knew that I was no more than human. Ceincaled was pure, fierce, wild beyond belief. He had no master and could accept none . . .

And he was glorious.

I stopped caring about past and future, about thought and

122

feeling. Aldwulf might hang me or I might fall from Ceincaled and be trampled, broken by the wildness of the power I had tried to master. But even as I saw these things they became as distant and unimportant as an abandoned game. There was a sweet taste at the back of my mouth, like mint in the middle of a rainy night. Ceincaled was leaping again, clothed in thunder, and death and life were both unreal. All that mattered was the sweet madness which possessed both the horse and me, madness which had swept on to me from within and changed the world to something I could no longer recognize, or care to. When I had drawn Caledvwlch there had been something of the sensation of light, but this was more a lightness, a blazing sweetness in my mind. I loved Ceincaled totally, and in mid-leap he felt it and returned the love, and we were no longer fighting each other but flying, dazzled with delight, filled with the same and equal fierceness.

Ceincaled reared one last time and neighed, a challenge to all the world, then dropped onto all four legs in the centre of the circle and stood tensely still.

Through the battle-madness that made the world seem sharp-edged, almost frozen, I saw the onlookers staring at me in wonder, Aldwulf frowning in a sudden unease, and Cerdic, eyes alight with greed.

'Good,' said the King of the West Saxons. His voice sounded far away. 'Now give me my horse.'

I laughed, and he started, flushing with anger. Aldwulf, realizing now what was happening, grabbed Cerdic's arm. Cerdic began to turn to him, an angry question forming on his tongue . . .

I had Caledvwlch out, and its light leapt up, pure and brilliant as a star. Ceincaled rushed at Cerdic. Someone was screaming in terror.

Cerdic flung himself aside, rolled, Ceincaled's hooves missing him by inches. Aldwulf, pressing back into the crowd, was less quick and less fortunate. He cried out before my sword touched him, blinded by its light, shrieking some curse – then screamed as the blade struck him. But Ceincaled struck the rope that bounded the make-shift-ring, breaking it, and my hand was jerked back. Aldwulf was not killed, though he would miss his left eye, and I wanted to go back and finish him, for he deserved destruction; but Ceincaled was stretching into a run and I forgot Aldwulf with the taste of the wind.

The Roman streets swept past, blurred with speed, and behind us someone was shouting to stop me, kill me. A warrior on the street ran into my path, dropped to one knee, his long thrusting spear braced against me. Everything narrowed to him as I approached. I saw his face, grinning in fear and excitement, sweat gleaming on it. I saw the sun flash off the tip of his spear, and loved the leap of it, loved him as well, knew that Ceincaled was only three paces away. I touched the horse with my knee, forcing him to swerve the barest fraction, and the spear-tip, flashing forward, missed us. With my left hand I caught the shaft and with my right swung down Caledvwlch. My mind was still dazzled with madness as the sword struck, blazing, and the warrior's neck spurted red as it was cut through. Then I was past. There were others, at the gate. I killed the nearest with the spear I had taken from the first, and cut through the spear-shaft of the second and let Ceincaled run over him. I found that I was singing, and laughed again. How could they hope to stop me? The Saxons were fleeing now. One threw a spear, but I swerved Ceincaled and it missed. My horse leaned into the race, and there were no others before me, only the open gate and the Roman road stretching into the west. We flew down it like a gull, like the hawk of my name. The Saxons were far behind. Even when they mounted a party to follow us, they were far behind. Too far to catch up again, I thought, remotely; too far ever to catch us again. We were free.

Eight

The rest of that race is not clear in my mind. It was a sweet rhythm of flying hooves and wind, and the empty hills of the plain before and about me after we abandoned the road. I sang for pure joy, laughing, loving the world and all men in it, even Cerdic, whom I would gladly have killed had he been here. Oh, the Light was a strong lord, a great High King. Any warrior would be proud to serve him.

It was late afternoon, and Ceincaled began to tire a little. I reined him to a canter. We still had a long way before us, I reminded myself.

How long a way? I could not guess. I was totally uncertain of distances in Britain, and had no idea of how far we had come. A great distance, surely, at such a speed. Some of the blindingly bright light died down within my mind, and I looked about myself.

I was nearing the western edge of the plain. The land to either side of me looked something like the Orcades in that it was open and hilly, but these hills were wider and greener. Checking by the sun I discovered that I was going north as well as west, and realized that I must have been doing so for some time. I had a vague recollection of the Roman road following the curve of a hill and Ceincaled galloping off it on to the plain, north-west. It was good, I decided, that we had turned west on the Roman road. If we had not – and in that madness we could easily not have – Ceincaled and I would have gone tearing off east, into the heart of the Saxon kingdoms. The thought made me smile, and the rest of the ecstasy departed. I slowed Ceincaled to a trot and turned him due west again.

Westward the hills became steeper, and soon there was a dark line of forest before us. Before we reached this, however, we came upon a river. It was a small, sleepy river, still dark with spring mud, and it calmly reflected the oak trees on its further bank. I rode northwards along the bank for a way, until I found a place where the bank was low enough for Ceincaled to cross it easily.

When he approached the water, the horse snuffled

interestedly. I dismounted and let him drink, talking to him softly while he did. He was thirsty and wet with sweat, but, incredibly, not hot to steaming, as any other horse would have been after anything resembling our race.

Watching the horse drink made me thirsty. As I knelt by the water, I saw that I was still holding Caledvwlch. I smiled and began to sheath the sword – then realized that there was blood on it.

I remembered, with an almost physical shock, the Saxons who had got in my way. I remembered Aldwulf falling back unconscious into the circle of Saxons, the left side of his face cut open, and the others dying, and how I had laughed. I dropped the sword on the grass and leant back on my heels, staring at it, as though the killing had been its responsibility and not mine. Then I saw that the horse was drinking too much, and stood to pull him away from the water and walk him about to cool him down. I had killed. I had just killed three men, and horribly wounded a fourth, and I had not even been aware of it until now. No, killed four men, if one counted Connall. But that had been mercy, and this was . . . it was war, a battle.

I let the horse go back to the water and drink some more. Lugh had given me his blessing, to carry into whatever battles lay before me. Could that madness that had possessed me be such a blessing? CuChulainn, they say, went mad in battle, and he was the son of Lugh. There are kinds of madness which are said to be divine or sacred. Mine had felt so. But it frightened me, that I could kill and not care. But could I say that I had been wrong to escape as I did?

I cleaned the sword on the grass, rubbed it on my cloak, and sheathed it again. Then I knelt and drank from the river. The water tasted like its source's appearance: slow and rich, peaceful. It was calming, so I sat on the bank and watched. Ceincaled had finished his drink, and now waded in the stream, enjoying the feel of it. I went to him and unfastened the saddle, quickly, then rubbed him down with a handful of grass and allowed him to splash into the stream again, and again myself sat down.

I looked at my reflection, which trembled with Ceincaled's disturbance of the water. I had changed since I last studied my face, back at the pond at Llyn Gwalch. It was a strange face now, marked by strange things. The eyes, though, floating reflected on the dark water, were the same, and just as puzzled by what they saw as before. But now there was a kind of intensity to the face, the look of a warrior and something uncanny as well. I shook my head and looked at Ceincaled again. I, a warrior. I had killed three trained Saxon warriors and wounded a Saxon king. But how could I, Gwalchmai mac Lot, the worst warrior in all the Orcades, an utter failure in arms, do such a thing as that? The warriors had been frightened and off balance because of the size and speed of Ceincaled and because of the fire which blazed in my sword. Otherwise I would have been killed at once. Certainly, it sounded like a dashing exploit such as a famous warrior might boast of in a feast hall, but I knew better.

Knew what better? I thought of the fierce being I had been only an hour before and wondered. I remembered what I had seen in myself when I first drew Caeldvwlch, that darkness, and afterwards the power and certainty as I held the sword; and I remembered Lugh's warning. How, in that mingling of human passion and divine madness, to distinguish between light and darkness? The disturbing idea that I was something other than human returned to me. I knew now, though, that whatever had happened I remained as human as any, even if I could ride Ceincaled. The horse had shown me that. I had not mastered him, but he had consented to obey me, out of love. It would take an immortal to break that stallion, and I was only human; I could only persuade him. This was comforting to me. It is human to be in ignorance, to be uncertain, and assuredly I was that. I was only a man who had seen things greater than those most men have seen, and the essence of those things had touched me, as a warrior is touched by his work, and a king by his. (Morgawse, Mother, I wondered, how deeply have you touched me?) But that was all, that was the whole of the explanation.

I laughed at my reflection. 'You truly are a proper fool, do you know that?' I asked it. 'The answer was directly in front of you, and you turned your back on it. You worry too much.'

Ceincaled pricked his ears forward, listening, then tossed his head. I laughed again, stood, and went and caught his bridle. He snorted, then pushed his nose into my hair and nibbled at it, as horses do.

'Hush, brave one, bright one,' I told him. 'That is not

grass. It is not even the proper colour.'

Ceincaled nickered, and I ran my hand down his neck. It was a shock to recall where he had come from. Poor Ceincaled. Torn from the marvels of those islands beyond the sunset, subjected to Cerdic's speed and Aldwulf's spells, to whips and starvation, the bit and the spur, to Darkness and to death, when all that he should have known were the fields of golden flowers, the endless spring for all eternity. I picked another handful of grass and brushed him down again. He was beautiful, this horse, too beautiful for Earth. With him I had won my freedom. Now, I felt certain, the Saxons could never find me again (barring accidents), and I no longer needed Ceincaled. In fact, he could easily become a hindrance, since such a horse is noticed and remarked upon. Had there been a choice, I would have kept the horse and given him up to no one: I loved him, his beauty and his splendid spirit. But I had no right to repay the gift of freedom he had brought with the death which would result from my keeping him.

Slowly, I took off the bridle. Ceincaled stood very still, and his image in the dark water trembled only slightly. 'Go, friend,' I told him. 'You have won your freedom. Go home. Perhaps Lugh Master of All Arts will ride you, but you are suited to no lesser being. You fought well and bravely, and I give you my thanks.'

Ceincaled hesitated, as though listening and understanding, then tossed his head, snorted at the bridle, and plunged into the river. When he had crossed it he galloped off westward. I watched him vanish among the trees, then sighed, crossed the river myself, and headed west.

The forest was not so thick as the one near which I had woken. Still, it was thick enough to confuse the Saxons if they were still following me. I doubted, though, that they were. Cerdic must have sent men after me, but I suspected that they would not notice where I left the road. And I had crossed the plain which the thralls had said lay between Dumnonia and the Saxon lands, so I was certainly in British domains by now. There could be a raiding party in the area . . . no, the last raid the king had ordered had been to the north, into Powys. I should be too far south to meet with it. I was probably safe; if I travelled a little further west I should certainly be secure.

I walked until nightfall – no long time – then stopped where I was and slept under a tree root, wrapped in my cloak. The following day I journeyed on, feeling worn and dirty.

I had not gone far when I reached a road. It was no Roman road but a plain dirt track which wound along the hilltops. It was easier to walk on the verge or through the surrounding wood than on the road itself, so deep and thick was the mud. Nonetheless, I followed the track, turning south on it. There was some risk, but not much, and I wished to find someone who could tell me where to find Arthur. The land was inhabited, I knew, for I had seen the smoke of hearth-fires the evening before, but I judged it safer to meet someone on the road, and preferably someone travelling alone.

The risk was worth while. I had walked for only half an hour when I found a cart stuck in the mud. The man who strained to push it out was stocky, red-haired, and swore in British.

'Ach! Yffern's hounds run you down, horse, can't you pull harder than that?' he shouted at his mare. She gave a few half-hearted jerks, without success. The man cursed some more and kicked one of the wheels of the cart. He did not notice me as I came up behind him.

'Greetings,' I said, after watching his performance. 'Can I help you?'

He stopped pushing and whirled about, afraid. His eyes widened when he saw me, and his right hand flashed through a peculiar motion.

'Who are you?' he demanded, and his hand had now dropped to his belt knife. 'What do you want?'

'I do not want anything from you, certainly not your life, so you can take your hand off your knife. I was offering to help you with your cart.'

The man gave me another long, uncomfortable stare, then shrugged, ran a heavy hand through his hair, and rolled his eyes in exasperation. 'Ach! Well, you're no Saxon . . . Can you help me? No, indeed not. I drag my carts here for the sheer pleasure of pushing them out of the mud.'

I decided that I liked this man. I smiled. 'In that case, I am sorry that I have interfered with so enjoyable a pastime, and leave you to the pleasure of it.'

He frowned, puzzled, then grinned. 'There; but I was angry, and it is a most generous offer. If you can help me to

129

get this demon-plagued thing out from this thrice-damned hole, I can give you a ride. I am going south and east, to Camlann.'

Camlann!

'I wish to go there myself,' I said. 'Here, let me see this cart. How is it stuck?'

It was badly stuck, in a deep hole which had been disguised by a thin crust of drier mud. It took an hour of shoving and massed wood from the forest under the wheels before the cart finally lurched from the hole. The carter gave a crow of delight when it slipped free at last.

'It is lucky that you came along,' he said. 'I'd never have got it free alone. I'd've had to go back to my holding and ask my clan to help, and it's no safe thing, leaving a loaded cart on the road these days, what with the bandits and the thieves, and the Saxons in Din Sarum.' (another name for Sorviodunum/Searisbyrig, I remembered). 'And there's more work at the holding than we've men to do it, and we could ill spare the hands to drag loose a cart.' He climbed into his cart, untying the reins from the post he had fastened them to, and beckoned me to come up beside him. We started down the road, half on, half off the verge. 'My name is Sion, by the way,' the man said. 'Sion ap Rhys, a farmer. My clan's holding is up north of here, near Mor Hafren.'

Mor Hafren, mouth of the Saefern river? Had I come so far north?

'I am Gwalchmai,' I said, without adding my father's name. I should give little information, I decided, until I knew how the sons of King Lot of Orcade would be received in Dumnonia.

'A fine name,' said Sion, after a short, uneasy pause. 'A warrior's name. And you wish to go to Camlann?'

'Indeed. How far away is it? I have never been to Dumnonia before.'

He shrugged. 'We should be in Ynys Witrin tonight. It's not far, but I won't push the horse, and we'll need to spend more time digging this accursed Hell-axled cart out of the mud before we reach the west road. There are times when I think that no amount of profit is worth travelling for in the spring.'

'What profit do you expect, then?'

He grinned. 'Considerable. That is wheat flour in the back

130

there. My clan found we had more than we needed when the winter ended, so we decided to sell it. And what better man to sell to than the Emperor? With his warband he always needs supplies badly. If I find the right man to bargain with I should get twice the price I'd find at Baddon.'

We rode together for the rest of the day, and I enjoyed it. Sion was a talkative man and a cheerful one, which last was fortunate, for the cart became stuck three times before we reached the 'west road', the old Roman road. Sion must have consigned every inch of that track to Yffern a dozen times over, together with the cart and the horse, but he swore with great equanimity, and the horse merely flicked its ears back as though he were consoling it.

Long before we reached Ynys Witrin the forest vanished, and then the hills, until we were crossing a low marsh on a road that was elevated on an earthen bank. Narrow rivers of deeper water wound through the sodden marsh grasses. We saw the town of Ynys Witrin long before we reached it. The great hill on which it is built stands above the land like a fortress. Ynys Witrin is a holy city. It was sacred before the Romans came and it is still sacred, though now to a different god. They say the first church in Britain was built there, and the monastery has been there a long time.

I was very impressed by the road into the town, and tried to imagine the amount of work needed to build it. Sion noticed this, and asked if I were a foreigner, hesitating a little before the final word. I told him that I was from the Orcades. He was confused.

'The Orcades? Where is that?'

'The Orcades, the Innsi Erc, the islands north of Pictland,' I said, surprised.

'Oh, the Ynysoedd Erch! Where Lot is king, with the Witch-queen. A frightful place, they say, and terribly far away.'

'Very far away,' I said. 'But not at all frightful.'

'We-ell . . . did you ever see King Lot ap Cormac, then? Or the Queen Morgawse, daughter of Uther? They tell stories of those two which make the blood run cold. I wouldn't care to meet either of them, not at all, at any time. My son, of course . . .'

I smiled. He had told me all about his twelve-year-old son, who was a fanatic admirer of Arthur and who wanted to be a hero, told it in the middle of telling about the difficulties of farming and about a blood feud his clan had been involved in twenty years before. He was, as I said, a talkative man.

'Not that I believe the stories,' Sion added. 'Men will tell tales about anything, and the more marvellous it is, the more interesting they find it. There are tales they tell now about the Pendragon in every market-place which would have been laughed at ten years ago, but because he is emperor now and has taxed the Church, the fools all pull their beards and believe them. But I am a Christian, a good churchman, and I don't hold with such tales . . .' he trailed off, gave me a sideways glance, fell silent a moment, then continued. 'But I was wondering what the King and Queen of the Ynysoedd Erch looked like.'

'I have seen them,' I admitted reluctantly.

'Indeed? They tell me of the Witch-queen, the Pendragon's sister. She was born here in Dumnonia, but I have never seen her. Is she beautiful?'

I thought of Morgawse. Morgawse, with her black hair and her eyes like pools of night, Queen of Darkness, no longer human. I looked down at my hands, forgetting the road, the man beside me, Camlann and all Britain with the horror of the memory. The cart-rim creaked beneath my fingers as I gripped it. Light, can I never be free of her?

Sion muttered something under his breath and made the same hand gesture he had used when he first saw me.

'What?' I asked, waking from my reflections.

'Nothing,' said Sion, but he reined in his mare and looked at me. 'What do you . . .' He stopped again. 'There is something strange about you, Gwalchmai.'

'What do you mean?' I asked, meeting his eyes evenly.

Sion shook his head abruptly and shook the reins so that the mare started forward again. 'It's just the light,' he muttered. 'This late afternoon sun makes things look . . . well, I am sorry.'

I smiled, my fingers curling about Caledvwlch's hilt. It was something, at least, that he was sorry for thinking I was not human.

'Look there!' said Sion, cheerful again. 'There is Ynys Witrin.'

We had turned directly west again. since the road was built from the main road to the east of the town, and the long rays of the afternoon sun made the buildings of mud and wood look fragile, as though they floated above the marshes. The steep tor should have looked peaceful: instead, it made me catch my breath. It was certainly a place of power, and that power was of more than one kind.

Sion's little mare picked her way eagerly towards the promised shelter. It was for her sake that Sion wished to stop at Ynys Witrin, instead of travelling all the way to Camlann. The cart, loaded, was heavy for her to pull all day, and the farmer could not afford to wear her out. I considered with a pang that Ceincaled could have travelled the whole distance we had compassed that day in a few hours. But Ceincaled had the right to immortality. I could not have kept him.

We crossed a bridge – the river was called the Briw, Sion said – and entered the Island of Glass, Ynys Witrin. The great hill loomed over us, the fortress at its top keeping watch over the marshland. The fortress belonged to a minor lord, a subject of Constantius of Dumnonia. Sion did not intend to ask his hospitality, since the lord followed the usual custom of offering guest-rights to none but warriors and craftsmen. It was to the monastery that common travellers went. This lay on the flank of the hill, to the east of the fortress, at the centre of an old, largely abandoned Roman town.

Sion drove up to the gateway and, getting down from the cart, rang an iron bell that hung beside it. After a few minutes, a monk came and viewed us through a slit in the door.

'Who are you and what do you want?' he asked in an irritated tone.

'Sion ap Rhys, a farmer. Hospitality for the night.'

'A farmer?' The monk opened the door. 'You are welcome then. The hospitality of Ynys Witrin will cost you . . . what is in the cart?'

'Cost me!' exclaimed Sion. 'What kind of hospitality is that?'

'The hospitality of monks taxed beyond their means by a tyrant!' snapped the monk. 'What's in the cart?'

'Wheat flour,' replied Sion sullenly.

'It will cost you a sack of wheat flour.'

'A sack. A whole sack. Man, I could buy two chickens for a whole sack of flour, this time of year!' said Sion.

'Are you seeking to plunder the Church, the holy Church,

your mother? Do you not think that it pleases God to be generous to his servants?'

'I think it pleases God when his servants are generous. Ten pounds of flour is more than I can afford, but I'll offer that.'

'Three-quarters of a sack . . .' began the monk.

After a time, it was agreed that for half a sack of flour Sion could have a place for himself and his mare for the night.

'Now, who is that in the cart?' demanded the monk. 'You can't say that he is your son; he's nothing like you.'

'No,' I answered. 'I am merely a fellow traveller.'

'You pay separately, then,' said the monk, with satisfaction. 'Is some of the flour yours?'

'No . . .'

'Then what do you travel for?'

'I seek service with the Pendragon.'

The monk gaped at me, then snarled. 'The Pendragon! Arthur the Bastard has too many men serving him already. Far too many. And who supports them?'

'The Saxons have recently, by being plundered,' I said. 'All Britain, when there is no war. But have you ever met the Saxons?'

'Why would I have met the Saxons?' asked the monk, forgetting, in his surprise, to be angry.

'Never mind. What will you charge me? I have no goods.'

'None?' He looked at me carefully, decided that I must be telling the truth. 'Your sword then.'

'No.'

'Your cloak.'

Sion was outraged. 'What sort of hospitality is this, even for Ynys Witrin? To take the very cloak of a man who comes to you without a penny, and knows no more of bargaining than a three-year-old child? I will pay for him.'

'A sack of flour,' said the monk quickly.

'Half a sack, as for myself,' answered Sion firmly, 'And no more, you thief from a thieves' den.'

The monk complained further, saying that he was being asked to support the plunder of the Church by giving hospitality 'to a godless lover of tyrants', but he wanted the flour and eventually let us in.

'I am sorry,' I said to Sion, as the cart rolled through the gate. 'It is true that I know nothing of bargaining. You should have let him take my cloak; I am sure to get a new one

134

at Camlann. As it is, I have nothing else with which to repay your generosity.'

Sion shrugged, but he was pleased. 'Keep it. You'd've been a fool to give a new cloak for a night's lodging; it's worth at least a week's. And that man was a fool to even mention the sword, for I, who know nothing of weapons, can see that that sword could buy a holding, herds and all.' He gave me a shrewd look, and I felt foolish indeed, for I'd not thought of this at all. 'It is only one sack of flour,' he added, 'and,' he lowered his voice, 'the sacks aren't whole-measure sacks. They're smaller. That fool didn't even notice, and gave us a generous rate without knowing. Well and good, for monks ought to be poor in the world's goods, and, with God's help, I'll do what I can to make them so.'

We settled Sion's mare in the abbey stables and saw that the cart was safe in the barn, then gave the gatekeeper his sack of flour. We then went to the chapel, since it seemed that the monastery was crowded and the monks had set their guests to sleeping in the chapel porch. Sion threw down a pack in the porch, whistling, then marched on into the chapel itself. After a moment's hesitation, I followed him. I had never before seen a church, and I found it confusing. I stopped just inside the door, staring at the columned basilica and the carvings along the lintel. Sion, however, went immediately to the far end and knelt before the altar there. He made the same hand gesture I had seen him use twice before, and now I recognized it as the sign of the cross. I walked up to the altar, silently, and stood looking at it.

It was a plain altar, with a cross of carved wood standing against the white-washed inner wall. The cloth over the altar, however, was richly embroidered, covered with interlocked and interlacing designs, frozen and moving at the same time, like the designs I had seen on bowls and mirrors and jewellery all my life. This had also animal designs, though, strange winged beasts prancing through the interlace, seeming to dance in the light of the two candles on the table. Something about the place reminded me of the room where I had drawn Caledvwlch. There was something of the same feeling of banked power, rigid and vibrant as the designs on the altar cloth. There was a feeling of centrality, of being near the heart of something, and an intense stillness.

I drew a deep breath, shuddering with excitement like a

nervous horse, and forced myself to calm down. On an impulse I knelt behind Sion, who was muttering some prayer in Latin. I drew Caledvwlch and held it before me with its tip resting on the ground, so that the cross of the hilt echoed the cross on the wall. Light stirred within the ruby, rose to a steady flame, and I willed it to quiet, knowing that I would be unable to explain the sword to Sion or to the monks. It stilled, and I tried to follow Sion's example, and pray. Pieces of various songs floated through my mind, and the old druidical invocations of the sun and the wind, the earth and the sea. Then I brushed these aside, deciding that I wished, after all, to speak to my lord the Light, not to any mysterious and unknown god who was new to me; and I spoke to him silently.

'Ard Rígh Mor, my King ... I would keep my oath to you. I have killed since I pledged you fealty. Let that ... oh, I am lost and cannot understand it. Let there be forgiveness of it. My lord ...' I wanted to sing, suddenly, but did not know what to sing. 'My lord, I am your warrior. Command me. Aid me. Let me find Arthur and find service with him. Let me ...' What? I thought of Morgawse, of Lugh, of Ceincaled. 'Let me know your will in this, since it is yours to rule. God of this place, if you are my lord the Light, hear me.'

There was a moment of stillness, a silent, deep listening quite different from the exaltation I had known before. It was as though the troubled water of a deep pool had stilled, and one could look down into it through limitless depths, as if into a lake of glass. At the heart of that stillness was a light, quiet as the candle flames, and a sense like the first notes of a song. I felt only this, and only for an instant. But I knew that my prayer had been heard, and I could go to Camlann with a quiet mind. I stood and sheathed the sword.

Sion turned, looked at me, frowned, then grinned. 'Consecrating the sword?'

'In a fashion.'

'A good thing to have done, a very good thing. Come, let us see if they have anything to eat in this thieves' den.'

In the porch of the chapel there were three other farmers and a trader, all bound for Camlann, who greeted us cheerfully and began to complain of the monks. Sion joined them in this pastime with great enthusiasm, and outdid them all in eloquence. None of the men did more than glance at me, for which I was grateful.

Presently a young monk brought us our evening meal in a basket, together with some fine yellow mead that did much to mollify the anger of the guests. After the meal we unrolled the straw pallets which were kept there for travellers, and we spread out cloaks on these, wished each other a good night, and curled up to sleep.

I woke up in the darkness, some time near midnight, and lay very still. There was something in the chapel porch, something which had no right to be there.

It was very dark, too dark. Beside me Sion's breathing had taken on a laboured, drugged sound, and seemed to come from a distance. It had become cold with a soul-chilling empty cold, and the air tasted thin and flat.

Stealthily I put my hand to the hilt of the sword I had placed by my head. Caledvwlch was warm, and as welcome to my hand as a hearth fire after a winter drizzle. I rolled over, got my knees beneath me, ready to move.

Whatever had entered the chapel was definitely there. I could see nothing, but I sensed its presence. It was prowling, creeping along the line of sleeping men, searching . . . it was at the opposite end of the porch from me, a pulsating core of darkness, cold and desolation. And it was strong, frighteningly strong.

I waited for it, my pulse thudding dully in my ears and shaking me with the force of my life. I felt divided: I wished to run from the horror of it; I wished to leap up and destroy it.

The shadow had crept half-way along the line of men, still looking. Looking for me. It was not the one Aldwulf had summoned in Sorviodunum; it seemed, even, to be too strong for him to have sent, though I knew he must have sent it. He would want vengeance for what my sword had done to him.

I could see the creature now, a darker patch in the blackness, lying across the floor like the shadow of a tree, only there was no tree to cast it. I swallowed, and tasted again the sweetness that had been there when I rode Ceincaled, and I was glad that this demon had come.

. . . it had moved to Sion . . .

I cast aside my cloak and stood, drawing my sword.

It stopped, drawing in on itself, and for a long moment there was a thunderous silence.

Then it attacked, as Morgawse's demon had attacked: I was smothered in a cold darkness, falling, unable to see, unable to breathe. I staggered, sickened and chilled to the marrow – by the Light, it was strong! And sweet Light, I was glad, and raised my sword between us; here was an enemy worthy of destruction! The fire of the sword flared into the blade, heating it in my hands, and the coldness in my mind blinked from existence. The shadow flew across on to the wall, trembling like the shadow of a tree in a storm. It radiated confusion, anger . . . and fear. It had not expected this. Steel does not hurt such creatures, and they have no fear of helpless men. This was different.

I smiled and advanced. 'Come,' I said, my voice strange in the darkness and the unearthly silence which lay so close. 'Come, my enemy. You are bound to this, and cannot return to your place until you have performed that which you were sent for.'

It made a high, thin, keening sound and leapt.

I was ready. I brought Caledvwlch down, and the creature gave a voiceless scream, screamed again, twisting on the floor, but now with rage; and before I could recover the sword it had slid across the floor and touched me. I fell backward. There was a deadly cold and intense pain which clawed inside my skull, and a flood of hatred, a black tide like the hatred I had once felt for my brother Agravain, or the hatred Morgawse felt for the world. I was drowning in it; I could not tell what were my own feelings and what the desires of my attacker. I did not know who I was, or where; all time and all clarity were swallowed in one gulf of darkness. In the confusion I seemed to remember something: my mother, clothed in terror, commanding; then Aldwulf, his face covered with a blood-stained bandage, kneeling before the runes screaming, 'Come! Any power that will destroy Gwalchmai, the Light's servant! Come, take your price!' – and I heard, who had been wandering, trapped in the hated light of the world, and came, saying, 'Where is Gwalchmai, son of Lot, son of the Queen of Darkness? I seek him.' No. It was not my memory, it was the demon's. This was the power Morgawse had summoned that night on Samhain after I had fled, which had pursued me to Llyn Gwalch to destroy me. For nearly three years it had wandered the world, seeking me, unable to depart until it had carried out her command, and then Aldwulf had called, and it had found me again. The thought, the realization brought me to myself, as a man and apart from the dark power, and I brought the sword up, pressing the hilt against my forehead.

The demon released me, screaming, and fell across the floor. I got to my knees and slashed at it again, and it writhed madly, speaking to me now, pleading inside my mind without words and saying that it would obey me in everything if I would spare it. I laughed and brought the sword down.

The demon's death cry shook the air, seeming to penetrate into the very fabric of the world; then faded slowly with the cold and the silence into nothingness.

I raised the sword again, panting, and looked for something else to fight.

Silence. The soft breathing of sleeping men, now without the drugged, laboured sound of earlier. A night bird called outside, and the wind rustled in the eaves. I lowered the sword. The fire faded, both from the blade and from my mind, leaving peace and a great weariness.

My King, I thought. You are the greatest of lords, the most splendid of war-leaders. My thanks for the sword, and for the victory.

Then I went back to my pallet, sheathed Caledvwlch and lay down, too tired to stand.

As I settled, Sion stirred, woke, raised his head. He looked about the chapel porch for something, paused, then looked towards me uncertainly.

'Gwalchmai?' he whispered.

I was already half asleep, and did not want to talk, so I pretended to be wholly asleep. After a minute, Sion shrugged and lay down again. I closed my eyes. Sleep was like a boat, drifting lazily across a vast and peaceful ocean.

Nine

When I woke the next morning the feeling of peace remained. Sion, however, seemed anxious. He picked at the bread that the monks had provided and brooded. The other farmers discussed land and crops and the weather, laying plans, but Sion did not join them. Half-way through the meal he stopped eating, a piece of bread raised in one hand, and looked at me evenly. 'I had a strange dream last night,' he announced.

'Oh?' I asked, amused. 'What was it?'

Sion looked back at his bread, shoved it into his mouth and chewed moodily before replying, 'A dark thing came into the chapel porch.'

My amusement vanished and I stared at him. He went on without looking at me, or at anyone else, though the others were now listening with some interest. 'I felt it come in through the door and stand there a moment. At first it looked like a shadow, and then I blinked and saw that it was . . . well, a little like a man. Like a corpse, blackened and half-rotted. It started to come forward, shambling a little, like a trained bear, and I tried to wake up, because I was in a cold sweat at the sight of the thrice-damned thing, but I could not wake.'

'Ah,' said one of the farmers. 'I knew a man who had a dream like that, and when he woke up in the morning he found that his daughter had died. They are strange things, dreams.'

'They are indeed,' said Sion, 'but that was not the end of it.' He began addressing me again, refusing to be sidetracked. 'You did wake up. You stood and drew your sword, and the sword lit up like a pine torch catching light. You held it between yourself and the thing of perdition, looking like you'd just been given your heart's desire, and then the two of you began fighting.' Sion shrugged uneasily, eyed Caledvwlch, and continued. 'And then it was as though you were frozen, just beginning the fight, and I looked up at the wall behind the black thing, and there was a woman standing there.'

140

I found that my hand was somehow about the hilt of my sword.

'A dark woman, she was, with a white, starved face and terrible eyes, more beautiful than any woman I ever saw, but with something sick about her. I've seen such a look as that in a town beggar starving in a gutter and cursing the by-passers, but never in some proud beauty like that woman. She saw you about to fight the spirit of Yffern, and reached out to touch it; as she did, the darkness tripled. But then she looked up, and grew angry, and I looked behind me and saw there was a man there, a yellow-haired man cloaked in light, and he raised his hand, forbidding the woman to interfere.'

I sat and stared at Sion. I started to speak, could think of nothing to say. I had considered this man a simple farmer. A farmer he was, but not simple. Men are not simple, and I had forgotten that others, besides myself, might serve the Light. 'And that was the end of the dream?' I asked. Even to myself, my voice sounded strained.

Sion shook his head. The other farmers looked confusedly from one to the other of us, but Sion ignored them.

'No. But the dream changed after that. Suddenly I was not standing in the chapel porch, but on a great, level plain full of people. The sky was very dark in the east, as though a thunderstorm were about to break. In the West I saw the emperor with his warband, and suddenly the dragon broke from their standard and rose into the air, glowing like hot gold, and then it seemed that I was standing in the middle of a battle, for all the people on the plain had begun to fight. Near me there was a tall man, a Saxon, from his looks; the left side of his face was scarred, and he held a black flame in his left hand. The dragon passed over, and I shut my eyes for a moment, and when I opened them, the Saxon was dead, and over him stood a young man with pale hair, wearing a brooch in the shape of a lion. There were other struggles going on all about me, but I don't remember them now. Everything was in confusion.'

The trader snorted suddenly and shook his head. 'Indeed it is. Confused nonsense. Anyone who expects more from dreams is a fool.'

'I've not finished,' snapped Sion. 'Let me tell this tale to the end, and if you do not wish to listen, don't. It kept growing darker, and the shouting and clash of arms grew louder, and the dragon kept flying back and forth along the lines trailing fire; then there came a flash of lightning from heaven, and I saw the ground behind me scattered with bodies, and one I noticed especially, a man in a red cloak, lying dead. There came a burst of thunder, and darkness full of fires, and I turned away, because I was afraid. When I turned I saw a man standing there, and he caught my arm. He was the emperor's Chief Poet, Taliesin – when the emperor took the purple, I fought with the army, so I recognized the man from then. But in the dream he was wearing a star upon his forehead, and he was the only one, in all that dream, who saw me. He said, "Remember these things, Sion ap Rhys, and do not be afraid. Though they are terrible, no harm will come to you by them. Have faith." So I bowed my head and all became dark. And then,' Sion took a deep breath, 'Then I woke up.' He shrugged. 'But all was quiet, and you were asleep.'

The trader laughed at this, and Sion scowled.

'Dreams are strange things, to be sure,' said the farmer who had spoken earlier. 'But I cannot make head or tail of that one. I never heard of anyone fighting devils in dreams. But a dream about the Pendragon, that is plain enough. The thunderstorm would be the Saxons. Only I could not tell what they did, in your dream.'

'It is nonsense,' the trader repeated. 'Though to be sure, you had us listening. But a man cannot heed dreams. I knew an old fool once who . . .'

Sion stood abruptly. 'I think I will go into the chapel and pray.'

'Indeed,' said one of the other farmers. 'Light a candle, and perhaps have the monks say a masss. That may avert it.'

'Avert what?' asked the first farmer. The second shrugged.

'I will join you,' I said to Sion.

He gave me another of his steady looks, then nodded in satisfaction. The others looked at me uneasily, shook their heads. One crossed himself. As we left the farmers began talking in whispers, while the trader tried to resume his story.

There was a monk in the chapel, replacing the burned-out candles. Sion ignored him and knelt before the altar, crossing himself and beginning to mutter a prayer in Latin. I knelt slightly behind him, wondering. It was indeed a strange dream. Like the farmers, I could not guess at what most of it meant, but some of it was frighteningly plain. Sion was an unlikely prophet, but I wished I could better understand the dream.

'*Gloria in excelsis Deo*,' said Sion, as though reciting something, 'Glory to God in the heights, and in Earth peace to men of good will...' He went on in this vein for a bit, then stopped, and stared silently at the crucifix. I wished I understood his religion better. It seemed to worship the Light, and I did not know how to do that on my own. I knew just enough to disbelieve the rumours and strange tales about that faith, the stories of cannibalism and unnatural orgies which had been discussed at great length in the Boys' House. It would be comforting to have some fine words like Sion's to say to my lord now, after the victory of the night before and now this dream.

Not knowing what to say, I drew my sword again and rested it before me, one hand on each of the cross-pieces. I felt again, suddenly and stronger than before, that deep silent regard, and again wished to sing, but all I could remember was a song to the sun, in Irish.

> 'Hail to you, bright morning,
> Shattering the sky of night,
> Blazing fair, victoriously dawning,
> Ever-young, the new-born light!
>
> Welcome is this morning,
> Golden-handed, sunlight lender:
> Welcome is the day's High King,
> Light's liege-lord, morning's sender.'

It seemed appropriate enough. The monk finished with the candles and left, his feet making soft padding sounds on the wooden floor. The door closed behind him, and we remained, staring at the altar.

The ruby in the hilt of Caledvwlch began to glow, burned brighter; the light steadied and became more intense, casting a clear rose-coloured light brighter than the candles. Sion saw it cast his shadow before him and turned. He stared for a moment, then let out a long sigh.

'It is true, then,' he said. 'I was not certain.'

'I know that some of it is true,' I replied. 'The rest, though, is beyond my understanding. I am only human, Sion ap

143

Rhys.'

Sion blew out his cheeks. 'I know.'

I was surprised, and showed it.

'Oh, I know,' Sion explained. 'Indeed, I did think differently yesterday. You came from the forest out of nowhere, and I looked once and said to myself, "It is one of the People of the Hills." But you were obliging with the cart, and got yourself covered in mud pushing it loose on that Yffern-bent track, and I thought, "Perhaps not." All the way to Ynys Witrin I was uncertain. I have dreams, you see, and sometimes one has a sense of things. It runs in the family. Usually I ignore it – the supernatural is best left alone – but I know enough to pay heed when something strange is happening; and even those farmers can sense that there is something strange about you, and they knowing no more than a Saxon's sheep does. Yesterday, when I mentioned that witch, just before we came to Ynys Witrin, I was nearly certain that you were of the Fair Ones, and you had taken a human form for some purpose of your own. But when we arrived, and you tried to give me your cloak in return for half a sack of flour, and afterwards followed me into the chapel here and prayed, I knew that you had to be human. The People of the Hills don't pray. And besides, it made no sense that one of the Fair Ones would get covered with mud about a cart of wheat flour. Only you have had dealings with the Otherworld, haven't you? There is still something strange about you, though today it is less strong.'

'I . . . have. But what of your dream? You have had other such dreams?'

He shrugged. 'On occasion. Before my clan finished our blood feud, twenty years back, I had a dream. And I had another one before Arthur claimed the purple, and one or two others about smaller things. Nothing as long and accursedly frightening as the one last night, though. Tell me, Gwalchmai, how much of that dream was true?'

I looked down at the hilt of my sword, where the light had died now. 'I did fight a demon last night, and I did kill it, though to me it looked like nothing more than a shadow. And I know the man and the woman you saw watching, as well, though they were not here. The Saxon in the confused part, the one with the scarred face and the black flame – that was Aldwulf, King of Bernicia. But I don't know who the

144

man that fought him was. I know nothing about the rest.'

'Aldwulf?' asked Sion. 'I have heard of him, but never that he had a scar. In fact, it is always said that he is handsome as the devil, and proud of it.'

'He has a scar now,' I said. 'I put it there. It was for that that he called the demon to send after me.'

Sion's eyes widened. 'How? Aldwulf of Bernicia is said to be in Din Sarum, with Cerdic and the whole Saxon army.'

'He was, but I had been captured by the Saxons, and was pretending to be a thrall. Aldwulf had captured a horse as a gift for Cerdic, one of the horses of the ... People of the Hills, you call them. I tamed the horse and rode out over Aldwulf before anyone could stop me.'

Sion shook his head in wonder. 'Dear God. As plainly as that: "I rode out over Aldwulf." So; and who were the man and the woman I saw watching you, then?'

I hesitated. 'The man was Lugh of the Long Hand. I think you call him Llwch in British.'

He stared, off balance. 'A pagan god?'

'Not a god. Not a human, either. Beyond that, I do not know, except that he serves the Light. It was he who gave me this sword.'

'And the Light, I take it, is God. Very well, I can make no sense of it. What of the woman? I could see that she was a ruler of Darkness, but what connection has she with you?'

'She is my mother,' I said unhappily. 'Morgawse of Orcade.'

Sion went very still. 'The witch herself,' he said at last. 'Your father, then, is King Lot of the Ynysoedd Erch?'

I nodded.

'Well,' said Sion, after another long pause. 'It is not only dreams that are very strange, these days. You are not what I pictured for the son of a king and an emperor's daughter, especially not when both of them have such a reputation, and when I had heard that the younger sons of the Queen Morgawse were...' he broke off. He had heard, plainly enough, that the younger sons of the Queen Morgawse were likewise witches. Poor Medraut, if he had acquired that reputation now.

'And you are not what I pictured for a prophet,' I returned.

'I? A prophet? Do not talk foolishness!'

'What else was that dream but prophetic? I think that many

145

of the things you saw must be still to come.'

'It is only a dream, not to . . . damn,' said Sion. He had not thought of the light it cast on himself. I laughed. He glared at me for a moment, then grinned. 'I am a plain farmer,' he said, 'and I do not think that any such thing will happen to me again. I have no part in any of these great and terrible battles, nor want any part: it is trouble enough, more than trouble enough, to run a holding in these days, and see that there is peace and good order in my own house. Still, I am glad that this has happened, for how can one not wish, in times such as these, to preserve civilization and the empire and the light of Britain.' He frowned again, then said, in a very low voice, 'Remember me, Gwalchmai – Lord Gwalchmai, I suppose it is. I know that I have not done anything in deed, only told you a dream. But it would make me glad to know, ten or twenty years from now, that one of those in the centre of the battle might remember me if I went and spoke to him.'

'It is not likely that I will forget you or your dream,' I said. 'But I doubt that I have any great part in the things that are to come.'

Sion gave me a look of flat disbelief. 'You have. Someday, I will tell my grandchildren how I met you on your way to Camlann and gave you a ride in my cart, and they will not believe a word of it.' He stood, dusting off his knees. 'They will say, "There is Grandfather, pretending that once he knew all the kings in Britain and making himself foolish."'

I shook my head. What fighting I did would surely be in dark places, where there is no fame to be brought back to the sunlit world. 'Why don't you wait until Arthur has accepted my sword before planning what you will tell your grandchildren?' I asked. 'You might say, "And once I met Gwalchmai mac Lot," and they will only reply, "Who?"'

Sion shook his head stubbornly. 'That they will not say. Do you wish to leave now for Camlann?'

We were just leaving the chapel when we heard the sound of shouting and of horses from the abbey yard. We glanced at each other and hurried out into the sunlight, and found the other travellers, most of the monks, and a group of warriors standing about within the gate and shouting. There were about a dozen of the warriors; they were British, mounted on tall war-horses, and their arms gleamed.

One of the monks was doing most of the shouting. He was

the abbot, I guessed, from the quality of his clothing and the jewels on the gold pectoral cross he wore. 'What more?' he was demanding. 'We have had to ask more from our flock to cover what you have taken already, and we've barely enough to last us until the harvest even so . . .'

'Do you think you can put us off with plain lies?' answered one of the warriors. He was a very big man, so big that his war-horse looked small. His red hair bristled in all directions, and his light blue eyes glittered dangerously; he wore more jewellery than I had seen on one man before, and brighter colours. 'You have enough and more than enough to grow fat on, without taking double tithes of your miserable "sheep" and robbing every traveller who comes by expecting hospitality. If the Saxons came here, they would take all you have, down to the last rush and candlestick. Aren't you grateful to us for keeping them away?'

'The Saxons are only an excuse, a pretext put forward by a tyrant!' said the monk fiercely.

The warriors laughed. 'Perhaps now you prefer the Saxons to the emperor,' said another, a lean, dark, one-handed man in plain clothing. 'But you would think otherwise if the Pendragon ceased to fight them.'

The abbot snarled. 'It is the duty of Christian kings to protect their people; it is not their duty to rob them. We cannot give . . .'

'Oh? Hear him, brothers!' said the red-head. 'He cannot give. But we can take.'

'Robbers!' cried the abbot.

'Be careful, Cei,' warned the dark warrior. 'Arthur said we must not push them to breaking.'

Cei shrugged. 'But if we bend them a little? Perhaps with a little fire? Just a small one, on top of the gate house?'

The abbot looked at him furiously, decided not to risk seeing whether he was serious. 'You godless killers,' he said. 'We keep some supplies over there, only a few, but all we have.'

The dark warrior gave his comrade, Cei, a meaningful look. 'Yes, perhaps you keep the tenth part of your goods there. Truly, Theodorus, it does you no good to lie to us. Last time you said you had no gold, and then came to us wanting us to recover what you'd sent to Sorviodunum for safe-keeping. Very well, I suppose that that will have to do for now.' He turned from the abbot to Sion and the other travellers and announced, 'The Pendragon has won another victory, for he came across a large Saxon raiding party in Powys, and destroyed it. Praise to God.'

The farmers cheered. The Saxon raids would probably be eased slightly now, and their lands and herds were safer.

'It is good that you are pleased,' said Cei. 'In token of it, you can lend us any carts and horses you have. You can claim them in Camlann, and you'll be paid for any goods you've brought.'

The farmers fell abruptly silent.

'By my name saint!' said Sion angrily. 'I've a fine load of wheat flour in my cart, and my best horses harnessed to it. I'll not lend it to any before you pay me.'

The other farmers muttered angry agreement. The dark warrior shrugged. 'You will be repaid. The emperor will not cheat you.'

'You misheard me,' said Sion. 'I said, I will not lend you my cart and cargo without payment.'

'Yes you will,' said Cei. 'You will lend it for payment later, or lose it altogether.'

'That is not just,' I said, becoming as angry as the farmers. 'I do not think that your lord could approve of it.'

The dark warrior lifted an eyebrow. 'We need supplies,' he said, very calm and reasonable. 'We need carts and horses to move the supplies, and all of ours are damaged or being used for the wounded. My lord Arthur approves. You will be paid, never fear.' I continued to stare angrily, and suddenly he frowned and gave me a sharper look.

The other spokesman for the warriors, Cei, ignored the whole exchange and simply asked the farmers, 'Where are your carts?'

Sion spat and crossed his arms. 'First pay me.' The other farmers followed his example and remained stubborn.

'Give them some token now,' I suggested to the dark warrior, 'or at least mark down the value of the goods, so that they can be sure of their full payment when they reach the High King.'

Cei glared at me. 'Who, by God, are you? You're no farmer. What's your business here?'

'My name is Gwalchmai, and I was going to Camlann to seek service with the Pendragon.'

Cei laughed. 'Arthur has no need of swineherds. You had better go back to wherever you came from and leave warriors' matters to warriors.' He said it as a challenge, speaking as Agravain often had.

The dark one shifted uneasily. 'Cei, stop.'

'What? Bedwyr, you cannot want to defend this base-born meddler?'

Bedwyr shook his head dubiously. 'Let him be. If he speaks the truth, he may be our comrade soon.'

'Him? A warrior? Look at how he's dressed! He hasn't even a horse!'

'Nonetheless,' said Bedwyr. 'Let us take what we need and go, without fighting. We must reach Camlann quickly.'

'Bedwyr, my brother, do not turn moralist on me again. I swear the oath of my people, you Bretons are worse than Northerners, and almost as bad as the Irish.'

Bedwyr smiled. 'So, it is "bad as the Irish" again? There speaks a true Dumnonian. But I seem to recall that . . .'

'*Per omnes sanctos*! There are exceptions; I admitted that I was wrong about him. God in heaven, how you revel in my mistakes. Why am I cursed with such disloyal friends?'

At this the warriors began to laugh and Bedwyr smiled again.

'Truly, Cei,' he continued, 'you are over-fond of fighting; and it will hurt us here.'

Cei sighed. 'Very well.' He looked back to me. 'I will overlook it, you. Now, men, where are your carts?'

'Where is your justice?' replied Sion, but uncertainly now.

'Be quiet, farmer!' snapped Cei. 'Or I will teach you when to hold your tongue.'

My hand dropped to Caledvwlch's hilt. Cei saw the movement and drew his own sword with a ring of metal, his eyes lighting. The warriors fell silent.

'What do you mean to do with that, my friend?' asked Cei, soft-voiced now, and courteous.

'Cei . . .' Bedwyr began again, then stopped, seeing that it was useless.

'I do not mean to do anything with this,' I said, my voice also soft. 'But I will not have you threatening my friends as well as stealing their goods.'

Cei dismounted and came closer, grinning fiercely. Abruptly I realized what I had done and wondered what could have come over me. How could I fight a professional warrior, one of Arthur's men? The most I could hope for was not to be hurt too badly.

But I could not withdraw now, and something of the same lightness fell on me. I drew Caledvwlch. Cei grinned still more widely and took another step forward.

'Cei! Who is it now?' came a voice from the back of the group. The warriors glanced round.

Another of their number had ridden up, carrying some of the monks' supplies, and Cei's band made room for him. He was a tall man of about twenty-one, with long gold hair and a neat beard and moustache. He wore a purple-bordered cloak fastened with gold, and radiated energy and strength. His hot blue eyes skipped lightly over me to rest on Cei. 'If this man is all, he's not worth it.'

'He began it,' said Cei in an injured tone.

'The day someone else begins a fight with you, rivers will run backwards,' said the newcomer. 'By the sun and the wind, for once let us obey Arthur and simply take the supplies and go.'

Cei paused, glanced back at me. I sheathed Caledvwlch.

Cei sighed a little, then sheathed his own sword. 'Well enough. It is not worth it; and it is too soon after a battle besides.' He swung up on to his horse. The blond man grinned and turned his own horse. The tension was gone: the foraging party would take what it wanted and go.

'Wait!' I called. The warriors stopped, turned, looking inquisitive. I smiled, feeling a strange emotion, half joy, half an old envy and bitterness – bitterness which dissolved away, leaving only the joy.

'A thousand welcomes, Agravain,' I said to the blond warrior.

Ten

My brother sat motionless for a moment, staring at me with his old hot stare. Then he dismounted hurriedly, ran a few steps towards me; stopped; walked on slowly.

'It is impossible,' he said, his face growing red. 'You . . . you are dead.'

'Truly, I am not.' I replied.

'Gwalchmai?' he asked. 'Gwalchmai?'

'You know him?' demanded Cei in astonishment. Agravain did not even look round.

'I had not thought to see you so soon,' I said. 'I am very glad.'

He smiled hesitantly, then beamed, caught my shoulders, looked at me, and crushed me in a hug. 'Gwalchmai! By the sun and the wind, I thought that you were dead, three years dead! Och, God, God, it is good to see you!'

I returned the embrace wholeheartedly, laughing, and it seemed that finally all the dark years of our childhood were blotted out for me. We had both endured too many things to feel anything but gladness on meeting one another again.

'What is happening?' asked Cei, in complete confusion. 'Why are you jabbering in Irish?'

'Cei!' shouted Agravain, releasing me and whirling about to his comrades. 'This is my brother, Gwalchmai, the one who died—the one I thought had died! I swear the oath of my people, I do not know how, but this is he.'

The warriors reacted by staring in astonishment, except for Cei, who gave me a look of first embarrassment, then apology. But the farmers around me drew away a little, and the monks stared with increased suspicion.

'So he is the famous Agravain ap Lot,' said Sion, looking at my brother – the only one in the crowd who was.

'Is he famous?' I asked, remembering my old worries for Agravain's case as a hostage. Clearly, they had been wasted. 'Och well, it might have been expected.' Agravain grinned at that.

'Where have you been when you were considered dead, that you heard nothing of your brother's fame?' asked

Bedwyr quietly. I looked up, met his eyes, and felt respect for him.

'I have been to a distant place,' I said. 'And through strange things, too many to tell quickly.'

'Indeed,' said Bedwyr, not questioning at all, and shook himself.

'These are strange matters enough,' said another of the warriors. 'Come, let's finish our business here and go to Camlann. Arthur and the rest will be there soon, and there's nothing to eat there but pork rinds and cabbage.'

Most of the foraging party set about loading the monks' goods into the already loaded carts, and, at my insistence taking down the amount and kind of the farmers' goods. Agravain and I stood looking at each other and trying to decide how to begin. Then the carts rolled out into the yard, and Sion, who had been harnessing his mare, reluctantly jumped from the seat. 'You will see that my horse is well treated?' he asked me.

I nodded, then, realizing that it was intended that he should continue to Camlann on foot and that I might not see him again, I caught his hand. 'And I will remember you, Sion ap Rhys, if the thought of that gives you pleasure. If I do not see you at Camlann, remember that. And if ever you need any help, and I can give it, my sword is yours.'

'I thank you,' he replied, quietly. 'And . . . may God grant you favour with the emperor.'

'And may you walk in Light.' I climbed into his cart and took the reins. 'I will drive this one,' I told Agravain. He nodded, and I shook the reins. The little mare started off, trotting down the hill towards the causeway. Those warriors who had taken the other carts followed, and Agravain rode his horse beside me. We left Ynys Witrin and turned east for the main road and Camlann.

'Why don't you let the farmers drive their own carts?' I asked Agravain.

'They would go too slowly, and when they arrived in Camlann, drive the prices up by their bargaining. As it is we can have the standard price ready for them when they reach the gate, and send them off at once. You seemed friendly with that man; where did you meet him?'

'On the road, yesterday.'

Agravain checked his horse. 'Yesterday? What did he do

for you, that you let him take liberties?'

'He gave me a ride in his cart, and paid for my night's stay at Ynys Witrin. I had nothing to pay with.'

Agravain scowled. 'And for that you take his hand? You should merely have repaid him double, and not demeaned yourself. Why in God's name had you nothing to pay with?'

'In God's name,' I said. 'Have you become a Christian, Agravain?'

'God forbid!' he said, grinning, then frowned again. 'You should not let commoners become so familiar. They are always wanting favours, then.'

I sighed. 'Sion is a good man. I was lucky to have met him.'

Agravain's frown deepened, but he shrugged. 'Well, you can choose your own friends.'

'I think he is capable of that,' said a quiet voice on the other side. Bedwyr drew his horse in besides us. 'Come. We must hurry. I do not want Arthur to have to wait for his victory feast at Camlann.'

Agravain spurred his horse and I urged Sion's mare obediently, though she did not like the brisk trot with the heavy cart. We fell silent again, and Cei came up and rode beside Bedwyr, giving me interested looks.

'You destroyed Cerdic's raiding party, then?' I asked, finally thinking of something to say. 'That is good, but surprising. I would have thought his parties move too quickly for even the Pendragon to reach them before they returned to Sorviodunum.'

'It was more chance than foresight,' said Bedwyr. 'We were returning from fighting the East Saxons when we heard news of this raiding party from Sorviodunum, and we caught them only just in time.'

'That was a thing Cerdic hadn't planned for,' said Cei with satisfaction. 'They say that that sorcerer of his, Aldwulf Flamddwyn, has been telling him where Arthur is. But even Aldwulf cannot predict where Arthur will be.'

'Nor can we,' said Agravain. 'Even when we are with him. He is a great king, Gwalchmai. It shames me that ever Father fought him. We should have made alliance with him, and not with those Northern cattle.'

'Now, that is true,' said Cei, 'and it would have saved you time, as well.'

'But your brother must believe this, too, Agravain,'

Bedwyr added, 'Otherwise he would not be seeking to serve Arthur.'

Agravain frowned again. 'What were you expecting to do, Gwalchmai? Arthur takes only warriors and a few doctors with the warband. You could stay in Camlann, I suppose, if you are not planning to go home.'

'I cannot go back to the islands,' I said. 'But you, Agravain, how is it that you are fighting alongside Arthur's own warband? And gaining fame in it, as well? I have not heard any news of you, not since you were taken hostage.'

'Och, that,' said Agravain. 'That came of itself. The High King was kind to me, after Father and our kinsmen had gone; and I had some admiration for him already, because of his skill at war, though I hated him for an enemy.'

'But he let you fight beside his men?'

'Not at once.' Agravain suddenly grinned at Cei. 'This hard-handed lout of a Dumnonian decided to give me the sharp edge of his tongue, and that is a sharp edge indeed. I understood little enough of it at the time, for my British was still not good, but I understood enough. And so one day, when he and the Family, returned from a raid, were at Camlann, and he began to say, "The only worse men than the Saxons are the Irish", I up and hit him. So he hit back, and we were at it like hammer and anvil. Only, as you see, he is bigger than I, and got the better of me.'

'Only you would not stop fighting for all that,' Cei put in. '*Gloria Deo*! I was certain I was fighting with a madman.'

'And when he knocked me down for the fifth time, and I tried to get up again, and had to hold on to a table to do it, he said, "You mad Irishman, don't you know enough to stop fighting when you are beaten?" and I said, "I do not; and I wish my father had not either." And he said, "You're a wild barbarian, but by God, you've heart enough. I take back my words," and helped me up. And when the High King next wanted him to lead a raid, Cei said, "Let me take Agravain, then. It is the only way to keep him out of trouble."'

'Not,' added Bedwyr, 'that Cei wanted to keep out of trouble. On the contrary, there is nothing he likes better, and he was the more pleased that he had a friend to make it with him.'

'So I have fought for the High King,' Agravain concluded. 'And it is well and good. Father has sent messages, from time to time, saying that he is pleased to hear that I fight well. But what of yourself, Gwalchmai? For three years I have heard nothing of you, not from the islands, nor from Britain nor from anywhere else. Where have you been?'

I looked away, unsure. I owed it to my brother to tell him the truth, but what he would do with that truth I could not guess. Probably, refuse to believe it. Still, I would tell him. But how could I speak of Morgawse before Bedwyr and Cei? Agravain would have to believe what I said of her – he knew her just well enough for that – but it was not for the ears of others.

'Perhaps you should begin at the beginning,' suggested Agravain when the silence became awkward.

'There is time enough for you to tell the tale,' Bedwyr added. 'It is miles yet to Camlann.'

I studied Bedwyr. Here, I realized, was another man who served the Light, but one completely different from Sion. He had seen at the first that I had had dealings with the Otherworld, too, and his eyes were still doubtful. Now Cei too was giving me a peculiar look. Only Agravain noticed nothing.

'Agravain,' I said, 'I can tell you. But now now.'

'By the sun and the wind!' exclaimed Agravain, using his old oath, which touched me hard with memories, 'You have just returned from the dead, as far as I know, and you wish me to wait patiently and make light conversation?'

'That might be best,' I said. 'It is a family matter.'

'I have another family now,' replied Agravain, waving his hand towards the warriors around him. 'And what concerns me concerns them.'

'If you wish to join us,' Bedwyr commented, 'you will have to tell us as well. There is no vengeance taken for past blood feuds or such once a man has joined the Family.'

'Gwalchmai join the Family?' asked Agravain. 'That is as unlikely as his engaging in a blood feud. He is not a skilled warrior.'

Bedwyr looked thoughtful. 'Perhaps.'

'I am not,' I said. 'I hope to serve the Pendragon in some other way.'

'Arthur does not take many men with us,' said Cei, 'but he might make an exception, if you can ride well.'

'He was the best rider in the islands,' said Agravain. 'He

155

can join us in some fashion, then, if not as a warrior?'

'That is up to our lord Arthur,' Bedwyr said.

'But if you wish to, we have a right to know what you have done,' Cei told me. 'Shortly after Agravain joined us, he had a message from the Ynysoedd Erch saying that his brother had ridden off a cliff, and he went into mourning for weeks. Anything that affects him thus is my concern too. So, tell us now.'

I looked from him to Bedwyr to Agravain, then shrugged. 'As you wish. But it is a strange story, and I do not know whether you will believe me. And there are things Agravain and I can understand that you may not. I am not a skilled fighter, to be involved in duels and blood feuds, but this is a matter of Darkness . . .'

The doubt in Bedwyr's eyes flamed in suspicion. Agravain gave a start, like a frightened horse shying. 'Then it does have something to do with Mother,' he whispered.

'It does,' I agreed. 'Would you prefer that I wait, brother?'

He began to nod, stopped again. 'I had heard that you went riding at night, on Samhain. By the cliffs. It was a mad thing to do, but like you, and I had heard also that . . .' he trailed off, and I saw that he too was familiar with my old reputation for sorcery. Cei and Bedwyr glanced at each other, the same thought in their minds.

Then Cei snorted. 'Your mother, the famous witch, and an old pagan festival, and this is a reason for disappearing? I do not believe in such things. I did not think you believed either, Agravain.'

'I don't,' said Agravain. But he did not look at Cei. He believed, well enough. It was impossible to know Morgawse and not believe in her power.

'Shall I go on?' I asked.

'Yes,' said Agravain. 'Cei and Bedwyr are also my brothers now; they have the right to hear.'

Well, if that was how it was to be, I would tell the tale to the three of them. But I didn't want to. It would be painful enough to tell to kinsmen, let alone strangers. 'Agravain,' I said, 'what did you hear of my death?'

'Only what I said, that you went riding at night on Samhain, and your horse was found by the cliff next day, riderless. No one could expect you to turn up two and a half years later, eighteen miles from Camlann, dressed like a servant and picking fights with Cei – couldn't you have chosen someone else? He's the best foot fighter in the Family.'

Cei grinned and nodded his agreement with this.

'And you have grown! It has been so long since I saw you – you are seventeen now, and the last time was what – more than three years ago. Come, explain how it happened.'

I drove the cart in silence for a while, trying to decide where to begin, and praying that my brother would accept the story. 'You recall a certain summer, years ago, when I first began learning Latin?' I asked finally.

He thought back. 'Yes. A wise thing to do; they speak a deal of it here, and I still cannot understand a word of it.'

'That is where it began. We had a quarrel over my learning such a thing, and you called me a bastard and said that I was trying to learn sorcery.'

Agravain looked surprised. 'I did? I don't remember that.'

'I suppose you wouldn't. It didn't mean much to you. But I was foolish, and it meant a deal to me. I determined to truly learn sorcery.' I lifted my eyes from the road and met Agravain's hot stare. 'And I am certain that you did hear of those matters.'

He shifted uneasily, flushing, and looked away from me. He nodded. I looked back at the road.

'So I went to our mother, and she taught me many things, all terrible.'

Agravain's hands had tightened on the reins, and now his horse snorted, trying to stop and shying at the unsteady jerk. He quickly relaxed his grip and edged the horse back to the cart.

'She is very powerful, Agravain,' I said urgently. 'She is much stronger, probably, than any other on earth, so much that she is scarcely human now. At first she hated her father, and her half-brother Arthur, and then all Britain, and I think now she hates all the universe, and wishes to drown the world in Darkness.'

Agravain's horse started again, laying its ears back, catching fear from its rider. Bedwyr dropped behind the cart, then drove his horse up beside Agravain's, to steady it. Agravain closed his eyes for a moment, his face strained and white. 'No,' he whispered. 'She can't truly want that.'

'She does,' I said, wanting to reach out to him, but not

quite daring. 'You know her. Think.'

He turned his face away, shoulders shaking a little. For a long time we rode in silence, the hooves of the horses clattering on the causeway, the cart jolting in the sunlight. The marsh reeds shook in the wind. Cei was puzzled, Bedwyr withdrawn.

After a long time, shortly before we reached the main road, Agravain's hands slowly relaxed and he nodded. 'It is true,' he said, in a choked tone. 'I would rather not think of her, Gwalchmai. But it is true. By the sun, why?'

I shook my head. He expected no answer.

'Go on,' said Agravain, after another stretch of silence, when we had turned south on the main road. I noted that he controlled himself better. Three years before he would either have started a quarrel with me or driven his horse ahead at its fastest gallop.

'I said that our mother hated Arthur. She has cursed him many times, but her magic does not seem to work on him. Two and a half years ago, on Samhain, she wanted to try some other spell to kill him.'

'God,' said Agravain in a strangled tone. 'What affair is it of hers? What harm has he done her?'

'She hates him. You know that. And I think every black sorcerer in the West is seeking of the death of Arthur. Aldwulf Fflamddwyn certainly is.'

'What? – och, I know she hates the High King. But can she . . . ?'

'I do not think she can,' I said.

He stared at me earnestly for a moment, wanting reassurance, then nodded, relaxing. '*Laus Deo*, as they say here in Britain. But, by the sun, she should be destroyed. Someone should kill her; though she is my own mother, still I say that she should die.'

'Perhaps she should,' I replied. 'But who could kill her? She wanted me, and Medraut, to be there that night . . .'

'I had heard that Medraut . . . but I was sure that was false. No one was altogether certain that Medraut was . . . and it is unlike him.'

'It is true, though,' I said. 'Though I did not know it till that night.' Again I thought of Medraut with pain. She must have devoured him by now, sucking out all his innocence and love for life, replacing it with hatred and bitterness and more ambition. And there was nothing I could do.

Agravain looked at me miserably. He had been trying for years, I think, to forget Morgawse, as he had tried for years to ignore her. But he accepted this now.

'Do you remember Connall?' I asked. 'The Dalraid, the one in our father's warband?'

'Of course. A brave man, and loyal, and a good fighter, as I well know from campaigning with him in Britain. The first time I ever went whoring he took me back in Din Eidyn.'

'Morgawse was going to kill him,' I said. 'And, Agravain, I could not endure it. Not him and Medraut also. I killed him quickly and fled, and she tried to kill me.'

He looked sick. 'This is madness. Why can't people fight with swords, simply, instead . . .'

'People never fight simply with swords,' Bedwyr broke in. 'Even you and Cei do not do that.'

Agravain paused, blinking at Bedwyr. 'What does that mean?'

'No one takes up the sword without a reason. Even love of battle is a kind of reason. In the end, the reasons are never simple, and they are as important as the sword itself.'

'Philosophy,' said Cei. 'You read too much of it, Bedwyr.'

'The reasons remain important,' said Bedwyr imperturbably. 'Go on, Gwalchmai.'

'Our mother set a curse on me, and I fled from it, without thinking where I was going, until I came to Llyn Gwalch – that is the place on the cliff where I spent so much time, when we were children, Agravain – and let the horse go. The demon couldn't follow me there. I don't know why, except that I once believed in the place, and the Light . . .' I stopped. How could I tell Agravain about that? He could not possibly understand. I did not understand it myself.

'Our mother could not kill the Pendragon,' I began, 'because Arthur fights against the Darkness, with the force that is also against the Darkness. When I was trapped there, I called on that force, because I was very wearied with the Darkness and hated it. And an ancestor of ours, who serves the Light, sent aid.'

'An ancestor?' asked Agravain in confusion. 'This becomes more difficult as you go on. What ancestor?'

'Lugh of the Long Hand.'

He shook his head again. I saw that I was beginning to lose him. 'I do not know what to think of this, Gwalchmai. If anyone else came to me with a story like this, I would laugh at him. But you . . .'

'I think that you must believe him,' Bedwyr interrupted softly. 'I do not know that I have ever seen a man so deeply touched by the Otherworld.'

Agravain glared at his friend. 'There is nothing wrong with my brother. True, he is a poor warrior, but that gives you no right to insult him.'

'I am not insulting him.' Bedwyr seemed mildly amused. 'And I think he can look after his own honour. Gwalchmai, go on.'

'Lugh sent a boat from Tir Tairngaire, at the urging of the Light . . .'

'What is this "Light" you keep talking about?' asked Agravain irritably. 'The sun?'

'I think I understand,' Bedwyr said slowly. 'In a sense, the sun. As the sun is a type of Light, since all other lights are ultimately derived from it, by reflection or by dependence with the rest of the world, so the Light which your brother speaks of is the source of good and of illumination, and other goods are known only in it. Yes, Cei, I did read it in a book of philosophy. But am I right?'

'I . . . I think so,' I said, astonished. 'Yes, if I understand you. I do not know any philosophy. I know only that the Light sent a boat, and I embarked, and it took me to the Islands of the Blessed.'

'Oh God!' said Cei, at last releasing his growing anger. 'How many have made that claim? And how many have been to those islands? None, because those islands do not exist outside the songs of poets! Agravain, you are my brother, but this brother of yours is another matter. He has been spinning gossamer from clouds of lies this whole while, and you've been taking it for true yarn. But I can't. When you have had enough, I will be riding up ahead.'

'He is not lying, Cei,' said Bedwyr.

But Cei only gave me a look of disgust. 'No, indeed. He is merely giving a poetic form to the concepts of philosophers, and discoursing upon the *summum bonum* or whatever you call it. This is a fine enough tale for Breton mystics and philosophers, Bedwyr, but I am a Dumnonian and a Roman, and

I want no more of this.' He spurred his horse to a gallop and left us, reining in beside some other warrior.

'Go on,' said Agravain. 'I will listen.'

But he was beginning to agree with Cei. 'I am not lying,' I said.

'I do not say that you would, deliberately,' said Agravain, apparently deciding to be very honest. 'But after what had passed, you could easily have had some kind of dream.'

'I thought it was a dream, when I woke up and found myself in Britain,' I said. 'But I still had this.' I touched Caledvwlch's hilt.

Agravain looked at it, his brows knitting. 'A sword. I noticed it earlier. It looked to be worth a good amount. You think it was given to you in the Land of Promise?'

'It was, by Lugh, from the Light. When I woke up south-east of here, returning from Tir Tairngaire, I knew that I had not been dreaming or gone mad, because it lay beside me. Its name is Caledvwlch.'

Agravain glared at it. He was becoming angry now, and I dreaded the results of his anger. 'A sword. A fine sword, as far as I can tell. Let me see the rest of it.'

I drew Caledvwlch. His eyebrows went up and he whistled. 'Och, fine indeed; I should like such a sword. But it is not supernatural.'

Bedwyr stared at the bright steel for a moment, then looked away. He apparently did see something supernatural in it.

I considered making the fire burn in the blade, to show Agravain the power as well, but decided not to. It was too violent and obvious, an abuse of the power. Besides, I had no desire to be thought a witch, and I did not know the warriors. So, 'Lugh gave it to me,' I reiterated.

Agravain snorted. He was rejecting the story now. Perhaps he could simply not accept it of me, of Gwalchmai, his weak, ineffectual little brother. 'Go on,' he said, however. 'You woke up with the sword, east of here, after spending – how long? – in the Isles of the Blessed.'

'It was nearly three years. It seemed only a day. But time was strange there. I woke in the hills in the borderland between the kingdom of Dumnonia and the land Cerdic claims, and when I was walking west I walked directly into a Saxon raiding party on its way back to Sorviodunum.'

Agravain calmed at this; this he could believe. 'Couldn't you tell a Saxon from a Roman?' he asked.

'I did not know where I was. For all I knew, I might be going to Constantinople, though I thought it unlikely. So I told them that I was a thrall, and my master had died in a blood feud, and they brought me back to Sorviodunum and sold me to Cerdic.'

'Why should he buy you? Did he suspect that you were a king's son?'

'I don't think so. Aldwulf of Bernicia told him to, and Aldwulf, like Bedwyr, or Sion, or most people these days, was not sure I was quite human when first he saw me.'

'That is ridiculous,' said Agravain. 'Why should they think that? You did not, did you, Bedwyr?'

'Your brother is right,' said Bedwyr. 'I think you underestimate him.'

'I know him better than you,' snapped Agravain. 'Go on.'

'Aldwulf wanted to kill Arthur, as I said, and thought that if he killed me and used the sword, he could manage it, by sorcery. But he had conjured up a horse of the Sidhe for Cerdic, to prove his power in sorcery, a horse which could outrun and outstay any horse on earth. Cerdic was trying to break it, but could not. I could – you must remember that I was good with horses, though this one was different – and I did, and I rode it out of Sorviodunum as fast as possible.'

'Then where is it now?'

'I let him go. He was of the Sidhe; I had no right to keep him. That was the day before yesterday; and yesterday I met with that farmer you disliked and came to Ynys Witrin, where you came this morning.'

'A fine story,' said Agravain scornfully. 'Very fine, indeed. But you forgot a few details, Gwalchmai. What about the hill-fort full of armed Saxons? But doubtless you slew them by the scores as you rode off on the king's horse.'

'They did try to stop me, they just weren't quick enough – no, I am not claiming any skill at arms. We both know better. But the Saxons were afraid. They did not think that I was human, and I had the sword.'

'Your sword! Why should they fear that?'

'It . . . I imagine it can be frightening.'

'Gwalchmai,' said Agravain, his voice level and controlled, but plainly very angry, 'Cerdic's warriors are not children to run away from a reputed magic sword. And what of the king, and Aldwulf of Bernicia? You say that Fflamddwyn is a sorcerer, and so his name and fame are in all Britain; couldn't he have ruined that famous sword for you?'

'I do not think his power is that great,' I said. 'I do not think anything could quench Caledvwlch, except its bearer. If I turned against the Light, since it is by Light that the sword burns ... whatever. Aldwulf was unconscious when I left. I'd cut his face open with Caledvwlch.'

Agravain reined in his horse to a complete halt. 'And how many Saxons did you kill leaving the camp?' he asked quietly.

I stopped the cart. Sion's mare halted gladly, her sides heaving. 'Three.' I knew what was coming now. 'Agravain, I am not trying to claim that ...'

'You have said enough,' Agravain went on firmly. The entire foraging band was halting now, and the warriors were turning their horses back or driving their carts forward to see what was happening. 'The first part of your story I believe, the second is a dream or some confusion honestly and easily made, but this ... this can be nothing other than an outright lie. You, striking down a Saxon king, and killing three of Cerdic's warriors single-handed? You can't even throw a spear straight.'

'Agravain, I said it was not from skill but ...'

'Was it by magic, then? You said you'd rejected that, and rightly so.'

'No, it was not, but ...'

'Then your tale is a tissue of lies,' Agravain proclaimed fiercely, 'Nonsense you made up to give yourself some honour which you are afraid to win honestly in battle. You are hopeless as a warrior.'

'I've never said otherwise.'

'And I will show you how hopeless.' My brother ruthlessly thrust aside my attempts to fend off what was coming 'Get out of that cart and I will teach you not to lie ...'

'I will lend you my horse,' Bedwyr said to me, quite suddenly, 'and my spear and shield as well, so that you can fight as a warrior should.'

There was an instant of startled silence. 'Thank you,' I said at last, slowly. 'But I fear I will disgrace your weapons.'

'Perhaps,' said Bedwyr, 'and perhaps not.'

'I wager he will,' said Cei cheerfully. 'I stake a gold armlet that Agravain downs him. You are right, Agravain, to do this; no one could believe that tale but a Breton.'

'I would accept your stake,' said Bedwyr, 'only I do not share your taste for jewellery. I have my reasons for believing the tale, Cei.'

Agravain scowled. He had wanted to fight me in the way he was best accustomed to, with his fists. But he decided that this would do. 'Very well. Hurry. We must reach Camlann before too long.'

I climbed down from the cart, tying the reins to the corner post, and Bedwyr dismounted. He gave me his spear and shield, tying a rag around the point of the spear and telling me to use the butt end, then gave me the reins of his horse, which was a long-boned dappled Gaulish war-steed. I thanked him, feeling resigned to my inevitable defeat. It would be only another fall, I told myself. It could not hurt me.

I mounted Bedwyr's horse and rode it in a tight circle, seeing how it responded and trying to get an idea of its temper. It was a good horse, though of course nothing like Ceincaled.

We moved off the road to the cleared land about it. Now that we had left the marshes behind, the road wound through steep hills, covered with ploughed land and pasture. The pastureland by the roadside was soft, so a fall would not be very painful. The warriors of the band formed a circle, not really understanding what was happening, but interested. No one accepted Cei's wager.

Agravain rode to the far side of the circle, levelled the blunt end of his spear, and nodded briskly. 'I won't hurt you,' he warned me, 'But you must learn.'

I nodded, sighed, and raised my shield. He would be cheerful again once he had downed me, and it was a small enough price to pay for that. Still, I wished that he would believe me. It hurt a little that he could so quickly call me a liar.

Agravain urged his horse to a trot, angling his spear and following the line of the circle. I followed his example, trying to remember what I had struggled to learn in the Boys' House. My brother saw I was ready and swung his horse towards me, touching it to a canter.

Suddenly, everything narrowed, and time itself seemed to slow as I touched Bedwyr's horse to a gallop and rode to meet him. My heart soared, and I swung my spear out of line. Agravain saw it, smiled, confidently came in. The world narrowed further to his spear tip and right shoulder, and around these points all was blurred. He was almost upon me; I swerved my horse just half a step, caught his spear on the edge of my shield, sending it glancing off, dropped my own spear into line and thrust it against his shoulder, braced for the impact.

Time resumed its normal flow, and Agravain fell from his horse, his eyes wide with surprise, as I reined in and turned my animal quickly, dropping my spear to threaten him.

He lay still for a moment, then rose, slowly, rubbing his shoulder and scowling in bewilderment. I came to myself and stared, first at him, then over at his horse, which was now nibbling the thick grass. I could not understand what had happened.

'We will try again,' said Agravain loudly. 'Now.'

'It was an accident,' I said. 'I could not do it again. I know that you're the better warrior of us, Agravain.' Of course he was; it was his world.

'We'll do it again, damn you!' shouted Agravain. He went over to his horse, remounted it, jerked savagely at the bit and rode over to the opposite side of the circle.

'Cei,' said one of the warriors. 'Is the wager still on?'

'If you want,' said Cei.

'Fair enough; I've armlets too.'

Agravain lowered his spear, and began trotting about the circle again. I did the same, waiting for him when he turned his horse nearly backward and came up with a swerving course. This time I reined suddenly as we approached, bringing Bedwyr's horse rearing to a stop. Again everything contracted about us, and I felt even more clearly the wild lightness in my mind. Agravain was almost beside me, and his spear, aimed at my left thigh, was close. I beat it out of line with my shield, turning my horse and allowing his weight to join mine behind the spear as I thrust at Agravain's side. Again, he fell; again his horse ran on, this time into the circle of warriors where it was caught.

Agravain rose to his feet. He was no longer scowling, but staring in total bewilderment, like a man who has seen the sun rising in the west. The madness was still on me, and I did not wish to speak, so I sat silent and unmoving, spear ready, and waited.

Agravain went and got his horse, remounted, levelled his spear. I rode to the opposite end of the circle and nodded.

He came at me immediately this time, at a full gallop. I hurled my spear, blunt end first, as he came, and rode on drawing Caledvwlch.

The spear hit his throat and glanced off, though he would surely have a bruise to show for it; had I thrown it tip first he would be dead. He almost fell as it hit him, but recovered in time, keeping his spear straight. His thrust as we drew even would have struck me through the ribs to the right of my shield, had it touched me – but I hacked at the shaft with Caledvwlch, and it snapped. Time froze, and I lifted the sword before Agravain's horse could complete another step. The light was burning in the blade, and I was filled with a strength which seemed hardly to be my own. The world looked as though it had been etched on bright steel. I let all the force fall into my arm as I struck Agravain with the flat of the sword blade. He fell into the grass, his horse plunging slowly past me. He rolled over and lay still. There was a massive silence.

My head cleared a little and I sheathed the sword. Still Agravain lay motionless. The rest of the madness departed from me, and I dismounted hastily. 'Agravain?' He did not move. I ran over to him. By the Light, how hard had I hit him? 'Agravain?'

He shook his head groggily, then climbed to his knees, holding his arm where I had struck it. He stared at me. His face was white, beaded with sweat. He climbed slowly to his feet, still staring.

'Dear God,' he said, very slowly, each word falling into the ring of silence that was the watchers. 'What have you become?'

'I said that you underestimated your brother.' Bedwyr walked forward, still calm and unshaken. 'I think that you will find a place with Arthur, Gwalchmai ap Lot.'

'But the sword!' said Cei. 'Didn't you see the sword? It was burning. He . . .'

'The sword?' asked another, 'Didn't you see his eyes?'

Light! I thought desperately. Now they do believe that I am a witch.

'He has beaten Agravain of Orcade in fair combat, do any

of you question that?' asked Bedwyr sharply.

'I question it,' said Cei immediately. 'That was not fair combat. No ordinary mortal being could have . . .'

'It was a fair fight,' said Agravain. The warriors at once stopped glaring at me and stared at him instead. 'It was a very fair fight, and long overdue. Gwalchmai is no witch, I swear the oath of my people to that. If any of you thinks otherwise, I am willing to fight again today. My brother is a warrior. God! By the sun, I have never fought anyone as good!'.

'It was an accident . . .' I began, still bewildered.

'It was not. You are better than I, and we both know that now.'

'One fall might have been an accident,' Bedwyr stated. 'Three times constitutes proof. You are very good, Gwalchmai. Perhaps better than I.'

'That is absurd. You are the finest horseman in the Family,' objected Cei.

Bedwyr only smiled.

Cei shook his head violently. 'Nothing of this makes sense. Swords cannot burn like firebrands. His story is impossible; but if it is true, where does that leave us? He is a sorcerer . . .'

'I said, nothing more about that!' Agravain snapped. 'Whatever he was in the past, my brother is a warrior now.'

'How can I be?' I broke in. 'I never could fight. You know that, Agravain. You must remember how I was in the Boys' House, how I could not throw a spear straight . . .' Agravain rubbed his throat where my spear had caught it, but I plunged on. 'Everyone knew that I was no warrior. Father was disappointed in me, I was disappointed in myself, so much that I was willing to give myself up to the Darkness from sheer anger and the pain of failing. How can I be a warrior?'

'You say that you laid open Aldwulf's face with that?' Agravain began to point at Caledvwlch with the arm I had struck, then winced and clasped it again.

'I . . . yes, but . . .'

'And you killed three Saxons when you escaped from Din Sarum?'

'Yes, but Agravain . . .'

'There you are, then.' He turned to the others. 'He has ruined Fflamddwyn's good looks for him and fought against our enemies. Can you question that he is fighting for us?'

'We have only his account to rely on for that tale,' objected Cei.

'Do you accuse my brother of lying?' asked Agravain, trying to reach for his sword and wincing again.

Cei stopped, staring at my brother. Then he sighed and shrugged. He plainly thought that I was lying somehow, but he would not fight his friend for it. 'I accuse no one,' he said. 'But I will tell Arthur of this.'

Bedwyr nodded. 'And I will tell Arthur that I believe Gwalchmai.' The two looked at each other for another moment, and then Bedwyr smiled gently. 'You merely do not wish to lose that armlet, Cei.'

Cei looked confused for a moment, then remembered his wager. He grinned shakily, pulled the armlet off and tossed it to the man who had won it. That man sat his horse looking at it uncertainly, then put it on. Cei clasped Bedwyr's hand, remounted, and turned his horse back to the road. Slowly the others followed, and Bedwyr took his horse and shield from me and went after them.

'Agravain . . .' I began again.

'Gwalchmai.' He rubbed his arm, winced again. 'By the sun, I have a bruise here. Bedwyr has forgotten his spear; where is it?'

I picked it up. The rest of the foraging band had started off down the road at a walk; Sion's mare was cropping the grass by the roadside. Agravain caught his horse, gathered the reins up, awkwardly one-armed. Just about to mount, he stopped, looked at me again and caught my arm.

'Gwalchmai, I am sorry,' he said.

'I am the one who is sorry. Truly, I did not mean to hit you so hard!'

'I don't mean for this.' He had slipped back into Irish from the British of the warband. 'Though I am sorry, and should be, that I cried liar on you. But all your life I have been calling you names to provoke you to fighting, and beating you to make myself feel better; and I have pretended to help you with the arts of war while I ruined you for them, pretending, even to myself, that it was generous of me and for your own good – do not say anything. I know that it is true. I began to realize it after I was a hostage here, when I was no longer the first-born and leader in everything, and when I saw that it was hopeless to fight and still wished to. And when they told

168

me that you were dead, and all Britain said, "There is one witch the less", then I did understand, and wished myself dead as well. I remembered how you looked at me once after a fight, and I knew it was the part of a dog and a devil from Yffern to so humilate a brother, and I had done it, and gone hunting afterwards. Listen, perhaps there is no repayment for it, but I am sorry.'

I clasped his shoulders. 'My heart, I have said that I was a fool then, and took things over-much to heart. If I had been able to laugh at you . . . and it is past now. Forget it.'

He embraced me. I felt his chest shake, realized that he was weeping, realized that I was as well. 'From this time on, Gwalchmai,' he muttered, 'it will be different.' He released me, looking at me earnestly. 'I will boast of you before I boast of myself. From now on there will be only victories.'

I could say nothing, and he said again, 'Only victories, Gwalchmai. Forget all that I ever said about your skill as a warrior. You will be a great warrior, a man they make songs about.' He looked up the road then, and added, 'They are slowing the pace for us, but we will still be left behind. Come, help me on to this horse. My arm is still numb.'

When the cart was jolting and swaying down the road again, Sion's little mare trotting briskly to catch the others, Agravain fell behind. I understood very well why. He wished to be alone with his thoughts, as I did with mine, and, after such words as had just passed, we would have nothing to say to each other for a time.

I did not know what to think or to feel. I had beaten Agravain, Agravain had repented to me for the past. I had beaten Agravain, he said that I would be a great warrior. There had been a time when that was the focus of my dreams, but I had abandoned those dreams for the Darkness, and I had never thought to see them placed within my grasp. And I wanted to turn the cart about and ride away from Camlann as fast as the horse could gallop.

I looked at the worn leather of the reins, dark with the polish of use, and at my hands curled around the leather. I had sworn those hands to the service of the Light. What had Bedwyr said about the Light? Something about all other lights or goods being known only in it. And I had already come to see that the Light could do whatever he wanted, even among the Saxons. Surely he did not need my aid, and did not

169

need to have given me Caledvwlch, or to have sent me to Britain. Agravain had asked me why, when I spoke of Morgawse, and I knew that he meant not only 'Why does she hate?' but, 'Why must she be there to hate?' And I could not see why. If the Light could protect Arthur against her strongest spells, and could save me from her, he could certainly rid the Earth of Darkness. He did not need me or anyone to run about Britain and make war. I saw with a sense of shock that I did not like the thought of war, and I saw that I believed that it was wrong to kill. I had never heard of any such idea in my life, and yet, I thought again of those three Saxons and thought that there surely should have been some other way. And if it were sometimes right to kill, as I would have killed Aldwulf, or, in a different way, as I had killed Connall – when was it right? And how could anyone be always right? The Light of its – his – own nature must be always right, if what Bedwyr had said was true, and I believed that it was. But the world of men is mixed, good and evil together, and there was no simple and clear struggle, no one decision like the one I had made at Dun Fionn.

Yet men make choices, and must make choices. I had chosen Light at Dun Fionn. Medraut had chosen Darkness. Violently, I wished that I could have stopped him, and I remembered him standing in Morgawse's room, looking at her in adoration. If I had dragged him from the room after me? But he had been calling me 'Traitor', the shout had echoed behind me. If I saw him again, and spoke to him, could he still change his mind? Surely, the Darkness could not completely enchain his will – and then I thought that I and the Light could not either. But who would choose Darkness, if they understood what they were choosing, understood the hunger and fear, the hatred that consumes happiness, the loss? And yet sometimes it seemed plain that we could not help but serve Darkness. And if I fought for Arthur, I would have to make choices, and it was evident that in the nature of the world I would sometimes choose wrongly. I did not want to fight in the complex world of men. It was easier to fight in the Otherworld.

I stared up at the hills before us, and found Bedwyr looking back down the road. Our eyes met for a moment; he reined in his horse and fell back till he was level with the cart again.

'Your thoughts seem heavy ones, Gwalchmai ap Lot,' he

told me.

'They are heavy, lord,' I replied. 'Agravain says that I may be a great warrior now, and you have said as much also. And I am a hair's breadth from turning about and returning to the Orcades, a piece of foolishness such as I have never heard of.'

Bedwyr's eyes glinted slightly. 'And why is that?'

'You serve the Light, I think,' I said. 'Is it right to kill men and to make wars?'

'Ach!' He stared at me. 'I do not know.'

'But you are a warrior, and when I spoke of the Light you understood it better than I did myself.'

'I doubt that. I merely know the language of philosophy, and so could describe it better. You have touched on something, Gwalchmai ap Lot, which I have often questioned. I could only say what I know myself, from what I myself have experienced.'

'Then tell me that, if there is time. I am sick with thinking of it.'

'I think I understand that.' Bedwyr's eyes glinted again with the suppressed amusement. It was very strange, I thought fleetingly, that I could speak to him so easily, and that he had so quickly taken my part against Cei. Perhaps it was that we served the same lord that created this understanding.

With his shield-arm, the one with the missing hand, he brushed his hair back from his face. 'Very well,' he began. 'As Cei has mentioned several times already, I am a Breton, and my father has estates in the south-east – no, that is not to say I have a noble clan; in most of Less Britain, clans are less important than ownership of land and civic status. My father is a *curialis* – that is a title. Officially his rank is *clarus*, but he calls himself *clarissimus*, because he likes the sound of it.' Again came the glint of amusement. 'We are near the border of Less Britain, and while I was young, not a summer went by without the Franks, or the Saxons, or the Swabians or Goths or Huns breaking into our fields and driving off our cattle, and demanding gold for the municipality. So I learned to fight early, as men also do here in Britain. I also learned to read, but I considered this of less importance. In Less Britain, as in parts of southern Gaul, the old municipal schools are still run for the children of the nobility, and I went there and was taught the elements of rhetoric from the *grammaticus* there;

171

and very tedious it was. We had a textbook, though, one among the class of twelve, and it was written by a Marius Victorinus, who was a philosopher. When he wished to give an example of an exhortation, he exhorted to philosophy; of discussion, a debate about the *summum bonum* – that is, what is most excellent in human life. He thought it was philosophy. I thought he was a fool, for the Franks cared nothing for philosophy, and I enjoyed killing the Franks. Mind, I enjoyed it, not tolerated it, but took pleasure in showing off my skill. When I was seventeen, I enrolled some peasants from my father's estate, and took them off, with one or two other youths from the area, to fight for the *Comes Armoricae* – the king of Less Britain, you would say. After a few years, the Frankish king died, and the new king was busy with the Goths, and the wars seemed over for a time. Then I heard that our king's younger son, Bran, had made alliance with Arthur of Britain, and planned an expedition. I had never been to Britain, and had killed no Franks or Saxons for nearly a year, so I took my followers and went with Bran.

'You know of that campaign, I think, and how Arthur won the purple, so there is no need for me tell you of it. But for myself, I was wounded in the battle by the Seafern.' Bedwyr held up his shield-arm again. 'The blow was not bad in itself, but the wound took the rot, and I, who was not afraid of the Saxons, was afraid of the doctors, and did not go to them until I was sick and had to be carried. They took the hand off, but I was in a high fever from the rot, and I thought that I would die. I lay there in the monastery where they had brought us, and now I had time to wonder about how many men I had placed in this position, and the thought did not please me as it had before. All my renown was useless to me now. And I kept remembering the exhortation to philosophy from that textbook, and thinking that glory was not, after all, the *summum bonum*.

'For three days I lay between death and life. On the third, Taliesin, the chief bard of Arthur, came to the monastery – I still do not know why. When he walked past the rows of the wounded, it looked to me as though a star burned on his forehead, and I thought that I was dead. So I called out to him that I was not yet prepared.

'He stopped and came over and knelt beside me. 'For something you are prepared, Bedwyr ap Brendan,'' he said,

"But not for death." Then he turned to the doctors and said that he thought the fever would break soon. "So you regret your life," he said turning back to me – I had never seen him before, and still I thought him the angel of death. "With all my heart." I replied. "You live now," he told me, "and will for many years yet. But remember your regret when you recover, and, I warn you, things will turn out otherwise than you expect. Have faith, and do not wonder at what happens." With that he left, and the doctors put me in a heated room with many blankets, so that the fever broke, and I began to recover.'

'Who is this Taliesin?' I asked. 'His last words to you were the same as Lugh's to me.'

He gave me a dark, serious look. 'Indeed? I do not know where Taliesin comes from or who his parents were. No one does. He is a great poet, and a healer besides. There are other stories about him, some very strange, but nothing is known for certain. I know that he is not evil, and his words then were true. I recovered from my fever, but I remembered what I had felt then, when I had thought that I would die. I asked the monks who cared for the sick if they had that textbook by the philosopher Victorinus, but they had never heard of him. They had only a few books, and those gospels. So I read one of the gospels, that of Matthew, and I came to the place where the Christ was betrayed, and led off to execution; and one of his followers drew a sword to defend him, and our lord said, "Put your sword in its place: for those that take the sword will perish with the sword." Then I decided that it was wrong to kill and to make wars, and I resolved to return to Less Britain as soon as I was well enough to travel, and there enter a monastery, and contemplate the Good. I anticipated that my father would be angry, but I would not have yielded for all that. So, you see, I know what it is that troubles you.'

'Why did you change your mind again?'

He smiled, a quick but very warm smile. 'I met Arthur. I had seen him before, but never spoken with him. He came to the monastery to visit the wounded. I was sitting in the garden: it was summer, and evening, and I was trying to read. He came up to me, calling me by name, and asked me of my wound; then asked when I would rejoin King Bran. I told him that I did not plan to continue to live as a warrior, but to enter a monastery, and he said that Bran thought highly of me, and that he did not understand.

'I explained my reasons, and, surprisingly, he did understand. He had even heard of Victorinus – he had read of him in a book by one Aurelius Augustinus. "But I do not agree with your Victorinus on the highest good," he told me. "Do you think that it is glory, then?" I asked. "Indeed not," he replied, "But Augustinus says evil is not a substance, but an absence, being nothing more than the denial of good. And this my own heart teaches me as well, for I can see from it that evil begins in weakness, cowardice and stupidity, and proceeds to hatred and desolation, while good is active. So it seems to me that the highest good cannot be a thing that sits like a picture on the wall, waiting to be admired, but must be active and substantial." And I: "Victorinus says that the Good, that is, the Light, subsists in all things, for if it did not, nothing would exist. But because men do not consider it, and act blindly, they create evil." And he: "If they do nothing but sit and consider, they are bound to create evil, for they cannot create good." "But they might find it and know it," said I. And he stood and paced about the garden, then asked me, "Is justice good? It is active. Are order, peace, harmony good? Is love? – Augustinus says that love is a property of men but not of God, but I think that, if this were so, we would be superior to God, which is unthinkable; for I am certain that these things are good, love most of all." And I: "The Church says that God, that is, the Good, loved and acted once, in Christ." And he: "I say he did then and does now, in us. Tell me, is it good that the Saxons take away the land, the cattle of their neighbours, and that men and women, and children, too, are left to starve? Is it good that only a handful of nobles in Britain can read, and few of them have books? Is it good that men are reduced thus to the level of beasts, thinking of nothing but food and slaughter?" "Why do you ask?" I said, "There are evils, but they have come about because Rome has fallen and the Empire has gone from the West. What can we do but ourselves abstain from evil in such times?" "We can restore the Empire," he said, and stopped pacing, standing with the moonlight in his hair – for by then the moon had risen over the abbey wall.

' "Before God, I will preserve civilization in this land or die defending it, because I love the Good. And I think that to fight thus is the highest good for men, and not philosophy.

174

What would your Victorinus say to that?" "Victorinus had no emperor like you to follow," I said, 'or he would have spoken differently.' And I knelt to him, and told him, "I have only one hand to fight for you, but, in God's name, take me into your service, and all I can do, I will." He looked at me in surprise for a moment, for he had not realized how much his words had stirred me; then he took my hand and swore the oath a liege-lord swears to his follower. And I have fought for him ever since, and will do so all my life, God willing: for I now believe that to act with a desire for good, even if we may act wrongly, is better than not to act at all. But whether in the end we are justified in the eyes of God, I cannot say.'

I was silent for a long time. 'That is hardly comforting,' I said at last.

'Life is not comfortable,' he replied. 'Nonetheless, I think there is more joy in struggling for the Light than in retreat.'

'But the difference between us and the Saxons is not so great,' I objected. 'They are men too, and much like us. And I know that you are a Roman, but still, I cannot see why the Empire has anything to do with the Light. No British king had some miserable slave tortured to death to see whether his master threw stones at a royal statue, or had three thousand people massacred at a theatre because they had rioted, as did Theodosius, the High King of Rome. My mother told me of this, but still, it is true, isn't it? And I never heard of any king in Britain or in Erin having hundreds of innocent noblemen put to death, solely because their names began with "Theod-", as Valentinianus did because of an oracle he had received, though he missed Theodosius. Moreover, the Romans took Britain by force of arms, just as the Saxons are attempting to do now, and no doubt the people here then liked the Romans as little as we now like the Saxons – why are you smiling?'

'Because you can speak Latin and read and are probably a Christian, and still, if you do not object to my saying so, you are a barbarian. I mean no insult. It is true, the Empire caused much evil and misery. But no British lordling ever created as much of good and beauty, ever gave to the world so much knowledge, art and splendour as did the Romans. And no British king ever founded hospitals, or endowed monasteries to care for the sick, the poor and the orphaned; or again, relieved his domains when there was famine and restored them after fire or war, which the Christian emperors

175

did. The Empire is worth fighting to preserve. That I could never question.'

'Very well, I am a barbarian,' I said, beginning to laugh. 'You southern British – excuse me, Bretons – always say as much about the Irish. I still do not see that your Empire has much to do with the Light; but, from what you have said, I think the Empire Arthur desires would. And I have been given a sword, which, if it is a weapon of Light, is also a weapon of war. I do not fear perishing by it if I take it up, and if your Christ threatened nothing more than that, I would have no hesitations. Only . . . by the Light, it is too sudden. I never expected . . . I never thought that I could become a warrior, and would have to make such a choice.'

'Perhaps when you meet the Emperor Arthur it will become clear. Look, there is Camlann. We are almost home.'

Camlann is ancient, older than the kingdom of Britain, in fact. It stood empty and decaying while the Romans ruled, but after Londinium fell to the Saxons, Ambrosius Aurelianus had it resettled. Arthur had it refortified with the great walls, which, when we rode up that day, were only half-finished. As we approached, Agravain drove up his horse to ride beside me again; and Cei fell back, watching me as though he expected me to grow wings and fly off rather than enter the fortress. So I came to Camlann, driving a heavy-laden cart pulled by a spent mare, flanked by three warriors who viewed me in vastly different lights, fastening my hopes on a High King who was absent.

The gates had been thrown open for us before we reached them, and we drove up the steep hill, the warriors calling greetings to the guards and shouting that they had a victory. The High King was expected back, with the rest of the warband, at any moment, and Bedwyr wanted the supplies from Ynys Witrin to be unloaded before the Pendragon returned.

'I do not wish my lord to have to trouble himself with inventories, nor to wait for his victory feast,' he told one of the servants.

'Of course,' said the man, eyeing the carts with some eagerness – I gathered they had been short of supplies in Camlann. 'Did you bring mead from Ynys Witrin?'

'Seeing that the monks make the best mead in Dumnonia,' Cei replied, 'we were hardly likely to miss it.'

'Good. We've only that ale we saved from last winter, and I had no wish to give that to the Emperor after a victory.'

The carts and horses were brought to a stable, and I cared for Sion's mare and gave her some grain. I was finishing with her when Bedwyr entered, followed by Cei and Agravain. 'The Emperor is almost here,' he told me, 'if you wish to come down to the gates.'

The Family was still riding up when I went to the gates to see them. It was a long column, coming from the North, mounted men, some driving cattle; one or two wagons, spare horses on lead reins. They covered the road into the distance, glittering with weapons in the afternoon sun. At the front a rider carried the standard, a deeper glint of gold at that distance, and behind him came a man on a white horse. Arthur.

I thought of all that had happened to me up to that moment, of my mother and my father both, of Agravain, of Lugh, of the Saxons. The physical struggle and the spiritual struggle: they met here. My throat constricted and I stood, my eyes, like the eyes of all around me, fixed on the man who rode behind the standard.

The vanguard of the warband broke off from the slower-moving group which drove the cattle. Horses' manes and tails and men's cloaks streamed in the wind of their motion, and, through the dirt of hard riding, the sun glittered off weapons and mail and jewellery. The Pendragon wore the purple, gold-embroidered cloak of the Roman High Kings over his coat of mail. He rode well, and held his tall spear as though he knew how to use it. As he passed the gates, the inhabitants of the fortress shouted a welcome with one voice, and they shouted, 'Arthur!'

The king laughed and reined in the horse, and his followers pressed around him, catching his hands in greeting. I remained standing on the half-finished well, staring at him and wondering that so much doubt and deep thought could come to nothing in so brief and transient a moment. I knew that somehow I had already made my choice, perhaps made it when I fled from Dun Fionn. Somehow I had known all along that I would become a warrior, and fight for Arthur.

Eleven

Arthur rode on up the hill at a walk, now surrounded by the inhabitants of Camlann. He was smiling, laughing at his subjects and waving off their shouted congratulations on his victories. He was then thirty, old enough to make such home-comings commonplace, but he did not treat it as commonplace, but as a thing new and surprising. He did that all his life.

On reaching the feast Hall at the summit of the hill he dismounted lightly, catching his horse's bridle before anyone else could. He glanced back at the throng of welcoming servants and home-coming warriors who had followed him, then beckoned one of the servants – the steward – from the crowd and began talking to him, gesturing down the hill. Making arrangements for the cattle he had plundered from the Saxons, no doubt. The steward nodded, then gestured in reply to some other question of the king's. Arthur looked up, and for just an instant he reminded me sharply of someone else, someone with the same kind of wide grey-eyed stare, but I couldn't place the memory and was not really trying.

'Bedwyr!' called the king.

Bedwyr had been somewhere in the crowd and emerged from it as if from the air. 'Here, my lord.'

Arthur gave him a different smile, one separate from the sort he had given the others, and held his hand out. Bedwyr caught it, and Arthur clasped it with his other hand as well. 'Did you bring the mead from Ynys Witrin?'

'Yes. And food enough for a few days.'

'*Laus Deo* for that. How much is there?'

'Gweir is making an inventory now. And I have already ordered the victory feast.'

'Good man. Is there any ale here?'

'The sour leavings of last winter, nothing more.'

'It will have to do. Goronwy, some ale for the Family. And Gruffydd is bringing in the wounded; send someone to see that he has what he needs for them . . .' he went into the Hall, still giving orders to various of the servants. I followed with the rest of the crowd, going up nearly to the high table, then stopped, uncertain what to do. Everyone was so busy. I could say nothing to the king yet; best to wait. I found I was in the way of some of the returning warriors and looked for a quiet corner.

Arthur dropped into a chair at the high table, caught the horn of ale offered by a servant and took a deep drink from it.

'Welcome back,' said Bedwyr.

'Welcome back yourself,' returned the Pendragon. 'When did you arrive here?'

'About an hour ago.'

'What? For God's sake man, sit down and have some ale. Goronwy . . .' he addressed the servant with the ale in an undertone, and the man nodded. 'So, Bedwyr, and how is abbot Theodorus?'

'Dishonest as ever. But we did find the mead.'

'So. And what is the matter?'

'The matter?'

'The thing that is weighing upon your mind. Were things very bad at Ynys Witrin?'

Bedwyr shook his head. Goronwy came back with some more ale and whispered to Arthur, after giving Bedwyr a horn. 'Don't use all of it, then,' Arthur said, apparently in reply to the servant. 'Tell the men we're short and they can only have one glass each, but there's plenty of mead tonight.' I had never heard of a king running short of ale before and I blinked, but no one seemed in the least surprised. 'Well, Bedwyr, and did the monks throw stones and cry, "Death to the tyrant who steals our good yellow mead! Plague upon the Dragon and his Family, since we cannot get drunk on Sunday!"?'

Bedwyr smiled. 'No. There was no trouble. They were not pleased, but gave in. The matter is of a different kind.'

Arthur glanced down the Hall. 'Your whole party looks as gloomy as men the morning after a feast. Even Cei and Agra-vain – especially Cei and Agravain.' He leant forward a little and lowered his voice.

Bedwyr shook his head in response. 'No, no bloodshed, thank God. Where are Cei and Agravain now?'

'I sent them to help with the cattle. It concerns them, does it? Very well, we will wait. The walls have not progressed as far as I had expected. What do you think . . .'

More of Arthur's Family trooped in and settled thirstily

upon their ale, joking about it. Presently Cei and Agravain entered as well, and stood about, presumably looking for me.

'Here!' Arthur called. 'Bedwyr says that there is a matter you wish me to resolve.'

Neither of the two had noticed me, and Cei was frowning uneasily as they came up to the high table. I stood, uncertain whether to join them now or not. The warriors in the Hall ceased to talk and listened.

'My lord,' said Cei, 'We wish you to make a decision concerning Agravain's brother.'

Arthur sat up straighter, setting his horn of ale down in its stand.

'Which brother?' he asked, in a very low, strained voice.

Agravain paused, looking slightly surprised. 'My brother Gwalchmai, who I thought dead. We met him at Ynys Witrin, and he came with us to Camlann. He wishes to join us. My lord, he is a very fine warrior. I had a match with him on the way from Ynys Witrin, and three times he downed me.'

'My lord,' said Cei. 'There is some reason to suspect him of sorcery.'

'He is no witch!' snapped Agravain. 'I swear the oath of my people to that. He is a warrior, and a very fine one. Ask Bedwyr.'

Arthur looked at his friend, and the dark warrior nodded. 'He is a fine warrior, and, I think, a good man. I would take oath that he is no witch.'

'I have heard of Gwalchmai, son of Lot,' Arthur said. 'And what I have heard has not been good.' I closed my eyes, my hand clutching the hilt of Caledvwlch. Lugh had warned me that Arthur might be suspicious. 'But you would vouch for him, Bedwyr?'

'Yes, my lord.'

'Well.' Arthur looked at Cei again. 'I think the matter may need consideration, but I will consider it. Where is you brother, Agravain?'

Agravain began to answer that he did not know, and I forced myself to walk out of the shadows and stand before Arthur. 'Here,' I said.

The grey eyes widened just slightly and fixed me. He did not move, and his face held no expression, but it was as though a shadow fell across him; and I suddenly sensed that what I had thought was a neutral tone was coldness, and that what touched him now was horror.

I tried to strangle the sharp-edged misery which leapt up in me. I would not, after all, wish him to accept reputed sorcerers readily, and still I had that reputation. I did look something like my mother, and perhaps he had met her, and I had recalled her to his mind.

But within me something said that the Darkness must have touched me to the very bone, and I would never be free of it, that it blighted everything I tried to touch, and I would never outrun the shadow of my youth

I went down on one knee to Arthur and stood again. There is still hope, I told myself. This is what you have been led to. It must come about.

'So,' said Arthur at last, still in the neutral tone which was not neutral but cold. 'You are Gwalchmai ap Lot?'

'Yes, Lord.'

'I had not heard that you had . . . returned to the Ynysoedd Erch. Surely, if you had, your brother should have been told of it.'

'I did not return to the Orcades, Lord Arthur. I have been only three weeks in Britain.'

'The story came here that you fell into the sea on Samhain, more than two years ago. Now you appear suddenly at Ynys Witrin, convince the lord Cei that you are a sorcerer, and ask to join my Family. What is the truth of these matters?'

I stood silent for a long minute, trying to think of an answer that would be easier to tell, then realized that the actual truth was the only possible reply. I told my story, hesitatingly at first, and painfully aware of the listeners. I left some things out; I could not bring myself to speak of the real depth of Morgawse's evil. After a while, I found that I could ignore the watchers and concentrate on my own words, so that they said what I meant them to. No one interrupted me.

When I had finished Arthur shook himself. 'A tale like the tales of poets, both in the matter and in the telling, Gwalchmai ap Lot.'

'I know. Perhaps, Lord Arthur, if I wished to lie I would tell a story more easily believed.'

At this, Bedwyr smiled, but Arthur's face did not move. 'Perhaps. And perhaps you might expect it to be believed

181

because of its very strangeness, which matches a strangeness in yourself. Admittedly, that is a subtle ploy, but your father also is a cunning man and your mother is . . .' the shadow across him grew darker, and I saw that he must have known her at some point, for he finished in a whisper, 'very subtle.'

'Lord,' I began, uncertain of how he received me and afraid, 'I am neither my father nor my mother. I have told you the truth. I have admitted that I did indeed once study sorcery; but I have renounced it, and never again will have anything to do with it.'

'Why does Cei think that you are a sorcerer? He usually disbelieves such tales.'

'It was the sword,' said Cei. 'When he fought Agravain he drew it and it burned. I swear by Saint Peter, it burned brighter than a torch. Ask anyone who was there, even Bedwyr; they all saw it.'

'It burned with light,' Bedwyr said. 'But Gwalchmai has told you where he received the sword.'

'Swords do not do that,' returned Cei firmly. 'I would have said it was impossible, but I saw it. So, it must have been some sorcerous practice of the wielder that caused it to burn, a spell he worked against his brother.'

Agravain snorted. 'He needed no spells to defeat me. Even without the sword he downed me twice. And remember how Gwalchmai has fought for us already!'

'According to his own account. Tell me, Gwalchmai, if you have seen Cerdic, what does he look like?'

I described the Saxon king carefully. Arthur nodded, and asked some more questions about the Saxons, and about Sorviodunum, and how many men where there. I saw what he wanted and gave all the details I could recall. Cei and Agravain fidgeted.

'What is the point of this?' Agravain asked at last. 'We know this already.'

'But it is not common knowledge,' replied Arthur, smiling at my brother. He looked back to me and stopped smiling. 'You have been among the Saxons recently, so part at least of your tale is true.' He looked past me, down the Hall into nothing, a wide, grey stare, remote and infinitely piercing. 'And yet, that you killed Saxons proves nothing. Saxons kill Saxons. The Queen Morgawse your mother: do you think she is beautiful?'

182

I was taken completely by surprise. 'Yes.'

'Why?'

I looked about in confusion. 'Why? Lord, why do we think anything beautiful? She is as perfect and terrible as Death itself, and so say all who have met her.'

Our eyes met for a long moment, and the thing that was common between us was a shadow, a knowledge of Darkness.

'Your story has a great deal of the Otherworld in it,' Arthur said at last. 'And although Bedwyr thinks highly of you, and although by blood you are my nephew, little as your mother may like the idea, I do not think that I can trust you.' My heart seemed to stop, and I stood, staring back at him, swallowing. 'You are free to take service with any other king in Britain, or to return to the islands. But I cannot give you a place here.'

It could not be over with, not so quickly. It could not be. It was not just. I stood stupidly in the middle of the Hall, still staring at the Pendragon. He looked away from me and picked up his ale-horn.

'Lord, I protest!' exclaimed Agravain. 'Take my oath that Gwalchmai is no sorcerer; or at least give him some chance to prove himself. Wait until we have news from the Saxons, see if his story . . .'

'My lord, let him prove himself by fighting for you,' urged Bedwyr. 'I spoke with him on the way; I am certain that he is no witch . . .'

'Do you question my judgement?' asked Arthur coldly, looking up at them.

They fell silent. Bedwyr bowed slightly; 'Never, my lord.' Agravain stammered, fell silent again.

I bowed to the High King once more, turned, walked out of the Hall. It was true. It was over.

'Wait!' shouted Agravain, and hurried after me.

Outside the Hall, he caught my arm. 'I do not know what the matter is, but this is unlike the Pendragon. He will change his mind.'

'He has decided,' I replied.

'He has . . . but, Yffern! It is unlike him. I do not understand it.'

It is forbidden, I thought to myself, to know too much of the Darkness. How could I serve a king like Arthur, when I had such knowledge? But I had thought the Light wanted it. I had been so certain. Where was everything now? What could I do?

'Listen,' Agravain said. 'Cei and Bedwyr and I share a house, with two others. Come and rest there, and Bedwyr will speak to Arthur for you.'

'He said that he never questioned the High King's judgements.'

'And he never would, before the Family. But sometimes he disagrees with Arthur and argues the point with him, and sometimes Arthur changes his mind. The High King thinks highly of Bedwyr, he made him cavalry commander – *magister equitum*, he calls it. I told you they spoke a deal of Latin here. Come and rest . . . and you look as though you wish to be alone.'

'Yes.'

So Agravain took me to his house and left me there, muttering something about seeing to his horse. I was grateful for it, and grateful that Agravain was of high enough status not to have to sleep in the crowded feast Hall. I sat on his bed and stared at the rush-covered floor, gripping Caledvwlch.

But what was it for? I demanded silently of the Light. Why the sword, the power, the struggle, the voyage to the Otherworld, if, at the end of it, I can't fight? You wanted me to take service with Arthur – Lugh told me to. So why is it denied to me now?

There was no answer. I drew Caledvwlch and looked it. The sword remained dull as my own confusion.

I despaired. I was trapped, forever locked in the evil of Morgawse, damned by the road I had taken in my youth. And yet, I had refused to follow her, I had killed her demon, I had found Light – to be sure, no Darkness is defeated for ever, but I had truly conquered! That I could not doubt.

I grew angry. Sheathing the sword, I stood and paced the room. Why should Arthur refuse me so quickly, so completely? It was not just.

No, the fault of necessity was in me. My tale had too much to do with the Otherworld, and I still half-worshipped Morgawse, and had told him so when I said that she was beautiful. I sat down again, and again prayed, and again found silence.

So the afternoon passed, and evening came. Agravain came back and asked if I wanted anything to eat, and I told him, no. He went off to the feast.

There was nothing I could do, I decided. Arthur had rejected me. Oh, I could not simply sit and feel sorry for myself; I must act. What had Bedwyr said that Arthur had said about action? – How could I go to another lord now, after meeting the High King?

I wanted more than ever, now that it was denied me, to serve Arthur. I wanted to have some part in his Family, the colour and splendour of it, the glory mingled together with shortage of last winter's sour ale, which everyone seemed to treat as a joke. The Family was not like other warbands, and the Pendragon was not like other kings. I sat and brooded over it, locked, helpless, in despair.

Agravain returned from the feast, more than half drunk and bad-tempered. It had been a difficult day for him, as well. After a while, Bedwyr and the two others, Rhuawn and Gereint, also returned.

'I have spoken to Arthur,' Bedwyr told me quietly. 'He says that he does not think we can risk accepting you, not at such a time as this, and mentioned his distrust of the Queen Morgawse your mother, who by your own testimony is plotting against him. But more than this he will not say. I do not understand it: usually he is willing to give anyone at all a chance to prove himself.'

'Gwalchmai must be a sorcerer, then,' said Rhuawn, a lean, long-faced man.

'Be quiet,' said Agravain harshly. 'I have said that he is not.' I recognized the signs: my brother wanted to fight someone. Apparently Rhuawn recognised them as well, for he was quiet.

Finally Cei returned, quite drunk, but controlling it well. 'Hah!' he exclaimed when he saw me. 'Still here, are you?' He was very pleased, with himself and with his judgement. 'I'd've thought you'd've gone running from here like a whipped dog by now. Or a whipped hawk?' He snorted with laughter. 'But hurt hawks don't run, do they? Don't even fly. They just . . . sit. And brood. And glare. As you are. Hah!'

'Hush,' said Bedwyr. 'You have no cause for that.'

'That practice of sorcery is cause enough for cursing,' said Cei. 'And I think our lord judged well!'

Bedwyr shook his head. He came over to me and said, 'I am sorry, Gwalchmai. Understand, it is not Arthur's usual way, this decision. And this is Cei's way only when he is drunk.'

'I'm not so drunk as all that,' said Cei. He sneered again. 'Well, Hawk of May, where are your spells?'

I realized that I, too, would not mind fighting someone and having some release for my anger. It was absurd, and I realized the absurdity, but still . . .

'Let him alone,' snarled Agravain.

'Why?'

'Because I'll challenge you if you don't,' replied Agravain quickly. He would, and would enjoy it, though I thought that Cei was not too drunk to fight.

Cei blinked at him, then shrugged and fell silent. However, a few minutes later, noticing Caledvwlch leaning against the wall where I had set it, he went over and picked it up, holding the loop of the baldric and swinging it back and forth, whistling between his teeth.

'Stop!' I called, abruptly ending my fit of brooding.

'What? You don't want me touching your precious magic sword?'

'Put it down,' I said. 'It is not for you.'

'Are you still trying to say that it is . . .'

'It is. My story is true, even if Arthur disbelieves it.'

'Liar,' said Cei.

Agravain stood, clenching his fists.

I could not let my brother fight my battles for me, however much he wished to. 'Stop,' I said again, also standing. 'Cei, put my sword down before you come to some harm.'

He laughed, eagerly. 'So, at last you are willing to defend yourself! *Laus Deo!* Do you want your magic sword? I will show you how magic it is . . .'

'No!' I shouted, seeing what he planned. But he had already closed his hand about the hilt and begun to draw the sword.

The dormant fire leapt, once, like summer lightning or a falling star. Cei screamed and dropped the sword, stumbled back against the wall. I was across the room to catch the weapon as he dropped it; I closed my own hand about the hilt and, without thinking, drew it. The fire blazed, pure, cool and brilliant.

'Are you hurt?' I asked Cei. He stared, opening and closing his mouth, quite sober now. 'I said, are you hurt?'

He looked at his hand. It appeared slightly burned, as though by the sun, but otherwise uninjured. 'No,' he whispered. 'God. God.'

'By all the saints,' muttered Rhuawn.

I looked at my sword, then sheathed it. 'It is well,' I told them all. 'This sword is a powerful thing, and I think that, had you drawn it, it might have killed you. Let it alone now.'

'I will,' said Cei. 'God. I . . . I wish to sleep, now.'

No one said anything as we settled down for the night: I, on Agravain's insistence, on his bed, and he on the floor.

I held Caledvwlch beside me in the darkness. The power was real, real enough to burn Cei when he touched it, real enough to have killed him. The Light was real – my lord, how could I doubt it? And the Light had led me here, and I had come, with high hopes I only fully recognized now that they were gone, and the miracle, somehow, still, had failed, and my soul ached with darkness.

I closed my eyes and ran my fingers over the sword hilt, feeling the cool smoothness of interlaced metal on the grip and the hardness of the single jewel. Simple steel and lifeless stone, yet they could fire with an unearthly light, and burn the hand that ventured to touch them. So could I, all doubts and uncertainties swept away in that white fire that three times now had burned within my mind. And yet, why should such things have happened to me? The Light needed neither men nor swords. Nothing that I did could matter. I had been delivered from the Darkness, and that ought to be enough for me.

I rolled over on the bed and looked up at the thatching of the roof, letting the sword lie on the floor where my hand could easily reach it. It is not as bad as all that, I told myself. This will not kill you. You have only to seek service elsewhere, and there is doubtless much else you can do.

Why a sword? I asked myself again. Why not a harp or a brooch or a ring, as in some tales? If I am not to be a warrior, why an instrument of war? And if I am not to serve Arthur, why be a warrior? No other king has set out to fight the Darkness . . .

The Darkness. My mind touched it at last, and I remembered Morgawse, as clearly as if she stood there in the room, and the things I had learned from her worked in me like yeast. Morgawse's eyes found mine behind my closed lids, and she smiled and smiled. I turned my mind from the thought. Eventually, I slept.

I dreamt that night, the only such dream I have ever had.

In my dream I rose from the bed and opened the door of the house to look out at Camlann. I saw all of it at once, with the walls finished, glowing in a golden light, splendid and strong. Arthur was before the gates, sitting upon a white horse, and he held a torch in his hand, the source of the light which filled the fortress. A man I did not know held the horse's bridle, a dark-haired man on whose forehead blazed a star, and his eyes were filled with infinite knowledge. Arthur lifted his torch, and the light of it sprang across all the west of Britain. I saw the whole island, from the Orcades in the north to the southern cliffs, the forests, fields, mountains and rivers and proud cities, lying like a child's drawing in the sea. But the east and north was covered with a profound shadow. I saw Aldwulf standing in the north, a black flame burning above his scarred face, and Cerdic in the south, lifting his arm to command an attack, though with an odd expression of puzzlement on his face. No armies answered his command, but a great white dragon, the symbol of kingship, rose into the sky on cloud-like wings. In the west, Arthur's dragon standard twisted, became a true dragon, and rose to meet the other. Yet I did not watch the combat, for a shadow fell across Arthur and he dwindled to nothing. I looked up and saw Her, ruling in the north and east, Queen of Air and Darkness, Lady of Shadows. Beautiful she was in the flesh, but in the dream the flesh was gone, like a dimming veil, and she blazed in dark splendour across the universe. My heart came into my throat, and my terrible love for her returned. I wanted to fling myself before her feet and beg her forgiveness, but I reached for my sword. It was not there. She smiled, and my strength vanished, so that I could think of nothing but her.

'So, my falcon,' she said, in her infinitely soft, deep voice, 'the Dragon does not want you? It is most foolish of him, for you are a great warrior.'

I was filled with joy at this, and wanted to run to her and . . . but I forced myself to hold back. 'Arthur is free,' I answered. 'He may do as he wills.'

'Of course,' she whispered, 'though he obeyed me once. But your new Lord permits you also to do as you will.' She leant forward from her throne of shadows, her eyes drinking me, like wine. I remembered, with night-edged clarity, a word she had taught me to fend off spirits. I whispered it, and some of my strength returned.

She smiled, a very sweet, dark, secret smile meant for me alone. 'My clever falcon! Yes. You see why I wished to kill you? It can be used against me and for Arthur, to establish the High King's power in Britain.'

I tore my eyes from her and looked back to the island I stood on. Arthur seemed very small after the Queen, and his power only fragmentary. I felt a touch of pity for him. I saw the battle lines forming, saw myself ride up on Ceincaled, lift my hand and speak a word of command. Cerdic clutched his throat and fell to the earth, and Aldwulf died, amazed. The Saxons were swept by plague and famine, storms destroyed their ships, and Arthur conquered all Britain. He reigned in Camlann, and I stood beside him, his most trusted counsellor, honoured by all. My father came from the Orcades with words of admiration and praise, and chose me to be the heir of his kingship. The Light ruled in Britain.

I looked again at the Queen, and met her eyes fully. She smiled for a third time, and those eyes were full of promises. 'Ah, my hawk of spring,' she whispered. 'You were always my favourite, and now that you are older . . . you are a strong enemy, more powerful than Arthur, and a greater sorcerer than that fool Adlwulf.'

I felt deep pride and a searing black joy that she should say so. More than ever I longed to approach her. I could make Arthur accept me! I could use what she had taught me for the Light, instead of the Darkness. Then I thought of what she had taught, and remembered the look in Connall's eyes when he knew that she would kill him, and the black lamb struggling under my hands while she looked for the future in its entrails, and I felt sick again, and thought of how Medraut was lost. But I needn't use the worst, I told myself.

'Where is Medraut?' I demanded of the Queen.

'That is of no consequence.'

'He is your son.'

'I have plans for him that are no concern of yours, my falcon. He hates you, my hawk, because you left and betrayed us.'

He would hate me. I could see how she must be working

on him, slowly destroying him. 'And you hate me also,' I whispered.

She shook her head slowly, and the black fire in her eyes was only the edge of a vast sea. 'You are too powerful, Hawk of May, and too beautiful.'

Dizziness swept over me, and I reached once more for my sword. Her eyes were everything in the universe, they were death itself. I could be powerful, and if I were her equal, remained her equal, she would . . .

'No!' I screamed and flung my arm between us. She stood, terrible in her power, and smiled a final time.

'Ah, but what else can you do, my son?'

What? The Darkness was about me and within me, and I could not even find a sword with which to fight it. I fell back, thinking of Arthur, of Bedwyr, of Cei, Agravain, and then of Sion. Spinning on itself, my mind found the instant at Ynys Witrin, in the silence of the chapel, and abruptly the universe turned about again, and I saw the sun instead of the shadow. My vaguely groping hand found what it sought for: my sword. I drew it and held it between myself and the Darkness.

'I will fight for Arthur,' I said, my voice steady. 'He cannot forbid me to follow him, even unaccepted. I will fight for him until he sees plainly that I do not fight for you. However long it takes, and however difficult it may be, this I can be, and this I will.'

Her lies were gone and her plan again defeated. She lifted her arms and the Darkness leapt. But she was distant again, and I stood at Camlann. I looked up and saw Lugh standing in the west, opposite Morgawse, holding his arm above the island so that the Queen could not touch it. Behind him was light too brilliant, too glorious to be seen. For a moment I saw these two confronting one another, and then my field of vision narrowed. I saw the island and the figures of armies. I saw the Family and myself in it. The armies began to move, and the sounds of battle arose. I realized that I saw things that were yet to come, and was terrified. I covered my face with my arms and cried, 'No more!'

And abruptly there was silence.

Sobbing for breath I opened my eyes and saw the thatch of Agravain's house above me. Everyone was asleep. I lay still for a long while.

Twelve

After a long time there came a bird-call from outside, then
another. Beyond the door it was morning. I sat up and buried
my face in my hands, shivering. Then I rose, dressed, picked
my way across the room and opened the door.

The dew was heavy on the grass, and the earth smelled
damp and sweet. The first wings of dawn were opening
above the plain, over the black bulk of the hills. The bird-
song ran back and forth, like water over stones. I closed the
door behind me and leaned against it, watching the sun come
up from the east. It was full day before I moved again, and
when I did it was to sing, a famous song, one sung over all the
West, which Padraig made when he went into Erin.

> 'I arise today,
> Through the power of Heaven,
> In these forces seven:
> Light of the blazing sun,
> Radiance of the moon,
> Splendour of the new flame's run,
> Sweetness of the wind's tune,
> Deepness of the boundless sea,
> The hard earth's stability,
> Stone fixed eternally;
> I arise today,
> Through God's strength to pilot me . . .
> Through the power most mighty,
> Invoking the Trinity,
> Confession of one, belief in three,
> The Creator of Creation!'

I laughed then, though I did not really understand the
song, and I offered my sword to the morning light. 'I thank
you, my lord!' I said aloud, then added, 'And you also, for
your protection, kinsman. But do not send me any more
such dreams!'

I sheathed Caledvwlch and wondered if there was anything left over from the previous night's feast. I was very
hungry, for I had eaten nothing since the morning before,

and had been through a great deal since then. I was considering how to find some food when I heard noises within the house. I went back inside to find that Agravain was awake.

'There you are!' he exclaimed when he saw me. He looked even more tired than he had the evening before. 'How long have you been up?'

'Only a little while. I went outside to watch the sun rise.'

'You would.' He snorted and studied me, then grinned. 'By the sun, it is good to have a kinsman here. But you cannot go about dressed like that. A king's son cannot wear the clothes of a Saxon thrall. You've left a mark on Aldwulf; that ought to entitle you to a decent cloak at the least, even if you are not in the Family. Come, we will go to the storerooms and find some gear for you.'

He pulled his own clothing on and we went up the hill, past the feast Hall to the storerooms on the west side of the hill. Agravain was trying very hard not to disturb me by referring to Arthur's decision or what might happen next, but instead pointed out the sights of Camlann. But I could tell that he was thinking hard.

The storerooms were a sprawling group of buildings, low-roofed and dark, and mostly newly built to store the High King's plunder. They were clear testimony of Arthur's success as a war-leader, for they were filled with piles of clothing, with weapons and jewellery, imported pottery, dishes of gold, silver, horn and glass as well as wood, bronze and eathenware. There was not much food there, but there is not much to be had by raiding in the spring. All the goods had been taken from the Saxons, either on their own lands or returning plunder-laden from British kingdoms. Agravain told me that it would mostly be sold to whomever could pay for it with grain or other foodstuffs. 'The High King prefers grain, though,' he went on, 'for the horses. The Family's war-horses devour up the harvest of a kingdom, I think. Still, I have helped to win this, so I can help to dispose of it. Choose what you will. I will give you a horse, as well.' He hesitated, then finally met my eyes and asked his question: 'Where will you go?'

I was uncertain how to phrase it. 'I will not go,' I said at last, simply. 'I will follow the Pendragon Arthur on my own until he does accept me. He must see, eventually, that I am not a sorcerer and that I am a warrior worth my mead.'

Agravain stared at me for a long moment, then grinned fiercely. 'That is a warrior's decision, a decision worth a song! Indeed, show them all that they are wrong, and teach them not to slander you!' Then he stopped, frowning. 'But it will be difficult. Arthur is a noble king, and will not refuse hospitality to you, but Cei is your enemy now. You frightened him last night, and made him look a fool, and he won't stand for that. Moreover, he is the infantry commander, and has a Latin title of his own for it, and is a man to be wary of offending – though he is brave, and honest, and a good friend.'

'I must try it, whether or not Cei is my enemy. It is all I can do.'

Agravain was much happier as we chose some new, more 'appropriate' clothing from the heaps. When I had a good woollen tunic and leggings, my brother searched through another pile of goods to find a leather jerkin with some metal plates which he had won a month and a half before and which he thought would fit me. It did, and he pressed it on me, saying that it was his to give. Such armour is not as good as chain mail, but chain mail is rare and valuable. Agravain had only one mail-coat, which he would have given to me, except that it did not fit.

Besides the jerkin I found a shield, white-washed wood with a steel rim, plain, but good solid work; and a long, leaf-headed thrusting spear with a nice balance, as well as five throwing spears.

'Now you need only a cloak,' Agravain said with satisfaction. 'What kind . . .'

'A red one,' said a strange voice behind us.

'Taliesin,' said Agravain, greeting the man who stood in the door, watching us with mild interest. 'Why a red one?'

I stared at Arthur's chief bard, speechless. The other memory I had associated with that name came abruptly clear: he had sung in Lugh's Hall, in the Islands of the Blessed. And it was he who had held the bridle of Arthur's horse in my dream, and spoken to Sion in his.

But he was not wearing a star on his forehead now, and his face was human, without that disquieting radiance the faces of the Sidhe have – though he remained a very handsome man. His name, 'Radiant Brow', which is given to the morning star, was not wasted on him.

'I know you,' I said.

But he shook his head. 'No, you have never seen me before, though you may have heard some of my songs. There are plenty of them about.'

'What are you talking about?' asked Agravain.

'Your brother thought we had met before,' Taliesin stated pleasantly, sauntering into the room. 'And I corrected him. I never had the pleasure – your brother is a remarkable man, Agravain.'

'He is not a sorcerer,' snapped Agravain quickly.

Taliesin grinned. 'You are too suspicious, my friend. I never said he was. Welcome to Camlann, Hawk of May.'

I was certain that I was not mistaken. 'But what . . .' I began.

'I am sorry,' he said quickly, 'I cannot answer your questions, not now. You would not understand the answers. You are thinking of a dream which you had last night, and a dream a friend of yours had, and of what Bedwyr told you about me. But I cannot explain. There is something to all of them – but you know that already. The answer would be less interesting than the mystery, however, and I prefer things to be interesting. Also, unfortunately, you must discover truth for yourself. Someone tells you something: do you listen? Indeed not; you run off your own way, and in the end, knocked flat on your back (as Bedwyr was when first I met him) you say to yourself, "Taliesin was right!" But I am tired of being told the obvious fact that I was right.'

Agravain laughed. 'Oh, indeed? I wish I could understand your songs well enough to tell you that you are wrong.'

'But I do not intend that they should be understood!' Taliesin protested. He hummed a snatch of music, broke off. 'We poets have that privilege . . . A red cloak is the best. There is one in the middle of that pile there, a very fine one.'

I remembered Sion's dream, 'A man in a red cloak lying dead', and I felt as though I stood on the edge of some precipice in darkness, feeling the presence of the gulf I could not see. Taliesin stopped smiling.

'I am not ill-wishing you, Hawk of May,' he said gently. His expression was unreadable. 'It is only that what must be, will be. Your colour is red, like the dragon of Britain, or like the blood that lies upon the battlefields, and will lie there, when the night comes. When the shield-wall is broken and the gate of the strong-hold battered down.' He shook his head. 'The Empire now may be compared to a tapestry, woven in many colours, by many choices; your colour is red.' He stopped suddenly, blinking, then recovered himself and smiled again. 'Besides, red will suit you. That pile over there – and now I must find Arthur and explain to him why the walls have not progressed as far as he had expected. *Vale!*' He swept out of the room, letting the door swing shut behind him.

'By the sun,' said Agravain. 'What did that mean?'

'I was just about to ask you. Agravain, who is Taliesin?'

'Arthur's chief poet, one of his advisers, and occasionally a cavalryman under Bedwyr.'

'Beyond that?'

'Who knows? Who can tell, with poets? Sometimes, as now, he simply says things that no one can understand, and sometimes he says that a thing will happen and it does. Before the last raid, he suddenly went up to one of the infantrymen, Macsen ap Valens, just as we were setting out, and took his hand and said, "Good fortune after the end; hail and farewell." And Macsen died on that raid. Some say that Taliesin is a bit mad. Others tell stories.'

'What stories?'

'His father or his mother was a god, or a demon – the versions differ. He drank from the cauldron of Annwn, and knows all things. He is a prophet, magician, devil, saint, angel.' Agravain shrugged. 'Priests dislike him for his reputation, but he goes to the Christians' masses when he is in Camlann. The only certain thing is that he is a great poet. Urien of Rheged was his first patron, but Arthur persuaded him to come to Camlann. But he is not a northerner. You heard how he said "farewell" in Latin – that much I've learned. Some say he is from Gwynedd. I know that he has the Sight, at the least . . .' Agravain made a druid's gesture, one meant to ward off evil, and lowered his voice. 'But all poets must be touched, else they would not be prophets and preservers of the law. No one can ask Taliesin questions and receive an answer they understand, and no one wishes to insult him by asking too many questions, for if he made a satire on you, the only thing left would be for you to fall on your sword. Where did you think you had seen him before?'

'In Lugh's feast Hall.'

195

Agravain looked away and made his gesture again. 'He says that it was not he.'

'I suppose it could not have been.' The bright echoes of the song ran through my mind again. Taliesin's song. I could not tell what it meant, but no one who had made it could be evil.

'Truly,' said Agravain, looking at the door again. 'Do you want a red cloak?'

Sion's phrase ran through my mind again, like an ill omen. I remembered too how often my mother wore red – but then, it was an easy colour to dye things, and many men liked the brightness of it. And whatever thread Talisein saw woven for me in his tapestry, the pattern was not going to be affected by the colour of a cloak. 'As much as any other colour,' I told Agravain.

He went to the pile Taliesin had indicated and dug into it. 'Here it is,' he told me. 'It is a good one. Nice thick wool.'

It felt strange to wear the new things, to have the weight of the shield on one shoulder and of Caledvwlch over the other; and yet that weight was somehow right. Agravain nodded in satisfaction. 'Now you look to be a warrior, and royal,' he decided. 'They will be more careful of how they treat you, now. Do you want some breakfast?'

The Hall was full of warriors eating the remains of the previous night's feast which were set out upon the tables. I managed to ignore the hostile or merely curious stares of the other warriors as we ate. It was not difficult, as the food was good and I was very hungry.

Agravain was more cheerful than he had been the night before, and talked about Britain and the Family over the meal. He had certainly changed in the years since I had seen him. I felt uncertain with him, as though I knew him and did not know him. But I enjoyed his company. There were times, though, when I glimpsed another thought in his face, and it was dark. I guessed that it had something to do with our mother. But she was the last thing he wished to speak of.

We had almost finished when we heard shouting outside the Hall, then a cry of pain. The Hall fell silent, and through the suddenly still air came a loud neigh of an angry horse.

'What on earth?' said Agravain.

But I had recognized the call. 'Ceincaled!' I said, jumping up. 'It is Ceincaled.'

It was. He stood in the sunlight outside the Hall, even

more splendid and lovely than I remembered. He was angry, ears laid back and nostrils flared and red, and some of Arthur's servants surrounded him, holding ropes and lowered spears. One lay on the ground, white-faced and clutching his stomach, being supported by another. Directly in front of the horse stood Arthur.

'Lord, be careful!' called one of the servants. 'The beast is vicious, a man-killer. Look what he did to Gwefyl!'

Arthur ignored them and took another step towards the horse. Ceincaled reared, neighed again, tossing his head. Arthur smiled, a light kindling behind his eyes. He took another step forward and stretched out his hand, half in offering, half in command, and he spoke slowly, soothingly.

The stallion snorted, but his ears came forward. He surveyed the king with proud eyes. 'Be still,' said Arthur. The horse jerked his head, snorted again, impatiently. But he stood still and did not move when Arthur stepped nearer and caught his head.

'He is not vicious,' said Arthur. 'But he is proud, and mistrustful; and he prizes his freedom.'

Ceincaled stamped and jerked his head, but his ears remained pricked forward, listening to Arthur.

I released the edge of the door which I had clutched and began to breathe again. 'Ceincaled,' I called.

His head came up and he tossed off Arthur's grip and cantered over to me, nudged my shoulder. I ran my hand down his neck, again awed by his beatuy. 'Ceincaled,' I repeated, and added in Irish, 'why, bright one, have you come back? This is no place for you.'

'By the sun,' whispered Agravain, behind me, in great admiration. 'What a horse!'

'It is your horse?' asked Arthur, coming up. He had a look of disappointment, mingled with something else. 'I should have realized; the horse you stole from Cerdic, no doubt.'

'He is not mine. How can any mortal own such a beast? I released him, three days ago.'

'I think, nonetheless, that he is yours,' Arthur replied in a harsh voice. He hesitated, looking from me to the horse. He laid his hand on the stallion's shoulder, looked at me again, seemed about to shout some accusation, then stopped himself. 'Well then, take him and do what you please.'

'But he is not mine! I released him.'

'When CuChulainn was dying,' Taliesin said, appearing as if from nowhere, 'the Liath Macha, which the hero had released earlier that day, returned to die beside his master, although he was one of the horses of the Sidhe and an immortal.'

'That is only a tale,' I said, 'and that was CuChulainn. Ceincaled is real. Why should he die on Earth?'

'He came to find you;' Taliesin replied calmly. 'Horses are great fools when it comes to their masters, and will go where their rider is without thinking, assuming that it must be safe. Even immortal horses.' He smiled and held out his hand. Ceincaled tossed his head and sniffed the hand, flicking his ears forward again.

I looked at the horse, and thought of the wonder of the Land of Ever Young, and thought of this world. I remembered the instant when I had first ridden him, and our two spirits had met, and the astounded love he had offered, and I knew that Taliesin was right. I stroked the white neck.

'You are a fool,' I told my horse softly, in Irish. 'Oh my bright splendid one, you are foolish. You will find nothing here, in the end, but death.'

He snorted and nibbled my hair.

'As you will, then,' I whispered, and bowed my head. I wanted to weep for him.

'So now you have a horse,' Arthur said sharply, 'and I see that your brother has found clothing and arms for you. It remains only for you to find service somewhere, and you should be able to do that easily.' He looked at Ceincaled again, and his hand curled about his sword-hilt, then loosened slowly. 'Perhaps you will try Maelgwun Gwynedd. He wants warriors.'

I twined my hand in Ceincaled's mane, staring at the king over the horse's back. Arthur stared back with a level, cold anger, and I suddenly saw that he thought I had cast a spell on the horse. I shook my head in response to the unvoiced accusation. Arthur caught the gesture.

'Another king, then? Urien might not have you: he also has no love for sorcerers. But there remain Vortipor, and Caradoc of Ebrauc...'

As well announce my plan then as at any time. 'Lord Pendragon,' I said, quietly and formally, 'it is not my wish to take service with any lord but yourself. And it is not my wish

198

to go out into Britain with a sorcerer's name on me.'

'Your wishes are not the point. If you are a warrior, you must find a lord to support you, and I will not.'

'I think, Lord, that I can support myself after a fashion, at least until the next battle, when I may win myself some goods. I will follow you and fight for you, whether you accept my oath or no.'

The bystanders murmured in astonishment. Arthur gripped the hilt of his sword. For a moment I feared that he would draw the weapon, but he released it slowly. The cold anger in his stare had become white hot. 'You plan well, Gwalchmai ap Lot,' he said, evenly but with intensity. 'You know that I cannot allow it to be said that my own nephew hangs about my court like a stray dog, and so I must give you hospitality. Very well. You may stay here, and drink my mead and have a place in my Hall. But I do not, and will not – ever – accept you as mine. I require more than strength of arms, or cunning, or sorcery for that: I require a thing called honour.' He glanced about and saw Cei in the circle of watchers. 'Since you wish to serve me,' Arthur continued quickly, 'let us see how well you manage. Cei!'

'My lord?' Cei elbowed his way through the crowd, looking a trifle confused and still heavy with sleep.

'You are to head the band that will fetch the tribute from Maelgwn Gwynedd in Degannwy. Take thirty men – you can choose them – and take Gwalchmai here. You will leave tomorrow morning.'

'Yes, my lord, but...'

'Very good. If you are to be ready on time, you had better begin now.' The High King strode off through the crowd, his cloak flapping.

Cei gave me a surprised, then a speculative look, and whistled over Ceincaled. 'So now you have a magic horse to match your magic sword, sorcerer. Well indeed, for we will have a chance to see what use they are now. You'll need both on the way to Degannwy. Especially a fast horse, for...'

'Come,' said Agravain. 'Cei is very busy.' He turned and walked off towards the stables, and I followed, leading Ceincaled.

The stables were next to the feast Hall on the north, and, like most of the store-houses, were new, very large, and very full. But we found one empty stall, and I gave Ceincaled water at the trough, then poured some grain in the manger and coaxèd him into the stall. He did not like it at first, no doubt remembering Cerdic's stables and the trap, but settled eventually to eat the grain. I began to brush him down, and Agravain sat on the straw and fidgeted with a piece of grass.

'By the sun and the wind!' said my brother, after a time. 'I have never seen Arthur so angry. Even when Vortipor of Dyfed abandoned us last summer, and left us to face the Saxons without his army, he did not speak as sharply as he did today. It is so unlike him that I cannot even be angry that he insulted you. But Degannwy! With Cei in charge of the expedition!'

'What is wrong with Degannwy?' I knew of the place, a small and unimportant fortress in Gwynedd, north-east of the ancient port and royal stronghold Caer Segeint.

'Degannwy is where Maelgwn lurks for most of the year,' answered Agravain. 'Maelgwn, and half the Arthur-haters in Britain. You recall Docmail Gwynedd?'

'Of course. He killed himself rather than surrender to Arthur.'

'Even so. Maelgwn would not have killed himself. He would have pretended to surrender and then attack again as soon as Arthur's back was turned. He is a year younger than I am, and already he is one of the most cunning men in Britain. They say that when he is old enough he will be a match even for that fox Vortipor of Dyfed. He is too cunning to attack Arthur openly, and he will pay the tribute, but it will not be pleasant journeying. And Gwynedd, especially in the Arfon mountains, is thick with bandits and stray warriors of Maelgwn's, who all hate anyone who has anything to do with the High King. Arthur has been planning to send a band to collect the tribute for over a year, since Maelgwn keeps promising to send it himself and never does, or say that he has and it was all lost to bandits. But Bedwyr was going to lead the expedition. Now . . . Cei will make it as difficult for you as he is able to, and he is able to make things difficult indeed, especially since he can select the other warriors for the expedition.' Agravain began to beat the palm of his left hand with his fist. 'Yffern take all of this! Gwalchmai . . .' he chewed his moustache for a moment, then said, 'Perhaps you would do better to seek service with some other lord. Only to prove yourself, before coming back.'

'If I cannot prove myself here, how can I do so anywhere else?'

'But Cei will try to provoke you, to make you either fight him or go away altogether. And you must remember how anyone could bully you.'

'I will avoid trouble, if it is at all possible without losing honour. Agravain, I must go, or give up the hope of fighting for Arthur entirely.' And may the Light protect me, I thought, if it is bad enough to worry Agravain in this way.

Bedwyr came into the stable hurriedly, looked about, and came over to sit down by Agravain. 'I am sorry,' he told me. 'I spoke with Arthur again, but I cannot convince him. He believed that you have cast some spell upon the horse, which angered him, and that you then were playing the innocent, which angered him further.' He looked at Ceincaled respectfully, then went on. 'But now I am certain that there is some other matter weighing on his mind, something which he will not speak of. He wished to be left alone, and when I left, he was fighting with it. A thing that . . .' Bedwyr trailed off, groping for words to describe what he had sensed and finding none. 'Gwalchmai. Swear to me that you have indeed given up sorcery.'

'Bedwyr!' hissed Agravain, beginning to rise and reaching for his sword.

'I swear it, by the Light and as the earth is under me,' I told Bedwyr.

We held each other's gaze for a moment, and then Bedwyr sighed. 'Truly. I ask your forgiveness for doubting it. Arthur is my friend as well as my lord, and he is not a fool, nor usually wrong in his judgements. He has some cause which makes him wary, but it must be that it is in himself, and not in you. He will not speak of it, even to me.'

I nodded, but inwardly I thought that the cause might well be in me. I had seen that I was somehow still bound to Morgawse. It was as though her shadow lay within me, inside the marrow of my bones, too deep for me to shake off.

'Perhaps,' urged Bedwyr, 'it would be better if you left. Find another lord – not Maelgwn. Despite what my lord Arthur said, I believe that Urien of Rheged would accept you. He is not a brilliant king, but he is honest, and a fine fighter. He is married to your aunt and would be well disposed towards you. They say that his son is not of much value in battle, and he has no other nephews with him in Rheged, so you might do well.'

'It is not a bad idea, Gwalchmai,' said Agravain. 'You could advance quickly there, and, if you did, you could, perhaps, return in a year or so.'

I shook my head, tiredly. 'I will stay.'

Bedwyr began to speak again, but stopped himself. He did not like the way that I angered Arthur, and clearly felt bound to protect his friend's will and judgement, but also felt that I was telling the truth. He sensed my determination and did not urge me again to leave.

We sat in silence for a time, wrapped in our separate thoughts. After a time, Ceincaled finished the oats I had given him and came over to nibble my hair and demand attention. I caught his head.

'Why don't you put your Liath Macha out to pasture?' suggested Bedwyr. 'Or better yet, exercise him. It is a fine day.'

'He is not a Liath Macha; he is white, not grey,' I replied.

Bedwyr stared at me blankly.

'Liath,' I said, realizing that he could not understand Irish. 'It means "grey", like Llwydd in British. "Grey of Battle". CuChulainn's horses were a grey and a black, and both were horses of the Sidhe, though the Liath Macha was the better of the two.'

'Indeed?' asked Bedwyr. 'How did he come by them, then?'

I looked at him in surprise.

'I am only a Breton,' said Bedwyr, with the same glint of suppressed amusement I had seen the day before. 'I know little of your CuChulainn. I had not heard so much as his name, until I met your brother. Taliesin probably knows all the tales, but then, he knows Irish. Agravain insists that he himself cannot sing the stories properly when I ask him, though. I suppose that you will say the same?'

'He can tell them,' Agravain replied immediately, 'almost as well as a trained bard. No, better. He leaves out the dull parts.' His eyes grew brighter. 'I have not found anyone to sing the tales for me for over a year, Gwalchmai. Do you suppose that . . .'

Eager to take their minds off the present, they searched about to find a harp and told me to sing of CuChulainn. I was glad enough of the distraction myself, and I sang the tale of

CuChulainn's horses. By the time I finished, my audience had grown. Besides Agravain, Bedwyr and Rhuawn (who owned the harp), I had the grooms and a few other servants and warriors listening. They applauded when I had done.

'You sing well,' said Bedwyr, his eyes bright.

'You are better than the last time I heard you,' said Agravain. 'Much better. Sing how CuChulainn died.'

I hesitated, for the song is a difficult one; but I began the tune on the harp, and then tried to follow what the music said with fitting words.

I had reached the point in the tale where CuChulainn's enemies succeeded in drawing the hero out into battle alone, and there I faltered, for I saw that Taliesin had entered and was listening. He nodded for me to continue, but I stopped and, on impulse, offered him the harp.

He took it silently and began where I had left off. He used the old bardic style, but in a way I had not thought it could be used, so that each word mattered. It snared the listeners in a web of sound, so that they waited impatiently for each phrase, yet wanted the present one to last. Taliesin looked at no one, nor did he watch his hands on the harp, but stared into the distance. He did not use the old tune, but a new and difficult one: a dissonant thunder for the armies, a complexity of violence and rage; and against it a clean, pure thread of music for CuChulainn, a tune now lost in the thunder, now emerging from it, until, at the end, when the hero gave his spear to the man who asked it of him, the song suddenly drowned out the armies altogether. It was a renunciation of everything, and it was triumphant, proud, totally assured. The last lingering high note came, the hero's death; and then, through the stillness, the crop of the ravens on to the field of battle. The song ended, and there was an infinite silence.

I buried my face in my hands. I had wept, as had all the listeners. 'Lord,' I whispered to Taliesin, 'I thank you.'

He wrenched his eyes from wherever he had fixed them and looked at the harp in his hands as though surprised to find it there. 'Ach, no,' he replied. 'There is nothing to thank me for in the mere singing of it . . .' And then he laughed. 'You have made me serious, twice in one day! Will you ruin my reputation for me? Truly, my lord, there is nothing to thank me for. It is only a song, and I only sang it as a bard should. You yourself are able to sing well.'

That anyone could be thought to sing well beside Taliesin was impossible, and I said so.

'Well, of course!' Taliesin replied, a glint in his eyes. 'But do not insult me by using the same standards for others and for myself. Whose harp is this?'

Rhuawn claimed the instrument.

'You will have to sing more of the song about this CuChulainn,' said Bedwyr. 'He sounds a great warrior.'

'So he seems, from the songs,' said Taliesin. 'He killed his son, his best friend, hundreds of innocent soldiers, a few monsters and a druid who had aided him.'

'He had no choice but to kill his son and his friend!' Agravain protested indignantly.

'I did not say that he had. I said only that he did kill them. He did some other foolish things as well. There is one story . . .' he told an outrageous tale about a tryst of CuChulainn's which went awry, and strode confidently off, leaving his audience helpless with laughter. I shrugged my laughter off and ran after him. He stopped when he saw me following.

'I thought you might come. Well?'

'I . . .' I hesitated, then plunged on. 'Agravain and Bedwyr believe that I should go to Rheged.'

'Do they?'

'You know that they do. You knew what I had seen in a dream, and I think you know also what is to come. You must know that I am not a witch.'

He sighed, nodded.

'Then help me. Why does Arthur hate me?'

He looked at me, chewing reflectively on his lower lip. 'You are very young for this,' he said softly, more to himself than to me.

'I am old enough; I am seventeen.'

'That is very young. I know you are expected to be men as soon as you have taken arms, and you men of royal clans are to be able to deal with anything a king can deal with, but it is not right, to set so much on those who are so young.' He caught my shoulder. 'Listen. I would like to give you answers to all your questions, but how can I? I do not know all things. Some things I foresee, but dimly, like things under a moving stream, and some things come to pass and others do not. Other things I foresee as clear and fixed, but fitting into no pattern, without explanation. How should I dare to trouble the waters by answering a question, and perhaps, by doing so, change the shape of what is to come? And you yourself know, in a way, why the Emperor hates you, and one day you will realize it, but now you cannot. You must be patient and learn to live in uncertainty. More I cannot tell you.'

'Very well,' I said heavily. 'But Rheged?'

'You have already made your own decision on that.'

It was true, I had. 'Who are you?' I asked in a whisper.

He smiled, very gently. 'I am Taliesin, the Emperor's chief bard. Does any other answer mean anything?'

'Are you of the Sidhe?'

But he did not answer, only turned and began to walk on.

In the afternoon I remembered Sion's mare, went to check on her, and found that the farmer had arrived and collected his cart and his money the previous afternoon. I felt, on hearing this, more uncertain of myself than ever. It was almost a relief to set out the following morning with Cei and the band of thirty for Degannwy. At least then I did not have to think about what troubles would come. There were troubles enough on the road.

The journey was indeed a rough one, especially the first part of it. Cei's thirty were hostile and suspicious of me. They used any means available to them to force me to leave, and Cei was their leader in all such attempts. If there was an unpleasant task to be done, the sort usually reserved for slaves if any are about, I was assigned to do it. I was insulted fairly blatantly, and otherwise ignored. I was not wanted there, and the warriors made it abundantly plain. But I discovered that I could use my tongue to turn the point of the insults or turn them into a joke, and this, with patience and a certain amount of pretending that I hadn't heard, prevented a duel. There was nothing I couldn't stand – though I was glad Agravain was not with us. He would have felt obliged to kill half the party.

We took the Roman road from Camlann through the hills which the British call Gwlad yr Haf, Kingdom of Summer, which they say lie close to the Otherworld, then to Baddon, which the Romans called Aquae Sulis, and north-west up another Roman road to Caer Legion, and went again into the mountains of Arfon. It was awesome country, beautiful and harsh. The road was rough there: it had taken the Romans a long time to conquer the west of Britain, and they had abandoned it quickly. Degannwy was in the midst of the roughest part of the country, a small fortress but a very strong one. Everyone in it, from the king Maelgwn on, hated us almost tangibly, and gave us the bare minimum of hospitality demanded by the king's oath of fealty to Arthur. When we left, Maelgwn managed to cheat us of some of the tribute he owed, and the grain he gave us was adulterated with chaff, though we did not discover this until we reached Camlann. We were in a hurry to leave Degannwy, for we feared that if we stayed there would be bloodshed between our party and Maelgwn's men, or that perhaps Maelgwn would send his warband after us and claim to Arthur that the destruction had been the work of bandits.

The return journey was at once easier and more difficult than the trip to Degannwy. Riding up the north road with empty carts we had had no trouble with bandits. On our return journey we were attacked three times in as many days, and by large groups. The robbers attacked from ambush, using bows – a weapon no warrior will touch – and attempting to loot the tribute-laden carts before the whole party could bear up to protect them. Two warriors were killed in these attacks, and seven were wounded. We doubled the distance we had to travel by riding up and down the line of carts, wearing our shields on our arms instead of slung over our backs. I don't doubt that many of the bandits only attacked us because we were Arthur's; the whole countryside hated us. At the monasteries where we stopped to collect the tribute – they paid their taxes separately from the king – the men were full of mutterings, and of stone-throwing when we left. We scarcely dared to ask for hospitality at the larger fortresses, and, when we did ask, had to guard our carts and our backs.

But the difficulties combined to make it easier for me. I fought with the others against the bandits, cared for the wounded as well as I could, and with them shared the hostility of all around us. In such conditions they would have been less than human if they had not begun to trust me. By the time we rode back into Camlann, I was accepted as a member of the Family by everyone in the band but Cei. Stubborn Cei, the songs called him. It was easy to see why. He was stubborn in battle, willing to hold a position at any cost, never afraid, never unnerved, using his sharp tongue to drive on his companions and taking no thought for himself. He was a man in every way fitted to command Arthur's infantry. But he was stubborn in his opinions as well, and that included his opinion of me. A pity, for I learned to admire him.

We arrived in Camlann again just over three weeks after we had left it. It was very sweet to me, if strangely dream-like, to ride back through the gates at one with the band I had joined as an outsider. It was victory.

The warriors in Camlann also looked at me differently to how they had when I left. Agravain, grinning, lost no time in telling me the reason for this. News of the events at Sorvio-dunum had arrived. The incident had become slightly dis-torted in the telling – I was supposed to have cut down a good dozen Saxons when I fled – but it had won me the respect of the Family.

But not of Arthur. Cei gave the High King a complete report of the journey, of Maelgwn's forces and his attitude, and of the bandits. Arthur became thoughtful over Maelgwn, gave gifts to the wounded and praised the dead, and had a feast given in honour of the rest of the band. Both Cei and Arthur avoided mentioning me altogether.

I was not very discouraged, however. I had proved myself to Cei's band, and this was a long step towards doing the same with the rest of the Family. I was beginning to know the men, and to make friends. Bedwyr and Agravain both decided that I was doing the right thing after all – though Bedwyr was more uneasy than ever over his lord's attitude. It was my first real victory, and I exulted in it. I was certain that, with the Light's aid, I could prove myself now. I wanted only an opportunity.

Three days after the feast that opportunity opened before me. The Family was on the move.

Thirteen

Arthur and Cerdic had been contesting who could force the other into a pitched battle first, and Arthur had appeared to be winning, for Cerdic's followers were impatient for open war. Now came news that Aldwulf had returned to Bernicia with his followers, leaving Cerdic's men restless and still more eager to fight. The loss of his raiding party must have stung Cerdic, though he gave no sign of it, but it was expected that he would presently be pushed into raising the *fyrd*, the full peasant army, and marching on Camlann. Arthur had been unwilling to encounter the whole of Cerdic's army, which was much larger than the force he could muster, but, now that it seemed inevitable, decided to strike first. There was a risk involved, but the Pendragon was also concerned over the situation in the north and what might happen when Aldwulf returned and renewed his alliance with Deira, the other northern Saxon kingdom. He was willing to take the risk so as to have his hands free. The northern British king-doms were already in difficulties: Rheged still weak from the civil war, and troubled with the Irish raids along its coasts; Ebrauc and Elmet engaged in a blood feud; March ap Meri-chiawn of Strathclyde already paying tribute to the Dalriada to his north and unwilling to fight the Saxons to his south; and Gododdin, my father's old ally, still bitterly opposed to her neighbours. The northern Saxons were already begin-ning to raid their British neighbours heavily, and had seized some lands as well, and to stop them was a matter requiring an extended campaign, which was impossible if Cerdic remained strong and in possession of Sorviodunum.

Arthur had contacted his subject kings Constantius of Dumnonia and Eoghan of Brycheiniog and requested them to raise their armies. While they sent the spear about their domains, calling up all the townsmen and farmers, Arthur himself prepared for one of the lightning-swift raids which were so characteristic of him. With luck, Cerdic would be unaware that the Family was, in this case, backed by armies, and would lead whatever forces he had gathered into a trap.

It was a fine morning late in June when he left Camlann and

rode south to take the east road to Sorviodunum. The sun was dissolving the morning mist, and the day promised to be hot. Camlann looked firm and secure, set above the heat-haze on its hill, the fields were beginning to shade into gold, the sky was the palest blue imaginable, and the earth smelled rich. The Family was in a fine mood, joking and singing and boasting of the great deeds it would do. Ceincaled stepped lightly, eager to run, rejoicing in the day and in his own strength, and I felt as he did. I wondered whether it always felt so, to ride off to war, destruction and the threat of death.

We followed the east road until we came into the Saxon lands, and then cut across the plain. We travelled by night when nearest to Sorviodunum, and, as the land was not heavily settled, managed to avoid the notice of the Saxons altogether. We pressed on, concentrating on speed, right through the land of the South Saxons and into Cantware. There we sacked the fort of Anderida, which Arthur had taken once before, seizing what goods were there and burning as much of the fortress as we could. Then we turned north and spread out over the country, pillaging it.

The purpose of a raid, other than the taking of plunder, is to cause as much damage as possible to the enemy. It is thus a savage business, worse than a pitched battle where warriors are fighting warriors. In raids, as often as not, one is fighting unarmed men, old men and women and destroying their livelihoods. The only pleasant part is the freeing of the British thralls, who are usually overjoyed and sometimes wild for vengeance. Set free enough, give them their masters' weapons and give them liberty to take their masters' goods and go, and they do all the damage anyone could wish. Arthur wished us to be as gentle as possible, and usually we were able confine ourselves to firing the crops and driving off the cattle, without killing, but still it is an unpleasant business.

We cut a wide path through Cantware and began to work westward through the kingdom of the South Saxons. Cerdic had heard of this by then, and he gathered the army he had raised and came after us. Aeduin king of Cantware was nearer, but had not yet raised the *fyrd*. He began to do so – we encountered one of his messengers – and waited for Cerdic. We regrouped, sorted out our plunder and left the heavier goods, and pressed on towards the north-west. Cerdic's army approached from the south-east, following the trail of ruin we had left. We were nearly in Cerdic's lands, now, but instead of pushing through them Arthur turned northwards until we were nearly at the Tamesis river. There we again sorted out our plunder and even abandoned most of the cattle we had driven off, then turned and rode west as fast as we could. Our scouts reported that Cerdic had divided his army and left a part of it near the southern borders of his lands, but this we had avoided by travelling so far north.

The Saxon kings were enraged. We had entered their lands and done untold amounts of damage, and slipped through their hands when they tried to catch us. The three kings – Aeduin of Cantware, the king of the South Saxons, and Cerdic – now had a unified force. Cerdic was probably delighted, perhaps even thought that he had won his contest with Arthur. He would certainly have to lead his army on into Dumnonia now. He had a very great numerical advantage over our forces, even though he was unaware that we had raised the armies, but Arthur hoped our advantages of surprise and a battlefield of our choice would be enough to offset this. If his hope proved useless, then the Saxons would destroy the Family and be free to do whatever they pleased with southern Britain. But we did not like to think of that.

The Family rode as quickly as possible to the agreed-upon meeting place of the armies of Dumnonia and Brycheiniog, and found that the armies were in fact there, a thing which had been uncertain, since some of the British kings had failed their promises before.

We had scarcely arrived, and Arthur had only just leapt from his worn horse and embraced Constantius of Dumnonia, when, on the High King's orders, fresh horses were found for the Family and the armies struck camp. I kept Ceincaled, however, for the raid had not tired him enough to warrant a new mount. And I thought I would want him if we could trap the army of Cerdic of the West Saxons.

Arthur had set men to watch the main roads, and a post arrived from one of these reporting that the Saxons were taking the east road towards Baddon. We turned directly south, marching as rapidly as we could to meet them, and Arthur fretted at the slowness of the full army's pace.

Those two weeks showed me why Arthur was so great a leader. In the whirl of speed our campaign had become he remained steady, was able to understand every detail which was reported to him, fit it into its place, and take account of it in his own plans. When everyone around him was too weary or tense or confused to think, he remained steady, certain and in control. He fought well, without malice or hatred, and never lost sight of what he fought for, so that he never, even in the most difficult moments, commanded an action of vengeance or cruelty, nor was he ever unwilling to speak to his followers. The blood and dust and exhaustion could not hold us as could Arthur's vision; he was the kind of king who occurs once in ten generations or in ten hundred years. He demanded, simply by being, all of the best his servants could give; and we gave it gladly.

I say 'we', and yet I was not able to include myself among those who served Arthur. I wished to, more so than ever, but the High King trusted me no more than he had at first. I hung about the fringes of the Family, fought when I could, and puzzled over the reason why even the sight of me seemed to anger him. I set my hopes on the battle and what it might show, half-eager and half-afraid. Perhaps, I thought, I would not like what it showed me: nonetheless, it was the test, and I was eager for it. I prayed to the Light, grasping my sword-hilt, that I would not disgrace myself or the Family.

The day before the battle we camped near the edge of the plain of Sorviodunum, in a forest by a river called the Bassas. In mid-morning the following day the Saxons arrived and we were waiting for them.

Arthur had, as always, planned carefully. The road followed a curve beneath the slope of a hill to its south, and he posted the cavalry along this hill, hidden in the woods which covered it. He set the infantry of the Family, with the warbands of Constantius and Eoghan, in the centre, just around the curve on the road itself; and dispersed the less skilled armies through the wood on the flanks. The Saxon forces, if all went well, would march around the curve into the foot forces, which should break their shield-wall; after which, on a signal, the cavalry would charge through the Dumnonian lines to cut the Saxons off and to disrupt them.

I waited with the cavalry, beside Bedwyr and Taliesin. Agravain was fighting with the foot, near Arthur, in the manner he still preferred. The morning sun was hot, and we had already thrown off our cloaks and tied them over our saddles, and the sunlight filtered through the trees to glitter off the metal of arms and armour. In the camp behind us the camp-followers were preparing for the battle in their own way, filling buckets with water and readying wagons: we could hear the called orders and the creak of yokes and wheels. We were very happy, oddly tense and relaxed at the same time, and we laughed and joked a great deal while we waited for the Saxons to arrive. I felt very light-headed, and for a time wondered if I would disgrace myself by fainting, and wondered if the heat had anything to do with it. But I did not feel so much faint as full of an exultation which mounted as the distant shadow on the road, the Saxon host, drew nearer. I looked up at the blue sky and wanted to sing. I loved the sky, the warm-smelling earth, the sunlight through the trees: all the sensations which seemed sharper and clearer than they ever had before. I loved my comrades, Bedwyr, Taliesin and all the others, and I even loved the Saxons as well. I wondered how many of those beside me would die, and if I would be among them. Life was very sweet.

The Saxons marched up the road in good order, in a wide column which overflowed on to the verges, and the sun shone on their spears and helmets. Their scouting had been poor, for they were in a hurry to catch Arthur, and they did not know that we were waiting. They crossed the river; and then it seemed that their vanguard must have heard something or received a message from an outrider, for they began to halt. The rear ranks ran into the vanguard, questioning, and Arthur and the centre began to advance.

They saw them and, for an instant, there was silence; then the neat column twisted as the army tried to spread itself out to meet the threat, the leaders shouting orders which were relayed to the rear ranks, the common soldiers milling about trying to obey, trying to avoid panic and to form a shield-wall.

They had no chance to do so. The British army, which had approached slowly at first, swelled, like a wave before it breaks, gathering speed, the lines moving forward and suddenly charging, jogging along with their shields held high before them. There was a scream of war-cries down the line, the glittering of weapons being raised at once, and the air flashed with throwing spears, incongruous in the morning sun. It seemed unreal. The lines were closing; some Saxons were throwing spears back, sporadically, still trying to form a shield-wall, and then . . . .

The lines hit, with a tremendous clash of weapons that made the air tremble. The British went through the front Saxon ranks in no time, and the Saxons were swept back, leaving a line of dead like the high tide line on a beach. The odds, which had been against us, were being evened now. The shouting and screaming of the hosts were carried back to where we waited like the report of Yffern, and there was a robin singing in the trees nearby. Our line of cavalry edged forward a little down its length, longing for the battle. I felt still more dizzy. Ceincaled tossed his head, snorting.

'It will be a hard fight,' said Bedwyr contemplatively, standing in the saddle to have a good view down the valley, then dismounting again. 'They are not as confused as they should be; see how the rear ranks still march forward past us. They have not panicked; we had hoped for that. And it is very hot.' He laughed, as though this were very funny, and we all joined him.

Arthur's dragon standard waved in the centre of the battle, and the High King was now visible beneath it as the British line advanced. We caught glimpses of his now and then, recognizing him by his purple cloak. I saw Agravain at one point, too, fighting a Saxon with a gold-crested helmet. My brother thrust the other through the throat with his spear, then lunged past, and I lost sight of him. The standards of Constantius and Eoghan waved, to the right and to the left of Arthur's, but behind it. The Family fought better than the other warbands.

Now the Saxon rear ranks finally caught even with the leaders, and spread out into the wood, past us to the north-west. They engaged the armies of Dumnonia and Brycheiniog, under the trees. We could not see what was happening, but it seemed that the Saxons were unable to advance, for they did not re-emerge from the wood to encircle the centre.

'It is going well!' said Bedwyr, intently watching. 'We have them . . . no! Wait.'

I saw Cerdic, standing in a sudden stillness in the centre, standing high, on top of something, so that everyone could see him. He was shouting. I could not hear what he shouted, but I saw the Saxon ranks solidifying around him, and then attacking with fresh purpose, moving sideways off the road.

Someone threw a spear at the Saxon king, but he jumped down again and vanished. The battle dissolved into chaos. I twisted my hands in Ceincaled's mane, trying to see. The centre was now near the edge of the wood on the other side of the road.

'No!' hissed Bedwyr. 'We have lost them ... no, we still have them ... Oh Yffern! Why did Arthur have to fight with the foot today?' His horse danced nervously, and he caught the bridle more firmly. 'We cannot attack now. It is far too confused, and the Saxons have their shield-wall formed. But the balance ...'

Was swinging. Despite their losses, the Saxons were rallying, forming a strong shield-wall; and they had broken the momentum of the British charge. The forces had locked shields, the high tide line of bodies moved no further forward, but hung for what seemed an eternity, motionless. The British stumbled back a few feet, then pressed forward. The hosts swayed like a tree in the wind, like a huge panting animal struggling to give birth. It was hot, very hot. My leather armour was stifling, and in the centre the heat must have been nearly unendurable. I felt even more dizzy as the pressure mounted within my skull. It is undecided, I thought, it may turn either way, and Light, let the victory be with us!

But then, just when it seemed that the outcome would become clear, I saw the south flank, the Dumnonians, whose line had been thinned by the Saxon move northward, begin to collapse. If they broke, and the Saxons came through, they could encircle the centre and ... I looked towards that centre, where the dragon waved above the locked warriors. Arthur should be the one to signal us when to attack, but he was nearly in the forest now: could he see the danger on the flank?

The centre jerked forward, suddenly and again I saw the High King. Behind him the standard wavered; Arthur turned, small with distance, and seized the standard as it fell, and swung his arm forward. The war-cry rose to us, and the Family was shouting its lord's name. They thrust forward ...

But the Saxon flank movement broke through the British line, and the British fell back, trying to lock shields again, were forced back, falling, and then the shield-wall was in pieces and the Saxons were coming through, the light making their helmets look like the heads of so many insects. I clutched my spear uselessly. We could not charge them; their line was three deep, and they could brace their thrusting spears against the ground and destroy any horsemen who managed to pass the hail of throwing spears they would throw at us. And yet, if the cavalry did not charge, the Saxons would encircle the now rapidly moving British centre, destroy it, kill Arthur . . .

It was unthinkable. We all knew it. To attack against the shield-wall was almost certain death, but . . . 'We will charge,' said Bedwyr quietly, voicing the thoughts of all of us. 'Mount!' He vaulted on to his horse, drew up the reins and looped them about the cantle of the saddle; his shield was already strapped to his arm. 'For Arthur!' he called, nearly screaming it, and spurred his horse forward into a gallop.

'For Arthur!' we answered as one, and followed.

The light-headedness that had been with me all the morning suddenly transformed itself into a fire in my mind, the same blinding inward illumination, more powerful than ever before. The sun of noon was high, Ceincaled's pace flowed like music, and I felt light as air, as sunlight. I urged the horse on, no longer thinking of anything at all, past Bedwyr and out of the forest on to the Saxon lines.

They had had time enough to see us coming, and greeted us with spears. I loved them and hurled my own throwing spears in answer, instinctively concentrating on one place in the line and hoping to break it. The world was dissolving about me, leaving only a light and an ecstacy. I threw away my spear and drew Caledvwlch. The Saxons, holding their places, leaning back and bracing their thrusting spears, wavered suddenly as they saw it, their faces distinct, pale and vivid under their helmets now. I was on them, swerving Ceincaled from the tips of two spears and striking, hard and fierce; turning the horse along the lines and striking again. I was vaguely aware of shouts and of screaming, yet the action seemed soundless and detached. The Saxons moved so slowly, recoiling, hesitating, some turning; then the rest of the cavalry also was striking into them and they shattered. We were through their lines and turning back to destroy them. I think I was singing, the same song that burned in my skull. We had the victory within our hands.

The pattern of the rest of that day is lost to me in the fire.

The Saxon army was broken in two places, I was later told, and tried to retreat back the way it had come. But the cavalry had cut off the retreat by the road, over the bridge, and the retreat increasingly became a rout, a desperate run through the forest and across the river as the soldiers dropped their shields to run and most of their arms to swim. Cerdic managed to control his warband and some of his men and retreat in order, but by then most of the British forces had crossed the bridge, and the cavalry cut him off. He surrendered to Arthur late in the afternoon, while the British cavalry still pursued the remnants of the rest of the Saxon forces.

My own memories of the battle, as of most battles, are limited, blurred by too much light, sharp-edged fragments of passion and action. It only becomes clear to me again when, as evening was darkening the east, Bedwyr rode up beside me and caught Ceincaled's bridle.

I knew that he had been somewhere near for most of the day, and that made me pause; but nonetheless I lifted my sword to strike. He caught my sword hand.

'Softly,' he whispered. 'The battle is over, Gwalchmai.' I met his eyes, which were dark and calm, and my mind cleared a little. 'Softly,' he repeated. I took a deep breath, lowered my sword, and he released my hand and watched me seriously. I looked about.

There were no Saxons in the immediate area, except for dead ones. I did not recognize the place; it seemed to be on the plain. A little to the west, behind Bedwyr, stood a group of Arthur's cavalry, on horses whose heads drooped with weariness. They were looking at me with a kind of awe.

I shook my head, tried to sheath my sword and couldn't fit it in the scabbard. 'Where . . .' I began, and stopped. Exhaustion rolled over me in a great wave, and I caught Ceincaled's mane to stay in the saddle. My side ached, and I felt drained, like a cleaning cloth with the water wrung out of it. Everything seemed dark, and looked different to what it had been only a few moments ago.

'We are some three miles north and east of where we were this morning,' Bedwyr answered my unfinished question, steadily. 'And it has been hard fighting. Cerdic has surrendered, and tomorrow he will ask Arthur for terms for a peace, and that peace he will have to keep, for a year or two. We have succeeded. Now, let us go back to the camp and rest.'

It was dark by the time we reached the camp, but the place seethed with torchlight and activity. The dead and the wounded were being brought in from the battlefield by the servants and camp-followers of the army, the wounded being carried to physicians and the dead guarded from looters. Men and women hurried back and forth, bringing herbs and hot water to the doctors; carrying food, for men and for horses; leading horses stumbling to the picket lines and carrying still forms on stretchers to the physicians or to the heap awaiting burial. For many the battle had only begun. I was glad that my part in it was finished and I could go to sleep. Even Ceincaled was tired, though he held his head high; and the horses of the others stumbled, blind with exhaustion.

As we entered the camp the workers – servants, slaves, mistresses and wives and relations of the fighters – looked up, then pointed to us. Someone cheered, and some others took it up. Ceincaled tossed his head and a spring came back into his step. Some of the other warriors drew in the reins and straightened, beginning to smile back. Some of the early lustre of victory surrounded us as we rode to the centre of the camp, where the Family was and where we could give our horses to the grooms.

Agravain was in the central hub of the camp, seeing to some prisoners whom he abandoned when he saw me. He ran across, circling the great fire, and reached me as I reined in my horse. He caught my foot. He was unkempt and dirty, there was a smear of someone's blood on his cheek and his beard was bedraggled, but his eyes burned.

'By the sun and the wind and the sea, Gwalchmai!' he shouted in Irish. 'I have never seen . . . if Father could have seen you, he would have given you half the Orcades for that charge. Yffern, he would give you all of them! By the sun, you fought like CuChulainn. I swear the oath of my people . . .'

He was drowned out by a crowd of warriors and servants who thronged about us, shouting congratulations and praise. It was too much for me. I had felt worn and bewildered before, and could only shake my head vaguely.

217

'I think I must indeed have fought like CuChulainn,' I said to Agravain finally. 'He went mad in battle. And I . . . don't remember . . .' Lugh's blessing, I thought. Yes, this sweet madness was given also to his son, CuChulainn. Again I shook my head to clear it, wishing that all the people would go away. 'But I am not a divine hero like CuChulainn, Agravain. I am tired. Can you make them be quiet?'

He let go of my foot, spun on the crowd and snapped, 'By Yffern, let him be now. Can't you see that he is tired? There is time and plenty for praising tomorrow.'

The crowd did nothing. Agravain's face darkened and he began to shout. Bedwyr edged his horse away from the crowd a little – they still followed him – and said to Agravain, softly but clearly, 'Perhaps if you spoke British they would understand you.'

Agravain glared at him for a moment, then began to laugh. The other warriors began laughing as well, then the servants. The rest of the cavalry slid from their horses, and the crowd began to disperse, everyone embracing and congratulating everyone else.

I dismounted slowly from Ceincaled and caught his bridle. The horse nuzzled my shoulder, snorted in pride and content. I rubbed his sweaty neck, whispering some words of praise and gratitude; then a groom took the bridle from me and led the stallion off. I was about to follow, and care for the horse myself in my usual custom, but Agravain caught my arm and pulled me off to the tent we shared with Rhuawn and Gereint. I remembered what he had been doing and asked, 'But your prisoners?'

'The servants will take care of them. I was really only waiting for you.'

My beautiful new spears were gone, and my shield, still strapped to my arm, was hacked so badly as to be useless. I dropped it on the floor and Agravain helped me off with my jerkin. I muttered thanks and collapsed on the sleeping pallet. In the few seconds before I fell asleep it struck me: I had done it. Somehow I, or the fire in my head, had become the hero of the battle and saved the Family. Oh my King, I said silently, you are generous to me beyond measure. The meadow grass under me smelled sweet, of sunlight and flowers under blue skies. Arthur would accept me. I had won.

Fourteen

I woke towards noon the following day. I would have slept longer, but I had a raging thirst. I lay still, aching all over, and trying to remember why I felt so glad in spite of this. After a litle, the past day returned to me and I sat up abruptly, wondering if I could have dreamt it. But it was real, real. I sat there for a few minutes, wanting to sing and knowing no words to carry my joy. I think that that was one of the best moments of my life.

There was no one else in the tent. I rose, tried to straighten my clothes a little, and left to find some water. I noticed that I had a cut along my ribs, where a spear must have penetrated the jerkin. It did not seem to have bled much, and was a light wound for the kind of fighting I had been in for; I saw that my right arm was covered with blood. Still, I decided it would be best to have it cleaned. Even a small cut can be deadly if it takes the rot. First, though, a drink; and then I would have to see that Ceincaled was properly cared for. And find Agravain, of course. I had been glad of him the previous night and he deserved thanks and attention. Besides which, I admitted to myself, I wanted to hear what he had to say about my fighting.

I found a servant carrying a double yoke of buckets from the river, and asked him if I could have some water. He looked at me suspiciously.

'And who might you be? I was bringing this to the sick tents, where it is needed.'

'Oh,' I said. 'In that case . . .'

He gave me another look, then smiled. 'Ach, it is not that badly needed. You are a warrior, plainly, and if you are just now waking after the battle – I could give you some.'

'That is exactly what I am,' I said. 'That, and very thirsty.'

He slid the yoke off his neck and handed me one of the buckets. 'Drink some, and I think you had better use the rest to wash in. You are a sight. If you don't mind my asking, who are you? You look as though you were in the thick of it.'

I took a long drink before answering. The water was delicious. 'My name is Gwalchmai, son of Lot.'

He actually gasped. 'Sweet Jesu! Annwn, but you were in the thick of it indeed! My lord, I can tell my children of this, to be sure!' The man caught my hand and clasped it eagerly. 'Indeed, my lord, you are the hero of the camp!'

'Am I? I don't remember it. I was not even sure what I was doing.'

He gave me a puzzled look. 'That is not the talk of a warrior.'

'Well, I suppose I am not yet used to being a warrior.' I felt very pleased, though. Extravagant praises are given to the finest fighters in any battle, and, though it seemed unreal, I had earned that position. My father would hear of this, and be proud. Arthur would accept me. I felt as though some inner wound had finallly healed.

I took the bucket of water back to our tent, which was still empty, and there washed and put on a clean tunic. When first I saw my reflection in the water of the bucket I understood the servant's initial suspicious look. I was covered with grime and dried blood. I felt grateful to Lugh for the gift of madness that hid the memory of how that blood had got there. I vaguely remembered rubbing the worst of the blood off my sword the night before, but I took it out and cleaned and oiled it again now. Then, feeling still happier, I set out again to find Ceincaled.

He had been picketed in the best place in the line, well-groomed and watered and fed with grain, but he was very pleased to see me. While I checked him to see if he had been at all hurt, listening to the grooms congratulating me on the way I had fought, Agravain came up.

He shouted my name when he saw me, ran over to give me one of his bear hugs, then stepped back, grinning. 'I thought you would be here,' he stated cheerfully. 'By the sun, Gwalchmai, the thing appears no less splendid in the morning than on the night.'

I shook my had. 'I don't remember it. And what else could I have done? Bedwyr ordered the charge, not I.'

'But the charge would have failed without you. Don't disagree with me, brother – accept the credit. You deserve it!'

I grinned back. 'By the Light, it is a miracle. Arthur will accept me now.'

'He'd be an idiot if he didn't, and he is certainly not that. By the sun and the wind, though! There we were at the centres, slogging away, thrust and cut and push and getting nowhere, until around noon Arthur caught the standard himself and shouted for us to charge, and we thought we had them. And then we hear a sound like the sky falling, and look up, and there is the cavalry charging down. By the sun, Arthur was angry—he thought you had decided you could not wait—only then he saw what was happening. We all thought it couldn't be done, and the Saxons were even laughing, falling back a little to watch. But then you charged ahead of the rest, looking like CuChulainn, and drew that sword of yours – I swear the oath, it cast shadows all the way over to where I was—and you did it! You broke through their shield-wall, and the rest came in behind you and chopped them to bits.'

'That . . . yes, I remember that. But you; what happened in the centre?'

'We started to yell our lungs out, and ran at the Saxons and carried them back until they were falling over themselves to get away from us. And then I and some others had to run down to the bridge, because your lot took it and left it again, and Arthur didn't want the Saxons to escape by the road. Hard fighting there, for a time. But it was the cavalry charge that won the battle, and you were the one who won the charge. There will be songs about this, brother!'

'And I am glad,' I said, because to say more made the understatement even worse.

'What did you mean, then, that you don't remember it?'

I explained, and he listened carefully. 'Like CuChulainn,' he said, nodding. 'I wondered what you meant last night. Well indeed; there are plenty who become at least a little mad in battle.'

I nodded back and asked, 'Where is Arthur?'

He paused, considering. 'Probably, he is talking with emissaries from Cerdic and the other Saxons. That, or asleep. He was up until dawn.'

'Till dawn?' It seemed incredible, when I remembered the army's exhaustion, that anyone could have stayed on his feet until dawn. 'What was he doing?'

'Och, he was trying to find out what had happened to everyone. But we can go to see if he is free.' Agravain gave Ceincaled a wary pat on the neck, which the horse tolerantly accepted, and we set off. 'He always tries to account for each member of the Family before resting,' Agravain went on.

'He meets with Cei and Bedwyr and hears who was hurt, and tries to learn whether they are dying or dead or only wounded or missing. He goes to the sick tents and talks to the wounded, especially those that are dying. And he sees that the physicans have all they need and that the wounded are being properly cared for.'

'He is a great king.'

'The greatest in the West,' Agravain agreed, smiling widely. 'Which makes him the only fit lord for a warrior such as yourself.'

Arthur was indeed in consultation with emissaries from the Saxons when we arrived at his tent. We joined the crowd of men bringing matters for his decision, and waited.

Soon, I told myself, I would have a place. Morgawse would be proved wrong for ever and I could stop questioning and doubting. Whatever might come next, I would have something I could rely upon. I would be a part of the Family, a servant of the greatest king in Britain, the man who was the centre of the struggle raging on Earth. In my imagination I saw it: Arthur would come out of the tent with the Saxons, see Agravain and me and hurry over to us. He would smile, as he had not smiled at me before, and he would take my hand . . .

The tent-flap opened and Arthur came out, followed by four Saxon noblemen and then by Bedwyr, who had been holding the flap of the tent open.

'It is agreed, then?' Arthur said.

'The terms are harsh,' one of the Saxons said. I recognized him as one of Cerdic's men. His British was excellent.

'A matter of opinion; I think them mild. You have said this before, however. Is it agreed?'

The Saxon nodded glumly. 'Tomorrow, mid-morning, on the road by the bridge. We will bring the arm-ring of Thunor and swear the oath on it.' He paused again. 'My Lord will be displeased.'

'Tell him that I do him great honour by giving him another form of oath than that I use for the rest of my subjects. It is plain enough that to swear the Threefold Oath in the name of Father, Son and Holy Spirit means nothing to you.'

'The terms are fair,' said another of the Saxons.

'For you, perhaps,' snapped the first. 'You are not asked to surrender lands . . .' and he added something in Saxon.

222

'If the lord refuses to accept the terms,' Arthur said, 'he must propose others as good, or fight again. You have safe-conduct from my camp, noble lords.'

The Saxons took the hint, bowed politely, and left, escorted by some British warriors. Arthur sighed, watching them leave, and began to turn to Bedwyr with some comment. Then he saw Agravain and me.

Again, his eyes widened slightly, and the shadow fell over him. Again I could feel the Darkness between us, and his horror. For a moment we both stood as though frozen, and my hopes collapsed for a second time, crumbling into dust and leaving me dazed and bitter in their ruin.

Bedwyr followed his lord's gaze, saw us, and frowned. He touched Arthur's arm, and the High King nodded and started over to us.

'Agravain,' he said, clapping my brother on the shoulder. 'For holding the bridge yesterday, many thanks; it was well done.'

Agravain's eyes lit and he grinned. 'I think we managed to set them back a bit, my lord.'

'A little,' returned Arthur, smiling in return. 'By Heaven, you fought like a lion, like a wolf setting a herd of deer to flight.'

Agravain grinned still more widely. 'Perhaps it was so, indeed. And my brother also will be praised, for he fought like a falcon, stooping upon a flock of doves, and broke the shield-wall.' Arthur said nothing, dropping his hand, and Agravain only then noticed that anything was wrong. 'Gwalchmai, of any of us, deserves your praise,' he said, more hesitantly now.

'He has my thanks,' Arthur said, after a long silence. 'For his part in the battle yesterday.'

I bowed slightly, not trusting myself to speak. What with confusion and hurt I did not know what I might say.

'What kind of thanks is that?' asked Agravain, still confused as to what was happening. 'My lord, Gwalchmai saved the battle for us.'

'And he has my thanks for it. I expect that now he will find it easy to serve any lord in Britain.'

'Any but yourself,' I finished for him.

The High King looked at me again, at last, and his eyes were like the north sea in midwinter. 'I would rather any man 'out yourself had broken the shield-wall,' he said, in a very quiet, level voice. 'A defeat at arms I could have mended, but a victory by the wrong means is worse than a defeat. Without the dream, the war is pointless.'

'I agree, Lord Pendragon,' I said. 'And I fought for your dream, though I do not say I understand it entirely. Do you truly believe that I broke the shield-wall by the use of sorcery?'

He did not need to answer. His stare was enough.

Agravain seized his arm. 'What do you mean? Didn't Gwalchmai prove anything yesterday? He has earned the thanks of every man in the Family, and of all Britain, all that fear the Saxons!'

'I have given him my thanks,' Arthur said, still quietly, but with a sharper edge to the coldness. 'That alone is more than I wish; do not ask me to do more.'

'You have done nothing! By the gods of my people, where is your famous justice? Gwalchmai has proved . . .'

'Nothing; except that he can kill Saxons. The which we knew already,' snapped Arthur. 'It is not your place to speak to me so, Agravain ap Lot.'

Agravain flushed. 'By the sun! I've half a mind to seek another lord, with my brother, one who will . . .'

'You cannot leave. You are a hostage, whom I keep so that your father will remain faithful to his oath.'

Agravain went white, then red with anger. He seized his sword, and I caught his arm. Arthur merely looked at him, not moving, and Agravain slowly loosened his hand, dropped it from the hilt. He stared at Arthur.

'Why?' I asked.

The High King knew what I meant by it. 'You already know that, son of Lot. You know it very well, too well, and would God that it were otherwise!' He turned on his heel and left, striding back into the tent; and those who had business for him stood aside, not daring to speak to him.

But I did not know, nor did Agravain. My brother stood, staring after his king, clenching and unclenching his fist.

'By the sun,' he whispered at last, in a choked voice. 'That he should, he . . .' he turned away abruptly. 'Oh God. Why?'

'I do not know,' said Bedwyr, tiredly. He had remained behind.

'Hush,' I told Agravain. 'He meant nothing against you. He was only angry with me.'

'But why?' Agravain asked angrily. 'You helped to give him this victory; you fought for him, risking your own life. What reason did he have to think that you did it by sorcery? And yet, he distrusted you from the start. Gwalchmai, he had much more reason to hate me. I bore arms against him when I fought beside Father. But when I became his hostage, he was generous to me, and never himself mentioned or allowed others to mention in his hearing that I was a prisoner and the son of his enemy. Before I joined the Family, even, he provided me with a servant to help me learn British, and treated me with all courtesy and nobility. But when you came, never having fought against him, seeking his service, and giving him a great victory, he wishes to drive you off like a stray dog. I do not understand it. I cannot understand it.'

'Nor can I,' said Bedwyr. 'I saw him last night, when he came to ask me about my men, who was wounded and who was safe. He could not wait to praise me for commanding the charge. I have known him now for years, and think . . . No. It is not unknown, it is something that has always troubled him. Sometimes I have found him sitting silently and looking at nothing, not as he does when he plans something, but with the look he had just now; and then I do not dare to speak to him. Gwalchmai, are you certain you have not met him before?'

'Never.'

'I mentioned your name to him last night, praising you, and he stopped me. "I cannot," he told me. "The man is a sorcerer and the son of a sorceress. He has given me a victory, but by sorcery, madness and darkness. I cannot take him into my Family and trust him." He was so tired, so unhappy, and so certain. Agravain, he will apologize to you later.'

I stood looking at the other two and thinking hard. In a way, the High King was right. I had done nothing but kill Saxons, and the madness and the fire in the sword could easily appear sorcerous; indeed, appeared that rather than anything else. No one fights with the sword alone . . . Bedwyr had said that. In the end, the reasons are as important, and Arthur had no evidence of my reasons for fighting for him. But what could I do to show him? I thought of all I had seen of the Family, of Arthur. It was not an ordinary warband, and not only because the warriors were so skilled. There was a bond of pride among them, a common love, and a common, half-understood vision. How could I think to enter into a thing like that through strength of arms? I had been a fool to think that I could solve everything with the sword's edge.

I remembered the dream I had had in Camlann, and again saw Arthur in the Queen's shadow. Everywhere I turned, she always appeared, as though all shadows were her shadow. She still held a part of me, locked in bonds forged with blood, past commitment and present desire. I would not be free until I met her again, face to face, and either severed the bond or became snared in it for ever. How could I say to Arthur, "I am free of the Darkness"? Darkness had formed me. I had defeated it in the past, but by no strength of my own. Arthur had reason to feel as he did, and I had no way to change his mind.

I ached with the knowledge that I had lost again, now, perhaps for ever. Perhaps I should leave. As Arthur had said, I could easily find a place with any king in Britain. If I went to Urien of Rheged . . .

No. Here I had been led, here I had set my hopes. To leave would be to accept defeat and surrender. I struggled with the pain for a moment, then ignored it.

'What will you do?' asked Bedwyr, gently.

'I will go on,' I told the two, looking back to them.

I might have hung about and brooded futilely for the rest of that day, but I had to visit the sick-tents. I still wanted to have my cut treated.

As I approached the tents, I heard a strange sound, a kind of low drone like a hive of bees. I stopped and looked questioningly at Agravain, who was still with me. Bedwyr had left with Cei.

'The wounded,' my brother answered casually. 'They have settled down somewhat now. God, but the physicians must be tired!'

'What? Do you mean that they are still working, from last night?'

'Oh, they've done the worst. They work in shifts. Now, I think, they are checking the walking wounded and getting down to work on some of the men they were unsure of last night. You know, men who come in with a bad arm and they can't decide whether or not to amputate, so they leave them a while; or men who were uncertain to live, even if they were treated, who the doctors left in favour of someone their skill wouldn't be wasted on.' Agravain hesitated. 'To tell the truth, I've no love for such places, especially at this stage of the work. Do you mind if . . .?'

'No. I will join you later.'

I didn't, though.

There was not enough room for all the wounded inside the tents, and those who had already been treated had been brought outside. These lay on the grass, like fish on a beach after a storm. Their faces were chalk-grey, eyes glazed in resignation or abnormally bright. Some wore bandages, some did not. No one who has hunted, let alone fought, is shocked at blood, but it is different when it is a man who lies before you with his stomach open and entrails tied in, rather than a deer, and when you see him in the cool light of rationality. The badly injured lay still, moaning or mumbling every now and then – an awful sound. It was this moaning and mumbling joined together that caused the droning I had heard. Some men lay still, asleep or dead; others, less badly injured, sat apart from the others, talking in undertones. The place smelled, too, of dirt, sweat, vomit, excrement and the beginnings of rot, a smell of pain. I picked my way through the lines of men slowly, now uncertain why I had come. One of the men saw me as I passed, and waved his hand heavily. I recognized him as one of Cei's band of thirty, and went over to him.

'Water,' he muttered. 'Do you have water?'

'I . . . I will try and get you some.' Several of the men around him also began to ask for water. I nodded. I wanted to run from that place. When I remembered how lightly I had claimed some of their water that morning, I felt sick.

I went into the tent and stood for a while, staring. One of the doctors, finishing off an amputation, noticed me. 'Well, what do you want?' he demanded harshly.

'I . . . have just a scratch. I will see to it myself.'

'Thank you. Well, now that you have decided that, what are you waiting for?'

'There are some men outside who need water.'

'There are lots of men outside who need water, but there are more in here who need surgery, and not enough to help with it; and the servants need sleep.'

'Would you like me to help?'

He stared at me, taking in the rich clothes and the gold-hilted sword. Then he smiled slowly. 'As a matter of fact, warrior, I would – if you've any notion of how to use a knife to heal instead of to harm.'

'I do not know, but tell me what to do, and what I can do, I will learn.'

Learn I did, until about midnight that night. Few warriors know of the battle which takes place in the sick-tents when their fighting is done, except when their lives become a part of it. It is a hard struggle, as fierce and ruthless as anything one encounters in the field, and requires as much, or more, training than do the arts of war. It is not, as some warriors think, a simple matter any cattle butcher could perform. The surgeon who holds the knife needs knowledge, and even his helpers, who merely hold down the patient, must know, or be able to understand, how to hold and how to stop the bleeding and where to tie the cords. Morgawse had taught me of various herbs, and one of her books had dealt with the properties of plants, but I had not paid much attention to advice for medicine. I had learned to use sword and knife, but was almost unaware that they could be used to save the life of the man they are used on. Even learning it while holding down a screaming patient for his doctor, it made good knowledge.

Just before midnight I pushed my hair out of my eyes and looked around to find that there was no more to do. Servants and relations of the wounded had been busy taking away whomever they could and making the rest comfortable, and that work too was nearly finished.

'You had better go and rest now,' said Gruffydd, the surgeon I had first spoken with. 'Unless – you did have something you originally came here for?'

'Nothing – well, a scratch. I only wished to guard it against the rot.'

'A wise thought. Let me see it.'

He looked at the cut and shook his head. 'Indeed. What made you think that this was just a scratch? It goes down past the bone, here and here.'

'Does it?' I was surprised. 'It didn't look that deep, and scarcely hurt at all.'

'Well, it doesn't seem to have bled much . . . Cadwallon, some salve and a bandage.' He paused, glanced up at me. 'You are not a berserker, are you?'

'A what?'

'A berserker. It is a Saxon word; it means one who goes mad in battle. Their strength is double to triple what it is normally, so they are dangerous men.'

'I did go mad in the battle. How could you tell?'

He grinned. 'Well, we'd heard, even in here, that you charged a Saxon shield-wall' – we had exchanged names at a snatched meal – 'and that is mad enough. But besides that, the wound hasn't bled as much as it should have. I've seen it before, but only with men who go mad in battle.' He began to clean the wound. It stung. 'We've heard all sorts of rumours about you – otherworlds and magic, wild as you please. But such nonsense is frequently attached to men who are berserkers, so that explains that.' He rubbed some salve on the cut. 'Though it is a damned and uncanny thing, the berserkergang. Those who have it normally foam at the mouth, and can't tell friend from foe, though they may be the mildest of men at other times.' He looked up at me shrewdly.

'No one has told me that I foam at the mouth. I do not think that it is quite the same thing.'

'It is a dangerous thing, I should think. I saw a man once, who went mad in battle, and staggered in here afterwards with wounds you could put your fist into. Said he hadn't even noticed when he got them. It was a wonder he could even stand; he died about an hour later. No, not a pleasant thing, this madness.'

'I am glad of it. It is a gift.'

Gruffydd gave me a quizzical look, but I did not wish to speak of 'otherworlds and magic', so I said nothing. He finished bandaging the wound. 'Well, that is that,' he said, and straightened, stretched, then paused and looked at me again. 'Unless you want to come back and help another time, after a battle. No, not immediately after a battle; if you have the madness, you probably collapse afterwards – but later. We would be glad of you. You have the instinct of a surgeon, and that is needed in these times.'

'Thank you,' I answered. 'I will come.'

I left feeling very happy, and more warmed by those words than by all the praises given to me by warriors. Even if

Arthur had refused me, I had fought in two battles, and fought well.

Arthur fought another, private battle at mid-morning the next day, on the east side of the bridge across the Bassas. It was a strange fight, against an uncertain enemy.

The High King met Cerdic and the two other Saxon kings, taking his own subject kings Constantius of Dumnonia and Eoghan of Brycheiniog and forty warriors besides. Each of the Saxon kings had brought a dozen men, which Arthur had permitted, so the group was a large one. Yet one would think there were only two men there: Arthur and Cerdic.

I came with Arthur's party, on Bedwyr's invitation, but I tried to stay out of sight near the back. Cerdic's eyes, though, swept Arthur's men until he saw me, and remained fixed on me for almost a minute before he looked at Arthur. The High King had been studying Cerdic all the while.

Cerdic bowed in the saddle of his roan steed, smiling a little. '*Ave, Artorie Auguste, Insularis Draco, Imperator Britanniarum*,' he said, using Latin and all of Arthur's highest titles in a mocking tone.

'Greetings, Cerdic *cyning thara West Seaxa*,' replied Arthur. 'I am pleased to see that you recognize my status.'

'I recognize your strength, *imperator*,' said Cerdic, still in Latin. 'You have a victory.'

'Which you think you can reverse, a few years from now?'

Cerdic smiled and changed the subject. 'I do not like these terms you offer.'

Arthur smiled back, a certain lightness touching his eyes. 'Then offer other terms, king of the West Saxons. I will do my utmost to be just to all my subjects, even if they have been disobedient.'

'That is precisely the part of the terms I dislike most,' snapped Cerdic. 'The West Saxons are not a nation subject to the emperor of the Britains.'

'All the provinces of Britain are subject to one emperor,' answered Arthur. 'If you do not wish to be subject to me, you can always leave.'

Cerdic spat, the red look reappearing behind his eyes. 'I made a nation here, Dragon . . .'

'Which I am willing to recognize.'

'. . . and it is my own nation, not yours or any other Briton's or Roman's.'

'I have no more desire to be king of the West Saxons than to be Protector of Dyfed. But I am the emperor.'

'I have heard otherwise, and from Britons.'

'I have other disobedient subjects beside yourself, Cerdic.' Arthur smiled again, even more lightly. 'Come. You know that you will swear to my terms in the end, just as the other Saxon kings have sworn once already. Why must we stand here in the heat any longer than is necessary?'

Cerdic frowned angrily, but a faint look of puzzlement was beginning in his face. 'And I must swear to recognize your claim to the *imperium*, to support no usurpers nor make war against you, to withdraw my royal forces from Searisby-rig to Winceastra and leave no more than twenty men as a guard on the border, which is to be at Wilton? And I must yield all claim to any lands west of that border, and obediently render you tribute at every year?'

'Why not? Most of the land east of Sorviodunum is thinly settled as it is. And as for obeying me and rendering tribute, you will not keep that oath any more than your fellows did, but it will give me more excuse to war on you when you break it.'

Cerdic almost smiled in response to Arthur's quiet amusement, but stopped himself. 'And what of my fellow kings?'

'As agreed, they will renew their oath, in a new form, and pay additional tribute for the next few years in return for their sedition.'

The two Saxon kings snorted. They had paid no tribute since Uther had died, and obviously had no intention of beginning – though, should Arthur's northern campaign take less time than was expected, they might send something.

'If the Saxon nations are subject to the emperor just as the British provinces are,' Cerdic began again, 'they should swear the same oath.'

'I have recognized that Saxons are pagans, and that to swear by the earth, sea and sky in the name of the Father, Son and Spirit is meaningless to them. Now if you break your oath you will be able to explain it to your own gods and not the gods of strangers. It will be easier for you.'

Cerdic frowned again, and this time touched his sword. For a long moment he met and held Arthur's gaze. Then he smiled, not as he had smiled at first, nor as I had seen him smile in the two weeks I had been his thrall.

'You are everything I had heard you might be, Arthur ab Uther,' he said, speaking British now. 'I do not see why you bother to employ sorcerers.'

'I employ none.'

'Then . . .?' Cerdic looked to me again.

Arthur shook his head. 'Gwalchmai ap Lot is not my warrior.'

Cerdic raised his eyebrows. 'Indeed. I wish I had been able to be as firm. Sorcery may be powerful, but sorcerers are unreliable – and dangerous.'

I wondered how Cerdic and Aldwulf had parted. Not amicably, it seemed, for Cerdic spoke with some vehemence.

'I am glad we think alike on this,' said Arthur. 'Have you, then, further objections to my terms?'

Cerdic sighed and began to haggle over the wording of the oath, then stopped abruptly. 'No. Why continue with this? We both know that I will swear your oath and break it when it pleases me. When next I fight you, Pendragon, you can call it sedition instead of invasion. I think you will find small difference between the two.' Cerdic swung down from his horse and signalled to one of his men. The warrior rode up and dismounted, and Cerdic took from him a large wooden box carved with runes. Arthur dismounted and stood by his horse, waiting.

'This is Thunor's arm-ring,' said Cerdic. 'We brought it from Thunor's temple, north and east of Gaul. It is very old, and sacred.' He opened the box and carefully lifted out an immense ring of gold, also carved with runes, heavy, and about wo hands' lengths in diameter. He stood looking at it for a moment, then looked up and smiled gaily. 'Thunor is a warrior, if a god. He understands these matters of oaths.'

'Swear the oath, then, if you are sure of his forgiveness.'

Cerdic hesitated, turning the ring in his hands. Then he turned to the other kings and politely gestured them to go first.

They, too, dismounted and came forward, Aeduin of Cantware and Eosa of the South Saxons. Each in turn knelt, drew his sword, and swore on sword and arm-ring, by Thunor and Tiw and Woden, an oath that was essentially the same as the oath sworn by all kings to the High King. They were both older than Cerdic, well used to swearing oaths and breaking them, and oaths sworn to the British were particularly easily broken. It was more difficult with the new oath, but their Thunor had broken his word at least once, and they would buy new swords, in case the weapon they had sworn on betrayed them in battle. When they had finished, Cerdic drew his own sword, and stepped forward to face Arthur, who was now holding the arm-ring.

The day was cloudy, but at the moment the sun broke free of the clouds, and the bare steel of Cerdic's sword gleamed brightly in its light, while the arm-ring glowed with warmth. Cerdic smiled more widely, but his eyes held the dark brightness I had seen before. I became suddenly afraid, and ceased to worry over what the kings had said of me. I set my hand on Caledvwlch.

But before anyone could think, Cerdic stepped abruptly forward, lifting his sword to place its cold, gleaming tip at Arthur's throat. Constantius of Dumnonia gave a cry of horror, and Bedwyr dropped his spear into line and drove his horse a step nearer before realizing that he could do nothing and reining in, white-faced. Cerdic's party pressed forward, their swords drawn. Cerdic smiled, the darkness filling him, mingled with a strange brilliance.

'I came here this morning to kill you, Pendragon,' he whispered.

Arthur had flinched at first, but now he looked at Cerdic over the bright metal calmly, and the light in his grey eyes was astounding. 'It would solve most of your difficulties, if I were dead,' he said in a conversational tone.

'Indeed,' said Cerdic. 'And war is a great thing for the lowering of morals. Even Woden, king of the gods, believes this. You understand it, *imperator*?'

I heard Bedwyr's breath hiss in the stillness, saw him alter his grip on his spear, preparing to throw it if Cerdic stirred. Cerdic did not even glance away from Arthur.

'If you still meant to kill me,' Arthur said, 'you would have done it by now, quickly.' He stepped aside and caught Cerdic's sword-hand.

'True,' said Cerdic. He lowered the sword till its point touched the earth, Arthur's hand crossing his upon the hilt. 'Unfortunately, Pendragon, bastard or not you are too much of a king and too much of a man. Arthur of Britain, let us be enemies, but not fight like wolves.' He dropped to one knee, reached out his left hand to take the other side of the sacred arm-ring, and swore, by Thunor, Tiw and Woden, and by the earth, sea and sky, to fulfil all his oath to Arthur, High King of Britain, as a subject king to his lord.

Arthur smiled at the use of the Treefold Oath, and when Cerdic had finished swore the returned oath, not to infringe the rights of his subject king, and to preserve the kingdom of his tributary 'secure against all foreign enemies and invaders'. He ended in an oath of his own, 'And I swear to make your nation part of one empire, Britain, and to hold it so, in justice and in light, so help me God.' He released the arm-ring.

Cerdic took it, resheathing his sword. Cerdic's men seemed confused; Arthur's, limp with relief, and not a little confused as well.

'When next we meet, Arthur Pendragon,' Cerdic said when he had mounted his horse, 'I hope our positions will be reversed, and, by Thunor's hammer, I think they will be. Until then, farewell. I am glad to have met you.'

'If it is till then, Cyning Cerdic, I will fare well for ever. I too am glad we have met.'

All the way back to the camp Arthur kept smiling.

A few days later we brought wagons and loaded our wounded on to them, and the Family returned to Camlann, the other kings and warbands to their fortresses, and the armies to their fields. For a week and a half the Family feasted itself on plunder and ransoms from the Saxons, counted its losses, and recovered, and then we were on the move again, riding north on the main road for Rheged.

Fifteen

The journey should have been pleasant for me. My performance in the battle had won me the wholehearted approval of
most of the men in the Family. The warriors rejected, as
Gruffydd the surgeon had, my stories of 'otherworlds and
magic' as being a mere side-effect of battle-madness. They
offered me their comradeship freely, with admiration and
without fear. Sorcerous and supernatural events, they
decided, were to be expected with the madness, but it reflected nothing unnatural on me. My wound healed cleanly and
without trouble; we enjoyed fine weather and, in the lustre of
our victory, the friendship of the country we rode through.
We set a leisurely pace, stopping at every sizeable fortress
along the way and being feasted there. I had money, as well.
Although I was not a member of the warband and could
claim no share in the considerable amount of plunder the raid
had yielded, nor in the sums the Saxons had expended to
ransom prisoners, both Eoghan of Brycheiniog and Constantius of Dumnonia had given me gifts, and some of the
noble warriors had done the same. Eoghan in particular gave
me a large gift and lavish praise, and tried to persuade me to
join his warband. My refusal delighted the Family.

I had to refuse two more such offers on the way to Rheged.
One was from Rhydderch of Powys, with whom we stayed
for two days. The other was from Maelgwn Gwynedd. He
sent a messenger to Arthur while we were at Dinas Powys,
on the journey north, conveying congratulations on the
victory late and in insulting terms. After delivering the
message the messenger spoke to me privately, criticizing
Arthur's injustice and pretending sympathy before making
his offer. It pleased me to refuse that offer, as it did not refuse
Rhydderch's.

But these offers in themselves were one reason I did not
enjoy the journey. Arthur, still, simply did not want me, and
I could not follow him like a stray dog looking for a master
for ever. I had become a warrior and I had fought for him, but
a warrior must have a lord. That it was so easy to find any lord
but Arthur depressed me. All the kings in Britain were

hungry for warriors, especially warriors who could rival the Family. Rhydderch of Powys deserved his nickname, 'Hael', 'the Generous', and was, as far as I could tell, a fine king and a good lord. He fought the Saxons, even as Arthur did, though less spectacularly. I did not really want to refuse his offer, which was worthy of his name.

Besides this, I felt lonely. I belonged and did not belong. I wanted someone who could understand, who believed what I said to them. Before I had had Medraut, for whom I now mourned secretly, more so when I tried to explain to Agravain something or other, and he firmly and resolutely did not understand. I wished to speak with Bedwyr about his philosophy and books, but he was forever with either Arthur or Cei, and both of these avoided me as much as possible. Taliesin I could speak to for hours, but we seldom said much, apart from what he said about songs. So I lived, as Taliesin had said, in uncertainties, and brooded over my own thoughts, wondering about the men I had killed and Arthur's anger, and Morgawse, and the Darkness. It was not a pleasant journey for me.

Towards the end I enjoyed it more, however, when we crossed Hadrian's Wall at Caer Lugualid and entered Rheged. The road was much worse and the area was heavily forested, making travel difficult, but I liked the land more than I liked southern Britain. Northern Britain was never conquered by the Romans, and southern Britons call northerners barbarian, ignoring the fact the northern poets are generally better than southern poets and northern and Irish metalwork is sought throughout southern Britain whenever Gaulish goods are unavailable. Rheged is probably the strongest nation in Britain. For centuries it has suffered attacks of greater or less intensity by raids from Erin, which lies only a short distance away across the Irish sea. This continual warfare long ago forced the kings of Rheged to build strong fortresses, and a strong warband; and the clansmen and farmers are hard, slow-spoken men always willing to join with the army and fight. Now, besides the Irish, Rheged defends herself from Saxons, and from the Irish-speaking Dalriada to the north, who gave the land many goods and ways which were familiar to me from my own home. I liked the land. Despite its heavy forests it seemed familiar, and for all their hardness the people were open-handed and open-hearted, and never stopped singing.

We rode up to Urien's royal fortress, Yrechwydd, on a cold grey day in August in a heavy rain. The bare wood and stone of the walls were sharp against the sky, and the gulls called over the feast Hall, for Yrechwydd overlooks the Irish Sea as Dun Fionn does the North. I listened to the beat of the waves and remembered my father's fortress, and my kinsmen, and Llyn Gwalch, and my heart leapt as though I were returning home. I looked at Agravain, and he too was grinning. We laughed and began to sing a sea song in Irish:

> 'A tempest is on the ocean's plain:
> Boldly the winds awaken it,
> Winter sweeps the fierce sea again,
> By wind and winter are we slain:
> Winter's spear has overtaken it.
>
> When from the east the wind sets
> The spirit of the waves is free,
> They desire to sweep over all the west
> To reach the land where the sun sets,
> To the wild, broad green sea.
>
> The deeds of the plain, the ocean's rush
> Have driven alarm upon me,
> But what, of all, is as tremendous,
> Wonderful and as momentous
> As its incomparable story?...'

'Crazy Irishmen,' muttered Rhuawn, drawing his cloak higher about his ears. We laughed, and sang louder.

Arthur had, of course, sent messengers ahead. We were expected. Servants waiting just inside the gates took our horses and a fire roared in the Hall. Urien himself was waiting by the gates, a great brown-haired bear of a man with a loud laugh. He welcomed us warmly, congratulated Arthur on the victory, and thanked him for coming to the aid of Rheged, then hurried us into the hall, declaring loudly that no one should stay out in such weather. The warriors hung their sodden cloaks by the fire and sat down at the tables while Urien's servants brought them mead. The Hall was crowded, although Urien had sent some of his own men out to make room for us—but after some of the mead everyone forgot this. After the welcoming cups there was a feast and a great deal more mead. The harp was passed around, and the warriors sang boastful songs of their prowess and made loud talk of how they would destroy the northern Saxons. Taliesin sang a song about the battle of Bassas river, and was loudly cheered. I felt light-hearted for the first time in weeks.

After the song, Urien called for me and gave me a place at the high table on his left, on the grounds that I was his nephew. I thanked him, but pointed out that Agravain was also his nephew.

'Of course!' said Urien, snapping his fingers. 'That is the other one's name: I kept thinking "Avairgain", and knowing it was wrong.' Urien called Agravain up to the high table as well. 'Your Irish kings seem to have all the same names: it's either Niall or Eoghan or Laeghaire for all the royal clan.' Urien took a deep drink of mead and shook his head sadly. 'At least you have a British name, Gwalchmai ap Lot. And a name well-suited to you, if Taliesin's song is true—and it always was before, so there is no reason to doubt it now. It must have been your mother's idea.' Urien ignored the way Arthur, Agravain and I went quiet at this mention of Morgawse, and poured me some more mead. 'Sensible father you have, to marry a British woman, and my Morgan's sister. How did this battle appear to you?'

'I do not remember most of it,' I answered, hesitated, and added, 'I go mad in battle, Lord Urien.'

Urien looked momentarily puzzled, then shrugged the subject off. 'Indeed? I wish some of my warriors would go mad in battle, then. I think, Dragon,' he said, turning to Arthur, 'that you have stolen the finest fighters in Britain, and left the other kings with the dross – and that besides stealing my chief poet, alas for that! I will never find a bard to replace Taliesin – and I am fast becoming a toothless lion. No, don't laugh. When you meet my war-leader you will see it is no laughing matter, and my son . . .' the king paused. All Britain had heard of Urien's son Owain, who, it was said, could not tell the hilt of a sword from the point. 'Now, if I had had better warriors or a proper war-leader a month ago when I fought the Scotti at Aber yr Haf . . .' Urien launched into a description of this fight.

I sighed inwardly and only half listened. Urien sounded as though he wished to offer me a position in his warband. He was certainly no toothless lion, but he needed more warriors.

From what I had seen of him, moreover, I liked him; and I liked Rheged. If I took service with Urien I could win some honour and still fight the Saxons; I could fight Aldwulf, a truly dangerous man and one much more my enemy than was Cerdic. And yet, it was Arthur who was fighting to make real a dream, and, as he himself had said, without the dream the war was pointless. I watched the High King as he began to discuss with Urien what should have been done at Aber yr Haf, using knives and serving dishes to show the land and the forces. The shifting torchlight gleamed on his hair and glittered on the gold of his collar. His face, intent on the rough plan of the battle, seemed to hold steady in the moving shadows of the hall. Beside him, Urien looked as dull and dense as the oak table. I took a long, hard drink of mead and set the empty horn down, still watching Arthur.

We stayed at Yrechwydd for a day before setting out south-eastward, to raid the Saxon kingdom of Deira. Urien came with us, bringing twenty of his men. These were only an honour guard: he came to see how the Family fought. Most of his warband was left to guard the coasts.

We moved swiftly, as always. The Saxons were not aware of us in the north of their land until we were gone, taking with us a few hundred head of cattle and sheep, a good deal of plunder, and leaving one of their chieftain's fortresses and part of the countryside in ruins. When the news of our raid reached the king of Deira, Ossa Big-knife, he was angry enough to attempt to retaliate immediately. We were in Ebrauc when he marched on us with his warband and the few hundred men he had mustered by the *fyrd* in the short space of time since he had heard of us.

We gave the Caradoc of Ebrauc the sheep we had driven off, and in exchange received the support of Caradoc's warband. Arthur did not think we needed Caradoc, but the British king would have been insulted if we had won a victory on his land without him.

The encounter – it could not really be called a battle – was brief and fierce. The infantry engaged the Saxons first, as usual – it was a good downhill charge, led by Cei, and left the enemy reeling—and, as usual, the cavalry made a flank attack. The *fyrd* panicked and the shield-wall was gone, as quickly as that. Ossa and his warband, more skilled, managed to regroup and retreat, though with heavy losses, and we pursued them to the borders of Deira but no further. I cut down a Saxon chieftain and won a very fine mail-coat from him, with which I was pleased. The rest of the plunder, including what we had taken on the raid, we sent to Yrechwydd.

Both Caradoc and Urien were surprised and the speed and completeness of the victory. There was a great deal of congratulating and gift-giving and Caradoc gave a feast. It was an especially splendid one, and used a large amount of the Saxon mutton we had given Caradoc, as well as great quantities of mead and wine. Taliesin sang of the recent encounter, singing the praises of the living and of the dead. He gave a stanza to me: 'I will sing the praise of Gwalchami,/Whose sword was as lightning, a flash to the Saxon/ Shining in the red tide, the ride of battle...' and so on. Urien beat the table at that stanza, and Arthur frowned. Agravain, seeing the frown, tensed angrily, and Cei grinned at him sardonically. The two glared at each other for the rest of the night.

The following morning Caradoc sent a messenger to me and, when I had come to his rooms, offered me a position in his warband. I refused.

He frowned. 'I have heard stories which led me to expect this,' he told me in his dry, quiet voice. 'Still, I had not thought . . . what do you hope to gain?'

I leaned against the wall, fingering a gold brooch I had won in the fight. 'A place in the Family.'

Caradoc shook his head. He was a small, calculating man who looked more of a monk than a king. 'I do not think you will get that. Arthur has something that he holds against you. I discussed it with him last night.'

I dropped my hand and stood up straighter. 'Did he say what it was?'

'You do not know? No, he said only that he suspected you of witchcraft. For my own part, I think it absurd to suspect a warrior who has proved himself in battle of so weak and womanish a pursuit as that. I would be willing to give you second place under my war-leader, and the rank of tribune . . .'

'Thank you, Lord; it is a noble offer and more generous than I deserve, but I will wait for Arthur. He may yet change his mind.' I bowed to Caradoc.

He steepled his fingers, stared at me a moment, then smiled drily and nodded. 'You can afford to wait, I suppose. Tell me, is it only the desire for battle and fame which makes men follow Arthur ab Uther? I ask this as a king, and one who needs more men and is uncertain how to get them.'

I shook my head. 'It is not only the battle and fame. Bran of Less Britain was willing to risk his life and his followers for Arthur before he was High King, when he was still a usurping bastard. It is because Arthur is Arthur . . . He says that he wishes to restore the Empire.'

'You are not Roman: what is the Empire to you?'

'Very little,' I admitted, smiling. 'But the Empire that Arthur would create is a great deal, and I am willing to wait and hope until Arthur sees that.'

He sighed, a short, sharp sigh of exasperation. 'So others also have said, they would rather fight for Arthur and starve than have high advancement with another, and always it is because "he is a great emperor", or "he will restore the Empire" or "preserve the Light". Very well, Gwalchmai of Orcade, good fortune attend your waiting!' He rose and saluted me. 'But should you change your mind before Arthur changes his, and should you decide that you dislike Urien, the place will still be open. You are a brave man and a fine warrior, and I have said as much to the Pendragon. Now, I believe that your Arthur is preparing to leave again, so you had best go and join him.'

I bowed deeply and left, closing the door behind me.

Since Ossa could not expect a second raid so soon after the first we made a second, south of the first one, and concentrated on the newly settled border region. Ossa refused to make the same mistake twice and waited to gather his army before marching on us. In doing so he made a worse mistake, for he left his royal fortress, Catraeth (or Cataracta, as the Saxons call it) with only a light guard while he marched slowly up to when we had last been reported. But we circled around through Ebrauc as fast as we could press our horses, left the plunder from the raid there, and struck into the heart of Deira. We took Ossa's fortress, removed all the hoarded plunder, and fired as much of it as we could before retreating again to Caer Ebrauc. We were surprised at the amount of plunder; Ossa's raids had apparently been successful. Ossa had tried to follow us when he heard that we were again in Deira, but arrived in Catraeth too late, and had to disband his army for the harvest-sason and try to repair the damage and appease his warband, who had also lost their goods.

Urien was delighted.

'By the sun and the hosts of Heaven,' he told Arthur when we were again feasting in Caer Ebrauc, 'you'll have them beaten by mid-winter!'

Arthur shook his head. 'It will be harder from now on. They know how quickly we can move now. And we are still unable to meet their army, and they know that. They have learned, I think, not to raid too deeply into British territory, or to fear retaliation if they do. But they will guard themselves now, and probably try more short raids. Still, at this rate – perhaps by midsummer.'

Urien laughed. 'Midsummer. I have been fighting for years, and have felt glad if I can manage to hold my own. Ach well, you have fine warriors, who know how a war should be fought. Your friend Bedwyr seems capable of leading the Family on his own.' (Bedwyr, near Arthur as always, smiled at the compliment but made a disclaiming gesture.) 'And Cei ap Cynryr is a man who would be war-leader in any other warband. And Gereint and Goronwy and Cynan and my nephew Agravain have earned their fame as well, that is plain. I cannot hope to match them with any of my own followers. And then, I must guard my coasts, or those thrice-damned Irish would burn my fortress under me.' Urien paused, taking another sip of Caradoc's wine, and looked at Arthur with a gleam in his eyes. 'And Gwalchmai ap Lot, though not a member of your Family, fights in such a way as to make songs for the poets.'

Arthur shrugged and changed the subject.

Agravain glared at Arthur, then hacked savagely at the haunch of venison before him. Gei glared back at Agravain, then stared at Bedwyr, questioningly. Bedwyr was his friend and Arthur's, and Cei expected the Breton to take their side in the debate which had grown up about Arthur's continued refusal of my word. Many of the warriors, who admired my fighting and my refusal to serve any other, endlessly discussed Arthur's reasons and frequently blamed him, which caused others to grow angry with them. Bedwyr alone tried to remain neutral, and Cei resented this neutrality.

'Well, but it is true, Hawk of Battle,' Urien said, refusing to accept Arthur's change of subject and turning to me. 'How was it in that skirmish half a day's ride south-east of the border? I missed that one.'

Urien regretted it when he missed any good fight. I told him about the skirmish, and wondered when he would offer me a place in his warband. He was obviously awaiting his chance. I think that, like Caradoc, he had asked Arthur some questions in private, but did not believe the answers he had been given. Perhaps he was waiting for me to tire and leave Arthur before he made his offer. He had given me gifts, a cloak of embroidered silk, imported from Italy, and a very fine shield with an enamelled boss, far too fine to be used. He was a generous man, open-handed, courageous in battle, loyal, a lover of mead and music and women, a good man, a man to trust. But not a man I wanted to follow. He was blind to too many things. The only country he knew was his own clan, though he recognized a few vague responsibilities to the clans which owed him allegiance, and a few hazy duties to Arthur. He had nothing of Arthur's transcendent vision, his brilliance, his habit of giving himself as well as his possessions to the cause, or his gallantry and gaiety. Urien's warband, too, was not the Family. I knew the Family by then, that it truly was a family, a band of brothers. I thought that it must be like the Red Branch at the time of CuChulainn, a place where courage and honour were taken for granted, filled with glory and laughter. Even though Arthur was no closer to accepting me, I did not wish to leave.

Urien would have stayed with us longer, for he was enjoying the campaign, but while in Ebrauc he received some bad news from Rheged. His war-leader, in a truly spectacular piece of idiocy, allowed himself and most of the warband to be trapped by a group of raiders whom they outnumbered three to one. They lost fifty men in escaping. Beyond this, the sea raids were increasing in frequency as the summer wore on. Urien was needed at Yrechwydd. We sent some of the plunder back with him.

Arthur was very pleased with the plunder. It would support the Family for some time, and that we had been able to give so much to Urien and Caradoc would allow us to ask them for goods in return once our supplies ran out. Besides this, Urien and Caradoc had been enough impressed to promise to raise their armies whenever Arthur should request it, and the kingdoms, it was hoped, had beeen enough impressed to answer that call to arms. The Family was proud of itself, of its strength and reputation. But we were tired. It had been a hard summer's fighting, and winter would be welcome for the rest it brought. Our weariness made us tense, and there were arguments, almost fights, between members of the Family. Arthur could always stop them, but they disturbed everyone.

It was perhaps because of this weariness and tension that our next raid was a failure. More likely, though, we failed because we attacked Bernicia.

Bernicia actually lies closer to Rheged than Deira, but Ossa of Deira had been doing most of the raiding, and so Arthur had wished to weaken it first. Now that Ossa was rendered temporarily quiet we turned our attention to Bernicia.

We struck into the southern part of the country after riding at a fast pace along the border of Deira and Ebrauc. We had a good road across the hills, a Roman road, since we were still south of the Wall. All the land which was uncultivated was heavily forested, full of lakes, an easy country to hide in. It is rich country, too: we took over two hundred head of cattle in the two days of raiding which brought us to the Wall. We were confident, certain that Aldwulf would not dare to attack us without first raising the *fyrd*, and that, at harvest time, even if he was alert to the threat of invasion it would take some time to do so.

Then, on the third day of the raid, one of our scouts rode up to Arthur at a full gallop, reined in his worn horse and gasped out the news: Aldwulf was within half a day's ride to our west, and had raised the *fyrd*.

No matter how careful his planning or quiet his movements, we all knew that he should not have been able to do it. We had ridden from Caer Ebrauc too quickly; he could hardly have received even the news of our presence from reports more than a day before. And it took still much time to lead an army, at its slow pace, down from Gefrin in the north. To have done as he had he would have discovered our plans the moment we left Caer Ebrauc and have begun to move southward at once, collecting his army along the way. No messenger can ride so fast. We did not speak of it, but we could guess how Aldwulf Fflamddwyn had found out.

We turned south, hurriedly. Aldwulf did not have all the men he could muster, but his army was still a large one, over five thousand men, and he had his warband as well. There were six hundred and twenty-three in the Family, since some were sick in Caer Ebrauc and some escorting Urien and the plunder to Rheged. We were accustomed to fight against superior numbers, but the Saxons now had the advantage of the land and of allies in the south as well. To the north stood the Wall, to the east was the sea, and to the south was Ossa. We preferred to leave. However, we had not gone far south when we discovered that Ossa was approaching with part of his army and all of his warband. Their numbers were such that we could have defeated them, but that would have left us a prey to Aldwulf, whom our scouts reported as following us southward, keeping to our west. The whole land had risen against us, and sprang ambushes at every turn of the road, so that our speed was cut down. The only way to escape, Arthur decided, was to take the stronger enemy, and pass through the Bernician army.

We made camp by the river Wir, keeping it between ourselves and the Saxons, and Arthur called the Family together to tell us what we must do. He was silent for a while, looking at his warriors, lingeringly, and then he spoke calmly and quietly: 'Tonight at midnight we will lift camp and attack the army of Fflamddwyn.'

A murmur like wind in the trees swept the Family, then died down again. The prospect of death was always near us and could not make us afraid.

Arthur smiled, very gently, very brightly. 'We will go through them on horseback, if at all, so we will leave the cattle and the plunder behind. Fflamddwyn is camped upon the other side of the Dubhglas river, less than four hours' easy riding. He will doubtless know that we are coming, but we still will have the advantage of the dark, and, it is to be hoped, a good amount of confusion. We will ride in a spearhead formation, the best of the cavalry first, the rest about the edges, and those who normally fight on foot and doctors and such in the centre. If the point of our spear goes through we will escape, Aldwulf will lose many of his men and most of his credit, while we will be largely unharmed. If not . . .' again he looked at his warband. 'I have no wish to point out that there is no escape, and give you examples and arguments to prove how bad your condition will be. If our spear breaks on their shield-wall, I trust you to kill before you are killed, and to make such a battle that it will be sung of by all Britain, and be a light to hold against the dark. You are my warriors, my hearts, I know that you will not surrender.'

They did not even cheer; their stillness was an assent more total than any shouting. Arthur smiled again, a light in his eyes. The evening sun fell on him, on the river and its grassy banks, the forest behind, half-bare with autumn; on the ranks of men and horses with their harness and weapons dull with use, and everything was as quiet as a forest pool in the middle of a summer day. Everything seemed to be worked in gold, apart from the world, apart from time and war, one immortal, imperishable creation, and the dream was real. Then, one of our plundered cattle lowed, a horse nickered, bitten by a fly, and the spell was broken.

'I will ride at the head of the Family,' Arthur continued briskly, 'and with me, Bedwyr, Gereint, Cynan, Rhuawn, Maelwys, Llenlleawg, Sinnoch ap Seithfed, Llwydeu, Trachmyr, Gwyn ab Esni, Moren ab Iaen, Morfran ap Tegid and . . .' his eyes fell on me and he paused, then continued in the same tone, 'Gwalchmai ap Lot.'

He went on, assigning the rest of the Family their places and giving orders for the breaking of camp and the disposal of the plunder, where to cross the river and where to meet if separated, but I did not really listen. He had given me an order to ride near him with his best men, the spear-point of the warband, the position of greatest danger. He was not a man to command this unless . . .

I waited impatiently until the High King had finished, then hurried towards him. Most of the Family hung about, paying close attention. Nearly all of them had taken sides with either Agravain or Cei in the dispute about me, and everyone was interested in the outcome.

Arthur had been turning towards the fire, where we would roast some of Aldwulf's cattle for dinner, but he saw me coming and waited. His face was quite still, expressionless. I knew that look, and the beginning of my hope died again.

'Lord,' I said quietly, 'you commanded me to take a place beside you against the Saxons.'

'I did,' said Arthur coldly. There was a moment of tense silence, and one of the warriors almost spoke, but decided not to. 'If you wish, you can refuse. You are not my warrior.'

I shook my head. 'No, Lord Pendragon, I do not care to refuse.' Suddenly the bloody and exhausting summer, and all the bitterness of extinguished hopes rose in me at once, and I said, 'You know that I will not refuse. You know that I will fight for you. Haven't I shown you that a dozen times over? But I wish to know why.'

'I recognize necessities,' answered Arthur. 'If my Family is to live, we must break the shield-wall. You can kill from horseback very expertly, Gwalchmai of Orcade; and yes, I know that you will fight. So I use you, to aid my Family and Britian. I wish I did not have to.'

'That is not what I meant,' I said, softly and quickly. 'Why do you refuse my sword and use it at the same time?'

'I have said that I do not wish to use it,' Arthur returned, the coldness growing sharper with anger. Agravain's party among the Family stirred, muttering. The air was thick with tension. 'Why have you stayed? Any king in Britain would be overjoyed to have you. Yet, you hang about me, unasked, with your killing and your sorceries and your mother's curse and Darkness . . .'

My hand was somehow on my sword. 'You know nothing of that. Why do you insist on believing that I adore her? If I could work sorcery, Arthur Pendragon, I would not hang about you, plodding on and fighting and killing for you – for despite what you believe, I have no love for killing – but I would work such a work that all Britain would demand that you accept me. I swear the oath of my people, I hate witchcraft, more than you because I know more of it. Are you entirely in darkness?'

'In God's name, what do you want?' shouted Arthur. 'What have you done since you came to me except kill and divide my Family? Indeed, you have won fame, riches and honour for yourself – shall I make return to you for that? Do you wish me to accept these things as right, good and noble? Do you think that I will accept this knowledge you speak of, the knowledge of Darkness?'

'What do you know of my darkness?' I hurled at him.

'What do you know of mine?' he demanded. 'Too much, perhaps.' He drew himself straight, standing taller than me, and his eyes were so bitterly cold that it was more terrifying than any anger. 'Now you have divided my Family so that I seem hardly able to heal it, and yet I must ask you to risk your life with me, in a place where no sorcery can help you if the shield-wall holds. Therefore . . .' he took a deep breath, and I saw with surprise that the sweat came on to his face as though he struggled with his soul within him, 'if we break the shield-wall and live, I will accept your sword. That I swear, by the Light and as I hope for salvation. Be glad, son of Morgawse. You have won.'

And he turned away and walked off, stepping with a quick light stride through the gathering dusk.

For a while I stood, staring after him, even when he was gone. Agravain came up and caught my shoulder, but I shook him off. The other warriors, nearly as stunned as I, bewildered by the speed of the thing, hung about for a moment, then began to go slowly off to the fires, starting to talk.

I stood silent, one hand still on my sword, then walked away from the camp to the river and sat by it, laying my spear in the grass. Autumn flowers bloomed raggedly by the stream, and the evening star was appearing, a soft gold light which the dark water reflected. The calmness of the world seemed to make a lie of the deadly speed of the battles of men, and of my own inner confusion. I rested my arms on my knees and stared at the current.

Arthur would accept me if the shield-wall broke that night. It was what I wanted, wasn't it? Again and again I asked myself that question, and always I answered myself, 'Yes, but not like this. Not because he is honour-bound to do so.' But what, then? Perhaps I would die that night, and then I would not have to decide. But if that was not fated, if I lived, I would have to decide. And even if I should die, I wanted to meet my death with a clean heart.

The waters in the last dark glow of twilight showed me my face, wavering on the current. A face like Morgawse's. Always Morgawse. I thrust my fingers in the ground, tore up earth and hurled it to smash that reflection. The water shivered, but stilled again, and the picture returned.

Not only Morgawse's face now, I thought, but the face of a warrior. I studied the past months in my mind. Yes, beyond any question. No one would take me for a thrall, a bard or a druid again. What I had become was written on me for all to read. A warrior, but of what warband, acknowledging what lord?

It didn't really matter. A warrior is a warrior, and all war is a sport, a game. All wars but Arthur's and the Light's.

I turned my thoughts from the brooding over injury and the bitterness I had grown accustomed to, and looked at what had actually happened. And hadn't it been fine, as Arthur had said, winning fame and honour and riches, taking gold and silk and fine weapons from the hands of kings who wanted my sword, drinking sweet mead and listening to the praises of poets. Yes, and riding into a town on Ceincaled with my mail-coat and weapons shining, red cloaks and gold jewellery, smiling back at the girls who waved at me. War is filled with too much splendour, too much gold and swift horses, scarlet and purple silks. It is beautiful, and one forgets what it is for. I had forgotten.

I drew my sword. It had been given me for a purpose, and I had forgotten that purpose. It had been given me by a king, and I had ignored the king to whom I had sworn fealty. I tightened my hand about the hilt, feeling the way it fitted, like a part of me.

I had divided the Family, Arthur had said. I gripped the sword with my other hand and held it up, pressing the cold steel against my forehead. Yes. All the arguments, the tension and anger, the breaking of friendships which I had tried to blame on weariness – all my fault.

But it had filled a part of me that had been long empty, satisfied desires I had always had and never understood. I had wanted it. I still wanted it.

Now, wouldn't Morgawse be pleased with this, I told myself. Son of Morgawse, be glad. You have won. And now, Gwalchmai of Orcade, what will you do? Lugh warned you that you had not conquered your own Darkness, but you, thinking of it in its accustomed form, ignored him. Arthur will accept you because he is too honourable to do otherwise. Arthur. He had acted with some injustice at the first, but that was a small shadow on his brilliance. What did I know of his darkness, of the man within the king, of the forces that drove him, of his reasons? Suddenly I saw him as human, uncertain, and I knew that before I had not fought for him but for myself, done nothing to quell his suspicions and much to justify them. And now I did wish to fight, for him, and atone.

Light, Lord, I said silently. My lord High King to whom

my sword is first pledged, command me. The sword is yours, and the life you saved; you, more even than Arthur, are the one I serve and fight for; you are the one I will obey.

I already knew the answer to the problem. I stood, slowly, and saluted the evening star with my sword, the decision made. The warm red light I had not seen for months lit again in Caledvwlch's hilt, glowed brighter and more tenderly, lighting the darkness around me. I would fight for Arthur that night, and, God willing, break the shield-wall; then, if I lived, go to Urien of Rheged and request a place in his warband.

I walked back to the fires for dinner.

The meal was eaten quickly. No one was hungry, but everyone knew that they should eat; and moreover, the cattle were Aldwulf's, and those we did not eat we turned loose and he might recover. After the meal we tried to sleep: a few may have succeeded, I did not. Just before midnight we rose and broke camp, leaving the plunder. I went to the picket lines and saddled and bridled Ceincaled.

'This will be the last time,' I told him in Irish, as I swung up. 'After this, *mo chroidh*, we go with Urien, if we live.'

He pricked his ears and stamped, and I felt his eagerness and bright, swift pride more sharply than I had for the past months. I laughed under my breath, running my fingers through his mane. If we died, it was a good night for dying, and it would be a good death.

I rode to the front of the band, near Arthur, and, when all the Family was ready, we left without a word spoken. We forded the river—it was not deep—and rode through the forest, north-west, spread out for easier riding. The Saxons were camped on the other side of the Dubhglas river, in land that was actually British. We rode towards them for some three hours, then tighened our formationa and rode carefully, making little sound.

Aldwulf had watchmen posted, but had not needed them. His camp had been awake for at least an hour when we arrived, and was bright with torches tied to spears thrust into the ground. We had gone quietly and without lights so as to avoid giving any additional warning to the Saxons. Our eyes were accustomed to the dark, and the torchlight was bright enough to aim a spear by. Arthur drew rein briefly at the top of the slope that led down to the river, and pointed out to the 'spear-point' the route we would take, speaking in an under-tone. We all knew what would follow: we would gallop down the slope, through the trees into the torchlight and cross the river to attack the shield-wall which the Saxons would raise on the opposite bank.

Arthur dropped his hand, spurring his horse to a gallop.

We followed, in silence but for the pounding of the horses' hooves and the jingle of harness. My head was light with a different madness and I was at peace.

At first the Saxons did not realize what was happening. They expected us, but it was dark and they were sleepy, expecting some torches, some war-cry or warning. They heard the sound of hooves and started, picking up their spears and looking about in confusion. They could not see us for the darkness, the forest, and their torch-blinded eyes. I drew loose a throwing spear as we approached the bank, and flung it with all my strength. Confuse them. Get them off balance. Other spears fell among the Saxons doing little damage, but startling and frightening them. Their chiefs began to order them to form the shield-wall, and they obeyed, but slowly. We came out of the forest and plunged into the river – the water splashed high and cold about our legs – the torchlight gleaming and leaping from us, the trees casting long shadows that wavered like a mad dream; and across the river, hurling more spears, some of which found their marks. The horses swam briefly, hard, their eyes rolling and ears laid back, and the Saxon spears were falling all about us, and the horses were running again, coming at the shield-wall. Arthur was grinning, holding his thrusting spear levelled to strike. The shield-wall opposite us was three men deep, and more warriors hurried to support it, shout-ing, wild-eyed. We approached, charging in silence from nowhere against an army, and suddenly Arthur threw back his head and shouted, 'For Britain, my hearts! For me!'

And we answered, 'For Arthur!' with one heart and one voice, a sound more terrible than death; I hurled my thrust-ing spear and drew my sword, blazing with white light, as we reached the bank.

My old madness did not fill me, but I did not need it. Cein-caled reared, lashing out with his hooves, and I bent over his neck and slashed down, fighting from love and from a dream, as Arthur fought. It was a few moments, no more:

251

had we paused long enough for our speed to slacken, we could not have done it, but the Saxons were afraid, bewildered and uncertain, and they broke. We killed them on all sides as we went through, tearing the torches from their posts and hurling them into the camp, setting it alight, hacking through tent-ropes and charging on, leaving destruction behind us. We plunged into the safety of the woods, only a few spears falling about us now as we rode down the night.

'Well done,' said Arthur, softly, then shouted aloud with joy. 'Oh beautifully done!'

We reined in our horses to a canter, thinking of the miles yet to ride. Behind us the sky paled with the first grey of the still hour that leads to morning.

Sixteen

I did not have a chance to tell Arthur that I would leave the Family for almost a month. I had received a leg wound in the battle, a bad one which was made worse by my riding twenty miles with it afterwards. It couldn't be helped. We had no fear that the Saxons would follow us – they did not have the horses, and would be far too preoccupied with their own losses, besides busy trying to recover their plundered cattle – but we needed a place to stay. With a warband the size of the Family, such a place is not easy to find. In the end we rode north and west until we came to a clan holding near the Wall, headed by a man named Ogyrfan. He was a tall, black-bearded man, of some importance in those parts because of his wealth and some Roman title. He feared the Saxons and longed for the restoration of the Empire, and so welcomed Arthur. He gave the Family food and a place to put the wounded. I was glad of it. I was weak from blood-loss, faint, and sick with pain. Agravain and Bedwyr carried me to the cow-byre – the only building available for a hospital – where I collapsed and stayed that way for over a week. I had the wound-fever the first few days and remember nothing of them, and when I recovered enough to be aware of myself again, was told that Arthur and the Family were gone, off raiding. The warband had been weakened by the summer, but the opportunity offered by the present situation had proved to be irresistible. Aldwulf's credit with the other Saxons was, as Arthur had predicted, seriously weakened by our victory. They could not see how, when he had had the British High King trapped and outnumbered and had himself been forewarned, Aldwulf could have let us escape. Ossa of Deira blamed him; his own nobles blamed him; and his subjects, who had been raided and now were short of goods and angry, blamed him bitterly and deserted his army. The harvest season was nearly over, and Ossa's men also wished to return to their farms, and Ossa himself returned to his stronghold after some bitter recriminations with Aldwulf. The king of Bernicia was thus left with only his warband, and that a fractious one, and he too retreated to his fortress for the winter. The countryside was thus left unprotected, and Arthur attacked Bernicia and raided as freely as if there were no king in the land, destroying all the new farms on the border and taking away grain and cattle enough to last the Family a year, with some left over for gifts as well.

For myself, however, I stayed at Ogyrfan's holding until my wound had healed enough to ride with, almost a month. It was a pleasant place, and ordinarily I might have been glad to spend time there. The farm was set near the Wall which wound off across the sweep of hill and field which it formed a fence to on one side. A fresh, swift stream rushed by the houses and watered the pastures. To the south the land rose, forested valleys and heather-clad hills melting into the tall shadow of the mountains. Ogyrfan was a strong, intelligent man, unexpectedly friendly to the High King's servants, and able to read. He did not even mind the increased tribute which Arthur had caused, saying that the Pendragon took only a few cows, while the Saxons would take them all. It was true of course, but a truth one seldom heard from those who paid the tribute. Ogyrfan's eldest daughter, Gwynhwyfar, was also pleasant company. I had not really spoken to a woman since Morgawse, half afraid of all of them for my mother's sake. Gwynhwyfar taught me to think differently. She helped to nurse me and the others back to health, and, under her father, was manager of the holding. She was strong enough to help Gruffydd the surgeon with his work without flinching, and weak enough to be afraid of a storm, or laugh at the song of a bird. She was some four years older than I, with masses of deep red, wavy hair and smiling brown eyes. There was a warmth to her, and a grace that made her beautiful, and she too was clever, and had read even more than her father. I was not attracted to her as a man to a woman, but her warmth drew me, touching one of the places Morgawse had chilled.

But despite all this, I was impatient to leave. Caledvwlch felt heavy at my side, and I sharpened my spear until it had an edge to wound the wind. Ceincaled, lord over the other horses in Ogyrfan's fields, would race along the fence in the morning, snorting white plumes, eager to be gone, to Rheged, to the south, to the north, it did not matter: he wished only to be on the road again. And my decision had been made, and I did not wish to linger on the way.

254

At last there came a time in early December when my leg was healed enough to ride with, if not to walk far on, and I slung my shield across my shoulder, picked up my spear and mounted Ceincaled. Most of the other warriors who had been wounded were gone and Gruffydd gone with them; a few would have to wait longer. The wind was cold, blowing over the Wall from the north, whispering of snow. Not a good season for travelling. Still, perhaps I would not have to travel far. East first, to tell Arthur and my friends what I had decided, and then, west to Rheged. Or perhaps, I thought, north. There was nothing binding me. North, to Din Eidyn, where perhaps there would be ships willing to brave the Muir Orc, and take me further north again, to Dun Fionn. Home. A sudden, sharp pang of homesickness fell on me, and I remembered my father and my kinsmen, the scream of sea-birds by the cliffs, the tall banks of Dun Fionn, and Llyn Gwalch by the grey north sea. Lot and my clan would have heard reports of me, but could not know what to think. I should have sent a message. Morgawse would know, and she was herself another reason to return. I could not live forever half-bound to her but must meet her again, and resolve the thing. Yes. North, past Pictland to the Isles of Fear, my home.

'Give my praises and my good wishes to the emperor,' Ogyrfan told me. He had come to say farewell, and drew his cloak about him against the wind.

I nodded, saluting him.

'And a swift journey for you, Gwalchmai, and mind how you use that leg,' added Gwynhwyfar. She paused, then, smiling, added one of the Irish phrases I had taught her: '*Slán lead*,' 'farewell':

'*Slán lead*,' I answered, smiling back, then turned Ceincaled's head to the road. He pranced, tossing his head against the rein, eager to be off. I called out thanks to Ogyrfan and his daughter and then gave Ceincaled his head, letting him run, off down the good road in the cold bright morning. Off to sever all the ties that held me to the Family.

And why should I be unhappy about it? I asked myself. I am young, strong and skilled. I have Ceincaled, I have Caledvwlch, and my sworn lord is greater than any other. A place with Arthur, no, but I am free and the Light's warrior. And I am going home. Who would want more?

I leant over Ceincaled's neck, urging him on, and the winter-dull earth rolled away under his flashing hooves.

It was not a long journey. Arthur had turned north, and was raiding the Bernician border towards the central part of that kingdom. I crossed the Wall and took the old road along the hills after him. There is a Roman road running that way as well, a straighter road, but from the old road you can watch the land. I followed this most of the day, riding at a trot, uneventfully. Towards evening it began to rain. My fingers froze, and the wind seemed always to blow directly at me, no matter how the road twisted. My leg began to ache, first dully, then viciously. When I reached the crest of a hill and saw the camp below me it was a grand and welcome sight. The fires burned red-gold against the slate colour of the bare hills. In the dim light I could see the picket lines, and a huddled mass of cattle by a half-circle of wagons taken from the Saxons. I stopped Ceincaled and stared down at the camp. Down there were the dung fires and men singing around them, hot food and strong, sweet mead, warriors laughing and boasting of their own deeds, joking about the deeds of others. I knew that it was so. I had been a part of it. Now I was where I had began in the Orcades, watching, from a distance.

Be still, I told myself. You will easily find another warband.

And yet, how could there be another warband like the Family, or another king like Arthur?

Well, I could have it for this last night. I touched Ceincaled's sides lightly and he began to pick his way down the hill.

We had not gone more than a few feet when a figure dashed out before us, waving its arms. Ceincaled reared, wrenching my leg, and I snatched up my spear.

'No!' cried the figure. 'Chieftain . . . *Arglwyd mawr. . .*!'

I looked closer and saw that it was not a Saxon ambushing me, but a rather ragged British woman. A poor one, if she felt that I looked like a 'great lord'. I lowered my spear and held Ceincaled in.

'What is it?' I demanded, impatient for the camp.

'Chieftain, forgive me. I saw you on the hill and was afraid, but when you started towards the camp I knew that you must be one of the Dragon's men, so I thought, "I must stop him . . ."'

'What for?'

She came closer and caught my foot. She was in her mid-thirties, her hair grey and face lined. A poor farmer's wife.

'Chieftain . . .'

'What is it?' I asked again. 'The Pendragon does not take servants, if that is what you wish.' It was unlikely that she had come for that on such a night, but there was the possibility.

'No, Chieftain. It is my man. I have heard that there are skilled doctors in the camp of the Dragon of Britain . . .'

My heart sank. 'Your husband is hurt?'

'Yes, great lord. Some of the Saxons whom the Dragon is driving away came to our household, asking for food. My man would give them none, and they struck him with steel and fled. Our clan cannot help him. I have heard that the Dragon has skilled healers . . .'

'Where is your holding?'

She pointed down the steeper slope of the hill, to the east. I looked down the western one to Arthur's camp and sighed.

'When did this happen? Can your husband be moved?'

'No, great lord. It was today, around noon. The filthy murderers fled, after they had struck my man, and they took the horses. But he could not ride a horse, he is too sick, and we have no carts. Chieftain . . .' she shook my foot. 'My man is hurt. He will die, unless he has doctors. The doctors of the camp say that they have work, and cannot come, and that I must bring my man to them. You have a swift horse. Help me!'

'Very well. Show me the way back to your household.'

She held my foot with both hands. 'May the gods bless you, great lord! May Christ and all the gods bless you! It is that way, down the path, and on to . . .'

'You must show me the way,' I repeated. Country paths are impossible for a stranger to follow. 'Come,' I held my hand out. 'My horse can carry two.'

She stared at me. 'Chieftain, I have never . . .'

I sighed, dismounted, helped her up – Ceincaled disliked it, shying and snorting – and remounted behind her. She showed me the path, which was a hard one. It took nearly an hour to reach the holding, and the woman was greatly impressed by the speed of our crawling pace. Her kin were awaiting her.

'But this is not a doctor!' said one old man, apparently

expressing the unease of the whole clan, for they nodded and began to mutter.

'He is a great chieftain,' said the woman, sliding down from Ceincaled. 'I found him on the hill, after the doctors at the camp had said they had many wounded and could not leave. He has a horse that goes like the west wind off a mountain.' (Ceincaled tossed his head, shaking rain from his mane.) 'And he will help us to bring Gwilym to the doctors.'

'Gwilym cannot be moved now,' said the old man.

I shrugged. 'I know a little of medicine. Let me see this kinsman of yours – and take my horse out of the rain.'

As soon as I saw Gwilym I knew that it was hopeless. The Saxon spear had gone clean through his body, slanting down through the lungs. It was a wonder that he was still alive: he would certainly not remain so.

The woman looked at me hopefully. 'What will you do, great lord?'

I shook my head. 'I do not think that I can do anything.'

The old man nodded. 'See now? I said, pull it out yourself, and find a new husband if he dies, but don't run about soldiers' camps like a whore.'

The woman only looked at me, frowning in pain. 'But you said . . .'

'I had not seen him. Men with this kind of wound ordinarily die within an hour.'

'You should have asked him to bring a surgeon,' said the old man. 'This one is no use. He is a warrior. What can he know of healing?'

'The doctors would not come,' said the woman. 'Chieftain, he is my man, he cannot die! Perhaps it is not so bad as you think. You must help him. Please! He is my man.'

I studied Gwilym more closely. He was unconscious, luckily for him. The wound did look fatal. Still, one cannot always tell.

'You must help him!' pleaded the woman. 'Great lord, you must at least try!'

'He can do nothing!' snapped the old man. Silently, I agreed with him, but the woman was right. I had to try.

'Very well. I will try. Bring me some hot water, close the door, and build the fire up.'

I tried for an hour, fighting my exhaustion and the pain in my leg for concentration on the man. The spear-shaft still embedded in his lung was keeping him alive, but all it did was prolong his time and his pain. Still, the wound was straight and clean, and I thought that if I got the spear out, and if the other lung didn't go, he might live. I worked, got the length of wood out after a struggle, and for a while thought it would work, but then the other lung collapsed and Gwilym died. The woman, who had been helping, felt his heart stop before he coughed up his last breath in blood, and took his hair and began to beg him to live, then buried her face against his shoulder and wept. The other women in the clan began to keen, and the children howled, and the men cried. The old man only nodded and said, 'I said he couldn't do it.'

I could feel nothing, not even compassion, nothing except the desire to get away. I washed some of the blood off, put my tunic and mail-coat back on, and limped to the door. No one said a word to me, though one or two gave me stares of hatred, since their kinsman had died under my hands. I limped off hurriedly, found Ceincaled, and threaded my way back up the hill.

By the time I reached Arthur's camp the fires had burned down to embers. My leg ached violently, I was soaked and frozen by the rain, and I wanted nothing so much as some warm, strong mead. I was stopped briefly by a sentry, who, recognizing me, welcomed me warmly and inquired about my leg. I told him that it had healed, and also how the other wounded were, and passed through. I left Ceincaled, rubbed down and munching grain, at the picket lines, then limped up to the main fire.

The welcome the warriors gave me was everything I could wish for. They jumped up, crowded around me, welcoming me and asking about my leg and why I came in so late. Agravain gave me one of his bear-hugs saying, 'Indeed, so you finally decided to come back and earn your mead. Welcome! A hundred thousand welcomes home.'

I answered the questions and was given a place next to the fire, some mead, and some food. I settled down gratefully, worn out. Only then did I notice Arthur sitting across the fire from me, unreal in the heat shimmer and watching all of it coldly. I saluted him with the mead horn and took a deep swallow.

Arthur nodded. 'So. You have come back to claim my promise.'

I did not feel like stating my decision and having the inevitable argument, but it seemed that I had to. I saw Agravain and several of his party stiffen, saw the rest watch them tensely. Yes, it was definitely right that I leave.

'No, Lord,' I answered quietly. 'I have come back only to say farewell. Tomorrow I will ride north, to see if I can return to the Orcades this winter.'

Agravain drew in his breath with a hiss. 'Gwalchmai, what do you . . .'

'What are you saying?' demanded Arthur.

'What do you think you are doing?' asked Cei angrily.

'But the lord Arthur has said that he will accept you,' said Agravain. 'You have earned it; you have won.'

'Arthur will accept me because he has no other choice, in honour.' I looked at the High King steadily.

He nodded. 'I do not deny it. I used your sword, because I had to, and you were wounded in my service. What do you hope to gain by this talk?'

'Nothing. Not now.' I wished that I could have told them in the morning.

'You have earned acceptance a thousand times over,' said Agravain. 'What are you saying, you're going north?'

'I do not wish to be accepted because Arthur is bound in honour to accept me,' I answered. 'Call me too proud for it, if you wish.'

'This I do not understand,' said Cei loudly, his voice high with indignation. 'All summer you hang about, waiting for an offer from Arthur and turning down half the kings in Britain, and now that you have it, you will not accept it, like a falcon that goes to great trouble to catch a bird it will not eat. By the Hounds of Yffern, the Family is not to be turned aside so lightly!'

'Do you wish me to join, then? If so, you are like that same falcon, trying all summer to make me leave, and then, when . . .'

Cei glared. 'You insult us all, and me most of all. I have a fair mind to . . .'

'What would that solve?' I asked wearily. 'If we fought on foot, you would win; if we fought on horseback, I would win. Everyone knows that, so it would prove nothing. And I have never intended to insult you. You are a noble and courageous man, and I'd be a fool to try.'

Cei blinked as though I had struck him. 'You are mad.'

I shrugged. 'In battle, yes. No man could think that I want to leave the Family to find a better warband. There are none.'

'Then why will you go?' demanded Agravain.

'What else, in honour, can I do?'

'What do you hope to gain?' Arthur asked again. 'Or have you gained it already? Will you return to the Orcades now, and tell your mother that the High King of Britain offered you a place, and you turned him down, like a farmer refusing bad eggs?' His voice was level, but edged with cold fury.

I remembered all of his greatness, and his anger hurt. That, coupled with my pain and weariness, made me speak more plainly than I would have. 'Lord,' I said slowly, 'I am not the servant of the Queen of Darkness. I will go because I have acted as though I were, because I have divided your Family, on which the fate of Britain rests, even as Morgawse would wish. Lord, I cannot say that I understand these things, but I will not betray them or my lord the Light. It is simpler, Lord, if I go. You have offered now, and I have refused. No one can say that you have wronged me, for it is my own will. The Family will be healed.'

'But you are the best horseman in the Family!' said Agravain. 'You cannot go.'

'I can, and will be the best horseman somewhere else.' I swallowed some more mead and rubbed my face with my free hand. 'I will go, and that is all. Let us speak of something else.'

Everyone sat silently for a long, long minute, staring at me. I began to eat, trying not to look back at them.

Then the sound of a harp broke the silence. I looked up, and Taliesin smiled at me, then bent his head to his work, bringing the same pure, high notes like a silver thread across the air. It was CuChulainn's song, I realized, and it was also the song in Lugh's Hall, the strong, clear song of renunciation rising about the strains of battle. The rain fell down out of the night and hissed in the embers of the fire. I listened to the music, and, for the first time, understood it.

The song gave me a strength which sustained me the next day when I saddled Ceincaled to ride on. The Family clustered about me, urging me not to go, wishing me a good journey, and giving me gifts. Arthur watched, his face unreadable. I had a pack horse which I loaded with supplies and the gifts, wrapped in a blanket. It hurt to look at the warriors, and there was a tightness in my throat as I knotted the pack on to the bay pack-mare and straightened, holding the lead rope.

At this point, Gruffydd the surgeon came through the crowd, followed, to my surprise, by the woman of the previous night.

'Doctors receive no farewells, is it?' he asked. 'Or is it that you are afraid I will look at your leg and tell you to stay down for another week.'

I smiled, dropped the lead rein, came over and took his hand. 'Even if you told me to stay down, I would go.'

'And your leg will give you trouble all the way to the Ynysoedd Erch,' he said, nodding. 'Well, go berserk and you will not feel it.' He paused and added in a low tone, 'Why are you going?'

'Because I must.'

The woman, who had been staring about her, said, 'Great lord, I did not understand. Had I known who you were, I would not have stopped you.'

I looked at her curiously, hoping that she did not have a wounded son.

She drew herself up. 'My clan is poor, Chieftain, but we have honour. We do not let those who do us kindnesses leave thankless and without reward.' She flushed 'Payment I . . . you would not need. But you have my thanks, Gwalchmai of the Ynysoedd Erch, and the thanks of my clan.'

'But I could not help your man,' I said, much moved.

She shrugged, pushed the heals of her hands against her eyes a moment before replying. 'You came, and you tried. It is much.'

Gruffydd looked from her to me. 'She came in just now asking for a dark warrior with a limp, who wore a red cloak and had a white stallion. I think I remember her from last night – isn't her husband . . .'

'He is dead now,' I said.

'Spear through the lungs,' she said. 'I remember now. And you tried to help? That was foolish. Even I could do no good with such a case as that.'

'She didn't tell me that; and there was a chance.' I turned to the woman. 'You honour me over-much with your thanks, good woman. I did nothing, and your husband is dead.'

She shrugged again, blinking very quickly. 'You came,' she repeated quietly. 'A blessing on your road, Chieftain.' She curtseyed awkwardly and turned, still blinking at the tears, and walked through the warriors without looking at them, beginning the long walk home.

'What was all that?' asked Agravain.

'You heard it.'

'Just that? A beggarly farmer's woman, and a farmer himself who was surely dead?'

'She is an honourable woman,' Arthur said sharply, 'to come miles into an armed camp to return thanks for an attempt at healing: a noble and brave woman!'

Agravain stared at him in surprise. 'My lord?' Then he put the woman from his mind altogether. 'Gwalchmai. I do not understand it, but . . . by the sun.' He looked away. 'Take care, my brother. *Slán lead*'.

'God go with you,' said Bedwyr softly.

'A blessing on your road,' said Gruffydd.

I nodded to all of them, turned to Ceincaled. He bowed his proud head, blew at me softly, nibbled at my hair. It made me smile. I stroked his neck and caught up the reins.

'No,' said Arthur suddenly, in a strained voice. 'Wait.'

I dropped the reins, turned back. The High King stood behind the others, his face pale. 'Wait,' he repeated. I wondered if he would wish me a good journey as well.

He shook his head violently as if to clear it. 'Gwalchmai. I wish to speak to you a moment first. Alone.'

I paused, staring at him, then handed Ceincaled's reins to Agravain. Arthur had already set off for his own tent, and I followed, again in complete confusion. I did not see what there could be to talk about. Perhaps he still felt that he was in honour bound to do something for me. Yes, that was likely.

In the tent he caught up a jug of wine, slowly poured two glasses and offered me one. After a moment of hesitation I took it and stood with it in my hand, staring at him.

'Be seated.' he said, waving to a chair at one side of the tent. I sat, and he himself sank on to his bed. He took a swallow of his wine, then met my eyes.

'I am sorry,' he said, flatly and quietly.

I stared at him in bewilderment. 'Lord, there is no need to think that your honour binds you . . .'

'Forget that,' he said sharply. 'Ach, Yffern . . .' he stood, paced a few steps towards the door, stopped and turned to me again. 'I have misjudged you. Badly. And if it can be that you still desire a place in my Family, it is yours.'

I felt as though the sky were caving in. 'I do not understand,' I said at last.

'On the banks of the Wir, you asked me whether I was altogether in Darkness,' he replied quietly. 'And I was. An old Darkness, and one which I cannot shake off, try as I will.' He turned and began to pace the floor of the tent, looking at nothing with a wide grey stare. 'From the beginning, I fought with myself about you. I had heard of you, your reputation, and saw no surprising new reason to trust you, but that was not the thing which decided me against you. No: I knew that you had been close to my sister, deep in her secret counsels, and, by Heaven, you look like her. That was all that was needed. Everything which you did after that I twisted to fit in with my own ideas, twisted to keep you in the Darkness with my sister, and kept myself in the Darkness instead. For which now I say that I am sorry. And yet all of it, the killing, the way you are in battle, the division you caused, the horse which I thought you had captured by spells – all of it was secondary and mattered less to me than the single thought, "He knows". It was that that angered me, and filled me with such horror that I could not . . .'

'But know what, Lord?'

'Know about your brother, of course.'

'Agravain? I don't see. Why . . .'

'Not Agravain; of course not. The other one. Medraut.'

Our eyes met again, his hard and tortured, mine confused, and he stood suddenly still as the hardness ebbed out of his and they widened, a straight, grey stare of realization. Medraut's stare.

Arthur sank down on the bed again and began to laugh, horrible choking noises almost like sobs, then pressed his head into his hands. 'You do not know. You never did. She never told you.'

I felt coldness in the pit of my stomach, and a sudden black terror. Morgawse, Arthur's sister, and Medraut who looked like Arthur (why hadn't I seen it before?) – and then, laden with horror, the words of Morgawse's curse returning to me: 'May the earth swallow me, may the sky fall on me, may the sea overwhelm me if you do not die by your son's hand!'

'Oh, by the Light,' I said.

Arthur straightened and stilled. 'And now you do know.'

I jumped to my feet. 'My lord, how? I thought she must have touched you, somehow, but this . . .'

'I consented to it,' he said in a harsh voice. Again we stared at each other for a long moment, and then he said, 'I did not know, then, who my father was. I swear it by all that's holy, I did not know she was my sister. She . . . she . . .' he stopped again. 'She came to me, outside the feast Hall, when first I won fame in the warband of her father Uther. She was staying in Camlann while her husband, Lot, campaigned in the north of Britain. She had singled me out, before then, but then . . . I was drunk, and happy, and she was more beautiful than a goddess; I consented only to adultery, but I consented to it. And later, Uther asked me about my parentage. I had not talked about it; one doesn't. But I told him, and he remembered my mother, and was pleased that I was his son. When he had gone to tell the others, I remembered her, rushed to warn her – and she . . .' He stood again, not looking at me, looking back in remembered agony and horror on the moment when he discovered that he had been seduced into incest. 'She had known, all along she had known, and greeted me as Arthur ab Uther, and called me brother, and laughed, saying that she bore my child. And ever since I have not been able to so much as think of her without remembering that moment; and the thought that another knew, her son, and perhaps had planned with her – I could not endure it and felt that I must rid myself of you at any cost.'

'My lord,' I said, still staring in horror and pity. 'My lord.'

'Oh, indeed. Only you were innocent, and did not even know.' He took another deep drink of the wine, and set the cup down. The grey eyes focused on me again. 'You never knew, until I told you.'

I went down on one knee to him. 'My lord, I . . . I could not have guessed such a thing. I do not understand why you did not send me away forcibly; especially after I had divided the Family, and killed, and made your victories bitter for you. Forgive me, I . . .'

'Forgive you? It is I who need forgiveness. Stand up. In God's name, stand. Now . . .' he too stood again. 'I should have seen months ago that you were not what I thought you to be. You endured everything which the war and I together could throw at you and did not complain. And you worked as a surgeon. I knew nothing about that until Gruffydd told me, and shouted at me for being unjust to you. He thinks very highly of you.' I stared at the king, startled. Of course. He was always busy the day after a battle, but saw the wounded in the night, when I was sleeping off the madness. 'I should have seen enough, over the months you followed me, to make me realize; and I should have trusted Bedwyr's judgement, since I knew myself to be bound by the Darkness. But I persisted in wronging you. And then, last night, you said that you left so as not to divide the Family, and spoke as though you meant it. I told myself you did it only for pride, but I could not convince myself. I knew, definitely knew then, that I was wrong; and yet I could not bring myself to admit it to myself. I could have argued myself out of it, but then, that woman . . .'

'What?'

'The woman with the husband who died. A noble, honourable woman, but low-born, not rich or powerful. No one who obeyed the Darkness would have looked at her twice, but you went out of your way on a cold night with a wound which must have been troubling you, to help a man whom you did not know and who could not be helped.'

'I did not know he was so badly wounded when I went.'

'Yet when you did know, you still tried to help. There would be no advantage from it for you, nothing to gain. It was pointless, but honourable and compassionate. There could be no doubt, after that. You were what you had claimed to be all along, and I had played the part of a fool and a tyrant.'

He walked over to me and laid one hand on my shoulder. 'I have said that I am sorry for it, and say it now again. Perhaps you no longer desire a place in my service. Yet I think, now that you have offered to go, there would be no further division when I asked you to remain. And you have disarmed Cei very thoroughly.' He grinned suddenly, if rather shakily, something of the light coming back into his face. 'Insults he can cope with, but not being told that he is noble and courageous. I think he hopes that no one will find that out, if he is quarrelsome enough.' He became serious again. 'Thus, if you should still desire to stay . . .' he sought for the word. 'There is work enough and more than enough, and I would be very glad of you.'

I was silent a moment, and Arthur watched me steadily, half-challenging, half-hoping, his hand still on my shoulder, almost testing.

'My lord,' I said at last, 'if someone should offer you Britain, with the Empire restored, and all Erin and Caledon and Less Britain besides, and the roads open to Rome – would you accept it?'

He grinned slowly, then embraced me, clumsily, till almost testing, but I realized that it was not me he was testing now but himself. I returned the embrace, then knelt and kissed his hand, the signet ring he wore on his finger.

'My lord,' I said, 'I have desired to fight for you, for long and long, since I knew that you fight for the Light, and it would be better to die fighting against the Darkness than to live long winning victories to no purpose. How could I wish for more than this? From now on it will be victories only.'

'God willing, even so, for I think we have had victories of a sort already. Come.' He helped me to my feet, embraced me again, then walked rapidly from the tent.

The others were still waiting by Ceincaled and the laden pack-mare, discussing something which they refrained from abruptly when they saw Arthur and me coming. Arthur stopped, surveyed the horses, then announced calmly, 'You can see that they are unloaded again. Gwalchmai ap Lot has agreed to stay, and to swear the oath to me, at my urging.'

Agravain looked at Cei, then at Bedwyr, then at me. I nodded. He gave a whoop of delight. '*Laus Deo,* by the sun!' He embraced me, pounding me on the back. 'I understand nothing of all this – you change your mind; Arthur changes his; you change yours – but I like it this way, so long as you do not begin it again,' he said, in Irish. 'And now, indeed, we have won,' he added, in British, letting me go and glaring at Cei.

Cei shrugged, eyeing me; then, suddenly smiled. 'It is good news. You are a very devil of a fighter, cousin.'

Bedwyr looked from me to Arthur, then, when Arthur also nodded, he smiled slowly. 'I am glad.'

'Very good,' said Arthur drily. 'I am glad my decision meets with your approval. You three can be witnesses. Call the rest, and we will swear the oaths now.'

267

It was still cold, and the wind sent the clouds scudding across the dark sky, and whispered in the bare branches of the trees. The Family was a splash of colour and light on the barren landscape, gathered about in a circle to watch and bear witness. Arthur stood before his tent, tall and straight, the wind tugging at his purple cloak. Bedwyr stood on his right, Cei on his left with Agravain beside him. I stared at the picture, wishing to hold it for ever, then dropped to one knee, drawing Caledvwlch.

'I, Gwalchmai, son of Lot of Orcade, do now swear to follow the lord Arthur, emperor of the Britains, dragon of the island; to fight at his will against all his enemies, to hold with him and obey him at all times and places. My sword is his sword until death. This I swear in the name of Father, Son and Spirit, and if I fail of my oath may the earth open and swallow me, the sky break and fall on me, the sea rise and drown me. So be it.'

Arthur reached out his hand for the sword, and I suddenly remembered.

'My lord,' I began, 'the sword cannot . . .'

He ignored me and caught the hilt from my hand, lifting the weapon. The lightning did not spring from it against him as it had against Cei. Instead the radiance lit it, growing greater and whiter until it seemed that Arthur held a star. And he said, 'And I, Arthur, emperor of the Britains, do now swear to support Gwalchmai son of Lot, in arms and in goods, faithfully in honour, in all times and places until death. This I swear in the name of Father, Son and Spirit, and if I fail of my oath, may the earth open and swallow me, the sky break and fall on me, the sea rise and drown me. And I swear to use this sword, of Light, in Light, to work Light upon this realm, so help me God.'

The radiance faded from the sword as he returned it to me. I stood, sheathing it.

'Witnessed?' asked my lord Arthur.

'Witnessed,' said Cei, Bedwyr and Agravain. And then Agravain stepped forward with a wide grin, shouting in Irish, 'And now it is truly done, and you have won! Och, my brother, I swear the oath of my people I am glad!'

The rest of the Family was not far behind.

Notes

The historical background of this novel is partially but by no means entirely accurate: I have used some anachronisms and made some complete departures from what little is known about Britain between the Roman withdrawal and the Saxon conquest. My worst offence is in the Orkneys, where I have antedated the Irish conquest, invented places as well as persons, and described a situation completely unlike anything that actually existed there. But it is barely possible, if improbable, that some of the Britons whom the Emperor Honorius instructed to organize their own defences viewed these organizations as continuing the late third–early fourth century 'Empire of the Britains,' and could have maintained an increasingly Celtic Roman empire into the sixth century.

For the legendary background I have drawn first on various Celtic sources, second on everything Arthurian written up to the present. Some of the poems are loosely based, anachronistically, on Celtic originals: the one on pages 58–9 on a fifteenth-century Deirdre poem; on page 71, an earlier Irish poem; on page 78 on the eighth-century 'Voyage of Bran.' The song on page 191 is, in fact, the sixth-century (or earlier) hymn known as 'Patrick's Breastplate' or 'Deer's Cry.' A version of it beginning 'I bind unto myself today' is still sung, at least in the Anglican church, and has a lovely tune. The poem on page 237 is also Irish; but later. The others are my own, but represent the sort of poetry current in Old Welsh and Irish – except, of course, for the *Aeneid* passage, which is book VI.125–9.

On pronunciation, Welsh looks more intimidating than it is (Irish is best left unmentioned); 'w' is usually a long 'u,' except in a few cases such as after 'g' and before a vowel, when it is the familiar consonant; 'y' is usually a short 'u' sound: 'Bedwyr' is thus three syllables, and comes into later legend as 'Bedivere'; 'ff' is as in 'off,' but 'f' a 'v' sound as in 'of'; 'dd' is the soft 'th,' as in 'bathe'; 'll' something like the sound in 'little'; 'si' is a 'sh' sound – 'Sion' is the equivalent of Irish 'Sean' and English 'John,' and has nothing to do with mountains. The other letters are not too different from their traditional values: 'ch' is as in Scottish, German, or Greek; 'r' is trilled, and the vowels in general are pure, as in Latin. Accent is usually on the penultimate syllable.

I have used modern Welsh forms, on the whole, as I was uncertain of the old Welsh ones. Place names are in complete confusion, but I imagine they were at the time as well: I have used Celtic forms when these are recorded. Sorviodunum/ Searisbyrig is modern Salisbury (or rather, Old Sarum); Ynys Witrin is Glastonbury; Camlann, South Cadbury where the excavations are. Caer Segeint is Carnarvon; Ebrauc is York; Din Eidyn, Edinburgh; and Yrechwydd a name from poems which might be several places but which I have relocated to suit myself. This should be enough to give the reader some orientation, but, since the novel is only partially historical, geography is not that important.

Kingdom of Summer

In Memoriam
Lt Col and Mrs H. R. R. Rouquette

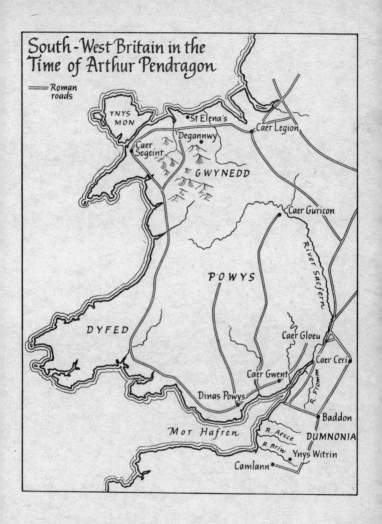

South-West Britain in the Time of Arthur Pendragon

— Roman roads

YNYS MON

St Elena's

Degannwy

Caer Segeint

Caer Legion

GWYNEDD

Caer Guricon

River Saffern

POWYS

DYFED

Caer Gloeu

Caer Ceri

R. Fromm

Caer Gwent

Dinas Powys

Baddon

DUMNONIA

Mor Hafren

R. Aesce

R. Briw

Ynys Witrin

Camlann

One

Dumnonia is the most civilized kingdom in Britain, but in the north-east, in January, it looks no tamer than the wilds of Caledonia. The fields are swallowed by the snow, with only the stubble tips showing pale above the drifts, and the sky is drained of colour and seems to weigh upon the heavens. Beyond the cultivated lands – in the case of my family, beyond the river Fromm – lies the forest, dark branches and white snow mingling to form a lead-grey cloud along the horizon, mile upon mile of silence and the panting of wolves. In the summer, men and women ignore the forest. Fields are tended and the produce is brought to market, the oxen draw the plough, the horses the carts – but in the winter the wilderness hanging beyond the river looms large in the mind. Life is quieter, and a ghost story which a man laughed at in the harvest season suddenly seems horribly probable, for humanity and civilization look very small and light against that ocean of the cold.

My cousin Goronwy and I had no love for going out to the forest in January, but it happened that our householding needed more wood. That meant a trip across the ford with the cart, and two grown men to make it, so we had gone, and spent the noon-tide hacking away at the loose brush, only occasionally pausing to glance over our shoulders. We were glad when we could turn back with the cart piled high. We crossed the river again, and paused on the home bank to let the oxen drink. Goronwy sat holding the goad, looking on the sleek backs of the beasts, who, since we were impatient, must needs take their time.

I looked back across the river. The water of the stream was dark with the winter, and the afternoon sun lay upon it and upon the heaped snow banks, casting horizontal beams that shone like warm bronze but gave no heat. The only sound in the world was the water whispering on the banks and the grunting of the oxen. It was three miles home, back to our householding, three miles back to the cow-byres and hearth-fires and the faces of men. The thought left my heart hungry for it, but I let my eyes drift slowly down the black river and along the trees of the opposite bank. And because of that, I saw the horseman there before he saw me. A glimpse of crimson drew my eyes from the water, and then, a mounted warrior rode openly out onto the river bank in the heavy sunlight.

He had a red cloak wrapped tightly round him, one hand half-extended through its fold to hold the reins. Gold gleamed from his hand, from the fastening of his cloak and the rim of the shield slung over his back; the spears tied to the saddle, and the bridle of his great white stallion caught the light like stars. He reined in his horse by the stream, and together they stood a moment as still as the trees behind them, white and crimson and gold. I felt as if I had just opened my eyes and seen a being from a song I had loved all my life, or a figure from a dream. Then the rider turned his gaze along the river, and met my own stare, and I came back to myself, and knew enough to become afraid.

'Goronwy!' I seized my cousin's arm.

'Well, and what is it...?' He followed my stare and froze.

The rider turned his horse and came up the far bank towards us, the stallion stepping carefully, with a light, clean stride, delicate as a cat's.

'Eeeeh.' Goronwy nudged the oxen with the goad and jumped out of the cart. The beasts snorted, backed up, breath steaming.

'Do you think we can outrun him?' I asked, annoyed with Goronwy and trying to prevent all the wood falling off with the jolts. 'Oxen, against a horse like that one?'

'Perhaps he cannot cross the water.' Goronwy's voice was low.

'You've laughed at tales of the Fair Ones before this.'

'I laughed at home. Sweet Jesu preserve us now!'

'Oh come! He must be a traveller. If he's no bandit, he will only ask the way. And if he's a bandit, there are two of us, and we've nothing more than death to fear.'

'I fear that enough, without the other.' The oxen shambled away from the bank, and Goronwy leapt back into the cart. 'But who'd travel in winter? This far from a road?'

The rider reached the ford and turned his horse to the water. The stream was not deep, and came no higher than the animal's knees, though the horse tossed its head at the coldness. Goronwy gave a little hiss and sat still again. If the rider could cross the water, perhaps he was not a spirit. Or perhaps he was. Either way, we could not outrun him.

He reached the home bank and rode up beside us and, as he did so, the sun dropped below the tree-line and covered us with criss-crossing shadows. I saw more clearly as the dazzle and glitter vanished, and could have cried for disappointment after such a shining vision. The horse, though splendid, had a long, raw gash across its chest, its bones showed through the hide, and its legs and shoulders were streaked with mud. The rider's clothes were very worn, the red cloak tattered and dirty, the hand on the reins purple with cold. His black hair and beard were matted and untrimmed, and he had clearly not washed for a long time. He might be a lost traveller, he might well be a bandit, but...

I met his eyes, and was shaken again. Those eyes were dark as the sea at midnight, and there was something to their look that set the short hairs upright on my neck. I crossed myself, wondering whether Goronwy might be right. My father always said that the tales of the People of the Hills were so many lies, and yet I had never seen a look like that on a human face.

The rider smiled at my gesture, a bitter smile, and leaned over to speak to us. He had drawn his sword, and rested it across his knees so that we could look at it as he spoke. It looked a fine, sharp sword.

'My greetings to you,' said the rider. His voice was hoarse, hardly above a whisper. 'What land is this?'

I saw Goronwy's hand relax a little on the ox-goad, and then he, too, crossed himself before replying, 'Dumnonia, Lord. Near Mor Hafren. Do you ask because you have lost your road?' He was eager to give directions.

The stranger said nothing to the question, only looked at the fields beyond us. 'Dumnonia. What is that river, then?'

'The Fromm. It joins Mor Hafren a bit beyond two miles from here. Lord, there is a Roman road some twelve miles eastwards of here...'

'I do not know of your river. Is the land beyond close-settled?'

'Closely enough.' Goronwy paused. 'Baddon is not far

from here. There is a strong lord there, and his warband.'

The rider smiled bitterly again. 'I am not a bandit, that you must threaten me with kings and warbands.' He looked at us, considering. 'What is your name, man?'

Goronwy rubbed his wrist, looked at the oxen, glanced back at the sword. 'Goronwy ap Cynydd,' he admitted at last.

'So. And you?'

'Rhys ap Sion,' I answered. It might be unwise to offer names, but we could hardly avoid it. I again met the man's eyes, and again I felt cold, and wondered if we were endangering our souls. But I thought the man human. He must be.

'So then, Goronwy ap Cynydd and Rhys ap Sion, I have need of lodgings tonight, for myself and for my horse. How far is it to your householding?'

'My lord, our householding is poor...' Goronwy began, a trifle untruthfully, since we are one of the first clans about Mor Hafren.

'I can pay. How far is it?'

'Three miles,' I said. Goronwy glared at me. 'We are not so poor that we must be inhospitable, Chieftain.' Goronwy stepped on my foot, as though I were too stupid to understand what I was saying, but goaded the oxen, turning them back onto the rough track home. The stranger urged his horse beside us at a slow walk, his drawn sword still ready. The hilt gleamed gold, and a jewel smouldered on it redly.

I looked at that jewel and wondered what would come next. The man might yet be a bandit, but would a bandit have a splendid horse and a jewelled sword? He must be a member of some warband, the servant of either our own king, Constantius of Dumnonia, or of one of the other kings and nobles of Britain. If he was Constantius's man, he probably would leave us in peace, and might even pay us, but if he served anyone else he'd be worse than a bandit. He had said, 'I can pay', but that didn't mean that he would. Still, if he intended violence, there were enough men in the clan to deal with him, even armed as he was and largely unarmed as we were. If he were human. No, he must be human. And he hadn't tried to kill us outright for the price of the cart and oxen, so perhaps he did only want a place to rest for the night. Perhaps he was a messenger, or on some special errand for his own clan, and had left the main road in his haste and become lost. Or perhaps he was recently outlawed. If he was a warrior ... I wondered if we could get him to talk about it. An old longing took hold of me, a thing most clansmen leave behind with their childhood, and which I had tried to leave behind and been unable to, something to do with gold and crimson and the glint of weapons.

'Lord,' I said, after a long silence, 'what road would you wish to be taking, come tomorrow?' It was as good a way as any to ask where he was from and where he was going.

He eyed me suspiciously, but I refused to be frightened. 'That is of no matter,' he said.

'Well, Lord, if you're in need of lodgings, we could tell you something of the roads hence.' Goronwy again kicked me quietly, not daring to tell me openly to be quiet and leave matters be.

'The roads do not matter to me.'

'Well, but they might to your horse.' Goronwy's kick had only made me angry. 'I seek only to be of service, Lord, but it seems your horse would walk the easier for a good feeding.'

He looked down at me, cold and proud, then looked at the arched, white neck of his stallion. He drew the hand that held the reins down the horse's crest, and the animal flicked its ears. 'My horse has strength enough for a charge,' the rider suggested meaningfully, and looked back to me. I thought, though, he seemed rather anxious for the animal. 'But tell me then, Rhys ap Sion, who seeks only to be of service, what way do you think the finest for horses?'

I was uncertain a moment, but recovered myself. 'There is the Roman road, the one from Baddon to Ynys Witrin, past Camlann – and the one eastward, if the road doesn't matter, to the land of the West Saxons, joins the first road to the south. Do you have no lord, Chieftain, to whom you are travelling?'

He smiled his bitter smile again. 'I am the Pendragon's man.'

Goronwy looked up at him sharply, catching his breath. The Pendragon was Arthur ab Uther, 'Imperator Britanniae', in the old title, 'Emperor of Britain'. His warband was said to be the finest west of Constantinople. Not two years before, the Saxon invaders had been stopped, their strength shattered for some generations to come, at the great battle of Baddon. This had been worked by the Pendragon and his warband, then and in the years before. Since that time, some members of the great warband had gone back to their own lands, some had been set by their king to fighting the hordes of bandits in the west of the country, and some had gone over to Gaul to aid Arthur's allies there, while many stayed with the Emperor at his fortress of Camlann. All the members of the warband were nobles, able to speak their mind to any king in the island, to command their share from the tribute paid to Arthur by the other rulers of Britain. Some of them were rulers in their own right. It was unexpected to have one of these men turn up in our own land, and that in mid-winter. I thought of what I had felt when I first saw this man, that he could have come from a favourite song. If he was of Arthur's Family he probably did.

'May the due honour be yours, then, Lord,' I said. 'And I am not one to withhold it.'

He looked at me keenly. 'You feel no anger, then, for the Pendragon who raised your taxes?'

'None, Lord, for the Emperor who broke the power of the Saxons.'

He smiled with a little less bitterness.

'If you are indeed the Pendragon's man, what brings you here?' Goronwy demanded, glaring both at me and at the other.

The rider glared back, cold and proud again. 'It is not yours to question, man. Mind your oxen.' He turned his eyes on the track ahead of us. Inwardly I cursed Goronwy, and I kicked him surreptitiously for his pains. He had shut the man up just when he seemed to be relaxing a little. I knew better than to suppose the direction about oxen was meant solely for Goronwy. Yet Goronwy surely had no more authority than I. My father, not Goronwy's, was head of the householding, and my father was generally inclined to support the Emperor, if with some reservations. Perhaps, if we gave him hospitality, the stranger would feel himself among friends and speak more freely. I wanted to hear him talk. Like a boy, I wanted to hear about Arthur's warband, the Family; about battles and kings and the struggle against the barbarian darkness. I wanted it like any child or like a man too stupid to know the difference between a pretty tale and the grasping, violent men whom kings and warriors are most like to really be. I had always wanted to hear about those things, even when I knew myself a fool for wanting to, even when I was good at everything a farmer and clansman should be good at, and was too old to want such things, and had no call in my life for wanting. I had even wanted to be a warrior. But men must be trained in that trade from their early boyhood, and they not infrequently begin fighting while no more than children of fourteen. Yes, and they die before they are twenty. But once I had thought that death might be worth it, and still, this man had but to ride across a river and I wanted it all again.

It would probably be better if this stranger said nothing. I had had trouble enough with my wantings before, and surely I was settling down now, with time. There was no call to stir the old demon up again. I was twenty-one, not old, but too much of an adult to run mad with the fancies of children.

The rest of our three miles passed in silence. The sun set in clouds, and the stars were clouding over. The wind was cold in our faces, stinging the eyes to tears. The warrior huddled in his cloak, finally sheathing his sword, though I noticed he kept one hand on it. My teeth were chattering when we reached the long, low-lying buildings of home and smelt the warm fires and food.

I jumped out of the cart at my own family's house, telling Goronwy to wait. He agreed with a grunt, though he looked at our guest nervously. The stranger merely held his horse steady and looked at Goronwy and at the door.

My mother and the elder of my sisters were by the fire, cooking. My younger brother Dafydd sat playing with the dog, while my grandfather talked to him. They all looked up as I opened the door.

My mother smiled. 'Well, then, Rhys. We had thought the forest swallowed you. But we've kept dinner despite that. Was it good wood you found?'

'Good enough. But we found more than wood, Mother. Where is my father?'

'In the barn. But what is it?'

'You'll know soon enough. Stay indoors.' At this suggestive statement, my brother jumped up and began demanding, and two cousins ran up from some corner to see what about, but I grinned and ducked back out.

When I came into the barn my father was brushing down our little brown mare, the one that draws the cart in summer. He was humming softly, his thick hands quick and sure and gentle. I paused a moment, hand on the door, looking at his thick-set figure and wondering what he would do. My father is the head of our householding, of our family: all the descendants, to the fourth generation, of Huw ap Celyn, some thirty-seven people in all. Our clan is not a high-ranking one, but we are prosperous enough, and recognized over the land south of Mor Hafren in Dumnonia. My father could speak in any quarrel and be heard, and men from other clans and householdings would come to ask his advice on crops and taxes and what to do about their neighbours' habits. He had always supported the policy of the Pendragon, and whenever others talked about refusing to pay the higher tribute which Arthur's warband required, he'd defend the Empire – but that was a different matter from taking a member of that warband as a guest, under constraint. My father never liked doing anything under constraint, and we were strong enough to dispose of one warrior. Still, we were a Christian householding, and my father was a Christian man, and believed in hospitality (within reason) and in courtesy. I shut the door quietly and walked towards him across the beaten earth floor.

'Well, Rhys, and have you stored the wood?' my father asked, without turning around.

'Never mind the wood. Father, Goronwy and I met up with a warrior. He says he's of Arthur's Family, and he wants lodgings for tonight. For himself and for his war-horse.'

My father set down the straw he was using as a brush, straightened and turned deliberately, meeting my eyes. 'Indeed. Where did you meet him?'

'At the ford. He crossed the river shortly after us.'

'From the forest? Alone?'

'Yes. But he is not equipped like a bandit.'

'Armed?'

'Well armed, I think. And I've never seen a horse as fine as his.'

'Where is he?'

'In front of the house, with Goronwy and the cart.'

My father caught up his lantern and walked out of the barn. I followed him.

The warrior was still sitting on his stallion, waiting, and Goronwy still looked uneasy. As we came up, I noticed that the door was open a crack, the firelight bright in it. My family was watching.

My father lifted the lantern high, trying to see the face of the dark, mounted figure. He was tense, I could feel it, but his face in the lamplight was calm and steady. The light made his red hair, grey-streaked as it was, look dark, and it cast his bright blue eyes into shadow. He looked young and strong, firm in his authority.

The warrior stared at him, eyes glinting through his tangled black hair. Then, slowly, he dismounted, steadied himself with one hand on his horse's shoulder. He half raised the other hand.

'Sion ap Rhys.' He named my father in his hoarse voice.

'Gwalchmai ap Lot,' said my father. 'Ach, I did not think you would remember.'

'I told you I would. This is your householding, then?'

'I am the head of it.' My father slowly walked closer to the other, stopped. 'And such as it is, Lord Gwalchmai, you're free and welcome to the use of it; indeed, the family is honoured. Rhys!' He half turned to me. 'You and Goronwy get the wood unloaded and the oxen stalled. Lord Gwalchmai,' he turned back to the other. 'Come into the house and rest.'

'My horse,' said the other. 'I must see to my horse first.'

'Rhys can . . .'

'I look after him myself.'

'Oh, very well. The barn is this way, Lord. Rhys, first tell your mother to get something special on for dinner – some of the ham, at least, and eggs, certainly eggs, and some of the apples – ach, she'll know better than I. But some hot water? Yes, hot water. Well, go on then!' He started back to the barn, and the other followed, leading his horse, limping a little.

I hesitated, then ran to the house, gasped out my father's message – unnecessarily, since the eavesdroppers had heard it themselves – ran back to the cart, leapt in, and told

Goronwy to hurry up.

'But I don't understand it,' complained Goronwy as he goaded the oxen, and then began to shamble towards the wood pile. 'My uncle Sion knows that warrior?'

I shook my head, in astonishment rather than in denial. My father had said many things about the Pendragon, his warband and his policies, but the strangest was that once, as he was taking some wheat down to Camlann to sell it there, he'd given a ride in the cart to a young man whom he later discovered to be Gwalchmai, son of Lot, king of the Ynysoedd Erch, those islands north of Caledonia. The two had talked somewhat on the way, and my father had paid the other's lodgings for a night, ignorant of the other's identity. Afterwards he discovered that the youth had just escaped from the Saxons, and was on his way to Camlann to join the Family. 'I knew, talking to him, that he would be a great warrior,' my father would say when he told the story. 'And I asked him to remember me. And that is pure pride, wanting to be known by a famous and glorious lord. But see, he is a great warrior. He was a good lad when I met him. Quiet, courteous, generous – perhaps a little uncanny, but . . . I wonder if he does remember me. I doubt it.'

It was nine years since my father first told that tale. Then he had just returned from the journey, and Gwalchmai ap Lot was still an unknown. By the end of that same summer he was spoken and sung of over all Britain. Numerous tales, of varying probability, were told of him. He was said to have tamed one of the horses of the Fair Folk, an immortal animal faster than the wind, that none could ride but he alone. He was said to have an enchanted sword, and to triple his strength in battle. He could, it was said, cut down three men with one blow; nothing could stand before him. He was a favoured ambassador of the Emperor, because of his courtesy and eloquence: they said he could charm honey from the bees or water from a stone. Whatever one chose to believe, he was one of the finest, probably the very finest, of Arthur's Family, which meant the best warrior in Britain, and, though it was generally agreed that there was something 'a little uncanny' about him, he was admired from Caledonia to Gaul. But he remembered my father Sion, and he would be staying in our own householding as a guest.

'You've heard my father's tale,' I told Goronwy. 'That is

the lord Gwalchmai ap Lot.'

Goronwy eyed me and muttered something. I didn't ask what. I knew well enough he thought me rather mad, and likely he was right, but I was too excited to care. I do not think wood was ever unloaded faster than I unloaded it then, and when the cart was empty, I left it and the oxen to Goronwy. They were, after all, his father's oxen, not mine. I ran back to the house and, finding that my father and the lord Gwalchmai were still at the barn, I ran there, ostensibly to see if they needed help.

Our brown mare had been moved, and the white stallion had her place. My father had poured out some grain and the horse was eating this as his master rubbed him down, slowly and stiffly as though the man were very tired. As I came up, he stopped, and asked me quietly if I could bring some hot water from the house.

'You don't need to bathe the beast,' my father commented.

'He has been hurt. I need to keep the wound clean,' Gwalchmai replied. 'Softly, Ceincaled, *mo chroidh* . . .' he spoke soothingly to the horse in a language which I guessed was Irish. The men of the Ynysoedd Erch came from Ireland a generation or so ago.

I brought the hot water from the house and he cleaned the slash across the horse's chest with it, still speaking to the animal in Irish. I wondered if it did understand, if it was truly one of the horses of the Fair Folk. It looked large and strong and swift enough.

'The cut is recent,' observed my father.

'We were fighting but yesterday afternoon.' The lord Gwalchmai finished with the horse's wound and began checking and cleaning the animal's hooves.

My father fidgeted. 'You did not have the horse when I met you.'

The warrior looked up, and suddenly looked less uncanny. Almost, he smiled. 'I had forgotten that. Yes, I let him go after I escaped from the Saxons with him. But he was a fool and came back to me at Camlann.'

'A fool?'

'Well, he is not a horse from this earth. He is a fool to stay here and have spears thrust into him for my sake.' He picked up the stallion's off hind foot and frowned at the rim of the hoof, checking the shoe. Even I could see that the metal was worn. The horse lifted its head from the manger, glanced back, then resumed eating. Gwalchmai sighed and, setting the hoof down, stood up. 'He is overworn.' He slapped the stallion's rump. 'Perhaps I should stay here with him tonight.'

My father was offended. 'You'll do no such thing. Haven't I just told my wife to cook a special meal, and all because we've you as a guest? The horse will be fine. I think, my lord Gwalchmai, you're more overworn than he is.'

The lord Gwalchmai stared at him.

'By all the saints in heaven!' said my father. 'Are you grown too proud to accept my hospitality?'

Gwalchmai made an averting gesture. 'Not so, Sion ap Rhys, indeed! It is only . . .' He stopped abruptly, then went on, 'Well, the horse will be fine, then, and I thank you for your hospitality.' He patted the horse again, said something else to it in Irish, picked up some saddle-bags, and the three of us walked up the hill to the house.

My mother had the meal nearly ready: fresh bread with sweet butter; apples, cheese and strong, dark ale were already on the table. A pot of ham and barley stew was cooking over the fire, and I could smell the honey cakes baking. Everyone in the house was waiting around the hearth: my aunt, with her three children (her husband had died some six years before); my two sisters, my brother, my grandfather and my mother. The rest of the clan, in the two other houses of our holding, were going to have to do without ham and barley stew, and come and see the guest in the morning.

My father introduced everyone, and the lord Gwalchmai bowed politely. There was silence and an uneasy shuffling of feet, and then my mother asked Gwalchmai if he wished to put his cloak aside, or wash before dinner. There was time, she said, before the stew was done. Gwalchmai stepped back a little, stiffly, shaking his head, so my sister Morfudd brought him some ale, and a place was made for him by the fire. My father seized a piece of the bread, smeared it with butter, and sat down, eating it enthusiastically.

'It's best while it's warm,' he told Gwalchmai. The warrior nodded, and leaned sideways against the roof-tree.

After a little while, he loosed the brooch that held his cloak, as though he felt the heat. 'More overworn than the horse,' my father had said. It was true: the man looked near to dropping. 'We were fighting but yesterday afternoon' – it was not good weather to be fighting in, nor to travel in, for that matter. I wondered whom he had fought. There are plenty of bandits about to the north-west. Even in the summer I would take a spear if I had to go up the north road very far.

The stew had finished cooking and, when my father had asked the blessing, we crossed ourselves and set to. The stew was delicious, the honey cakes as good as they smelled, and everyone except the guest ate eagerly. Gwalchmai, though he complimented my mother very nicely and asked courteous questions about the holding, ate very little, and that slowly.

When we were finished, and the meal had been cleared away, my mother looked at the lord Gwalchmai and shook her head. 'My lord, do give me that cloak a moment,' she pleaded. 'That's a great tear you have in it. I'll mend it for you.' As he shook his head and began a refusal, she wrinkled her nose and added, 'And the rest of your things could stand some mending and a good wash, my lord. Rhys, why don't you get some of your other clothes, so I can wash the lord Gwalchmai's?'

I was a bit shocked by my mother's forwardness, but the lord Gwalchmai only said, 'There would not be time for them to dry. I must leave tomorrow morning.'

'Tomorrow morning? Well, if I hang them by the fire, they can dry by midmorning, and certainly you can stay till then. But you must stay longer, indeed you must. You are not well enough to travel in such weather.'

'I am well enough. I must leave early. Just show me where I can sleep.'

'Let me mend the tear in your cloak, then, at the very least. Come, it lets in the wind to chill you, and the snow to drench you, and I can mend it in no time.'

When Gwalchmai began another polite refusal, my mother, exasperated, seized the cloak by the front, unpinned it, and took it away from him. He stood back, hand dropping to the gold hilt of his sword. I noticed the glint of his chain mail under the woollen over-tunic – then noticed that the tunic was slashed and unravelling across the ribs, and that the edges of the tear were stained a darker red. My father also noticed it.

'So-o-o,' he said, surprised. 'Your horse wasn't the only one to take a spear thrust.'

Gwalchmai backed quickly to the roof-tree and drew his sword half out of the sheath. The blade gleamed with an unnatural brightness in the flickering light.

My father stood where he was, the blood slowly rising to his face, making it dark with anger. My mother looked at him, not at Gwalchmai, the cloak still in her hands. I looked around for a weapon.

'You have your hand on your sword,' my father pointed out in a level voice. I knew that voice: when I was a boy, it had usually preceded a thrashing for me.

Gwalchmai made no reply. Only his eyes moved, quickly checking the room, fixing on my father.

'You can put the thing away,' said my father. 'I knew you for two days, nine years ago, but I believe that in that time you consecrated the thing at Ynys Witrin. You should not be so ready to let blood with a consecrated weapon. Especially the blood of your host.'

Gwalchmai flushed slightly, and stared at my father for a long moment. Then, abruptly, he sheathed the sword. His hand dropped from its hilt and hung loosely by his side.

My father hurried over to him. 'Let me see this wound of yours.'

The warrior looked at him a moment, then made a helpless gesture and began unfastening the tunic. My mother, lips pressed firmly together in disapproval, put some water over the fire to heat.

It was a painful-looking wound, a slash across the ribs on his right side. Gwalchmai drew his under-tunic off over it carefully, and set the garment on top of the mail-coat. His torso was criss-crossed with old scars already, more than I cared to think about receiving, mostly on the right side of his body. My mother shook her head, took a clean cloth and began cleaning the cut. She paused a moment, and he sat down by the fire. He was thin, and shivered a little. The look on his face was terrible: exhaustion and humiliation and, almost, despair.

'Why did you try to hide it?' my father demanded angrily. 'You can't go travelling with that. You will have to stay here.'

Gwalchmai shrugged, winced at the movement. 'I have already travelled with it. Most of today. I . . . well, most . . . farmers would . . . kill a man of Arthur's, if they knew it were safe to try. Ach, almost everyone this side of Britain hates the High King.'

My father's face again grew dark with anger. 'I would not kill a guest of mine if he were my worst enemy, even if he were fit and strong and ready to do me injury, and not sick and wounded. I am not like to kill a man I met as a friend, no matter who his lord is. And I support the Emperor.'

Gwalchmai looked up at him steadily, then, very slowly, he smiled. 'Forgive me. I did not even think, nor pause to look at you. You would not.' He drew a deep, sobbing breath. 'It has been a long, long time.'

'Since I met you?'

'I was not even a warrior thén. One forgets how people act. Ah God, Sion, I am weary.'

'Stay here, then, till you are rested.'

'I will pay you.'

'Sweet Jesu be mèrciful! When a guest of mine pays me, I will sow my fields with salt, so witness me Almighty God, and all the saints and angels.'

Gwalchmai smiled again, and a light seemed to touch his dark eyes. 'I had forgotten such people,' he said, very softly, to himself more than to us. 'And I deserve nothing of it. Sweet Jesus is indeed merciful.'

I sat and looked at him as he sat cross-legged in the red light of the fire, with my mother bandaging the wound. Not what I'd expected for so glorious a warrior. I realized, as I looked, that he could not be too much older than myself. His face, under the dirt and matted hair, was still young and very good-looking. But it was already marked by pain and disappointment. He seemed so much older, so suspicious and controlled until now. I looked about at my family, a close circle in half-light and warm shadow. Yes, it was good. I could afford to be young; I had one place, a good place, a place worthy of love.

But yet something in my heart felt like a sparrow caught in a house, which flutters about the eaves, looking for the clear sky and the wind.

Two

The lord Gwalchmai slept very late the next morning. When he woke, he bathed, washed and trimmed his hair and beard, and put on some of my clothing to go and look at his horse. My trousers and tunic were loose on him, and just a bit long as well, but my mother had confiscated his own things and was working on them, shaking her head over their condition as she worked.

The white stallion stood comfortably in our barn, devouring our grain and ignoring all the other animals there except our brown mare. Gwalchmai argued with my father about the grain.

'The cost of the grain must fall to me, Sion. Warhorses are costly to keep, a luxury for their owner. No host is obliged to provide luxuries for his guest.'

'A warhorse is no luxury for a warrior who fights from horseback. I have the grain; let him eat it.' And my father kept his stand, despite the other's persuasive arguments.

The warrior also checked his mount's hooves again, and again looked concerned over the shoes. 'Is there any blacksmith nearby?' he asked, hopefully.

'None professionally, at this time of year. Some come by when the weather's warmer, and set up their stalls on market days. But we could shoe your horse for you. My nephew Goronwy's a fair hand at that.'

'It would be well if he could. And could he also, perhaps, mend my coat of mail?'

'Ah, that's harder. Very hard, I should think.'

'It need not be a complete repair just now. Simply a few links worked in sideways to keep the rest together, on the line where the spear broke it.'

'You can tell Goronwy what you want, and see.'

Gwalchmai nodded, and we started back to the house. My father excused himself outside the barn and went to check on the cattle in the byres.

'How did the spear break the mail?' I found myself asking, as we trudged up the hill. 'I thought chain mail would keep a man safe.'

'It was a thrusting spear.' I must have looked blank, because Gwalchmai suddenly smiled and explained. 'Chain mail will keep off throwing spears, provided you're not too close to the thrower of them, and it can turn the edge of a sword or knife if the blow is shallow. But a thrusting spear, or the point of a sword, or a hard straight blow with a good sword, will cut mail like leather. You'd expect more of the stuff, knowing the price of it, wouldn't you? Still, it's a deal better than the next best.'

'How much did you pay for yours?' I asked, curious.

'I didn't buy it. I took it from a Saxon chieftain.'

After killing him, of course. A hard, straight blow with a good sword? I looked at the jewelled hilt of Gwalchmai's sword, glowing against the grey of my second-best over-tunic. The gear of war has a beauty which had spun a glitter of steel and bronze and bright banners over all my thoughts of it, ever since I first saw a party of warriors ride down the south road from Caer Legion to Camlann one summer morning. But, after all, that gear and glitter were only the tools of a trade, and that trade was killing or being killed. Why should I consider it glorious? I was old enough to know better.

The sword was still very beautiful.

Gwalchmai ate somewhat more that evening than he had the night before. He thanked my mother for the meal, very courteously. The hoarseness was gone from his voice, but he still spoke softly. Morfudd, the elder of my sisters, was very quick to notice anything he might need, and watched him, demurely but with a glint in her eyes. I knew she would discuss him with my other sister later. I could see why a woman would. I suddenly thought of my own face in contrast. Not the sort, I feared, to inspire that kind of look from women. More the kind that evokes sisterly confidences, and from women other than my sisters. No, not ugly, but big-boned, red-headed and blue-eyed like my father, and irregularly freckled in summer. Everyone always observed that I looked honest. An honest farmer, of a reasonably prosperous clan, of an age to settle down with some honest wife and continue the clan. Gwalchmai's face was fine-featured, with high cheek bones and dark eyes, his beard, now trimmed down close to the jaw, making his face look even narrower. He looked like what he was, a warrior and twice royal. Why should I feel that that was so much more than what I was? Britain could do without warriors more easily than without farmers, and kings and their clans come and go, while my clan had farmed the land around Mor Hafren before the Romans came.

But with Britain as it was now, if the warriors had not fought, the only farmers about Mor Hafren would be Saxons, and I and my clan, if we lived and stayed free, would be looking for land among the mountains of Gwynedd, or across the sea in Less Britain. The Pendragon had saved us, and the man who sat across the table from me refusing the ale Morfudd was offering him, he had fought against the darkness. . . .

I was the one who ate only a little at that meal. My mother gave me a hard look as she took away my plate, a 'come-and-tell-me-about-it-later' look. I wondered if I could. 'Mother, when this warrior goes off again, I want to go with him. I want to see Camlann and Saxons and war; I want to abandon my family for the sort of thing this Gwalchmai has embittered himself with.' No, it would not do. It was a child's plea, an absurdity, and it was impossible anyway. It was just as unlikely that Gwalchmai would be willing to take me as that my mother would be willing to let me go.

We sat down by the hearth fire, and Gwalchmai asked my father polite questions about the householding and the clan, and the land around Mor Hafren, and the last harvest, and listened very attentively to the answers. It took my father a while to work the talk about to his own questions. He eventually did it, though.

'. . . set them out to pasture when the snow isn't too deep, even in the mid-winter. But now, well, too cold for anything of the kind, and they won't leave the byre. Cleverer than humans that way. Or than some humans.'

'I am not clever, then?' Gwalchmai looked serious, but his eyes were a trifle too bright.

'You are travelling at a time when sensible men sit by the fire.'

'I am sitting by the fire now.'

'But what we had to do to put you there! Truly, lord Gwalchmai, when did you set out, and why?'

'As to the when at the beginning of November; as to the

294

why – I am looking for a woman. She may have come this way, eight years ago, in the late autumn. A fair-haired woman, who rode a brown mare and was followed by two servants, one of them an old man with half an ear missing. She had blue eyes, may have worn blue, and spoke with a northern accent.'

'A noblewoman?' asked my father. 'No, I've not seen nor heard of such a woman. But why are you looking for her?'

'I . . . owe her something. I have not had the opportunity of repaying her, while the war lasted, and now that we have peace in Britain, I am trying to find her again.'

'In the middle of winter? Who is she?'

Gwalchmai looked down. 'Sion, it is a complicated tale, and a long one, and one not greatly to my credit.'

My father shrugged, fumbled at the foot of his stool, and picked up a piece of wood he had been carving into a cup. 'As you please. But, if the tale is long, we've this night and the next, and on till that wound of yours is healed, my lord.' He stopped, his eyes meeting Gwalchmai's. 'Why does it trouble you so?'

Gwalchmai smiled. 'Because it is a bitter memory.' We were quiet for a moment, and then he went on abruptly. 'I loved that woman once, and wronged her.'

My father eyed his cup, and began to whittle at the rim, studiously avoiding Gwalchmai's eyes. 'And you still love her?'

'As God witnesses me, yes. But I must seek her forgiveness at the least. I did not ask it when we parted, and I had brought great suffering onto her.' There was another long silence. Gwalchmai looked at his hands, the long fingers twined together on his knees. 'You've a right to hear the tale, Sion ap Rhys, if you wish it. I've no right to conceal the matter to save my pride, or to preserve an honour which I forfeited to her. And I also owe you a debt.'

'Mm. Of trust,' said my father, beginning to carve properly. The knife made a soft *chk*-ing sound. 'I should like to hear the tale.'

Gwalchmai looked up and into the fire, as men do when they summon their memories of an event, and wonder how to set the words to it. He rubbed the palm of his sword hand against his knee, slowly, as though something clung to it.

'I suppose, then, that it began in the spring, eight years

ago,' he said. The wind rustled in the thatch, and my mother's needle glinted as she sewed. Gwalchmai straightened and sat motionless, eyes still fixed on the fire. 'Eight years ago, in the spring of the year, my lord Arthur sent me on an embassy to Caer Ebrauc. The old king, Caradoc, had died, and his nephew Bran ap Caw, the eldest of the twelve sons of Caw, succeeded him. All the sons of Caw were enemies of Arthur over some blood feud begun when my lord seized the High Kingship, so my lord feared that Bran might begin a rebellion. This was during our northern campaign against the Saxons of Deira and Bernicia and the other northern kingdoms. The campaign had till then gone well, and the Saxons were feeling the force of our raids, but to no greater degree than that which made them determined to have revenge on us. They were as much stronger than us as they ever were, especially when they leagued together, but we had moved about, striking where they least expected it, and raided until they had had to go hungry a bit that winter. It would take another year at least, though, before they would have to make and keep terms, and a rebellion by one of the British kingdoms at that point could be fatal to us. My lord had to send an ambassador to Bran to try his mind, and to conciliate him. He chose me.'

'You were fairly young at the time.' My father gave him a sharp look. 'That was only a year after I met you.'

'I was just eighteen.' Gwalchmai smiled. 'But my lord had to send one of his best warriors, or Bran would be insulted. He couldn't send Cei or Gereint or my brother Agravain, because they'd be liable to throw wine in Bran's face the moment he hinted any insult to Arthur, which would hardly conciliate the man. He couldn't send Bedwyr, because he is a Breton and only moderately well-born – though a nobler man never breathed upon the earth – and Bran could be insulted at that, if he chose to be. He told me all this when I pointed out that I was too young. He sent me.'

'Gwalchmai the Golden-tongued,' murmured Morfudd coyly.

He laughed, glancing at her. 'Cei first called me that as a joke. Well, I set out for Caer Ebrauc from King Urien's fortress in Rheged, I, and two others from Arthur's Family. The roads were bad, and it took us some seven days, though we all had fine horses. The apple trees were beginning to blossom, though, and the woods were becoming green. My horse Ceincaled ran like the sun on the waves. I thought it very good to be alive, to be young, to be Arthur's warrior – the last was still new to me. I had no great concern for Bran of Llys Ebrauc. I could not in my heart see how any man in Britain could oppose Arthur and his Family. There is no one like my lord Arthur the High King, and no war-leader so great in all Britain.

'But, when we reached Caer Ebrauc, I began to see that Bran might be a danger after all. The city is one that the Romans built to keep their legions in, and it has a great wall, still strongly fortified, and a great deal of room for war-riors, while the land about it is rich and well populated. The town behind the wall is more than half abandoned, like any other town this age, but it is prosperous enough. The king's warband stays in one of the old Roman barracks, instead of in a feast hall or their own houses. It is a large warband. Mostly foot fighters, not cavalry, but still, some five hundred trained, well-armed warriors. And Ebrauc could also raise an army from the subject clans, while Arthur had to rely on his subject kings for that, and they are not easily to be relied upon. I rode into Caer Ebrauc with greater care than that with which I had ridden up to it.

'Bran lived in the palace of some ancient Roman com-mander, which had last been repaired by some vicar of the north a century or so ago. I and the others would stay with him, as fitted our rank. We stopped in front of this palace, gave our horses to the grooms, and tried to see that our luggage was put somewhere safe before we went in to see Bran. While we were busy arguing with the servants, a girl came out of the palace and went over to the grooms to see that the horses were stabled.'

He fell silent for a moment, then shook his head. 'The sunlight was as clear as spring water over clean sand, and the doves were cooing on the broken tiles of the roof. She walked like the shadow of a bird on a clear stream. Her hair was the colour of broom flowers. When she reached the horses, she felt my eyes on her, and turned around, and blushed when she saw me watching. Then, the servants had the luggage, and we were being shown in to the king.

'I felt like a harp-string which has just been plucked. I

wanted to make a song about the way she moved. I think my blood was singing. But I had to still myself to speak with Bran.'

'Was she very beautiful?' asked Morfudd eagerly. My mother looked at her sharply. Gwalchmai stared a moment, then looked away and shrugged.

'She seemed so to me. Others have told me, no.' He paused, and added harshly, 'Her nose was too long, her teeth too big, and she was thin as a fence post.'

'But you said . . .'

'I said! Well, but there was the way she moved, the way she lifted her skirts to run a little, and turned her head, and the light that slid across her face when she smiled. Let her stand still, and you might call her plain; but when she moved, or spoke, she was like a skylark above the hills. She it was that made herself beautiful, not the beauty given by nature.'

He looked back at the fire, clenching his fists, and spoke as though it caused pain – which, for a man such as he, it doubtless did. 'And that was all. I wanted to see her again, and thought that I desired her, but I didn't particularly care if I knew her name. It was the way we talk of such things. I had never . . . well, she made me feel a great thing, but I had no thought that she could feel, too. God forgive me, but I wanted to enjoy myself and give nothing.'

Gwalchmai gave my father a straight, fierce look, then unclenched his hands, rubbed them together and went on. 'I went and talked to Bran of Llys Ebrauc. It was a fine combat of words. He kept suggesting or hinting deadly insults, and I kept twisting them about into straightforward questions or harmless comments, and both of us hinted at the political implications unceasingly. In the end, Bran asked me how long I intended to stay. My lord had told me, "Stay there as long as the situation requires", and it was plain to me that the situation required me to watch Bran constantly. So I replied, "By your leave, I will stay until my lord enjoins my return." Bran didn't like it. He knew that he couldn't prepare any rebellion while I remained in Ebrauc, and he did not dare to order me killed, for fear of my lord's vengeance. I could see him trying to think of some way he could say that I had insulted him, so that he could command me to leave; but he had no reasonable pretext. So he told me he would give a feast that night, to welcome me, and that all of his were mine for the using, and so on. I was glad to get away from him. But, when I lay down to rest before the feast, I thought again of the girl. It seemed to me that she must be one of Bran's servants: she had been plainly dressed, and had seen to the horses. Bran had made an offer of hospitality, and I thought, "If we must stay a while, perhaps I will take him up on it." I fell asleep wondering what she would look like when she smiled.

'She was, indeed, at the feast. She came in on the left side of the hall, to pour the wine for the high table, and she wore a dress of blue silk fastened with gold, and more gold in her hair. Bran smiled at her, and said, half-laughing, "Why, the moon is rising!" and she smiled back and filled his glass. The man next to me whispered, "That is Elidan, daughter of Caw, the king's sister."

'And that, I told myself, is that. I could spend my time with serving girls, if I pleased, but Elidan, daughter of Caw, the king's sister, was not to be touched, and most especially not to be touched by her brother's enemy.

'She poured the wine, and sat down beside Bran, taking the queen's part, since his own wife was dead in childbirth. After a little while, she rose again to refill the glasses, and when she came to pour for me, some of the wine spilled. She gave a little gasp and nearly dropped the jug. I caught the side of it to steady it, and my hand touched hers, my eyes meeting hers as I looked up. She blushed again, and I could feel the trembling in her hand. The wine shivered, light and dark rippling on its surface.

'I let go the jug. After a moment, she filled my glass, curt-seyed and went on down the table. I watched her as she went, and my blood was singing again.

'We stayed at Ebrauc, and Bran and Bran's people by and large ignored us. Some tried to quarrel, but both the men I had chosen to come with me knew how to pretend they hadn't heard, or even that they didn't care. Still, it was no pleasant place for us, and I wished fiercely to be back with my lord Arthur, fighting. I knew that the Family had been gathered, and had raised the standard and ridden off to war. They were all there, my brother Agravain, my friends Cei, Bedwyr and the rest; and I sat about at Llys Ebrauc, a dead weight on the earth. I knew that Arthur wanted me where I was, and that it was an honour to be trusted with such a task – but it was early May! I could have killed from sheer frustration.

'And then I had a chance meeting with Elidan, and forgot all else.

'About a week after my arrival, I went to the stables to see to my horse, and she was there, looking at the horse. I had not seen her since the feast. When I came up, she blushed again, and backed off from the stall.

'"You needn't be afraid," I told her, "he won't hurt you." She looked at me, gave a little bow with her head, and stood still. I went into the stall and caught Ceincaled's halter, and he snorted and nuzzled my wrist. "See?" I told the girl. "He is very gentle." Still she said nothing. "Would you like to come and see him?"

'She edged closer slowly, coming into the stall on the opposite side of the horse. Very carefully, she put out a hand to pat his neck. He eyed her and flicked his ears forward, and she smiled. I thought it was the first time my eyes opened, when I saw her smile.

'"Is this Ceincaled?" she asked, in a low voice like the sound of a soft note on the pipes. "Is it true that he is of no mortal breed?"

'I told her yes, it was true, and, when she questioned me and smiled again, I told her the whole story. I am not in the habit of telling it, and certainly not as I told it then, to impress. But it had charm enough for her, and she listened with her eyes shining and her lips slightly parted.

'"So I am blessed with the finest of horses," I told her, when I finished the tale, and, before I myself knew what I was saying, I went on, "Though he needs exercising, as any other. Do you know of a good place to ride, my lady?" "There's Herfydd's Wood," she replied. "A very lovely place. There are open meadows in it, too, where horses can run." And then she paused, and added, "I am taking my mare there this afternoon, if you wish me to point out the way." "I would indeed wish it, and would be grateful," I said. "And grateful also if you would show me this wood." She stammered an assent.

'There was nothing in this beyond courtesy, nothing to make anyone suspect. She had her servants with her the while. But we could talk. It was a glorious ride. I have no recollection of what we spoke of, merely that I talked a great deal and made her laugh. Her laugh was like the flutter of a bird's wing, and it set my mind flying. When we returned to Ebrauc, I asked her if she knew of other good places to ride in, for, though I had enjoyed Herfydd's Wood, variety is a pleasure. She said yes, there was Bryn Nerth, which she could show me, if I wished. Thus we rode together the next day, and the next, and the next as well. The world seemed to me like the laughter of sunlight in the trees, all shimmer and light dancing.

'But after five days of this, at the time we had set for our ride, she appeared with a set, chilled face and told me that she could not take her mare out that day. I argued with her, and she made excuses and left. I went out alone in the end, very angry, and rode at a full gallop until Ceincaled was sweating and eager to stop, and that is a long way. It was plain enough why she had not come. Bran had begun to suspect – not remarkably – that this riding together was not just courtesy; and he had spoken to Elidan, had warned her or commanded her against me. I told myself that I shouldn't have asked her to come with me in the first place. It was madness to desire her, and to cherish the hopes I did. Her brother was very fond of her – and she was fond of Bran, if it came to that. Even if my interest had been in anything permanent, which it was not, still it would have been impossible. One cannot contract marriage alliances with one's lord's enemies. And if it were not a marriage, Bran would have good reasons in his rebellion. I owed it to my lord Arthur, to my honour as a guest and an emissary and her respect as a Christian noblewoman to leave the girl alone.

'I resolved to be no more than courteous, and I kept my resolve, too – for a week or so. But I held her at night in my dreams, and when I played the harp alone I found myself singing of her, and I began to wonder how we could fool Bran; and I could think of many ways. And then one day I saw her in a corridor in the palace, alone, and without thinking I seized her wrist and said, "I will be riding in Herfydd's Wood tomorrow after lunch," very softly into her ear. I let her go and walked on, feeling her eyes on me as I went. I cursed myself afterwards for saying that, and resolved that I would not go to the wood the next day. But I went. I spent an hour or so riding about the wood, alone, then turned back in disgust – and met her near the wood's edge. She had only one servant with her, an old man with half an ear missing, and he wore a look of great reluctance.

'I leapt from my horse and ran over to catch her mare's bridle. "You came," I said: it was all I could say. She looked down at me gravely and nodded, then let go the reins, kicked one foot from the stirrup and jumped from her horse. I caught her as she jumped. The wind touched her hair, but her eyes were still, stiller than the sky and as deep. I felt as though the force that drives life itself had touched us, that we stood between earth and heaven. I could feel her heart beating through her ribs as I held her, like the heart of a wild swallow, and I was filled with the wonder of it. All was astonishment. We stood and looked at one another, and it was as though we looked into a gulf of light, a fire burning beyond the deep places of the world, or gazed at each other through the blur-edged reality of some vision. But she was there, and in my arms, a thin, strong body and solemn blue eyes and straight fair hair. "You came," I said again, and I kissed her.

'"Yes," she said. "I came." She turned to the servant and said, "Hywel, could you stay here and watch the horses?"

'The old man nodded unhappily, and we walked off together into the green silence of the forest.'

Gwalchmai fell silent, and sat resting his head on his arms, leaning forward to stare at the low fire on the hearth. My father was motionless, his carving knife a still line of brightness in his hand. Only the wind still made its hollow sound in the thatch.

Morfudd stirred first. 'I think that is beautiful,' she said dreamily. 'Beautiful.'

Gwalchmai straightened abruptly, throwing his head up and giving her a fierce dark stare. 'Beautiful! Och, King of Heaven, beautiful? Woman, it was a very terrible thing.'

'You loved her very badly,' said my mother matter-of-factly, beginning to sew again. 'And it seems that she loved you. You were both young. Such things are terrible enough.'

'It was badly that I loved her,' he replied bitterly. 'And the worse because she did love me, while I, what did I love? A beautiful feeling! Dear God, I didn't care if it destroyed her, and, if it came out, it would. I took advantage of my position as a guest in Bran's house, I betrayed my lord's trust, I betrayed her and I betrayed my own honour. I treated a king's sister like a common whore, and it was the worse because she loved me. Afterwards, that first time, she cried. She wouldn't tell me why until much later, and then she said, "It was because I knew I loved you so much more than you loved me, and because of my honour." She risked everything for me, and I . . . beautiful! Lord of Light, have mercy.'

'You're overstating it,' my father said.

'I wronged her greatly.'

'You wronged her, yes. But there was no need for her to come and meet you. Any girl would know what you meant, and any girl of sense would not have gone.'

Gwalchmai looked back at the fire, linking his hands together and only replying with silence.

'If you feel that way, why didn't you marry her?' asked my mother.

A shrug. 'Later I wanted to. Much later. Too much later. After I had killed her brother.'

'So there was a rebellion?' asked my father.

He looked up at us. 'I thought all the world knew of that. Well, the north must be more aware of these things than Dumnonia.'

'I have heard that you killed Bran of Llys Ebrauc,' I volunteered. He gave me a questioning look. 'There was a song,' I explained.

'Trust Rhys to listen to songs,' muttered my father. 'Well, so Bran found out?'

Gwalchmai leaned forward again, his elbows on his knees. He still spoke carefully, anxious that we should see the worst of it. 'No. The rebellion had nothing to do with it. We were very discreet. After the first time, we didn't see one another for a while. I was angry with her for crying, and because the thing we had was so much more solid and mortal than the vision of it I had at the first. But, after a little while, when I had been thinking of it and of her for a time, I sent her a message through her servant Hywel, the old man. He had been with her since she was born, and didn't like the business at all, but she'd told him she'd go alone if he didn't come, and I gather he wished to protect her reputation as much as he was able to. She was accustomed to go riding with only one or two servants – Ebrauc is safe enough that a woman can do that, near the fortress – and we would ride out in different directions at different times, meet at a set place, and then return, again at different times. We were very careful. We spent most of the summer in this, until about the middle of July. Then one of Bran's men successfully picked a quarrel with my companion Morfran. He is a fine man, brave and steady and quick with his tongue, but has no looks at all and is well-used to hearing of this, which is the reason I chose him for this mission: I knew he would not fight over every trivial slur. But some insult was offered which no nobleman could ignore, and there was a fight. Bran's man was killed. Bran summoned me to see him – summoned me, as though I were his own man and sworn to obey him. He demanded reparation, and by that he meant not a blood-price, but Morfran's life. I refused, of course, and Bran then had the excuse to command me to leave Ebrauc. He added to this command some Roman sentence of exile, by which I and my companions could be killed if we returned. I knew very well that, as soon as we had gone, he would summon his warband, equip it, and raise his army for a rebellion.

'I spent a great deal of time wondering whether I could have prevented it by closer attention to Morfran and the other. I had not precisely ignored them, but I hadn't known of the fight until it was done with and Bran's man was dead. There was nothing to say, "This you should have attended to; thus it could have been prevented", and yet I do not know, and cannot know, whether I could have managed it better if it had not been for Elidan. I was angry about Bran's order, and angry with myself when I left. I was angry with Elidan on both accounts, and yet I longed to see her to say farewell. But our departure was hurried, and though I looked for her until I almost forgot discretion and went about asking for her, I could not find her, and rode out of Llys Ebrauc angrier than before. And I was thus angry when I met her on the road.

'She rode out of the wood beyond the wall, on her brown mare, with Hywel after her. She was wearing blue, and the wind caught at her hair so that she looked like a feather blown on a bright gale. My companions stared at her. I had not told them about her, afraid that they might make jokes, and that to the wrong people.

'She drew rein on the road, and her mare champed at the bit and sidled towards the bank. She patted its shoulder with one thin hand.

'"So you are going," she said.

'"I am going," I replied, angrier than ever because she was so beautiful and so daring. "By your brother's order."

'She looked down and fidgeted with the reins; looked up again. "God go with you, then, my falcon," she said.

'It hurt me that she should call me that. I had once asked her not to. Though my name means "hawk", my mother used to call me by it, and the memory of that is most bitter. She is very terrible and dreadful, my mother Morgawse. "God may well go with me," I said, "for certainly he will not stay with the injustice of Ebrauc."

'At that, she too flushed with anger. Morfran looked at her and suggested that we take her hostage, which made her straighten and glare at all of us; but I shook my head.

'"Oh, indeed," said Elidan, "I am not to be a hostage, by your mercy, my lord. Come, I know that there will be war, Gwalchmai ap Lot. My brother wants it. It would be better if I could, as a hostage, prevent it; but no one can prevent a warrior from killing. You care for blood too much." I did not know where such words came from, and I stared at her in astonishment. She urged her horse closer, and then leaned over to catch my hand and press it to her forehead. "But I love you, and I love my brother, Gwalchmai. Do not you fight him. Promise me that you won't hurt him. Promise me that you will speak to your lord the Emperor about him, and tell Arthur that if Bran ap Caw swears a peace, he will keep it. But promise me that you won't kill Bran, most of all promise me that."

'I snatched my hand away. I was thoroughly enraged by this slavish pleading for her brother. "If your brother wishes to play the treacherous fool, that is his affair, and he must be prepared for whatever consequences my lord imposes," I said. "My lord knows far better than I how to deal with rebels." But when she turned white, and looked at me with a strange, chill look, I had to add, "But for my part, I will not kill him. I swear by the sun and the wind, I swear the oath of my people I will not. And . . . my lord Arthur is merciful."

'She pressed one hand to her forehead, drawing the hair aside, as though her head ached, and she nodded. "God and his saints preserve you then, Gwalchmai." We looked at each other for another long moment, and I tried to find words that would make it a sweet parting, but I could think of none. So I nodded and urged Ceincaled on, and he started into a canter and left her there. At the first bend of the road I looked back at her, a quiet figure in blue on a quiet brown horse, and I thought of what it meant for a woman to hazard herself thus to say farewell, and wished I had been kinder.

'"And what was all that?" asked Morfran, driving his horse next to mine. I shook my head, and he smiled at me knowingly. "Her falcon, she calls you? The daughter of Caw, the king's sister. Well, well, and that should be a thorn in the shoes of our friend Bran. You golden-tongued goshawk, why didn't you tell us? I'd like to make a song for the beauty of it all. A song about the hospitality of King Bran of Ebrauc!' And he began to make jokes about Elidan. I felt awkward, angry, and, after a while, I laughed.'

Gwalchmai had been playing with a piece of kindling: he threw this suddenly into the fire, and drove the heel of his hands against his eyes. My father set down the cup and his carving knife and stood, took a step towards our guest, then stopped again. 'Lord Gwalchmai,' he said gently, 'you need not tell us this tale.'

Gwalchmai looked up again. 'It is well that I should tell it. It is right that the shame of it should be known.'

'Say nothing further tonight, then. It is late, and you are tired.'

'I am. And I thank you for your hospitality, Sion.'

'What we have, you are welcome to. Sleep well, my lord.'

'Sleep well.'

Three

The next day my father again sent me out across the river, this time to cut down saplings to repair the cow byres. I did not think they needed repair, but I went, this time with my brother Dafydd. I thought about our guest and his tale all the day, and hardly glanced at the forest. I tried to picture this Elidan riding out of the wood, dressed in blue silk and looking like the Queen of the Fair Folk in the songs; and then I remembered that she was thin and a bit plain, and the nonsense became impossible to believe in. No, it was non-sense, the whole of it, and Gwalchmai was making a deal too much trouble over it all. My father had always said that, if a wrong action can be repaired, one should go about repairing it at once; if not, trust it to God. Gwalchmai seemed to be far too fierce about it either way. But warriors had to be fierce. I recalled all the tales I had heard about their violence, cruelty and licentiousness, and decided that our guest's scruples were exaggerated and absurd for a man in his position, since that position doubtless included murder and pillage on a wide scale. I managed to feel fairly detached about his presence by the time I returned home, worn out and chilled to the marrow of my bones.

I went to the barn to look after the animals, and found Gwalchmai there. To my astonishment, he was rubbing down our mare. I stood frozen, pitchfork in hand, until he turned and smiled at me. Then I closed my gaping jaw, leaned the pitchfork against the wall and said, 'You shouldn't be doing that, my lord.'

'Och, I know well enough how to look after horses. I will not hurt yours. She is a fine little mare.'

'I didn't mean that! You're . . . well, you're sick, and a guest.'

'This would be no trouble to a newly weaned child. But I cannot look after the bulls. You must do that; I know nothing about cattle. Well, perhaps a very little about sheep.' He turned back to the mare, humming softly to himself. She snorted and closed her eyes. His war stallion tossed his proud head and nickered, and his master laughed and spoke to him in Irish. After watching a minute or so, I picked up my pitchfork and went to look after the cattle. Gwalchmai's scruples no longer seemed quite so absurd.

I was tired after supper, and my mother suggested that I go straight to bed, but I would have to be much more tired than a single day's work could make me before I would do such a thing. I sat down at the right of the hearth and scratched the ears of our hound-bitch while the talk began. The dog occasionally grunted with delight, and licked me furiously every instant that I stopped.

'I've been thinking of what you said last night,' my father told Gwalchmai, 'and I can see why you didn't wish to tell the tale, and also why you did. Did you kill Bran, then?'

'I did. Deliberately, and when I might have spared him.' The warrior's voice was very level.

'In battle?' asked my father, his voice equally level.

Gwalchmai nodded. 'Yes, but I might have spared him just the same.'

'I've heard that you go mad in battle.'

Gwalchmai paused. 'Yes. But I was not mad then; or at least, not mad as I usually am . . . I will tell you the rest, as I said I would.

'The rebellion did not begin until September. We had some hard fighting before that, not pitched battles, but ceaseless raiding. Raiding is a sad business, and hard on the horses – but my lord's wars are always hard on the horses, since we must move at least twice as fast as our enemies. My lord gave me work, enough so that I had no time to think about Ebrauc and Elidan. Indeed, I did not think much at all, except to wonder when next I could rest.

'Then, in September, my lord called me aside for a private conference. We were at a holding near Gwyntolant on the Dyrwente, a clan headed by a man named Gogyrfan – yes, the Queen Gwynhwyfar's father. The clan supported us, and we had used the holding as a hospital for most of the northern campaign, and the lady Gwynhwyfar had attended our wounded better than a doctor. Arthur married her before the campaign was out, but he never, for that, failed in his attention to the war.

'My lord called me to the private room he had been loaned, and sat down at the table. There was a map there – there always is, with Arthur – and he began checking over the roads. I wondered why it was that he always seemed to have more energy than I, when I knew that he worked harder.

'"Bran of Ebrauc has rebelled," Arthur said, "or will do shortly."

'I dropped into the chair opposite him, again wondering, out loud, if I could have prevented it.

'My lord looked back up from his map and told me, "Enough of that; it wasn't your fault. The question is rather, how to stop Bran without the Saxons finding out that he's rebelled. We're a good hundred miles from Caer Ebrauc; still, with the south road we could do it in four days, or three if we pushed hard . . . though we'd be in no condition to fight then. Bran is still raising his armies now. He hoped to catch us off-guard by rebelling at the harvest season, but he has the disadvantage that it will take him longer to gather his forces, and they'll disperse more quickly if the war is drawn out. He won't have all his forces yet, and I think we could risk a pitched battle." I shifted in my seat, and Arthur grinned at me. "I could wish I was so eager for it. Very well, I plan to ride to Ebrauc tomorrow, force a battle, and be back north in two weeks, which shouldn't give the Saxons time to do more than realize we were gone. We can leave King Urien to make some raids on his own to confuse them – but only if Bran hasn't found too many allies. He's been gathering supplies all summer, but allies . . .' Arthur frowned at the map, and began discussing all the kingdoms that neighbour Ebrauc, asking me how the various kings and nobles were disposed towards Bran and towards himself – I had been ambassador to most of them by then. They none of them seemed to me the sorts to risk their crowns on an uncertain rebellion, though we'd have cause to worry if Bran had some success. There were other kings, of course, like Maelgwn Gwynedd, who would be only too eager to rebel, but they were far away from Ebrauc, and, if we moved quickly enough, should be unable to help.

'"Then we will force a battle," Arthur concluded. "But, Yffern! Bran would choose now as the time to rebel. Aldwulf might have decided on battle, and it only takes one more defeat for him and he's broken. Bran must have thought I'd be unwilling to leave the campaign just now."

He sighed, and began tracing a line on the map with his finger, thoughtfully looking into nothing with a wide grey stare. I waited.

'"I want you to leave this afternoon," he said at last. "The Family can't be ready to leave before noon tomorrow, but you leave now and take Bran my terms. Give him the impression that the rest of us are still north of the Wall, and waiting for his reply before we act; hint that the Family is scattered, and will be unable to assemble for at least a week. But see if you can talk him round: unlikely as it may be, it's worth the trial. Bran is an honourable man, and unlikely to dismiss a herald with violence, unless – there's no truth in the rumour about you and his sister, is there?' His eyes focused on me for an instant. I did not meet them. I stared at my hands, and at the scarred wooden table. I had asked Morfran and the other to keep the matter quiet, but it had come out despite that. When it came up, I would laugh, make a joke of it, and change the subject as though it were only a mad harper's tale, but I could not lie to my lord. "There isn't, is there?" he demanded again, impatiently. I was silent. He put both hands flat on the table and looked at me. "Before Heaven, there is." I did meet his eyes then, knowing it would be worse if I did not. The shame of it cut deeper than a spear point. I had dishonoured him in Ebrauc, since I was his emissary and ambassador, sent in his name; I had betrayed his trust. "There is," I said.

'"Why didn't you tell me?" my lord asked, his face very calm.

'I shrugged, not knowing what to say. "You have kept me busy. The matter did not arise. But if you wish I will go as your herald to Bran."

'"I do not want you killed," snapped Arthur. "I will send Rhuawn."

'"There is no need to send anyone else. Bran had no idea of this when I left, and he should have none now. The girl is not so foolish as to tell him."

'Arthur studied me, his face still so calm; I have seen it look like that when they tell him, after a battle, who of his men are dead. I could no longer look at him, and so pretended to study the map, furious and ashamed because he was disappointed. "Was she very beautiful?" he asked at last, and I looked up and saw that the set look had softened. I opened my mouth to say no, and instead said, "As a birch tree is, with the west wind blowing; as a lark singing." And as I said it, I wanted to see her again. I would have given the bright world, all of it, though it were an unequal bargain.

'At this Arthur smiled. "Is she?" He folded the map slowly, thinking of something else – of Gwynhwyfar? "Then you are fortunate. You believe that Bran does not know?"

'"My lord, I am certain that he does not. Even in the Family most people do not believe it, and I doubt that Bran has even heard the tale."

'"Then I will send you," Arthur said, and told me what terms he was willing to offer Bran for peace. I went out from the room, saddled Ceincaled, and turned him southward, my heart full of Elidan.

'But when I came to Caer Ebrauc, I had not even a glimpse of her. Bran kept me at the gates of the fortress, waiting until he came down from the palace to meet me there. He listened to the terms Arthur had proposed with a cold lack of interest, and when I had done, said only, "You were exiled from this land. I could have you put to death for coming here." I felt for my sword, but he continued, "You came from the north very quickly. See if you can do better going back, and tell Arthur ab Uther, that bastard who lays claim to the imperium of Britain, that Ebrauc has her own king, that Bran ap Caw has more title to the Pendragonship than he, and that we will bow our heads to no yoke, least of all to his. Go, and tell him!" He shouted it with a kind of delight, and, drawing his sword, struck my horse with the flat of the blade. Ceincaled reared up, but I checked him, drew my own sword and saluted Bran with it. The light that dwells in the blade kindled, and it burned like lightning – it is not an ordinary sword – and Bran's men fell back. "I will tell these things to my lord the High King," I said. "And may the end be to your account, Bran of Llys Ebrauc." I turned Ceincaled and set my heels to him, and we were off down the road like a falcon swooping. I was angry enough to weep, and all my thoughts turned on Elidan.

'I rode north until I met the Family on its way south, and told Arthur that Bran had turned me back from the city gates with boasting and insults. My lord was not surprised, and only sighed and shook his head, and told me to ride in the van. We rode in silence. No one liked leaving the northern campaign for this rebellion. We were worn by a summer's fighting, and not eager for a pitched battle.

'We reached Caer Ebrauc some three days after I left it. Bran had had no more than a few hours' warning of our approach, but he had room enough in the city for armies larger than his, and time enough to bar the gates and set a watch on the walls. We spent the night camped before these, wondering what to do. We could not support a siege without forfeiting the northern campaign, but no one knew how to take a city. Whatever the Romans may have done, no one fights from a city now.

'In the morning, Arthur came out of his tent in the grey dawn, and walked about the walls, looking at them. Then, while the camp was breakfasting, he returned and gave orders that, as soon as we were done, we were to move off and burn and plunder western Ebrauc. The corn stood in the fields then, thick and white for the harvest, and all the men were with Bran since the army had been called up. There were none to stop us.

'It was barely two days before Bran left the city, with his warband of three hundred cavalry and two hundred infantry, and an army of some fifteen hundred: as Arthur had thought, he could not afford to lose the harvest. At that time the Family numbered under six hundred, since some of us had been raiding far afield when Arthur assembled the warband, and many were dead or wounded from the summer's campaign. About half of us were cavalry: the odds were not bad. But Arthur called a parley first.

'We held it in the middle of a field we had burned, with untouched fields across a pasturage shimmering in the wind to remind Bran of the cost of war. We did not dismount, and Bran looked at nothing with a hot blue stare while Arthur talked. Arthur's terms were generous: he offered to return the plunder we had taken and provide transport for grain from other parts of Ebrauc to the region we had pillaged, if Bran would swear submission and agree to pay the tribute. But Bran didn't even wait for Arthur to finish before saying, "So you will return the goods which you stole from me. Will you return me my sister?"

'Arthur did not look at me at all. "Speak plainly."

'"My sister, I say, my sister Elidan, the brightest, the purest woman in all Britain until your whore-mongering sorcerer corrupted her. Can you redeem that wrong, Imperator Britanniae? I will make terms with you if you give me the man you sent upon that mission, so that I can..."

'"Enough!" Arthur said. "As before, when you set your men to quarrel with mine, you dredge up excuses, and fasten on a private grievance as the pretext for rebellion."

'"A private grievance, a pretext? When your emissary makes a whore of his host's sister? I know that there is no faith in you, or any of yours. Truly, I will be protecting my women if I make peace with you!"

'"Enough," Arthur said again, and Bran stopped. "Your mind has been set on this, King Bran, since first you came to power; and when you turned my emissary from your gates with insults a week ago, you had no such pretensions."

'"If I had known then," Bran cried, 'then I would have given him the edge of my sword, and not insults!" He looked directly at me for the first time, where I sat my horse at Arthur's right. "You witch's bastard, I will see to you before the day is out. Mark me in the battle."

'I could answer him at last, but I did not answer him, only asked, "Where is your sister?"

'He glared at me and said, "I have shut her up where you cannot defile her again. For all your sorceries, you will die today, if my sword hand has any strength."

'"I may, if mine has none," I said. I felt completely calm, and I knew that I would kill him that same day. I studied him carefully: the brown hair, beard cleft by an old scar, eyes the colour of Elidan's, the grey stallion and the purple-edged cloak. I was sure I would know him in the battle. It seemed to me entirely reasonable and necessary to kill him, not because he had insulted me, but because he was Elidan's brother and determined to keep me from what was mine.

'We rode back to our own lines. Arthur had already settled the dispositions. But as he dismissed Bedwyr – who was in charge of the cavalry, as always – and me to our places, he caught Ceincaled's bridle and said in a low voice, "Do not kill Bran unless you have to." I said nothing. Arthur shook the bridle a little, leaning over in his saddle and forcing me to look at his face. Then he let go, turned his horse, and raised his voice to encourage the men to fight well.

'It was a battle like most of our battles. Arthur had chosen hilly ground, which scatters a charge, and makes numbers of less weight. Our foot faced Bran's centre, where he had stationed the infantry of his warband, flanked on each wing by the irregular forces of his army, and, on the right wing, by his cavalry opposed to the drawn-out line of our own. Our foot charged before Bran was quite ready, and forced his centre to retreat. The army was thrown into confusion, some of the men trying to encircle us, the rest, afraid of a flank attack from the cavalry, trying to retreat with the centre. When Bran's warband managed to slow its retreat, the army was further confused, and our cavalry charged, caught Bran's cavalry – which had been trying to outflank our foot – and struck through them into the right wing.

'I go mad in battle, and this is a gift of sorts, and not a frenzy such as berserkers have. Everything seems as clear as spring water over sand, and everyone around me seems to move under water, slowly and without force. If I am wounded I cannot feel it, for I feel nothing but a sweet joy, and I can never remember killing, though I know I must have. My memories are fragmentary, once the charge has begun, and so I remember the first part of this battle. From the time I threw my first spear it is like the memory of a dream. And yet some of the fragments remain. I remember seeing a brown-haired man on a grey horse fighting his way towards me, but in the madness it meant nothing, though something in me seemed to remember him. And then I was face to face with him, fighting, still as in a dream. I remember striking at his hand, and that he cried and dropped his sword, then turned his horse and rode off at a gallop, clutching his hand to his chest.

'But something of the madness was gone from me, and, though I still scarcely knew what I was doing, I drove Ceincaled after him. Others crossed my path and I cut them down, but after striking, again looked for Bran.

'It was late afternoon. Later I found that the cavalry charge had shattered both Bran's cavalry and his army, and that the warband surrendered after their king had fled the field. At the time I saw only the purple-bordered cloak retreating over a hill, and a black thirst came over me to see it dark with blood. He had·a good start, but there is no horse like my Ceincaled, and I gained on him quickly.

'The afternoon sun lay richly over the autumn trees, and the din of the battle blurred behind us as we left it behind a hill; the loudest sound became the pounding of our horses' hooves and the jingle of harness and gasp of breath. He had a good horse. It kept running after most beasts would have dropped, but it could not keep running for ever. It stumbled, stumbled again, and Bran drew rein before I reached him and leapt down, his shield on his right arm, gripping a spear in his shield hand. He grinned at me, all teeth. His face was a mask of blood and sweat and dirt.

'"Well, sorcerer," he said. "Your sword isn't burning now. Does the magic fail before human courage?"

'I didn't understand a word of it then. I reined in Ceincaled and slid to the ground, my sword in my hand. I cared only to kill Bran. I was mad, but it was not my accustomed madness: nothing was clear, there was a red mist over my eyes and a salt taste in my mouth. I cried out, howling like a dog, and rushed at him.

'He blocked my first thrust with his shield, clumsily, turning as I circled him and tried to get to his right, wounded side. I struck at him again and again, and once or twice shallow blows went past his guard, but he fought. By Heaven, he fought bravely, and never dropped his savage grin. "I . . . am not afraid . . . of your magic," he told me, working hard to get the words out. He must have wanted very badly to say them. "I am a king, a king, may Yffern . . . take you . . ." His shield drooped a little, and I saw my chance and thrust forward, driving the sword through his ribs to the heart, so that he fell forward onto me and died, and was silent, his words unsaid. I stepped back and let him fall to the earth. The fine linen of his cloak began to darken with his blood. I kicked the body twice, hard, then left it for the plunderers and went back to Arthur and the Family. And that was how I committed murder.'

Gwalchmai was silent for a very long time, looking at nothing at all. In his eyes was an old, weary pain that I did not want to think about, and he rubbed the side of his sword hand with the thumb of the other hand, leaning forward above the fire. My hand was frozen in the neck fur of our hound-bitch.

After a little, the dog whined and nudged my hand, and Gwalchmai straightened and looked up at the smoke hole. 'And no one in the Family said anything about it,' he said, as if he had not stopped. 'Arthur asked me where Bran was, and I told him that the man was dead. He said nothing, only looked at me. Not angrily, only . . . I do not know. He has trusted me no less since that time. I swear the oath of my people, he is the greatest of all lords on the green earth, and I do not deserve him.

'The day after the battle we rode to Caer Ebrauc and the people there opened the gates for us. Bran's half-brother Ergyriad ap Caw had been chosen as his successor by the royal clan. Bran had designated his full brother Heuil for that position, but Hueil was a trouble-maker, and Ebrauc apparently wanted no more wars with Arthur. Ergyriad was too pleased to be king to risk his position by greater ambitions, and swore submission to Arthur without trouble. Arthur returned all the plunder we had taken, re-leased all our prisoners without ransom, and helped arrange for provisioning the regions we had pillaged, and Ebrauc was reconciled to us. So the rebellion ended. My lord planned to leave for the north the next day, and raid in southern Deira on the way. I went to look for Elidan.

'Bran had said that she was shut up somewhere, but I knew that she must be in the city, and roamed about the place threatening the servants until one of them, an old woman, told me where she was. I ran there desperately, getting lost twice on the way through very eagerness. Since I had killed Bran, it had seemed as though all the world were stricken and bloodless, and I was broken with weariness and sickness of heart. I could only think of Elidan.

'Bran had locked her up in a little room above one of the palace stables. She knew nothing of the battle until she saw me. The old woman in the palace, the one who told me where she was, had brought her food once a day, and other-wise she had been left alone.

'I cut the bolt from the door with one blow of my sword and burst into the room without even calling to see if she was there. She was standing in one corner of the bare room, her back to the wall, ready to fight – until she saw that it was me. Then her face lit up, like the sunlight flooding through a lake, turning everything to shining colour. She cried,

"Gwalchmai!" and ran across the room into my arms. I held her and held her, kissing her hair and neck, and something of the black ache went out of my soul.

'But finally she pushed herself away from me a little and looked up at me, her hands against my shoulders, and began asking me questions. "How are you here?" she asked. "Was there a battle? Is my brother safe? Has he sworn fealty? Where is he, and where is the Emperor?"

'And I had no answers. I tried to pull her close again, but she kept her hands braced against my shoulders, smiling with shining eyes. "When was the battle?" she asked. "My brother found out, and he was very angry. That is why he shut me up here. I fainted when I heard how he sent you away from the gates, and he noticed . . . is he safe?"

'"What does it matter?" I asked.

'She frowned. "He is my full brother; how could that not matter? Where is he?"

'There was nothing I could say. She stared at me, her eyes widening. "He's not . . . hurt . . . is he?"

'I could not look at her. "He is dead," I told her.

'"No, oh no. He can't be. You promised; he can't be."

'Then I remembered that I had promised, and I was horrified. I had broken my sworn word, and, until that moment, had not even thought of it. I became furious with her for binding me with that oath, and, as I thought, making me forsworn. "Promises like that are meaningless," I said. "They are impossible to keep in a battle. Your brother came at me to kill me. What was I to do? Offer him my sword?"

'"Gwalchmai," she said, and something in her tone made me look back at her. Her eyes had become very large and dark in her face, a face grown pale and stricken as the whole world. Something in me twisted and grasped desperately at the edge of an inner abyss. "Gwalchmai, *you* didn't kill him?"

'I was quiet for a long instant, and then I was enraged, desperate. "Yes, I killed him," I shouted at her. "And every inch of the steel was deserved: he was a traitor and a rebel, a brute who would lock you up and part us and insult me, yes, and I did kill him!"

'"You perjured, murdering liar." Her voice was even and savagely cold. "You . . . sorcerer. You are just what

Bran said you were. Oh, my brother, oh, Bran, Bran." She turned from me and walked abruptly to the wall and leaned her head against it, pressing one hand against her mouth. Her shoulders shook beneath the thin dress. In the stable beneath us the horses shifted in their stalls, and the doves cooed in the thatch. I stood in the middle of the room, and the light was black in my eyes.

'"Elidan," I said. She did not move. "Marry me." I had not till that moment thought to ask it, but as I did, I saw that I desired it with my heart's blood.

'She whirled on me, her face twisted, but her eyes bitterly cold, like Bran's. "Marry you?" she said. "Marry the man who murdered my brother, while the blood is still hot on his hands? Marry the perjurer, the liar . . . I wish I had died the day I saw you first! Leave me!"

'I crossed the room in two strides and caught her by the shoulders. "Don't command that. Tell me anything else. I swear the oath of my people, Elidan, anything else and I will do it."

'"Go away! Let me mourn in peace. Go! I never want to see you living again. You warriors are all the same, all thinking of nothing but your own fame and glory. You care nothing for the pain you cause, if you get what you want and make a name in a song. Well, you won't get me. For all your skill at murdering, and all your looks and your noble blood, you can find another whore to worship you; I've been whore enough . . ."

'"Don't call yourself that!"

'"Go!" she screamed, and tore one arm loose to strike me, then lashed out again with the same furious determination. I let go.

'"Go away," she repeated. "If you come near me again, I swear I will kill myself, and I do not break my oaths."

'I stood back and looked at her, and she stood still, straight and proud, her lips parted for breath, eyes too bright, face wet with tears. I felt that if my eyes parted from her, my soul would part from me as well. But in honour there was nothing else which I could do. So I did the hardest thing of all I have ever done, and walked back across the room and out of it, closing the door very quietly behind me. As I left the stable I heard her begin the keen for the dead and quickened my step. I have not seen her from that hour to this.'

Gwalchmai stopped. I had ceased to scratch our dog's ears, and she whined and nudged me several times hopefully, until I slapped her. Gwalchmai suddenly stretched out his hand and called her, and she came over, sniffed the hand politely, then settled at his feet while he began scratching her ears as I had.

My father was frowning. 'You did nothing more for the girl?'

The warrior shrugged. 'I sought out the old man, Hywel, and gave him all the money I had with me, and borrowed more from the other members of the Family, and told him to let her use it for whatever she wanted. I don't imagine he told her where it came from, or she would not have accepted it, but I know she received it. I went to her half-brother Ergyriad, the new king, and virtually begged him to let her do all that she pleased. I had to give him presents; I borrowed from Arthur for that. When we left, I had someone watch to tell me what she did. It seems she left the city the same day we did, that afternoon. She took her brown mare, Hywel and another servant and a mule laden with goods. No one knows where she went, except that she turned south. I had had a large enough share of the plunder in that campaign, so she could have bought some land, and had men to work it for her. I do not think she would go to another king, for she was not overfond of the court and its plottings.'

'Then why are you looking for her?' my father asked. 'Seeing that she is probably settled and happy?'

'To ask her forgiveness. I did not even admit to her that I had done any wrong.'

'In the middle of winter?' My father looked at him. 'My lord, it's a noble enough objective, and I can see how a man such as yourself might think it needful, but couldn't you have sought her in the summer?'

Gwalchmai smiled again, and began rubbing the dog's ears with both hands. 'There was never time. Before Baddon there was the war; since Baddon, I have been trying to get away from my lord for this task, and first he sent me to Deira, and then to Gwynedd, and then to Caledon. I was on my way back from my embassy to Aengus MacErc of the Dalriada up in Caledon when I stopped for the night at

Caer Ebrauc. When I was seeing to my horse I began talking with one of the servants at the court, and this man said he thought that she had gone to eastern Gwynedd, away from the road in the Arfon mountains. I considered the matter, and decided that I would have time to look for her. I wrote my lord a letter, and sent it to Camlann with the man who was accompanying me, and myself set off for Gwynedd with the servant who had told me of it.'

'I have heard that King Maelgwn Gwynedd is Arthur's enemy,' my father pointed out.

'It is true that Gwynedd is no friend to the Pendragon. But there was no reason to see Maelgwn the king, and I am not wholly helpless. But the servant from Caer Ebrauc was wrong: she was not there.'

'Hmm. The man probably only wanted protection on his journey.'

'It is possible. He needed protection, for he was from Gwynedd, but had killed his cousin years before and fled. His clan took him back when he appeared, though. But he had worked in the stable at Caer Ebrauc, and had heard one of her servants say that they rode to Gwynedd. And she did pass through Caer Legion, for I met a man there who remembered her. But in Arfon there was no trace of her. I looked, from near Castel Degannwy to the springs of the Saefern, and no one had seen or heard tell of any such person. So I returned to Caer Legion, and tried to discover where else she might have gone, and . . . well, I have been looking since.'

'I do not see why it was so important,' said Morfudd. She had grown increasingly restless as Gwalchmai spoke, and now she gave Gwalchmai a smiling, light-hearted look. 'So, this woman was offended at you; well, you provided for her. I don't see why you should go running after her any longer, unless you still want to marry her.'

Gwalchmai looked away from her. 'It is possible,' he said. 'Though I do not think she would. She is not a light-minded woman, but proud, willing to do all in love and no less serious in hate. But can you truly not see that this was a terrible thing?'

'What was so very terrible about it?' asked Morfudd, tossing her hair. 'You were in love. Oh, I'd be very angry if someone had killed Rhys here, or even Dafydd, but you did kill this Bran in battle, and he was a rebel, and had tried to kill you first. If Rhys had done all that, and had even shut me up in a stable for a week, I'd be perfectly willing to forgive you for killing him.'

'Thank you,' I said. 'It would do you good to be shut up in a stable.' But I muttered it.

Gwalchmai did not smile. 'I was a guest, an emissary, and I betrayed my host and my lord. I dishonoured her, broke my word to her, and murdered her brother. I disobeyed my own lord and broke faith with God. By the Sun and the Wind! I deserve to die for it.' Gwalchmai's hand was hard on his sword-hilt, suddenly, the knuckles white. 'I have forfeited my own honour, and I must go to her, and admit as much. I have not acted for the Light, but I must at least deny Darkness or I will never be free of it. Even if she is justly angry, I must; and if she is angry, it is so much the better, for her anger is deserved.'

'You are too fierce with yourself,' said my father levelly.

'I cannot be.'

Their eyes met. The dog whined and crept over to my father, seeking reassurance. 'You are too fierce with yourself,' my father repeated. 'It is the nature of men to commit sin, and it is only in God's mercy that any are forgiven.' He crossed himself quickly and went on, 'You killed a man in battle whom you should not have killed, but it was not murder: you did not creep up upon him, but killed in combat, in the heat of passion. Very few men would have done otherwise, and very many have done the same and lived peaceful lives after.'

'That does not make it right.'

'Your lord, from what you've said, does not see fit to blame you.'

'That is my lord's mercy.'

'Your lord Arthur's mercy, as I have heard the tale, extends only so far as is safe for Britain. I do not believe he would be so quick to trust you after this if you were so blameworthy as you think yourself. I wonder how serious his order not to kill Bran ap Caw was, and for whose sake he said it. You said that you deserved to die for what you had done. You didn't, by any chance, think of administering that justice yourself, did you?'

Gwalchmai flushed and raised his hands in a gesture of

321

helplessness, suddenly smiling again. 'You are a shrewd man, Sion ap Rhys. The night after she told me to go away I walked about the walls of the city all night and wished never to see the morning. But I know and knew that my life was owing to my lord and to Heaven, and if I could still be of use to either, it was not mine to escape so easily.'

'Indeed. You might apply the same notion to your guilt. Do what you can to make reparation, and by all means go and ask the girl's forgiveness, but do not make yourself sick with self-hatred over it, and travel in the winter. It will not do you, or her, or your lords one bit of good.'

Gwalchmai smiled sadly rubbing the palm of his hand again. 'Perhaps.' He looked up, the lines of weariness, pain and tension for an instant leaving his face, as his eyes followed the smoke from the fire. 'Perhaps.' Abruptly, 'I would sell my sword to see her once more, Sion. She was like an aspen, standing caught in the brilliance of its shadowing leaves. I have thought of her so often since we defeated the Saxons at Baddon.'

'Have you no knowledge where she might be now?' I asked.

He shook his head. 'There are a few roads I might ride down yet. But they are not truly possibilities, only safeguards.' He was silent another minute then said, softly, 'It would be better for me to go back to Camlann now. My lord the High King has had no news of me since November, and he may need me. I know I will not find her on this journey; I will have to wait, and try again. Tomorrow I will leave for Camlann.'

'Not for at least a week,' my father said. 'Stay with us as long as you desire.'

Gwalchmai again shook his head. 'I am near well enough to travel now, and it is not far.'

My father began to argue, and Gwalchmai argued back, eloquently and interspersing deep thanks to all of us. He and my father both stood up, the better to express themselves. My father seemed solid, his stocky frame unshakeable. Gwalchmai was thin and dark and graceful and equally inflexible. The thought suddenly occurred to me, as I looked at the warrior, that it would not be intolerable to be his servant. When I had been younger, the idea of serving was the one thing that kept me from running off to join a warband, and when I had day-dreamed about it, I had always had to devise some improbable means of escape from that humiliation necessary to a farmer. But Gwalchmai had a kind of a humility, an outlook that saw nothing worthy of scorn in farming, or, I suspected, in service. If only . . . but why not? The thought chilled me. He might not want a servant, but I could offer to be one. It was possible; it actually was possible. I had only to speak a few slight words to him alone, and I might be off and away. Did I want it? It was absurd at my age, but . . . would Gwalchmai take me? Even if he didn't, he might know someone at Camlann who would . . . should I?

In spite of my tiredness, I lay awake a long time that night.

Four

My father persuaded our guest to remain for three more
days and, for the same three days, contrived errands to keep
me away from the householding. I was certain that he did it
deliberately. He first sent me out to check on the sheep and,
as soon as I had done with that, my mother sent me down to
the river to fetch sand for the oven. When the sand had been
fetched she found that she needed some clay, and so on and
off away from the house, and I had no chance to talk to
Gwalchmai. I wondered if my parents knew the question I
kept rephrasing in my mind or if they were simply determined to restrain my talk of war and the affairs of Britain.
As Gwalchmai had said, my father was a shrewd man.

The rest of my family busied itself with Gwalchmai's
gear. My mother mended his cloak, and as much of the rest
of his clothing that she considered worth mending. Some
she simply tore apart and replaced from ours. She tried to
make him accept some spare clothing and a new cloak as
well, but he adamantly refused this with the warmest expressions of gratitude. My father and Goronwy set up a
forge and Goronwy shod Gwalchmai's stallion – and our
mare, for good measure – and patched up the mail-shirt
with a few flattened iron rings. The rest of the houses of our
holding approved of the warrior and discussed him with
great interest and curiosity, and recounted to me how courteous he was, how little the sort of man one would expect the
Pendragon's nephew to be.

Gwalchmai himself was busy, cleaning and sharpening
his weapons, and offering assistance with any work, his or
ours. For myself, I slunk in and out of the house on my
errands, and said barely five words to him in a day. And
then it was the afternoon of the day before he was to leave,
and the man had scarcely met me. I was horrified at it.
Almost I decided not to talk to him after all – but I knew that
I would have no second chance, if I let this one pass me by. I
could stay with my clan, and perhaps be head of our householding after my father; I could marry, and would soon
enough, no doubt, if I could find a girl to take me; I could

farm the land by Mor Hafren, as though the world were as it had been in my grandfather's time. As though Rome had not fallen, and in the time of my grandchildren all would be the same. As though all these things were life itself, and not just a way of life. I had to go. I knew that I had to go to Camlann, though why my heart had seized me thus I could not say, and to go to Camlann I had to talk to Gwalchmai. So, when I came back from one errand I did not even go into the house, but instead went down to the stable, hoping.

He was there, cleaning his horse's harness and singing in Irish. He had a fine singing voice, a strong, clear tenor, and sang well. But he stopped when I came in and stood quickly, catching up a rag and drying the soap from his hands.

'Greetings to you, Rhys ap Sion,' he said politely, and waited for me to get what I wanted from the stable. I came over a little closer to him, looked at him, and felt my heart settle like a wine-skin with a puncture. I did not see how I, Rhys ap Sion ap Rhys, could ask him to take me. But I shuffled my feet, looked at the horse in the stall behind him, and blurted out, 'There is a thing I wish to ask of you, Lord.'

Without looking at him, I knew that he smiled. 'That is well indeed! Any service I can render to your family, after the grace you have shown me, I will do most gladly.'

I shuffled my feet again. The horse was fine-looking, and much easier to watch than this chieftain. 'Lord,' I said again, and there was no hope for it, I had to go on, 'I have had all my life a great hunger for . . . for the world of kings and emperors,' and finally I had to meet his eyes, 'and I would like to go with you to Camlann.'

He was shocked. The black brows contracted. 'You do not know what you are saying,' he told me. I did not reply. 'Ach, most boys want to be warriors, I think: yet it is not the way of life you may think it to be.'

'I am not a boy,' I pointed out. 'Farmers may not age as quickly as warriors do, but I'm twenty-one, and no silly child. And I think, Lord, I can see what your life must be from the way it has used you. I still want to go.'

He looked at me carefully, then leaned against the horse's stall, shaking his head. After a moment he began to laugh quietly.

At this I grew angry. 'I'm not as ridiculous as that! I know how to ride, and how to look after horses, as well as other cattle. I can throw straight, so I think I could protect myself if you gave me a spear. I can't read, but I know Latin as well as British, and no one's ever got the better of me in a market place. I'm no fool, whatever you think.'

'I did not think you were.' Gwalchmai was abruptly serious again. 'Only . . . I am sure that you are an excellent farmer. But being a warrior is a hard task, and a bitter one, and I should think that serving warriors is worse still.'

'But all warriors, especially when they go on embassies, have servants.'

'I never have. And there is too much fighting I must do to take a servant with me, and if I travel more to look for her it will be worse.'

'I can fight,' I said. 'I've not been trained at it, but I can hold my own against any clansman from Baddon to Caer Gloeu.'

Gwalchmai shook his head again. 'Can you throw a spear?'

I looked at the throwing spears that leant against the wall with the rest of his gear, ready for the morning. They were made of light, straight ash wood with leaf-shaped heads of fine steel, the butt ends sheathed with bronze. They did not look particularly difficult to hurl, unless one was on horseback. I picked one up and hefted it: it weighed a bit more than I had expected, but it seemed well balanced for throwing. Gwalchmai considered me, then pointed to the wall of the barn.

'That plank with the double knot-hole in the middle. Hit that,' he told me.

I shifted my weight, brought my arm back and threw the spear. It wobbled unevenly through the air and struck near the base of a different plank, sticking out sideways. Gwalchmai said nothing. I picked up another spear, and threw that with no better results. I threw the third, then went and pulled all of them out and tried again.

'Stand with your weight on your left leg,' Gwalchmai said, after a while, 'and shift it to your right as you throw. That's it. But stop trying to throw with your arm. The force comes from the shoulder. Don't move your wrist at all; it only makes the spear wobble . . . there.' My hurled spear finally flew levelly and struck straight into the wall. I felt elated until I noticed how far it was from the designated plank. Gwalchmai went and drew it out, came back, and then sent all three spears into the plank, just by the knot hole, with really astonishing speed. He collected them again and set them against the wall before turning back to me. I knew that my face was red, and I said nothing.

'You really do know how to throw things,' the warrior said. 'It took me months before I could throw that well. I was a slow learner – though I can throw spears from horse-back as well, which may compensate. If you'd been properly trained, you'd've made an excellent warrior.'

I looked at the plank I had hit. 'How much training does it take?'

Gwalchmai shrugged. 'In the Orcades – the Ynysoedd Erch, that is – we start when we are seven. The training lasts until we are fourteen or so, and then boys of high rank can begin to go raiding, though they still need some practice for the rest of their lives. And then, fighting from horse-back is another matter entirely.'

I'd heard it before, of course. Warriors begin training at seven, fighting at fourteen or fifteen, and, usually, die before they are twenty-five. Gwalchmai was over that. I was too old to begin. I had known it, but I had never really realized how much that training meant without that accursed plank staring at me. I glared at it.

'I never said I was a warrior,' I told him. 'And perhaps I would get skewered in a battle. But I know that warriors have servants, and their servants do not fight, and other warriors do not harm the servants.'

'No, they don't. Servants are valuable property, if sold to the right buyer,' Gwalchmai observed dryly, then, in a serious, tired voice, added, 'You are your own man, and of a free and prosperous clan. Your family can only be called a gift from Heaven. Why, by all the saints, would you wish to cast all that aside, be subject to another man's will, and wander about Britain with every man's hand against you?'

'I know it is mad, I know.' I stood there, groping for words. 'I know. I only . . . Lord, Rome has fallen, and the Emperor in the east left us to defend ourselves. My grandfather told me of it when I was a child. I . . . ' I struggled with myself, trying to explain something I didn't understand myself. 'And your lord is defending us. Yes, and we are the last Christian land in the West, the last fragment of the Empire – and the Church does nothing, and the kings of Britain do nothing but pretend that the world will go on for ever as it is now, when already it has changed so that the last Emperors would not be able to recognize it.' At this something seemed to give, and I found that I could speak quickly. 'Lord, the West is in Darkness. The Emperor Arthur has given the Saxons one great defeat, but still we are fighting a war, the battle is still continuing, isn't it? Is Britain at peace, Lord? Is the world?'

'The world never will be,' murmured Gwalchmai. But he watched me with a quiet intensity.

'Ach, no, of course not. But now less then ever. Now we have a war between the law and chaos, between Light itself and Darkness. And perhaps Arthur is, as they say, a violent man, but even if he were as corrupt as the king of Gwynedd paints him, it is something to go out and fight against death and ruin, better than sitting up in Arfon like a vulture waiting for the end, or working on a farm near Mor Hafren and pretending that the world's at peace!'

Gwalchmai's face was expressionless. I drew a deep breath, not really knowing what I'd said and feeling weak and exhausted. 'Well,' I said, trying to calm myself, 'is it a reason?'

'It is. You sounded exactly like my lord the Pendragon.' He sighed and ran a hand through his hair while I gaped. 'It is a good reason. Something of that was my reason, as well.' He sat down on the straw and gestured for me to sit next to him. I sat.

'You have reason to join with the Family, Rhys ap Sion.' Gwalchmai laid one arm across his knees, the hand limp. Chain mail glinted at his wrist where the mail-shirt projected from under the tunic. 'Though I suppose it is for every man to fight for my lord the Light in some way, still it is true that my lord and the Family fight in a way special to this age. If you cannot be a warrior, then, you must be someone's servant. I have never wanted a servant, but there is sure to be someone else who will, someone who knows that he fights for the Light of Heaven. There is only one matter that is against you.'

'My family,' I said. I was trembling. He had agreed, I was

going.

'I owe them a great deal.' Gwalchmai picked up a piece of straw and began splitting it. 'I am indebted to your father for more than a few nights' lodging, I think. He is a wise man, your father. It would not be just of me to steal his son. And I think he does not want you to go.'

'I think the same. But if he agrees to let me go, you will take me?'

'If he agrees, and willingly lets you come, I have no choice.'

I put out my hand and, after a moment's hesitation, Gwalchmai took it.

When I went to look for my father I felt neither exalted nor utterly lost.

My whole family was by the hearth, with dinner nearly ready.

'There you are, Rhys,' said my mother. 'Did you bring the salt?' (That had been her latest errand.) 'You did take your time at it!'

I gave her the salt without comment and turned to my father, who was sitting by the hearth. 'Father, I need to talk to you.'

Something in my voice made both my parents go still and glance at each other.

'If you have need to talk, I must have need to listen.' My father walked to the room he and my mother shared with the youngest children and opened the door. I went in and he shut it behind me and sat on the bed, looking at me expectantly. I felt even less inclined to speak than I had under Gwalchmai's eyes.

'Well, what is it?' asked my father.

It was best to say it quickly. If I delayed, I did not know that I could say it at all. It is a terrible thing to part from one's own clan, and worse when it is plain that the parting is not a light one. 'I have asked the lord Gwalchmai to take me with him when he leaves here. I told him that I wanted to be servant to some man of the Pendragon's. Gwalchmai has agreed to take me with him, if you will freely let me go.' My father's hands clenched into fists, and I added, 'Father, he didn't want me to come at first. He tried to talk me out of it. He said he didn't want to "steal your son".'

The fists relaxed. My father looked at me for a long

moment, then, suddenly, put his hands to his face and turned his head away. 'How could he steal what I had already lost? You went to ask him.'

There was a horrible roughness to his voice, and it cut me as nothing had done before.

'I am asking you,' I said, 'to let me go freely.'

'Is there something more you wanted here?' he asked, in a quiet voice unlike his own. 'Is there anything we should have given you and held back?'

'Father,' I said, and I was shaking with the hurt of it, 'you've given me more than I needed, you know that as well as I. But it's that I myself wish to give more.'

'There is the land, and the clan. You can give all of yourself to them, and they need more. It is no easy thing to run a householding, especially in these times, and it is no small thing to run one well.'

'But I want to go to Camlann,' I said. 'That is a bigger thing. It is the greatest thing in all Britain, and I want to be part of it. I want to serve God . . .'

'You can do that anywhere.'

'But in a special way at Camlann.'

'They will fail,' my father said, his voice shaking, but still quiet, angry. 'They are trying to fight darkness when they have too much darkness in themselves. Not so much Gwalchmai, nor the Pendragon, either, but do you think the Family is made up of such men? Warbands in general care nothing for the fight to preserve civilization or for the Light – oh yes, I know what you're after, I've felt the pull myself – but warbands care for plunder and for glory. Civilization is here, in the order and peace of this householding, and not at Camlann. Look at Gwalchmai. He is a fine man, sensitive and honourable, and even in so pure a warband as Arthur's he's dragged into a crime and made to wear himself away with suspicion and doubt. If he had given himself to land and a clan, and kept them in order, and if the Pendragon had done that, they could have made a place where the crime could never have occurred.'

'Which the Saxons would have destroyed,' I said. 'Father, I must go. Maybe you are right, but still, I must go.'

He jumped up, caught my shoulders and shook me. 'Do we mean so little to you?'

'Oh no, no.' I could barely speak, and I was appalled that

despite it all I still wanted just as much to go. 'You mean so much. But I must go. Give me your blessing on it.'

He looked at my face, and I looked at his. It was a strong face, as I remembered. But there were lines about it, and the blue eyes were tired. He was getting older. I had not noticed.

'If I did not let you go willingly, you would run off on your own, wouldn't you?' he asked.

It made me grow cold. I had not even thought of that. But I nodded. He was quite right. Once I had explained why I must go, it had become impossible to avoid.

'Well, then. Go, with my blessing. You are a good man, Rhys, and the desire is, in the end, honourable and just. Perhaps you are right. Perhaps we are not strong enough here. Perhaps the sun rises at Camlann.' He put his arms around me and gave me one of his bear hugs. 'But remember that we are here,' he whispered, 'and if ever you can, come back.'

He let me go and strode abruptly to the door to call my mother.

My family was astonished and appalled. They clamoured with questions which I didn't know how to answer. Gwalchmai arrived from the stable into the midst of it, and they clamoured at him as well. All through supper, all the evening it was the same – 'But why, Rhys?' and 'What will you do, Rhys?' I couldn't say to them the fine words I'd said to Gwalchmai, nor could they understand without my saying anything, as my father had.

My mother cried quietly. I think she did understand my reasons, though, because she asked me no questions, only went about the house packing things for me. She did it quickly and deftly, not missing a thing I might need, and carefully considering space and weight, all the while brushing away the tears. My sisters were anxious and plaintive, my cousins vociferous, with a tendency – restrained by my father – to be accusing. My brother Dafydd was unhelpfully thrilled, grabbing a broom and threatening to spear everyone about him.

I don't think anyone slept well that night. I know that for my part I lay awake long after even the rest of the house had settled. I listened to the logs drop in the fireplace, the wind in the thatch, and to my brother's even breaths beside me. I thought of my whole life, and wondered if I would ever come home again. I prayed a bit, as one does. But I did not cry. There were no tears in me for that departure, greatly though it hurt; and that I had no tears perhaps hurt most of all.

The next day was damp and cold. The clouds hung low, pale and swollen, and in the distance the hills looked like ledges of grey stone. The sun was not fully up when we left, and the earth was hushed. The entire holding huddled outside the barn to see us off. My father saddled our mare's three-year-old foal Llwyd, a shaggy little grey gelding, and handed me the animal's bridle without comment on the gift. Gwalchmai bound most of our baggage behind Ceincaled's saddle, and readjusted the strap that held the shield across his own back. He wore his crimson cloak again, and in the early light looked as strange and otherworldly as he had at that first moment by the river. He turned to my father.

'I am sorely in your debt, Sion ap Rhys,' he said in his soft voice. 'Any thanks I may offer you are shallow and useless indeed.'

My father shrugged, scratched his beard. 'I've done no more, Lord, than provide common hospitality.'

'You have done a very great deal more than that.' Gwalchmai hesitated, then, drawing his sword, dropped to one knee in the snow, graceful as a hawk swooping. He held out the sword, hilt first, to my father. 'If ever this sword may be of any use to you and to yours, Sion ap Rhys, if I should then refuse it, may the sky break and fall upon me, may the sea rise up and overwhelm me, may the earth gape and swallow me. Witness it.'

My father, staring at him, slowly lifted his right hand and let his fingertips rest upon the ruby in the sword's pommel. The blade glowed as though some bright light were reflected from it – but there was no light. And that picture took hold of my mind, so that now it sometimes leaps before me at things that have nothing to do with either Gwalchmai or my father: the warrior in his gold and crimson, kneeling, and my father in his grey homespun accepting the pledged trust, half in embarrassment, and half in assurance; a proud humility and a humble pride, and the sword burning with light between their hands.

Then my father dropped his hand, and Gwalchmai stood and sheathed the sword. 'Use it to protect my son,' my father said, a little hoarsely. Gwalchmai nodded and mounted his stallion. He began adjusting the spears tied alongside the horse, checking that they were in easy reach. I swallowed and tried to say goodbye to my family. I did a sad job of it, and was glad to scramble onto my horse. It had all taken too long, I thought, this farewell. Such things should be done as quickly as one is able to say the words.

Gwalchmai gave one final half bow from the saddle, turned Ceincaled's head, and rode down the hill and away from the holding. I gave Llwyd a kick, and the horse started, shied, and trotted after the stallion. I did not look back at my family. Not until we had gone over the next hill and left the house out of sight did I look back. Then I turned just long enough to take it in: the slope of the pasture land, the pale stubble of the snow-covered field, the grey of the forest beyond the river under the leaden sky, and the streaks of smoke hanging motionless on the damp air. Smoke I had seen so many times before, coming home from a day's labour, eager for the hearth. I turned my eyes to the grey morning ahead of me. Gwalchmai's cloak was a splash of crimson against the heavy sky.

'Makes himself damnably conspicuous,' I muttered, to distract the gloom from my heart.

The warrior stayed silent. We rode on towards the old Roman road that leads southwards, to Ynys Witrin, and beyond that, runs onward past Camlann.

Five

We reached the Roman road about mid-morning. Gwalchmai drew rein as we turned onto it, and looked down the
length of it. Ceincaled tossed his head, breath steaming
about him, and then was still. I stopped Llwyd and looked
down the road as well. I had seen it before, and it seemed
even less worthy of observation than usual. It followed a
straight line through the curve of the hills, and had once had
a cleared space around it which was now grown over with
scrub. It looked cold and deserted, and there were no tracks
in the snow that covered it, but it was a good road. Gwalchmai, however, continued to look at it.

The wind was cold, and I saw no reason simply to sit in it
and suffer. 'Lord,' I said, after a while, 'this is the road.'

He glanced at me quickly. 'Oh. Indeed, it is. Only . . .
would you object to making another day's journey north,
before turning to Camlann? It would be good to check one
more road she might have taken.'

I looked southward down the road and rubbed my hands
together, understanding why no one travelled in the
winter. 'We go where you want to, my lord.'

'I am not your lord. You are a free man yet. Only . . .'
He looked to the north.

I looked south again. 'We'll go north then, lord.'

He turned Ceincaled north and urged the horse into a
trot, eagerly, and I followed with a great deal more reluctance.

We rode north for some fifteen miles with no other occurrence worthy of note except that it began to snow. I had a
good warm cloak and warm clothing, but my ears and feet
and fingers froze. Llwyd, who was used to better treatment
than this, became stubborn and bad-tempered, shying at
nothing and trying to slip away and go back home. I had my
hands full to control him. Gwalchmai seemed not to notice
the cold and rode easily, setting a fast pace despite the snow.

We reached Caer Ceri in the early afternoon. It is an old
Roman town, walled, one I had been to once or twice before
when our holding had some trading to do and the market at

Baddon was closed because of the Saxons. Caer Ceri was deserted when we came to it, though, and the market square was occupied only by a flock of sheep. I expected that we would stop and buy a meal by some warm hearthside. I had been looking forward to it for the last five miles, to getting off the horse I hadn't ridden since autumn, and sitting down by a warm fire to eat warm food and drink hot ale. But Gwalchmai rode straight through the town without pausing, and turned left onto the west road to Powys. When the walls fell away behind us and he urged Ceincaled into a trot again, I realized that he had no intention of acting in a rational fashion, and I must resign myself to the cold sausage and oat cakes my mother had supplied for lunch. These were half frozen. I offered some to Gwalchmai, who took them with thanks and some surprise, and we chewed the food slowly as we rode.

Llwyd was growing tired, since he was as much out of the habit of being ridden as I was of riding, and, while it made him less troublesome, I began to worry. If he went lame or grew overworn, where could I get another horse?

'Lord,' I said to Gwalchmai, 'how much further do you want to go today?'

'To Caer Gloeu, above Saefern Hafren. It's another ten miles or so, I think.'

That was quite a distance for a short winter day. It would be nearly dark by the time we reached the town. We had done some twenty miles already, by my reckoning. I remembered all the songs I had heard of Arthur's campaigns sweeping from one end of Britain to the other. Hard on the horses, Gwalchmai had said. Very hard, I thought, and hard on the warriors as well.

'Lord, my horse is unused to so much travel. He has not been ridden this winter since the snows began.'

Gwalchmai stopped, dismounted, and looked at Llwyd. He checked the gelding's legs and hooves, then straightened, chafing his hands together. 'He needs the exercise, that is true,' he commented. 'But he will not go lame or be overworked – though he may consider himself such. He has a strain of the pony in him, hasn't he?'

I admitted it, and Gwalchmai nodded and remounted his war stallion. Ceincaled seemed as rested as he had been that morning. We rode on, and I felt as thoroughly outclassed by the warrior as Llwyd was by his mount. I had always considered myself a good horseman.

Caer Gloeu was more twelve miles distant than ten, and the sun was setting when we reached it, a dim copper disc half-smothered by clouds. It was still snowing, in fits. I was chilled through and ached all over. Llwyd plodded with his head drooping, not caring where he was. I cared: I still wanted the hot ale.

Caer Gloeu was slightly larger than Caer Ceri, but equally deserted. It might almost have been the same flock of sheep milling in the market square. Gwalchmai stopped Ceincaled in a street opening to one side of that square and sat motionless, as though waiting. I huddled my shoulders and felt wretched and angry, too tired to care whether we were standing about for some purpose or just looking at another road.

After a few minutes, however, the door of one of the old houses opened, and a man came out, carrying a spear and pulling a threadbare cloak around his shoulders. He stood on his door step and gave us a steady, hostile stare. This, apparently, was what Gwalchmai had expected, for he dismounted and walked over near the man, keeping both hands up at shoulder height in plain view.

'I need a place to stay the night, for myself, my servant, and our horses.' His voice was quiet, but clear enough to carry across the square. The townsman continued to stare, holding his spear ready to thrust. He was a tall, pudgy man with thin brown hair and no beard. He glanced towards me with narrow eyes.

'Your servant?' he said to Gwalchmai. I suddenly realized that it should have been my task to ask for hospitality. Too late. I already looked a dolt, and Gwalchmai was going on.

'My servant and our horses; the horses will need grain. I can pay, man.'

At this, the man spat, but he lowered the spear and nodded. 'For the one night?'

'For this one night only.' The man nodded again, and Gwalchmai walked back to the horses and caught Ceincaled's bridle. The townsman gestured for us to follow, and we went back down the street, through an alley, and back up a smaller street to what I supposed was the back door of his own house. There we were led into a ramshackle stable, very draughty and dirty, with a small donkey and a cow, a few chickens and a pig occupying what space was not filled with wood and rubble. Gwalchmai looked about it and asked the man to move the cow, so as to make room in the stall for the horses. Our host argued a bit, swore some, and complied. Then Gwalchmai silently began to clean out the stall while the townsman stood about watching him suspiciously. I was furious. Any decent man would bring his guests inside by the fire and give them some hot ale, not make them clean his own filthy stable.

Deciding that I had better behave like a servant, I dismounted, stiffly. My legs shook when they touched the ground and I had to steady myself against Llwyd's shoulder before going to a corner of the stable to get fresh straw and the grain. Our host tried to give us less grain than the horses needed, and I had to argue with him. He claimed that we were being extortionate and trusting in our strength of arms to get away with it. 'But this is a town,' he told me. 'We have a civic government, a Roman government, and we enforce the laws. You can't rob citizens here.' I supposed his Roman government consisted of the levy of all the able-bodied citizens, ready to perform whatever extortion they could agree on. I felt revolted by the man, and then thought to wonder if he would have acted in the same way if I had come as a farmer, and not as the servant of a warrior.

We settled the horses and left them hungrily chomping the grain. Llwyd rarely got such food at home, but if he was to do more travelling he would need it.

Our host's house was nearly as dirty as his stable, and, besides wife and numerous children, it also contained chickens. No householder that I knew would have tolerated such a place, but things are different in the towns. Few people live in them any more, since only the very rich and the craftsmen can afford it. Our host's house was filled with drying pottery and wet clay, so plainly he was a potter. I picked up one of the plates and examined it. He was not a very skilled potter. Nonetheless, he snarled at me and told me to leave his valuable ware alone. Well, it was probably valuable enough. Potters can usually make a living.

The potter's wife had apparently begun to make porridge as soon as her husband had agreed to let us stay the night, and she now set this before us. It was lumpy, badly cooked, and had neither meat nor eggs in it. I put down the bowl after my first spoonful. This was too much for my temper.

'Since we're paying you might give us some meat,' I suggested to the potter's wife, quietly. She looked as surprised to find me speadking to her as she would if one of her chickens addressed her. 'Or an egg,' I added.

Gwalchmai looked up from his porridge, also in surprise. He had apparently been willing to eat the lumpy porridge without a word. But I was in no mood to let anyone cheat me of a much-desired meal. 'Bring us some bread, with butter, mind you, and some cheese!' I ordered, slamming my bowl down. 'And if you have some ham, bring that. And ale. Hot ale. My lord and I have been riding all day, and if you think we'll settle for poor porridge at the end of it, you are much mistaken.'

The woman glanced nervously at her husband. One of her children snickered. Gwalchmai coughed behind his hand, not looking at me, and the potter became red in the face. 'I've no need to offer you hospitality!' snarled our host, 'Any mongrel warrior thinks he rules the earth. Well, you don't, and you're no warrior even, servant. I take no talk from servants. I . . .'

'My lord, though, is a warrior, and no mongrel about it,' I said, and was going to tell the man that this was Gwalchmai ap Lot, the Pendragon's nephew, son of the king of the Ynysoedd Erch and so on, when I noticed Gwalchmai's look of alarm, and recollected that he had not mentioned any names at all to the potter. He knew more about it than I, and I would do well to tread carefully. But I was not going to give up my hot ale and ham. 'My lord happens to be a very good warrior, as you may hope you will not discover,' I finished. It seemed so easy to threaten the man.

'We're a town here! We have a government here!' said the potter. But he looked uneasy.

'Of course. And you are our host, even if you're paid for it,' I replied. 'And since you're a civilized man, and a host, you might give us some civilized food.'

The woman suddenly ran off and fetched the food, good wheat bread, butter, cheese and ham, and began to heat the ale. Her husband swore at us for a while, then grumbled into silence. Gwalchmai gave me a look I could not read – irony? annoyance? amusement? But the food was delicious and worth the effort, and I didn't care who was offended.

When he had finished his bread and ham, Gwalchmai began asking whether the potter and his family had lived in Caer Gloeu long. Yes, the man admitted sullenly, he had. Had he been there eight years before?

'I've been in Caer Gloeu all my life,' said the potter. 'What of it?'

'Only this: some time in mid-autumn, eight years ago, a woman may have come this way, a thin, fair woman, probably riding a brown horse and perhaps wearing blue. She had two servants, one an old man with half an ear missing.'

The potter listened attentively, then shook his head. 'Never seen any such woman. What kind of a whore was she, travelling like that? Must have been good.'

'She is not a whore.' Gwalchmai's voice was still quiet, but there was a chilling edge to it. The potter looked at him, and suddenly crossed himself. The dark warrior looked dangerous and completely uncanny, though he sat very quietly with his emptied plate on his knee. 'She is a lady of high family.'

'Well, I never seen her. Never heard anyone tell of her, either.'

'Neither here in town, nor on the road north, nor from the west, across the Saefern?'

'If she went by there, I never heard of her.'

Gwalchmai looked at him a moment steadily, then sighed. The whole journey suddenly made sense to me. Caer Gloeu stands between Powys, Dumnonia, and the southern wilds of Elmet. Anyone who travelled to any of these lands was likely to stop for the night at Caer Gloeu, and a woman travelling alone, with only a few servants, would probably have been remembered. Our host did not seem to be lying, so it was plain that Elidan had not come to Caer Gloeu, and we could turn back to Camlann in the morning. I was relieved; Gwalchmai was plainly disappointed. He took another drink of his hot ale, then set the mug down.

'I thank you.' He actually did say it, and I was amazed. So was the potter, who blinked at us as though he had heard a ghost. Gwalchmai continued matter-of-factly, 'My servant and I will sleep in the stable, by our horses. Have you any extra blankets?'

'You can sleep in here by the hearth,' said the potter. 'Won't need many blankets. A good fire, there.'

The warrior glanced at the smokey fire and said, 'We will sleep in the stables.'

I wanted vehemently to protest. The thought of going out into that draughty and filthy building, just when I was beginning to get warm, made me want to hit someone. But I couldn't, so I worked on getting good blankets from the potter. In the end I managed to make him give us a rug, though he wasn't happy about it.

When Gwalchmai had said we would sleep by our horses, he had meant it, and we settled for the night in the very stall, near the manger. It wasn't too cold, after all. Gwalchmai began to unfasten his baldric, so as to set the sword where he could reach it in the night.

'Why couldn't we stay in the house?' I asked.

'I do not trust them.' He said it simply. He frowned, loosening the fastenings of his chain mail, but not taking it off. 'This way we can guard ourselves and the horses at once.'

It made sense, if one could conceive of the potter slipping a knife into his guests for the sake of two horses and some valuable weapons. But who would do that? Or would he? If he thought we might leave without paying him, since he hated us so much as it was? The thought frightened me, not even so much for the danger, as for the appalling amount of suspicion and mistrust it demanded. But the potter . . . just might.

'Should I have said those things?' I asked, suddenly aware that it might have been an activity of questionable worth.

The warrior laughed. 'You know better than I.' We lay down and drew our cloaks and the rug over us. 'I would not have said such things,' my companion added after a moment. 'But the ale was very good on a night like this. Sleep well.' The straw rustled as he felt for his sword, and a horse shifted its weight in the dark above us. I knew that Gwalchmai would wake instantly if anyone came into the stable. It was safe here. Not comfortable, though: the floor was hard and cold even through the straw, and I ached quite enough as it was. Probably, I thought, I will sleep badly . . . and fell asleep on the thought. I slept the whole night without so much as a dream. Too much riding in bad weather will do that.

When I woke the next morning, dim sunlight was filtering through a crack in the roof, making a patch on the staw near my head. I lay awake for a while trying to determine what I was doing in a barn, then remembered that I had left home and sat bolt upright. My head cracked against the manger above me, and the two horses paused a moment and looked down at me, then began to munch their grain again.

I sat up again, more cautiously, and straightened my cloak and tunic. Gwalchmai was not there. I picked up the rug and blanket and began folding them to take them back to our host. Just as I stood up, Gwalchmai came out of the back door of the house.

'Good morning,' he said, smiling. 'You are a sound sleeper, Rhys. Our hostess has made breakfast, and it is inside.'

I was ready for breakfast. My bones ached from the damp and chill of the stable and from the previous day' riding, and warm food by a fire seemed a provision from Heaven. 'I am glad of that,' I said feelingly. I picked up the rug and draped it over my arm.

Gwalchmai was fidgeting with his cloak. 'Have you a spare brooch?' he asked.

I had one, at the bottom of my pack, a plain bronze clasp identical to the one that fastened my own cloak. I went and dug it out. The warrior thanked me and pinned his cloak with it. He seemed to have lost his own brooch, and I wondered at it: I'd noticed the clasp, and it was a valuable one if I was any judge of the thing. It seemed hard that he needed mine, which wasn't worth a tenth of the other, but was valuable enough to me. But he was doing me a great favour, I reminded myself, in taking me to Camlann, and I ought to be generous with my possessions.

Morning apparently improved our potter's temper, for he was almost pleasant, and his wife had produced bread with egg and sausage for breakfast. Gwalchmai had eaten already, and stayed in the stable to tend to his horse, so I settled down to my eggs alone, but with enthusiasm nonetheless. The potter leaned against the wall opposite, actually humming, and turning something in his hand. I was nearly done with my meal before I realized that what he held was Gwalchmai's brooch.

I knew the potter could not have taken the brooch. That

meant that Gwalchmai had given it to him as payment, but it was a vast over-payment, especially given the potter's sullenness. No wonder the man was cheerful now. He'd made a very fine bargain indeed. But I didn't like the thought of a pudgy-faced townsman profiting from his extortion. I finished my eggs thoughtfully and put the plate down. 'I see my lord gave you his brooch.'

The potter smirked.

'You can give me the change from the payment,' I said. He eyed me, pretending not to understand what I meant. 'Well, you don't think my lord meant you to grow fat off what he won on the field of battle against the Saxons, do you?'

'He gave it to me.' But there was a defensive whine in the man's tone. He didn't believe for an instant that Gwalchmai had meant him to keep the brooch.

'Of course. He gave it to you, and you can give me more goods to make up the value of it. Or, if you prefer, you can give me the brooch back and I'll give you the value of your hospitality – or rather, the value of a night's hospitality, since I wouldn't give a sick chicken for yours.'

'But this is a small brooch. It's not worth a hen.'

'Not worth a hen!' I wondered if the man thought me an imbecile. 'Man, you could buy an ox with that, and easily. Irish gold work! And those are garnets, not your Gaulish enamel.'

'Well, there was grain for the horses. That warhorse is a waster of grain, my expensive grain.'

'Not that expensive. All that you gave us and the horses together is worth no more than a scrawny capon.'

'It's worth a pig at the least!'

'Well, the brooch is worth an ox, and you yourself admit that your goods are not worth that. Give it to me.'

'A crafty look came into his pale eyes. 'Stealing it from your lord?'

I tired to look unconcerned, though the man turned my stomach with his suppositions. 'If you think that, I'll call him and you can tell him that.'

The gleam faded from his eyes, and reluctantly he set the brooch down on the table. 'What'll you give me, then?'

I hadn't thought of it. I looked down at the clasp for a moment, then unfastened my own bronze brooch and set it down beside the other. 'That.'

'That? I wouldn't give a dozen eggs for it.'

We bargained for a while, and eventually the man accepted my bronze pin and a bronze ring, and gave me the brooch and a flask of his ale. I collected my gains, and fastened my cloak with Gwalchmai's brooch.

'May you prosper,' I said to the potter, standing up.

'*Vale*,' he returned, speaking, like a true townsman, in Latin. Then he added, 'You're a farmer, aren't you?'

I paused at the door 'I was that.'

'I knew it. Only farmers, and of them only householding clansmen, drive a bargain like that. God deliver Britain from such!'

I grinned and went out into the stable. The potter knew he'd got the worst of the bargain.

Gwalchmai had already saddled both horses and was waiting, and we mounted and were moving out of the town in short order. The sun was still low, and it glittered off the new snowfall with a jewelled brilliance. There were more clouds in the west, however and I judged we'd have more snow before long. I ached with every step Llwyd took, but I felt cheerful despite it all. I waited for Gwalchmai to notice the fruits of my bargain.

He did, before too long. Soon after we had reached the road to Caer Ceri, just beyond the walls of Caer Gloeu, he suddenly frowned and reined in his horse. His eyes were fixed on the brooch.

I grinned inwardly, but put a serious look on my face. 'Would you like your brooch back, Lord? I found it for you this morning.'

'Where did you . . . I gave that to the potter.'

'That I know. I'm wondering why. He could have bought an ox with it, and he deserved a thrashing.'

Gwalchmai rubbed his chin. 'Could he? I didn't know it was worth so much. Oh, I know I overpaid him, but what else? I am the Pendragon's servant, and it is honourable to be free of what I own, and I haven't any more gold, except what's on my Ceincaled.'

'You didn't know it was worth so much? Then how did you get it?'

'From a Saxon I killed a few years ago – now this potter will be confirmed in his opinion of warriors. Did you tell him I would kill him unless he gave it to you? That is a wrong.'

So much thanks I had for saving his money. 'Threaten him? Well, God knows, the man deserved it. But no, I gave him my brooch and a ring, and he gave me this and a flask of ale. I have the best of the bargain, and the man is busy thinking how warriors are cleverer than he thought them to be, or, at least, have clever servants.'

'You bargained?'

'How else does one buy things?'

Gwalchmai looked at me. No, I realized, he would never bargain. He would give, mostly, if he starved himself to do it, and from his lord's allies or enemies, take without payment.

'Well,' I said, sighing a bit because men are so different, 'well, for those who are not warriors, bargaining is the only way to buy, and those who do not bargain are fools. I told our potter that I was collecting the change from your payment, and have this,' and I lifted the flask of ale, 'as well as the brooch to show for it, and our host is cursing the bargaining of farmers. Is it wrong?'

Gwalchmai shook his head. 'You did not threaten him, but still left him cursing?'

'I left him a plucked goose. All that food, and the grain for the horses, for one bronze pin and a ring not worth half a dozen eggs!'

Gwalchmai gave me the same ambiguous look he had given me the night before, then suddenly burst out laughing. 'Ach, *righ rearach!* It is wonderful, it is a miracle! A flask of ale as well? I do not see how it was done, but Rhys, it was done well.'

I grinned back. I thought so too. 'So,' I said, 'here is your pin back, and you can give me mine.'

He shook his head, throwing up one narrow hand, palm out. 'Not so. You made a fine bargain for it; it is yours.'

I looked at the pin, glittering red and gold against my plain woollen cloak. An ox would be a low price to pay for it. I could not think of myself casually wearing something worth so much, it seemed almost scandalous. 'That would not be proper, my lord. You won it in battle; I merely talked to a fool. You take it back.'

But Gwalchmai shook his head again. 'I will not. Yours

will hold my cloak, and if someone takes exception to it, I can get another at Camlann.' He touched Ceincaled's sides with his heels and the horse broke into a flowing trot, and I kicked Llwyd until he jolted into the same gait. 'I have never seen a townsman bettered in my life, except when it is a matter of making them pay the tribute at sword's point, and that is no sweet thing. When we reach Camlann I will give you a ring to replace yours, and, by the sun, the tale is worth more than that.'

A ring, I thought, I did not want. I did not want the brooch, either, but I had it now. Well, I could always trade it for some less flashy gear. Or, if I found someone I could trust going that way I could send it home. Or even ... sometimes my father himself brought grain to Camlann to sell, and I could give it to him, perhaps with some gifts for the rest of them. A good thought, that.

We rode no fewer miles that day than we had the day before, going all the way to Maeldyfi and the monastery there (Gwalchmai would, I think, have gone to Baddon if he had been alone, but Llwyd was tired and could not keep the pace of the war stallion). It was even colder than the day before, and it began to snow around noon, when we again ate as we rode, and, what's more, I ached more than I had the day before. But my heart was a deal lighter. I was not an utter dead weight on my lord – my lord until we reached Camlann, at least, when I'd have to find some other master. I could get the better of townsmen, which my lord couldn't, and provide ale to go with the sausage and oat cakes we had for lunch. I could not only go to Camlann, but I could provide something there.

The monks at Maeldyfi where we stayed the night were in the custom of providing food and shelter for travellers, though they asked for a 'donation', by which they meant as much as they could get from the travellers. Too many monasteries in Britain are thus. I have heard that the Irish monasteries are different, and have been since Patricius brought the Faith there. I have met one or two Irish monks who have come to Britain in voluntary exile, desiring, for their love of Christ, to be parted from all that is familiar and secure and devote their lives to God. Most British monks seem to want to devote their lives to the prosperity of their community, and ignore God as much as possible. My father used to shake his head over them and try doubly hard to out-bargain them – for their own good, he would say – relieve them of some excess possessions, and explain to me that the fault was not of the Church, but of the man who ran it. Whatever the fault may be, monks will try to take more from their guests for a night's hospitality than either towns-men or farmers. Some people, awed by the candles and chanting, will pay it. I saw to it that in Maeldyfi we did not – for their own good, of course. I had to give them my spare tunic, but I got in return some bread and cheese for the next day's lunch, as well as the night's lodging and grain for the horses. Gwalchmai, to his own keenly felt shame, had no spare tunic to give (my mother had thought it not worth mending), and awkwardly promised me a better one than the old, when we reached Camlann.

The monks were hungry for news of the world, since they had few visitors in winter, and treated us much more hospitably than the potter, but Gwalchmai was as sus-picious of them as he had been of the townsman, and again insisted on sleeping by the horses. I remembered that the Pendragon was generally unpopular with the monasteries. He had insisted that they help the war either by paying tribute or by converting the Saxons. Being unwilling to take the risks involved in converting the Saxons, they paid, and hated. Gwalchmai, I noticed, again avoided mention of his name or loyalties.

We left Maeldyfi early next morning and took the road on southwards towards Baddon, which is some eighteen miles from Maeldyfi. My family's lands lie some fifteen miles west of the road, and about as far north of Baddon. I began looking for the familiar turning onto the rough track that led home, and was overcome by the strangeness of passing back down the same road only a few days after leaving home, and this time, truly knowing that it was all changed, that I was not turning my horse onto that side road.

Gwalchmai began singing, primarily in Irish, after leaving Maeldyfi. After a little, however, he stopped his verses and slowed his horse until it walked beside mine. He said nothing about this, and I was busy enough with my own thoughts to let it pass without question. But late in the morning, about the time I first began thinking of lunch, Gwalchmai suddenly touched his horse to a full gallop and tore off towards the wood at the side of the road. I reined in Llwyd in astonishment, looking after him, and only then saw the arrow sticking upright in the snow that covered the road. For a moment I could not understand where it had come from; and then I thought 'bandits', and looked back up to Gwalchmai.

The scrub there had been cleared back from the road and Gwalchmai was half-way to the line of trees, his white stallion running like a falcon swooping on a swallow, weaving back and forth to throw off the archer's aim, a dazzle of speed, mane tossed like light off water. Someone screamed, and then a body staggered out of the woods and fell with a spear – Gwalchmai's spear – jutting from it. I think I cried out. I know I must have clapped my heels to Llwyd's sides and started towards the struggle, not knowing what to do, but somehow thinking that I must stop it, as though it were only a quarrel between my cousins. But now there were other men running from the wood, yelling, men in tattered cloaks, carrying thrusting spears and bows. One more staggered back, spitted on a spear; and then there was a flash like lighting sweeping from the horizon, only holding, holding: Gwalchmai had drawn his sword, and it was incandescent with light.

There was more yelling. I think some of the bandits must have tried to flee, but they had no chance to. Some were trying to fight, at any rate, and it was useless.

Llwyd ran like a horse in a nightmare, crawling across the snow, but finally I reached the edge of the wood and did not know what to do. There seemed to be blood and dying men everywhere. Their eyes stared up at me, reflecting the morning sun. I later realized that there were only six bandits in the group, but at that instant there seemed to be fifty at least, and the shadows swung wild across the snow, cast by the burning sword.

One man backed up against a tree, holding his spear ready. I had time to look at him. His face was white above his brown beard, but his eyes were terrible and dark, and they were fixed on the sword. Gwalchmai swung his horse about, and the stallion reared, splendid as fire and wind, plunging towards the bandit.

'Don't!' I shouted, unable to bear it. 'My lord, don't!' and somehow I drove my horse up against his and caught his sword arm.

His head whipped about when I shouted, and our eyes met when I caught his wrist. Looking at him, I became terrified. 'I go mad in battle', he had said. Despite what he had added, I had thought of berserkers, men who foam at the mouth and rage like dogs when they fight, and had thought he had meant that – but Gwalchmai was not berserk. He was smiling, not with savagery or irony, but with a kind of ecstatic joy or even love, and there was a light, an exaltation in his face that should not be discovered on any human face. His hand was raised to bring down the sword, and I knew that it was nothing to him whether or not he killed, because in that madness, the difference between death and life was finer even than the sword's edge. He could kill me where I stood and not even notice. Somehow, it was not the threat of death that was terrifying, but the total foreignness of his eyes. I knew, meeting them, why those who saw angels were so afraid.

'Gwalchmai,' I said. His sword hand under mine did not move, but his lips parted as though he would speak. 'My lord,' I repeated.

Slowly, the glory began to fade from his eyes, and a kind of bewilderment crept into them. He dropped his gaze, the smile falling from his face, and looked down. His arm relaxed, and I released his hand. The light was gone from the sword, leaving it a mere piece of edged metal, cold in the winter sun.

Gwalchmai lowered the sword until it pointed to the ground, and drew away towards the bandit without looking at me. The robber stared at him, holding his spear level; then abruptly threw the weapon aside and flung himself on his face in the snow and began to beg for mercy, gabbling his pleas. I looked around and saw that around us were only corpses, lying on the snow. Five corpses.

'Sit up,' said my lord levelly. The bandit grovelled. 'Come, sit up.' The man rose to his knees and stared at us, his lips trembling, blue with cold. 'Why did you seek to kill us on the road just now?'

The man licked his lips. 'For money,' I said. The man bobbed his head in agreement. 'Arglwyd Mawr, Great Lord,' he said, 'I have no land.'

'Have you not? Then you should choose another craft

than this. What is your clan?'

He licked his lips. 'I have none.'

'Because you have been disowned by it, kin-wrecked, for the murder of a kinsman?'

He stared, then bobbed his head again. Most robbers are kin-wrecked.

Gwalchmai sighed. 'Is there any reason why I should not kill you?'

'Great Chieftain, I am a poor wretch and helpless, and you, you are the lord Gwalchmai . . . yes, yes, I heard your servant say so, and who else has such a sword, and such a horse, and fights so? Is it fitting, Great Lord, Master, that a falcon strike at gadflies?'

'If the gadflies strike at him. Get up. Come, get up. I will not kill you now.' The robber stood, shaking. 'Your companions here are dead. Have you others in your band?'

'One other, Chieftain. He is sick.'

'Then take what goods you have, and what you will from these bodies and buy oxen. There is land enough lying vacant; and if you will not farm, set up in a trade, you and this other. The Saxons have been defeated, man, and my lord the Pendragon is already sending men out to hunt down wolves such as yourself who prowl these roads. Do you hear me?'

'I hear you, Great Lord.'

'Then give thanks to God that you live yet, and take steps to avoid another encounter like this one where the numbers as well as the skill will be against you, and there will be no mercy shown.' Gwalchmai turned Ceincaled and rode off at a gallop. I followed, silently, wondering. I had begun to think that I knew Gwalchmai. I had put him down as a gentle, over-sensitive man, brave, honourable, over-conscientious. I had forgotten the first thing I knew about him: that he was the deadliest cavalry fighter in all Britain, Arthur's sword hand on almost numberless battlefields. I told myself, as I rode behind him and looked at his crimson-cloaked back, that the deadliness made his gentleness and self-control all the greater. But I felt sick. For all the songs I had heard, I had never understood what it means to see men killed, and the eyes of those five corpses still burned in my brain like glowing coals.

We rode thus for another half hour, and then Gwalchmai

drew his horse back beside mine. He still carried his naked sword, and there was blood on the blade. He lifted the hilt in a little gesture towards me. 'Rhys, have you anything I could use to clean this off?'

In silence I stopped, dismounted, and dug out of my pack a cloth my mother had meant for me to clean harness with. Gwalchmai also dismounted, rubbed his sword with snow, then dried the clean blade with my mother's cloth and slid the sword back into its sheath. The gold and ruby of the hilt glittered as he handed me the cloth back. There was only a little smudge of human blood on the material. I looked at the smudge for a moment, then put the cloth back in the pack and remounted. I gathered up Llwyd's reins, and saw Gwalchmai still standing, frowning a little.

'There is something the matter, then?' he asked. I tightened my grip on the reins, and Llwyd fidgeted and shied a little sideways. Gwalchmai caught his bridle, and the horse suddenly became very nervous, laying his ears back, rolling his eyes and snorting. I could see the reason.

'There is also some blood on your hand,' I told him. Gwalchmai glanced at his hand, and dropped it from the bridle so that the smell should cease to frighten my horse. He stooped and picked up some more snow to clean his hands. 'And that, also, is what is the matter with you?' he asked, without looking at me.

I did not know what to say. I looked at the reins, and Gwalchmai dried his hands on his cloak, then rubbed them together for warmth and wrapped them in some rags.

'My lord,' I said at last, 'I have never before seen a man killed, but I have just seen you kill five men. I am a fool, for I know that they would have killed us, and I knew from the beginning that you had killed many, but still, I am sick to see them dead, and you drying your sword and smiling.'

Gwalchmai looked at me thoughtfully a moment, then walked over to his horse and vaulted easily to the saddle. 'And they were poor wretches, too, were they not?' He straightened his cloak around him, the sword disappearing under its folds, and picked up the reins with firm hands. 'Outlaws, those, from Elmet, who starved in the north and so came south hoping to do better where the roads are more travelled but where they are not so much travelled as to be dangerous. Hardly equal opponents for me, hardly men with any chance of saving their own lives.'

I had heard of northerners coming south to practise robbery in the winter, so I nodded. If he did need to travel in the winter, my father always avoided the good roads. I had, in fact, heard of travellers killed by robbers on the south road, people in clans I knew. 'My lord, I know that they must have killed innocent men freely, and that they had no care for whether or not the fight was equal.'

'But we should care.' He touched Ceincaled's sides and started off at a walk. He stared down the road, looking tired. 'If I am to fight for my lord the Pendragon and for Britain and the Light, I ought to care.' He looked at me again, smiling a very little, almost questioning. 'And yet, it is not right to let them continue to kill when I can stop them. I let that man escape today. Perhaps this afternoon he will kill someone, because he did not die this morning.'

I looked at Llwyd's neck, and twisted my fingers in his coarse mane. If the bandit killed someone this afternoon, I was partly responsible, for I was the one who had prevented Gwalchmai from killing him. What if someone I knew, someone from a householding in the area, had to travel the road? What if someone from my family did? 'And yet, the man might buy some oxen. There's land enough that needs workers.'

'And he might not.' Gwalchmai looked back down the road. 'Well, I have killed the other five, and I frightened him, and it may be enough. But I do not see that I could have done anything but fight them.'

That was true. He could not have simply sat still and allowed the robbers to kill us both.

'I do not know,' Gwalchmai said abruptly 'I am used to the fighting and the killing now, and I do not think of it much, unless someone should ask me. And I do not remember killing. Only Bran; I remember killing him. But I killed him for myself, and the others I kill because I must. A servant of the Light gave me a sword, and it is meant to be wielded. If the Darkness is to be turned back, surely the sword is the means? I am ready to kill for my lord, to order and defend, and yet I do not know if it is wholly right. But there is no other way open to me, so I must fight, and trust Heaven for the rest.'

For some reason, I felt tremendously comforted. 'You

are right. If I wish to fight for civilization, I suppose I had better get used to it all. Forgive me, my lord.'

Gwalchmai gave me a strange look, then smiled. I smiled back. We rode on, under a clear sky. The sun stood in the middle of the blue arch, and the snow glistened around us. Gwalchmai began to sing a long, slow, melancholy song in Irish, his voice rich and clear in the silence which weighed over the forest about us. A strange world, I thought, and people the strangest thing in it. A complicated world, where to act might be to act wrongly, and not to act be even worse. It would take some getting used to.

Six

Gwalchmai was eager to reach Camlann, and from Maeldyfi wanted to press on as far as Ynys Witrin, a good fifty miles. At Ynys Witrin we could claim hospitality from the local lord, who would be bound to offer it freely to the Pendragon's nephew. But Llwyd was tired, and could not go fast, and the distance was too great – or so I said – and we eventually spent the night at a farm some ten miles south of Baddon. The farmer was a hard bargainer, unwilling to accept any of our goods until Gwalchmai took the gold-worked headstall from Ceincaled's bridle. Then he began to offer us more than we needed, eager for more gold. I took two bronze armlets and a silver ring in change (a better bargain than the other hoped for), and Gwalchmai knotted a rope to improvise a headstall, though he was not pleased with it. He would sooner have sold all his own gear than have touched the horse's.

The next day we rode on to Camlann, arriving at the fortress just after noon. At mid-morning we turned from the Roman road onto the raised track that goes through Ynys Witrin and the marshes, and made good speed towards the irregular hills that fill the horizon. The land about us was well settled, clear of forest, and the fields were well tended. It was another bright, clear day, and sheep and cattle were out in the pastures, giving the land a cheerful, inhabited look welcome after the long road and the forest. As we went west, Camlann slowly resolved itself from the surrounding hills, seeming to grow taller as we approached it. Gwalchmai urged his horse to a trot, then to a canter, and the stallion ran with a light step and pricked-up ears. He knew well enough where he was going. Llwyd had no such eagerness, but he followed the other horse. He had grown used to doing that.

The feast hall showed clear against the sky, crowning the great hill. Only after I had noticed that did I discern the walls and the ring and bank defences of the fortress. But the walls were large enough when we came to them, and had been strongly re-fortified, unlike the walls of any town I had ever seen. The gate we approached was also new, with a single guard tower set above it, and it was made of oak and iron. But it opened before we reached it, and Gwalchmai reined in just inside it to greet the guards, while his stallion danced in eagerness to be properly home. I drew in Llwyd, who was sweating from his run. Both the guards posted there came down from the guard tower and began shouting to Gwalchmai.

'A hundred thousand welcomes home!' said one of them. 'Man, we were wondering who we could send out to avenge your death. Your brother said no, it was like you to go travelling in winter – but he was the readiest of all of us to begin any revenging.'

Gwalchmai laughed. 'Was he? That is like my brother. He is well? And my lord Arthur? And the Queen?'

Yes, yes, they were all well, and there was news, and certain things had happened so, and Cei had said to Agravain – 'But you will hear all this soon enough,' the guard interrupted himself. 'And it is a cold day to stand about talking. I will see you at the feast tonight.'

'Is there a feast tonight?'

'There will be now. There's been no excuse for one these two weeks. Oh, and who is this fellow with you?'

'My servant. Rhys ap Sion.'

The guard cocked one eyebrow and looked at me as though I were someone's new horse. 'Gwalchmai the Golden-tongued has taken a servant? Do you plan to stay in one place, then?'

Gwalchmai simply laughed. I was ready to tell the guard that the job was not mine, and that I was to find another master in Camlann, but the man went on, 'Good for you, servant, and good luck! I hope you like to travel.'

Gwalchmai laughed again, wished the guard a happy watch, and started Ceincaled off up the steep hill at a canter.

Camlann is a huge fortress. There are seven hundred men in Arthur's Family; about four hundred of these sleep in the feast hall, while the rest have houses inside the fortress. Some of the men are married and have their families at Camlann. Besides these warriors, the servants and their families make their homes in the fortress, and the doctors, smiths, carpenters and masons, the grooms and the trainers and breeders of horses, and all the tradesmen who have settled in the fortress. There is also some farming done, since a number of cattle are pastured in the fields around, with flocks of sheep, while some pigs and chickens are kept in Camlann itself, and vegetables are grown there, but the rest of the food – all the grain, and much of the meat – has to be purchased. A fortress that size requires a great deal of grain, and warhorses must eat more grain in great amounts; it takes a good deal of care to keep the food coming in. There must be wealth, and a safe market, so that people can bring their goods in. There must be a steady flow of tribute from the other kings of Britain, who in turn take tribute from the clans subject to themselves, and this requires civil peace enforced by the authority and power of the Emperor. But this power and authority and peace existed, and Camlann was not only huge, but thriving. I looked at the people we passed as we rode up the hill. A girl stepped carefully through the snow, carrying a basket of eggs; some boys ran by hurling snowballs at one another with savage warcries; a man chopped wood; two women stood in a doorway, gossiping. Most of them waved or yelled at us cheerfully, and I thought of the dreariness and bitterness of Caer Ceri and Caer Gloeu, and knew that I was right, after all, to come to Camlann.

The stables at Camlann adjoin the feast hall, and it was to these that we rode first. Gwalchmai was again greeted with delight. There was a great deal of pounding one another on the back and joking when we dismounted. I did not know anyone, and everyone was too busy to pay attention to me, so I hung about, smiling to show that I sympathized with homecomings.

Gwalchmai handed Ceincaled's bridle to one of the grooms, saying, 'You can see to him just this once, Celli. I wish to go to greet my lord and my brothers. He has had some grain already this morning, but I have used him hard, these months, and more would not harm him. Ach, but you know your business – but he needs a new headstall, a good one, if there is one about.'

The groom took the horse's bridle as though it were set with diamonds, grinning. Gwalchmai caught up the saddle-bags and slung them over his shoulders, so I hastened to do the same with my gear. I stood for a moment, holding Llwyd's bridle and trying to think what to do with my mount, and then Gwalchmai remembered my existence, and again explained me as 'Rhys ap Sion. My servant.' I received more curious stares, but someone took my horse. Gwalchmai strode from the stable with a quick, eager step, limping only a little, and I had half to run to keep up with him, for all that he was carrying his spears and shield as well as his luggage, and wearing a mail-coat, which is no light burden.

The Hall at Camlann is high-roofed, and the swallows nest under the eaves in summer. Torches set in brackets along the walls burn even in the daytime, and in winter the fires in the hearth-pits down the centre of the Hall keep the place warm. It is always half-light, and usually glitters, since it is full of whitewashed shields hung against the wall, and spears, and warriors wearing jewellery. When we arrived the place was half full of men playing some board game or knucklebones, talking or listening to a harper. It had that sleepy, comfortable air peculiar to winter afternoons. No one really noticed us as we came in. Gwalchmai set his saddle-bags down by the door and leaned his spears carefully upright beside them. As he was unstrapping his shield, someone looked over, then leapt up crying, 'Gwalchmai!' and at once the whole place was up and crowding around us.

The enthusiasm of the welcome we had had from the guards and the grooms began to look rather dim. A few greetings stood out from the crowd here, however. One tall man with hot gold hair and beard and hot blue eyes thrust his way through the other warriors and flung his arms about Gwalchmai, shouting in Irish. My lord hugged him back, and began speaking in the same language. The one word I caught was the name 'Agravain', and I realized that this must be his brother. The two did not look very much alike. From what I had heard, they did not act much alike, either, and Agravain was renowned as an infantry fighter.

While Gwalchmai jabbered away at his brother in Irish, I hung about at the door, smiling to show that I still sympathized with homecomings, though in fact I was getting a bit tired of them, and wondering whether anyone would offer us food, which we'd had none of since dawn. After a little, I noticed a slight, dark, serious-looking man watching me. He was quietly dressed, only a silver chain around his neck proclaiming high rank for him. I smiled, and he smiled back and stepped over to join me.

'Greetings,' he said, courteously. 'Are you looking for someone, man?'

'Not yet, Lord. I am Gwalchmai ap Lot's new servant, and I am waiting for him to finish greeting everyone.'

The man looked at me with interest. 'Gwalchmai's servant. That is very unexpected, for Gwalchmai.'

'So I have been hearing. Actually, Lord, I'm only temporarily his servant. He said that he would find me a place at Camlann when I asked him to bring me here.'

'You asked him?'

I found myself grinning. 'Well, Lord, he was staying with my family, so I seized the opportunity. I have wanted to come here.'

'Indeed,' began the other, and would have asked something more, when Gwalchmai broke out of the crowd to clasp my companion's arm.

'Bedwyr,' he said, 'here you are, then. How is it with you?'

I stared at the man, trying to believe he was who he must be. Sure enough, his shield hand was missing at the wrist. Bedwyr, the man whom the Emperor had appointed his warleader after he had been his cavalry commander for years, his closest counsellor. I had not pictured him so plain and quiet.

He smiled at Gwalchmai, a deep, glad smile that filled his eyes. 'It is well. Camlann is much the same. But how is it with you? Did you find what you were seeking?'

My lord's smile stopped, and he shook his head. 'Not yet. It must be tried again.'

Bedwyr gave him a considering look. 'Then see that it is tried in summer. This winter quest has worn you, I think.'

Gwalchmai laughed. 'It is just being away from home. Where is my lord Arthur?'

'In his room, talking to a messenger from Gaul about the situation there, and about trade. If you wish to see him, it is not an urgent meeting.'

'I will wait for him. Where is Cei, then?'

'Out hunting. He has been bored.'

'I imagine. No one to fight.'

Agravain pushed back through the crowd to Gwalchmai

and caught his elbow. 'Since you will wait for Arthur, come have some wine with us and tell us where you have been.' He swept his brother off towards the nearest table, calling for the wine. Bedwyr, however, looked back to me.

'Why did you wish to come here, then, Gwalchmai's servant?' he asked.

I looked at him, quiet and calm and paying attention to me, and blurted out, 'Lord, I wished to serve the Light.'

He nodded, thoughtfully. 'A very good reason. Welcome to Camlann, then.' He turned and strolled over to the table where Gwalchmai was now seated with a glass of wine and a ring of friends, being talked to by his brother. I followed, hesitantly. Gwalchmai looked up to welcome Bedwyr, then noticed me and set his glass down hurriedly.

'Rhys! I had forgotten you. Agravain, this is my new servant, Rhys ap Sion.'

'A servant?' Agravain looked at me fiercely. 'Good. I've told you for years that you needed one. Can he look after horses?'

'I will not let him look after Ceincaled,' said Gwalchmai, smiling. 'No one will do that but I myself, whether or not it is dignified. But Rhys is a clever man, *mo chara*. He outbargains townsmen and leaves them cursing and admiring the astuteness and business sense of the Pendragon's warriors.'

'Mistakenly, in your case.' But the other seemed pleased at the thought of outbargained townsmen. 'Well, servant, go fetch your lord some food.'

I looked around, wondering which way to go to do this, and why Agravain should be the one to tell me to, but Gwalchmai whipped his feet off the bench and exclaimed, 'Ach, no. Come here, Rhys, and have some wine. Agravain, he's done a fair piece of riding, and that in bad weather, since he joined me. And he has never been to Camlann before; is he to go running about now?'

Agravain shrugged, bellowed for someone else to fetch the food, and I, after hesitating and looking around to the lord Bedwyr, came and sat down on the bench at Gwalchmai's left, feeling very out of place. A thin, long-faced warrior handed me a glass goblet of wine, and Agravain began talking again about what all the warriors in the Family had done since his brother left. I held the goblet gingerly, looking at it. Glass, like wine, is a great luxury, and neither are made much in Britain these days. The goblet was blue-green, with a sheen over its surface, and the red wine glinted through it with a purple colour. I sipped the stuff very carefully, trying to decide whether I liked it or not. I had never had any before, except for a little at Mass, and that had not been heated with spice and honey.

Agravain and the other warriors went on talking, prompted by eager questions from Gwalchmai. A servant came and set a platter of meat and bread before my lord; he broke off one edge of the bread, stabbed a bit of meat with his knife, and pushed the platter in my direction, nodding to what someone was saying. I glanced around, saw that no one was paying the slightest attention to me, and began eating. The meat was broiled venison, richer fare than I was used to, and very good.

After a while, Gwalchmai told his friends a little about his own journey. Most of it concerned his embassy to Caledon, and he managed to describe his wandering in search of Elidan very briefly and without mentioning the girl. But he did speak of my father. He had had a fight with some bandits, he said, and this had made him decide to seek shelter for the night. Before that, apparently, he had been sleeping in the open, and he would probably have continued to do so if I had not been there to be horrified at the hardship of sleeping in stables. 'So I went off through the forest, thinking that it would be safer if I reached Dumnonia, and by chance I found Rhys here by a ford. I had met his father before and found him a good man, so I stayed five days at the holding. They saw to it that my horse was shod, my cloak mended, and gave me such hospitality as travellers pray for, and Sion ap Rhys refused any payment, though I offered it him again and again.' This brought looks of astonishment. 'He is a man as generous as a king, and more generous than a king like Maelgwn.'

Agravain gave a snort at that. 'So you asked his son as a servant?'

Gwalchmai looked at me and smiled, as at a secret joke. 'Not so. His son asked me as a lord.'

'That sounds more like you,' Agravain commented, scowling. But his eyes rested on his brother with delighted pride. I wondered if Dafydd would look at me that way if I came home, and shivered.

'And you will treat your servant the same way you treat your horse,' Agravain concluded.

'I hope not. Rhys is not over-fond of oats, even in porridge.' Gwalchmai grinned at me.

Agravain shook his head and began to go on, and I was anxious for him to explain his remark, but just then someone at the front of the Hall shouted, 'Gwalchmai!', and my lord nearly tipped the bench over in his haste to get up.

'My lord,' said Gwalchmai. He went up the centre of the Hall, half running, to meet the man who had just entered it. When they met, the other clasped Gwalchmai's forearm, and Gwalchmai caught his hand, kissed it and pressed it to his forehead.

'Good indeed,' said the newcomer. 'A hundred thousand welcomes home, at long last. We have expected you since Christmas; where have you been? If you have told the others already, you will have to repeat it to me. Macsen–' to a servant – 'we must have a feast tonight. Go tell my lady that the lord Gwalchmai is back, and ask her to prepare it. And see if you can find Taliesin, and ask him whether he's finished that epic he was working on.' And to Gwalchmai, 'Did you find what you were seeking?'

Gwalchmai shook his head. 'It was a cold trail that vanished in the mountains of Arfon, a word I could not find again, and a bitter search after it. My lord, it is good to be home.'

'And yet, you will search again.' The voice was quiet, creating privacy in a public place, and not questioning.

'By your leave, my lord.'

'If you must. But not in winter, and not alone.'

At this, Gwalchmai smiled. 'If you are concerned that I travelled alone, my lord, it will please you to know I have found a servant.'

I had stood up as soon as I had heard Gwalchmai call the other 'my lord', and when the man followed Gwalchmai's gesture and looked at me, I did my best to bow. I was not very skilful at it. The other looked at me appraisingly, and I looked at him. He was tall, of average build, with light blond hair beginning to grey at the temples, and he wore his beard cropped close to the jawline, in the old Roman fashion. He had grey eyes, wide-set, and the kind of stare that seems to look beyond what it is fixed on. He wore a gold collar about his neck, and his cloak was of the imperial purple. But he did not require the purple to proclaim him Emperor and Pendragon of Britain. He was the kind of man so accustomed to command that it is unconscious, the sort of man men obey without thinking.

'You are Gwalchmai's servant?' Arthur asked me. 'What is your name, man?'

'Rhys ap Sion, Great Lord, of the clan of Huw ap Celyn.'

'The clan of Huw ap Celyn. You live in Dumnonia, do you not? Up by Mor Hafren?'

'I . . . yes, Great Lord.' I was astonished that he should know. Arthur smiled, a quick instant of pleasure at my astonishment.

'I am also Dumnonian by birth,' he explained. 'And we have wheat from near Mor Hafren every harvest.'

I knew that, because my father took the cart up to Camlann every harvest, with some other holders from our area, and sold the wheat, but I had not expected the Emperor to know. 'My father, Sion ap Rhys, grows some of that wheat, Great Lord, and he is glad to sell it to the Pendragon, as I am glad to be here.'

Arthur grinned suddenly. 'Prettily said, man. You'll have no trouble when your lord takes you on an embassy.' He sat at the table, took a glass of wine, and nodded for the rest to sit as well. 'And, as regards embassies, I must see you,' he said, addressing Gwalchmai again, 'regarding that journey to Caledon, for there are a few things I wish you to explain further. Dear God, you need have no fear; I won't send you back there yet.'

'I thank you for that, for once. My horse needs a rest.'

'Less than you need one. Rejoice: till the spring comes I will give you nothing to do but write letters, confer with ambassadors, translate Irish into good Latin and *vice versa*, and look after your horse. My friend, you were a fool to swear your oath to me.'

'I consider it otherwise. Am I not to do accounts, copy your books, or give advice on the new building plans, then? How are the plans going?'

'If you wish, I will let you do all of those, except the accounts. Gwynhwyfar has taken to saying that everyone else makes chaos of them, and does them all herself. But the plans – well, we will begin the new store house after the thaw; I decided not to put it next to the old one, but down the hill . . .'

'Near Gereint's house?'

'No, eastwards . . .' After a few minutes of this, Arthur tired of trying to sketch the planned building on the table in wine lees, and leapt up offering to show what he meant. The idea of tramping about the fortress gave me no great pleasure just then, however, for my legs were sore from all the riding. I offered instead to carry our gear to wherever Gwalchmai wanted it carried. Agravain, rather surprisingly, offered to show me the house he and his brother shared with another prestigious warrior. So while Arthur, Gwalchmai and Bedwyr swept off to inspect the building site, I picked up the two sets of saddle-bags and began to collect spears.

Agravain watched me impatiently and finally exclaimed, 'My brother's servant, and you don't know how to carry a spear! Here.' He picked the spears up in a way that I could not see differed from my way in the slightest, and walked off briskly. I fumbled around to find the shield and ran after him, nearly dropping one of the saddle-bags as I hurried to catch up.

The house was a pleasant one, soundly built of mud and wattle, neatly whitewashed, and with a thick thatch. It stood to the east of the Hall, and from the doorway one could look out at the tor of Ynys Witrin standing like a watch tower against the marshy plain that leads to the Saxon kingdoms. Inside, however, it was a mess, with bedding and clothing and weapons strewn over everything. I later found out that Agravain had had a servant till the year before, when the man died of a fever, and no one had cleaned the place since. I set the saddle-bags down and wondered where to put things. Agravain leaned the spears against the wall with satisfaction.

'There,' he said. 'And now, Rhys, or whatever your name is . . .'

'It is Rhys.'

'Whatever it is, you are my brother's servant, and there are one or two things I will tell you.'

I wondered what. He looked at me, rubbing the knuckles of one hand.

'I gather you persuaded my brother into taking you on.

Well and good, for he needs a servant; he is always doing things a warrior ought not do, and takes no care for himself. But what he needs is a servant, one who will do as he is told and not give himself airs. You came into Camlann as though you thought yourself some kind of guest, and sat at the same table as the noblest warriors and the High King himself. My brother will not stop such behaviour. He will be inclined, if I know him, to treat you as he treats his horse – better than he treats himself – merely because you are dependent on him. It is a privilege to serve him, servant, remember that.'

I swallowed the anger that was rising in my throat and nodded, trying to look as though the privilege impressed me.

'And listen, servant.' Agravain stepped over and seized the front of my cloak, twisting it so that it choked me and forcing me against the wall. 'My brother will do nothing to punish you for insolence, but if you serve him badly, and let him do without while you live in luxury, and take advantage of his courtesy – I will see to it that you are beaten as much as you deserve. Do you hear me?'

'I hear you,' I croaked. I longed to tell him that I was a free-born clansman, a servant by choice only, and that I could throw his privileges in his face and leave; but the thought that I could stopped me, and made me hold my tongue. I had chosen, and I had had no expectation that all warriors would be like Gwalchmai or Bedwyr.

'Good,' said Agravain, and hit me across the face, just to show me what he meant. I had my fist up, ready to hit him back, before I remembered that if I did hit him, he might do anything, and he was a trained warrior. And also, I had chosen ... I forced my hand to relax. Fortunately, Agravain had not noticed it. He hit me once more, with the flat of his hand this time, and let me go. I began to straighten my cloak.

'Where did you get that brooch?' Agravain demanded suddenly.

My hands froze. 'My lord gave it to me,' I said, trying to keep my voice deferential. 'He gave it to a townsman as payment for a night's lodgings, and I got it back by bargaining. Your brother told me to keep it.'

'That's no brooch for a servant. Give it here.'

I had not thought it a brooch for a servant, either, but I would not be told so by Agravain ap Lot. 'Lord, my lord told me to keep it. If I gave it away, I would be disobeying him.'

'You can give it to me. I'm his brother.'

'I will then – if he tells me to.'

Agravain grabbed one of the spears and held it upside down, by the neck like a cudgel. 'By the Sun! You will do as you're told.'

'I am, Lord. I was told to keep it.'

'Greedy fool.' Agravain glared at me a moment longer, and I braced myself for a thrashing with the spear. But he lowered the weapon. 'I will speak to my brother about this. He should not give such things away.' He tossed the spear aside. 'Get this place in order,' he flung at me, and strode from the house.

I sat down on one of the low beds, shaking with anger, and beat my fist against the mattress from sheer frustration.

'You should have expected this,' I told myself, out loud. But it did no good. I hadn't expected to feel like this. I had always been able to stand up for myself; for that matter, I usually won any fight I stood up in. But now any noble dog could treat me as he pleased, and I would have to smile and say 'Yes, Lord'. Gwalchmai and, it seemed, Bedwyr and the Emperor were pleased to treat me honourably, but I had a strong feeling that Agravains were more common. I slammed the bed once more, and hit my hand against the wooden frame.

I sucked my knuckles and looked at the frame, and then the pounded mattress, and had to laugh. Still laughing, I straightened the dented bedding, and got up and tried to set some order to the mess that filled the room.

By the time Gwalchmai arrived, at twilight, I had managed to put everything in a place. The wrong place, un-doubtedly, but it was improbable that anything really had a right place. It was hard work, because I was no more used to it than the warriors were, but I was beginning to feel that I was winning the fight.

Gwalchmai opened the door quietly, looked around at the place in surprise, then shot me a questioning look.

'Your brother told me to put it in order,' I explained.

'Ah.' Gwalchmai closed the door, went over to the fire,

caught up a taper and lit a hanging lamp. A warm glow fell over the small room, and Gwalchmai blew out the taper. With the glowing end still raised, he turned and looked at me. His look was a little sad, his eyes attentive on my face.

'How many times did my brother hit you?' he asked quietly.

I stared.

'Oh come, you will not tell me you got that bruise across your face by running into a door, will you?'

I shrugged. 'Only once, hard.'

Gwalchmai sighed and sat down, twirling the taper with his fingers. The end made a little circle of red as it spun. 'Agravain came and told me I should not give servants valuable brooches, and warned me against insolence. I am sorry if I have got you into trouble.'

I looked at Gwalchmai as he stared at the end of his taper, his fine, thin face looking worn and worried, and suddenly, without thinking about his name and his troubles, I liked him very much.

'He only noticed the brooch after he hit me,' I said. 'My lord, some men talk with their fists, and I expected it when I asked to come with you.'

Gwalchmai shook his head. 'Agravain is a good man. He merely feels that he must ... maintain a position. And he doesn't know how to talk to people.'

I thought to myself that Agravain might be a good man to those he considered to be 'people', but I felt that that included only a small segment of humanity. However I nodded in reply to Gwalchmai's statement. 'My lord, it is nothing to worry about. I've had worse fights with my cousins.'

'But Agravain hits hard, and you couldn't hit him back.'

'He doesn't hit that hard.'

'Yes he does. I remember his thrashings. Vividly.'

At my look of surprise, Gwalchmai added, 'I wasn't always a good warrior, you know, and Agravain is more than three years older than me. And he knows how to humiliate. I hadn't thought of that when I agreed to let you come.'

'My lord,' I said, exasperated, 'the fact that one man feels that he must maintain his position at the expense of mine is no reason for me not to stay here.'

'But there are others who might feel the same way. There is Cei. I've known him to bully servants on principle. And he lives here, in this house.'

I'd heard of Cei. If Gwalchmai was famed as the finest warrior in Arthur's cavalry, Cei ap Cynyr was the finest in the infantry. There were nearly as many songs about him as there were about Gwalchmai, and most of them mentioned that he had a heavy hand and a hot temper. If I stayed with Gwalchmai at Camlann, to live in the same house as Cei and Agravain might be a bit tiresome. But then . . . 'My lord, if I won't be living here, what does it matter where Cei lives, or Agravain either for that matter?'

Gwalchmai looked up sharply from the taper, which had finally gone out. 'What? You're not going back home?'

'No. But you said you would find me another lord at Camlann.' Gwalchmai was silent. 'You told me you didn't want a servant.'

'Oh. So I did.' He tossed the taper in the fire, stood and leaned against the wall, watching it burn. 'I'd forgotten that.' His eyes lifted from the fire and met mine. 'Would you be willing not to go to another lord? To stay with me instead?'

I sucked in my breath and fidgeted with the cloak-pin. I knew my own wants well enough. For all that I had only known this man for a week or so, I knew I could trust him with my life and honour. I knew that, serving him, I would be required to do nothing demeaning or dishonourable, and that I would most certainly be able to work hard for the Light. And it would be hard, too, with more long journeys, and sleeping in stables – and probably in the open as well – and no food and long hours and plenty of enemies. But I wanted it, God knows. And besides the rest, I liked the man.

'My lord,' I said, 'I would be very willing to do that thing. But only if you want me to. I do not wish to do what your brother threatened to thrash me for, and take advantage of your courtesy. You are not responsible for me, just because you agreed to bring me here.'

'My courtesy! Man, this is scarcely courtesy. I am calling you to a hard life. If you served some other master, you would have an easier time of it. No, it is because you are a good servant and a good man to have at one's back.'

I wondered what, other than out-bargaining the townsman, I had done to deserve that description. But I grinned. 'It is your courtesy, my lord, as far as I'm concerned. Is it settled, then? I stay with you?'

'It is settled.' He stepped quickly from the fireplace and put out his hand, and I clasped it. He smiled, and I grinned back. Agravain or no Agravain, I had a place for myself.

Seven

We stayed in Camlann about a month and a half before we set out again. I think it was probably the longest single period Gwalchmai had stayed there. The war and Arthur's embassies had kept him busy before. And, as Arthur had promised, he had work to do in that month and a half. Unlike most of the other warriors, Gwalchmai could read and write, his Latin was excellent, and he knew Saxon and Irish as well as British and was familiar enough with the web of British affairs that he could work a way into any tangle of alliances and enmities without offending the allied or hostile parties. All this was very useful to Arthur, who, I discovered, spared nothing that was useful to his ends, himself least of all. But he never asked more than his followers were willing to give. He was a man obsessed with a dream, a vision of the Empire arising again in Britain, and taking into itself all the barbarians, to create a new order, working with justice in peace; and to create it he worked with his whole life and the lives of those around him. He had the gift of making other men see what he meant, and the whole fortress assumed nothing else than that we were about restoring a Christian civilization to a world that was growing dark, though most of the people there would not have put it that way. It was an exhilarating assumption.

Not all the warriors were worked as hard as Gwalchmai, however. Most of them knew only how to fight and, when not fighting, played knucklebones, hunted, or were bored. Agravain and Cei were in this group, and, once I got to know them, I found them sometimes humiliating, frequently infuriating, but on the whole tolerable. Indeed, I quite liked Cei, though his temper was worse than Agravain's, and his tongue sharper. He was a very tall, heavy-muscled red-head with a thick red beard, and he wore more jewellery than any other man in the Family. His treatment of servants was all I had heard it would be, but he was not by nature a bully. He enjoyed being talked back to, though he might offer, and occasionally provide, a thrashing for it if one went too far. He liked arguing, and was a fine bargainer, and we had some grand disagreements about how I arranged matters in the house. He had an acid wit and a fine sense of sarcasm, but he knew how to laugh.

Agravain was completely different. He was indeed trying to 'maintain a position', and, seemingly, felt that he had to defend it at any cost. I wondered whether it might have something to do with his having come to Camlann originally as a hostage for his father's oath of peace. While there was little he would not do for his friends – and, more especially, for his brother – he would not lift a finger for anyone else, or stir by a quarter of a step from the lofty and glorious standing of warrior and first-born son of a king. On some days he was moody, and would fall into a rage at the imagined implications of a look – this with his inferiors, of course, not other warriors. The only way for us to handle him was to give him what he wanted, and that immediately. Still, after the first day he left me alone. I gather that Gwalchmai had had a serious talk with him, although neither Gwalchmai nor Agravain ever said so.

I was glad to be left to work, because I had more than enough work to keep me busy. The house had to be looked after: the fire kept burning, the place kept clean and orderly, the thatch repaired. Then, Agravain and Cei assumed that, since I was living there, I would naturally do all their personal work as well as Gwalchmai's. I had to see that their clothing was taken to a washerwoman, their small wants for this and that were satisfied, and that their weapons and armour were in good condition. (Another servant, Amren, showed me how to do this last.) The horses were looked after by grooms, which was a mercy, but I still had to exercise Llwyd, and sometimes Cei and Agravain's horses as well. Gwalchmai very rarely let anyone else near his Ceincaled, and, to tell the truth, was in other ways the least work of the three.

When I had finished looking after my lot of warriors, there was still much else to do in the fortress. Because the Family had for so long wandered over all of Britain, few of the warriors had personal servants, and the servants who worked at Camlann were adequate for a smaller community only. There were only about a hundred and fifty men and a hundred women for the whole fortress, and all of us were busy. The public places like the Hall and the guard tower and store-rooms had to be kept clean and ordered; the cattle had to be butchered, and the hides cured for leather; the kitchens had to be supplied, mead to be fermented, and so on and on. But I did not dislike the work, as I had thought I might. The pleasant thing about service is that, unlike farming work, it can be done in company and while talking. I found the other servants at Camlann good company. Perhaps two-thirds of them were either former townsfolk or descended from a long line of servants. But there were also a fair number of clansmen like myself, farmers who had lost their land to the Saxons, and had been unable or unwilling to find land and settle elsewhere. There were even a few Saxons, men who had been captured on a raid and had sworn to serve some lord or other in exchange for their lives. The others came from every part of Britain, and even from across the sea in Less Britain, and to hear their tales was as good as listening to a song.

The management of the household of Camlann was under the supervision of the Queen Gwynhwyfar. She was a thin, brown-eyed lady like a candle-flame, warm and shining, topped by masses of red hair. She never seemed to sit still, and always seemed to know where every man and woman in the household was and what they were doing. She never seemed to walk anywhere: she ran; some said she danced. She determined how much wool we had and how much we needed by buy and how much each person could take; she saw to it that the cattle were slaughtered in the right numbers and that we had enough grain; she ordered major repairs, like thatching, and kept all the accounts. Her instructions were administered by Gweir ap Cacwmri, who ran practically everything, and his wife, Tangwen, who ran everything, including Gweir.

Of the other servants – it would take weeks to tell. Amren, who showed me how to look after weapons, was Bedwyr's servant, and a Breton like his master. He had travelled in Gaul before he took service with Bedwyr, and could tell tales of the south, of Lugdunum and Massilia and the ships that leave for Rome and Carthage, tell them all night, if he was allowed to. And then there was Aegmund, a Saxon from Deira: he'd sworn to serve the lord Rhuawn at the beginning of the war with the Saxons, thirteen years and more before, when Rhuawn first went raiding. After the battle of Baddon, Rhuawn freed him and offered to help him return to a Saxon kingdom, but Aegmund had become a Christian, married, made a home, and wanted to stay. There were others – but enough of that. Suffice it that, by and large, despite Cei and Agravain and some others like them, Camlann was better than I had hoped it would be. I was sorry when Gwalchmai told me that we were to leave it again.

It was a day in mid-March, chill and rainy. I was in one of the store-rooms whitewashing a shield, and my lord sought me out there to tell me that we were to ride on the morrow.

I set my brush down in confusion. 'Where are we riding, then, my lord? And for how long?'

'Just to Gwynedd.' Gwalchmai dropped into a crouch beside me and studied the shield with interest. The months since our arrival had done him good, taking the gaunt, bitter look from his face, but leaving a kind of restlessness more plainly marked. He was wearing a gold collar, and the collar of his cloak was of embroidered leather, very fine, so that he looked more kingly than usual, and he could look fairly royal in a homespun tunic. Nonetheless, he picked up the whitewashing brush and frowned at the pot of lime. 'Whose shield is this?'

'Constans's,' I said automatically, wondering what next.

'You shouldn't be doing his.' Gwalchmai dipped the brush in the lime and began to dab it on the shield. 'I've told you, you're doing more than your share of work as it is.'

'Well, Macsen had to go and find some more thatch for the Hall today, and Constans wanted the shield done this week, so what's wrong in offering help? Don't you start doing it. Did you say we were going to Gwynedd?'

He nodded, painting carefully around the shield-boss.

'Just to Gwynedd.' Gwynedd was ruled by Arthur's greatest enemy, King Maelgwn ap Docmail, and the whole kingdom was a refuge for all who hated the Pendragon. 'Just' to Gwynedd.

'For how long?' I asked.

He shrugged. 'As long as is necessary.' The side of the brush grazed the shield-boss, leaving a white smear on it, and Gwalchmai looked about for something to clean it. I picked up a rag and rubbed the stain off myself. Gwalchmai leaned back on his heels. 'My lord had been planning to send someone to Maelgwn this spring; we had only about two-thirds of tribute due us from Gwynedd last year. As usual. It was necessary for us to deal with the man; and now there is this new matter of his reported guests, and the matter has become urgent. My lord wishes us to leave at once.'

'Guests? More outlaws?'

'No – at least, the reports do not seem to suggest that.' Gwalchmai smiled, but his right arm, resting across his knees, stretched out so that his fingers brushed his sword-hilt. 'One of my lord's men in Caer Segeint sent that some foreigner's came to the port, sailing in curraghs, which they were permitted to draw up high onto the beach. There were horses and wagons provided to convey them to Degannwy. The visitors spoke Irish.'

I let out my breath in a little hiss. 'Aengus of the Dalriada? Surely even Maelgwn would not make alliance with a king of Erin!'

'Why not? He hates Arthur even more than he hated the raiders. But Aengus is more likely. We will find out soon enough. My lord wishes to impress Maelgwn with the fact that he is watched, and that Arthur can move quickly.' Gwalchmai began painting the shield again. It was never any use telling him not to.

I stared at him, tightening and trying to relax my grip on the cleaning rag. 'Won't Maelgwn . . . isn't it dangerous?'

Gwalchmai paused a moment, then shook his head. 'Maelgwn will hardly have us killed, if that is what you mean.' He resumed painting. 'Such a killing would be sure to come out, and Arthur would break him for it. Maelgwn is cautious, a cunning fox of a man. He never takes un-necessary risks. He will try to find some way of outwitting us instead.'

I knew that Gwalchmai must be right. He knew a great deal about the ways of kings, far more than I did. But I had been raised on stories of border clashes with Gwynedd, and did not like the thought of living among enemies. But, I told myself, what else have you come for? You wanted to fight for the Light, and here is a chance. The Emperor's enemies plotting against him, and you and your lord ready to ride off into the midst of them, like Constantine in the songs . . . I still didn't like the sound of it. But I told myself that I should be eager for this chance to do something and asked, 'What time tomorrow do you want to leave?'

'As early as possible. An hour or so before dawn would be good. I would like to reach Caer Gwent by nightfall.'

'But that's a good fifty miles away, and across Mor Hafren!'

'We will press the horses, and the ferry will run at evening. And if your horse is too tired, you can change horses at Caer Gwent.'

Yes, in such a case we could stay at a fortress. No sleeping in the open this journey. And the snow was over, though it was by no means warm. It wouldn't be unbearable.

Gwalchmai noticed my sour look and suggested, 'They will treat your horse well at Caer Gwent, and you can pick him up on the way back.'

He would think of worrying about something like that. I sighed. 'I'll do that, then. What will we need? Do you wish to travel light?'

'Light as we can, but take enough to impress. Is that shield of mine with the enamelled boss in good condition?'

'I cleaned it last week.'

'I'll take that, then. And my other shield, in case there is any fighting. Rhuawn is also coming: there must be at least two warriors on such an embassy as this. We'll take one pack-horse for the three of us, and change horses at Caer Gwent. You will need to talk to Rhuawn's servant Aegmund about that.'

'Is Aegmund coming?' I asked hopefully. I liked the man.

But my lord shook his head. 'No. One servant is enough. Besides, the man's a Saxon, and can't ride to save his life.' He painted over the last blank area of the shield with a flourish and leant back to consider it, then set the brush down and stood up.

I also stood, rubbing my hands with the cleaning rag, as though I'd done the work.

'If you need me, I am going to talk to Bedwyr, and then to my brother, and after that I will see to my horse,' Gwalchmai informed me. I nodded, and he slapped me on the shoulder and limped off.

I stood a moment, still clutching my cleaning rag, making a mental list of all that would have to be done. The first thing, I decided, would be to find Macsen and tell him that I couldn't fix any more of Constans's armour.

By that evening I had almost everything ready. Aegmund was a great help in it. He was horrified at the thought of riding from Camlann to Caer Gwent in one day, although his lord Rhuawn only nodded and said he thought it a fine idea. When the two of us began packing, we were a bit unsure of what to do: how is one to pack for three men, using one pack-horse which must be burdened lightly for a fast journey but still carry enough both to impress and to last out a stay of indefinite duration? In the end, though, we managed something, and I felt triumphant as I cinched down the last buckles on the pack.

'And an hour before dawn tomorrow,' Aegmund said gleefully, 'you will already be up and off. If I wake up, I will think of you.'

'If. Not likely, my friend, not likely. And we will not reach Caer Gwent until after nightfall. I wish you were coming.'

Aegmund shook his head. 'Though I will have much care for you, and for our lords. Well, God go with you.'

'He will have to, if I am to stay awake on this journey. But there, I wanted it.'

Aegmund grinned, and we slid the loaded pack up onto the wall of our pack-horse's stall, ready for the morning. We turned to leave the stable, then saw the Pendragon himself walking towards us, the dim light from our lamp glittering on his golden collar. We both bowed respectfully and stood aside for him, but he stopped when he came to us.

'Aegmund,' he said, smiling, 'I hoped you would still be here. I have a gift for Cynyr, lord of Caer Gwent. It is up in the Hall; ask the Queen for it. It is only a cup, man, you can easily fit it onto the top of the pack.'

Aegmund grinned, said, 'Yes, *myn kyning*,' using one of his rare phrases of Saxon, and was off to fetch the gift. I was ready to bow again and disappear too, but Arthur snapped his fingers for attention, and said, 'Rhys, I wish to speak with you a moment.'

'As you will, my lord,' I said, surprised.

Arthur walked on up the stable a little way, and, after a moment's hesitation, I followed him. He stopped at Ceincaled's stall and leaned over it, looking at the horse. 'Do you know,' he asked me, softly, 'where Degannwy is?'

'In the mountains of Arfon,' I said.

Arthur made a clucking sound to the horse, and Ceincaled came over and sniffed at his hand, scattering the dim lamplight. Arthur let his hand rest on the horse's withers. It was a strong, square, sensitive hand, an amethyst ring glowing purple on the ring finger. 'Has Gwalchmai told you the story of the daughter of Caw?'

I suddenly remembered why Arfon was significant. 'Yes, Great Lord,' I said, and, feeling that this needed some explanation, added, 'by way of penance, I think.'

Arthur smiled at that. 'He desires to do penance rather more than is good for him.' The hand dropped from the horse's shoulder and rested on the wall of the stall, the light dying in the amethyst as it parted from the lamplight. The emperor turned, and looked at me a moment. 'You have some liking for Gwalchmai, I think,' he told me.

'Great Lord . . .' I said, surprised again, then went on, 'he's a good man.'

'Then I will speak freely.' Arthur crossed his arms, leaning against the stall. 'I once commanded your lord not to kill Bran of Llys Ebrauc, not because I particularly cared to save Bran's life, but because I knew Gwalchmai, and knew him to be too proud to easily endure knowing that he had killed from hatred. If you know the tale, you know the outcome of that command. Gwalchmai is hard on himself, and will yet insist on seeking this woman. I cannot give him another command, to forget it and her, since there are some things that cannot be commanded. But no king ever had a better warrior than I have in Gwalchmai, and I do not want him to be too hard on himself. Nor do I want him to find the woman.'

He saw the question in my face, for he smiled. 'I only met that woman once, but from what I have heard, and from what I know of her brothers, I doubt that she will be willing to forgive. Their father, Caw, died fighting for the king his brother when I took the *imperium*. It was in the field of battle, yet, because I wished to have the good will of the royal clan of Ebrauc, I saw that Caw was buried with full honours, and returned all his goods to his clan, with praises of his courage and expressions of good will. It is reasonable that children should hate the man who caused their father's death, but the children of Caw went beyond the will of the royal clan, and returned to me many expressions of pride and desire for revenge, saying that while the weak and cowards may forgive a wrong, the glory of the nobility is to avenge it. They were brave men, the sons of Caw, loyal to their friends, but implacable enemies; they are yet enemies, those that live, and for all that I do they will not be reconciled. I do not think that Elidan daughter of Caw will differ in this from her brothers.' He uncrossed his arms again, his eyes fixing on nothing, as they sometimes did when he was thinking. 'And if Gwalchmai finds her, and she accuses him again – it will be worse for him than before.'

'Wouldn't it still be better than uncertainty?' I asked.

Arthur's eyes fell on me again, and he smiled quickly. 'Possibly, and possibly not. I will not ask you to prevent him from seeing her, if she is indeed somewhere in Arfon. Only this: if your lord orders you to stay with Rhuawn or return to Camlann or Degannwy or any such place, while he goes questing for the daughter of Caw, do not obey him. Tell him that I have told you this, if he asks the reason. Do not let him see her alone, and take care for him. If he has someone with him, he will exercise some restraint on himself.'

I thought of my father telling Gwalchmai to use his sword to protect me, and here I was being told to protect Gwalchmai. I had to smile at it.

'Great Lord,' I said, then stopped, and decided that his Latin title would be more fitting: 'Imperator Arthurus, I would have had some inclination of my own to do as you say, at least as regards his not questing alone; I am glad to have a command for it.'

Arthur smiled slowly. 'A very insolent and insubordinate servant indeed! Excellent.' He gave the horse one more slap on the withers, and then we walked back down the darkened stables. The spring stars looked out through a wrack of cloud, and Aegmund was coming back down the hill with the golden cup and a lantern which cast a warm buttercup-yellow glow against the dark sky.

It was more than an hour before dawn when we left the next morning, and Camlann was eerily still under a faint moon. Everyone spoke in whispers as we saddled the horses and led them from the stable, their hooves loud in the silence, the jingle of their harness muffled by the moist air. The Emperor Arthur and the Queen Gwynhwyfar, half-seen forms in the dusk, bade us God speed and then we mounted and trotted off from the Hall, down the hill to the main gate, and out onto the road.

We did not take the usual path and ride down to Ynys Witrin to follow the Roman road north. Instead, we took one of the old, rough tracks across the hills directly north from Camlann, crossed the Briw river, and took a smaller Roman road up north to reach the ferry. The small Roman road does not go all the way there, but only up to the hills, where the Aesce river has its springs. The roads were thus bad all the way, but we had good horses, and to go by Ynys Witrin took us fifteen miles east, which we would have had to double by another fifteen miles back westward.

We set a fast pace, trotting steadily. I was half asleep, and slouched on Llwyd's back, thinking of my warm bed, cursing Aegmund in his, and vaguely wondering why it was necessary to go so far in one day.

We forded the Briw about seven miles downstream of Ynys Witrin. The water was cold and came up to the horses' bellies, so that we had nearly to sit on our legs to avoid drenching. It was still dark then, though the moon was low and the east grey. When we crossed the river, Ceincaled tossed his head and neighed, loud and clear and triumphant. Gwalchmai laughed. 'A fine day for a journey!'

I grunted.

As we went on up the winding track, the moon set, and the whole earth became grey, while the birds and animals of the land round about began to stir. Then the sun rose slowly, fiery and immense over the flat lowlands. I looked at it and thought, 'Bad weather coming,' but said nothing.

By the time we reached the Aesce, the birds were singing over the whole earth, and the wet grasses shone with amber and silver. Geese cried overhead, streaming towards the marshes, and before us lay the great mass of the hills, blue-grey and green.

'A fair country,' said Rhuawn. 'I wonder if the stories are true.'

Gwalchmai shrugged. This part of Dumnonia is called Gwlad yr Haf, Kingdom of Summer, which is also one of the commonest names we in the south have for the Other-world. It is said that men have found doors into the hills, and wandered through them into strange worlds, where the

Fair Ones feast in halls thatched with silver and the feathers of birds. There are the common tales of persons who are rescued from the hills, and the stories of those who spend a night there, and find that a hundred years have passed when they come out again, and so on.

'They say that the Kingdom of Summer is more beautiful than the earth,' Rhuawn murmured.

'It is,' said Gwalchmai. 'And yet I am not sure that it is wholly distinct from it.'

Rhuawn gave him a steady, serious look. Gwalchmai turned Ceincaled westward, following the Aesce to find the branch of it which would take us up its gorge into the hills. We walked the horses to give them a rest from the rapid trot which had taken us from Camlann, and their hooves sounded soft on the marshy ground, while the river gurgled beside us. Gwalchmai looked at the hills, his eyes very dark, but with a kind of light in them. After a few minutes, he began to sing, first in Irish and then, after a while, the same song in British. It was a strange song, and seemed to make a stillness about itself, almost frightening, though it was sweet and lovely.

> '. . . The sheen of the sea you sail on,
> The dazzling white of the sand
> Extend in azure and saffron
> As an airy and radiant land.
>
> A sweeping plain for a countless host,
> Where the colours glow into glory,
> A fair stream of silver, plains of gold
> Welcoming all to their bounty.
>
> Along the leaves of a forest
> Your curragh swims, and by hills
> Where branches dip, fruit-laden
> When your prow is parting the swell.
>
> A wood shines with fruit and with flower
> And the sweet wild scent of the vine,
> Flawless, remote from death's power,
> Gold-branching beyond touch of time . . .'

The sun touched the heaped hills northward, and the green glowed into emerald, while the blue-grey of the bare

trees shone with highlights of silver from the damp.
Rhuawn shook his head thoughtfully.

'That is a strange song. What is it?'

Gwalchmai smiled, and a little of the glow went from his
eyes. 'It is a song about a man who sailed to the Land of
Youth, which is one of our names in the Orcades for the
Kingdom of Summer. They say that if you sail far enough
west, you will reach it. The song is called "The Voyage of
Bran mac Febal".'

'I remember. You sang some of it once before.'

'That is so. This part comes later. When Bran had set sail,
he met the son of Lir – whom they call a god, in Erin –
riding across the sea in a chariot, and the son of Lir sang that
song, to show that the sea was not a barren plain but a fertile
kingdom, if one has the eyes to see it . . . We should turn
right here, and we can follow the Aesce up to the hills.'

We forded the Aesce and started our horses to a trot
again. The willows were yellow and green, and the air was
almost warm. Almost. I thought about sailing the bitter salt
plain of the sea, and finding then a fertile wood in the beauty
of spring, and seeing the whole sensible world as another
world. I shivered. A world as shining as a dream, more real
than waking, which men might slip into in a moment's
insight. Had Gwalchmai been there? I had heard some
songs that said so, and which said that his horse and his
sword had been brought from the Kingdom of Summer,
the Island of Apples, the Land of Youth, or any of the other
names of the Otherworld. A world which lay somehow
beneath and behind our world, and which broke through
upon us unexpectedly, yet was always there to those who
had eyes for it.

I shivered again, but from cold, and thought to wonder if
it could be warmer in the Otherworld. I snuggled my raw
hands into my cloak, and checked the packhorse's lead-rein.

The Aesce enters the plain by a great gorge, flanked by
jagged, sky-tearing cliffs. We had to dismount and walk the
horses part of the way, for the river, swollen with its spring
waters, had overflowed a section of the path. We were all
drenched up to the knees by the freezing stream, and
Rhuawn slipped and was soaked to his waist. We stopped at
the head of the gorge to put our boots back on and to wring
out our clothes, but then remounted and headed off at a fast

trot, and soon reached our Roman road. We were some fifteen miles, as the crow flies, from Camlann.

We ate our lunch in the saddle, about as far north as the Ciw river, which joins the Afen west of Baddon. It was then beginning to cloud over, and in the afternoon it began to rain, while a fierce March wind battered the drops against our faces. We didn't really mind. Rhuawn told an exceedingly long and complicated tale about a man who caught the north wind in a fishing net, and what came of it, and had us all laughing.

We had to make the horses swim a few paces when we crossed the Afen, which was high with the spring floods, and this made us even wetter than the rain had. We trotted fast to keep the horses warm, and their sides steamed. We had lost our Roman road some time before, and the way was winding and muddy, but for all that we made good time, and reached the main west road from Baddon, not far beyond the Afen. This we followed direct to the inlet where one can take a ferry across Mor Hafren to the shore of Powys and to Caer Gwent.

We arrived at the ferry at evening, and dragged a boatman from his supper to take us across. The water was rough, and gleamed with white in the darkness, smelling strongly of salt. Our horses, except for Ceincaled, stood with drooping heads, too tired to be nervous. I felt quite seasick by the time we put in on the west bank in Powys, and made no argument when Gwalchmai gave the boatman the excessive payment of a gold armlet. Then it was remount, and drive our horses on another mile to Caer Gwent. But there were fires there, and hot baths and hot food, warm beds and a warm and courteous welcome.

The next morning we presented Cynyr, lord of Caer Gwent, with Arthur's gift, and he thanked us very prettily, and asked us to stay for a few days. Gwalchmai declined the invitation for us, and so we were provided with fresh horses – except for Gwalchmai, who wanted and needed none – and set out on the main west Roman road to Gwar Uisc. My fresh horse was inclined to be skittish. I had parted from Llwyd with only a twinge of regret. I knew that Cynyr would have him treated well, and he was welcome to any work he could wring from the lazy beast. I would pick the horse back up on the way home.

We did not go quite so far that day, since we would not change horses again until we reached Caer Legion in the north. We crossed the Uisc river on the bridge at Gwar Uisc, and then rode north through Powys. We spent that night at a farm near the river Dyweleis, and set out again early the next morning. Three days after leaving Caer Gwent, we reached Caer Guricon, just over the border of Gwynedd. Both Caer Gwent and Caer Guricon are old Roman towns, but the differences between them are astonishing. There were fewer people in Caer Guricon than in any Roman town I had seen, and those that did live there huddled close to the building which the local lord used as his feast hall. But the great difference was not this, but the hostility. The local lord gave us the hospitality we demanded, since it was our right as the Emperor's warriors; but he gave it glaring and grudgingly. No one in the town, from the lord's warriors to the Hall servants, would speak to us, and they had all a silent, vicious stare that set one's teeth to grinding. The lord wanted us to stay and sleep with his warband in the feast hall, but Gwalchmai insisted on a separate house. We were eventually given a small, narrow townhouse, with broken roof tiles, which had not been swept or cleaned for a long time.

Gwalchmai looked around it and laughed. 'Well, cousin,' he said to Rhuawn – members of Arthur's Family call each other cousin, when they aren't calling each other 'brother' – 'we are back in Gwynedd.'

'And a grief it is, too,' Rhuawn replied. 'Shall we keep watch?'

In the end we did not keep watch, but settled in the middle room of the house. Gwalchmai dragged his sleeping mat in front of one door, and Rhuawn pulled his over by the other, and no one slept in the middle of the room, in case anyone tried to drop things on us. If I had not been so tired from the journey I do not think I could have slept at all, and, as it was, it took me an hour to drift off, all the time expecting to hear stealthy footfalls creeping into the house. But nothing happened. Nothing was really expected to: it was simply wise to take precautions in Gwynedd.

We left as early as we could the next morning, and did a hard day's riding, reaching Caer Legion after nightfall. The town was a little more hospitable than Caer Guricon, and we changed horses there – again, except for Gwalchmai, who kept Ceincaled – and the next morning, our sixth day from Camlann, we rode westward into Arfon. The heights of the mountains were still white with the winter snow, while their flanks were green and grey. The sun struck their peaks, flashing from ice, glowing on mists, glittering on streams and cataracts. I could not keep my eyes from them. They tell the same kind of stories about Arfon as they do about Gwlad yr Haf, and it is easy to see why.

In the late afternoon we turned off our Roman road, pushing our horses hard, and followed a mountain track southward. It was the last step in our journey, the road to Degannwy itself. The sun began to set, turning the mountains rose and lavender. I was tired enough from the journey to be wide awake, but I felt like a rope that is drawn too tight, and quivers at a touch. At every bend in the road I half expected to ride clear out of the world, and find that the snows in Arfon were turning into apple blossom, and the trees to silver. Then, finally, we rounded a bend in the road and saw Degannwy far in the distance. There was nothing Roman about that fortress. It was built before Claudius came to conquer the east of Britain, before Julius Caesar ever invaded. The legions of Rome had never really conquered Arfon, for all their centuries and legions in Britain, for all their roads and towns and discipline. Looking at the green, twilit dark slopes around me, I could not think that anyone, even Arthur, could come into Arfon in war and bring his warband out intact and alive. No doubt the same thought had occurred to Maelgwn Gwynedd, and caused him to move his royal fortress from the Roman port town of Caer Segeint up to this small stronghold in the mountains.

It was fully dark when we reached Degannwy and demanded entrance at the gates. The guards kept us waiting, watching us with that vicious stare I was coming to expect in Gwynedd, while one of their number sauntered back to their feast hall to tell the king Maelgwn that some emissaries of the Pendragon had come. The stars were bright by the time the guard strolled back and told the others to open the gates and let us in, and we could ride our stumbling horses up the hill towards the Hall, with its lights and sound of music. The stables were a low-lying mass a short distance down the hill from the Hall.

Gwalchmai swung down from Ceincaled in front of these stables, and caught the stallion's bridle while he began to talk to one of Maelgwn's grooms. Rhuawn and I also dismounted, stiffly, and I began to check the packs on the pony we had brought from Caer Legion. A group came down from the feast hall with torches, and I was glad of it, since I had light to see that everything was still in its place, strapped firmly down on the little beast's back. I looked back to Gwalchmai, awaiting directions.

He finished his interrogation of the groom, and turned to the party with the torches, ready to question and explain in his quiet, eloquent fashion. But he froze half-way through that turn, and stood moveless as a wild animal that has seen some predator. The torchlight glowed on his crimson cloak and gold jewellery, but the uncanniness suddenly filled his face so that he looked scarcely human. His eyes were very wide, lips half parted. One hand still held his mount's bridle, the other was raised, held forward in an arrested gesture.

I felt cold and shaken to see him so abstracted from himself, but I didn't want to look at what he was looking at. I glanced to Rhuawn, who looked puzzled, then over to the party with the torches, and finally at what Gwalchmai was staring at.

My first thought, looking at the woman who stood with the torch-glow red on her, was that she really did look very like Gwalchmai, as much as a woman can look like a man. The resemblance must have been even closer when he was younger. She had the same fine bones, the same high-bridged straight nose and thin, expressive mouth. Her hair, fastened behind her head and bound with gold, was the same deep black, and her eyes . . . but when I saw her eyes, I felt that she did not look much like him after all. Like his, they were black, but black in such a way that they seemed to drink all the light around them, and quench the colour in everything that surrounded her. Black enough to drink your life like a thirsty man gulping down a cup of water, and she would do it, and smile as she did it. She stood very straight, wearing a low-cut crimson gown which left her pale arms bare. She was extraordinarily beautiful, ageless, and she was smiling, but she looked at no one but Gwalchmai. Slowly, very slowly, she walked forward, and her shadow fluttered in the torchlight, and still my lord did not stir.

'So, my falcon,' she said in a low, soft voice. 'Are you then displeased to see your mother?'

He lowered his raised hand and straightened slowly, as though struggling to do so; and then he bowed, very gracefully. 'Lady, I had not expected to find you here.'

She gave a low laugh. 'Indeed not. But now we are a pleasant family party: you and your brother and your father and I.'

'My father? And my brother? Agravain is at Camlann.'

She laughed again. 'Agravain! Have you forgotten that you have two brothers? Your other brother has greatly wanted to see you again.'

'Medraut.' Gwalchmai's face was expressionless. 'So.' He raised his head a little and spoke in a different voice, proud and cold. 'I have come to Maelgwn ap Docmail, king of Gwynedd, as the emissary of Artorus Augustus Caesar, Imperator Britanniae, Insulae Draco.'

'Well, indeed. Maelgwn is in his Hall, feasting with your father. Do you wish to come and greet him now?' She took another step nearer, her eyes never leaving his face. 'Your father, for all that you have done, will still no doubt be glad to see you. I myself am glad to see you, my spring-tide falcon; very glad . . .' her voice grew lower. I could not think, nor move, and the torchlight seemed dim and colourless. She took one more step nearer, her eyes fixed as a cat's.

Then, suddenly, Ceincaled reared, screaming, and tore his bridle from his master's hand. The horse towered a moment, wild and white and shining, and descended, flinging himself towards the lady, ears back and teeth bared. She hurled herself to the side, and some of the men who had come with her drew their swords. Gwalchmai cried out and ran to catch his horse's bridle.

The lady picked herself up from the ground and turned and walked back towards the Hall without saying another word and without looking at her son once. Gwalchmai held Ceincaled's head, stroking the stallion's neck and speaking to him quietly in Irish. Both horse and man were trembling.

Rhuawn, after another moment's immobility, jerked his own mount's bridle and started into the stable. I took my horse and the pack-pony, and Gwalchmai followed us with Ceincaled, still whispering to the horse.

We found stalls for the animals, rubbed them down and gave them some grain. Our horses fell to at once, but Ceincaled stirred uneasily. He nickered when Gwalchmai left him, and neighed loudly when we left the stable, so that Gwalchmai turned and called something in Irish which must have meant 'Be still'. We looked at the feast hall.

'I do not understand,' said Rhuawn at last, speaking in Latin so that Maelgwn's men would not understand. 'That woman is your mother, the Queen of the Orcades, the daughter of the Emperor Uther?'

'*Illa'st*,' Gwalchmai replied, tiredly, 'She is. And the King of Gwynedd is not plotting with Aengus of the Dalriada, or with any from Hibernia, but with Lot mac Cormac of Orcade, my father. Or rather, he plots something with my mother, for, when I left Dun Fionn, she governed most of the plotting, and I imagine that she is doing all of it now. My father is a strong man, but she is a subtle designer, and will outlast him.'

'I have heard, and now believe it,' Rhuawn said, very slowly. 'I have heard – but be gentle to me, and forgive me that I speak of it to you – that the Queen of Orcade is a great witch.'

Gwalchmai nodded. 'She is. By her skill in sorcery she has made herself a Queen of Darkness. And she hates my lord Arthur most bitterly, more bitterly than Maelgwn Gwynedd does.'

Rhuawn gave Gwalchmai a steady look. 'Although she is the Pendragon's sister?'

'Rather, I think, because she is the Pendragon's half sister than in despite of it, and because her mother was the wife of the Pendragon Uther, while Arthur's was some country girl. But it is no matter. We must find what it is that she and Maelgwn plot together, and tell Arthur, and stop them. They are more dangerous than Cerdic and the Saxons.'

Rhuawn nodded, very thoughtfully, and we began walking up the hill, accompanied by some of Maelgwn's servants, who had been waiting.

If the Hall had been friendly, it would have been a joy to enter. It was filled with music and light and warmth, and with a rich smell of roasting meat and strong, warm mead, triply welcome after the cold, wild air of the mountain twilight. It was a small Hall, and would seat no more than four hundred men, and he rarely had many guests. But it seemed both large and unfriendly when we walked up the length of it with all eyes fixed on us. The music stopped when we came in, and the only sound was the wind in the thatch, the crackling of the fires, and our own footfalls. Gwalchmai walked very straight and proud, his head held high, cloak thrown back from his left shoulder to show the hilt of his sword, and the shield with the enamelled boss gleaming over his other shoulder. He ignored the stares completely. Rhuawn also looked calm, but I was near enough to see how tightly his hand was clenched on his sword-hilt. I had no sword to clutch, and had no wish for these barbarian nobles to see how nervous I was, so I spent the walk up the Hall looking at the faces of the men at the high table.

Maelgwn held the centre of the table, of course, looking down the Hall at all his warband. He was a slight man, with gingery red hair and a thin beard. He wore a purple cloak, more than his status permitted him, and a gold circlet around his hair. The purple did not suit him. He pretended to talk to the man on his left, but something about the angle of his head told me that he was all the while looking at us. He seemed the sort for that, the kind of man I would not trust in a market place, or leave to guard my flock. But he looked lower than his reputation as a great enemy, a petty miserable little schemer who only chanced to be a king.

The man on his right was of another sort altogether. Though still not above average height, he had plainly been taller than Maelgwn, and something told me that once his hair had been like hot gold. It was grey now, and his face was lined and haggard, his eyes sunken. But those eyes were still a fierce, hot blue. They were like Agravain's eyes. I did not think that Agravain resembled his father quite so strongly as Gwalchmai did their mother, but there could be no doubt as to his paternity. I could just remember the days, more than twelve years before, when every movement of Lot mac Cormac, king of the Ynysoedd Erch, had been a source of gossip and debate in every kingdom in Britain; when many British kings would do nothing which had not been commanded by Lot at Dun Fionn. Those days had ended when Arthur seized the imperium in Britain, and compelled a Lot defeated in battle to swear peace and give hostages. It could still be seen that Lot had once been a great man. As we approached the high table, however, I thought how worn he looked now, and how much older than his wife.

We stopped before the high table, the main fire pit warm at our backs, and Gwalchmai saluted Maelgwn, drawing his sword and lifting it, hilt first. Maelgwn finally turned from his feigned conversation. As he did so, the man on his left also turned. This was a young warrior, a man about my age. His blond hair was lighter than Lot's, his first beard a soft, shining down on his cheeks, eyes a clear grey. He was very handsome, and smiled in welcome. It was a pleasant smile. I wondered who he was and what he was doing there, but only briefly. Gwalchmai was saying to Maelgwn, 'To Maelgwn ap Docmail of Gwynedd, greetings, in the name of the Pendragon Arthur ab Uther, High King of Britain and your king.'

Maelgwn drummed on the table with his fingers. After a deliberate, awkward moment's silence, he said smoothly, 'It gives me pleasure to greet the emissaries of my lord the Pendragon, especially when they are led by so illustrious a nobleman as yourself, Lord Gwalchmai. Be free, Lord, of anything that is mine.' He gestured to one of the servants, and additional places were made at the high table to his right and left. 'All that my hospitality can offer you is yours. You would be welcome to me, Lord Gwalchmai, for the sake of your royal family alone.'

Someone in the Hall laughed, but fell abruptly silent. Again there was silence in the Hall but for the crackle of the fire and the whine of a hound.

Gwalchmai bowed slightly, and said, with a smoothness excelling Maelgwn's, 'And I am welcome, I hope, for the sake of him who sent me here, by whose service I hold such honour as I possess. Though, indeed, it is a pleasure contrary to my expectations that I should meet my kin here You, my lord father, I greet in my own name, and not in my lord Arthur's, and so also do I greet my cousins and my brother.'

Lot leaned forward, his hot eyes fixed on his son. He licked his lips nervously, but did not speak. The fair young man smiled again. Gwalchmai looked at him directly a moment and the smile faded, the eyes turned elsewhere. My lord lifted his sword-hilt and bowed once more, before sheathing the weapon and walking about the table to take his seat beside his father, on Maelgwn's right. Rhuawn drifted off to the left, and I followed him hurriedly, not wanting to stand in the centre an instant longer.

There were a few servants coming and going about the table and I grabbed a flagon of mead from one, and hurried to pour it for Rhuawn and Gwalchmai. The alternative was to go and sit down at the far end of the Hall with Maelgwn's servants, and the idea did not enrapture me. After the mead, I managed to grab a trencher of meat and offer that; Gwalchmai, however, ate nothing. I took the trencher back to a quiet corner on the right, and sat down with it and the remnants of the mead. The meat was lamb, cooked with plenty of mint and parsley, and was very good. I sat, eating it and watching my two warriors, plainly ready to serve their needs. I was close enough to hear what they spoke about, and I thought that, of the three of us, I was the most comfortable.

Maelgwn began the conversation by asking both Gwalchmai and Rhuawn about the health and plans of everyone at Camlann, listening attentively and offering encouraging comments, as though he were a great friend of Arthur's. Lot said nothing. The fair young warrior, who was now seated next to Rhuawn, attended him carefully, offering him water and salt and listening to whatever Rhuawn had to say, not looking at Gwalchmai at all.

After a while, Maelgwn ran out of questions, and the conversation at the high table slithered to a halt, though the rest of the Hall was still noisy enough. In the silence there, Lot leaned suddenly forward, shook his head as though to clear it, and asked Gwalchmai, 'And what of your brother Agravain?'

Gwalchmai lifted his mead horn and studied it. 'He too is at Camlann, and in good health.'

'He is happy there?'

My lord shrugged. 'Happy as he may be, while the weather keeps him still. You know that he does not like to sit idle. In another month or so, my lord Arthur will probably set him to chasing bandits, and then he will be happy.'

'Your lord Arthur.' Lot rested his chin on his hand,

looking to Gwalchmai; his face was also turned towards me as he did so, and I could see that his eyes were narrow and fierce. 'Your lord, Arthur. It is true that you have sworn that bastard warleader the Threefold Oath of allegiance?'

'It is true, yes.' Gwalchmai set down his mead horn on its stand, firmly, and looked up at Lot. 'For him, and for the cause we serve, I will live and die.'

Lot's mouth contracted, lips twisting as though in pain, but all he said was, 'And Agravain?'

'He has not sworn.' Gwalchmai hesitated, then added, 'And yet he too would fight and even die for my lord Arthur.'

Lot's hand clenched to a fist, then relaxed, and he laid his palm flat against the table. 'But still, he is not sworn to it. Well.' He gave Gwalchmai a long look, then smiled, a smile like the sun on a wave in summer. 'You have changed since you ... left Dun Fionn. They say that you are the finest warrior in Arthur's Family.'

Gwalchmai smiled back. 'Only on horseback. Agravain can still lecture me on where to put my spear when I fight on foot.'

Lot laughed. 'The horses, the horses! That has always been our downfall with Arthur. Oh, his men fight well on foot, but it is the cavalry charge that breaks armies: and I hear that these days you lead the charge.'

'Since we are at peace, no one leads the charge these days.'

'But you have been leading it, which I never expected of you. Well enough! Let us have a song about our shame and Arthur's glory, the High King's horsemen.'

One of Maelgwn's poets struck up a song on the harp, and began to sing of one of Arthur's battles, a song I am sure was not often sung in that Hall. For the rest of the evening mercifully little was said.

At some unreasonably late hour of the night the feast ended, and we were escorted to a small hut Maelgwn had allotted us, apologizing as he did so for the poverty of the accommodations. Degannwy, it seemed, was crowded, as well it might be with the King and Queen of the Ynysoedd Erch and their retinues packed into it. Our hut had but a single room with two low beds, but it was nonetheless both clean and warm, and had its own fire.

Gwalchmai dropped onto one bed and sat with his head

in his hands and his elbows on his knees. Rhuawn, after a moment's hesitation, took the other bed and began to untie his leggings. Since I, obviously, was to sleep on the floor, I began unpacking.

After a little while Gwalchmai sat up and began to build the fire up for the night. Rhuawn took off his mail-shirt, wrapped it in an oilskin, then pounded the bed a couple of times before lying down and arranging his sword by his head. 'Do we keep watch?' he asked Gwalchmai.

My lord shook his head. 'There is no point keeping watch against what we have to fear now. We must sleep, and trust God that we will wake again.'

'So there is danger.'

'Great danger.' Gwalchmai sat back down and began to untie his over-tunic. 'I . . . my mother tried to kill me when I left Dun Fionn.'

'Ah. I had heard that was the case.' Rhuawn rolled over onto his stomach and looked at his friend. 'Tell me, was it by sorcery?'

Gwalchmai drew off his over-tunic, then nodded, folding it.

'Well. I never thought to fight devils. I was told it was a privilege of the blessed angels.' He smiled. 'I don't qualify.'

Gwalchmai smiled and shook his head. 'Cousin, I am glad of you.' He looked around for another oilskin for his chain mail, and I handed him one from the pack.

'Will you go back to Camlann as soon as your horse is rested?' asked Rhuawn.

With his mail-shirt half off, Gwalchmai froze. 'Go back? Why should I?'

Rhuan shrugged. 'I would not care to fight against my own blood, and my own father. In all loyalty to our lord, a man cannot oppose his clan.'

Gwalchmai took the shirt off hurriedly. 'It is not like that.' Rhuawn and I both looked at him, and he spread his hands. 'It is not a question of my family against Arthur's family. It is a question of Darkness against Light, and I am for Arthur.' When Rhuawn still said nothing, he went on, 'Don't you see that this is my mother's work? My father never visited Britain except when one of his allies summoned him to fight, and then he came at the head of an army. Otherwise, he plotted and dictated letters and listened to his spies. He would not of his own accord be here with a fox-faced schemer like Maelgwn. And because it is my mother's work . . .' He took a deep breath. 'Listen. The Saxons desire our lands. Well; and we try to prevent them from taking them. But the Saxons do not desire to see the lands empty, swallowed by wilderness, while the people flee and starve or go in fear. My mother does. If the Saxons put out the light in Britain, they may make some light of their own; but my mother wishes to see all drowned in Darkness, and revenge herself. Can one make peace with that?'

'Why should she desire such things?' I asked.

'Perhaps at first she did not desire them. But now she does. I know. No one knows her as well as I do. Perhaps my brother Medraut knows her well, but I think not as well. She taught me sorcery. That is my guilt, for I asked her to, when I was young, but from this I know that desire she has, the desire to drink up all the world into her own will, and to break all that will not be devoured. I know her . . . why do you think I speak British with a Dumnonian accent, while Agravain sounds as though he had just left Erin? I spent time with her.'

'Your brother Medraut speaks British with a Dumnonian accent,' observed Rhuawn softly. I realized that the fair young warrior must have been this Medraut. 'He seems a good enough man.'

'Ah God! Poor Medraut. I do not know how it is with him now, whether he has escaped her or not; but if he has not, she will use him up, as she has used up my father. We must fight her, Rhuawn.'

Rhuawn fondled his sword-hilt. 'In that case, brother, let us sleep with a calm mind, for we will need our strength when it comes to battle.'

'Good advice, my lord,' I suggested. 'You yourself have said that Maelgwn would be unlikely to kill us, and this is still his fortress. Go to sleep.'

Gwalchmai sighed and lay down, but left his hand resting on his sword-hilt, the sheathed blade lying beside him. I decided to leave the rest of the unpacking for the morning, and made myself comfortable in front of the hut's door, then blew out the lamp. With a few blankets under me the floor wasn't too hard, and I was, at all events, too tired to care if Morgawse of Orcade herself had dropped through the smoke hole with half a dozen demons in her train.

But I dreamed all that night, dreamed that I struggled in a vast, black ocean, thrashing desperately towards a light which receded endlessly away. After an aeon, it seemed that my feet hit solid stone, and I stood and staggered towards the light, which glowed brighter, like a star came to earth. But just before I reached it, it vanished with a sound like thunder, and I saw only Medraut ap Lot, holding a naked sword in his hand, and smiling.

Eight

Perhaps it was because of the nightmares, but I woke very early the next morning, feeling tired and depressed. The fire was low and the house very dark; both my warriors were still asleep. I dressed and went to the door. The morning was misty and cold. I looked back into the house. Rhuawn turned his head away from the light and muttered. I noticed that Gwalchmai's fingers were still curled about his sword, but he was smiling, as though his dreams were better than mine had been. I sighed and went out, closing the door behind me.

I wanted some hot water to wash in, and decided that it must be possible to get something to heat it in right in our own hut, so as not to compete with all of Maelgwn's warband in the Hall – if they washed, which I wasn't sure of. Breakfast could be eaten in the Hall, but it would be pleasanter to find some bread and bacon in the kitchen and bring it back. For both needs I'd have to take on Maelgwn's servants, and find the kitchens.

After getting lost three times in the mist and the unfamiliar stronghold, I finally found my goal, in the back of the Hall. A few servants were lounging about the low-roofed room, heating water and kneading bread, but there did not seem to be anyone who was in charge. Nor did anyone wish to pay any attention to me. Everyone I advanced on seemed suddenly to remember something which had to be done, and vanished, or else stared at me stupidly, as though they couldn't understand my Dumnonian accent. Exasperated, I sat down directly before the main fire, in everyone's way.

After a little while, a plumpish, rather pretty flaxen-haired girl marched up to the fire with a large copper dish held over her arm. There was water in it, and it looked about the right size. I eyed it appreciatively.

The girl halted in front of me and glared. 'Move over, if you please,' she ordered. I started: she had an Irish accent.

'Who's that kettle for?' I asked.

'The Queen,' she replied shortly.

Maelgwn was not married, so there was only one queen

in Degannwy. I reluctantly gave up my designs on the kettle, and moved over. 'Where did you get the kettle?' I asked her.

'A hen laid it in the rafters, having been affrighted in a coppersmith's shop,' said the girl. 'Who are you?'

'I, woman, am Rhys ap Sion, the lord Gwalchmai's servant. We need a kettle.'

'Indeed?' said the girl. She hung the kettle over the fire and stood back, her hands on her hips. 'And what do you want with a kettle?'

I grinned. 'I need to make a brood-nest for your hen. Come, who's in charge here? My lord will want some hot water for washing when he wakes up.'

She shrugged. 'There is an old man named Saidi ap Sugyn – you British have such strange names – whom I was told to mind about the kitchens.'

'Where is he, then?'

She tossed her head. 'Och ai, he is minding his bed. He will not rise until noon, and he goes to bed at nightfall, and all the while he is awake he complains that he is tired. It is not in my mind to mind him at all, and the rest of the servants are like minded.'

'I mind that he is not here when I want him. Where does he sleep?'

'His house is just behind the kitchen. But I would not wake him, or he will be angry, and stint you on bread.'

'He may try that as he pleases, but he will not succeed,' I boasted, and gave a slight bow to the girl before striding off through the kitchen. Only for an instant: my Irish servant girl shouted, 'Hai! Rhys ap Sean!'

I stopped. She was still standing at the fire, rocking on her heels a little. 'You are heading into the feast hall, Rhys ap Sean, lord Gwalchmai's servant. Saidi's house is behind the kitchen, the other way.' She gave me a self-delighted smile. 'Come, I'll show you myself.' She tripped off, and I followed, feeling ridiculous.

Saidi ap Sugyn was annoyed at being woken. He swore at me, complained about his age and general health, complained about southerners, the Irish, and the Pendragon, but eventually told me to take any kettle I wanted and go to Yffern with it. The serving girl giggled at me when we came back to the kitchen, so I made her go out of her way to show me where the kettles and the food were. I took an extra loaf of bread, beyond what we needed for breakfast, just in case.

As I walked back to our house I considered Degannwy. I suspected – and later knew for certain – that the place was badly run. The servants, from the steward on down, were overworked and underfed; and, from the steward on down, they made up for this by stealing and cheating whenever they could, and afterwards blackmailing each other with having done it. In consequence, everyone was ill-equipped and miserable. Eggs would disappear before they were needed in a cake; knives and pots vanished steadily, often reappearing, no one knew how, for sale on a market day. A woman would set out to weave a cloak, and when she was half-finished, discover there was no more wool to be had, and when she did get some more wool, there was no dye or the wrong dye for it. Maelgwn's warriors knew what was happening, and beat the servants freely, and the servants beat each other and the dogs, and cheated even more. And yet the place held together remarkably well, for everyone blamed their troubles on the high tribute demanded by Arthur, and held the Pendragon's wars against the Saxons to be the root of all their own wretched little difficulties; and everyone was afraid of his neighbour and his superior, and did not dare to carry his dishonesty to its extreme. So Degannwy was a strong fortress, but it was no joy to anyone. Its strength was of opposition only, as I saw it, without an instant's unity of mind or charity of thought to bind it into a civilized living place like Camlann.

I had more time to myself at Degannwy than I had had at Camlann. I was recognized as the Lord Gwalchmai's servant, and, as such, had no part in the life of the fortress. That left only two warriors and one house to worry about, with the horses from Caer Legion, and Rhuawn helped with those. Gwalchmai was at first very busy waiting upon Maelgwn, or, occasionally, talking to his father. He wrote Arthur a letter the afternoon of our first day in Degannwy, informing the Emperor about the situation. He rode from Degannwy with this sheet of parchment hidden under his shirt, telling the guards at the gate that he wished to exercise his horse. I am still not sure exactly how it reached Arthur. The Emperor has men in Gwynedd who report Maelgwn's movements to him, and Gwalchmai knew where to leave a message, though he could not speak directly to any of these men without endangering their lives. At any rate, he came back without the letter. He then spent his time talking to Maelgwn and Maelgwn's men, at least once a day. The matter of the tribute was settled – Maelgwn admitted he must have 'made a mistake', and would give an additional amount the next year to compensate – but very little more was learned of what Lot and Morgawse were saying to Maelgwn privately. There did not seem to be any preparations for a war: no messengers rushed to and from the Ynysoedd Erch or the various chieftains of Gwynedd; no one was gathering supplies; there were no long training expeditions of the warband into the countryside – but it was plain enough that two such kings would not be meeting unless they had something of the sort in mind.

In all his conversations with Maelgwn or with the warriors from the Islands, Gwalchmai avoided very thoroughly any encounter with his mother and his younger brother. When finished with his official work he usually rode out into the mountains and did not return until nightfall. When he was present, he was rather unnerving. While unfailingly courteous, remotely willing to oblige, and well able to be charming with Maelgwn, I could never feel that he was really there, caring about what anyone was saying. He had abstracted himself to some terribly silent place behind his eyes, and, from that first night on, refused to drop his guard with anyone. I could dimly see that his mother's presence at Degannwy might disturb him, but I didn't like it. And I could not see why he so avoided his brother. Rhuawn and I agreed that Medraut was a surprisingly likeable man.

On our second day at Degannwy I came into the stables to look after the horses, and found Rhuawn and Medraut hanging over the door of a stall and discussing one of Maelgwn's stock.

'These mountain horses are simply too small,' Rhuawn was saying. 'And they've no withers – look at this one! Nothing to hold onto in a battle. The first time your spear hits anything, off you fall; and even if you do not, you're too low to use a spear to any advantage. No, Maelgwn will never match any southern king for cavalry unless he buys some stock from Gaul.'

'On the other hand,' returned Medraut, smiling, 'those southern horses of yours, those Gaulish warsteeds, fall over their own feet in hilly country. This little mare could take you clear up Yr Widdfa in the middle of winter, or carry a charge downhill in the mud. Show me a southern cavalry band that could do that!'

'We've done it, in the Family.' Rhuawn stroked his moustache. 'It isn't easy, but we did it once, in the north. Once, in fact, we carried a charge downhill, across a river, and up the opposite bank into a Saxon shield-wall. Of course, your brother led that charge . . .'

Medraut laughed. 'Gwalchmai could saddle the North Wind, if he set his mind to it. He always could. He's the one who first taught me to ride, actually, though I'll never be as good as he is.'

'In cavalry charges there's no one on earth that good.'

Medraut smiled again. 'I am ready to believe you. Of course, when he . . . left . . . Dun Fionn, no one knew he was so much of a fighter, but I've heard the songs since. Strange, hearing that kind of song about a brother you haven't seen in years. Why doesn't Arthur let him command the cavalry?'

Rhuawn turned to lean against the stall, and noticed me. He interrupted the conversation to call, 'Oh, Rhys, I've already seen to that miserable beast of yours – Lord Medraut, this is Gwalchmai's servant, Rhys ap Sion, a good man.'

I bowed a little, and Medraut ap Lot straightened, smiled widely, and beckoned me over to join them. My dream flashed into my head for an instant, but dreams are ambiguous things, and usually mean nothing at all, so I came over and leaned against the stall.

'So,' Medraut began again, 'why doesn't the Pendragon give my brother command of his cavalry?'

Rhuawn yawned. 'Because he is so wild a fighter. Gwalchmai goes mad in battle, and will cut through anyone in front of him. If he is ever killed in battle, it will be because someone strikes him with a throwing spear from behind. No one will ever beat him, face to face. No one. But as for directing others in a struggle – once he's begun he doesn't understand plain British and can't recognize his best

397

friends. Bedwyr, now, keeps his head in any circumstances. He is a philosopher, can hold the whole plan of battle in his mind, and see where everyone is and where everyone has to go. He can even direct Gwalchmai.'

Medraut looked thoughtful. 'He really does go mad, then? That might explain . . .' he stopped.

'What?' asked Rhuawn.

The other smiled. 'Oh, nothing. How does he go mad? I haven't had a chance to talk to him, and I don't know that I could ask him, anyway. It's hard to ask an older brother questions like that.'

'Mm. I imagine. Well, he just . . . goes mad. He pulls out his sword and rides down whatever is in front of him. He doesn't even feel it if he's wounded, until afterwards. Then he usually collapses. But during the battle he has the strength of three men, and moves faster than you can think.'

Medraut looked very intent. He nodded. 'Collapses afterwards. Yes . . .'

'He isn't berserk,' I put in. Somehow, I thought Rhuawn was giving the wrong impression. 'I wouldn't even say that he was "mad", if that wasn't the word he uses himself.' I hesitated, groping for some way to communicate the ecstasy I had seen in his face during this battle madness. But Medraut nodded and said, 'Of course,' and began to talk about horses again. He was pleasant company, especially after the hostility of the rest of Degannwy, and I enjoyed listening.

Eventually the conversation turned to music, and he asked us to come to his house the next afternoon and listen to one of the Irish harpers, and both Rhuawn and I accepted willingly. I was flattered at being asked, and was glad that Rhuawn wasn't the sort to take offence at Medraut's asking me.

The lord Medraut was staying with a few other of the warriors from the Ynysoedd Erch, in a house a deal larger and finer than ours (though no less crowded), which adjoined another house where the Queen was staying, alone. Her husband did not share her room, which surprised me, but Medraut made no comment on the situation.

When we arrived, however, none of the other warriors were there, and Medraut explained that they were in Maelgwn's hall playing dice. 'And, alas, the harper is there too, playing songs to the rhythm of knucklebones clicking. But we have a harp here, if you can play it. I can, a little.'

Rhuawn also could, a bit (though I couldn't, not at all), and we settled by the fire. I sat off to the side, feeling awkward. Medraut rapped against the wall and, after a moment, the door to the adjoining house opened and the Irish serving girl from the kitchens appeared.

'Ah, there you are, Eivlin,' said Medraut. 'Does my mother still have any of that Gaulish wine lying about in there?'

'My lady does, but . . .'

'Then fetch it, like a good girl. Come, these are guests.'

She shrugged a little and turned to go, but, as she did, she lifted her eyebrows at me, plainly commenting, 'What are you doing as a warrior's guest?' But she came back with a jar of wine and three goblets, and poured for all of us. I was still not much of a judge of such things, but I thought it good wine. Eivlin apparently did too, for she didn't give me much of it, and left the jar with Medraut only very reluctantly.

Medraut took one swallow of his wine then set the goblet aside and began to tune the harp.

As members of noble clans, both Medraut and Rhuawn had of course learned harping, and both were good. Medraut sang a few songs about some highly favoured Irish hero named CuChulainn ('But Gwalchmai used to sing them better,' he commented); and Rhuawn responded with a song about Macsen Wledig, and an older song about Pryderi ap Pwyll. They began passing the harp back and forth, sipping the wine while they listened, and the damp afternoon was forgotten.

After a while, Medraut called Eivlin back, and asked her to fetch some bread and cheese from the kitchen. This brought a worried look, and I wondered if she had some work of her own we were distracting her from. I offered to go with her – I needed to clear my head a little by then, anyway – and she accepted the help with a surprised air.

We had a job to find the cheese. Someone had stolen the great round that morning, and Saidi ap Sugyn, who was up and about, did not want to cut a new one. I threatened him with Medraut, Rhuawn, Gwalchmai, the Queen of Orcade, and my fists, and he finally yielded. We exited triumphantly. Eivlin laughed.

'I am glad you came, Rhys ap Sean,' she said. 'Indeed, I would have threatened him with my lady and the lord Medraut, but that withered ram cares no more for them than he does for his own lord. You argue like a farmer.'

'I am one,' I said.

She raised her eyebrows again. 'In*deed*? Lost your land?'

I snorted. 'It would take a fine army indeed to take land from *my* clan. No, I'm here because...' I didn't think I could tell her my tangle of reasons. 'Because I support the Pendragon, and because I'm fond of my lord Gwalchmai.'

She looked very startled at this declaration of free choice, so I asked her whether she had been born a servant.

She tossed her head. 'In a manner. My father was kin-wrecked, and fled from Erin for his life, and took me with him. He's no kin in the Orcades, so there he went, and found service with King Lot.'

'What was he kin-wrecked for?' I asked, before I could think better.

'He killed his brother,' she said shortly. She took the cheese from me and opened the door of Medraut's house, before I could understand what she had said.

Medraut and Rhuawn had stopped singing and were talking. Eivlin set the bread and cheese down firmly and swept into the next room. I sat down, thinking about fratricide. They say that there is a curse on those who do such things, on them and on their descendants. Poor Eivlin. I wondered how old she had been.

Rhuawn absently cut himself a slice of bread and some cheese, and ate it, listening to Medraut, who was talking about harping.

'...twenty-three major songs, one has to learn, and the genealogies, which are worse...' Rhuawn snorted and nodded vigorously. 'All to be told in the bardic style, which is tedious as a summer afternoon and far less relaxing. Gwalchmai liked it, but he never sang in it. He used to sing me the stories straight, which was wonderful.'

'He's a good harper,' Rhuawn agreed.

Medraut laughed. 'I used to think he was good at everything. But then – well, do you have an older brother?'

Rhuawn shook his head. 'No.' He grinned. 'But I've a younger brother, so I can imagine.'

Medraut smiled, but the smile drooped suddenly with hurt. 'But then, of course, Gwalchmai . . . left. We thought for years that he was dead: not a word about him. And then reports that he was alive in Britain and fighting for Arthur, fighting brilliantly. We didn't believe them at first, but finally we had to. I don't know why he left, unless he . . . my poor mother was very worried.'

Rhuawn and I sat very still, awkwardly. Medraut looked at us sharply. 'Well, she was. Come, you don't believe all that nonsense about her being a witch, do you? She's simply a clever woman, and that makes men distrust her.'

I thought of her advancing on us that first night and shuddered. Rhuawn coughed and asked for the harp. After listening to the music for a while, Medraut cheered up.

When we returned to our own house it was growing dark, and Gwalchmai was sitting cross-legged on the floor, looking in the fire. He looked up and nodded to us when we came in, but that was all. Rhuawn seated himself on the bed.

'A very enjoyable afternoon. How was yours?'

Gwalchmai slowly traced designs on the ground before him with one long-fingered hand. 'Maelgwn says nothing more. The mountains are beautiful, in the spring.'

'Indeed?' Gwalchmai did not reply. 'We spent the afternoon with your brother, Rhys and I. You might join us next time, instead of riding about the mountains alone.'

Gwalchmai looked up sharply. 'With Medraut? What were you doing with Medraut?'

'Playing the harp, mainly. He talked a deal about you.' Rhuawn paused, then went on, carefully, 'Cousin, I do not think your brother knows much about the doings of the rest of your family, and he speaks as though you were once close. There is no reason to act as coldly towards him as you have done.'

'Medraut knows why I left Dun Fionn.'

'He said otherwise.'

'Did he? Then he was lying.'

'Cousin, he is not a bad man. I have found him very courteous, pleasant, and generous.'

Gwalchmai gave both of us a long, dark look, then shrugged. 'When I left Dun Fionn he had . . . taken certain steps in my mother's direction.'

'Couldn't he have changed his mind?' I asked. 'You say

that you did.'

Gwalchmai rubbed his face with his hands, tiredly. 'I don't know,' he said, after a long while. 'Perhaps. But he did know why I left . . . you think that I should talk to him?'

We told him he should.

'Then I will. Privately. But now I am going to see to my horse.' He rose and left us, vanishing into the cold twilight.

'He's just finished seeing to his horse,' muttered Rhuawn. 'He spends more time with that beast than with his friends and kinsmen.' He picked a straw from the mattress and tossed it angrily into the fire. It was true, and I too was annoyed, and said nothing.

The next few weeks proceeded in the same fashion. I saw a fair amount of Medraut ap Lot, and he and Rhuawn became friends and went hunting together. Gwalchmai, however, made no further mention of his brother until Rhuawn finally dragged the matter up again. Then he said, very coldly, 'I did talk with him. You are much mistaken if you think he has any love left for me, and I think he is also intimate in my mother's counsels.' And when Rhuawn shook his head and protested, Gwalchmai insisted: 'He does not seek you out either because he loves you or because he cares for the Light. I urge you, cousin, not to speak with him. I do not trust his motives.'

But neither Rhuawn nor I could believe this of Medraut. I decided that when my lord spoke with his brother they must have quarrelled, which was understandable after so much separation and reunion in such circumstances.

I had become somewhat busier than I had been. On another visit to Medraut's, the serving girl Eivlin had again had to drop her own work to fetch things for us, so I again had offered to help. While we were walking back from the feast hall with the jar of wine Medraut had asked for, she turned to me and said fiercely, 'And you are not afraid of the curse?'

'What curse?' I asked, though I was thinking about the curse on fratricides myself.

'Stars of the heavens! The curse that is on me from my father's deed; what other curses do you think I carry about?'

'Oh, that curse. I do not believe in curses.'

She stared at me, stopping in her tracks, and,

setting her hand on her hip, she put her head back and looked up at me. 'A fool, is it? You do not believe in the magic of blood and iron?'

I put my head back, too, and declaimed, 'I am a Christian man from a Christian kingdom, and if blood and iron can curse, blood and water atone. I'm afraid of no sorceries.'

'Not even my lady's?' she asked, very quietly. I felt cold, and was silent a moment. 'You believe, well enough.' She began walking again.

I hurried after her. 'Your lady is able to terrify, but that doesn't change what I believe, and no curse is stronger than Christ's power. It wouldn't trouble me if your father had killed all his brothers and his parents as well.'

She shivered. 'Your Christian sorceries are so powerful? I had heard they were . . . and you are really a Christian?' I nodded, and she stopped again, looking at me with a closed face. 'Is it true that you drink blood?'

I was shocked. I had known that the Ynysoedd Erch were a barbarian, pagan kingdom, but this idea passed belief. 'Holy angels, no. Where did you hear that?'

'Why, everyone says that. You mean it isn't true?'

'It is not. We Christians are not permitted any sorceries, let alone the drinking of blood or whatever.'

She shrugged. 'Well. I had heard that Christians had a rite where they killed babies, and ate their flesh and drank up their blood. All the servants at Dun Fionn say so. I had thought it a sorcery to match my lady's; and indeed, it seemed likely enough, for she has been trying for years to kill the Pendragon, and failed. But if Christians have no sorceries, it must just be that she cannot kill him because of the distance, unless someone else is protecting Arthur. Are you certain that there are no such rituals, and that you had heard nothing of them?'

In a flash of insight, I knew where the idea had come from. 'There is a mystery, a ritual I have taken part in,' I told her. 'But we use bread and wine, not flesh and blood. At least, it looks like bread and wine; my mother has baked the bread for it, sometimes. But we say that after the mystery, it is really flesh and blood.'

'Oh,' said Eivlin. 'And me thinking it was powerful. Well.'

'It *is* powerful,' I insisted. 'It is a mystery . . .'

'And it is because of this little dinner,' she snapped her fingers in contempt, 'because of this make-believe sorcery, that you sneer at curses? Indeed, you are a fool.'

'I am not afraid of curses,' I said, setting my teeth, and I tried to explain about the sacraments, and about Christ, and his victory over death and Hell. This led me into insisting that he was God and Man both, and I became confused, and thrashed about in the creeds. Eivlin eyed me sceptically and made acid comments, and I finally gave up in disgust, and retreated to reaffirming that I was not afraid of any curse.

'So you say, so you say,' she said. 'And yet you are afraid of my lady. Indeed, and you will be afraid of me, too, because I am accursed, and you will be certain to avoid me in the future.'

'I will not. Didn't I offer to help you today? As for your lady – did you say you had to turn the bed today? Well, I will help you with the heavy work.'

She raised her eyebrows, but assented in a meek tone. I helped her then, and afterwards had to help her some more to prove my lack of fear for curses. I was angry at first, then pleased that I was proving myself. It was not until the end of the afternoon that I noticed her smug smile and began to suspect that I was being made a fool of.

Nonetheless, over the next few weeks I helped her whenever she asked me to, to prove that I was not avoiding her, not afraid of curses, and not afraid of Morgawse of Orcade. I intended to back out eventually, but Eivlin, for all her plump fairness, was as cunning a bargainer as any I've encountered, a woman to fear in a market place. She was as convincing as a dealer in sick cattle, and twice as witty. The only thing that ever seemed to bridle her was her lady. I had occasionally also to see Morgawse, and I liked her no more on second glance than on first. She paid no attention to me at all, beyond the first sharp question to Eivlin, but Eivlin was subdued when the Queen was about, and always quiet for a time even after her lady had left.

And yet, when I had seen her room and helped to clean it, I could find no evidence that the Queen practised sorcery. She had a few books about, but nothing else, and I could not tell what the books were. Medraut insisted that she was no witch, and that her reputation was merely an envious legend, begun because she was beautiful and intelligent and skilled at governing. 'And because she has a certain air about her. My brother has the same look, sometimes.' But I could not think that she and Gwalchmai were at all alike in their respective otherworldliness, and I knew that Medraut was wrong. Probably, I told myself, he says what he would like to believe.

As a few weeks passed, Rhuawn became determined that Gwalchmai and Medraut should speak to each other properly, and reconcile their differences. He asked Medraut over to our hut one afternoon, and kept him late, without warning Gwalchmai of what he did. Most of the afternoon was the usual pleasant, relaxed conversation; and then the door opened and Gwalchmai appeared. It was twilight behind him, and raining, and my lord's hair was plastered down from the wet, while he was dripping and tired looking. But he took one look at Medraut, and both froze. For a moment I thought Gwalchmai would back out into the rain again, giving some errand as an excuse. Rhuawn stood hastily, greeting Gwalchmai and offering him mead. Gwalchmai did not even look at him, but stood and stared at Medraut.

Medraut stared back. The two faces, the dark and the fair, were still as the sky, only their eyes brilliant and cold. Then, between one blink and the next, Gwalchmai strode across the room and stood above his brother looking down at him. The open door let in a wet night smell, and the rain dripped from his cloak onto the floor.

'What are you doing here?' Gwalchmai's voice was quiet, but something in his tone told me that here was danger.

Medraut uncurled himself from before the fire and stood, brushing wood ash from his shoulder, then smiling hesitantly. 'I was asked here, brother. If you don't want me, I will go.'

Gwalchmai glanced at Rhuawn, at me. 'Truly. You were asked. But what were you doing, Medraut?'

The other smiled, nervously, apologetically. 'I was playing the harp, the way you taught me once. What is wrong in that?'

'That is not what I meant.' Gwalchmai stared at his brother steadily. Some water ran from his hair and crawled down one cheek, shining like red bronze in the firelight. 'Medraut.' His voice had changed, become earnest. 'Once you wished to be another CuChulainn for strength and skill, and for courage and honour, and I thought you might be such a one. Is it all nothing to you beside a whisper in the dark, and the hope of a purple cloak in the daylight?'

For just an instant I thought I glimpsed something strange in Medraut''s face, a chill, bitter darkness rushing behind his eyes. But that was only for an instant, and then he was smiling, ruefully and painfully, and I doubted whether I had seen anything. 'Still unyielding?' he asked Gwalchmai. 'Are we nothing to you, your family and your homeland, whom you loved once? Are we sold, for a white horse and a sword and a place behind the Pendragon?'

'I sold nothing, only gave it, and to the Light first, not to Arthur. And for all the grief, it is worth it. Is your bargain the same, Medraut?'

Medraut moved quickly to the door, caught it and stood with his hand on the latch. 'I can do nothing here.' He did not look at his brother, and his voice was strained by some inner pain. 'If you still wish, Rhuawn, we can go hunting tomorrow. Good night, Gwalchmai.' He slipped out, closing the door behind him.

Rhuawn stared at Gwalchmai angrily, but said nothing.

Gwalchmai sighed, unpinned his cloak, and stood a moment holding it, the crimson vivid against his thin, dark frame. Hesitantly he sat down, looked at Rhuawn, looked at me.

'You must not believe Medraut,' he said at last. 'Whatever he is planning, it is not to your good.'

Rhuawn said nothing. I did not know what to say. My lord had not treated his brother prettily. But after a while, I offered Gwalchmai some mead, simply to break the silence. I thought for a moment he would go on talking about Medraut, but he only took the mead, ran a narrow hand through his wet hair, and began to sip the hot drink slowly.

The following day, when I went to meet Eivlin and rapped on her door, she did not at once call out 'Come in!' I waited a moment, then rapped again. This time a voice did call, 'Come.'

I pushed the door open and stopped short. Morgawse of Orcade was sitting with her back to me, tying her black hair up with a strand of gold. She was wearing only a shift of crimson linen through which every line of her body was visible, and she sat looking into a bronze mirror. I could see her face in the mirror, and the opened door with my own form reflected frozen there. Her imaged eyes met mine, and her mouth contracted. She turned. I let my eyes rest on her reflection, afraid – I will admit it – to look into her face.

'What are you doing here?' Her voice was softer than thistledown, but cold to freeze the marrow of my bones.

'Eivlin,' I gasped. 'I . . . I was going to help her mend the thatch.'

'Your help is unnecessary. Go – no, wait.' She rose and came towards me, and I had to look away from the mirror. I heartily wished myself elsewhere, and wondered why I had ever left my home. I cannot explain it, but this woman froze my blood. 'You are Gwalchmai's servant, aren't you?'

'Yes, Great Queen,' I mumbled.

She smiled sweetly. 'Then it is most generous of you to help us with our business. What is your name?'

I licked my lips, not wanting to speak of anything which might give her power over me and mine, but I had to say, 'Rhys ap Sion, Lady.'

'Rhys ap Sion.' She toyed with a gold pendant about her neck, her eyes fixed on mine. I felt dizzy, and squirmed inwardly, but I remembered my boasts to Eivlin, and just managed to stand straight and stare back.

She dropped the pendant. 'It is most generous. Does your lord, my son, know that you do this?'

I nodded, then shook my head.

'Perhaps he commanded you to,' she said, still smiling. 'I think that he did.' She reached out and rested one hand on my shoulder, then leaned forward, her lips slightly parted, still smiling. 'He is welcome to whatever you see. Tell him so. But be warned that I do not like to be spied upon, Rhys ap Sion, and those who do so . . . well.' She dropped her arm. 'Eivlin is in the kitchens for the day. Perhaps you can seek her there.'

I bowed deeply and left. As I stepped out of the door I nearly walked into Maelgwn of Gwynedd. He snarled at me and struck out, and I ducked, turning the movement into a bow and a muttered apology, and strode off as fast as I could. But behind me I heard him greet Morgawse, and I heard her low laugh, while a glance over my shoulder showed me that she was closing the door, and his arm was about her waist.

I walked half-way to the kitchens and stopped and stood on the clean grass with the clear sky over me. Gwalchmai had said that it was Morgawse who led the plotting, and truly, withered old King Lot did not look capable of it. Lot had worked in a world of armies and alliances, but Morgawse was more subtle. Morgawse would dominate her allies' minds and subjugate them not to a cause, but to herself, and she would start with Maelgwn. No matter who had invited whom, she was sleeping with the king of Gwynedd, and was going to dictate his counsels. The Ynysoedd Erch were simply too far away for her to work as she pleased, and so she had come to Gwynedd to hunt for a tool. Lot mac Cormac probably knew nothing about any of the plans, but there were probably others who did . . .

I turned from the kitchens towards the stables, hoping to find Gwalchmai.

As it happened, he was not there, but in the practice yard nearby, throwing spears at a target from horseback. Ceincaled swooped about the yard as lightly as a swallow darting about a barn, and Gwalchmai seemed to be a part of him, while the flung spears flew straight and steady. It was a fine sight, but I was in no temper to sit back and admire it.

'My lord!' I shouted. He glanced at me, then turned Ceincaled in an easy semi-circle and cantered over. He reined in before me and leaned over, elbow on knee, to listen to me.

'My lord,' I repeated, 'do you have any business in the next hour? There is a matter I need to talk to you about.'

He sighed. 'There is nothing urgent. Maelgwn is engaged this morning. Only . . . must you?'

I glared at him irritably. 'I must. And privately.'

He straightened. 'Och ai, in that case – does your horse need exercise?'

I soon had my wretched beast from Caer Legion saddled, and we rode out of the gates and into the mountains. It was early April, and the snow had melted. All the earth was green and misty, and sounded with streams. It made me think of the planting season and the green corn, and young lambs and calves to worry about at home. A deal of work, spring, but a good season.

Gwalchmai hummed abstractedly for a while, and sang a little in Irish. I tried to piece my thoughts together, and wondered how to communicate them. After all, she was still his mother, and warriors kill men for making such suggestions.

'My lord,' I said at last.

'So,' replied Gwalchmai. 'You wish to talk about my brother.'

I was taken aback. 'Indeed not, my lord. About your mother.' And I told him what Morgawse had said to me that morning, and that I had seen Maelgwn going to her, 'to talk'.

Gwalchmai heard me out with patience, and when I ground to a halt he said, 'And you think she commits adultery with Maelgwn?'

'My lord,' I drew a deep breath, 'in due respect, I do.'

To my surprise he smiled a little, bitterly. 'She does, if you doubt it.'

I stopped my horse. 'You know?'

He nodded. gestured with open hands. 'I know my mother. I have been watching Maelgwn. The whole fortress knows, though they wouldn't mention it before us, of course. She has been quite open about it. I could almost be sorry for Maelgwn, only I so pity Lot.'

My face felt hot, and I looked between my horse's ears. To have come to my lord in such high haste, with such urgency, and such stale news! 'Lot knows too?' I asked.

'He probably knew before ever they set sail from the islands.' I looked up sharply, and he added, quickly, not looking at me, 'No. He is not indifferent to it. He would not assent – only he cannot any longer deny her any whim that enters her thoughts. He cannot decide anything for himself, Rhys. He still desires, and wills, but he cannot act. He . . .' Gwalchmai extended one hand vaguely in the air, 'he has withered away. He is only a shadow now, a ghost among his own warriors, who stares and cannot speak. I go to speak with him, and I tell him how things stand, with Agravain and with myself, and he is glad of this thing or that, but to act,' his hand clenched convulsively, 'he is like a dotard. And he is the one who was the shield of his people, the bulwark of the warband, leader of a thousand spears; the lord of Dun Fionn and the Orcades and all the islands to the north and the west of Caledon, ruler by his own strength and cunning and courage! Sweet heaven, how she has used him!' He brought his hand down against his thigh, half raised it again, then straightened the fingers with an effort. He rubbed the worn leather of the reins, looking off towards the mountains. Ceincaled tossed his head and walked on. The hooves of our horses made a steady rhythm against the earth.

I sat still, knowing that I couldn't say anything, and that it was best to leave him be for a while. It no longer surprised me that he spent so much time by himself, nor that he was remote when he was in Degannwy. He had quite enough worries as it was, without additional difficulties from Rhuawn and myself. Sweet Jesu, what a family! Except for Medraut, my lord could well afford the loss of the whole royal clan of the Ynysoedd Erch.

Except Medraut ... and Gwalchmai asserted that Medraut was as bad, close to the Queen and following in her road. Medraut, however, asserted – though never in so many words – that Gwalchmai was indifferent to his family and to natural affection, cruel, and concerned primarily with his own honour. Well, Medraut didn't properly understand the circumstances.

But could he, in his position, really not understand them?

I found myself weighing the two brothers in my mind. Gwalchmai, I knew, was accomplished in eloquence and courtesy, and, having seen him being persuasive with Maelgwn and his nobles, I knew that he could be very persuasive indeed when he set his mind to it. Medraut had a double measure of the same eloquence, and a graceful, amiable charm as well, a very real and forceful charm. I could not believe that he was what Gwalchmai asserted him to be, and yet I suddenly wished that I spoke Irish and could question Lot's servants about Medraut, to see if his deeds matched his words. No, I liked Medraut, I was sure there would be a good report of him ...

On the other hand, I was not quite as sure as all that. The manner in which he treated Eivlin leapt before my mind. No matter what task she was engaged in, he expected her to drop it at once if he told her to run and fetch something; indeed, I'd originally offered to help the girl precisely because of that. And I had a nagging awareness that he treated her better than he treated most servants. And yet, I argued, for a nobleman to be unaware of servants' feelings meant very little. Medraut was royally born and, unlike his brother, he had never left his privileged position. He could simply assume that servants were there to do things for him, and so be annoyed when they failed to, because that was what he had always known. I liked Medraut. There was some way, I was sure, in which it could be seen that both Gwalchmai and Medraut spoke the truth, and the whole problem was a misunderstanding.

But still, I might do well to ask Eivlin about Medraut, and perhaps even ask her to interpret what Lot's other servants had to say.

I looked back to Gwalchmai. He had settled somewhat after his outburst, leaning back in the saddle, one arm crossed under the other. I cleared my throat. 'My lord, since you know that Morgawse is ... scheming with Maelgwn' (after all, that was the significant part) 'do we know what they're planning? At all?'

He sighed a little and shrugged. 'They have written letters, some of which were sent to the north. That much I know. But it is not likely to be open war, not now.' He hesitated, then said quietly, 'I should have told Rhuawn, and you, that we knew so much; and yet I could not. I fear I have been poor company, this last month. Forgive me. It has been a distraction to me, my family, and there has been this trouble about my brother.'

I nodded to indicate sympathy, and bit my tongue to stop myself asking more about Medraut. He straightened and tightened the reins a little, and Ceincaled pricked his ears forward.

'We've a fine hillside here,' said Gwalchmai. 'Why don't we gallop?' He touched his stallion and was off, and I kicked my own beast into following him.

We rode directly north from the fortress, heading towards the main east–west road, keeping the highest mountain peaks behind us and to our left. The land was wild, but much of it only seemed to be deserted, and in the summer was used for pasturage. It was a sweet country, if not a rich one, and it was a fine day to be away from Degannwy and out in the clean bright air. After a little while, Gwalchmai turned off the track we had followed, heading as though for a cleft between two large hills, and we slowed to a walk again. Gwalchmai glanced back at me, smiled, and checked his mount until I caught up.

'Rhys,' he said. 'Can you climb trees?'

I opened my mouth, then closed it again like a fish. 'My lord? I mean, yes. Ordinary trees, that is, not ash trees. But . . .'

'That is well. I am not good at it myself. We do not have many trees in the islands.' He smiled again and explained, 'There is a tree where one of my lord's men here in Gwynedd leaves the letters and messages which my lord sends me. But one must climb to reach the place, and, as I said, I am not good at climbing trees.'

We rode on for a little way, then Gwalchmai stood in the saddle, peering at something, and then turned Ceincaled to the right. Soon we came to the edge of a wood, and there, huge and pre-eminent, stood a large oak tree. My lord reined in his horse and dismounted. 'This is the one,' He said, staring at one of the branches. 'And there is a message.'

I looked at the branch. It looked like a branch, to me. 'How can you tell?'

He glanced back to me. 'There was a sprig of holly back where we turned off the road. That means that I am to check the tree. If the message is urgent, there is a sprig of pine as well. When I have the message, I take the twigs away.' He placed one palm against the oak and looked up it again. 'Can you climb this?'

It had wide-spreading branches at some distance from the ground, but a large fork within grabbing distance. 'Certainly.' I jumped from my horse and clambered up. Just like the apple trees in my clan's orchards.

'Where do they put this letter, then?'

'There's a hollow where that big branch joins the larger fork, to your right . . . yes, there.'

I leaned over and searched the hollow with my hand. Something prickly. I pulled it out: it was a pine cone. I held it in my other hand and reached again: only rough oak bark and the sodden remains of last year's leaves.

'There's nothing here,' I told Gwalchmai.

'Nothing? What's that in your hand?'

'Only a pine cone.'

'That's the message. You're sure there's nothing more?'

I said I was sure, and he told me to climb down. When I reached him he took the pine cone and turned it in his fingers.

'Do you break it open?' I asked, intrigued by the ingenuity of the system.

He shook his head. 'No. It only means that Arthur received my last letter safely.' He sighed, tossed the pine cone into the wood and walked back to Ceincaled. 'I was hoping for more.'

I could see that, when a letter was sent for such a distance, there would have to be some sign that it had reached its destination, but it still seemed a complicated system. I said so.

'It has to be,' said Gwalchmai. 'any message passes through several hands on its journey, and any one of the men could be bought by Maelgwn or some other ruler, or be killed, and the message lost. As it is, those who bear the message do not know what it is they carry. The man who put the pine cone there was told only to do so much. There are a few other signs; Arthur and I agreed on them before we left.'

I suddenly realized that Gwalchmai was trusting me with a great deal. If I told Maelgwn, he could set watchers on the oak and capture the messenger, and perhaps through him find the rest of Arthur's supporters in Gwynedd. And even if I did not do that, it would be a simple matter for me to substitute any message I wanted. If Medraut told me to leave something there, I could drop his letter in that hollow, leave a sprig of holly by the track, and Gwalchmai could think that Arthur commanded him to be more charitable towards his brother.

But I could not. Gwalchmai must have known that, to trust me so far. While I thought it would be a fine thing if my lord were a little gentler with Medraut, I could not use trickery and deception to make him so. That would be the same as no gentleness at all. And then, even as I thought of it, I suddenly noticed that I did not quite trust Medraut. I would have to see about him. Truly, I would.

Nine

When I returned to Degannwy an hour or so later, I went to look for Rhuawn. It took some looking, but I eventually found him. He was with Medraut, and the two sat together in a quiet corner of the feast hall, near a fire, playing the harp in turns. Both looked up when I walked over to them, and Medraut smiled and indicated a place to sit. I sat, leaning against one of the benches. Rhuawn was singing a long song in praise of the spring, 'when warbands are splendid before a bold lord', and, while it was not exactly what I had been enjoying the season for, it was still a fine song.

When Rhuawn finished, Medraut took the harp. He began to pluck it idly, as men do before they've decided what to sing, bringing out light ripples of sound like the wind on a pool.

'We have songs such as that in Irish,' he told Rhuawn. 'There is one which is supposed to have been made by the greater warleader, Fionn mac Cumhail. It is the longest and dullest of the lot, so, of course, everyone has to memorize it.' He played a little more, the runs of music sliding into each other with a rush under his fingers, while he gazed dreamily into the fire. 'My brother was born in the spring,' he said, after a little. 'He will be twenty-seven this May.' A kind of tune began to grow out of the music, then faded again. 'I wonder if I could give him a present.'

Rhuawn snorted. 'I don't think you should; and I think, if you did, he would not receive it from you.'

'I might show him my care by it.'

'I don't think he'd pay any attention. He does not listen to me when I try to speak with him on your behalf. He keeps very much to himself.'

Medraut smiled warmly at Rhuawn. 'I thank you deeply for your efforts. It is good to have a friend in this ... but truly, I think he only misunderstands me. If I remain patient and generous, he will see that I at least am not his enemy.'

Rhuawn shrugged. 'Hawks may swim and salmon may fly.'

'My brother can swim, and his name means hawk. I wonder...'

Rhuawn straightened and leaned forward, putting out his hand for emphasis. 'Your brother will remain obstinate. He's already made that plain to me, abundantly plain. I don't know why, but he's set against you and will never change his mind.'

I opened my mouth to say something in Gwalchmai's defence, but Medraut was already speaking. 'I can't simply give up his friendship. He is my brother.'

'He has abandoned you. He has sworn the Threefold Oath to Arthur, and he holds that above his own blood. He tells people that you and your mother are sorcerers, and he tramples your kinship. In your place, I'd have no qualms about letting him discover his own condemnation.'

I stared at Rhuawn, astonished. But Medraut was shaking his head. 'It isn't Gwalchmai's fault.' He stopped his harping for a moment, then began again with a different rhythm, and went on, 'Listen, Rhuawn. I will tell you a thing I have thought of.'

Rhuawn listened attentively. I shut my mouth tight and chewed on my lip, to remind myself to keep quiet.

'It is about this battle-madness of his which you have told me of.' Medraut's harp thrummed steadily. 'When my brother was young, and as I remember him, he had no such thing. He used to have fights with Agravain, and Agravain always beat him, and there was no sign of madness. The first time I heard of it was in songs, and in reports from Britain.

'Now, when Gwalchmai left Dun Fionn, he left suddenly. He took his horse from the fortress on a stormy night and rode off at a gallop across to the cliffs westward. He says – I have heard it, Rhuawn – that our mother tried to kill him that night. He has even said that I . . .' he hesitated, fighting with it, 'that I was with her, and assenting. But I know that no such thing happened. The idea is madness – me, to kill my brother? For a long time this confused me. I could not see why my brother, who had always been so close, should say such things. And yet, I think he truly believes them; and moreoever, I have heard that he says he journeyed to the Otherworld after he departed Dun Fionn, and tells of many other impossibilities. What I think is that he had a fit of this madness you tell me of, for the first time, perhaps, and that he rode off in it, raving and seeing visions, and that his mind has been warped by this demon ever since. So you see, it is not Gwalchmai's fault that he thinks of me as his enemy. It is only this disease.'

I had been searching for some way in which both brothers might be seen to be speaking the truth. Here, now, was a way. Madness and delusion, and it was undeniable that Gwalchmai did go mad in battle. It made sense, excellent sense, and neatly accounted for the situation.

And yet I was certain it was a lie.

But Medraut plainly believed his theory. He bowed his head over the harp, and the music went on.

Rhuawn rubbed his sword-hilt with one hand. 'Do you think so, truly?' he asked Medraut. 'If it is thus, this is a dreadful ill for him to suffer.'

'What other explanation is there?' asked Medraut.

'That something did happen that night,' I said. Both the warriors looked at me, and I looked back at Medraut. His harp-playing faltered a minute, almost became a tune, then resumed in a different, wilder key. It was an infernal distraction, that plunking. 'You wouldn't have had to know anything about it,' I admitted. 'Or, even, remember it.'

'But I would know,' Medraut said simply. His grey eyes were wide and grave.

'Of course he would,' snapped Rhuawn. 'Rhys, this makes a great deal of sense. I've never liked battle-madness, because it doesn't always happen in battle. Sometimes those Saxon berserkers go mad in the feast hall and murder half a dozen of their comrades. And if someone has the berserker-gang, I have heard that it gets worse with time.'

'My lord Gwalchmai is not mad,' I snapped back. 'You must have seen him fight. You know he's not a berserker.'

Rhuawn looked uncertain a moment. Medraut kept on playing the harp. 'I have seen Gwalchmai in battle,' Rhuawn spoke slowly. 'He is a very great warrior, but he is uncontrollable. And he collapses afterwards, just as the Saxon berserkers do.'

'I didn't say that Gwalchmai was mad,' Medraut added hurriedly. 'Only . . . touched, at times. Ill.'

'If you'd seen his face when it is on him, you couldn't believe that,' I insisted.

'Well, I have never seen his face at such a time, it is true . . .' began Medraut.

'I have watched him fight, and this is the only explanation for his treatment of Medraut. And when did you ever see his face when the madness was on him, Rhys? No one dares to meet his eyes then.'

'When we were coming down to Camlann we met some bandits on the road and he killed them. And even in the madness, he is still himself, only . . . only . . . ach, I can't say it. But your own servant, Aegmund, has told me tales of Saxon berserkers, how they foam at the mouth and howl like wolves. Gwalchmai is not like that at all.'

'But it must be the same kind of thing,' returned Rhuawn. 'We can't say what he sees in the madness.'

I couldn't answer this, and simply glared.

'It is a hard thing to believe of one's lord,' said Medraut, still hesitant. 'And, God knows, a hard thing to believe of one's brother. But I have no other explanation. I know that Gwalchmai desires glory and honour – as what warrior worth his mead does not? – but he would not, for that, spread lies about my mother and me. No, he has believed a thing proceeding from madness, and, having believed it, sought glory among foreigners instead of with his own kin. While one must honour the Pendragon,' Medraut nodded to Rhuawn, 'still, my brother forsook his own blood for Arthur's service, a thing no right-thinking man would do. And once he had given his oath to Arthur, whom political necessity had made our enemy, he could not but keep to the delusion. And now he thinks that my mother and I – and my father, too, I imagine – are fighting for some great darkness, while he and the Pendragon fight for some kind of light. But, in fact, all my father wanted and wants, is to have power in Britain, which is just what the Pendragon wanted, and has. And my father's rights are as good as the Pendragon's. He married the legitimate daughter of a Pendragon, and he is the legitimately born king of a royal clan, although he is Irish, while the Pendragon – and I say this not to disparage him, for, indeed, I greatly admire him for overcoming it – Arthur is only one of the Pendragon Uther's bastards, and legally clanless and unable to succeed to the High Kingship. Arthur is High King, as we know, and a great one: and that is a fact in the real world. It is not as though he stood for some pure light, while my father and my mother, who once with an equally good claim opposed

417 .

him, must perforce stand for darkness. Such notions are fine in a song, and lend elegance, but what have they to do with the world in which we live? My poor brother confounds Britain with the Land of Youth, the Kingdom of Summer. Och, by the sun, I have missed him, these years, and wondered, again and again, when I would see him: I see him, and find that he is still mad, and hates me. If only he were free of it, and could come home!'

Unable to command himself, Medraut turned his whole mind to the harp, and finally began playing some kind of tune, a weird thing in a minor key. I sat, bewildered, wondering where the bottom of my world had dropped to. It was true enough: Arthur had scant legal right to the imperium of Britain. Could the struggle I had seen so clearly, the struggle of Light and Darkness, be merely the clashings of dishonest kings? The idea was solid, easy to consider, without any vague indefinites and worlds within worlds depending upon it. And if it was true, then Medraut, and Morgawse, were quite innocent, and Gwalchmai was quite deluded, and I with him. Medraut's harp kept on steadily, and I thrashed about in his words, trying to find some way out.

'My friend,' said Rhuawn, 'you are right. This is a sickness which has come upon him. I wish to God that he were healed of it, for it is a dreadful thing for a man to be separated from his own clan and his own blood. I thought so at the first, and now that I am sure you are innocent ... but what can be done? Are there treatments for madness?'

Medraut drew a deep breath, his eyes very bright. 'Yes. There are some treatments for madness.' His voice was soft. 'One can read of them in books, works written by learned Roman doctors. But I could not mention it to him. He would never trust me to help, though I have ached to try them.'

'These methods,' said Rhuawn slowly. 'Could I help?'

'Would you be willing?' asked Medraut in a surprised tone.

I struggled silently with Medraut's argument, trying to find the flaw in it. But my thoughts were confused, and all I could do was stare at the whole and think what sense, what excellent sense, it all made.

'Anything,' said Rhuawn. 'Gwalchmai saved my life in battle, once, and all my loyalty is due to him, together with the friendship I bear for him and for you, and, in honour, I will help him to a cure in any way which you show me.'

'He would not accept our aid,' said Medraut. 'We could never convince him that he is wrong, and probably he would think I devised some sorcery against his life. If we even suggested anything, he will write to his lord, and Arthur would listen to him.'

'Arthur trusts Gwalchmai above his own right hand,' said Rhuawn, 'and he does not understand the situation.'

'If I should give Gwalchmai some medicine, then, would you keep it secret from the High King?' Medraut asked, almost pleadingly. 'It would only take a little while.'

Rhuawn held out his hand. 'I will help you in any treatment you plan, and I will set Arthur's mind at rest that all is well with us.'

Medraut took his hand and clasped it gladly, then looked at me. 'Will you also, join us?' he asked.

I licked my lips, trying to find a way out, and looked at Medraut. He seemed humble and earnest and excited: no help. He must be wrong. He must be, but where?

'Perhaps Gwalchmai has spoken to you about me, or about this struggle he believes is going on. I know that he can be very convincing. But think carefully, and see if this does not seem more likely than those fantasies he spun for you.'

'Come, Rhys,' put in Rhuawn. 'We don't call him Gwalchmai the Golden-tongued for nothing. But Medraut is talking about real things.'

'Will you help us?' Medraut asked again.

I again licked my lips. Where, where, where?

Suddenly, there flashed before my mind the image of Gwalchmai kneeling to offer his sword to my father. There was no one to impress there, no advantage to be gained. The gesture was a pure gift, as Gwalchmai had given to Arthur and as Arthur gave to Britain: and it was real. The image was quickly followed by others: my lord laughing with admiration and telling me to keep the brooch; unthinkingly helping with a task unbefitting to his rank; talking earnestly with Arthur; singing that unearthly song in the marshes before Gwlad yr Haf. I dropped my half-lifted hand. There was really no question. Medraut was lying, and he had lied all along. While Gwalchmai's eloquence and courtesy were real things, expressions of his whole life, Medraut's came from words alone, fine paint over rotten timbers. Even without asking Lot's warriors, I realized that I had never actually seen him do anything courteous, noble or gentle unless he stood to benefit from it. I could weigh the two men together, and their two visions of the world, and there was no question whom I should believe.

'No,' I said. 'I will not.' And I stood abruptly and faced them both. 'I will not because my lord is not mad, nor deluded, and you, Rhuawn, you know that he is not, but you find it more likely and comfortable to believe Medraut. I will not have any part in certain un-named things done to "cure" him, things suggested by a reputed sorcerer who has made you swear not to tell his enemy and your lord, the Emperor Arthur, about any of this.'

Rhuawn leapt up in a rage. 'Do you accuse me of disloyalty to my lord Arthur?'

'That's as may be. You are disloyal to your friend Gwalchmai. A month ago he's cousin and brother to you, and now you're ready to forget this, and forget that he saved your life even as you speak of it, because of a few words from a man recently met, a man who openly admits that "political necessity" makes him your lord's enemy, whose father we came here to hinder in a plot, and whose mother is a famous witch. Tell me I lie!'

Rhuawn hit me across the face hard enough to make me stagger back. I stumbled into a bench, fell over it, and cracked my head against the floor. The world went black for a second, and then I scrambled around until I managed to stagger up into a crouching position, clasping my skull.

'You forget your place,' said Rhuawn. 'I should kill you for daring to speak so to a warrior. You need a thrashing to remind you that you are a servant, and that servants do what they are told, without back-talk. You have been honoured very much above your desserts as it is, and it has made you proud.' He took a step forward, drawing his sword so as to beat me with the flat of it. Medraut, who by now was also on his feet, caught his arm. 'Indeed, you must not thrash him, Rhuawn. He is Gwalchmai's servant, not yours.'

'Gwalchmai will not thrash him.' But Rhuawn halted. I rose to my feet, the feast hall wobbling about my ears. I was vaguely aware of some others down the other side of the room staring, but I was too angry to care. I wished that Rhuawn would come, even with his sword, so that I could hit him, just once.

'If Rhys chooses not to believe the truth, it comes from no evil nature, but only from a misplaced loyalty,' said Medraut, 'and it need not hinder us. If we can cure my brother, Rhys will be glad enough, I am sure. Come. Leave him be.'

I realized then that Medraut was making certain of Rhuawn for some scheme. He had hoped that I would have a part in it as well, but I was not essential. Rhuawn was . . . to reassure Arthur? I looked at Rhuawn. He was still fuming. I could not talk to him now. I glanced around the Hall, then turned and walked off, still holding the back of my head where I had hit the floor. Medraut and Rhuawn sat down again behind me, and I heard Medraut's voice begin again, softly.

One of Maelgwn's warriors jeered as I left the Hall: 'Oh, had enough of your betters' company?' and the rest laughed. I wanted to hit him, too, but I wanted more to find Gwalchmai, to find and warn him.

He was not at the house. Rather than run about looking for him I sat down and fingered the back of my head. A lovely lump I would have there. I had cut my mouth against my teeth, too, and I rinsed the blood with some stale, once-boiled water, then sat on the bed and waited for Gwalchmai.

I had not been sitting very long when there came a knock at the door. I called out 'Come in', and checked that I had a knife handy. But it was only Eivlin.

She looked about the room with some interest, then came and stood over me, hands on her hips. 'Truly, I hope the other man is worse off than you,' she said.

I glared and wiped my mouth. I supposed that my lip must be swollen, and there, it was bleeding. 'What do you want?' I asked her.

'Well, as though you had not promised to help me with the thatch today! "What do you want?" he says, bold as a bad dealer.'

'I went to your house, and your lady turned me out. I don't think she will want many people around today.'

Eivlin took her hands from her hips and crossed them before her. 'Perhaps she did,' she said in a different tone, then, 'indeed, I was working in the kitchen this morning like a common drudge. But she is finished now, and gone

421

out hawking with Maelgwn Gwynedd. I'd be glad of your help, Rhys.'

'Let the thatch wait. I must speak to my lord about a matter.'

'A matter of import?' she began lightly, and I cut her off: 'Yes, a matter of great urgency.'

She stood staring at me a moment, then suddenly sat down beside me and took my head in her hands. 'Och ai, you've had a blow here,' she said, touching the back of my head very gently. She looked about, saw the kettle of once-boiled water, and picked it up; then took a kerchief from her pocket and soaked it. 'Let me bind it up for you.'

I grunted, but let her. She did it deftly and gently. 'Now, I wonder who he was fighting,' she said. 'Saidi ap Sugyn?'

I had to smile at that. 'Sadly, no. More sadly, it was not a fight. It was nearly a beating.'

She hissed a little between her teeth. 'Not your lord? Is that why you must speak to him?'

'Not my lord, no, of course not Gwalchmai. Another warrior.'

'May they be damned, the lot of them, for their swords and heavy hands,' said Eivlin, bitterly and without a trace of mockery. I looked at her sharply.

'Do not be so easy with your damnings. Yffern is a heavy place to send a person ill-advisedly, and some do not deserve any such thing.'

'May they be damned nonetheless.' Eivlin dropped her hands to her lap and looked at me coldly. 'They've no thought for any but themselves and what pleasures them.'

'My lord is different,' I said. 'And I know others that are good enough men.'

She shrugged and sighed. 'I have never known them, then.'

I caught her wrist to get her attention and asked, 'What of Medraut, my lord's brother?'

'Him!' she said, then stopped abruptly, her face closing. 'Well, as you say, there is your lord's brother Medraut.' She stood, pulling away, and I let go her hand. 'So you are waiting for your lord here,' she said, her back still turned to me. I nodded, realized she couldn't see me, and said, 'Yes.'

'Well, do you expect him soon?'

There was the problem: I didn't. 'He will be back before

nightfall, if not before twilight.'

'And you would not be caring that he is at Medraut's now?'

'He is? What is he doing there?' I jumped to my feet, and my head twinged. Eivlin turned and caught my arm as I winced.

'Do not be touching that! The lord Gwalchmai is talking to the lord Ronan mac Suibhne, one of Lot's warriors, about some political matter. Ronan is a member of the royal clan, and so is staying with Medraut. It seems that your lord knew him before ever he came to Britain, and hopes to learn something of him now, since Medraut is not there.'

'Oh,' I said, 'That is all. Well, I will go and see him there, then – and maybe I will see how much thatching needs to be done, afterwards.'

'Don't do any thatching with that head,' advised Eivlin. 'You've a fine knock on the back of it, and thatching will make you dizzy.'

We set off across the stronghold, Eivlin walking beside me and chattering about the kitchens and the fools there. She made me laugh, which made my head ache, but I had to laugh even when it ached. When we finally reached the house, low and sprawling against the wall of the stronghold, rotten-thatched, Eivlin gave a little curtsey and opened the door. 'Do you go in first, since you have the headache,' she said.

I smiled at her, liking her a great deal, and stepped inside.

I heard only one soft movement from behind the door, and then, before I had time to turn my head, the world splintered in pain, went first red, then dark as I fell under the blow from the man behind the door.

I am not sure when I woke up. It could not have been too long, an hour at the most: but it does not make much difference, as I promptly fainted again when there was some jolt. My head hurt horribly, and I was sick to my stomach as well, and I heartily wished that the world would go black again and leave me alone. Instead, it swam in and out of my awareness as though I were on that thrice-damned ferry, come from Camlann to Caer Gwent and Degannwy. I could hear voices which my brain first understood and then didn't, and there was a good deal too much motion. When I opened my eyes, I could see nothing.

But after what seemed a long time, the jolting stopped, was succeeded by a few jerks, and then I felt hands on my shoulders dragging me up. The dark was replaced by light, and I found myself standing, or sagging rather, between two men and staring stupidly at the horse they had just lifted me from. Someone behind me said, 'Take him inside,' and I was dragged off to a dimly-seen little hovel and dropped on a mattress. Then, thank God, everything was still and I could lie down and be quiet, closing my eyes so that my head hurt less.

After a little while longer, someone else came and looked at my head, and then began to give me a drink of water. I was thirsty and drank greedily, if slowly, until the face of the woman who was holding the cup registered somewhere. Eivlin. Yes.

And then I realiized that she had lied to me and betrayed me into some trap of Medraut's making. Of course, I told myself dully, you were a fool to believe her so quickly, a cursed fool to walk right into Medraut's house. You should have known that Medraut would have no intention of leaving you free to warn Gwalchmai. And yet, that Eivlin should . . . I stopped drinking and turned my head away from her.

She realized what I meant and said, 'Oh Rhys, I am sorry, I am sorry. I did not know that they would hurt you. Please, have something more to drink. It will make you feel better.'

But I wanted nothing from her, least of all her sympathy, and I gritted my teeth and did not look at her. After a while she went away.

It could not have been very much later when someone came over and dragged me up into a sitting position, and I found myself looking at Medraut ap Lot.

When he saw my eyes focus, he drew his hand away from my shoulder and smiled. 'So you are again to be numbered among the enemy,' he said lightly. 'Good. Mother has a use for you which I would like to see you serving.'

'Go away,' I moaned hopefully. I did not feel up to dealing with him.

He only laughed. 'Not feeling well? You'll recover.' Then his fine eyes narrowed, and he said savagely, 'I am glad it worked this way, whatever Mother says. I do not like having to be gracious to insolent servants.'

'And I don't like being smiled at by treacherous sche-mers,' I replied.

But he only smiled again. 'That conclusion is recent, I think. You thought me a fine nobleman until this morning. Admit it.'

'I thought so, until I started comparing you to your brother, yes,' I said.

That did hit him. He slapped me hard, and my head hit the wall. I promptly fainted again. After a few minutes I came groggily to myself, and Medraut was still there. I felt very ill, and leaned against the wall, wishing he would vanish.

'My brother is a fool,' hissed Medraut, 'and a traitor to the Queen our mother. He had the chance to win power offered him, by her, and he chose Arthur instead. He sold us all, scorned us, and ran away. He was not worthy of the honour she gave him. He is a fool, a deceiving, care-less...' he stopped and stood abruptly. I looked up at him unenthusiastically and restrained myself from the comment I had sitting on my tongue.

'You, now,' Medraut went on in a different tone, smiling his pleasant, open smile, 'you are fortunate. Mother wishes to speak to you. I will tell her that you are recovered well enough to answer, and she will honour this place with the glory of her presence.'

I wished she would honour some other spot, but Medraut strode off, calling some order to another man who was sitting by a door. I looked about me for the first time. The place shortly to be glorified appeared to be one of those huts which shepherds use when their flocks are in the summer pasturage. Four walls of mud and wattle, a plain dirt floor with a fire pit in the centre and, for a bed, the heap of bracken I was sitting on. One of Lot's warriors sat on a three-legged stool by the door, watching me impassively.

'Do you speak British?' I asked him, without much hope. '*Loquerisne Latine?*' He simply stared. I groaned and lay down again.

My head throbbed, I still felt nauseous and generally con-fused. And Morgawse of Orcade was going to come and ask me questions. I could think of nothing to do except to pray for the grace to answer her fitly, and not yield; and so that much I did. As I prayed, I found myself wondering whether I could have avoided this. Well, there was Rhuawn. He was not a bad man. I knew that, in ordinary circumstances, he was as generous and even-tempered a warrior as any living. If I had spoken to him more gently, or at least spoken privately, he might very well have listened to me. Unless . . . I wondered again at Medraut's harping. Sorcery? Well, if so, it had not worked on me, and so should not have worked on Rhuawn.

But even if Rhuawn had supported Medraut, I began to think that I should have kept silent. Pretended to agree, and then gone and warned my lord when I knew the whole plot. More efficient and far less risky. If I'd used a little discretion, a little common sense! And common sense had always been supposed a strong point of mine. I groaned again, and resolved to be more careful in the future. If I had a future. Which was by no means certain.

Choices are strange things. Not three months before I had chosen to fight, actively, for the Light. I had asked a visiting stranger to take me to Camlann. And now here I lay waiting to be questioned, or God alone knew what, by a notorious witch, and wondering whether I would see another morning. The thought shook me. Never again to see the faces of my family, never again the warm hearth fire with my own place waiting there, or the fields white with the harvest or the oxen drawing the plough or the skylarks flying. To die in a strange land, with no one knowing of it.

But then, I had made the choice, and made it honestly, so it was no use thinking what might have happened. And everyone has to die some time, and it is good enough to die for the Light, keeping one's faith with a good man. Things might have been otherwise, I might have held my tongue with Medraut – but I hadn't, and, being who I am, I wasn't sure I could have. So I thrust all distractions from my mind and started praying again.

When I heard hoof beats outside, I pushed myself up to a sitting position and crossed myself, then waited. It had grown dark in the room, and I realized that it must be night outside, though whether it was the night of the same day that I was hit on the head I was not sure.

Medraut entered the room first, holding a lantern with a horn shield for the flame. He barely glanced at me, and raised the lantern high, standing aside from the door.

Morgawse entered the room like a flood. She wore a long, dark travelling cloak over her crimson gown, and to my still addled eyes it looked as though she trailed in the whole night after her. She stood very still inside the door, looking down at me. She was smiling a little, but her eyes froze my heart's blood. I braced myself and stared back.

'Light the fire,' she ordered, without moving her gaze.

I saw Eivlin creep from behind her back and slip to the fire, fumble about with the tinder. It made me sick to look at her, and I looked hard. She was very pale, and carefully avoided turning her eyes towards me.

The tinder caught, and a little more light flared up, making Eivlin's hair glow like ripe wheat fields in the wind. The shadows leapt, then steadied in the lamplight as the fire began to bite into the wood. Morgawse unclasped the silver brooch of her travelling cloak and let it fall from her shoulders. Medraut caught it and handed it to the guard, with a short order in Irish. The guard bowed slightly and left. The Queen looked neither at him, nor at Medraut, but only gestured slightly with her right hand. Medraut glanced about, and hung the lantern from the thatched roof, then picked up the three-legged stool the guard had used and moved it closer to the fire. He stepped over to me, caught my left arm and dragged me to my feet. My head swam, and I felt a wave of sickness, but I stumbled over to where Medraut pulled me, and flopped down on the stool, facing the Queen.

She crossed her arms. They were bare, free of her rich, dark crimson gown, and looked very white and strong. I would almost rather have looked at her eyes than her arms, but I tried to stare straight in front of myself and pay her no attention. Eivlin, I noticed from the corner of my eye, had crept back against the wall and huddled there, pale and dark-eyed and miserable.

'S-s-o-o,' said Morgawse at last, her voice very soft and cold. 'You do not believe that my son Gwalchmai is mad.'

I had not expected to hear that tale again. I shut my mouth more firmly and glared into space.

'Well, perhaps you are right.' The Queen's dress rustled as she moved. 'Now, perhaps, you are right. But tomorrow you may be wrong.'

I didn't like the sound of it. Did she plan to drive Gwalchmai mad? Could she? He had said that she had tried to kill him by sorcery. Plainly enough, that attempt had failed. Perhaps she would simply fail again.

But perhaps she would not.

'Look at me, slave,' said Morgawse. I looked. Her eyes were even colder and blacker than I remembered, and I felt as though I were trying to swim at mid-winter. But I met them. I would not be afraid; especially, I would not let my betrayer Eivlin see how much afraid I was.

'You are going to help in the treatment Medraut will give my son for his madness,' Morgawse stated.

I set my teeth. 'Lady, I will not.'

'Whether or not you will, by your help it is going to be done, and done tomorrow. Living or dead, you are going to help.'

I could feel my heart pounding very hard, and I felt sick again, but this time not from the blow on my head. I swallowed several times. I once heard a story about a man who fell into the hands of witches, but managed to slip away from them. Some time later he dreamed that they came, cut his throat and tore out his heart, draining away his blood and sealing the wound with a sponge. He dreamed that then they commanded him to do dreadful things, robbing the graves and churchyards, and that these things he did. He woke next morning in his own bed, shaking, and was glad it was only a dream, glad to travel on his way – and then, when he stopped at a spring to drink, a sponge fell from his throat and he fell over dead, 'with no more blood in him than a bled duck'. My sister Morfudd had told the story with relish, and I had laughed, but I could not imagine at what. Looking at Morgawse's eyes, I was certain that she could do, if not that, then something of the kind. Living or dead, she said, living or dead I would help her in whatever she and Medraut plotted against Gwalchmai. Something in me, the very fabric of my flesh and blood, began to shriek at me to assent to whatever she asked. If I would betray my lord, living or dead, surely it was better to do it living? Then at least I might be of some help afterwards. Then she would not tear my heart out with that strong white hand, so that afterwards I fell over dead like that other . . .

'Lady,' I said, 'whatever you can compel my body to do, I will not help you in any scheme of yours. And don't think that you can terrify me into obeying you, for I know that, for all your sorcery, you cannot damn my soul any more than you can save your own.' And I put my head back and looked her in the eyes.

To my surprise, my words struck her. Her face flushed a very little, and her smile slipped only slightly, but some quaver seemed to pass behind her eyes, a horrible ravaging loneliness and a sick desire. She took a quick stride closer to me, and caught my hair, dragged my head back and stooped until her face was bare inches from mine.

'Bravely spoken!' her voice was almost a hiss. 'Keep your soul, then; but I will have your mind and your body for my purposes. And those I can have, slave, I can.' She thrust me violently away and snapped upright again. The thrust pushed me off the stool, and I scorched my leg in the fire before I managed to get onto my hands and knees and crawl away. Morgawse, Medraut and Eivlin watched me thrash about. The first two were scornful, almost amused, but a glance at Eivlin showed me that she sat against the wall with her knees drawn up, biting her lips and looking utterly wretched. I wondered what she was thinking.

I sat back on my heels, deciding that I was safer on the ground, and managed to look back at Morgawse. She still made my skin crawl with a black horror, but I no longer felt so afraid of her. I knew that her power was limited. More than that, I knew suddenly that I could die, and still keep the faith: and this knowledge was victory.

But her face was impassive again, deathly white except for those terrible eyes. She began speaking in her normal soft voice: 'You will go back to Degannwy tomorrow morning, and you will ask your lord to come and speak with you, away from the stronghold. You will bring him here, and say that there is something he must see here; and you will advise him to tie his horse securely outside. When you have him in this hovel, ask him for his sword. Tell him that you wish to swear on it. When he has given it to you, freely, you will throw it out the door as hard and as far as you are able, and you will then block the doorway if he tries to go out after it. Then Medraut and Rhuawn will come and bind him, and your part is done.'

'I couldn't do that, even if I were willing,' I said. 'Gwalchmai's sword is an otherworldly weapon, and they all say that it burns the hand of anyone else who tries to draw it. It even has some otherworldly name.'

'Its name is Caledfwlch,' Medraut broke in. 'May it soon be shattered! But it will not burn the hand that draws it when it is given freely. *You* will do as you are commanded.'

'Be silent,' Morgawse told him, very softly and sweetly. Medraut stopped as sharply as a fox when it hears a hound, and slunk back in silence towards the wall. I realized that he was terrified of the Queen, and felt bolder myself.

'It is no matter whether or not the sword burns my hand,' I told Morgawse. 'I will not help you. Try Rhuawn – but you can't be too sure of him, or you wouldn't be asking me. Is it that you have to keep him deluded? Well, try your sorceries on me, if you think they will work. But I say this, that I am a Christian man from a Christian kingdom, the servant of a good lord, of a great Emperor, and of the most high God: and I will not grovel to the mere Queen of Orcade.'

Medraut gave a slight jerk, as though about to rush forward and strike me, but he checked himself and looked at Morgawse. She merely smiled once more. 'Again, fine words. But say what you will, for all of your lords and gods I may do what I will with you now, and I will that these things be done, and I will make you do them. Medraut!' She languidly raised one arm and extended a forefinger, a thin, fine, strong finger like Gwalchmai's.

Medraut was only too ready. He rushed forward, grabbed me, set me back on the stool and began to tie my arms behind me. I looked at Eivlin out of the corner of my eye. She was huddled by the door, her hand pressed against her mouth, her blue eyes wide with misery. 'I didn't know they would hurt you,' she had said that afternoon. For the first time, my anger with her lapsed. She certainly wasn't pleased with the results of her treachery. Could I believe that she had not been lying to me all along, as Medraut had, but that she had merely obeyed her lady's orders without questioning them, because of her terror? My eyes had been sliding more and more fully upon her, and they met hers directly. She put her hand down and stared, stricken, her lips moving faintly. I looked away quickly. But I could believe that she had been merely a tool, frightened and ignorant. It was some comfort to know that such a person as Eivlin existed, and that she was not just a performance intended to deceive. And yet, she was still a tool.

And Morgawse wanted to make me a tool for betraying Gwalchmai, as Eivlin had betrayed me. Medraut finished with my hands and tied my legs to the legs of the stool. I set my teeth and waited.

Morgawse unfastened the gold bands that held her hair, and it fell over her shoulders and down her back. She ran her fingers through it, tossed her head. Very black, her hair looked.

'Pretty,' I commented, trying to ease my terror – and annoy Medraut – by being insolent. 'Do you pull out the grey hairs every morning?'

She did not trouble herself to reply, but spread her hands and chanted something to begin the rite.

I have never been able to tell anyone exactly what happened in the next few hours. It is not that it was so painful or so disgusting as to be unspeakable – it hurt to some extent, and was unpleasant, but no more than some sicknesses. Nor is it even that I found it shameful and revolting – though, God knows, I did, and still feel hot when I think of it. But my memory of it is blurred and, to tell the truth, I have never tried very hard to remember, since such things do no good to anyone, neither the sufferer, nor the hearer, nor, in fact, the performer. I fought Morgawse. She sang, and threw things on the fire, and made patterns, and tried to glare me into submission with her eyes. I set my teeth, knotted my fingers together behind my back, and fought her harder. She went on with the sorceries. I felt as I had in my dream, as though I were struggling in a black ocean, a numbingly cold force that drove down on me or tried to drag me under. I thought of my family and our farm, picturing them down to the cattle in the barn and the swallows in the thatch. I thought of Camlann. I thought a good deal of Gwalchmai, whom I could not betray. I thought of all of them at once, holding them like the words of a prayer: everything I knew of light and order and joy and love; and I looked back at Morgawse with my teeth set, and did not give in.

But she went on with it, on and on, and I began to feel that I was suffocating, and had to gasp for breath. My mind grew blurred about the edges, chilled. I twisted my fingers in the ropes around my hands, feeling my palms slick with sweat. The dim little hut swam in my eyes, and the fire blurred the way it does if you watch when you're half asleep. It all seemed unimportant and remote. I had trouble remembering names – who was the Emperor? my brother? my lord? I felt a great way away from all of it, and my life seemed the merest hair-line distinction from my death. Almost it seemed as though I could step out of that dim hut in Gwynedd into a whole bright and lovely universe, the Kingdom of Summer from Gwalchmai's song. I felt as though, if I looked, the wooden walls would burst into leaf, and the birds of Rhiannon begin to sing. But that feeling I fought as well. It was necessary (why?) that I resist, for someone (who?) would be hurt if I didn't. My head drooped; I raised it again and looked at Morgawse. Her eyes beat at me like waves beating against a cliff. A crumbling cliff. But her face was dripping with sweat, her hair wild and dishevelled. She held a long dagger with both hands, and the blade was smeared with blood. It was my blood, from some while before, but I looked at it indifferently. Nothing mattered. Only to hold . . . on . . .

'You will set the trap for him,' she said, for the thousandth time, 'and then, then, finally we will be revenged on him, Medraut and I. And when his mind has snapped we will give him back to Rhuawn, who will take him to Arthur. And Medraut will go too, very loving and concerned. And then! Rhuawn is ours in some measures, Gwalchmai will be a cruder sort of tool, and there will be others. Medraut will bring them. Just as others will join Maelgwn in his secret alliance, and wait until the Family is at war with itself. Then will the shield-wall be broken and the gate of the stronghold be battered down; then Arthur will die.'

She stood, radiant of darkness, horribly beautiful and appallingly certain. But nothing she said seemed to mean much beyond the confines of that hut. I stared at her and was unable to think or feel anything at all.

She began to smile, triumphantly, and raised the dagger. The walls flickered like a candle in the wind. I drove my heels against the floor and stared numbly back. Morgawse seemed to brush the ceiling, a black wave cresting and about to break.

'Medraut!' said the Queen. 'Now!' I leaned back, scarcely able to see her. 'Medraut!' The tide ebbed a little. Dimly, I was aware that Morgawse was glancing about. I slumped on the stool. 'Medraut! Where are you?' The Queen lowered her arm, only the dagger blade flashing as it moved. Then she turned away, crossed to the door, and left. I could not even think that she had gone to look for him. I could not think. The world before me was all dark, but I felt as though that other world lay under and around. I looked at nothing, waiting to see it flower around me.

The door opened again, but it was not Morgawse. It was Eivlin; somehow, even in the dimness, I recognized her. She darted across the hut, dropped to her knees behind me, and the next instant I felt her hard, desperate strokes against the ropes. I went on looking at the wall. I could neither understand nor care about what was happening – and yet I remember it very precisely.

She had my arms free, then my right leg. My right foot was asleep, and I curled my toes until they tingled painfully. The half-sensed music in the air seemed to grow dimmer, fading away. I shook my head.

The ropes holding my left leg gave, and Eivlin jumped to her feet, grabbed my right arm and pulled at me. I stood, wavering, beginning to wonder what was happening. Eivlin stooped and picked up something she had set down when she cut the ropes. It was a sword. She drew my right arm over her shoulder and half-dragged me over to the door and out of it. The moon was shining down on the threshold, and the night air was chill and damp. I stopped, looking at the sweet light.

'Come on!' hissed Eivlin, and dragged on my arm furiously. I began to stumble forward again. A little distance from the hovel a small pony was tied. There must have been horses, something told me, and there should have been a guard watching them; but there was only the one shaggy mountain pony. Eivlin rapidly untied its reins and caught the bridle.

'Come on!' she hissed again. 'Get on.'

Still not quite sure what was happening to me, I tried to mount, became dizzy, and had to stand leaning against the pony's side, pressing my hand over my eyes to clear them.

433

The little beast flicked its ears back and looked pleased, and I began to laugh. Eivlin exclaimed angrily in Irish and tried to pull me into the saddle by force, and, eventually, with her help, I managed to scramble up. Eivlin took the bridle, looped the reins under her arms, glanced hurriedly back over her shoulder – and froze. I looked back too, and saw Morgawse standing in front of the hut.

Something stirred in me, and I leaned dizzily from the pony, seizing the sword from Eivlin's motionless right hand. Eivlin shrank against the pony's side.

Morgawse began walking towards us, slowly.

I lifted the sword as though it were a cleaver, noticing for the first time that it was Medraut's. I would fight, I thought – and then noticed that I was not tied hand and foot this time. I grabbed Eivlin's hair and drove my heels into the pony's sides. He snorted, shied so that I nearly fell off, and started away. Eivlin was dragged along, abruptly coming to herself and staggering up against the pony, shivering like a scared rabbit.

'You will die!' Morgawse screamed from behind us. 'Both of you. You, vixen, you will die before the evening of this coming day. And he will die too, this lover of yours, soon enough!'

I kicked the pony into a trot, glancing back. Morgawse was not following us, only shouting, 'Do you think you can return to Degannwy? Maelgwn's men will keep you for me.' Her voice rose, climbing into a shriek of rage. 'Go, by all means! You have merely delayed his death, little fool, and caused your own. Go!' Eilvin jerked the pony's bridle and began running, and he started to trot a little faster.

I could feel the little animal warm between my legs, and the smooth-worn leather of saddle and harness. Eivlin's hair was pale in the moonlight. I looked up. The moon was softly blurred, a half-moon of spring, like a yellow apple, and the night sky was deep and soft, hazed with a little mist. The mountains lay about, silent black bulks, with only a few of the far peaks still ashimmer with the last snows. Over the smell of horse and leather I could catch the scent of wet grass, and the air told me that it wasn't long before dawn. And something in me leapt into heaven like a skylark as I realized that, contrary to all expectation and probability, I was actually alive and in possession of my own senses, headache and all. I wanted to sing, but the only song I could think of was Gwalchmai's song about the Otherworld, mixed up with hymns from home in a ludicrous fashion because I couldn't remember the words to it. It made me laugh, and once I began laughing, I couldn't stop. Eivlin looked at me sharply, her eyes gleaming in the dim light, and I laughed harder, which gave me shooting pains in my head.

'It is no matter,' I at last managed to gasp to her, by way of reassurance. 'Morgawse has not stolen my wits. Oh Eivlin, Eivlin, what did you do with Medraut? And what about the guard?'

'There is nothing to laugh at!' She was sharp and unhappy. 'Medraut went to see why I was so long in bringing wood for the fire, and I hit him on the head with a piece of firewood: I do not know whether he is alive or dead. As for Ronan, the guard, I first of all told him that my lady wished him to take the horses back to Degannwy and return at sunrise, but that he must leave one horse. Ach, I couldn't even think of what to say what the one horse was for – but he didn't ask, only left at once. He was unhappy to be there at all. Then I went back to the hut and waited behind the door until my lady came out, and I hit her on the head too, but I couldn't hit hard, because I was afraid of her.'

'Two horses, you should have said, and we could have ridden off like rulers of the world. Eivlin, you are the signet-ring on the hand of Daring, you adorn the earth as the moon adorns the night...' I wanted to quote more songs to her, but she only snapped, 'Enough of that. We must be far, far away from here by morning.'

I fumbled for the pony's reins, realized that Eivlin had them, and looped my hands in its mane instead. What with the headache, the sorcery and the escape, I was light-headed enough to want to try galloping. With Eivlin up on the saddle. As though the pony could gallop with both of us. 'Go where?' I asked, restraining myself.

'Caer Segeint! Caer Legion! Anywhere! But we must find the main road first, and then you must ride away as fast as you can.'

I was going to ask, 'And what about you?', when something else hit me and I asked, 'But what about my lord?'

She stopped, and the pony took another step, then halted,

tossing its head in disgust. Eivlin stared up at me. 'Your lord? It isn't his life I'm selling my own to save. Let your lord find his own way of escape.'

I frowned at her. 'I was in danger because I would not betray Gwalchmai. How can I run off and abandon him to Morgawse?'

'Och, Rhys, Morgawse cannot still have the same plan, if you are gone, and Medraut is dead.'

'We don't know that Medraut is dead. I'd stake my head he isn't. And they still have Rhuawn.'

'My lady has said that your lord no longer trusts Rhuawn as he did. Come, he's in no more danger than you yourself, and what's a lord? You can find plenty another man to serve, or you can go back to your clan. Didn't you hear my lady? We cannot go back to Degannwy. Maelgwn's guards would not let us through the gate.'

My better sense told me that she was right about Degannwy, though I felt ready to fight it single-handed, and me too sick to walk far. But I knew one thing. 'I will not let Morgawse do as she pleases with Gwalchmai. He must be warned.'

'Man, man, you are mad! Do you throw away our lives for this warrior, this man who only uses your service?'

'He is my lord, and I serve him because I chose to; and he is worth my loyalty. I like Gwalchmai. I would even call him my friend, if a lord can be called a friend. He must be warned. And besides, I am his servant. If I flee when he needs my service, where is my own good faith?'

Eivlin was shaking her head. 'Not so, not so. Rhys, my lady is most terribly powerful. We must get very far away. That is, you must, for I know that my lady will kill me by a curse, before the evening of this coming day, just as she said. By the sun, by the earth and the sky and the sea, by your own god, Rhys, don't let it be that I die for nothing. If we go back to Degannwy, you will die, he will not be warned, and Morgawse will kill me when I have accomplished nothing. Let us hurry. Come, we must reach the road before it is light. Morgawse will surely send Lot's men after us, secretly.' She tugged on the bridle again, and the pony moved forward.

I again fumbled for the rein, wanting to stop the animal. 'Eivlin, my lord must be warned. What do you mean,

Morgawse will kill you by a curse? She can't do that. We must get a message to my lord...' I stopped suddenly, remembering what I had seen – had it only been that morning?

Eivlin halted again, and the pony jerked impatiently on the bridle. 'But I will die!' she said, angrily and tearfully. 'And you will die too, and all for this warrior who cannot look after himself! But if we must...'

'We don't have to,' I said. 'Gwalchmai has a place he looks for messages sent to him from the Emperor. We can leave a message there. It is on the way to the main road.'

Eivlin looked at me, astonished, then hopeful. She began walking again, in silence.

The world was a pre-dawn grey when we reached the forked oak, and the first birds were beginning to give experimental chirrups. The exhilaration of the escape had worn off, and my head hurt a great deal, so much so that I felt sick. I was tired, too, tired enough to want to collapse under a tree and not get up for a week. I looked at the oak. I had told Eivlin to leave a sprig of pine by the track where we turned off. I thought that Gwalchmai had said pine for an urgent message. Yes, pine for an urgent message, holly for an ordinary one.

'The place is the hollow where that big branch joins the main trunk,' I told Eivlin. She dropped the reins and skipped over to the tree, then looked up it. 'Can you climb?' I asked hopefully.

She looked at me as though I had said, 'Can you fly?' Gwalchmai had said there weren't many trees in the islands, and what trees there were, I supposed, would be climbed by boys more than by girls. I wearily struggled off the pony and staggered over to the tree. I didn't know whether I could climb it. I could try.

'What will you write your message on?' asked Eivlin.

'Write?' I said, and suddenly I realized that I didn't know how to leave a message. 'I can't write,' I exclaimed.

'Och, indeed! He cannot write, but has come here out of the way to leave a message! I thought all Britons could write, all that speak Latin.'

'Maybe most townsmen can, but I'm a farmer,' I said. 'Where would I learn to write? Can you write?'

She only snorted. I gathered that writing was uncommon

in the Ynysoedd Erch.

I stared at the oak and dredged my aching head for ideas. I had never really wanted to write before, but I wanted it then. But it was no use wishing. A pine-cone meant that Gwalchmai's letter had been received; what would mean 'Beware of Rhuawn. Medraut and Morgawse tried to kill me, and will try to drive you mad"?

Gwalchmai would have to know that the message was from me; that meant I must leave something of mine. The brooch. He would remember that. I fumblingly unclasped it and balanced it in my palm. Medraut and Morgawse were the real danger; what did I have of theirs? Eivlin still had the sword.

'Eivlin, give me Medraut's sword.' She hesitated, looking at me questioningly, and I said, 'I don't know how to use it properly, and nor do you, so it's no use to us.'

'It's worth money. You'll need that.'

'This is worth more.' Eivlin reluctantly handed me the sword. I weighed the hilt of it. It was indeed a good sword, for as much as I knew about swords – which, after my time in Camlann, amounted to something. The blade was narrow, of fine-tempered steel. I looked at it, and at the brooch, then slid the sword blade over one side of the ring of the brooch, under the central pin, and over the other half of the ring. It bent the brooch a little, but I hoped I made my meaning evident. Now, how to warn him of Rhuawn? I felt about my belt, but I had nothing of Rhuawn's. Rhuawn was Dumnonian. Was there any way I could use something specifically Dumnonian? No, and I was Dumnonian too. Not that, then.

I stood, my feet growing wet from the dew, cold and sick and sleepy, trying to drag an answer out of a murky mind. The birds sang more loudly. The pony stamped.

Rhuawn was a member of the Family; the Family was . . . was . . .

Members of the Family sometimes wore a sprig of hawthorn through their cloak pins, to remind themselves of Baddon, where the hawthorn had bloomed when they drove back the Saxons. As plainly as if he stood there, I remembered Bedwyr's servant Amren telling me the tale of the hawthorn at Baddon. I looked around.

'Eivlin,' I said, 'I need a sprig of hawthorn.' She stared.

'It's part of the message.'

'I will bring it, then. You put the rest of your ... message in the place.'

'Give me a leg up, then. I do not think I can climb it.'

With some struggle and a great deal of dizziness, I managed to clamber into the fork of the tree, and Eivlin went off to find the hawthorn. I leant back against one branch to rest a minute.

'Rhys. Rhys. Wake up.' I opened my eyes and found that the east was touched with the palest rose. Eivlin stood under the oak with a branch of flowering hawthorn, white in her arms. She looked lovely as a day in spring. I muttered something, and she handed me the hawthorn. I twined it about the hilt of the sword and put the whole arrangement in the hollow of the branch. The sword stuck out a little, so I smeared some of the old leaves over it so that it would not shine, and jumped down. I collapsed when I hit the ground, and Eivlin helped me up.

'I need to sleep,' I told her.

'Indeed, if you fall asleep while I'm down to the end of the meadow and back, you do. But we must reach the main road first.' She helped me back onto the pony, and we continued on.

When we reached the main road it was nearly midmorning, and the sun had dried the dew. We found a hard bank and led the pony across it and into a brake, hidden from the road. Eivlin took some bracken and swept the bank, unnecessarily, I thought, so that anyone following would not be able to tell that we had left the road. She seemed certain that Morgawse would send some of Lot's warriors after us. I dragged myself off the pony and lay down. My head was throbbing but, for all my weariness, I no longer felt sleepy. Eivlin came back from sweeping and lay down beside me.

'We must not rest long,' she whispered. 'We must be away this afternoon. And do wake up before evening. Rhys, I want to talk to you before I die.'

'You're not going to die,' I said irritably. 'Why should you die?'

'My lady will send a demon to kill me,' she said simply. 'Ach, I know you will tell me that she tried to kill your lord and failed. Well, but your lord, perhaps, can fight demons.

439

They say his sword is magical. I cannot fight so. I was cursed before ever I was born, from my father's deed I was cursed.'

'You're not going to die,' I repeated. 'Morgawse is not the only power in this great world. Eivlin, if you are so sure you are going to die, why did you save me in the first place? Your lady is just as sure to kill me!'

'It was my fault you were in danger,' she said, in a very small voice. 'My lady told me to bring you to Medraut's house, and to tell you that your lord was there. I knew that she meant you no good, and yet I brought you there, and told you that, and then . . .' Her breath caught on itself. 'She wished to . . . do dreadful . . . things. And I was to help her. And when she was beginning, I said to myself, "Eivlin, here is the one man who has taken no notice of your curse. Here is a man, no warrior, but a servant like yourself, who has helped you freely, who can turn a phrase just so, and has just such a smile: and because of you, and his trusting you, he will be dead and damned."'

'But she couldn't damn me,' I broke in. 'Kill she can, but the other is beyond her.'

Eivlin shrugged a little: I felt the movement through the bracken. 'Well, I knew that she would kill you horribly. And I could not endure it. So I went and told Ronan to take the horses home, and I hit Medraut on the head and cut you loose. It is better to die honestly, at least. And you keep saying that you are a Christian and have your own magic, so hers cannot hurt you; I think you will escape her.'

I turned my head and looked full at her. There were tears on her cheeks, runnelling the smudges on her face. Her fair hair was limp, dirty and dishevelled. I thought her more beautiful than any woman on earth.

'You won't die,' I said, and hauled myself up on one elbow. 'As God in Heaven is just, you will not die. Believe me . . .' I put out my hand clumsily to touch her shoulder, just to comfort her, and suddenly she came into my arms and began to cry. I held her, and she put her head down on my shoulder and sobbed loudly while I stroked her hair and made soothing noises. For all the danger and weariness, for all my aches and sickness, that was one of the fullest moments of my life.

Ten

Eivlin fell asleep in my arms, still crying, and I was asleep very shortly afterwards. I had wanted to stay awake and just hold her for a while, but it was a matter of minutes before I was snoring. When I woke up the late afternoon sun was lying heavy on the brake and the road beyond it, and Eivlin was not beside me. I sat up and looked around. Neither Eivlin nor the pony were there. I had a moment of sick terror, thinking that Morgawse had sent a demon and that Eivlin was gone – but then I tried to imagine what a demon would do with the pony, and the bad minute passed.

I stood up carefully. My head still hurt, but not as badly. Gingerly, I fingered the back of my skull – there was one big lump, caked over with dried blood, which was exquisitely agonizing when I touched it. That must be the result of Medraut's blow, if Medraut had indeed been the one who hit me. Above it was a smaller lump, doubtless from hitting the floor after Rhuawn hit me. My sister Morfudd always used to say that I had a thick skull. Well, with such treatment I needed it. I wondered how Medraut's head felt.

There came a crackling noise in the bushes. I set my hand quickly to my knife and backed away out of sight. But it was Eivlin, leading the pony. I sighed with relief and stepped back into the open.

'You frightened me, when I woke and found you gone,' I told her.

'Did I indeed?' She brushed a strand of hair out of her eyes, smiling. She had washed her face and carefully straightened her hair, and had stuck a wild rose in the clasp of her dress. Very pretty she looked. 'I only wanted to find some water for the pony.'

'For us too, I hope.'

'Oh, to be sure. There is a stream just down the hill. Come, I can wash your head.'

I took a couple of hesitant steps forward, and she waited, holding out her hand. I took her hand, feeling at once embarrassed and very pleased, and we strolled down to the stream, leaving the pony tethered to a bush.

'You look very pretty,' I told Eivlin, remembering how my sister liked to have this commented upon.

'Do I?' she asked, in the tone that means 'So! You noticed.'

'Truly,' I responded. Eivlin smiled smugly and checked the rose to see if it was falling off.

The stream was fresh from the mountains, fast running over a rocky bed, and cold to make your teeth ache. After I drank from it Eivlin washed my head, which hurt and made me dizzy again, though she was gentle. When she finished, we sat a few minutes looking at the stream and listening to it gurgle.

Eivlin sighed and leaned against me. 'It is a fine day to die on,' she said softly. 'I could almost be glad. I am glad: I am away from her, at last, and I am with you, and it is a fine, honest way to die.'

'You're not still dreaming about that!' I said, irritated. 'I have told you, you're not going to die.'

She only laid her head on my shoulder and tickled the palm of my hand. I became a little more irritated.

'You won't die,' I repeated. 'Why do you think you should die?'

'My lady said I would.' She sat up straight again. I wished she hadn't.

'Well, your lady said I would die, too, but you don't seem to think I will.'

'You! Well, but you fought off her spells and her witchcraft for hours, right in her very presence. She thought it would be easy to govern you; she thought it would all be done in half an hour, but at the end she was so tired she could not even slay us both when she saw us escaping.'

'Maybe that means her spells aren't all that you think they are.'

'Not so! Rhys, I have seen her...' She stopped, then went on more quietly, 'And besides, I am cursed from my birth, and I have been her servant. For her to kill me is nothing, a snap of her fingers. And I do not have any of my own magic to protect me, as you have magic.'

I wondered what she meant for a moment, then understood. 'If you mean Christ, you can be protected too, if you believe. Here, we can stop at the first monastery or hermitage we come to, and you can be baptized, if that will stop

442

your talk of dying.'

'What? What's that?'

'It's a . . .' I remembered my previous disastrous explanations of another sacrament. 'It's a kind of magic to free someone from past curses.'

Eivlin looked dubious. 'Is it a complicated spell? Can't you do it? Is there much blood?'

'I could do it, I suppose. I think it's allowed. But it's better if a priest does it.'

'One of your Christian druids?'

'No, a priest is . . . never mind. But there's no blood at all. All that is necessary is that you believe in Christ – I told you about him, didn't I – and they pour water on your head.'

'Where's the magic, then?'

'It's not exactly a spell, it's a . . . well, the water means that the curse is washed away. I had it done to me when I was a baby. My mother says I howled, but I can't remember it, of course, though I've seen it done for my cousins.'

Eivlin sighed and brushed a strand of hair away from her face. 'I do not see how it would help against my lady. But if you think it is a strong magic, perhaps it may.'

I thought of Morgawse, and for all my well-learned catechism I wondered whether Eivlin was right to be afraid. Sacraments are not magic spells, and, whatever they may mean to her spiritual state, could I be sure anything would alter the effect of Morgawse's very strong earthly magic? But firmly I told Eivlin, 'It's a magic against Morgawse. You won't die.'

Eivlin looked at me steadily, then sighed and stood up, brushing off her skirt. 'Ai, perhaps. But we must be gone, then, to find one of your priests, because it is late in the day.'

Reluctantly, I too stood up, and we went back to where we had left the pony. He was busily consuming every blade of grass within range, just as though he had not grazed most of the day.

'Your turn to ride,' I told Eivlin. 'I can walk.'

'"I can walk", says the man, and he with a lump on his head as big as my fist! Indeed, you will not walk; you will ride and try to get better.'

I protested, but not very convincingly. My head did ache, and the short walk up the hill had started it throbbing. The advantage of my sickness was that I didn't notice how hungry I was, although the last meal I had eaten was breakfast, the day before. But I wondered how Eivlin felt, and if she had had any supper. She was doing all the walking, and I could not think it good for her.

We started off down the road westward. 'We will go to Caer Segeint,' Eivlin said firmly. 'It is a big town, and a port, as I well know, having spent the night there when we first arrived in Gwynedd. If my lady has sent messages there, it is a good place to avoid messengers, and most of the men there spend their lives doing nothing else.'

I assented to the plan, though I would have preferred to go to Caer Legion, which I knew. But I could see Eivlin's point, and it was a good one. 'And after we reach Caer Segeint, what?' I asked.

She was quiet a moment. 'Perhaps we could sell the pony and take a boat down the coast?'

I groaned inwardly. 'How much would it cost?'

'What kind of boat are you used to using? For myself, I know a bit about curraghs, but that is all.'

'It is better than I can do. I was in a boat once in my life, crossing from Dumnonia to Caer Gwent, and I had no liking for it then. We'd have to hire a boatman as well as a boat, and, for myself, I know I have no way to afford it.'

'You have only once been in a boat? How . . .'

'I am not an islander. My family's holding is near the Mor Hafren, and the only water we need to cross is a river. I think we should take the pony on down the coast into Dyfed, and claim protection there in the Emperor's name. Dyfed isn't too friendly with Gwynedd, and they've fought invaders from Erin enough to hate anyone who speaks Irish – though they'll have to make an exception for you.'

Eivlin shook her head. 'We travel too slowly. The ones my lady has sent after us will certainly catch us if we try to go all the way to Dyfed with only one pony. Do we have enough for a horse?'

I checked my possessions. Three bronze arm-rings, one enamelled; and one gold ring Gwalchmai had given me at Camlann. Then there was my cloak – the weather might be warm enough to sell it. If we made the pony a rope bridle and sold the leather one, and rode bareback, we might have enough to buy one horse. But then we would have nothing to buy food with. I sighed. 'We can travel fast and not eat, or we can have our bread and ale and a slow journey.'

'Even so? Perhaps we can steal a horse.'

'Steal? We will do no such thing.'

'Och, Rhys, we need a horse. Come, if you will you can see that the horse's owner is paid afterwards.'

I didn't like the idea of stealing from some poor farmer, but she might be right. I struggled with my conscience a moment, and wondered what my father would say about it. If he were in my position, I decided, he would take the horse.

'Very well, if we pay him back. But don't you think we could avoid anyone Morgawse sent? If the south road's as empty as this one, we'll know someone's coming long before they reach us.'

'Unless Medraut comes.' Eivlin became very serious.

'You do not think he might be badly hurt, then?' I asked hopefully.

She shook her head. 'If he is sick, my lady will find some way to heal him quickly. And he can use sorceries to find us...'

It had the sound of truth. 'Then we will have to steal a horse. Or two horses, and leave the pony; and we can hope that they haven't passed us already.'

Eivlin nodded. 'Unless you only need one horse,' she added in an undertone.

'You are not going to die, remember? Come, let's hurry and see what we can find before dark.'

The afternoon was one of those long, slow afternoons of late spring that make one realize the summer is not far off. The mountains were all green, or blue with distance, with no snow to be seen anywhere. When the land to our right fell away we could see the Irish Sea, calm and blue-grey in the sunlight. Eivlin eyed it wistfully. She still preferred the idea of a boat.

It is a strange thing, but for all that we were flying for our lives in a foreign land, tired, hungry, sick in my case and afraid of imminent death in Eivlin's, we were cheerful as a pair of larks. The afternoon was beautiful, and it seemed as though it might well last for ever. We had escaped and were free and in love, so why not be happy? The sight of the sea started Eivlin telling stories about the Ynysoedd Erch, and I responded with tales about my family, and we laughed like a couple of idiots at a fair. The sun slipped down the sky only gradually, slanting into our eyes and lengthening the shadows behind us.

'And so,' Eivlin concluded one story, 'Eoghan fought a great and mighty and terrible fight against Ronan, to make up for the boat race, and he thrashed him thoroughly; for, except for Medraut, he's the finest fighter in Lot's warband.'

'Medraut's really a good fighter, then?'

'By the sun! From the time he first entered the Boys' House for training, he seemed a greyhound among housedogs, or so say all the warriors. And yet ... he does not fight much. Those he wishes to use, he charms, and through them he makes all the other warriors obey him. They are all afraid of him, because he can ruin a man's standing with a few words, and set all the others against anyone he wishes, and then there is the sorcery. Why once, to be sure, he ...'

Eivlin abruptly stopped, and also stopped walking, staring ahead of her.

'He what?' I asked.

'Rhys ...' she said. I looked ahead of us. I could see nothing but the empty road in the evening sun. I wondered if she'd forgotten something and left it in the brake where we slept.

'What's the matter?'

'What's the matter? Don't you see it?' Her stare was fixed, her head back so that the shadows trembled in the hollow of her throat.

I looked again. I could still see only the road. But Eivlin's hand was shaking, and the pony laid its ears back and began to shift its weight uneasily. It snorted.

'There's nothing there,' I said. 'Come on.'

Eivlin made a whimpering noise and took a step back. 'A shadow,' she whispered. 'There's something in the road.'

'There's nothing there. With this sun, all the shadows are behind us.'

'No! A shadow, another. By the green earth!' She spun about, letting go the pony' bridle. The animal sorted and half reared, and I grabbed the reins, tightening my knees. 'Rhys!' Eivlin screamed it. 'It is behind us, too!'

'Eivlin, there's nothing there. Eivlin!' She was not listening. I slid off the pony, seized her arm. 'There's nothing there.'

'My lady's curse. It has found us. Ahhh, it is coming nearer. Rhys, help me!'

I grabbed her shoulders. 'It is only a shadow. She's trying to frighten you.'

She suddenly flung her arms around my neck and pressed her face against my shoulder. 'Don't let them near me! Ai!' Her arms tightened till I could barely breathe, but I held her; and then she went rigid. She flung herself back from me and began to scream. I caught her arms. She tried to tear away from me. Her eyes stared horribly at nothing, so wide that the whites showed all about the blue, and her face was like that of a woman sick with a deadly fever. The pony neighed loudly, reared and jerked away, its eyes rolling. I let go of Eivlin with one hand and tried to grab its reins, but missed, and it bolted off down the road. Eivlin kept on screaming, an awful high rhythmic wailing. Foam flecked the corners of her mouth.

'Merciful, holy Christ!' I cried out loud. 'Eivlin, Eivlin, listen!'

She struggled harder, nearly wrenching free, striking at me with her free hand. It seemed to me that we were struggling in the midst of a choking black cloud, and I felt the same sick dizziness that I had meeting Morgawse's eyes. Eivlin kicked and clawed, and her scream shivered into short shrieks which frightened me even more.

'Eivlin!' I said again, but I knew that nothing I said reached her. A rage swept over me that Morgawse should be able to do this. I managed to grab Eivlin's other hand again. Morgawse had no right, not in Heaven or Earth, no right at all. I dragged Eivlin over to the edge of the road. Whatever I could do, I would.

There was some water in the ditch by the roadside, a shallow puddle from the spring rains. I dragged Eivlin over to it. She wrestled with me. I kicked her feet out from under her and we both went down. She splashed up, gasping and shrieking. I let go one of her arms, picked up some water in my palm, and poured it over Eivlin's head. 'Eivlin,' I said, 'I baptize you in the name of the Father, the Son and the Holy Spirit. And to Hell with you, Morgawse!'

Eivlin let out one long, high shriek and lashed out, hitting me on the side of the head. The world turned red a minute, and I let go of her altogether. She crawled off, collapsed, half lifted herself a few times, only to flop back into the water and lie still, face down.

I stumbled over and turned her right side up so that she could breathe. Her head fell back limply, eyes half-opened and glazed. I felt sick in the marrow of my bones. Shaking again, I realized that I must be sobbing.

I knelt in the puddle and drew her shoulders up onto my knees, resting her head against my arm. I was praying 'Lord God, don't let her be dead!' – over and over again. Very carefully, I set my fingers against the hollow where her jaw joined her throat. Her skin was cold and wet, and for an aeon I seemed to feel nothing . . . and then, very faintly, the pulse beat against my fingertips. I closed my eyes, feeling the course of her life throb slowly again, again, pause, again. Still alive. Thank God.

But she could die any minute. I had to find somewhere where there was warmth, fires and food and people who could care for her. I had to get away from the sunset and the empty road. I looked up the bank, prodded my memory. Yes, it seemed that the pony had bolted west. Good. If he had gone east, he would probably have continued all the way back to Degannwy and his own stall. As it was, he would probably stop and wait for his masters. Ponies are sociable beasts.

I dragged Eivlin's limp form up and pulled her over my shoulders like a sack of flour, then stood up. She was not light. She was also dripping wet and slippery with mud. Well, so was I. If only the pony had not gone too far. I staggered up the bank and onto the road.

By the time I had gone a hundred paces my head was throbbing violently and I felt faint. Clearly, I could not carry her far. Damn Medraut, or whatever that guard's name was; damn him for hitting so hard. But there was nothing for it but to keep on, and pray for strength.

I was lucky. It was not too long before I cam across the pony. He was standing in the middle of the road, trembling, his ears flat against his head. He shied away from me, but did not run. I set Eivlin down and walked over to him. He skittered off, eyeing me. I darted at him, and he shied.' I nearly fell and had to stand still, holding my head. 'Be calm,' I told myself, aloud. Animals are tense and afraid when humans are. I put out my hand and began to talk to the pony soothingly. Eventually the little beast let me take his bridle and pat his neck. He even pricked his ears forward a bit. I led him over to Eivlin, picked her up and piled her on his back. Her hair had come out of its fastening and fallen over her face. I stroked it back before starting on, holding the pony's bridle with one hand and balancing Eivlin on the saddle with the other.

The sun was almost down, though it was still light. Part of me was all rage at Morgawse, but I began to pray, for strength to keep walking, for somewhere to stop, praying mostly that Eivlin would not die. The pony's hooves clopped steadily.

The road faded into a blur just in front of me, a place to put my feet. My headache was nearly blinding. The tired pony was stubborn and nervous. I had to talk to it, both for its sake and for mine.

'Come along,' I said. 'Just a bit further, and we'll find you a place in a nice stall, with lots of grain and some bran mash for being such a good beast. Come along...' The sun sank, but the western sky was still bright. Eivlin looked ghastly in the half light. I wanted to stop and check her pulse, but I was afraid to stop. 'Come along...' I told the pony.

And then there came a swish, a flash and a thud, and a throwing spear was standing upright in the road before us.

I stopped, staring at it blankly. I felt as though I could cry like a child, from sheer anger. It was not just that Medraut should catch us now, after so much, it was not right. The pony snorted and set its ears back.

I turned and looked behind us. The road stretched empty, wild and desolate. The spear must have come from the side. They must have been waiting for us.

I clenched my teeth, rested Eivlin's head against the pony's neck so that she wouldn't fall off, and strode forward to pull up the spear. I clutched it hard to stop my hands shaking, and I shouted, 'If you want this back, come and take it from me!'

Silence. The mountains lay green and still all around.

Then, off on one hillside came a flash of motion. I pulled up the spear point. Best use it as a thrusting spear, so as not to waste it.

The movement came again, then resolved itself into a figure running down the slope through the trees. The runner burst into the open at the foot of the slope, and hurried onto the road, and I wanted to sit down on the road and laugh, or, alternatively, weep. It was only a little boy, a white-blond child who could be no older than nine.

The boy ran out onto the road and looked at me with challenging eyes, startling dark eyes under the pale hair. 'Did I scare you?' he asked, hopefully.

I set the end of the spear against the ground, shaking my head. I did not dare to speak. The boy took a couple of steps nearer.

'Are you sick?' he asked anxiously. 'Is something wrong?'

'No, no, I'm not sick. But she is. Where do you live, lad?'

'Ohhh.' The boy stared at Eivlin. 'Did you fall in the river? You're drenched.'

'No, no. But this woman is very sick, and needs to be taken to a warm place quickly. Where do you live?'

'St Elena's Abbey, near Opergelei Monastery,' he replied quickly. 'My mother's a nun. The nuns know about sick people. I'll show you the way; I know all the quickest ways there.'

I remembered the sort of 'quickest ways' boys enjoy taking, and I hastily said, 'A way that won't be too hard on the pony, I hope. Or the woman. She is sick.'

He looked disappointed, but nodded. 'There's the way Father Gilla takes his mare. I'll show you, Lord.' I handed him his throwing spear, and he darted ahead of me. 'It's this way.'

'What's your name?' I asked, following him.

'They call me Gwyn. I don't have a father.'

'Gwyn' – 'fair', for his hair, of course. A nun's bastard. And he liked to practise throwing spears at travellers, thank God, and lived an an abbey where someone knew how to treat the sick. I could almost be overjoyed that his mother had defiled her vows to have a bastard, and raised him with the rest of the orphans which people would necessarily leave at an abbey.

My guide led me to a rough track which branched off from the main road towards the sea. 'This is a lovely way for horses,' he told me. 'Sometimes Father Gilla lets me exercise his mare, while he's saying Mass for the sisters. I can't go to Mass yet, you see. Are you a warrior, Lord?'

'Neither a lord nor a warrior,' I said, watching my feet.

Talk to the boy, ignore the headache. 'I'm only a servant. My name is Rhys ap Sion.'

'But you're not from here. You have an accent.'

'I'm from Dumnonia.'

'Oh! Have you been to Camlann? All the nuns at the abbey say that Camlann is a haunt of devils.'

They would. Monastics, and living in Gwynedd: they were doubly Arthur's enemies. 'I'm a servant at Camlann,' I said firmly. 'And there are no devils there. If you want devils, try Degannwy.'

He was pleased. 'I didn't think there were devils at Camlann. My mother says that all warriors are devils, but I think they're beautiful. I want to be a warrior when I grow up. Have you seen the Emperor?'

'Yes.'

'What's he like? The nuns say he's a devil and a traitor and has cloven feet, and that he will ruin everyone with his taxes.'

'No cloven feet, I'm afraid. The Emperor Arthur is – well, he's about as tall as me, with hair about the colour of yours, and ...'

'Does he wear a purple cloak? And a diadem? Hywel made a picture of an emperor in a gospel, and he said you could tell it was an emperor, because only emperors can wear purple cloaks.'

'He has a purple cloak. I've never seen him wear the diadem. But he is a good man, courteous and just, and a very great king.'

Gwyn bit his lower lip, his odd dark eyes shining. 'I would like to see him. Have you seen all his Family? Sometimes bards come by and sing songs, and I ask them to sing songs about warriors. But my mother won't let them, and she gives me a thrashing when she finds I've asked the bards to sing.' He went on rather ashamedly, 'I know I'm wicked to disobey my mother – but have you really seen them? Gwalchmai and Bedwyr and Cei and ...' the boy stopped suddenly, peering anxiously at my face. 'You're sick!'

I was. The 'lovely way for horses' was, as far as I could tell, composed entirely of vertical hills. It was dark, and I kept stumbling on things until my head felt ready to split.

'Is it much further?' I asked, my voice hoarse.

'Oh no, no. Let me take your pony, Rhys ap Sion. You lean against him and walk slow, and I won't ask you any more questions. Here.' He confidently took the reins, and I dropped back and leaned my forearm against the pony, supporting Eivlin's head on my shoulder. She was warm. I was glad: she could not be dead yet, for the night was chilly.

We walked on and on, and I could only set one foot before the other blindly, past thinking of the way. It did cross my mind to wonder that anyone would let a boy as young as Gwyn roam about alone in such wild country. But he was evidently familiar with the way, and it must be habitual with him. A nice little boy, for all his shocking parentage. He kept quiet so as not to disturb me, though he was plainly thrilled enough to want to shout questions. And he wanted to be a warrior when he grew up. Well, at that age I had wanted the same. A good lad. How far could this abbey be from the road?

Gwyn paused, and I nearly stumbled into him. Lifting my eyes, I saw a dark mass of buildings, with the amber of lamplight glowing before its gate and in two or three windows. I was too spent to feel anything much.

'Rhys ap Sion,' said Gwyn nervously, 'you see my throwing spear?'

'Yes.'

'Could you say it's yours? You see . . .' he paused, looked up at my face, and went on with a rush of candour, 'I'm not supposed to have it, and my mother would be very upset. I ran off after lessons today, so I'll get a thrashing anyway, but Mama would cry if she thought I had this!'

I almost grinned. So he liked to run off. 'Certainly. You can say that you're carrying it for me.' I thought of something else and added, 'And don't tell them that I'm a servant at Camlann. It might upset them.'

He nodded, began to lead the pony on, then paused again. "But you will give me the spear back again after, won't you?"

"Of course."

He nodded, reassured, and led us to the gate with excessive enthusiasm. After a minute or so, an upper panel opened, and I had a brief glimpse of a pale face; and then the whole gate swung open and a thin woman stalked out, eyes flashing.

'Gwyn!' she scolded. 'You've been gone since terce, and . . . oh,' she added as she saw Eivlin, me and the pony. She

452

stopped, staring.

'This is Rhys ap Sion,' announced Gwyn proudly. 'He's very sick and the girl is even sicker. I met them on the big road. He let me carry his spear.' Gwyn gave me an in-on-the-secret look that the nun must have noticed if she hadn't been staring at me.

'Sister,' I said, trying to collect my splintered thoughts, 'the boy's speaking the truth. For the love of Christ, give us the hospitality of the abbey, or this woman may die.' She kept staring. 'I will give you all I have,' I added, desperately, 'and I serve a rich lord, who can give you more. But, as you would be saved, let us in and see that she is cared for!'

'Wh – why yes, yes. Sweet Jesu! Come in. Gwyn, run and fetch Sister Teleri – yes, and find your dear mother too. Oh, give me that spear!' Gwyn reluctantly surrendered the weapon. 'Your poor mother's been worried; go at once!' He darted off, and the woman ushered me into the abbey.

Things began happening quickly. The pony was led off to a stable, and I was led off to a kitchen, trailing along behind the women who were carrying Eivlin. A small, brown, middle-aged woman appeared from nowhere and began fussing over Eivlin. She shook her head.

'Not good,' she said, turning to another woman who appeared to be her assistant. 'She seems near drowned. You,' the woman rounded on me. 'What happened to this girl?'

'I . . . uh . . .'

'She's soaked through, poor child. Were you ship-wrecked?'

'No, she got wet when I baptized her.'

'You what! There was no need to be so thorough, and you should have asked a priest.'

'I couldn't! She was dying, and going mad, and I was afraid for her.'

'Going mad? She doesn't have a fever.'

'It was a curse.'

'What?' The woman eyed me. 'Well, leave it for now; you're sick yourself, and making no sense. Is this woman your wife?'

'My wife?' I blinked vaguely. 'No. I . . . I love her . . .'

'Indeed.' She said it a bit acidly. 'Well, behave with more respect in this house. You stay here, and this poor girl will have a hot bath and a warm bed – I think we can put her in

453

Myfanwy's cell. Yes, there's a fire there. Come along,' – to her assistant. She picked Eivlin up lightly in both arms.

'Wait!' I said. 'Who are you?'

'I am Sister Teleri, physician for this house, and I trust you will respect that.' She swept out of the room, her assistant following her with a lantern.

I sat down by the fire and leaned against the wall. Well, this Teleri seemed to know what she was doing, and there was nothing more I could do for Eivlin.

Someone shook my arm. I tried to push them away, then opened my eyes; realized that I had been asleep. Groggily, I looked around. Teleri was back.

'How is Eivlin?' I asked.

'If Eivlin is your . . . friend's . . . name – she is ill, and very weak. But she should recover. Now, what is the matter with you?'

'With me? I'm not very sick. I was just hit on the head a few days ago – no, it wasn't that long ago – it was . . . yesterday afternoon?' I had to stop. It couldn't be only one day?

'Mm. Let me see. Oh, come.' Teleri caught my hair and pulled my head down, very gently examined the lumps. 'Hmmm. You're as sick as your friend. Look!' – this to her assistant. I looked at the other woman vaguely; she only looked at what Teleri was showing her. She was a tall, thin, long-faced blonde. 'Do you see his eyes?' Teleri asked. The other nodded. 'Pupils dilated and unfocused. You see that after head injuries. We'll clean him up, put him to bed and make him stay there. Come along.'

Teleri and the other woman hauled me to my feet. I wondered if the assistant were Gwyn's mother, the one the woman at the gate had also sent for. Their hair was near the same colour.

Teleri was very deft and gentle, and chattered cheerfully about head injuries the while, telling her assistant all the awful consequences she had seen. But I didn't care. They finally settled me in some quiet monastic cell, with lots of blankets, and told me to lie quiet.

'Look after Eivlin,' I told Teleri. 'She must not die.'

'I should think not! Come along,' she said to her assistant, 'let him sleep. They whisked themselves from the room, taking the lantern. I lay still in the warm, quiet dark. I must pray for Eivlin, I thought, and fell asleep thinking it.

Eleven

I woke up when the morning sun poured through the window onto my face, but I rolled over on my side and went back to sleep. I woke again when the abbey rang its bells for something or other, but resolutely kept my eyes shut. However, after a while I heard footsteps, and the door of the room creaked stealthily open, and I had to sigh, open my eyes, and sit up.

Gwyn stood frozen in the door, his dark eyes wide with remorse. 'Did I wake you up?' he asked mournfully.

'No. I was already awake.'

'Oh.' He closed the door behind him, smiled a little, shyly. 'Are you feeling better?'

'Very much so. Do you know how Eivlin is?'

'Who?'

'Eivlin. The woman who was so sick.'

'Oh! She's still asleep.' He thought a moment, added, 'Teleri told my mother she's never seen anything like it before, that the girl doesn't stir at all when there doesn't seem much wrong with her. Teleri says she hopes your friend wakes soon.'

'So do I,' I said, feelingly, 'so do I.'

Gwyn looked at me steadily and seriously. 'I'll pray for her,' he said at last. 'Father Carnedyr told me to pray when I'm doing my lessons, and I'll pray for her.'

'Thank you,' I said.

Gwyn shuffled his feet awkwardly. 'I should be at lessons soon,' he blurted out, 'but . . .'

'Come and sit down,' I told him, having to grin, despite everything. I would have done exactly the same thing.

He sat down next to me on the bed. 'Tell me about Camlann! Does everyone ride warhorses everywhere? Is the feast hall roofed with gold, like Tegid says?'

'The Hall is roofed like every other hall, with good thatching straw. No one rides warhorses all the time, and they certainly do not ride them everywhere. But . . .'

Gwyn smiled. '*That* would make a mess, if they rode them everywhere. Once I rode Father Gilla's mare into the

455

refectory, pretending that it was a feast hall, and she knocked over the tables and broke a lot of crockery. I was thrashed for that three times – Oh. I'm sorry. Father Carnedyr says I always interrupt, and ought to be thrashed for it. But is the Queen very beautiful?'

He wanted to know everything, and could scarcely sit still to hear it. I could say barely three sentences before he would pour out more questions. It was not that he was without manners, but was simply quick-minded and excited. He wanted to be a warrior, he told me again in a confidential fashion, even though, 'My mother says I am going to be a priest.' But Hywel had given him the spear, and he practised with it every day; and had he really scared me on the road? I was glad he was there. I had no chance to think about Eivlin or the rest of the troubles, and he made me feel almost as if I were at home. I told him fine and splendid things about Camlann. I was still telling them when the door opened again and Teleri's assistant stood there, a tray of food in one hand.

Gwyn, who had been leaning eagerly forward, eyes shining, abruptly stood up. His face dropped. 'He was awake already, Mama,' he told the woman. 'Truly, I didn't wake him.'

The woman set down the tray. 'Indeed? But he's a sick man, my dearest, and you should not have come troubling him with your questions. And why aren't you at lessons?'

He shuffled his feet.

'He came to see how I was,' I put in, hurriedly. 'Since he was the one who found me, he felt responsible. And I've been glad of his company.' Gwyn shot me a grateful look.

The woman began to smile, but suppressed the smile, though her eyes glinted. 'It is good that you should worry about the poor man, my white heart. But you must remember that he needs rest – and you need lessons. Off with you. Father Carnedyr must be waiting.'

Gwyn did not look pleased at the thought of his schoolmaster waiting for him, but he brightened again when I said, 'Thank you for coming. If your mother doesn't mind, come again later.' He looked at the woman and she nodded assent, so he ran off cheerfully. The woman laughed when he was gone, and carefully closed the door.

'Gwyn is your son?' I asked her.

'Mine,' she said. 'Would you like something to eat?'

'I thank you. He's a very fine boy.'

She sighed, brushing a strand of yellow hair away from her blue eyes, the gesture as graceful as a willow tree. 'He is a fine boy, but a wild one. I hope he has not tired you.' I shook my head and she picked the tray up and brought it over. The food consisted of a bowl of porridge with honey, bread and butter, and fresh milk. The smell of it was magnificent. 'Gwyn is clever. He is good at his lessons, and sweeter-tempered than a day in June. But he is imaginative and too high-spirited, and is always running off. He will get himself into trouble.'

'He says that you want him to be a priest.'

'And so he should be. He is bright enough, and it is a noble vocation and much needed in this age. And it offers its own kind of honour and glory to those that follow it.'

I said nothing, but began eating the porridge. It was delicious.

'You dislike the idea,' she observed. 'Well, many men do. Gwyn, now, wants to be a warrior. If you will, do not encourage him in it, or tell him tales that might feed his desires.'

I looked back up at her, surprised, spoon in mid air. She stood straight and calm by the wall, smiling a little, plainly dressed, but her tone had something of command in it. I wondered where she was from. By her accent, she was not born in Gwynedd.

'All boys enjoy such tales,' I said. 'And there's no harm in a song. All they can do is make a boy want to be brave, and that's no evil.'

'That is no evil, no. But they can also make boys love war and conflict, and value gold and strength of body above virtue and honesty. They have much to say of the glitter of worldly power, and little of kindness, peace, and nobility of soul. I would not have my son listen to them. I tell you this because you were telling him about Camlann.'

I looked carefully at the porridge, embarrassed. 'Well . . . he asked me.'

'And you have been there?'

'I have been a servant there.'

She was quiet a moment, considering me, then said, 'Your own loyalties are your own affair, but I must ask you

457

to keep silence about them to my son. I have trouble enough with Gwyn without having him admire – and perhaps run off to – the Family of a man I consider a usurper and a tyrant.'

'Arthur is a very great king,' I said, stung. 'A man given to the protection of his people, to the creation and defence of order and justice. And many of his warriors are good men.'

'Have you found them so? We differ then.'

I swallowed. 'You are very fierce, Lady.'

She did not notice my use of the title, but shook her head slowly, meeting my eyes. 'I have cause to be. Gwyn's father was – is – a warrior.'

'Oh,' I said. 'He . . . he didn't disgrace your vows?'

She shook her head again. 'No, at the time I had not made my vows. All I lost was my honour, though, God knows, that is loss enough.' She moved to the window and looked out. 'All I am asking is that you tell my son no stories about wars and warriors,' she said, more gently.

It was reasonable, since he was her son and responsibility, and anyway could be no more likely to become a warrior than I myself, so I agreed and ate my porridge in silence, wondering who she was.

When I finished, the woman turned from the window, smiled again, trying to lighten the air. 'Here, let me look at your head.'

I let her. She looked, then put on some salve and bandaged it. When she finished she stood back, wiping her hands.

'How is Eivlin?' I asked her. 'The woman I came with?'

'Still asleep. We are keeping her warm and comfortable.'

I was quiet a moment. 'Will she wake up?' I asked.

Instead of answering, she looked at me closely. 'Does it matter to you so very much?'

'Yes.' I had to say again what I had said the night before. 'I love her.'

She looked at me for a moment longer, then smiled in a way that made me realize that she had distrusted me before. It was an open, warm smile that made her face breathtakingly beautiful. 'You are speaking the truth,' she said. 'Forgive me – there is so much evil done to women in these dark days that one is inclined to suspect it when there is none. Your . . . friend is fortunate.' She picked the tray up again. 'Now,' she said, briskly, 'you must stay in bed and rest. Teleri says that that is the best treatment for head injuries.'

'I'll stay in bed, then.' Though, without Gwyn, it would be maddening for very long, and if Gwyn came I thought it might be difficult to stay off the subject of Camlann. 'Are you going to send a priest to give me the sacrament?' Gwyn's 'Father Gilla' sounded sympathetic.

She smiled again at that. 'I'll speak to Father Carnedyr when he has given the children their lessons. Teleri will probably come by later, and you can talk to her as well, for that is what you're wanting, is it not? You can tell Teleri that I – that is, that Elidan – is seeing about the priest . . . what's the matter?'

Elidan.

After all my lord's searching, I was the one who had found her, and quite by accident. But it had to be her. If she had taken her vows after Gwyn was born, or just before he was born, that made it eight years or so, the right time . . .

And it meant that Gwyn was Gwalchmai's son, and it explained how Bran had found out about Elidan's well-kept secret. Dear God.

'Lady,' I said, 'I have heard your name before.'

She was startled, and for a moment, I thought, afraid; but if she was afraid she hid it quickly. Only her eyes narrowed a little as she said, 'It is possible. My name is not common, but neither is it unknown. But I do not know where you could have heard of me. I am only a sister at St Elena's.'

'Whose father's name was Caw, and whose brother was once king of Ebrauc.'

Her face froze. 'That is nonsense,' she said at once, making amends. 'You have heard of someone else.'

'Lady, I knew that you were thought to be somewhere in Arfon, and your accent is northern, however much you imitate the speech of Gwynedd. And you must have made your vows at the right time. Why should you deny that you are Elidan, daughter of Caw?'

She set the tray down again, hurriedly. 'Very well,' she admitted, then bit her lip, straightened and went on more quietly and with great dignity, 'I am Elidan, daughter of Caw. But I have renounced the world and the things of the world and . . . I have enemies. You must not betray me.'

'There's no question of the world at large, Lady, but I fear I must tell my lord.'

'Your lord? Why, whose servant are you?'

'Gwalchmai ap Lot's. He has been looking for you, Lady.'

'No!' she cried, 'Not . . . no, I will never see him again. I swore to die first! You . . . listen, he deceived me, lied to me, perjured himself, murdered my brother, dishonoured me and my house. I swore never to see him again. Tell him I keep my oaths!'

Her anger and horror left me speechless for a moment. Then it struck me that, if Gwalchmai had been there, he would have knelt at her feet and agreed with her, and this made me angry in turn. 'He treated you badly,' I said, 'but not as badly as all that. There are two sides to every quarrel, and your dishonour was as much your fault as his.'

At this the vehemence vanished and she looked at me coldly. 'I forgot myself. Of course, you are only his servant. No doubt he told you some pretty story where I was all to blame. That was not the way of it . . .'

'He told me the story, but gave himself the blame. The only thing he couldn't claim was that he won you by force.'

'So I am to be blamed as a willing harlot? That was what they said in Caer Ebrauc. My brother was kinder: he believed I was ensorcelled.'

'You are no fool, Lady; you cannot believe he cast some spell on you. And if you thought him a sorcerer at the time, that makes it worse.'

'But he was so beautiful!' she cried, then stopped, pressing her hands to her mouth. I stared, and she lowered them again, looking at me with a return of the anger. 'Well, then, I have said it, and so he was. And he was nobly born, and famed, famed all over Britain though no older than myself. Every girl in Caer Ebrauc fell to sighing whenever his name was mentioned. But he looked only at me, as though I were more than the whole earth in his eyes. Dear God! He needed no other sorcery than his eyes and his words, I will confess it to you. I wished I could give him my soul. How could I refuse him anything in the bright world? But it was nothing to him. He took what he wanted, swore me an oath and rode off. Then he broke his oath and killed my brother. He used me. But I am of no ignoble family, and I will not be used again. He deserves to die!'

Her voice was sharp with pain, but her eyes were fierce, hurt but clear, tearless. I remembered what the Emperor Arthur had said of her, that she would not forgive.

'Lady,' I said helplessly, then, resolving to persevere, 'Lady, my lord nearly killed himself when he left you last, so he felt much the same. No, he didn't tell me that. He barely admitted it when he was charged with it. I first met him because he was searching for you over all Britain, alone, in the dead of winter, simply to beg your forgiveness.'

She stared at me in disbelief for a moment. 'To beg my forgiveness?' Her hands clenched, then relaxed. 'To beg *my forgiveness*? How . . . no. How can he expect such a thing of me? I am not so weak and frail as to fall on his neck again when next he beckons. I will not say to him, 'Very well, it was nothing, I will marry you.' He wanted to marry me. After he killed my brother. I should have died the first day I saw him come riding into Llys Ebrauc with the sun behind him: and may I die truly if ever I see him again and give him my "forgiveness".'

'But he has repented of it most bitterly!' I pleaded. 'And, in Christ's name, Gwyn is his son.'

At that her eyes froze me like the wind in January. 'Not Gwyn,' she said, evenly but with greater force than any she had used yet. 'Gwyn is my son. *He* will not take my child away. I will not let my Gwyn grow up a warrior in some fortress, to his own destruction. I will fight Gwalchmai with my bare hands if he tries to take Gwyn away from me.'

'You'd rather let your child be called a nun's bastard?' I demanded, trying to get out of bed to face her.

'Yes, yes, far better "nun's bastard" than "warrior's bastard"! You stupid fool of a servant, haven't you learned yet that courts are cruel, dangerous and cruel? As earth is under me, heaven over me and the sea round me, I will not let my son meet his father!'

As the words of her oath resounded in the small room, the door flew open and Teleri rushed in. She stopped in the doorway and looked from me to Elidan, then back to me. She came fully into the room and pushed me back into the bed with one hand. 'You,' she said. 'Sit down and be quiet. You should not go about shouting at your physicians.

Now, Elidan, just what is happening here?'

Elidan glared at her, then drew a deep breath, almost a sob, and shook her head. 'He . . . he is the servant of . . . of Gwyn's father.'

Teleri's eyebrows shot up and she stared at me in astonishment. 'Indeed?'

'And he says that his lord is searching for me.'

'It's true enough,' I said. Common sense was returning to me, and I saw, with a cold weight in my stomach, that they could very easily force me to leave. Which was all very well for me, but unthinkable for Eivlin. I realized, moreover, that the lady Elidan had some cause to fear discovery, and that my language had not been tactful. 'It's true that I'm his servant,' I said, 'but my lord was not as guilty in the matter as this lady may have thought. And he repented very bitterly of the way he treated her. I have just told her that he searched for her all over Britain, and that in mid-winter, all to ask her forgiveness. I could swear to it that he means no harm to her, and certainly none to this convent.'

'Oh, indeed?' said Teleri. 'Travel in mid-winter is a harsh penance for any man – but this is not to the point. I do not care, Elidan, whose servant this man may be. He is sick, and our task is to heal the sick. That is that, even if he does bring his lord down on us.'

'I am afraid for my son,' said Elidan.

'Ach. Your son. Yes.' Teleri's frown deepened. 'But, my dear, what is to be done? You cannot suggest that we throw this great ox out to die.'

Elidan flushed. 'I . . . but no, I do not make war on servants. Only . . . Rhys ap Sion, you owe us something for the care we have given you and your friend. Swear that you will not mention my name to your lord when you see him again. Swear as you hope for salvation.'

'How can I swear an oath such as that? My lord Gwalchmai will certainly continue to search for you.'

'What was your lord's name?' Teleri asked in a different tone.

'Gwalchmai ap Lot.'

Elidan turned away abruptly and went to the window. She held the sill, and I saw how the bones showed white with the force of her grip.

'You never told me your lover's name,' Teleri said to her.

'You never said that he was the Emperor's nephew.'

'There was no cause to,' Elidan said wearily. 'And I was afraid then that the sisters might reject me, if they knew how powerful my enemies were.'

'We would not have rejected you had your lover been the Emperor himself. But I see why you are afraid. Such a man might bring a whole warband to take you away, and to appeal to our king would be to ask the fox for shelter from the dragon.'

'Gwalchmai would never do such a thing,' I protested.

'I once thought that Gwalchmai would never break his oath,' returned Elidan. 'But he did, and my brother is dead. Now I do not know what he might do. If I went to my clan, to my half-brother Ergyriad, he would be pleased that the matter turned out so well. He would be honoured if Gwalchmai were to marry me. But I will not. I cannot forgive him. I will not fall so low as that.'

'Gwalchmai only wishes to speak with you,' I insisted. 'He is a good man, the best lord I could ask for. If you cannot find the Christian charity to forgive him, you ought at least tell him so to his face!'

'I have heard a great deal of Gwalchmai ap Lot – as who hasn't?' Teleri said cautiously. 'I have certainly heard, what with magic swords and horses and battle-madness, that he has more dealings with the Otherworld than is safe or fitting; but I have heard also that he is kind, a protector of the weak, and God-fearing. I do not know: it is hard to be certain of anything to do with the Emperor, here in Gwynedd, for there are men enough to tell evil tales to any who will listen. But if he were a common man, child,' and she went over to stand by Elidan, 'I would say, forgive him and forget him.'

Elidan said nothing, only stared out the window.

'I swear to you, my lord will do you no harm,' I repeated again. 'But if you disbelieve me – well, you will do what you wish anyway, and there's nothing I can do to stop you. But Eivlin, none of it reflects on Eivlin. She is a brave woman, and honourable. Nor have I dishonoured her, so you need not fear to keep her in this place. And if I haven't married her yet, there's nothing to say I won't.'

That last surprised me, for I hadn't thought about it before. And yet, I could do much worse for a wife, and not much better. I was quiet suddenly, considering the thought.

Teleri snorted, then laughed. 'Bravely spoken! But none of us are threatening your sweetheart. Of course she will stay until she is better, and you as well, for I can't answer even for a farmer's thick skull if you go running about as you have been. Elidan, did you look at his head this morning?'

Elidan pressed the heels of her hands against her eyes, nodded. Teleri checked again. I was sure that Teleri had been raised a farmer's daughter.

'It is better, a little,' Elidan said while Teleri examined the lumps. 'Or so I think. But you are right, he must stay and we can demand no oaths if he will not give them. We cannot punish him for another's crime.'

Teleri nodded, retying the bandage. 'Much better today. A good thick skull.'

'That is what my sister says,' I told her. 'How is Eivlin?'

Elidan walked over to the bed and sat down, looking exhausted. 'Her we could not have sent away. She ought to be well. She has no fever, is not chilled or shivering. She is not injured and has no signs of illness. But she feels nothing, responds to nothing, and her heart beats very slowly and unsteadily.'

Teleri pressed Elidan's hand a moment, smiling at her, and I looked at the woman, understanding why Gwalchmai had loved her. She would not let hatred cloud her sense of honour, and had the courage to risk a great deal for what she willed; and the strength of will and nobility showed through her like a stone under the current of a river, unyielding. But she would be unyielding, I thought, if Gwalchmai came and pleaded with her. Arthur had been right. The children of Caw accounted it a dishonour to forgive.

'Indeed, and we wished to ask you about that,' Teleri said briskly. 'What happened to this girl, to cause this? And no nonsense about curses.'

'But that is what caused it,' I said. Elidan's face stayed quiet and expressionless, but Teleri leaned back, thin black eyebrows again raised up on her forehead. 'It seems nonsense, and yet is true,' I insisted. 'My lord had nothing to do with it, though, do not think that. Eivlin was the serving maid of the Queen Morgawse of the Ynysoedd Erch. Morgawse, and King Lot, are at Degannwy, plotting with

Maelgwn Gwynedd, and my lord was sent there as an emissary by the Emperor. Morgawse had some plot against my lord, and wished to use me in it, but Eivlin helped me escape when I was captured, and for that the Queen cursed her.'

'You are saying strange things,' remarked Teleri. 'But well; a curse. And the baptizing you were babbling about?'

'Eivlin was never baptized. She was born in Erin and raised in the Islands. When she started screaming, and raving about shadows attacking her, I thought it might be some help. And she did stop screaming. She fainted, and became as she is now.'

'It is certainly less noisy.' Teleri studied my face carefully. 'But you believe this tale.'

'How could I not, when I suffered it?'

She looked thoughtful. 'I have never held much with ghost stories. And yet, I would not call you a fool, and I have never seen anything like this illness. But still . . .'

'But still, it rubs against the grain to believe it. Sister, I do not like believing it myself. When it comes to fighting, I prefer real things to shadows on an empty road. But Morgawse's power is real, and dangerous, as I have reason to know myself.'

'If there is sorcery about, it explains why Gwalchmai is here,' Elidan said bitterly.

'Lady, if you think Gwalchmai would worship devils, you do not remember him at all. But his mother, and his brother Medraut, and Maelgwn Gwynedd and all at Degannwy, all wish to destroy Gwalchmai as a part of some plot against the Emperor. And if they can, and if they do destroy the Emperor as well, how much longer do you think Britain will be safe? Merciful Christ, this is a struggle of Light against Darkness, not a tale to win your sympathy!'

'Stop!' commanded Teleri, holding her hand up. 'You go too deep. Now I,' she stood up, 'I am inclined to believe you when you say that the girl's trouble is a curse, though God help me for believing such a thing. I will have Father Gilla say a Mass for her, and we can all pray. It is not a means of healing I usually approve of, but it will at least do no harm. Beyond that, I do not know what to do. If she does not wake, she will die of thirst, since we cannot get her to swallow anything. But for the rest of your tale – your lord, and King Maelgwn and the Emperor and this famous witch Morgawse of Orcade – all this we will leave aside. The struggles of kingdoms are beyond us. Our task is to heal the sick, care for orphans, copy books and farm. So much our abbey has ever done, and so much we will ever do, God willing.'

I could say nothing to that. I nodded my head, thinking about Eivlin, and then about Gwalchmai. Had he got my message? Had he understood it? Could he do anything about it?

'Perhaps,' I said, slowly, 'perhaps my lord Gwalchmai might know what to do about Eivlin.'

'No!' cried Elidan. 'He must not come here. He must not know that Gwyn exists.'

'Elidan!' Teleri faced the other woman. She was a good five inches shorter and far less regal, but Elidan's firmness melted away. 'Elidan, if this tale is a true one, what has happened is beyond us. It would be a grave sin to let an innocent girl die for fear of this man who might heal her. If he can help, he must come.'

'But what of my son's life? What if he takes my son away?'

'Don't tell him about Gwyn. Keep the child a secret. If you cannot forgive the man, do not. But I do not believe he will force you to anything, and you must consider the girl's life.'

'Of course,' Elidan said after a long moment. 'May it be for the best. Rhys ap Sion, if you think Gwalchmai can help the girl, bring him here. I will speak with him. But, as you would be saved, do not tell him about my son.'

I hesitated. 'I do not know even that I can reach Gwalchmai,' I muttered, evading the issue. 'I can't go directly back to Degannwy. The guards would not let me through the gate. But if I do reach Gwalchmai...'

'Swear that you will not mention Gwyn to him. I will trust you with it, you must see that.'

I looked at her. If she did forgive Gwalchmai, she might release me from that oath. If she did not, or if she forgave him only in a form of words... It would probably be better, then, that Gwalchmai never knew of his son's existence. There would be nothing he could do about the child. He could hardly drag him away from Elidan. She had said she would fight with her bare hands to protect the boy, and I believed her. And she was doing what she thought right. And if Gwalchmai knew that Gwyn was his son, and was unable to keep him, it would merely be another load of undeserved misery.

'I swear I won't mention Gwyn to Gwalchmai unless you yourself give me leave,' I told Elidan, looking into her solemn eyes. 'So help me God and all the saints and angels. As I hope to be saved, I will not.'

'Then tell Gwalchmai to come. I will speak to Abbess Maire and tell her the whole situation. I will ask her to support you, and give all the help she can, for I believe your tale of Morgawse's sorcery, and it is fitting to us to oppose it.'

'I thank you,' I said.

'Well!' Teleri put her hands on her hips. 'Well done! And now that you have decided to seek this lord's help, how is he to be reached?'

'I will go,' I said. 'I can try and climb the wall at Degannwy by night. It should not be impossible.'

'You will do no such thing,' declared Teleri. 'You will stay here and rest.'

'You can send a messenger with a letter,' Elidan suggested. 'He can enter by the gate, as though he would sell something to the fortress.'

'I don't know how to write,' I said.

She smiled. 'Then dictate it to one of us. This is an abbey. We do teach writing here. Father Gilla can take the message in, if he's willing; his little mare is the best horse we have. I will speak to him, and you can dictate the letter this afternoon.'

'But sleep now,' Teleri added. 'You look as though you could do with the rest.'

She swept from the room, pausing only to stoop upon the food tray and bear it off with her. Elidan followed without a backward glance.

I sighed and lay back, looking at the ceiling. There were too many things to think about, and I could not rest. Every time I managed to turn my mind from Eivlin, telling myself that worrying helped nothing, I found myself wondering about Gwalchmai. Perhaps it was absurd to ask him to help us; perhaps he needed help himself. He was surrounded by

467

enemies, with only Rhuawn as a treacherous support. I
knew that Rhuawn would side with Gwalchmai against
Maelgwn, but Medraut's more subtle opposition had
escaped him. He was a good man, Rhuawn, but deluded,
and unlikely to come to his senses unless Medraut did something foolish. Unless Eivlin had hurt Medraut badly with
that piece of firewood. That blow might delay Morgawse's
schemes for a while. I trusted Eivlin to have hit hard, and
thought that Medraut's headache might be worse than
mine; and perhaps even Morgawse felt unwell. It was a
cheering thought, and eventually I managed to relax and
drift off to sleep.

Perhaps it was because of my head injuries, but I had
nightmares.

It seemed to me that I saw Morgawse of Orcade, standing
in a small, dark place, braiding her hair in a strange pattern
and singing. After a while, beyond her singing, I could hear
a keening, faintly at first, then louder, breaking into a dirge
sung without measure in a foreign tongue. Morgawse
stopped her song and laughed, her teeth showing white as
she tossed back her head with pleasure. Her image faded,
and the dirge grew louder. I saw a funeral procession,
walking in the dark with smoky red torches wavering
about. In the midst of the torches was carried a bier, with a
still form lying on it, covered by a cloak. Of a sudden, the
ring of mourners was broken, and Agravain ap Lot burst
into the middle and flung himself down beside the bier,
weeping. He buried his face in the cloak. The whole began
to recede, the wailing growing fainter, and I struggled to go
nearer, to know who it was on the bier because I was terribly afraid, deathly afraid that it was Gwalchmai. But the
dirge faded until it was only a faint hum, like the wind, and
the torch light seemed to recede back and back away. I sank
into a black ocean, still struggling to follow. Then there
came a crash like thunder, and I opened my eyes and saw
Medraut. He was smiling.

'He appears well enough to me,' said Medraut smoothly.
I looked behind him and saw that he was speaking to Teleri.

'You cannot take him,' said Teleri. Her hands were
knotted together, her eyes too bright. 'For sweet mercy's
sake, do you expect us to simply hand him over to you?'

'I expect that you will do what I tell you to, or else see

your abbey here burned to the ground. Get up!'

I sat up, impossibly confused. I was in the same room at St Elena's, and it was afternoon. The same rushes lay on the floor, the stone walls had the same chipped rocks. It was not a dream: Medraut was really standing before me.

He smiled again. I noticed that his head was bandaged. 'I told you to get up.'

I stood, gathering the bedclothes about me. I had only my underclothes on, since the nuns had taken my tunic and trousers.

Medraut laughed at me. 'Bring him his clothes, and hurry,' he ordered Teleri.

'In Christ's name, you cannot take him!' she said.

I was awake enough to know better. 'He can. And he will fire the abbey if you don't. Better go.'

Almost, she didn't. She stared at me for a long moment, twisting her hands together; but then she turned and ran from the room. Medraut laughed again, looked about and sat down comfortably on the bed.

'You've found excellent care here,' he commented. 'Not, perhaps, healing as rapid as my mother's: but then, no doubt the treatment is pleasanter. Where's the other slave, the one responsible for this?' He touched his bandage.

'She's dead,' I told him, praying that he couldn't tell otherwise. 'She died yesterday. Just before sundown. She started screaming, and fell down on the road, and she is dead.'

'I thought as much.' He drew one knee up and locked his arms around it. His fair hair caught the afternoon sun, and his soft new beard gleamed against his face. Gold shone on his brooch and collar. 'Mother defends her honour. The little vixen should never have dared defy her. I hope she suffered.'

I said nothing, hoping that Teleri had not mentioned Eivlin, hoping that Medraut neither knew nor was able to sense anything about Elidan and Gwyn. Teleri came back with my clothes, and I dressed rapidly and in silence.

Medraut stood, brushed off his cloak. One hand rested lightly on his sword, and I stared at the weapon. Either he had two swords with identical hilts or he had somehow recovered the one Eivlin took from him. He noticed the stare and flashed his easy smile.

'Yes. I have it back again.' He slapped the sword hilt. 'A useful thing. I could show you more of it.'

I had no particular wish to see more of it. I felt sick. Had he, or Morgawse, somehow trailed me and found the message before Gwalchmai? Or had that still form in my dream indeed been Gwalchmai?

It is no use to rely on dreams and guesses. Whatever had happened to my message, it did not change the fact that I had to leave quietly with Medraut, drawing no attention to anyone at the abbey, and be prepared to fight the whole fight over again. I was glad that the thought numbed me. If it had not, I do not think I could have left the room without falling down and begging him to spare me, which might have meant disaster. The final end, I told myself firmly, is not in our hands at all. We can only do what seems to be right, and trust God for the rest.

Medraut stood beside the door and gestured for Teleri and me to leave first. Teleri passed him proudly and briskly without looking at him. When I stepped after her, however, Medraut clouted me full on the ear. I stumbled against the door, hit the other side of my head on the frame, and fell to my knees on the floor. Teleri cried out. Medraut bent over and dragged me up by the front of my tunic.

'And that,' he said, his eyes savage, 'that is for running off and shaming my mother. I can't give you the full payment, slave, since that is her right, but it is not forgotten.'

The world was swirling about me in circles, so I closed my eyes, counted to ten, and managed to stand on my own feet. Medraut let go of me. 'Show us the way out,' he commanded Teleri, who stood, frozen, her hand lifted – whether to strike or help I was unsure. Her eyes flashed and she almost retorted, but managed to check herself. We walked out of the abbey.

Medraut had a dozen mounted warriors waiting in the yard. From the corner of my eye I noticed a huddle of nuns against the wall, and Gwyn, staring at the men wide-eyed with awe. My little pony was out and saddled, and at Medraut's order I mounted, wearily, and submitted to having my hands tied while someone else took the pony on a lead rein. Medraut swung up onto his own mount, a sleek, long-legged grey. He nodded to the nuns. 'It is good that you were sensible.' He gathered up his reins. 'As it is, all you have lost is one insolent servant, and not your home and your lives.'

'What are you doing to Rhys?' bellowed Gwyn. Abruptly, the boy dashed from the wall and ran towards the horses. Someone shrieked. Medraut whipped out his sword.

'What's this brat?' demanded Medraut. 'One of your bastards?' he looked contemptuously at the nuns.

Elidan walked out of the huddle after her son. 'Mine,' she said, her voice calm and very clear.

'He showed me the way here,' I said, not daring to look at either of them. 'He's too young to have any sense.' I did not care to think what Medraut and Morgawse could do with the lad.

'Out of the way, brat, or I'll cut your ears off,' said Medraut in a pleasant tone.

Gwyn glared at him. 'What kind of warrior are you?' he demanded 'When I'm grown up I'll come and fight you. You can't take Rhys away like this: he's sick. Teleri and Mama both say so. Mama!' She had reached him and caught him by the ear. 'Mama, he can't!'

'He can,' said Elidan. 'And nun's bastards never become warriors, which is something to thank God for, for you will never be tempted to vulgar brutality.'

Medraut was too surprised to react, at first. Elidan dragged Gwyn out of his way. The boy protested, 'But Mama, he's . . .'

'He is a dog, but we have no power.' She thrust him out of the way.

Medraut drew his sword with a rasp of steel, and Elidan turned to him, graceful as a deer, her head lifting and her eyes clear and brilliant with contempt. I wished, wildly, to do something to distract Medraut: to laugh at her, or point out the ridiculousness of her gesture. But it was not ridiculous. She knew exactly what she was doing. She was making Medraut absurd by the purity of her own courage and honour; she was showing his act at its worst, and letting him see it too, and she smiled at his sword now, completely scornful of her danger. She was astonishingly beautiful.

Medraut swore, inarticulately, knowing what she had done; then clapped his heels to his horse and rode at her. He only used the flat of the sword, but the blow caught her on the head and she fell; and Medraut touched his horse to a canter and rode off without looking back. I risked one glance, as someone jerked the pony's lead rein and dragged me off after them. Gwyn was screaming, but Elidan had risen to her knees, her forehead streaming blood, and was putting her arms about her son and soothing him. Her eyes met mine over his shoulder, still brilliant, but now full of a profound grief and helplessness. Slowly, she shook her head.

The track up from the abbey seemed much shorter than the agonizing trip down to reach it. Medraut insisted on moving at a fast trot, which was about the best speed my pony could manage. When we reached the main road he ordered one of his men to ride ahead of us with some message. They spoke in Irish, and I understood nothing they said except for one word: *Riga*. I had already learned that this was the word the men of the Ynysoedd Erch used to refer to Morgawse. *Riga*, 'the Queen'. The messenger nodded to Medraut, called a greeting to his comrades, and touched his horse to a gallop, off to find Morgawse and tell her that Medraut had recaptured me. The rest of us followed him along the road at the same jolting trot. My head, which had been feeling better, began to throb again. I stared ahead blankly, trying not to see the men around me, trying not to feel. After so much, to be returning to Morgawse. After everything! If I thought of it, my hands began to shake and it became unbearable.

But at least Eivlin was safe – if she lived. Ach, Yffern take Morgawse, and Medraut and the lot of them, Eivlin had risked her life to save me. And now she was probably dying, but she wasn't Morgawse's tool. Nor would I be. And yet, I had been nearly spent when Eivlin had broken in to rescue me. Morgawse had very nearly succeeded. I remembered her smile of triumph.

But perhaps by now she did not need me for any plot against my lord. If Gwalchmai were dead, all that Morgawse would want with me would be to punish me for my presumption. If Gwalchmai were dead – I had no reason to believe that except a nightmare. A nightmare, and Medraut's sword, and the whole situation. What was Rhuawn doing? Still deluded? Ready to go back to Camlann with Medraut, leaving Morgawse with Maelgwn and . . . what had Morgawse said? 'Others will join Maelgwn in his alliance, and wait until the Family is at war with itself. Then will the shield-wall be broken and the gate of the stronghold be battered down; then Arthur will die.' All that order and unity, strength and laughter, all that Light, to fall and be broken. And there would be nothing, then, nothing but a wilderness which used to be a kingdom.

I looked down at the road. Could I throw myself off the pony head first and break my own neck? To kill oneself is a sin, but with nothing before me but a painful death, the act must be justifiable in God's eyes.

But I couldn't do it. It was sheer idiocy not to, but I couldn't even think of it seriously. I sat silent, clenching my hands against their bonds and looking at the mountains which stood calm and joyful in their spring green.

We did not ride to Degannwy, but headed off up another track, deeper into the mountains. Something in its curve touched my memory, and I recalled that I had ridden down it in the moonlight with Eivlin, laughing uncontrollably with the joy of our escape. Now Medraut sent half his men back to Degannwy, and the rest of us trotted up the narrow track in single file, riding in the last of the afternoon sun. We had made good time on the journey. My little pony was sweating from the pace. I was sweating too, but I felt cold, as cold as if it were February instead of late May.

We saw the shepherd's hut before us, and Medraut turned his grey steed over to the place down the hill where the horses had been tied before. There was a horse there now, a chestnut mare with fine trappings: Morgawse's horse. I closed my eyes, unwilling to keep on seeing it. We stopped.

'Get down,' Medraut commanded me. I slithered off, stood looking at my bound hands on the pony's thick mane. The beast tossed its head, sides heaving. Medraut gave some orders to his men, again in Irish, then turned back to me. 'Come,' he commanded. I took a deep breath, turned, and came.

All but one of the warriors remained by the horses. The one who came was that same Ronan who had stood guard before. It was almost more than I could bear, and I bit my tongue.

If the ride from St Elena's had seemed short, that march up the hill seemed to take years, and I was ready to scream by the time we reached the door. I bit my tongue harder, tasting my own blood. Medraut opened the door and shoved me in first.

Morgawse stood in the room, dark in gold and crimson, but there was someone else there as well, someone standing behind the door, because her eyes were fixed there. I saw that that was how it must be as I took another step in, as Medraut followed me; and then the door slammed in Ronan's face. Medraut whirled about, his hand on his sword, his face astonished, and I turned too.

Gwalchmai stood against the bare wooden door, his sword a streak of fire in his hand, mail-coat gleaming. His eyes were steady on Morgawse's eyes, his face without expression.

Ronan behind us pounded on the door, exclaiming angrily in Irish. Without moving, Gwalchmai gave some order in a low voice, in Irish. The pounding stopped, and Ronan queried.

Morgawse nodded, her eyes not stirring. She repeated what Gwalchmai had said. There was a long silence. Then I heard Ronan's footsteps retreating, and the air in the hut lay thick and still.

'So.' Gwalchmai spoke at last, his voice cool and detached. 'You had no notion where my servant might be.'

'Why is *he* here?' demanded Medraut, looking towards Morgawse. He eased his sword from its sheath, ready to attack. Morgawse said nothing, and, after another moment's hesitation, Medraut dropped back towards her.

Gwalchmai took a quick step forward and caught my shoulder, brought down his sword with a single swift stroke that cut my bonds in half. 'Rhys. Are you well?' His voice held expression again: concern. I was shaking. For one awful moment I had believed that Morgawse had carried out her first plan against Gwalchmai and succeeded. But this was clearly not the case, and I was too confused to think.

'I am fine,' I stammered. 'But you – you're not dead.'

'Of course not. Why should I be?' I shook my head, unable to explain, resolving never to trust a dream again. Gwalchmai gave my shoulder a soft shake and took another step forward so that I stood behind him.

'Lady,' he said to Morgawse, 'I have found my servant, and will not trouble you further. We will go.'

Incredibly, she smiled. It was a smile I had no liking for, an intimate, secret smile directed towards Gwalchmai alone. 'You have conquered, my falcon,' she said, very, very softly. 'Never would I have believed it, once. Always I thought you were a fool: first because you could be used, and then because you rejected power when it was offered to you. Now I see that you are wiser than I.' She stepped nearer. Medraut stared at her, bewildered. Gwalchmai stood motionless, just looking at her as he had that first night we came to Degannwy.

'It makes me like you the better,' the Queen went on. 'All the men I have known, and all my sons, they have always been weak. I am very glad, my spring-tide falcon, that you are stronger . . .'

'Mother!' said Medraut in an agonized whisper. She did not turn, but only took another step towards Gwalchmai, smiling that smile. It made my hair stand on end.

'My lord,' I said, 'let us leave.'

He didn't seem to hear. He kept looking at Morgawse. The point of his sword drooped, slowly, and she came closer.

'And yet I should have expected things of you, my second son. Born not to please Lot, nor for my plans, but for myself.'

Gwalchmai stepped back, almost stepping into me. I caught his arm. 'My lord, don't listen to her.'

She came nearer, lifting her arms as though she would embrace him. Her eyes were too dreadful to look at. Gwalchmai was shaking. He drew the sword up and side-ways, the edge turning towards her.

He might kill her. He might not. If he killed her, his mother – what would it mean to him, what would it do to him, afterwards? I became very afraid. And if he did not kill her, she was coming to claim him, very plainly dragging up whatever dark memories she had left in his heart from his earliest years. Whatever he felt for her, he could not simply oppose her with his will. He was pulled by her into an unholy murder or a worse love, and I could see it all plainly when I looked at her.

Morgawse took one step nearer, and I looked away. Gwalchmai's sword gave a little lift, and I knew that he was going to strike.

'Mother!' said Medraut. She did not look at him, only at Gwalchmai. The sword swung back the merest hair, and I grabbed my lord's wrist with both hands.

He gave one heave that nearly tore his hand loose, but I was holding tightly. Morgawse did not move. Gwalchmai whirled and looked me in the face. His eyes were wide and furiously dark.

'Gwalchmai,' I said. 'My lord, let us leave. There is nothing more to do here.'

He spun back, looked at Morgawse.

'Come along,' I insisted. 'There are things to be done, and we must not waste our time.' I fumbled behind me for the latch of the door. Morgawse began to frown.

'What must be done?' asked Gwalchmai, like a man in a dream.

I risked it. 'I have found Elidan – and beyond that, there is the work your lord set you.'

His fingers went white on the sword hilt. 'Elidan?' he looked back at me.

'Stop,' said Morgawse.

'Lady,' Gwalchmai said, recovering himself, 'Rhys is right. There is nothing we must do here, and very much to do elsewhere.'

Morgawse, frowning, dropped back towards Medraut, not turning about. She lifted one thin, dark hand and held it palm up, fingers pointing at Gwalchmai.

'You will not leave,' she said. 'Medraut, assist me.'

Gwalchmai gave one long, sad look at Medraut, and looked back to Morgawse. Medraut dropped to one knee and held the hilt of his sword with both hands, the point slanting upwards before both his mother and himself. He did not look at Morgawse, but he was biting his lip in a kind of frenzy, so that it bled.

'Is that to be the way of it?' asked Gwalchmai, very quietly. He almost said something more, but checked himself. He drew himself up, raised his sword and held it point down, his right hand on the hilt and his left hand clasping the naked blade. He lifted it until the cross-piece was level with his eyes. A light stirred along the steel, and the ruby in the pommel began to glow with a deep radiance.

Medraut glanced at Morgawse, looked back at Gwalch-mai, and seemed to brace himself. The Queen's face was taut, pale, her eyes fathomless and too wide. Slowly she raised her other hand and placed it, palm down, on top of the first.

I gripped the latch of the door, ready to fling it open. But Gwalchmai showed no signs of moving, so I merely held my place, waiting. The silence grew denser.

Morgawse spread her fingers, shifted her hands a very little. Her face was like a lightning bolt, vivid and inhuman with strain. As though with a great effort, she drew her hands apart a very little. I heard my own voice gasp: darkness boiled between her hands, seeped out to blacken the dimness of the room. I closed my eyes, opened them. The darkness still seethed between the Queen's thin hands. It trickled downward along the blade of Medraut's sword and flowed onto the floor, piled about Medraut's knees into a mass.

The sword in Gwalchmai's hands began to burn brighter, the deep crimson glow running from the hilt down the blade, paling to an almost white shade at its tip.

'Do you truly believe that will be sufficient?' whispered Morgawse. Her voice in that stillness was like the first breath of wind stirring the air before a thunderstorm: it made everything shiver. Her fingers arched about the darkness, curling with effort till they resembled claws. 'Behold! I am Queen and Ruler of Air and Darkness, and all Earth will be my domain, and all flesh obey me. Do you think that sliver of steel enough to restrain me? Fool!' She tossed her head back, and her hair swirled about the night, seeming to draw in the blackness, or to hurl it out.

I saw Gwalchmai tighten his grip on his sword, the bare blade cutting into his left hand. The radiance deepened. 'Darkness does not have sole dominion over Earth,' he said, his voice hoarse with effort. 'It is by Light that this sword was formed, and by Light it will hold, not as steel, but as the image of a will.'

Morgawse flung wide her arms, and utter blackness swallowed the hut and the very ground beneath our feet. I could no longer feel the latch of the door, and I could not tell where we were. It was as though we hung suspended, or fell through a huge gulf into which all light and life were pouring. I fumbled before myself and found Gwalchmai's shoulder. For all the blackness we could still see Morgawse, but as if she were the centre of that blackness, though she seemed ghastly pale, standing beyond the brink of that abyss before us, painfully near, appallingly remote. Gwalchmai's sword still burned, steady as a hearth fire on a winter night, or a candle standing before an altar: but his shoulder beneath my hand was knotted with effort, hard and cold as any stone.

'And what is Light?' asked Morgawse the Queen. Her voice was thin and cold, not a woman's voice, not a human voice. 'All things began in Darkness, and all things will return to Darkness, though you may struggle your brief moment on the edge of the abyss. All things are touched and shot through with Darkness. See how in this present age the darkness engulfs the world: Rome has fallen, and all the West has followed her. Can a little light hope to live in Camlann? Darkness has gripped the hearts of all who fight for Light. The heart of Rhuawn your friend has listened to it; Arthur your lord has obeyed its impulse; it holds its place in your own heart. All must fall back to the Darkness, break and return to where it began. Night comes, and there will be no day again. Light is illusion; Darkness alone is true and strong. Know this!'

For a moment the light from Gwalchmai's sword seemed to grow paler, fainter, seemed to illuminate nothing. I felt him stir, bracing himself. I wished to cry out to him, tell him to leave the struggle and flee, if there was anywhere we could flee to. But I could neither move nor speak. My body seemed locked in chains of ice, and my mind was full of darkness. Dear God, I thought, only let me see the sun before I die. Only let there be something besides the darkness.

'And God said, "Let there be light", and there was light,' replied Gwalchmai, his voice ringing clear and strong and glad. 'Though Rome has fallen, and though Camlann should fall; though I, and Arthur and Rhuawn have been shaken by Darkness to our souls, you cannot shake the stars, or call back the March winds when the spring breathes upon the orchards. Light is the first-born of Creation, by Light and in Light the world was formed, and Darkness is only that which Light illuminates, not force, but only its absence.'

Morgawse flung her arms above her head, the blackness

moving about her like water, her eyes distended and unnatural. Medraut's sword moved up like a wisp of shadow, and I glimpsed him, saw that he knelt before Morgawse on both knees now. In a high flat voice the Queen cried in a strange language, syllables I had not thought a human tongue could shape, sounds that made me want to cover my ears. Gwalchmai staggered, dropped to his knees. His eyes were shining in the light from the sword, his face streaked with sweat or tears. I crouched behind him, afraid to stand, to move, to breathe. I watched Gwalchmai's hands on the sword shaking, saw the blood from his left hand trickling across the blade. The light flickered.

Morgawse cried again. I saw that Medraut's head was bowed as if in exhaustion, but still he held the sword up, his arms shaking as though it were a terrible weight. At Morgawse's voice the night flowed upon us like a wave cresting, breaking. For an eternal instant I could see nothing at all, nothing but a faint glimmer where the sword had been, dimming as though it were receding into the dark.

But the glimmer did not vanish. It brightened, faded again, brightened and continued to brighten. I felt Gwalchmai tense, gather his strength, rise. The darkness ebbed, fading, and with a shock I realized I could see the beaten earth floor of the hut. I would not have exchanged that sight for any rose garden on the green earth.

The Queen held her hands out, palms towards Gwalchmai, mouth framing words that came without sound. But the light stirred again in the blade, grew bright, clearer, the crimson brightening to rose, glowing almost white. The Queen managed to cry out one last time, but the darkness was fading. Medraut gave one sob and collapsed on the ground at his mother's feet. His sword fell on the earth before him, and the darkness vanished. The room was filled with scintillating light from the sword, light that broke like sunbeams through unquiet waters.

Gwalchmai drew his left hand away, his palm bloody from clasping the blade, then lowered his right arm, the sword swinging level again. The light faded to a ripple along the steel.

Morgawse lowered her arms and stared at us over Medraut's motionless body. Her crimson gown was crumpled, and the corners of her lips and eyes drooped. For the first time I saw lines in her face and white in her hair, and I knew that, like any other woman, she grew old. I turned away and unlatched the door. The mountain breeze was sliding along the heather, and the last of the sunset transfigured the mountains.

Gwalchmai's hand dropped to my arm a moment, fell away. 'Let us go,' he said, quietly, and, to Morgawse, 'Mother, much health.'

'No!' shrieked Morgawse. She stumbled forward, nearly tripped over Medraut. 'No!' in desperation. I turned my back and stepped out the door, and Gwalchmai followed silently. 'No, no!' she cried again, and began to sob. 'Do not leave me, I beg you! Still I am powerful, I can recover – give me time, a few days only . . .' And I thought she no longer spoke to us, but to some demon she had long served; but I did not look back. Behind me Gwalchmai gently closed the door.

Twelve

It was not as easy to leave as I had assumed. Beside Morgawse, Medraut's six mounted warriors had seemed an insignificant detail; but when we were outside and facing the road home I realized that six armed men are never insignificant. We went only a little way down the hill before Ronan saw us and began giving us orders in Irish, presumably to stop and go back. Gwalchmai gave a high, clear whistle, and Ceincaled cantered about the hill to him as he started to argue with the other. I should have expected that he had the stallion nearby. Medraut's men leapt onto their own horses, and Gwalchmai was fighting them before either of us had time to think about what was happening. The fight was not, however, fiercely contested. Medraut's men were nervous to begin with, and when Gwalchmai put a spear through Ronan, then drew his sword and cut down one other man, the rest turned their horses and fled. Too much had already happened for me to think or feel much about it. I simply caught Ronan's warhorse, mounted, and Gwalchmai and I set off. The first stars were kindling in the east.

'My lord,' I said, after a few minutes. 'We are taking the same path the Queen's warriors took. How far do you mean to follow them?'

He shook his head. He looked drained, haggard with weariness and strain – as he ought to, after what had happened in the hut. 'We do not follow them. They have friends in Degannwy. Let them hurry to reach the fortress. We must find a place to camp tonight.'

I nodded, then asked, 'How did you find me? What has happened in Degannwy?'

He raised his left hand in a gesture of protest, then frowned at the blood on it. 'Please,' he said, lowering the hand and staring at it. 'It is late tonight. There is too much to ask and to answer, for both of us, to do it now. The morning will come soon enough.'

We did not go very far that night. We turned north on the road to Degannwy, riding towards the main road since we

481

did not trust our welcome at the fortress. But we turned aside shortly before the Roman road and found a good, sheltered camping place in a wood. There we built a fire and hobbled our horses, turning them loose to graze.

The air held a sharp chill, and it seemed damp in the wood. I did not anticipate sleeping well. But I could not consider looking for shelter at some farm holding nearby. Something of Gwalchmai's wariness had forced itself upon me, and I could not trust the world at large. I thought of my family, and suddenly felt horribly lonely. Morgawse was defeated, Gwalchmai still alive, and it was all too much for me. These vast conflicts were too absolute and lofty and remote from the texture of my life. I wanted home, the cow byres and the fields green with new grain, the warmth of the hearth fire and the voices and faces of my family: I was sick with the want of them. Sitting there in a wood in Gwynedd, with the huge mountains brooding around me, I thought of everything familiar and longed with all my being to go home.

Gwalchmai came over to the fire with his saddle-bags, and the hilt of his sword caught the light for an instant, as though about to burn of its own accord again. What, I wondered, did I have to do with him? There he was, royally born, Morgawse's son, perfectly accustomed both to dangerous battles and otherworldly conflicts. He belonged to all this. I did not, and I wanted to go home. Most simply put, I was tired.

Gwalchmai set down the pack and dropped beside the fire. 'I have some bread and cheese here,' he offered, softly. 'Also, some ale. I remembered how you liked it.' He opened the pack and handed me the ale.

I looked at the flask a moment, wanting either to laugh or sob. 'Thank you, my lord,' I said at last. He smiled and began to pull out the bread and cheese.

It was not much of a meal. I could have eaten good red meat, and the cheese was sad stuff. But I imagined Gwalchmai trying to coax it from Saidi ap Sugyn in the kitchens at Degannwy, and was amazed that he'd managed to get the ale. Saidi must have made him pay for it. If I had been there – well, but Gwalchmai was Gwalchmai, and I couldn't be annoyed with him for that. And I enjoyed the meal. Any food would have tasted delicious just then.

Despite my forebodings I slept soundly, though when I woke I found my neck stiff, my limbs aching from the damp, and my head giving the odd twinge now and then. Well, the way to cure that was to move about. I got up to find Gwalchmai saddling the horses. He gave me a smile and greeted me, and I managed to reply without being rude. The sun was just up, drawing the chill, damp mists out from the mountains, and I was glad to get on my horse and trot out onto the road. The motion at least was warming. Gwalchmai handed me the remainder of the bread and cheese, and I hacked off some of each and gave the rest back to him. I liked the food even less than I had the night before, but I was hungry. Gwalchmai apparently was too, for he finished what I'd given him, which I had not entirely expected.

We reached the main road very quickly and drew in our horses to stand for a moment, seeing how the line of it curled off into the mist. The morning sun was a brilliant blur eastward, and I thought the air should clear before too long.

Gwalchmai sighed and turned his eyes from the road over to me.

'Rhys,' he said, then stopped.

'My lord?'

'You said, yesterday, that you had found Elidan.'

So I had. I had forgotten about that. 'I have, my lord. She's at an abbey called St Elena's, the sister foundation of Opergelei monastery.'

'An abbey?'

'She's become a nun, my lord. I found her because Eivlin was struck by some curse from the Queen, and sick, and we could not go far, and this St Elena's was the nearest shelter.' I could not mention Gwyn, I reminded myself.

'Who is Eivlin?'

I realized that he must have been unaware that she existed. I thrashed about for a bit, trying to explain, and we turned down onto the road, following it westward at my direction. Then I simply told him all that had happened from the argument with Rhuawn until Eivlin had collapsed. I concluded by saying, 'I put her on the pony and went on until we met a person from this St Elena's, who showed us the way to the abbey. Elidan was working in the infirmary there, with another sister. Eivlin was still asleep when Medraut came to bring me back to the Queen, and she wouldn't wake, whatever the healers did to her. I had intended, my lord, to send you a letter and ask you to come and see if there was any way you could help her.'

'Of course,' said Gwalchmai. He looked westward along the road eagerly, his eyes very bright. 'Opergelei is near the sea; and you say that St Elena's is near it?' He touched Ceincaled to a canter. 'Elidan! To see her once more! Did you speak to her?'

Kicking my beast savagely to make it keep up, I became angry. Elidan, Elidan, but it was Eivlin who was hurt, Eivlin who'd risked her life. 'I did. But can you help Eivlin?'

He shrugged, noticed my look, and slowed Ceincaled to a walk again. 'Och ai, this is a great burden to you.'

'And it ought to be, seeing that she saved my life and that I intend to marry her.'

His startled look slowly gave way to a delighted smile. 'So that is the way of it. I am glad for you, cousin.' He looked down the road again. 'It is probable that I can help her. Or rather, that she can be helped by my being there, with the sword. I do not know. I have never practised such things. But you can have hope, and I will do all that I can — but forbear me, Rhys, because I am sick to see her: what did she say to you, Elidan?'

He was saying nothing more than the truth, I knew, when he promised to do all he could for Eivlin. But he was wild for Elidan, and could pay attention to little else. It was a hard question to answer, and I sat a while, rubbing at a spot in the saddle. Eventually, I looked back up to him. He was watching me like the hawk of his name watching an intruder. It was best to meet his gaze evenly and say only the truth. 'She was . . . angry, afraid, when she found that I was your servant, though she did not hold me responsible for what you did nine years ago. But she has not forgiven you, and I think that she has made the thing worse, in imagination, than it actually was. She grieves over her honour, which she thinks she has lost. She says that she will not forgive you, but she will see you.'

'Ah.' he looked away. Even without repeating her bitter accusations, it was bad enough. After a while, 'Well, I will

ask her forgiveness, for all of that. And still it will be sweet
to see her again. Is she well? Does she seem happy?'

'She is in excellent health, and, if I read things correctly,
likely to be the next abbess of the place. I think she is content
with her life, and happy enough.'

It pleased him. 'I had feared that she would be reproached
all her life. It is a dreadful thing for a king's sister to be
known to have slept with the man who killed her brother.
Good. I am glad you found her.' He fell silent, beginning to
brood over what I had said.

Well content with her life, I thought, looking at him. I
remembered her suppressed smile at Gwyn when I had first
seen her. Well, she had success after a fashion, she was comfortable, and she plainly loved her son. Her life was less
ruined than Gwalchmai's, I thought. But then, she did not
really blame herself for it, and he did. I wondered how
Gwalchmai would like Gwyn, and how the boy would take
to his father. Very well, no doubt.

Perhaps Elidan would change her mind when she saw
Gwalchmai again. She had loved him very passionately
once.

Gwalchmai was rubbing his sword hand against his
thigh, and I was sure he was reconsidering all that he had
done in the light of what I had just told him, and I knew that
he would soon conclude, with Elidan, that his actions were
unforgivable. God preserve me from a conscience like his.
Partly to distract him and partly because I wanted to know,
I asked, 'How did it come about that you were with Morgawse when Medraut brought me back, my lord? Did you
find my message?'

He came back to the present, ready to be courteous.
'Your message? Oh, the sword and the brooch. Yes. Here.'
He fumbled under the collar of his own cloak and pulled out
the same brooch, still a little bent from having the sword
pushed through it. I took it, untied the knot I'd used to hold
my cloak, and secured the wool with the pin. Much better.

'Did you understand it all, then? Come, my lord, tell me
what happened at Degannwy.'

He shrugged, patted Ceincaled's neck and thought for a
moment before he began.

'I was concerned the evening when you first disappeared,' he said at last. 'Degannwy is a hard place, and many

things could have happened. I asked Rhuawn whether he had seen you, and he was affronted and uneasy. 'He was insolent to me,' he said, 'so I gave him a blow. Probably he has run off because of that.' And he told me that I should thrash you.' Gwalchmai smiled sadly. 'Ach, Rhuawn. He is a good man, brave and honourable and generous, but he is too much of a clansman and too much of a warrior, and it distorts his vision of things. Some other warriors of Maelgwn's told me that Rhuawn knocked you down in a quarrel, but no one had seen you since. I did not think you would have run off, but there was nothing to do. Yet I mistrusted Rhuawn. Medraut had lied to him and lied to him, and I no longer knew what Rhuawn might be thinking or feeling. Medraut lied to you, too, but I thought I could trust you further...' He noticed my look and added, 'Well, but you are not one to plot behind a mask or listen to fine justifications of what is not true. And perhaps, when a warrior is sent on many missions to foreign kings, even if he is honest in himself, he grows able to wear a face not his and suspect all his companions. So I mistrusted Rhuawn. I left the fortress early on the next morning, thinking you might have left the stronghold, and hoping you had left a message. And I found the message. The sword and the brooch were plain enough: Medraut had threatened you; but for a time I did not understand the hawthorn. I sat in that tree and fingered it and wondered what you could mean. And then I remembered the hawthorn flowering at Baddon, and the warcry and the Saxon shield-wall breaking, and I knew that you meant Rhuawn.' He looked at me, and I nodded. He went on. 'It darkened the sun for me. I have known Rhuawn very many years, and liked him well since the first day I joined the Family. Mistrust him as I did, I had not thought he would league with Medraut to kill or ensorcel you...'

'He didn't. I just wanted you to be wary of him.'

'So you say now. But at the time I thought he was plotting against us, with Medraut and my mother. I threw the hawthorn away and trod it into the ground, and rode back to Degannwy at a gallop, taking the brooch and the sword.

'I went to Rhuawn first; he was still in our house. I opened the door quietly and found him sitting on the bed, sharpening a spear. He gave me a greeting, cheerful but a bit forced. I only closed the door and looked at him until he asked what the matter was. Then I showed him the sword and the brooch, and told him how I had found them. He took the sword in his hands, turning it over, looking at the brooch. I said: 'There was a sprig of hawthorn bound to the sword, which I have taken to mean you. Do you claim to know nothing of this?' He set it down again, too quickly. 'I know nothing about it. Where is Medraut?' 'I do not know,' I replied, 'nor do I care: where is Rhys?' And then he accused me of not caring for my brother and for my own clan. And I said that my brother plotted against me, and Rhuawn had joined him, betraying Arthur and myself.' He paused, and added, 'I must ask his forgiveness for that word. But I was very angry. He became angry as well, but frightened. He said 'You *are* mad'; and I did not know what he meant . . .'

'It's what Medraut had been suggesting to us,' I said. I had not told him the details of the quarrel. He gave me a sharp look and I added, 'Medraut said that the Darkness was all a delusion of yours, born of the same madness that touches you in battle. He made it sound very plausible.'

'So that is it. Rhuawn refused to talk to me. I asked him about the hawthorn again, and he said that the whole message was two-edged nonsense and impossible to interpret, and that anyone might have stolen the brooch and left it. I do not think he believed it, but his honour was at stake because I had accused him of treachery. I finally told him that I would seek out Medraut. He angrily insisted on joining me.

'Medraut did not return until afternoon. I think my mother must have worked to heal his head and then left while it was still night, because she was already at the fortress, and he came back alone. We caught him before he could slink into his house, while he was still leading his horse into its stall in the stables. I gave him the sword, saying, 'This is yours, I think.' He took it, stared at it, and I think he was troubled, but then he smiled, trying to be charming. 'It is indeed,' he said. 'I lost it yesterday afternoon. I was looking for it; where did you find it?' I told him, and he shook his head. 'But Rhys was not there?' he asked me. 'Very strange.' He looked at Rhuawn and said, 'Rhys wanted to leave the fortress and had a quarrel with some of Maelgwn's men at the gate, and they followed him to stop him. I heard about it and went after, but the men thought he had been insolent to them and were stubborn and we came to blows. I was hit on the head, and I do not know what happened to Rhys after. Perhaps this was left by one of Maelgwn's men.'

'Rhuawn heard this tale with attention, and, after a moment's pause, nodded eagerly. I saw that he would accept it. But I asked Medraut which men of Maelgwn's had been responsible. He named names without hesitation, but he would not meet my eyes. And I knew that he lied, but that he could have the men he had named ready to join him in the lie within an hour, and that there was nothing I could do to stop him. So I let him keep the sword, and told him that I did not believe his tale, and left him there with Rhuawn. But Degannwy was unsafe for me, and I thought in my heart that I would leave as soon as I was able to without giving insult to Maelgwn.

'However, Agravain arrived from Camlann that night, and . . .'

'Agravain?' I asked in astonishment.

Gwalchmai nodded, tiredly. 'Agravain wanted to come when first my lord Arthur received news from me. He wanted to see our father. Arthur was reluctant to allow him to come, fearing that he would be forced into a position where his loyalties were divided; but eventually my lord yielded, and Agravain rode from Camlann to Degannwy as fast as his horses could take him. He arrived that night. The feast hall was very loud and ugly that night, with Maelgwn's men and my father's about to quarrel, and plenty of mead poured out to help them. But when Agravain burst into the hall it was like lighting a lamp in a dark place. Agravain was always popular with Lot's warband, and everyone murmured as he came up the hall. But my brother paid no attention to anyone but Lot. He walked directly to him, and they embraced the way friends do after a battle, when each has thought the other dead and devoured by wolves. But Lot and Agravain were always close: their wills held the same rhythm and they delighted in the same joys. When Arthur demanded Agravain as a hostage for my father's peace, it was a heavy grief to Lot, a thing that stole the colour from the earth.' Gwalchmai hesitated, then went on, 'My father always intended Agravain to be king of the Islands after him, and the royal clan and the warband had always favoured him, he was so plainly what a warrior should be. Now . . . I do not know. But after embracing our father he turned to me, and then greeted all the men in the warband with great delight. My father had him sit on his own right and called for a harper. It was very good to see my father so. He became more what he used to be. He began by asking Agravain about Arthur, and then about all our battles; and then they talked war and hunting and laughed together. But Medraut left shortly after Agravain arrived. He bowed to Lot, and said that his head ached from its pounding, and that he must lie down. I did not like the fact that he left, and I was sure he went to tell Morgawse that Agravain had come, if she didn't know already – but, on the other hand, it seemed likely that his head did ache, and I had no desire to leave the feast hall myself.

'My father and Agravain also left the hall early, to talk, my father with his hand on my brother's shoulder. Their gladness was as sharp and bright as a sword's edge, and it cut me to joy when I looked at them. I have never been able to be what my father wanted, but Agravain . . . well, it was very good. So I watched them go, and smiled as I watched them, and it was the last time I saw my father living.'

I stared at Gwalchmai in shock. I had not imagined that anything so huge could have happened to him. He looked down the road without turning, tapping the fingers of one thin, strong hand against his knee. 'My lord . . .' I said.

He shook his head. 'It is better so. Dear God, Lot could not go on thus. He was a proud, strong man, and he knew where he had fallen to. Better to have died now, than years from now; best to have died before this.' I looked away from him. Whether or not one was close to him, whether or not it was a good time, a father dead is a piece of one's universe missing. He couldn't feel what I would, if it were my father, but he felt something nonetheless, and I did not think he wanted me saying anything about it.

He began the tale again. 'Agravain was with him when it happened. He said Lot stopped in the midst of a sentence, clutched at his head, cried out and fell over. Agravain tried to help him, then ran back to the feast hall to fetch me, but there was nothing either of us could do. And there was a sense of Darkness in that room to chill the heart's blood, with my father lying stiff and grey by the hearth. I knew how he came to die so quickly.'

'Morgawse?' He still did not look towards me, but he nodded. His face was intensely expressionless. 'But why?'

He gave a shrug. 'I think she feared that Agravain would cause difficulties in her affair with Maelgwn. And also, Agravain was a rival to Medraut in winning the loyalty of the warband and the succession to the kingship of Orcade. But I am as certain that she blotted out my father's life as I am certain that the sun sets to rise. If I had thought sooner, when Medraut left the hall! But he was dead. We laid him on a bier to mourn him, and raised the coronach – that is an Irish dirge – by torchlight, most of the night. Agravain was wild: he flung himself beside the corpse and swore ... what is the matter?'

'Nothing,' I said. 'Just a dream. Go on.'

He gave me a steady, serious look. 'I remember that your father also has dreams. I would be grateful if you could tell it me.'

'Only that the day after your father died I dreamed that I saw the Queen casting a spell, and then a funeral procession with a covered body on a bier and Agravain as a mourner. I thought the body was yours. But go on.'

He nodded, apparently calmer about it than I was. 'Agravain swore that any person who had any part in killing Lot should die by his sword, and that Lot was the greatest king in all Erin, and all Britain, and all the Islands.'

'What about Arthur?'

'Arthur is not a king; he is High King,' my lord replied, a very faint smile touching his lips and vanishing again. 'Well, we stayed up all the night. When the first sun made the world breathe again, Agravain took me aside. That was yesterday morning. I felt as though the day were made of fine, bright, brittle glass and might shatter at any instant. I could tell from Agravain's eyes that it was the same to him if the sun rose or if it was swallowed by the earth for ever. 'Mother did this,' he said. I shook my head. 'Do not seek to deny it or explain it away; you know as surely as I that she killed him, she and that white-haired bastard half-brother of ours ...'

I was a bit shocked. 'Can't he accept that Lot was

Medraut's father as well?' I asked.

Gwalchmai gave me a very startled look. 'But he wasn't. Everyone knows that.'

I felt stupid and confused. 'I didn't know that. Why do you say so?'

'Everyone always knew. Medraut was born in Britain. My father came down to do some fighting in the north, and he left my mother at the court of her father, the Pendragon Uther. My father was gone from May until December, and Medraut was born in the next June. And besides that . . .' He stopped himself sharply.

'You know who his father is?' I asked, even more astonished.

He said nothing, shaking his head. 'But you do,' I insisted.

'Yes, I know. But let it rest there, Rhys *mo chara*. Ach, it is not that I do not trust you, but that secret is not mine to give away.'

'But who . . . does Medraut's father know?'

'He knows. But there is nothing he can do. Morgawse always had plans for Medraut. I do not think that Medraut knows, though, and he is happier so. Let it rest.'

We rode on silently for a little while. I tried to adjust the fact that everyone had always known Medraut to be a bastard into my picture of him; and then, for some strange reason, I thought of the Emperor Arthur, his straight fair hair and wide-set grey eyes. But no, Arthur was Morgawse's half-brother, and it was impossible.

'So, Agravain spoke very wildly,' Gwalchmai continued. 'He made me afraid for him. Our mother never liked him, and he is defenceless in too many ways to defy her openly. The rest of our father's warband knew it. It is strange: I could have sworn that Medraut held that warband to command it as he pleased, but it was plain to me that most of the men would follow Agravain, if Morgawse were not there. They never liked Morgawse, but they feared her greatly. Enough men have defied her only to disappear from the green earth for any of them to disobey her. But they hated to be ruled by a foreign woman and a witch, and Medraut was too near her and too close to her for their tastes. Many of the men had fought beside Agravain many years ago, and they wanted to be loyal; but they would not dare to support him against Morgawse.

'Maelgwn Gwynedd came to see Lot's corpse, and ordered the rest of Degannwy into mourning, from sympathy, but it was clear that he was pleased that our father was dead, and expected to have the warband and my father's possessions freely his. Agravain wanted to kill him at once. It is a good thing that Maelgwn speaks no Irish, or there would have been a fight between the warbands on the spot. As it was, I had to calm Agravain, and stay with him for hours. Finally I promised him that I would go and talk to our mother, and I made him promise not to act until I was done with that.

'I had been intending to see her since I first realized that Medraut and Rhuawn would give me no information about what had happened to you, but I'd looked for a public place to catch her in. Now, I knew, I had to speak with her privately. Medraut had vanished – I suppose he was off fetching you. I did not know what to do.

'Then, in the middle of the afternoon, Rhuawn came and sought me out. I left Agravain for a little and talked with him instead. He gave me a very strange look and said, 'So you have care for some of your family.' I replied, 'I have care for all of them, as far as I may for each, but some are my enemies. Medraut has hated me since I left the islands, and hated our lord Arthur even longer. Why have you listened to him?' He grew cold again. 'Medraut is not your enemy nor mine,' he said. 'He left Degannwy out of trouble over your father's death. But he sent me a message to say that he has found Rhys.' 'Where?' I asked. 'At a shepherd's hut, up in the mountains. He is hurt. Medraut says he wants you to come. I can show you the way there, this evening.'

'I almost agreed. I was tired, and my father's death made me want to see Medraut again. It is true, that much of what he told you, that we were close once. That is probably why he hates me so deeply now, because he truly feels that I have betrayed him. And Rhuawn was asking me to come with him, and I had already resolved to face my mother, so why should I fear Medraut alone? But as I was about to say that I would go then, I suddenly felt that Rhuawn was too quiet, and I recalled your message. I looked at his face, and it was as though I glimpsed another's face reflected there, like the bottom of a pond glimpsed through the bright mirror of its waters. So, instead of agreeing, I said, 'Perhaps. Speak to me again this evening.' Rhuawn gave me a cold look and left without another word, and I went back to Agravain. You have told me that Rhuawn was not as guilty as I first thought, and now I do not know how much he understood when he made that suggestion, and how much he believed Medraut. I had said some most bitter things to him the day before, and I do not know how far my anger may have driven him. He is not a wicked man.'

'He knew better than to betray you,' I said. 'He knew you for years, and by your life and actions, and he knew Medraut only by his words, and that for a few weeks only. A man may be deluded by another's eloquence, but, by all the saints in Heaven, anyone with any sense ought to know better than to accuse a sane friend of madness.'

Gwalchmai only shook his head. 'Rhuawn is a good man... At any rate, when he had left, I thought for a time, and decided that I wished to see for myself what was happening. As you know, I have done a good amount of riding, and I knew of several shepherds' huts which Rhuawn might have meant. But they had earlier said that you left the fortress. That meant that it was probable the place they thought of was to the north, towards the main road. I gave it some more thought, then told Agravain what I intended, and prepared myself for as long a journey as might be necessary. And the second shepherd's hut I found had my mother's horse tied up before it. The rest you know. But, cousin...' He reined in Ceincaled suddenly and caught my forearm with his sword hand, so that I had to stop too. He met my eyes very seriously, and spoke deliberately, very quietly, 'I owe you a very great debt. My mother's shadow has lain across my whole life, but now I am free of it. Yet, if you had not stopped me from killing her, she would have bound me in it for ever. That alone would give me gratitude enough for a lifetime, but you have taken this whole struggle when it was not by nature yours, and you have fought and suffered to hold the faith when...'

'My lord Gwalchmai, for God's sake no more of that! When it comes to people being saved, you saved me a good deal more than I saved you. And if the conflict between Light and Darkness is not my struggle, whose is it? I have never heard that only warriors are allowed to serve God. I've done no more than I should have.' And I looked down at the spot on the saddle leather to avoid his eyes. Ronan, or Ronan's servant, really should have cleaned that.

Gwalchmai gave my arm a slight pressure, then released it. 'Indeed?' I looked back up, matter-of-fact as I was able to be, and he smiled, then suddenly touched Ceincaled, and the horse leapt to a canter. I kicked my rather bad-tempered warhorse into following. Gwalchmai called back, 'How much further is it to this St Elena's? That beast of Ronan's is supposedly a warhorse: we ought to be making better time.'

We made good time, actually, and reached St Elena's shortly after noon. I nearly missed the turning, but managed to remember a tall ash tree, and we picked our way down the path used by Father Gilla and his mare.

We had to rap repeatedly on the high wooden gate before the little window in the top of it opened and a thin, brown-eyed face peered out. 'We've no room for travellers,' said the woman.

'We're not seeking hospitality,' I said. 'But my friend Eivlin is sick and staying with you, as I did myself until yesterday afternoon . . .'

'Sanctam Mariam Matrem! You're the one they dragged off yesterday, those terrible warriors. How is it that you're here?'

'My lord here rescued me. He's come now to help heal my friend: you can ask Sister Teleri if you doubt me.'

The face vanished and the window closed. We waited a while, me standing by the gate, Gwalchmai on Ceincaled, leaning forward with one arm across his knees. Eventually the window was flung open again and the sharp dark face of Teleri peered out.

'Rhys. It is you then.'

'It is me, returned and in one piece. And I have brought my lord here.' Teleri looked behind me for the first time, and her stare fixed. Gwalchmai leapt from his horse, paused an instant to catch his balance, then gave a slight bow.

The gate opened. 'Come in, then.' Teleri surveyed Gwalchmai with intent interest, but spoke to me. 'Your Eivlin is no better, which is what you were gaping your mouth to ask, I suppose. Ach, man. I am glad to see you whole, and to know that you gave the slip to those wild Irish devils. Can your lord help the girl?'

I shrugged. Gwalchmai, just entered through the gate

and looking about himself, answered for me. 'It is possible, though not certain. I will try.' He paused, then earnestly asked his own question, 'My servant Rhys has told me that my lady Elidan, daughter of Caw, is of your sisterhood.'

'She is,' said Teleri flatly. 'Will you see this Eivlin lass now?'

He nodded. 'Yes. Where may I leave my horse?'

With Ceincaled and my warhorse left standing in the yard, we followed Teleri into the low-roofed building. A number of nuns had already gathered about to see, and they all stared very hard at Gwalchmai. His crimson cloak and war gear marked him out very plainly. But he only gave a courteous nod to those he passed and ignored the stares. He was probably used to it.

Eivlin had been brought to one of the nun's cells, and she lay on the bed, wrapped in blankets, looking very pale and lifeless. Only her hair lay over the mattress, and one sunbeam touched it, bringing out its ripe wheat colour. It cut me to the bone to see her so, and I stopped in the doorway, so that Gwalchmai nearly bumped into me. I stared at Eivlin.

Teleri, already by the bed, looked about impatiently. 'Well, stop staring like an ox and come in,' she snapped, 'if indeed you wish to see if your lord can help her.' I started and came in, standing aside. Gwalchmai entered and walked over to the bed. He dropped to one knee, caught her wrist and laid the back of his other hand against her forehead. He frowned.

'There is no fever,' he told Teleri.

'Truly? That I found out at once.' Teleri put her hands on her hips. 'No, there is nothing wrong to be found with her, except that, for all we do, she will not wake or stir. Now, Rhys says that he baptized her, and I've heard tell that baptism is death to sin; but if so, she's been rather thorough about it.'

'Did you try giving her hot mead with mint?' asked Gwalchmai.

She looked startled and dropped her hands. 'We did. A fine shock that, to wake sleepers. But she can't swallow, and didn't stir.'

'Her heart beats very faintly.'

'And grows fainter. You have some knowledge of medicine, I think.'

'A little. Mostly the care of wounds.' Gwalchmai took his hand from Eivlin's wrist and knelt, looking at her. 'I have worked with Gruffydd ap Cynan after my lord Arthur's battles – except when I was wounded myself, of course.'

'Indeed?' asked Teleri, a different note in her voice, one perilously like respect. 'Now there is a physician I have heard much about.'

'He is very skilled.' Gwalchmai brushed a strand of hair from Eivlin's face and shifted his hand to his sword. He frowned again.

Teleri took a step closer, then knelt beside him, straightening her gown. 'Your servant Rhys ap Sion believes this sleep to be the result of a curse. I have no knowledge of curses and less liking for them as causes of sickness, but if it is not, I do not know why she does not wake.'

'It is a curse. But now – the force of the curse is gone, and only the sleep is left. The Darkness struck her very hard and deep before it vanished, and life has gone very far away from her. And yet . . .' He chewed his lower lip, then deliberately drew his sword.

Teleri looked at him sharply, one hand ready to seize his sword hand. He smiled a little, apologetically. 'I wish to try something. I do not know whether it will help or not. This sword is no common weapon, so it may.' Teleri lowered her hand, still watching him suspiciously.

Gwalchmai laid the flat of the sword across Eivlin's forehead. She did not move or stir. He shifted his grip on the hilt, settling it, nervously rubbing his mouth with his other hand. I took another step nearer to see, looking at Eivlin's pale face under the cold steel. Gwalchmai bowed his head, his shoulders hunched.

Slowly, the sword began to glow. I heard Teleri's gasp loud in the small room, but I only looked at Eivlin. The wavering, submarine light flickered down the edge of the steel, traced a sinuous line along the centre of the blade, and focused in the hilt to a deep rose shade.

Gwalchmai dropped his free hand to his thigh, bracing himself. 'Dulce Lux,' he said clearly, but almost to himself, 'Care Domine, miserere . . .' and, changing his languages, 'O Ard Rígh Mor . . .' He straightened his shoulders, and the light shot down the sword, flaming into white brilliance. 'Lighten our darkness, we pray you, Lord...'

'Amen,' said Teleri, wondering. I barely heard her, for at that moment Eivlin drew a deep breath. I dropped down behind the other two and reached between them to catch her hand. Her fingers were cold, but I had a shock from them like the shock one gets in cold, dry weather. Gwalchmai caught the sword's hilt in both hands, sweat streaming into his beard, and threw his head back, eyes focused on nothing. He said something in Irish, poetry I think, his voice almost singing it. Eivlin's breast heaved, and I thought the colour was returning to her cheeks.

'Eivlin!' I said, and she opened her eyes, looked over the sword and the other two, and saw me.

'Rhys!' she answered, and pushed away the sword to sit up. The light flashed out, and Gwalchmai bowed his head, letting the blade drop to the floor. He held the hilt limply with both hands.

'Rhys,' repeated Eivlin, and got out of the bed. 'What is all this? You should not be up like this, with your head. What have you done with the pony?'

'Eivlin.' It was all I could say.

'Eivlin, Eivlin, he says. But what has happened? Where are we? I have had a nightmare and a sweet dream, and then you wake me from the second with your "Eivlin", and we are nowhere. Ach, how is your poor head?'

Teleri laughed, and Eivlin looked at her for the first time, then let her eyes slip to Gwalchmai. They widened, very blue, and she looked back to me. 'It was not a nightmare, was it?' she said. She began to shake a little, and I got up and put my arm around her. 'My lady sent a ... but I am alive! We are alive, and it is gone! Did you work that Christian sorcery of yours?'

'Well, I did,' I replied.

Teleri gave me a very dubious look, and stood up briskly. 'The man says that he baptized you. In a most irregular fashion, near drowning the both of you, which is not required. And you have slept for two days, and would have slept for ever, if this lord had not woken you.'

Eivlin looked to Gwalchmai again and turned crimson. 'I thank you, lord Gwalchmai ap Lot.'

Gwalchmai looked up, then slowly stood, sheathing his

sword. 'Any service I have rendered you is slight in comparison with the great gift you have given to me and to my servant Rhys, in risking your life to oppose the Queen my mother.'

She flushed an even deeper red. 'I did not save him for you, but for myself.'

'I know. He has already told me that you plan to marry.'

She whirled on me, and I felt my face grow hot. 'Indeed, Rhys ap Sean? And when did you ask me if I would marry you?'

'I . . . well, it merely came out so, when I was speaking to my lord.'

'You should not be saying such things without asking first. It is I that you would marry, not your lord.'

'I – I . . . does that mean you won't?'

'Now, did I say that?' She looked proudly at the wall, crossing her arms. 'Think yourself, though, how it is to be told that you are going to be married, and not knowing it. Indeed!'

'Forgive me. Will you, then?' I had not meant to ask her so bluntly, but I had to, to appease her.

She gave me a very bright look. 'It may be so.' And then she threw her arms around me and said, 'Och, Rhys, Rhys *mo chroidh ban*, I am alive!' She began to cry. I stroked her hair and patted her on the back, carefully not looking at Teleri or Gwalchmai.

Teleri coughed. 'The girl should have something to eat.' Eivlin did not move. I didn't want her to, either. Teleri sighed. 'Well, then, I will find Elidan, and we will bring her something.'

'Elidan,' said Gwalchmai. Without looking up, I could sense how his eyes fixed on Teleri.

'Yes, your lady, Elidan,' Teleri said, then, rather sadly, 'you may speak to her, but I do not think she will wish to speak long.'

'If all she will give me is a short while, it will be enough.'

Teleri's light steps lingered in the doorway, and I knew she nodded; and then they passed on down the passageway. I glanced up. Gwalchmai moved over to the doorway and leaned there, looking out, and I could turn my attention back to Eivlin.

Eivlin stopped crying and began to demand to know

where we were and what had happened. I got as far as telling her about Medraut, when Gwalchmai stiffened, moved aside, and Teleri returned with a tray of food. Elidan entered, slowly, behind her.

Teleri set the food down by the bed. Elidan merely stood, calm, straight, looking at Gwalchmai.

He dropped sweepingly to one knee. 'My lady.'

She faced him, eyes narrowing a trifle. 'Lord Gwalchmai.' She glanced over to us. 'I am glad you succeeded in healing this girl.'

'It is cause enough for gladness. But, my lady, I have searched for you over all Britain. Allow me the favour of speaking what I have long desired to say to you.'

Her face did not change. 'You wish to ask my forgiveness – or so your servant says.'

'Yes.' He bowed his head, his hand tightening on his sword hilt.

Eivlin, staring in astonishment, glanced quickly at me. I shook my head. I did not want to stir; we were quite outside any of this, and I think all of us sensed it.

'Lady,' Gwalchmai began, when Elidan's silence became too heavy to bear, 'I know that I wronged you. I treated your love, which was beyond price, as a thing of little value, and I brought dishonour upon you before your clan and your kingdom. I swore you an oath, and broke it, and I killed your brother, disregarding both you and my own lord's command. These things are true, and surely they give me need of repentance. They have grieved me, since first I realized what I had done, more bitterly than any wound. And because you did not know this, I felt I must say it to you, that I know it was wrong, and that . . .' he stopped.

'You would say?' asked Elidan.

'That I loved you then, and love you now, and I beg that you, of your own nobility, pardon the wrong.'

'That is not nobility,' said Elidan. Her voice was even, but rough with strain. She clenched her hands by her sides, unclenched them, drew a deep breath. 'I never thought to see you again, after you left Caer Ebrauc. I never believed you regretted your crime. I believe you now, that you regret it, and . . . it helps. And yet . . .' She turned from him, braced herself against the wall. 'When first I knew that you had betrayed me, I thought I would go to my brother

Hueil and ask him for vengeance. But I knew that that request would destroy him, as the desire for vengeance had destroyed Bran; and I could not do that. Against my own desire, I bore the wrong without striking back, accepted dishonour, and left Caer Ebrauc. Slowly I came to accept the shame as my own penance for assenting to sleep with my brother's murderer, and I accepted the helplessness. You must accept the same.'

'My lady . . .'

'No!' she turned back to him, and there were tears on her face now. 'No! I once said I would kill myself before I would let you come near me again; and though I have bent that oath for this, I have not broken it, nor will I break it. I am not your lady; I am Elidan of St Elena's Abbey, and nothing to do with you.'

He looked up at her then, and her face did move. She bit her lip, as in pain, jerking her hands up as though she would press them against her face, forcing them down again. 'No,' she repeated, in a whisper this time. 'The sight of you is like a knife to my heart, and makes me remember things I would rather forget: love, too much love; and betrayal and callousness and murder and dishonour. Go away.'

'I know the truth of my own will in this,' Gwalchmai replied in a low voice. 'I will go, if you desire it. But can you not be merciful?'

She shook her head. 'I cannot be weak. I will not believe you and accept you again. I trusted you once, and was betrayed, and I will not be made a fool of again. It is a lie. The world is a lie, its beauty a deceit. I trusted it once, and I will not do so again. Such honour as I have, I will keep, here, and so let the rest perish, miserably as it is evil. I must be strong; I am the sister of a king, daughter of kings . . .' She gave a long sob, looking at him desperately. 'For God's sake, go!'

Gwalchmai bowed his head once more. 'As you will.' He stood, and said quietly, 'Rhys, I will wait for you by the horses. When you and Eivlin have decided when you wish to leave, come and tell me, and we will arrange the travelling. Elidan . . .' He lifted one hand towards her, then dropped it. 'I wish you joy.' He gave a bow which included all in the room, and left. The quiet was heavier than a tombstone.

500

Elidan sat on the bed and buried her face in her hands, shoulders shaking again.

'You're a fool,' said Teleri.

The other shook her head.

'Child, you love him yet, and he loves you to doting. What are you wanting, to refuse to forgive him?'

'I love him,' Elidan said in a muffled voice. 'I had not thought I did. I thought it was all dead within me and yet ... but oh God, God, how can one trust the world? What would my clan say?'

'Your clan!' That brought an edge of contempt in Teleri's voice. 'What does that matter?'

Elidan looked up, her face wet, eyes terribly steady. 'They would be right. One cannot make peace with the world.'

'If one cannot forgive evils, how is anyone to live?'

'I must be strong,' Elidan said to herself, ignoring Teleri. 'Thank God I was strong ... The world's evils are the truth of the world. Let it fall back into the night it came from!'

Her words suddenly recalled another voice, a thin, cold, inhuman voice saying 'All must fall back to the Darkness ... Light is illusion, Darkness is true and strong.' The memory made me shake. 'Lady,' I said, slowly, 'that is not a very Christian thing to say.'

She stood, eyes chilling, still wet with tears. 'Be quiet!' she said, her tone that of a king's daughter. 'Let me alone!' And she fled the room, slamming the door behind her.

Teleri looked at the closed door, her face worn and old and very sad. 'And what have you shut yourself away from in honour, I wonder,' she whispered, to herself. 'You know, poor lady, but you will not yield for all that. You want to shut it all out, but you've only shut yourself in, and oh, child, will you ever get out again?' She shook her head, then turned to Eivlin with a shadow of her usual briskness. 'Come. I've brought you some sausages, and oat cakes with honey. You must eat them all, for you're sadly in need of food and drink.'

Eivlin shook her head, still staring at the closed door.

'Eat your oat cakes, and have some of this milk,' Teleri ordered. 'There's no point in talking about it.'

The milk was drunk and the oat cakes consumed in

silence. Once she had begun eating, Eivlin discovered that she was hungry. Teleri noticed me eyeing the food, sighed, and departed to return with more, and with a little package. 'For your lord,' she said, handing the latter to me. I thanked her, wanting to say more to her than I was able, and started eating. For all the strong feelings and high commitments on earth, one still has to eat, and that bread and cheese at day-break seemed a long way off.

When Eivlin was scraping the last of the honey off the plate with a fragment of oat cake, I finally asked her when she wanted to leave.

'Now.' She popped the crumb into her mouth and dusted her hands off.

'Ach, don't be silly,' said Teleri. 'You were near to death an hour ago.'

'Indeed, and perhaps I was, but now, thanks to your god and Rhys's lord Gwalchmai, I am fine again and ready to leave.'

Teleri shook her head. 'You would faint on the road.'

'I will not. I have just eaten, and I will ride a horse, and there is nothing the matter with me, since the curse is done with. I feel better than I have for long and long, and Rhys wants to leave now.'

'I didn't say anything,' I objected.

'And why should you need to, what with mooning at the door like a cow about to bellow for her calf? You've no wish to stay here with me and see your lord ride off alone.'

'I'm concerned for him,' I admitted. 'He deserved better than that.'

Eivlin looked at me evenly a moment, then shrugged. 'I think he did. He must be a fine man.'

I bit my lip and stood up. 'Eivlin, it's only for a while. If you want it, in a month or so we can go back to my clan's farm and settle there. You will have my whole clan there, and the finest holding near the Mor Hafren, and all manner of things will be well.'

Her eyes lit up. 'A sweet thing, that, to have a clan, to be no outcast and have no curse. But now. To be sure, I do not know all that has happened yet: you say it has been days, you say he freed you from Medraut and defeated my lady – a great thing that! – and now he will ride off on an unknown course. But I know enough to know that you will follow him, the more so because he has been hurt. And I will not be left behind. If I must steal a horse and ride after secretly, I will. If you are going to travel into a hostile land, with no certainty of coming back alive and whole, I swear by the sun and the wind – no, I swear by Christ – I am coming with you. We will leave now.'

Teleri shook her head. 'Neither of you should leave. Rhys ap Sion, I have not forgotten your head injury. You need the rest as much as she.'

'And Gwalchmai?' I asked. 'And if I stay here, what must I say to Elidan?'

Teleri frowned. 'There is that.'

'I do not think I am likely to be tactful to her; I think she is being a fool.'

'I do not think you are a great one for tact,' she agreed drily. 'Well, but this girl?'

'I am coming. I am not to be got rid of so easily.'

Teleri crossed her arms and frowned at Eivlin. Eivlin stared insolently back, and crossed her arms with an identical air. Teleri's lips quivered, and she fought for a moment to stop herself, but finally yielded and smiled. She sat down on the bed beside Eivlin and patted her arm. 'Less sick by far than you are wilful, my girl. But ach, I was wilful myself at your age, joining the sisters with my whole family howling at me no; and there's no harm to wilfulness in the right place. Go then, and when you've married this man of yours, be sure that the two of you aren't stubborn at the same time, for I think you and he could make the North Sea in February look like a quiet lake. Rhys, go tell your lord that we'll be out when I've found some things for Eivlin.' When I gaped, she snorted and snapped, 'Go along.'

I left, wondering. If I had looked at Teleri that way, I felt sure, I would not have convinced her of anything, but all Eivlin did was look insolent, and all was smooth sailing. The North Sea in February?

Gwalchmai was, as he had promised, waiting by the horses. He stood leaning against the abbey wall, idly stroking Ceincaled's neck while the stallion nibbled at his hair. When he saw me coming, though, he straightened, gave the horse a slap on the withers, and limped across to meet me.

'We can all leave together now – or as soon as Eivlin

comes out with Teleri,' I told him.

'But she was near to death. She cannot be ready to travel.'

'She will leave now, she says, if she must steal a horse to do so. I think she will be well enough. Any weakness she had was from hunger and weariness, and the hunger should be much better now. And, since we speak of hunger, Teleri gave me this for you.' I held out the package.

He blinked at it vaguely and made no move to take it. 'But you should wait here a few days. I can go back to Degannwy alone, and rejoin you later.'

'To Degannwy?' I stared at him. 'I thought we decided that that would be too dangerous.'

'And it would have been, arriving on the tail of Ronan's friends. Considerations of policy matter little to warbands when some of their number are newly dead. But it should be calmer now. Maelgwn should have less reason to wish for my death, with my mother defeated, and Agravain is there to calm down the warriors. I must go back to see Agravain. He knew I might be a few days, but he will not be peaceful until I am back, and I fear what he might say to Maelgwn.'

It was reasonable. Degannwy sounded safe enough. In fact... 'Very well then, we can all go to Degannwy,' I said.

He looked dubious.

'My lord, it is not far, and Eivlin can ride with me. If your elder brother has a following in Degannwy, it's safer than St Elena's here. Medraut knows where this place is, and, if he's still alive, he might track us here again.'

Gwalchmai shook his head. 'He wouldn't. I doubt he will care for anything for long and long. The image of his god was broken with my mother's power.'

'As you say, then. But we will leave, regardless. Eivlin and Teleri will be out in a minute.'

Gwalchmai shook his head tiredly, tried to object again, then suddenly smiled a slight, almost apologetic smile and threw up his hands in surrender. I wanted to clasp his shoulder, talk to him as I would have talked to my brother or my cousins, and get him to talk the pain out. But I knew he wouldn't, that he would only retreat into attentive courtesy; so I nodded and went to put Teleri's package of oat cakes into the saddle-bags of Ronan's warhorse.

Teleri and Eivlin took their time. I had an uneasy feeling that Teleri was supplying provisions for any conditions of weather or the roads, and I could picture Eivlin cheerfully packing it all. Well, Gwalchmai certainly wouldn't want to stay at Degannwy very long, and if we travelled with him we'd need anything Teleri could think of to give. Eventually the two emerged from the building carrying, as I had anticipated, a huge pack. After some struggle, Gwalchmai managed to tie this onto Ceincaled in such a way that it did not render it impossible for him to pull out his spears.

Teleri watched him check those spears, then snapped her fingers and turned to me. 'We still have that spear you brought when you first came here,' she said. 'Do you want it back now?'

I looked at her blankly.

'Come, the spear you gave Gwyn to carry!'

'Oh! That is his spear. He didn't want anyone to know he owned one, though, and so said it was mine. Perhaps you could give it back to him – secretly.'

Teleri compressed her lips, but her eyes glinted, and she nodded. I explained to Gwalchmai, carefully casual, 'Gwyn is the boy who showed me the path here. He's one of the children the abbey raises out of charity. He's marked out to be a priest, so naturally they don't want him to play with spears.'

Gwalchmai nodded and rechecked the fastenings of the pack. Teleri shot me a slantwise look, but said nothing. She understood what I was doing, and why.

Everything tied in its place, Gwalchmai turned to Teleri and bowed. 'Sister Teleri, I think the three of us owe you much.'

She snorted. 'For healing this girl and her ox of a man? What else is a woman who purports to be a healer supposed to do? But I think you intend to thank me for it.'

He smiled. 'I do so intend, if you will permit it. Most persons in your place would consider our loyalties once and immediately become enemies, and I have hurt a friend of yours. The debt we owe is the greater because of this. I cannot speak of payment, and yet...' he tore the gold armlets from his arm and offered them to her. 'If you would take these, as a token of my gratitude and your worth, I would be honoured.'

Her eyebrows went up, and she stared at the armlets, as well she might, for they were heavy and worth a good deal. She put out her hand slowly and took one. 'This I'll keep,' she said, and then, taking another, 'and this goes to satisfy the other sisters for the things I have given you. Keep the rest, Lord. You may need money. So: go, and God's blessing be upon you, with a smooth journey.'

Gwalchmai slid the remaining armlet back over his wrist, gave another bow, and mounted. I caught Teleri's arms, told her thank you, kissed her – which surprised her – and scrambled onto Ronan's horse. Teleri embraced Eivlin and helped her onto the saddle in front of me. Then she opened the gate, and we rode out from St Elena's.

We had not reached the main road when we had to make another farewell. Gwyn burst from the wood carrying a sword made of two sticks, and shouted delightedly, 'Rhys! You're safe!'

Gwalchmai reined in Ceincaled hastily as the horse shied from the movement. 'Is this the boy that led you to St Elena's?' he asked me.

'Yes, my lord,' I said, not looking at him. If only Gwyn made no mention of his mother.

'You escaped?' asked Gwyn eagerly. 'Was there a fight?'

Gwalchmai sat, tall and graceful on his splendid stallion, smiling at the dirty and enthusiastic boy. 'There was a fight,' he said. 'And Rhys and I escaped. Your name, I think, is Gwyn.'

The boy looked at Gwalchmai fully for the first time, and his dark eyes widened. I could tell that he felt, as once I had felt, that here was a song come alive. He gave a deep and extraordinarily clumsy bow. 'Y-yes, Great Lord. Are you Rhys's lord, a great warrior, in the Family?'

'I am Rhys's lord, Gwàlchmai ap Lot. I think I must thank you for showing my servant the way to St Elena's.'

Gwyn's face lit like a torch. 'It was no matter, Lord Gwalchmai.' In an undertone, 'Rhys, you didn't tell me that you served *him*.' He edged closer to me, then looked at Eivlin. 'And your friend is better, too, and everything's come out well, then!' He caught my foot and smiled radiantly at me. 'Rhys, did your lord rescue you, and kill all those evil warriors, like in the songs, with a fiery sword?'

I shook my head. 'Not all of them. Only some of them.'

The thought delighted him. 'I wish I had been there. I can throw spears. I would have fought them when they came, only ... His face fell. I remembered Elidan falling under the blow from the flat of Medraut's sword.

'Perhaps when you're older,' I said.

'I would have fought them,' Gwyn said fiercely. 'I wish they had let me. I had nightmares last night. I dreamt they were doing terrible things to you, and to Mama.'

'I'm sorry,' I said, awkwardly.

He smiled again. 'It was all right. I screamed so that I woke everyone up, and Mama gave me warm milk and sang to me until I went back to sleep; she hasn't done that since I was little.'

Gwalchmai laughed, and Gwyn remembered him, and went awkward again. 'I am glad you rescued him, Lord Gwalchmai.'

'You may be glad that he rescued me, as well, for he did that.' Gwyn gave me a highly impressed look, fastened his eyes back on Gwalchmai. My lord leaned forward, resting one arm across his knees. 'I think you lost a spear in helping Rhys.'

Gwyn nodded regretfully. 'A good one. Hywel gave it to me. I can make other ones, but I don't know how to make the points properly.'

'Perhaps you will get it back when you go home.' Gwalchmai drew one of his throwing spears from its strap and extended it towards Gwyn, butt end first. 'But in case you do not, take this.'

Gwyn took it slowly, scarcely daring to breathe. He clutched it tightly. 'Thank you, Lord Gwalchmai.' He made another attempt at a bow.

'You keep it carefully,' I said. My voice was too harsh; well, better that than to have it shaking. 'Practise with it. Become a good warrior, and then come to Camlann. The Emperor Arthur himself was a bastard raised in a monastery. It can be done.'

Gwalchmai gave me a surprised look. 'Study well, too,' he advised Gwyn. 'To be a priest is a noble thing, and I've heard that you're to be one.'

Gwyn shrugged off the notion, stroking the spear. 'I'm going to be a warrior. Do you really think I can be?' – earnestly, and to me.

'Yes,' I said firmly, 'If you work at it.'

Gwalchmai smiled, gathering up his reins. 'Well, the best of fortunes to you, then, and a welcome to Camlann, if you come there. Again, my thanks.' He touched Ceincaled's sides, and the horse started off at a trot. I followed, riding past Gwyn, who watched us with an exalted face, clutching his spear. When we had gone up the path a short way, I heard a triumphant whoop behind us and looked back to see him dashing down the path.

Gwalchmai was still smiling. 'He is a brave and spirited lad, that one. But you cannot think, Rhys, that he will come to Camlann.'

'He might.' I did not look at my lord. I could sense his curious glance, so I added, 'I like the boy, from what I've seen of him. I think he's being wasted at St Elena's. It makes me angry.'

Gwalchmai nodded again. From the way his smile faded as we rode on I could see that he was again thinking of Elidan. It made me bitter sick to think of him carrying that burden all his life, and sicker to think of Gwyn. But there was no answer for it. The world's a mixture, and something always goes wrong. And, on the whole, something at the back of my mind insisted, I would rather be Gwalchmai than Elidan. I did not think she would forget now, and, as Teleri had said, she was shutting herself in to shut the world out, and her spirit was too fierce to be content with that darkness.

Thirteen

The second time we entered Degannwy was like the first in
that it was again dark by the time we arrived, and
Maelgwn's guards again made us wait at the gates. Eivlin
jeered at the one who was sent to Maelgwn, which made
him walk off stiffly but in more of a hurry. I tightened the
arm I had round her waist. There should be no reason for
them to talk to Maelgwn. Perhaps they were only doing it
to annoy us. Eivlin leaned back a little into my arms, comfortably smiling. She at least seemed unweakened by the
journey. After I had managed to make Gwalchmai eat some
of Teleri's provisions, I had given Eivlin the rest, so she'd
no cause to go fainting from hunger.

Maelgwn's guard returned, another warrior with him.
The guard nodded, and we were allowed through the gate,
but the other warrior caught Ceincaled's bridle as soon as
we entered. He addressed Gwalchmai in Irish.

'What is he saying?' I asked, whispering into Eivlin's ear.

She tilted her head back, looking at me. 'He's asking
whether your lord will come at once to see the lord Agravain . . . he says that Agravain locked himself into his room
last night, and has spoken to no one since.'

Gwalchmai questioned the other, and he responded.
Eivlin continued to translate: 'Your lord says he will come
at once, but asks if my lady, or his other brother, are also
there. Brenaínn – that's the warrior – says that Medraut is
here, but that he also has locked himself into his room, since
last night. My lady has not returned. Brenaínn is afraid, and
he says he mistrusts Maelgwn.'

I didn't like the sound of it. Agravain, little as I liked him,
was still a security for us when he held control, but it did not
sound as though his control extended very far at the moment. I had thought Morgawse soundly defeated, but what
if she'd recovered? And I did not like the sound of Medraut shutting himself into his room and doing God alone
knew what. And that fox Maelgwn Gwynedd still held
Degannwy and all the lands about, and all his men still hated
Arthur and the Family. It might be better to exercise discre-

tion and investigate before we entered the stronghold.

Gwalchmai, however, thanked the warrior and trotted Ceincaled up the hill, head held high. I sighed and followed.

Agravain had apparently been given one of the anterooms of the feast hall, a more honourable location than our hut, though probably less comfortable. We had to pass through the hall itself to reach it. There was no proper feast that night, but Maelgwn and some of his warriors sat morosely about the high table, drinking. Gwalchmai paused to go up the hall and greet the king.

Maelgwn smiled unpleasantly. 'So, you are back then, just as my guard reported. With your servant, too. Well, well, some here are going to lose money.' Someone snickered, and Maelgwn eyed his warriors viciously. 'Myself included, then. There was high wagering that you would not return. Where is the lady, your mother the Queen?'

Gwalchmai shook his head. 'That I do not know. I last saw her yesterday. Ask of my brother Medraut.'

Maelgwn chuckled. I realized that he was drunk. 'I would have done that very thing, but no one can ask anything of your brother Medraut, any more than of your brother Agravain – or of your father Lot, though he may be in a different category. A most silent family. Do your affairs prosper? Tell me, is it true that you are a sorcerer?'

'It is not true,' Gwalchmai nearly snapped.

'Ah. I wondered, you see. You and your mother, at odds, and both . . . you ought to be a sorcerer. You look so much like her, and I think your family's bespelled. But if you see your mother, tell her I am waiting, hm? – but now you wish to talk to your brother, to your elder brother, since you will not speak to the younger. Go ahead.'

Gwalchmai bowed, freezingly courteous, and strode off to find Agravain.

The door, round the side of the feast hall, was certainly locked. My lord rapped on it, knocked again. No reply. He called, 'Agravain?' Silence. I shuffled my feet, about to suggest that Eivlin and I go off somewhere else, when I remembered that we were not safe in Degannwy. A pity. I had no wish to meet Agravain if he was in one of his rages.

Gwalchmai called again. After a moment came a sound of movement, then a short, cold command, in Irish.

'"Go away,"' Eivlin translated. I nodded. I had guessed.

'Agravain. It is me. What is the trouble?'

'Gwalchmai?' came from behind the door.

'Who else?'

An oath, footsteps; the door was flung open and Agravain stood in it staring at us. He was not a pleasant sight. He wore a mail-shirt over a badly crumpled tunic, and carried a naked sword. His bright hair and beard were matted and filthy, his eyes blood-shot and darkly circled. He had bitten through his lower lip, and the blood was smeared across his chin and cheek. He stared at Gwalchmai as though he couldn't recognize him.

'Agravain!' My lord stepped into the room, catching his brother's arms. 'God in Heaven, what has happened?'

'I killed her,' said Agravain in a horse, flat voice. 'I killed her, Gwalchmai. But she deserved it. She ... she ... och ochone, where have you been?'

'Never mind that, man, sit down. Rhys, find some mead.' Gwalchmai guided his brother into the room. I stood a moment before the door, then ran to find the mead. Eivlin looked at the other two, at me, then picked up her skirts and followed me, shouting, 'Rhys! Wait!' I stopped, waited until she caught up, and we went on together. We said nothing to each other.

Saidi ap Sugyn in the kitchens was not pleased to see either of us, but he had learned better than to argue with us. He gave us the mead, with some bread and ham I requested. If Agravain had locked himself in since the previous night, he ought to be hungry. But my brain kept repeating the words, 'I killed her'. No one needed to tell me whom he meant, and yet ... I looked at Eivlin, who was frowning deeply and carrying the bread. Her father had been under a curse for killing his brother, but this was something worse.

When we got back to the room, Gwalchmai had persuaded his brother to sit down and put the sword away, and had himself sat down beside him. He was talking, quietly and smoothly, in Irish. Agravain replied with a few incoherent words in British. My lord glanced up and nodded when I came in, so I found some goblets and poured the mead. Agravain drained his cup at once, while Gwalchmai set his down untouched. I thought Agravain had the better idea.

Agravain glared at me savagely, glanced down at the sword. Gwalchmai caught his arm again and shook him, saying, 'It is fine. Rhys is our servant; he will do no harm.'

The other shuddered and put his head in his hands. I edged over, picked up his empty cup and refilled it. When I gave it to him he drained it as quickly as he had the first, then sat staring at the bottom, clutching the empty vessel with both hands. I was afraid to disturb him. Gwalchmai signalled, so I handed him the flask of mead, and he poured more for his brother.

Agravain took only two swallows of his third cup before looking up at Gwalchmai. 'Why did you take so long coming back?'

'There were some matters of importance to me. And I had killed Ronan, you know. I could not come back at once. But you must tell me what has happened.'

Agravain began to shudder again. 'I told you. I killed her.'

'You killed our mother.' Gwalchmai's voice was clear and calm as he named the act.

'Yes. Yes. She . . . I . . . she killed Father. You know she did. She was playing the whore with that fox-haired bastard Maelgwn, so she killed Father.'

'Agravain.' Gwalchmai's hand clasped his brother's wrist, steadying, but his voice was raw with pain. 'You promised me that you would wait, that you would not act until after I had seen her.'

'Well, you went away to see her.'

'Till I'd come back, till you knew! There was no need, what have you done?'

'I killed her. She deserved it.'

'You've destroyed yourself. No, no, be still. Have some more mead.'

'I have been here, waiting for you to come back. I thought I would kill myself, at first, then I said, no, wait for Gwalchmai. Do you think they will kin-wreck me?'

Gwalchmai shook his head. 'That . . . oh. No, I think not. They may even make you king yet, and say that she was not of the blood of the clan, so that you have not murdered any kin. But *ochone, ochon, mo brathair . . .*'

'Speak British! If I try to talk of it in Irish I will go mad. It's too close to think about in Irish.' He took a deep swallow of mead and looked at his brother, more evenly now. 'I have called down the curse, haven't I? They say it is a terrible curse to kill your mother. But she deserved it.'

'But you did not, Agravain. Why did you act?'

He threw the nearly empty cup of mead across the room. 'You went out to find her. And I said, "Here am I, too cowardly to dare what my brother dares, afraid even to think of her." And then I realized, "Well, I have been afraid to think of her for years, afraid to look at her, much less fight her. But she has murdered my own father, used him up and tossed him aside and murdered him." So I got my horse and rode out. I found your tracks leaving the main road. When it was dark I found a shepherd's hut, and she was there. So was Medraut, but he was asleep. She looked very strange, as though age had touched her or her magic failed. She screamed and begged and wept and screamed. And I killed her. Medraut started waking before I could, could . . . bring down the sword; so then I had to, or he would have stopped me. So I killed her, and ran out, and came back here to wait for you. But she deserved it.'

Gwalchmai said nothing, merely embraced his brother. Agravain put his head down on the other's shoulder, clutching his arms. His shoulders shook as he began to weep. I knew that, whether or not it was dangerous to wander about Degannwy, the room was not a place for Eivlin or me. I touched her arm, and we slipped out, closing the door.

By the time I realized that I was not sure where to go, habit had brought me to the hut Maelgwn had first given us. Well, it was as good a place as any. I opened the door. Rhuawn was not there and the place needed cleaning. I went over to the hearth and built the fire up, while Eivlin sat on the bed and sliced the half loaf of bread which she'd kept. The day was too warm to warrant the fire, but the flames and the soft sound of it were comforting. When it was burning well I went and sat beside Eivlin, putting my arm about her, and we watched the smoke go up. I tried not to think of Agravain's face.

'What sort of a man was this Agravain?' Eivlin asked, after a little while.

I took a piece of the bread, thinking it over. 'A true warrior, of the sort you once told me you hated. Violent, moody, bad-tempered, though cheerful and generous enough with his equals. A fierce fighter, a fiercer feaster, and a great believer in thrashing servants to keep them in their place. God forgive me! I never liked him.'

'And now he has killed my lady, his own mother. And the thought of that act will eat into his heart, like rot eating into a wound.'

I nodded. 'My lord was right: Agravain has destroyed himself. Eivlin, my heart, it is a bitter cold thing to think of. He did not deserve it. He had enough that was noble in him: courage, honesty, great loyalty towards those he loved. You know the royal clan and the warband of the islands; do you think he will be kin-wrecked?'

'Och no. The warriors always wanted Agravain back, and spoke of him whenever they were frightened by Morgawse. King Lot had already named him as his successor. And the royal clan always hated Morgawse, though they feared her more than they hated her. They will be quick to find excuses for this lord now that my lady is dead.'

Good. He could go home and be with his clan, honoured by the warband, and perhaps even be king for a few years. But something of that mad misery in his eyes gave me a cold certainty that it would be no more than a few years. A curse? Not, I thought; in the sense of some black spell like the one that had nearly killed Eivlin. But the woman had been his mother, and he had never come to terms with her, and now he had murdered her and never could. Morgawse, dead. I remembered her terrible eyes and soft voice. Darkness, still present, threatened no less savagely with Morgawse of Orcade dead.

The door of the hut was flung open, and I started out of my brooding to see Rhuawn. He stared back, astonished, then grinned.

'Rhys! You are safe, then. I am glad. And you are the Queen's servant, Eivlin . . .'

I stood, carefully dusting off the bread crumbs. Eivlin also stood, eyeing Rhuawn suspiciously. 'Much health, Rhuawn,' I said.

He nodded briskly. 'But what has happened to you? How have you come back? I tell you, Rhys, these past few days have been as confused as some nightmare. I heard that Gwalchmai had come back. I told Medraut, through the door – he has locked himself into the Queen's room, and he will not speak to anyone. He said a few days ago that you had had trouble with Maelgwn's men . . .'

'Rhuawn . . .' I interrupted.

He frowned. 'Come. I know. I gave you a blow and some hard words when you were insolent. But do not hold that against me still.' He dropped onto the other bed, waving a loose hand for us to sit as well. Leaning forward, hands locked together between his knees, he went on, 'You were insolent, but, God knows, you spoke from loyalty. You are not to blame for misunderstanding the situation, and I lost my temper, and went further than I meant to. Is it well?' He put out a hand, smiling a little. After an instant's hesitation, I took it. Deluded still or not, Rhuawn's apology, such as it was, was sincere.

'It is well, if well with you, Lord. Though I think I did understand the situation.'

His smile vanished, but he shrugged. 'As you say. But come, tell me what has happened. I do not know whether I stand on firm earth or on ocean. Medraut said he fought some of Maelgwn's men, who were a bit over-hasty when they tried to prevent you from leaving. Did you escape from them?'

I shook my head. 'There is no way that I could escape from them, seeing that they were never there. I did escape, though, but from Medraut, the Queen Morgawse, and a warrior they had with them to guard the horses. That was Eivlin's doing.'

Rhuawn frowned, and began tapping his knee with his sword hand. 'Are you still unreasonable about Medraut?' he asked.

'Lord, I am saying nothing more than the truth. Medraut is a sorcerer and a liar. He charmed you, and nearly charmed me, into believing him honest. He and the Queen had some plan against your lord the Emperor which involved getting my lord Gwalchmai out of the way first. That was why he chose us to practise his lies on . . .'

But Rhuawn was shaking his head. 'This makes no sense. I like Medraut ap Lot. I have known for years, too, that Gwalchmai has a kind of madness in him.'

'You have also known that Morgawse was a witch.'

'So it has been said. But it is much more reasonable to believe that she has merely excited envious rumours.'

'Lord, you cannot believe that! Think of her a moment.'

He paused, uneasily, then shook his head again. 'This makes no sense. Why should I listen to a runaway servant?'

'Because I am speaking the truth. And I'll swear to it by any oath you choose.'

He studied me, and looked at Eivlin. She nodded her support. He stood abruptly, walked over to the fire. Not a stupid man, I thought, and basically a good man. Caught in his own confusions.

'If I believe you, Medraut is a subtle, treacherous, dangerous schemer.' He found a stick and prodded the fire savagely. 'While I am a fool.'

I wanted to agree, but it would be better to let him keep his place, that carefully won position of important warrior. 'Not a fool, Lord. Just a man who is honest enough to believe others honest, and experienced enough to know about court manoeuvrings and think of men's words and policies rather than their actions and characters. That is no dishonour.'

'In other words, Rhys, a fool.' His stick had caught fire, and he raised the tip out of the flames, watching the end burn. 'But there are good, arguable reasons for believing both sides here.'

'You have known Gwalchmai for years. Think about actions and personality instead of reasons.'

He shook his head. 'But I like Medraut. He is less . . . less unwordly than Gwalchmai, more careful of his clan and position. Or so he has seemed. You have never struck me as a liar, Rhys, and yet – you could be mistaken. Gwalchmai . . . yes, he is as generous, as noble and courteous a man as any I know, and yet . . .'

'Gwalchmai has murdered our mother.' The voice broke in like a sword stroke, and we all spun about. Medraut stood in the door, watching us. I had not heard him come.

There was nothing wild about him, as there had been about Agravain's appearance. He was too calm, almost, well dressed in a purple-bordered cloak, gold-studded baldric at a precise and elegant angle. But his eyes were too bright, and very, very cold.

'Well?' he asked, addressing no one. 'A fine madness, isn't it, Rhuawn, to bring a sword down into your mother's neck, and sheath it again all bloody with the source of your own life.'

'What are you saying?' asked Rhuawn, horrified at the words.

He smiled, brightly, mockingly. 'I think I was plain enough.' Dropping his hand from the door frame he strolled into the room. 'Gwalchmai and Agravain between them have murdered Morgawse of Orcade, daughter of the Pendragon Uther, their mother and mine. They killed her because they thought she was having an affair with Maelgwn.'

'Agravain killed her,' I said. Rhuawn stared at me, shocked. Medraut's clear grey eyes also fixed on me, and looking at him was as chilling as looking at Morgawse. 'Agravain killed her because she murdered Lot by sorcery.'

Medraut laughed. 'Agravain! A whimpering puppy, a cur that should have been drowned at birth! If she had been herself she could have blotted him off the face of the earth with one snap of her fingers. Oh, he may have held the sword, but the heart that forged the deed and the mind that framed it belong to Gwalchmai, may the hounds of Yffern devour his heart and mind down all the eternities we can dream of, asleep or waking. He killed her.'

Rhuawn was shaking his head in confusion. 'Rhys,' quietly. 'Rhys, is this true?'

'Agravain killed the Queen,' I insisted. 'He did it to revenge his father. Gwalchmai was there before Agravain arrived, but he only talked to her, and left again. I was there, and left with him. Medraut was there too. My lord did not kill her, though it would have been easy and desirable for him to have done so.'

'No.' Medraut laid one palm flat against the wall, looking at me with a fixed bright stare. 'No. He merely crushed her, kicked her aside, and left. He killed some men from his father's warband, his cousins, and left. With you. Why should I dispute it with you? I came to ask you where he is.'

'He is talking to Agravain.'

'And together they wash their hands in her blood and gloat, saying how well done it was, how now the earth is free of a great sorceress. Rhuawn!' Medraut whirled to him, face pale, but eyes even brighter. 'I told you he was mad. Do you see what has happened, now that he has gone unchecked? Murder, murder of his kin, murder of his own mother, my mother, who made all the world look pale beside her beauty. She who commanded, and the stars bowed in heaven! She is dead. Oh by the sun, the blood, and the sword, and . . . but it is better. He would have done worse things. She talked to him, and he would have done worse things to her. But ahhh . . .' the words died into a cry of pain, and he stood motionless, blinking. He was not pretending the pain for Rhuawn's sake. It was real enough, and more convincing than even his best acting had been. It called Rhuawn over to him, to catch his arm.

'Come, sit down,' Rhuawn said. 'The thing is appalling, I know, to lose both parents within three days' time; and yet, cousin, one must live on. Rhys, get him something to drink.' When I did not move, Rhuawn jerked his head up and glared. 'Do you still believe Gwalchmai, after this?'

'I was there,' I said. 'Gwalchmai did not kill her. And I'm certain she would have killed him – or killed Medraut, for that matter, if she thought it would help.'

'You lie!' Medraut jumped up again. 'She would never have killed me. She told me so. Not me! She, she . . . God, but I will kill you, and Gwalchmai, and Arthur. Especially Arthur . . .'

'Hush. My lord Arthur has nothing to do with it.' Rhuawn was confused. 'Rhys, fetch him something to drink. Medraut, my lord Arthur is not your enemy.'

Medraut looked at him and began to laugh. I left to fetch some mead, and Eivlin left with me.

Saidi ap Sugyn was even less pleased to see us this time, but gave us another flask of mead. I took the flask and two more cups and started back to the hut, but I told Eivlin to find Gwalchmai and tell him what had happened. Agravain ought to be calm enough now to go to sleep, if he were not dead drunk, and I did not trust Medraut. He might do anything at all.

Except for the hissing of the fire, the hut was completely silent when I got back. Medraut, apparently, had no wish to be consoled. Rhuawn again crouched before the fire, prodding at it with his stick, while Medraut sat on the bed, looking relaxed and controlled again, eyes fixed on the door, fingers curled loosely about the hilt of his sword. When I came in, Rhuawn threw his stick into the fire, took the flask of mead from me, and poured a cup for himself and for Medraut. Medraut barely glanced at the offered drink, so

Rhuawn set the cup down beside him and went to the fire.

Gwalchmai came only a few minutes later, Eivlin trailing in behind him. He stopped in the door, waiting.

Medraut stood slowly, hand still on his sword, eyes unwavering. Gwalchmai met the stare evenly, though his hand also drifted to the gold of his sword hilt. 'Medraut.' He spoke the name very gently. 'You wished to see me.'

'Rhuawn.' Medraut still did not look away. 'I wish to speak to my brother privately.'

'Of course.' Rhuawn stepped towards the door, then stopped. 'Cousin, if you wish to come to Camlann with us, my lord Arthur offers rich hospitality to all. There would be a place for you. And friends, myself among them. It might be good for you to see another land, and to forget the past . . . . I will be waiting down the hill. Shout if you need help.'

Medraut nodded, not looking at him, and Rhuawn slipped past Gwalchmai out the door. Eivlin looked at me, pale-faced, and, when I nodded, followed him out, closing the door behind her. I stayed. Perhaps there was little I could do, but to wait down the hill seemed too far away.

Gwalchmai glanced at me and frowned a little. 'It is not necessary, Rhys.'

I crossed my arms and leaned against the wall by the fire.

'Let your mastiff stay and guard you, then,' said Medraut. 'It is unimportant whether he or anyone else hears what we say.' He took a deep breath, and the gold glittered on his baldric and collar. 'I wanted to see what you would say to the truth, the simple truth. You killed Mother.'

'I?'

'You. Oh, I know, Agravain carried the sword. But if you had not broken her with that other sword, your sword, she would be alive. Is it sweet to you, to have destroyed the most splendid thing the world ever held?'

'Medraut. It is not sweet, but very bitter – and yet I did not kill her.'

'Death and defeat are the same, especially for her. And the guilt is yours, evade it as you will, yours. And I know it. That is what I wished to tell you.' He was infinitely cool, elegantly calm.

Gwalchmai approached him slowly, stopping when they were only a foot or so apart. He too was completely calm, but with the kind of calmness the sick man has when the pain is so great, so wearing, that he ceases to struggle with it. His voice was entirely steady. 'Before God, I swear that when I left, my heart held no malice towards her. Earlier I might have killed her, but you yourself saw what became of that. Medraut, she is dead. And you saw, before we fought her at the last, how little you meant to her. Leave her be. It was a long, dark dream, brother, but it is ended now. If you will waken, the night is over.'

'The night is real, and your day is a delusion. What I told Rhuawn is true: you are mad, brother, chasing after an illusion and destroying the reality. One day I will take your Camlann, your lord Arthur, your beloved Family, and break them all to fragments, and the night will have its own.'

'Then you will break the most splendid and lovely thing in this dark West. Forget the Darkness, Medraut. You cared about other things once. I know, once you loved other things than power and her. Medraut, I have cared. I have thought of you, since I left, again and again, wondered what she did to you, prayed that you would break free. Can't you wake even now?'

'I have woken. She is dead. As for love, brother, I loved you once, and it makes me hate you the more now.' Medraut's mouth began to curl into his mocking smile again, and his eyes glittered. His hair shone in the lamplight. Facing him, Gwalchmai looked like a shadow. 'But perhaps I should go and see your sweet dream of light, brother. I think I will. I will accept Rhuawn's offer. I will go to Camlann, to visit my father.'

Gwalchmai's eyes widened only a fraction, but a jewel flashed on his collar as he drew in his breath too quickly. Medraut noticed and laughed.

'Yes, my father. I know now, you see. Mother told me. After Agravain used that sword of his.' He struck the hilt of his own sword abruptly, hard enough to hurt his hand, but no pain showed in his face, only an intensity near to desperation. 'Agravain was frightened, you see, and did it badly; and then he was more frightened, and ran out. I had just woken from the half-death your sorceries sent me to, but I came to her. He had cut her deeply, from the base of the neck through the collar bone, down towards her heart. But she was still alive. And she spoke to me. She said she had always loved me, only me, and never anyone else – she said that, do you hear.' Gwalchmai was shaking his head sadly in denial. 'She said that. But then she said, "So now, fulfil our plans, if you love me. Go to your father." And I said, "The man they called my father is dead; who do you mean?" And she smiled.' For the first time, Medraut's eyes left his brother's face, and stared out the door into the night. 'She smiled that smile of hers that made your heart stop, the smile that no one will ever see again. But when she spoke, her voice bubbled over the blood. She said, 'Your true father, who begot you in Britain, that summer when Uther was Pendragon. Go to my brother Arthur at Camlann. Go to your father.' At first I didn't see what she meant. Then I did see, and she knew that I saw it, and she died, still smiling. Then . . . then I put wood about the hut and fired it, and watched it burn until it was only ashes. She is dead, my mother. Shall I go to my father?' He smiled again, but the smile twisted into a grimace of pain. His shoulders were shaking, hands clenched, but the unwavering cold eyes were fixed on Gwalchmai again. I felt sick.

'Medraut!' Gwalchmai raised one hand in a helpless compassion.

'Death to you all!' Medraut whispered, then, his voice rising to a shriek of agony and fury, 'Death and ruin to you all, you traitors, you murdering, raping, unsurping . . .' The cry trailed into a scream of frenzy, and he turned, rushed out of the room into the night. The door slammed shut behind him.

Gwalchmai looked at the door, hand still lifted. 'Medraut,' he whispered, then slowly lowered his hand, fingers curling, straightening. 'Medraut.' I couldn't move. The fire hissed loudly in the silence, and the shadows flickered about the hearth.

After a minute, Gwalchmai sat down on the bed. He looked at me. After another moment, 'It is true,' very quietly.

'Arthur is his father?'

'Yes.'

'Incest? And Arthur her great enemy, as well as her brother?'

'Yes.' Gwalchmai nodded tiredly, rubbed one hand down his thigh. He looked at the fire. 'My lord did not know at the time that he was Uther's son. It was a month or so later that he led some raid for the Pendragon, and did it so well that he attracted Uther's attention. When Uther sought him out, it was discovered that my lord was his own son. My mother knew it beforehand. That was why she seduced him.' He looked back to me and said calmly, simply, 'You will say nothing of this to anyone. It would do harm to my lord.'

'They will guess, if he goes to Camlann. He looks like Arthur.'

'If they only guess, it will do no harm. Rumours can be ignored.'

'But will Medraut go to Camlann? Can he? You know, and can tell Arthur, that he means to destroy us all.'

'The High King must give hospitality to any noble who comes. He certainly can't refuse it to the son, or the brother, of the king of the Orcades. Arthur wanted to send me home when I first came, but he couldn't. Medraut will go to Camlann. And he will find many friends there, though he will still in himself be friendless.' Gwalchmai rested his elbows on his knees, rubbed his hands across his forehead. 'Maelgwn will let us go now, but he will continue to scheme on his own. Agravain will go home to Dun Fionn in the Orcades. We agreed that this would be best. The warband will probably name him king in the next few days, and the rest of the clan will doubtless confirm it when he gets back. We will visit Arthur first, of course, and he will swear loyalty. But he will die, Rhys. This thing will kill him. And...' He pressed his hands against his eyes. 'And...' His shoulders began to shake, as though something within him were breaking, and he gave one quiet, racking sob.

I stood against the wall a moment, looking at him. 'We can go home to my clan,' I had told Eivlin. And if I left him to ride out his own grief, we could. He had managed without me before, and doubtless he could manage without me again.

But to walk away from suffering is the act of a coward, and a selfish coward, and it is following Darkness instead of Light. I could not close the door behind me. I had only one choice to make, and I had already made that one.

I crossed the room, dropped to my knees beside him and

caught his arm. 'My lord.'

He looked up, mouth set with pain, eyes dark and exhausted.

'My lord,' I repeated, holding his shoulder. He caught my wrist, looking away, and began to weep with quiet, hopeless, tearing sobs, half-choked off, as though he feared to tear up his own heart. I held his shoulder. There was nothing at all to say.

In the end I could not do much except convince him to drink some of the mead and go to sleep. He could not talk the pain out, or cry loudly or shed numerous tears. I knew that the next day would find him courteous, rather remote, attentive to Agravain, ready to fence eloquently with Maelgwn about the journey back to Camlann or the tribute due to the Emperor.

When he was asleep I took the mead and went out to look for Eivlin.

She was still waiting down the hill, though Rhuawn was gone. She sat with her knees pulled up, looking at the moon. I came up behind her, then stopped, looking at the moonlight in her hair.

'Eivlin?' I said.

She turned, the light gliding over her face and shining on her eyes, and her smile made her wondrously beautiful. 'Rhys.' She patted the grass beside her, and I came and sat down.

'Isn't the moonlight lovely on the mountains?' she asked. 'Though on the sea it is even more beautiful. At Dun Fionn you can look out from the cliffs and see the crests of the waves all silver and traced with foam, and the hollows of the waves all black and shifting.' She stared up at the moon itself, a waxing moon in a deeply blue sky. 'How far away the moon is, the gem of the night. I wonder if she can see us.'

I shook my head. 'Would you like some mead?'

She smiled, tossed her head. 'Ach, everyone else has been having some. Yes.'

I poured it, and we drank it together, looking at the moon. 'Eivlin,' I said, when the cups were empty.

She looked at me, her lips half parted, eyes gentle. 'You are going to say that you cannot go back to your family and your farm,' she stated calmly.

I blinked. 'No. I can't now.'

'Because you love him?'

'That too. But because he needs me now.' I pulled a blade of grass and studied it by the moonlight. I could see the crease down its centre, and all the delicate little lines of its growth. 'You see, he never used to have a servant, until I came and asked him to take me to Camlann. He has a damnably proud humility which makes him always be at someone's service – Arthur's, Agravain's, Elidan's, whoever's. He could always be depended on, but depended on no one. So I began to do things for him without waiting for him to ask me, and because he is courteous and gentle he made room for me, until now he has come to depend on me. And, now, he needs me. Now especially. Dear God, he's suffered enough to break any man. I can't go. I've committed myself to him, and to what's happening at Camlann, too far to pull back. Rightly or wrongly, the only thing I can do now is to live for the Light, and pray God that Camlann survives Medraut and the things ahead. But whether or not we succeed, whether or not we actually keep the Light burning, the only choice I have now is to stay with it.' I let the blade of grass drop, thinking of what I was tying myself to and thinking of Morgawse's words.

Eivlin reached over and took my hand, cradling it in both of hers. 'If that is the only choice, my heart, at least it is a good one. And he's a good lord.'

I caught her hands in turn, with both of mine, turning to her. This was the thing that made it hard. 'But I still want you to come. Perhaps it's no world to marry into, to raise children in, but if you could . . .'

'"If I could!" Listen to the man! Do you think I am so easily put off, Rhys? Let your clan farm all the land on both sides of the Mor Hafren and let them root in it: I am coming with you. Always. Without asking me, you said you would marry me; and now, without being asked, I say I will. For ever.' She paused, then added briskly, 'But you must be sure we get our own house in Camlann, and be sure it is a good one. Your lord should be able to manage that, at the very least. And I will be the mistress of my own house, and it will be a very fine thing.'

'Yes,' I told her, grinning at her. 'Yes. A very fine thing indeed.'

In Winter's Shadow

To Robin

for Akko and the Adirondacks,
Cambridge, Caesarea, and Chartres
and much more.

'Brief as the lightning in the collied night,
That, in a spleen, unfolds both heaven and earth,
And ere a man hath power to say, "Behold!"
The jaws of darkness do devour it up:
So quick bright things come to confusion.'
                        A Midsummer Night's Dream

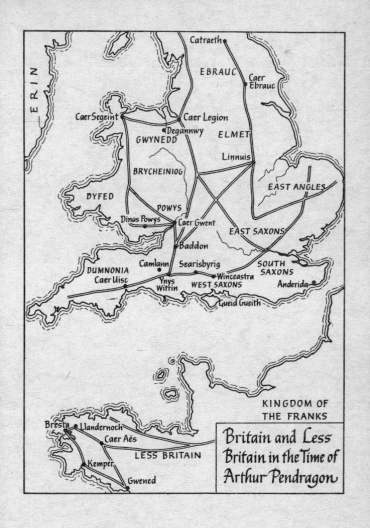

ERIN

Catraeth

EBRAUC

Caer Ebrauc

Caer Segeint

Caer Legion

Degannwy

GWYNEDD

ELMET

BRYCHEINIOG

Linnuis

DYFED

EAST ANGLES

POWYS

Dinas Powys

Caer Gwent

EAST SAXONS

Baddon

DUMNONIA

Camlann

Searisbyrig

Caer Uisc

Ynys Wittin

Winceastra

WEST SAXONS

SOUTH SAXONS

Anderida

Gueid Gueith

KINGDOM OF THE FRANKS

Bresta

Llandernoch

Caer Aës

LESS BRITAIN

Kemper

Gwened

Britain and Less Britain in the Time of Arthur Pendragon

One

'To Gwynhwyfar daughter of Ogyrfan, Augusta, Empress of Britain,' the letter began, 'from Menw son of Cynan, lord of the noble clan of the sons of Maxentius, many greetings. Well, cousin, by now you have heard that your father is dead, and you know that I am his successor to the lordship of our clan. You must not expect that I will, as he did, humour you and let our own fortunes take whatever course they will. I mean to better them, as you, for all your protestations of love and virtue, never have.

'When last we spoke, you told me that I spoke like a beggar, and commanded me not to mention this subject to you again. But I am a chieftain now, and lord of your own flesh and blood, and, though you have married above us, now I can demand this of you, and need no longer beg. Those lands I spoke of would be the easiest thing in the world for you to win for us. Your husband the Emperor dotes on you – or so they say – and you have only to get him to mention the matter to our king for Ergyriad to give us all that we ask, were it lives instead of lands.

'If you refuse us this service, do not trouble to write again. I will know that you have chosen to be no part of your clan, and, if I have any power here, I will see to it that you are treated accordingly. You are no better than us, however high you may have risen in the world, and you have no right to keep to yourself riches and honours which ought to be shared with your family. Accept that you are one of us, do what I ask, and I will forget the past. But if you prefer the imperial purple to your own blood you must suffer for it.'

I set the letter down on the table and stared at it, then pressed the palms of my hands against my eyes, as if that would ease the dull burning there. If I could sit still, if I could not think or feel, even for a little while, perhaps the rage and grief would not crush against my heart so closely.

I remembered the time I had told my cousin Menw that he spoke like a beggar. Three years before, I had accompanied my husband on a visit to the northern kings, and had stopped at my clan's holding, meaning to stay for a week or so. It was the first time I had been home since I married Arthur and went south to hold his fortress for him; my father had ridden out miles to meet me, and treated me like the blessed mother of God the whole time I was there. He had always enjoyed spoiling me – I was his only child, and my mother had died giving birth to me, so he had no one else to spoil. Menw was right when he said that. And yet, it was not to the point. He should be able to see that.

When I had been home two days, Menw had offered to escort me to the house of an õld friend whom I wished to visit. I might have taken some of Arthur's warriors instead, but I was touched that my cousin offered, and agreed at once. He had been something of a bully when we were little, and I thought he wished to make amends. But no sooner had we ridden from our holding than he began to speak pointedly of the power I must have as wife of the Emperor, and I grew uneasy. I had heard that tale from too many petitioners, as preface to too many pleas for justice, money or revenge, not to recognize it immediately. And sure enough, on the way back, Menw reined in his horse on a hill and looked out over the land in a calculating fashion.

'Pretty!' he observed.

I nodded. The dusk lay purple across the hills, and the soft summer stars were coming out eastward over the holding. To the north the Roman Wall leapt into the sunset behind us, scaling the boundaries of the old Empire.

'That land there,' Menw went on, pointing southeast, 'is the only part not ours.' His tone gave particular significance to the words 'not ours', and when I looked at him sharply I saw that he had a sly, insinuating smile. Menw was a big man, with thick dark hair and heavy eyebrows, and the smile suited him very badly.

'Is there something you would say?' I asked, hoping that my coldness would discourage him.

But he seemed pleased, and frankly proposed a scheme for obtaining his neighbours' lands by official fraud and deceit. 'No one would be surprised,' he told me. 'Through you we are not only noble and Roman-descended, but the Emperor's kin as well. The sons of Hueil are scarcely more than peasants, and rebellious ones at that – you know they fought in Bran's rebellion? And they are dishonest, and give short measure when they trade, and are of no use to anyone. We have more right to the land than such as they.'

'But what have they done that is criminal enough to deprive them of their fathers' lands?'

He looked startled. 'What do you mean, what have they done? It is what they are, and what we are, that matters.'

'The laws are clear, Menw. I cannot help you.'

He began to glower. 'You mean you do not wish to help us.'

I shook my head. But it was no use trying to pretend I had misunderstood him and thought he wanted legal advice. He knew I understood, and began angrily to claim that I was indifferent to my family's welfare. It was no use to tell him of the ties of justice and the laws: he did not wish to understand anything more than the tie that binds each to his own clan. Eventually I simply turned my mare and rode on towards the holding, but he refused to leave the subject and rode after me, shouting that we needed the land. It was then that I told him that he spoke like a beggar. At that he forced his horse against mine and seized my arm, his face dark with anger, and I had to stop my mare for fear of being pulled from her back.

'You selfish vixen! What do you want with all those riches and honours? Great lady you may be, but you've no children to pass them on to. If I were your husband I would divorce you and marry any slut that could give me an heir. I'd divorce you at once, do you hear? And if he divorces you, you'll need your kin. Better think who you call a beggar, "noble lady"!'

I struck him across the face, jerked my arm free, then, not trusting myself or him to say anything more, spurred my horse to a gallop. He galloped after me, shouting, but my horse was faster than his, and he arrived at the holding several minutes after I pulled my mare to a halt in the yard. I waited for him to dismount, then dismounted myself. I tossed him the mare's reins as though he were a groom, said, 'Never mention this subject to me again,' and left him holding the sweating horse, glaring at me, his eyes bright with a powerless hatred.

And now my father was dead and Menw was chieftain of our clan. *Father*, I thought, still trying to understand it. I had only heard of his death the week before, and I still did not really believe in it. It is hard to believe that someone is dead when they have lived far away. They form no part of the pattern of one's life, and are not missed in the common things. It seemed as though, if I could only go home, he would be waiting there, as young and strong as in my earliest memories, and not even bent and feeble as he had been on that disastrous last visit. Only my father was not, never again would, be waiting for me at home. And now, after this, I could not go home at all.

I took my hands from my eyes and stared at the letter. Home. That was a strange name to give that remote holding in the North which I had left eleven – no, twelve – years before to come to this fortress of Camlann. I tried to remember it. The house had been built by my great-grandfather's grandfather, who had received his lands from the Emperor Theodosius, the last of the Roman emperors to die with the Empire still whole. That ancestor – the Maxentius we named ourselves after – had been a military official of the British province of Valentia. He had fought bravely for Theodosius the first time the province had nearly been overrun by the Saxons, and our lands had been his reward. He had built the house of grey fieldstone, partly in the Roman, partly in the British fashion. His Roman atrium had been thatched over by my great-grandfather to make a central hall, and that same grandfather had also dug up the mosaic floor of the atrium and built a firepit instead. The firepit still had a rim of patterned tiles: I could remember playing on them when I was small, while the older members of the clan sat by the fire and talked. My father once told me that the mosaic had been of a man driving a fiery chariot through the stars, and I used to try to imagine that picture. The idea stirred me. I was not sure what a chariot looked like – sometimes I pictured it as a cart, at other times as a kind of wheelbarrow – but I could always imagine it riding in fire across the wide sky and along the winds of heaven, brushing the stars. I played at driving the chariot when I rode my pony out into the hills, or when we took a cart from our holding south to fetch grain.

The land around our house was wild, if beautiful, and sparsely settled. The nearest holding was three miles away, and the nearest town – Caer Lugualid on the coast – a full day's ride. Once there had been other towns closer to us. The Roman Wall passed about a mile from our holding, and at intervals along it were the ruins of towns and garrisons, all long abandoned. From the time I was old enough to ride any distance I used to go out with some of my cousins and look for treasure in the ruins, crawling under the fallen roofs and walking through the grass-grown streets. For a long time I accepted the ruins as simply as I accepted the hills, and only wondered over what I found in them – a broken glass bottle iridescent with age; a copper coin with the head of an ancient emperor; a tiny bronze statue of a god. But when I grew a little older I began to wonder what it had been like when those towns were full of people, how they could have lived in a land where so few lived now, and where they had all gone. One day I asked my father.

'They were protecting the Empire, my own darling,' he told me. 'They were soldiers like our father Maxentius, stationed on the Wall to defend Britain from the Saxons. As for how they lived, why, the Emperor had grain shipped to them from the south. Hundreds of ships brought it up the coast to Caer Ebrauc, where our king Caradoc lives now, and from there it was taken to all the people living on the Wall. And the ships didn't bring only grain, my girl, but those treasures you are always seeking. Glass, and gold, and silk and fine dyes, and spices from the East, carried all the way from Constantinople where the Emperor reigns.'

'But Uther Pendragon is the Emperor,' I pointed out, 'and he doesn't live at Con— at where you said, but at Camlann, in the South country.'

'Uther Pendragon is the Emperor of the provinces of Britain, true. He is king over the other kings of Britain, and to him chiefly falls the task of defending Britain against the Saxons. But once there was an Empire over the whole world, and all the provinces of Britain together were only its furthest western boundary. And the eastern part of the Empire is strong yet, and is ruled from Constantinople, which is so far away that a ship might sail from now to Michaelmas, and not reach it.'

'Why doesn't that Emperor still rule Britain, then? And what happened to all the people on the Wall?'

'He never used to rule from Constantinople; he ruled from Rome. The people on the Wall, Gwynhwyfar, left it and Britain and went to defend Rome, but they failed. And because they failed there is no emperor at Rome, only the one in Constantinople and the one in Camlann.' And my father explained to me carefully about the fall of Rome. I was young: I had never heard that tale. But my father was a learned man, and owned books of history and philosophy, from which he knew something of the stretch of time and space beyond the small present we inhabited. It awed me. I had learned to read, along with my cousins, because we were noble and Roman-descended, and my father insisted that we ought to learn to read, but until then my knowledge of letters had been confined to crude messages and to accounts, with some stammering over a gospel imposed between the two. The idea of Rome struck me like a vision. I could not look at the Wall, or the tiles round the fire-pit, or my collection of bits from the ruins, without that vast Empire leaping up before my mind like the world revealed by a lightning-bolt. With my father's help I began to struggle through the cramped pages of his books till my eyes ached.

I suppose that that is one of my chief memories of home: my father's room with its wolfskin rug and copper lamp, myself sitting next to my father, his arm around me, and both of us bending over some book opened on the table before us, struggling with complicated Latin abbreviations and laughing at each other's mistakes. My father had been a lonely man until I showed an interest in his books. In a gentler age he might have been a scholar; had he been an unimportant member of the clan he might have left it to become a monk. But his father had designated him as his successor to the chieftainship; the clan had confirmed it, and he was left to do his best to meet the responsibility and to feel guilty when he spent time with his books. He had no one to talk to about them but me. My male cousins were not much interested in reading, beyond what was obviously useful. It was not surprising, really: we were noble, which meant that they were kept busy learning the arts of war, while at the same time they had to master the proper way of caring for our lands. Occasionally the older ones went off and fought for our king, Caradoc of Ebrauc, and came back boasting of their accomplishments and rousing the younger ones to envy. As for my female cousins, they had to learn to spin and weave and sew, to butcher and cook an animal or to heal it of various common ills, to make cheese and mead, to keep bees, keep house, manage servants, and see to the holding accounts. I had to learn the same things, but shamelessly ran off, especially from the cooking and housekeeping (I quite liked accounts, and, God help me! managing servants) and my father never punished me for it, though perhaps he should have. Sometimes he would reluctantly say, 'Gwynhwyfar, you ought to be helping with the poultry', but I would reply, 'Of course, Father, but first could you explain...' and two hours later he would still be explaining.

Sometimes I would feel ashamed of myself for avoiding the work, and yet more ashamed for manipulating my father in such a way, and I would resolve to be better in future, and work very hard at the things I most disliked. But always wonder or astonishment at the past would stir in me again, and I would go back to the books looking for an answer to one question, and stay to answer twenty while the day's concerns sank into the centuries.

Our clan was always fairly busy. Most of our land was only good for sheep, but we received wheat from dependent clans further south, and raised cattle and horses in the valley pastures. The lands my cousin Menw now coveted were good cattle lands. But we did not need them to make us wealthy. Our family had always been one of the most important in the north of Ebrauc. To the south and to the west, and even north across the border into Rheged, we were respected, honoured, feared. About the east we did not speak when I was young, for there lay the Saxon kingdom of Deira, from which, at any time, bands of raiders might march to burn down holdings and drive off cattle. An eastern dependency of ours suffered such a fate, one bad winter, and there was very little we could do to aid the survivors. Sometimes whispered accounts spread that such-and-such a holding had been taken, and with what deaths, rapes and brutalities the victims had suffered. Sometimes wretches would turn up begging at our holding, half-starved and desperate: they had lost lands and livelihood to the Saxons. It grew worse as I grew older. While Uther Pendragon remained Emperor there was some degree of order, but when he died the kings of Britain fought over who was to succeed him, and were too busy fighting to pay much heed to keeping out the Saxons.

Then, in the autumn of my twenty-first year, the new Emperor Arthur rode with his men from the east, leaving a Saxon army shattered behind him. He asked my father for hospitality and for a place to leave his wounded.

I was awed by it. I had been listening to reports of him for as long as I could remember. At first he had been the leader of the imperial warband under the old Emperor, then, when the civil war broke out, he had been the one man who continued to fight the Saxons. But after the war had dragged on for several years, and after a massive Saxon invasion in the South, Arthur claimed the imperial purple for himself, and defeated the other contenders to win the title of Emperor. He had no legal right to it. He was the Emperor Uther's son, true, but a bastard son by an unknown peasant mother, and a clanless man, an orphan raised out of charity at a monastery. At first all Britain was outraged by his usurpation. But he was an incomparable warleader. He not only defended the borders of Britain against Saxon invasions, but actually invaded the Saxons, and compelled their kings to become his tributaries and subjects of the Empire. Many of the British kings continued to hate him because of his birth, and the Church called him anti-Christ and devil because he taxed it to support his war against the Saxons, but my father said, 'I don't mind if he is a devil so long as he rules like an angel of God,' and began to support him. So, when Arthur turned up at our holding one grey morning with the whole of his warband after him, my father spared nothing and no one to make them welcome.

I was shaken awake by one of my aunts, given a babbled account of what was happening, and told to come and help. I went out into the dawn and found the yard full of armed men on tall horses, looming out of the mist. Their spears looked like a forest in winter. I saw my father in the centre of the yard and hurried over to him. He was talking to a tall, fair-haired man who glanced up as I came over; his eyes were the colour of the mist. 'Ach, there you are,' my father said. He sounded calm, but I could tell that he was very excited. 'This is my daughter Gwynhwyfar, your excellency. She is a sensible girl. You can give her charge of the wounded.' And, to me, in an undertone, 'This is the

Emperor, my girl. He has just defeated Fflamddwyn. Do you think we could put the wounded in the cow-byre? There's no room for them all in the house.'

I had expected Arthur to be middle-aged. I had pictured him as a grey, gaunt old warrior, wearing the imperial purple as clumsily as the crow in the fable wore its stolen peacock feathers. But he was barely thirty, with hair and beard the colour of wheat before the harvest, and his eyes seemed to have the sun behind them. When I stammered out that all we had for the wounded was a cow-byre, he smiled, said, 'It will do,' summoned various men out of the mist like a conjurer calling them from the air, and told me to tell them what to do. Of course, on the whole, they told me what to do, and Arthur strode in when it was half done and most of the wounded were cared for, to see them settled. He had already settled the rest.

I had seen wounded men before, the times being what they were, but not so many, fresh from a battle. I was confused, horrified, and could scarcely manage to tell Arthur's surgeons where the supplies were, or give reasonable orders to the servants. The world beyond our holding, the remnant of the Empire of my visions, had burst in upon us like a storm.

Arthur did not stay long, as he was eager to continue his campaign against the Saxons before the winter closed the roads. But he left his wounded with us, and asked if he might use our holding as one of his bases, promising (with a glint of dry humour) to find his own supplies and not borrow from us. That was essential. However welcome he was, his warband, the Pendragon's 'Family', numbered nearly seven hundred trained warriors, as well as doctors, grooms, armourers and a few servants, with more than twice their number of horses. It required a kingdom or two to support them all, and most of the kingdoms of Britain were notoriously reluctant to contribute to that support, with the result that, while the Family relied principally on plunder from the Saxons, it also tended to take supplies wherever it could find them. Most men in my father's position would have done their utmost to persuade the Emperor to take his Family elsewhere – one cannot refuse an Emperor outright – but my father hesitated only for a moment before agreeing to provide a base. It was plain that

Arthur was surprised by this, and more than a little pleased.

The Emperor was in and out of the holding at intervals over the next year, continuing his campaign against the northern Saxon kingdoms. He could not hurry the campaign because his force was far smaller than that which the Saxon kings could raise, so he did not dare meet them in pitched battles. Instead he tried to wear them out by raiding, and would turn up suddenly when they thought he was a hundred miles away and had sent most of their army home. When he judged that the time was ripe he would ask his British subject kings to raise their armies and risk a pitched battle against the Saxons, but for a long time they would be too strong for that. He had used these tactics against the southern Saxons with some success, but he told us that they were not defeated, as we had thought, but merely stalled. 'It will take another three or five years to settle them properly,' he said. He had time to talk to us on the later visits. He talked mainly about the Empire. Defeating the Saxons was, to Arthur, only the first step towards the goal of preserving the Empire. His monastic education had forced him to read books, and he knew that the Empire had once meant more than just a man in a purple cloak leading a force to crush the Saxons if they invaded too often. He had thought about the value of peace and of impartial justice, and could imagine what it might be like to live in a world that was not constantly at war with itself. He and my father were soon talking easily, eagerly. When Arthur spoke of the Empire his eyes shone, and when he thought out some new idea he would be unable to sit still, but would leap up and stride about the room, his purple cloak flapping, and stop suddenly when he understood what he wanted to say. I used to watch him and think of the man in the mosaic I had never seen, driving the chariot of fire. A chariot like Arthur's Empire, whirling precariously through the dark ruins of the West. I only prayed that it would not break among the winds.

If I had been a man I would probably have begged Arthur to allow me to join his warband. As it was, all I could do was try to see that our holding was a smoothly managed, effective base for him, and listen while he and my father talked – occasionally forgetting the modesty required of an unmarried woman, and joining in. Once, on his third visit,

Arthur and I found ourselves speaking alone together while my father watched us, and we stopped, embarrassed, and, on my part, suddenly afraid. We watched each other out of a great silence. Afterwards I saddled my mare and rode out to the Wall, recklessly alone in the grey afternoon. I walked the horse along the ruined fortification, trying to be reasonable. Why should the lord Arthur, Augustus, Emperor of Britain, take any notice of the daughter of an obscure northern nobleman? I would be sensible, I resolved, and eventually the constriction that had locked about my heart when he looked at me would go away.

But when I returned to the holding and turned my mare out to pasture – there was no room for her in the stables, which were full of Arthur's men – I met Arthur again. He saw me carrying my saddle back, and hurried over to me and took it from me. Then, arranging it over his arm he frowned, looked at me and said, 'You must have ridden some distance, Lady Gwynhwyfar: the saddle cloths are damp. That is no safe thing for a woman to do, in times such as these, and so near the border. You especially should not do it.'

'Why me especially, your excellency?' I asked, before I thought.

For a moment he stared at the saddle, then looked up suddenly and directly at my face. Without answering he turned away and took the saddle into the stables, returning it to its place. I stood outside, realizing that I had had no need to reason with myself, and feeling even more afraid.

We were married after the harvest, the year after Arthur's first visit. My father could not but be glad at the marriage. He had put my worth very high, which was why I was unmarried until I was twenty-two, an age when most women have two or three children. But now I was the wife of an emperor, and in a strange way it confirmed my father's love for me, and proved his devotion to the old Empire as well. He was proud and happy. But his grief went deeper than the gladness, for I left him alone. I went south to Camlann with an escort of wounded and cripples whom Arthur was sending home from the war, to hold Arthur's fortress for him and to find supplies while Arthur completed his campaign in the North.

Menw had spoken with bitter envy of the 'riches and

honours' I had received. But, God knows, honours were few those first years, and as for riches, I was hard put to it to find enough to keep the fortress and the army alive. Most of the kings of Britain still hated us as usurpers, and refused to pay the tribute, and our allies we had to conciliate with gifts. Arthur took plunder from the Saxons – cattle and grain, sheep and woollen clothing, arms, armour and cooking pots – which were very useful. Occasionally he sent me some uninjured men whom I could send to various kings to demand the tribute – but it was desperately hard! And I was at first an intruder in his fortress, a northerner among southerners, a woman of twenty-two suddenly put in authority over men who had served at Camlann since the Emperor Uther's time. Moreover, there had been a bad harvest that first year, and food was scarce. I remembered one of Arthur's grim letters to me, that first winter: 'The alliance with Urien wears badly. He begins to complain that he cannot support his own warband these days. I will need him to raise his army for me in a few months: make him a gift of six hundred head of cattle and something golden – I have given all my own plunder to Ergyriad. We have nothing to eat and are living off the land. The horses are sick. Ten men have the fever; I pray it does not spread. Beg Urien to send something, especially grain, to supply us at Yrechwydd, for I have told the men there will be food there. We will be there in three weeks.' And I, who had been making the servants at Camlann live on boiled cabbage, wrote madly to every king between Camlann and Caledon to produce those wretched cattle, and wrested a gold crucifix from a monastery. It worked. Arthur got the supplies, and his campaign was able to continue to its eventual success. But the cost of it, the cost! Kings and the Church offended, less tribute received the next year, and, at Camlann, a sullen anger poisoning everything. You cannot blame a man for being angry when he has lived on cabbage for a month, only to see six hundred head of fat cattle sent north, and not even to his own king, but to a wealthy ally. After one appalling day, when I really feared that half the servants would run off and rob the local farmers, I had to lock myself into the empty house and weep until I was sick. I was alone, distant from my family and from my new husband, and the people in Camlann appeared to hate me. I do not know how I survived that first winter, and the winter that followed was worse. That was the year I lost my baby, the only child I ever carried. Perhaps I had been working too hard, or perhaps my body had always been at fault, but I lost the child, a boy, in the sixth month, with a great deal of pain and blood, so that I was very sick for a month afterwards.

The war in the north ended; Arthur came back and campaigned in the south, all the second year of our marriage. That campaign took another four years, and ended at last in victory. We worked together on the peace, thinking that now all our hopes would be realized, believing that now all would be well. But the hope that had been dearest to me receded slowly, and when I was thirty I had at last to admit that something was wrong, that I would never conceive, that I was barren and would die so. It was just over a year later that Menw flung my childlessness in my face and I gave him the blow he regarded as a dishonour and would never forget.

Riches and honours. In these years of peace, there might be some things that Menw would recognize under that name. Most of those kings who had hated us were reconciled to us now, and even the Church was growing less vehement. The Saxons showed some signs that they began to feel part of the Empire, no longer sullen and conquered enemies. The tribute came in regularly, and we were able to set the warband to sweeping bandits from the roads of Britain and to protecting trade and good order. But even now there was little ease or comfort in wearing the purple. It was like trying to walk the edge of a sword. And there were new problems now, splintered alliances and, worse, internal quarrels, so that I sometimes wished we were back in the years of the war, when at least one had open enemies and a plain solution to the problems.

I had no time to sit staring at a letter. This very afternoon I must buy grain to feed the fortress – undoubtedly the grain-sellers were waiting for me to come and bargain with them. I had to arrange a feast for the emissaries from the kings of Elmet and Powys. I must allot some wool from the stores to the weavers of the fortress, if all the Family were to have their winter cloaks in time. Soon, if not today, I must find a new supply of iron for the smiths, as we had bought none for some time, and there might be a shortage soon. There would doubtless be some petitioners asking for a hearing. And there was the question of what our emissary must say to the king of Less Britain

Yet I sat staring at the letter, re-read it. *If you prefer the imperial purple to your own blood you must suffer for it.* It was typical of Menw to phrase it that way, I thought bitterly. An extreme sentence and a violent one.

I had never expected to go home. Even when I knew that I would never give Arthur a child, an heir, I knew that he would not divorce me. He had relied upon me in the long war with the Saxons, often for his very life. We had seen each other rarely while the war continued, and since the peace we had generally been too busy to talk of anything but the concerns of the Empire, but the bond between us went as deep as life itself. Arthur and I knew each other as only those who together have spent themselves to their limits can, and he would as soon cut out his heart as divorce me.

No, I had never expected to go home. But I had always had my home behind me, forever a possibility: the house and the hills, the Roman Wall leaping off into the west, the patterned tiles around the firepit. Though I had preferred the purple to my blood, and suffered for it, in a way it was my blood, my home, all that I had been, which had chosen the purple. To be cut off from it all was to have my father die all over again.

And if I refused Menw's demand I could never go home. I would be as good as kin-wrecked, exiled from my clan. Most of he clan agreed with Menw, and thought I ought to do more for them. Moreover, I had been gone a long time. They would not oppose him to support me.

Best to get it over with. I picked the letter up, rose from the desk, and dropped it in the fire. It uncurled slowly, wrapping itself around the coals, and the ink darkened even as the parchment went brown, standing out sharp, clear and absolute. Then the coals ate through, here and there, and it darkened to illegibility, while the air was full of its burnt leather stink.

My eyes stung and I wiped them with the back of my hand, finding that my hand shook. But it was over now, and the only thing I could do, done. I must get back to work, and not brood over it.

I picked up the light spring cloak which I had draped over a chair when I sat down to read the letter, then picked up my mirror to check that I appeared dignified and composed, as befitted an empress. I saw instead that I was crying. 'It's the smoke,' I told myself, aloud, but I had to set the mirror down and stand a moment, wrestling with myself. I went into the adjoining room, found the water pitcher and washed my face. The cold water was soothing against my hot eyes, and I felt calmer when I went back and checked the mirror again. Better. I could not afford to show weakness, not when Camlann was as tense as it was at present.

There was more white in my hair, I noted absently, when I looked to see that it had not come down when I washed my face. Well, red hair does not suit purple cloaks. I turned the purple border of my own cloak inwards so that it would not clash as much. If my hair were white I could stop worrying about that, at least. There, there was the picture of the woman I had to be: still looking younger than thirty-four, thick hair pulled back severely and piled behind her head, gold necklace proclaiming wealth; poised, controlled. My eyes were red, and I could not smooth the lines of tension on my face, though I smiled at the reflection, trying to lie to it. But probably no one would notice, if I acted assured. I took a deep breath and went out.

The house Arthur and I shared was next to the Feast Hall of Camlann, on its west. It had three rooms: an outer room for conferences, with a firepit; a bedroom, and a washroom. The servants who looked after it lived down the hill to the north, so that, though we had to fetch our own wood and water at night, we had privacy. The house faced north, looking over the most crowded part of the fortress: the road from the gates past the stables to the Feast Hall. The Hall covered the crown of the hill, set east of the centre of the walled enclosure. The hill slopes very steeply on the east, and the houses on that side cling to the slope at an angle. Standing in the door of the house I looked out at the huddled houses along the side of the road, with their chickens scratching in the dust around them; at the stables sprawling along the north slope, and some horses, being worked on a lead rein, circling in the sun of a practice yard.

The green patches between the houses grew larger further down the slope, and then the great grey bulk of the walls broke the pattern, firmly set stone with a wooden rampart above them. The gates were guarded by a single watch tower, but, because it was a time of peace, were left open. Beyond them the road stretched away, turning eastward across the patchwork of fields, fallow and pasture and ploughed land. It was April, and the swallows, returning from the remote south, were beginning to wing circles about the eaves of the Feast Hall, while dandelions flowered in the grass, and apple trees scattered here and there were budding. That morning it had rained, but now the sun was out, and everything glittered, the light so sharp it seemed to cut into the soul. Here was Camlann, here was my fortress, the strong heart of the visionary Empire. I took another deep breath, then turned from the view and walked along the west wall of the Hall to the south, where the storerooms were.

The fortress was generally short of grain by the end of the winter, and many farmers, finding that they had some surplus left, took advantage of this to sell the old grain at a high price. A number of them had arrived that morning, and I was expected to bargain with them for their produce. The steward could have done it, but he was a bad bargainer, and could make no use of the information we could obtain from them about the state of things in the countryside, which was invaluable to me. When it came to buying large amounts of goods, later in the year, the price paid by Camlann set prices for all the South, and the amount taken by Camlann checked availability everywhere, so it was very important for me to understand what was happening outside the fortress as well as what was happening within it.

There were half a dozen carts drawn up before the main storeroom, with their owners, all tight-lipped, independent clansmen, sitting in the carts in a row, looking sour because I was late. Normally I enjoyed bargaining with them because they enjoyed bargaining, and practised it as a great art. Now I found it maddening, and wished I could simply impose a reasonable price and have done with it. Instead, we worked through the preliminary stages of the poorness/richness of the previous harvest; the amount of seed corn available to the farmers; the amount the grain would sell for in an ordinary market; the relative scarcity/surplus of grain at Camlann and in the countryside; the value of the goods Camlann offered in return for the grain; the relative scarcity and value of these, and their cost in terms of products other than grain. We were finally approaching the vital question of whether the farmers wanted payment in cattle, woollen goods or metal, and how much, when the Family's infantry commander, Cei ap Cynryr, came storming along the wall of the Hall, saw me, and made his way towards us. Cei was a very big man, the largest in the Family. He had a great mass of sandy red hair, and wore large quantities of garish jewellery and brightly coloured clothing so that even when he was in a quiet mood it was impossible to overlook him. Now he was plainly in a temper. I braced myself.

'That golden-tongued, oily-mannered bastard!' he exclaimed, pushing aside a farmer. 'My lady, you must speak to Rhuawn and make him offer me an apology, or I will fight him, I swear it by my sword, and not spare him. And yet it is not his fault, but the fault of that weasel from the Ynysoedd Erch.'

I took his arm and hurried him aside. I knew who 'that weasel' was, but it would be better not to let the farmers, outsiders, know the details of quarrels within the Family – though by now most of Britain must be aware that Arthur's invincible, formerly indivisible force was torn in half by violent factions. The quarrel had been going on long enough to become notorious. Almost since 'that weasel' arrived in Camlann.

'What has Medraut done now?' I asked.

Cei spat. 'Ach, he has done nothing, not directly. Would you expect it of him? No, he will never confront a man to his face. He will leave some lying story behind his back, and let someone else fight for it.'

The farmers looked very interested at this, and I made hushing motions. Medraut ap Lot was the youngest son of Queen Morgawse of the Orcades Islands, which in British are called the Ynysoedd Erch, the 'Islands of Fear'. His mother was the legitimate daughter of the Emperor Uther, and Arthur's half-sister. Medraut had adored his mother, who had intended him to become king of the Islands on her husband's death, though it was widely believed that he was not her husband's son, but born of an adulterous love affair. However, Morgawse was dead, murdered by her eldest son Agravain in revenge for another of her affairs and for a rumoured connection with her husband's death; and the royal clan of the Islands had chosen Agravain as its new king, despite the murder. The Queen had been reputed a witch and the clan had not loved her, though they were too much afraid of her to deny her anything. They were not so afraid of Medraut, and he had come to Camlann, while the new king, his brother, who had long fought for Arthur, returned and ruled in the Islands. Medraut was very bitter against Agravain. But the immediate cause of quarrels was generally his other brother, Gwalchmai, who was also at Camlann, and was one of Arthur's most trusted and valued followers. Gwalchmai seemed to be hated by Medraut even more than Agravain was, though he had had no part in the murder, and most of the quarrels were between his friends, of whom Cei was one, and Medraut's.

Cei glanced at the farmers and lowered his voice. 'Rhuawn has taken to blaming Gwalchmai for the death of that witch from the Ynysoedd Erch. He has been repeating that tale for years now, like a catechism, so that half the Family thinks that Gwalchmai murdered his mother – as though the witch deserved to live in the first place! Whose tale is that but Medraut's? Ach, but it is an old story; so old that I must listen to it in silence and say nothing. But when Rhuawn dared to say that Gwalchmai is hindering the negotiations with Less Britain, and deliberately obstructing the conclusion of a peace there, because of some imagined weak-mindedness – when I heard Rhuawn saying this to his friends, I went to him as he spoke and told him that it was he who was weak-minded, to believe such ravings. And Rhuawn leapt up with his hand on his sword, and called me a blind, stubborn fool who could not see what was before his eyes, and accused me of flattering the Emperor into believing falsehoods – and this in the presence of four others! My lady, I could ask Arthur to demand that Rhuawn apologize to me, but I do not wish to humiliate the man. You can persuade him to offer it: do so, for God's sake, or I will fight him tomorrow, and, though he is a fool, I do not wish to harm him.'

I nodded, feeling sick. The quarrel was typical. I had had to wheedle too many warriors into offering apologies, and I could not disguise the fact that my sympathies were entirely with Gwalchmai, which meant that it grew increasingly difficult for me to win over members of Medraut's party, which included Rhuawn.

Warriors tend to quarrel in the best of years. They are taught to regard an insult, or an admission of weakness, as a dishonour, and the only remedy for dishonour as the sword. They quarrel most in the winter, when they are kept in a narrow space together – the three hundred men who slept in our Hall had more space than most – and have little to do. In the summer they can go to war if there are any wars to be fought, or else fight bandits and form escorts, or, at the least, go hunting; and then they tend to be good-natured. But the quarrels at Camlann were more serious. They were not easing with the warm weather. For years they had been growing steadily worse, and the ordinary methods of soothing them – flattery and pleas on both sides – were working less and less well. I was afraid for the future.

'If Rhuawn apologizes,' I told Cei, 'you must beg his pardon for calling him weak-minded.'

'Must I, by God? He is weak-minded, to believe such slander!'

'The slander is Gwalchmai's affair. If anyone accuses him to his face, he can demand an apology, and we can see to it that he receives it, at least as far as the negotiations with Less Britain are concerned. But it is not your affair to fight Rhuawn on his behalf, noble lord. Let Gwalchmai guard his own honour. He is not exactly helpless.'

'He is too courteous. And no one will accuse him to his face if they must fight him: he either escapes the insults or turns them.'

'It is still his affair. And if you do not wish to fight Rhuawn, noble lord, you will have to apologize.' I said it more sharply than I meant, for I was growing impatient.

Cei again began to protest, but one of the farmers, also impatient, came over and suggested a price for his grain, asking if it was acceptable. It was too much, and I knew it, but I snapped 'Perhaps,' and went back to make arrangements. Cei hung about behind me like a large red thundercloud, waiting for me to finish.

When we had fixed on a price – and the price was still too high, since I was in no mood to bargain patiently, and these southern farmers are not to be out-bargained at the best of times – I was further distracted by a petitioner. A boy who had been sitting in one of the carts jumped out and knelt before me.

'What is it?' I asked wearily.

'M-most n-noble queen,' he began, then switched to a surprisingly good formal Latin. 'Your grace, I have come here hoping to find a place in the Emperor's service.'

I had expected some complaint about a neighbouring clan, and I looked at the farmer whose cart the boy had been sitting in, surprised. 'Isn't he your son?'

The farmer shook his head. 'No, noble lady. I only gave him a ride from Baddon. He is a good, biddable lad, though; listen to him.'

I sighed and brushed back a loose strand of my hair. Another petition for service at Camlann. People came all the time, offering to practise any imaginable trade, and many of them we accepted, and many we did not. I did not feel like weighing this boy's qualifications now, after the letter and with Cei looming behind me. But I reminded myself to be strong, be gracious, and smiled at the boy. Cei snorted impatiently.

'What manner of place, young man?' I asked, also in Latin, studying him. He looked about thirteen, of average height for that age, with a mass of pale hair above a thin face and a pair of surprisingly dark eyes. He was not a farm lad, I decided. His Latin was too good, and there was a nervous sensitivity to his face which argued some education.

'I . . . your sacred kindness, I am willing to do almost anything. But I wish to learn how to be a warrior.'

Cei snorted again. 'Boy, do not trouble the lady. Go back to your family and don't run away from it in future.'

The boy flushed deep crimson. 'I . . . I . . .' he stammered.

I smiled again to reassure him. 'What is your name?' I asked. 'And where is your family? You are young to seek service on your own.'

'They call me Gwyn,' he said. 'I don't know my father's name. And I have no family, except for my mother, and she

552

is in a convent in Elmet. Your grace, I am willing to do almost anything, if you will let me stay here and train to be a warrior. I know you must train boys to be warriors here. All the sons of the great warriors – like this lord here' (with a nervous, appeasing smile at Cei) '– they must become warriors as well. Surely it would be no trouble for one more to join them?'

'So he is a nun's bastard, raised at a nunnery,' said Cei. 'My lady, send him away. We have more servants than we can feed already, and don't need some half-grown dreamer of a nun's bastard.'

The boy had gone an even deeper red when Cei began, but went white at the end of his speech. He jumped to his feet, began to stammer a reply, then was quiet, blinking miserably. He evidently was a nun's bastard, and must be a dreamer, if he wished to be a warrior so badly that he was willing to leave what home he had, alone, and travel to Camlann to offer to do 'almost anything' to learn the arts of war.

'My lady,' Cei began again, going back to the subject which had been his sole concern all the while, 'how can I apologize to Rhuawn after his slanders?'

But I felt sorry for the boy now. 'You are too old to learn to be a warrior,' I told him gently, for a moment ignoring Cei and the farmers. 'Most boys begin their training between the ages of seven and nine.'

'But I did start then, noble lady, on my own!' he cried, slipping back into British. 'And a monk at the brother foundation to my mother's convent, he taught me, too – he used to be a warrior, you see. Only I need to know more.'

'Be quiet, boy,' Cei snapped, but I raised my hand for him to wait.

'Can you read, Gwyn?' I asked.

He nodded eagerly. 'Yes, noble lady. And I can write, book hand and cursive both. My mother wanted me to be a priest, and made certain that I learned how to write. She taught me herself.'

I looked at Cei, lifting an eyebrow. 'There is a shortage of servants who can read, even here,' I said. 'I could use a copy clerk to take down inventories and keep records for me.'

Cei shrugged. 'As you please, my lady. It is a waste of

time to teach some priestly little bastard from a convent the arts of war, but if you need a clerk, by all means keep him. Will you speak with Rhuawn?'

'You may stay,' I told the boy. 'Go to the Hall and ask for Gweir the steward; he will look after you, and tonight I will ask my lord Arthur to confirm you in a place as a servant. Yes, Cei, I will speak to Rhuawn, but I will promise him that if he apologizes you will as well. Good fellows,' to the farmers, 'if you will come with me I will arrange for you to receive the price of your grain.'

The farmers were satisfied, Cei grumbled agreement, and the boy Gwyn was overjoyed. The next matter, then, was to talk to Rhuawn – though while I was in the storerooms I ought to see about the wool for the weavers. And then there was the feast for that night.

I spoke with Rhuawn before the afternoon was half over, and eventually persuaded him to apologize to Cei. But I knew that neither of the warriors would be content. Their reconciliation was like the forcing together of two fragments of a broken dish, which might hold together for a little while if undisturbed, but which left the break as deep and unremedied as before. And at first Rhuawn had not listened to me, but only eyed me with a kind of suspicion and given polite, noncommital replies. By the end of our talk he had grown warmer, and told me how he regretted his harsh words, but that Cei's insult had been too much for any honourable man to endure, and so on and on.

Yet when walking back up the hill towards the Hall I kept remembering the way his eyes slid sideways from mine at the first. The mistrust was growing. I could scarcely bridge the gap between the two factions now, and if things continued as they were, Rhuawn and his friends would soon regard me as an enemy. Indeed, I was aware of rumours about me circulating, conversations suddenly hushed at my approach. Only up to now no rumours about me had been believed.

As I approached the kitchens, where I would check the arrangements for the feast to be given that night, my name was called and I found Arthur's second-in-command, the warleader and cavalry commander Bedwyr ap Brendan, hurrying towards me.

'My lady Gwynhwyfar!' he called again. 'My lord

Arthur asked me to find you. He wishes to have a conference upon the situation in Less Britain before the feast tonight.'

I stopped, trying to order my thoughts and rearrange my plans for the afternoon. 'Very well, lord,' I said, after a moment, 'but I must give some orders to the kitchens first or there will *be* no feast tonight.'

He nodded, smiling, and fell in step beside me. As Arthur's warleader, Bedwyr would naturally be at the conference as well, so he had nothing to do but wait for me.

Bedwyr was a complex man. He was Arthur's best friend, and Cei's as well. But he was as different from Cei as a man can be, and different from most other warriors as well. He dressed plainly, without any of the bright colours or jewellery they love. He had very dark brown hair, brown eyes, wore his beard close-trimmed, and his usual expression was one of quiet attention. Very little escaped his notice. He was a Breton, from the south-east of Less Britain, of a noble, Roman-descended family. He had had a Roman education, for the Roman ways are stronger in Gaul than in Britain, but he had not paid much heed to it. He joined the warband of Bran, the younger son of the king of Less Britain, who became Arthur's ally. There he quickly gained in fame and authority, for he was a dangerous cavalry fighter, and had the clarity of thought, the self-possession and the force of personality that make a leader in war. When his lord Bran crossed the sea to help Arthur in his struggle against the kings of Britain for the purple, Bedwyr was one of his captains. But he was wounded in the battle in which Arthur won the title, and lost his shield hand – he had since fought with his shield strapped tightly to his arm. This brush with death had put an end to his former ruthlessness, and he was converted to the philosophy he had read as a boy, and intended to return to Less Britain and become a monk. Instead he met Arthur, and after one conversation had decided that it was better to fight for God than to contemplate him in a monastery. Some dozen warriors had followed him in swearing the oath of allegiance to Arthur, and Lord Bran had ruefully remarked that he had come to Britain to help Arthur to a title, not to his own best warriors. But Arthur smiled and made Bedwyr his cavalry commander.

Yet even as commander of Arthur's cavalry, and later, when Arthur relinquished that position. as warleader, Bedwyr had kept a philosophic detachment. He was a very good man, who had never since his conversion had one base or cruel action reported of him, and he had a passion for honour, but when I first met him, that seemed his only passion. I found him cold. He was never discourteous, but he had had very little to say to me, and would not even look at me for long. After trying for some time to be friends with him and achieving nothing, I presumed that, like many philosophers, he had little use for women. I found this the more irritating because he was only four years older than I, and no grey-bearded sage. I was puzzled that so many others, whom I loved, loved him, and I began to return his coldness with an (equally courteous!) dislike.

When Medraut arrived in Camlann, however, and the quarrels began, I decided that the fortress could not afford this quiet enmity between the Emperor's wife and his warleader, and once again set out to be friends with him. For a long time, again, I made no progress – and then, one afternoon over something quite trivial, Bedwyr smiled at me. His smile transformed his face in a way I had never noticed before, perhaps because I had never received a smile from him before. The dark eyes were warm and delighted, fixed on my face with an attention which had ceased to be quiet and considering and had become alive, eager. Then I saw that I had been wrong all along: he was not cold. His detachment was the protection of a proud and honourable mind against a passionate nature. He had once been ruthless and violent, swayed by impulse, and was now determined to trust his mind alone. And I decided that his philosophic honour had led him to avoid women, so that he scarcely knew how to speak to them, but that he had never consciously been an enemy to me. I began to like him then, and he had ceased to be cold and distant with me, so that I came to love and trust him as Arthur did. It was the one good thing that came out of Medraut's presence at Camlann.

Bedwyr waited while I gave some orders to the steward's wife about the feast, then escorted me out of the kitchens. 'My lord Arthur must have been waiting for us for some time now,' he commented, without anxiety. 'Where were you, my lady? I expected to find you at the storerooms;

indeed, I was told you had gone there.'

I sighed. 'I left the storerooms to visit Rhuawn – yes, another quarrel. With Cei!'

'Ach! And will Rhuawn apologize?'

'Yes. As will Cei. But God knows how long it will last.' And I thought again of Rhuawn's eyes slipping aside from mine, the distrust, the suspicion.

Bedwyr looked at me another moment, then said, 'And?'

'And? And I am concerned for the future. Soon I will be able to coax no more apologies from Rhuawn or from any of . . . his party. But for the quarrel itself, it was no worse than the other quarrels.'

'Well. And yet you look troubled, my lady, more than by the other quarrels.'

I walked on a few steps before looking at him. His eyes were on my face, waiting. 'I am troubled, yes,' I told him. 'But it is a personal matter.'

His expression cleared. 'Your father. Forgive me. I should have remembered and kept silent.'

'Even you cannot remember everything, noble lord. There is nothing to forgive.'

'You have heard from your clan since?'

He was trying to ease the grief of the death by reminding me that I had other family, trying to be kind, and I confused him when I stopped abruptly and clenched my hands together, struggling with myself. I was tired, I thought, or I would not weaken like this, not be so subject to my grief and anger. There had been too much to do in the past month, and the mood of the fortress had been so embittered that often I had been too tense to sleep.

'My lady?' Bedwyr had stopped, facing me, and was watching me with concern.

I waved him back. 'I had a letter from my cousin Menw. He . . . we quarrelled, years ago. He is now clan chieftain. He . . .' I stopped, because I was ashamed that Menw had demanded what he had, and ashamed to accuse him, my own cousin. I did not want to talk of that letter.

Bedwyr's jaw set. He turned and began to walk on, not looking at me, and I joined him. 'You should not allow small-minded men to distress you, my lady,' he said.

'More easily advised than done, Lord Bedwyr. Like most philosophic advice.'

557

He looked at me again, not smiling, not distracted by my attempt to divert him. Half unwilling, I began to tell him about the letter.

We arrived at my house before I finished. The spring sun was still high, although the afternoon was drawing on, and it fell warm and heavy upon our heads and sides. Inside the house someone was playing a harp, and the soft sound carried clear and liquid into the silence when we stopped and I hurriedly ended my account. Bedwyr and I looked at each other.

'It was bravely done, lady,' he said softly. 'It was no doubt a most bitter thing, to accept exile from your home, but it was bravely done. If there were time – but our lord is waiting.'

Arthur was indeed waiting, sitting and staring into the fire with his feet propped against the grate. Lord Gwalchmai ap Lot, who was to be the emissary to Less Britain, was also there: it was he who had been playing the harp. Arthur could not play, for harping is a noble skill not taught at monasteries such as the one where he was raised – but he loved to listen. When Gwalchmai saw us, however, he at once set the harp down and stood to greet us, and Arthur straightened, took his feet off the grate, and waved to us to be seated.

'My lady,' said Gwalchmai, bowing his head; then took my hand and smiled, at me, at Bedwyr. 'And Bedwyr; we thought you must have ridden clear to Ynys Witrin, so long have you been in arriving.'

'Lady Gwynhwyfar was resolving a quarrel between Rhuawn and Cei,' Bedwyr said quietly, taking his seat on Arthur's right.

The corners of Arthur's mouth drew down in pain and he looked at me. 'Another quarrel?'

I nodded and settled wearily into my own place at the desk, opposite Arthur. Gwalchmai resumed his seat, all smiles gone, and stared at the fire. He knew whom the quarrel must have concerned. I watched him for a moment as he sat very dark and still in his crimson cloak with his jewelled sword, his black eyes seeming to look through the flames into another world, as they always did when he was troubled. He had lost weight recently. Part of that had been in travelling – he had returned from Less Britain only the week before, and neither that embassy nor the voyage had been an easy one. But the situation at Camlann must have been almost unbearable for him. I longed to reach past that withdrawal and unearthliness and ease the hurt, to mother him. But it was impossible. He was only four years younger than I and difficult to mother. As Cei had said, he was too courteous. I must watch him suffer the enmity his brother had raised against him, and say nothing.

And it is only enmity to him, now, something in the back of my mind added. *Some day it will be enmity to me and even to Arthur. Medraut will turn the fortress against us. And soon, it will be soon.*

I looked at my husband, who was waiting for me to give an account of the quarrel. Already it hurt him as much as it hurt Gwalchmai, for he loved the Family even more than he loved his Empire, if such a thing were possible, and the division in it was a constant torment to him.

'Cei overheard a comment Rhuawn made to one of his friends,' I told Arthur, 'and he called Rhuawn a fool because of it. Rhuawn returned the insult. But there were no swords drawn and no blows given, and they have agreed to be reconciled.'

Arthur nodded, but his eyes were cold and bitter. 'What was the comment?'

I hesitated, looking at Gwalchmai.

'We will agree that I am not here,' Gwalchmai said, giving an ironic half smile. 'I never heard the comment and need fight no one because of it.'

I hesitated again – but, after all, it did concern the very problem we had come together to discuss. 'He accused you of deliberately obstructing the negotiations with Less Britain. I am sorry.'

Gwalchmai shook his head. He touched the hilt of his sword briefly, for reassurance rather than in anger, then locked his hands together on his knees, staring once more into the fire. He felt responsible for the quarrels and had once asked Arthur to send him away from the Family to avoid them. Arthur had refused.

'There is nothing more we can do to disprove that,' Arthur said, looking at his warrior. 'We are already sending you back to Less Britain. No one can say that I mistrust you.' Gwalchmai nodded, looking no happier.

559

'And the accusation will be the more firmly refuted if we can achieve a settlement with Macsen. So, to the matter at hand.' He fixed his eyes on Gwalchmai until the warrior looked up, smiled ruefully, and bowed his head in agreement. 'Tell us again what Macsen claims.'

Macsen was the king of Less Britain, in Gaul. His kingdom was originally colonized from Britain and was closely bound to it, subject to the same laws and enjoying the same privileges. While Macsen's younger brother Bran was king, all had been peaceful, for Bran was Arthur's ally, joining with him against most of the kings of Britain when Arthur first claimed the purple. But Bran and his brother Macsen had long been rivals, and had nearly come to armed conflict when their father died. Only Bran's alliance with Arthur and Arthur's power had prevented that war, and won Bran the election to the kingship which Macsen thought ought to be his. Now Bran was dead, killed in a border skirmish with the Franks the previous autumn, and Macsen had been chosen king in his place by the royal clan of Less Britain. He was understandably hostile to Arthur, and the whole web of law and custom that bound Britain and Less Britain together was all under challenge. We had sent Gwalchmai as an emissary to Macsen as soon as the weather permitted the voyage, and he had listened to Macsen's claims and justifications for two weeks before sailing back to consult us on the responses we were willing to make. Gwalchmai was invaluable as an emissary: he was of royal birth, and so must be received honourably anywhere; he had been brought up at a scheming court and could find his way through any maze of political intrigue without difficulty; he was literate and could speak good Latin, as well as British, Irish and Saxon, and he was an eloquent advocate in all four languages. None of this had been of any use with Macsen, and I could not help suspecting, as we again plodded over Macsen's claims and our possible responses, that on this mission as well Gwalchmai would achieve a limited success at best. Macsen was unlikely to risk war with us, but he would undoubtedly try every trick short of it to have his way. And if Gwalchmai was forced to return for more consultations, the accusation against him would grow and gain strength, and with it the question: 'Why does Arthur do nothing?' and its insidious answer:

'Arthur is deceived, a fool; Arthur is partial and blind.' I shivered.

The conference ended. It was agreed that Gwalchmai would leave again for Less Britain in two days' time, and he and Bedwyr took their leave, allowing Arthur and me to prepare for that night's feast. I began to take my hair down, as it was to be a formal feast for which I must look impressive and tie my hair up with gold. Arthur looked at me wearily.

'So much for King Macsen,' he said. 'Though, indeed, I think we have no more seen the end of our troubles with him than we have of our troubles with that fox King Maelgwn of Gwynedd. Gwynhwyfar, my heart, I am sick to death of these kings.'

I looked for my comb, found it. 'Unfortunately, these kings cannot be abolished.'

He snorted 'Any attempt would abolish us instead. And they have their rights to their kingdoms.' He stood and moved restlessly about the room, then stopped, leaning his hands on the table, and asked the air, 'What am I to do?'

I knew that he was no longer thinking of Macsen of Less Britain, or of any king. I had heard that note of pain before. More and more often over the past year he had woken at night rigid and soaked with sweat, crying 'Morgawse!' It was always Morgawse, always his dead half-sister who filled his nightmares, and never the waking cause of them, her son Medraut. But there was a reason for that, and he had told it to me the night he had heard that Morgawse was dead. He had told no one else, not even Bedwyr. Gwalchmai knew, but that was because Morgawse had been his mother as well, and Arthur had once assumed that he knew already.

'What am I to do?' Arthur asked again, turning from the wall. 'I must prove things which ought to be obvious, prove that I trust Gwalchmai, whom the worst tyrant would not suspect of disloyalty. And if I can disprove one lie by some public gesture, disprove it without giving it the substance that acknowledging it would give it, I am no better off, for ten more have sprung up. And yet I cannot charge the source of them with anything, for he speaks no treason, and denies originating the rumours with a face of perfect innocence. He uses even my questions against me. If

I could sentence him with exile! But on what charge?'

'I thought we had decided to weather the storm as well as we could,' I said.

'I decided. Bedwyr agreed with me, you and Gwalchmai disagreed. Send him to the Islands, you said, even if it does seem a criminal breach of hospitality. But it is too late for that now. He has friends.'

'He has friends.' I set the comb down; it felt very heavy in my hand. 'Nor would it be safe to send him to the Islands. His brother is . . . ill.'

The eldest son of Morgawse, Agravain ap Lot, king of the Orcades since his father's death, was in fact a broken man. His act of matricide had destroyed him, and now, by all accounts, he was drinking himself to death. His father had had a large degree of control over Pictland and the Western Islands as well as the Orcades, but this was slipping through Agravain's lax fingers, and his clan and countrymen were not pleased. To send Medraut to the Islands when they were so ripe for intrigue would be at once dangerous to ourselves and cruel to Agravain, who had, after all, followed Arthur and fought bravely for him for many years, and who had suffered enough already.

'Even if it were safe, I could not exile him. I have nothing to charge him with. Gwynhwyfar, how did you know that this would happen? You warned me, the first night that he came.'

I thought of Medraut on that first night, sitting at the high table during the feast we had given to welcome his brother, the new king Agravain. He had worn a saffron cloak, and the torchlight caught and glowed in his fair hair. He was a beautiful young man – of average height, like his brother Gwalchmai, strong, graceful, a fine horseman and a skilled warrior. Most of his features were like Gwalchmai's – or, I suppose, like Morgawse's – the straight nose and finely moulded cheekbones, the same narrow long-fingered hands. But his wide-set grey eyes and square jaw were like Arthur's, and I had sensed in him the same passionate dedication I knew so well in my husband. But the dedication, I had been sure, had been to a very different end. And even when Medraut smiled I had been afraid.

I shook my head, then rose, went over to my husband and put my arms around him. He did not move; only his heart beat steadily against mine. 'I did not know,' I whispered into his shoulder. 'I was merely afraid. I do not know why. You and Bedwyr wanted reasons, and you were right. It would have been unjust to have condemned him untried.'

'You had reasons.' Arthur pulled away from me and sank into the chair. 'You have dealt with people enough; I ought to trust you when you say that someone is lying. And I should have listened to Gwalchmai – he knows Medraut better than any living. But I thought he was too close to his mother's death to think clearly yet, and I thought you were being over-cautious and perhaps jealous, and I determined to take the risk. I should not have. The stakes are too high.'

'You couldn't simply have rejected him. He is your son.'

Arthur flinched and looked away from me, leaning against the table and staring at the smoke stain left by the lamp upon the wall. Medraut was his son, born of incest committed twenty-six years before with his sister Morgawse. He had not known, then, that she was his sister; he had not known who his father was. She was a married woman, staying with her father the Emperor while her husband fought a war in the north of Britain. He was one of her father's warriors, a bastard raised at a monastery, who by skill and good luck had found himself a place in the imperial warband. She had paid attention to him, pursued him, told him that her husband was cruel, and eventually seduced him one night after a feast given in honour of his first victory. He had been eighteen at the time. Shortly afterwards, he had discovered that Uther was his father, and discovered from Morgawse that she had known all along. The black horror of that discovery had ridden him ever since.

Arthur had told me this when he heard that she was dead, speaking as though he tore the story from himself like a monstrous growth buried in his flesh. I had wept, but he had been dry-eyed, brutal with himself. 'I knew what she intended when I came out of the Hall and saw her waiting in the shadow,' he said, 'and I agreed to it. I agreed only to adultery, but that was enough, and that one instant of agreeing will extend for the whole of my life, and, if God is just, endure for all eternity. And she is dead, now, and I cannot confront her, cannot ... escape from her.' He picked up the letter that contained the news, stared at it, and said, quietly, so quietly I barely heard him, 'Her son – our son – adored her.'

And yet, when Medraut had appeared at Camlann, he had seemed more confused than hostile. We knew from Gwalchmai that Morgawse had told Medraut the secret of his birth, and Gwalchmai had insisted that his brother was now Arthur's deadly enemy. But Medraut seemed more bewildered than anything else: very bitter against his brothers, but uncertain what to do now that his adored mother was dead. This had given Arthur hope that we might win him over. Gwalchmai had told us that Medraut had once been a sweet-natured child, and that they had been very close. Gwalchmai himself had once worshipped Morgawse, but afterwards broken free of her hold on him. Arthur had hoped that Medraut might do the same. Perhaps he had even hoped to confront and escape the shadow of Morgawse through her son. At any rate, he had given Medraut a place at Camlann. And I could not blame him for hungering for this child of his enemy, this golden youth. I had given him no son, no child at all. There might even be some truth in his idea that I had feared Medraut because I was jealous of him. I could not believe it was so, but on such a matter I might easily lie to myself. Arthur's enemy had given him a son out of hatred, while I, who would have given up my eyes and hearing to bear a child, I was barren.

I sat on the edge of the table and caught Arthur's hand, held it in both of mine. My heart ached again for him, and I was very weary. 'My own,' I said, 'we have decided to try to weather this storm. We have endured worse. Do not torture yourself with it.'

'There will be fights soon. My men may begin to kill each other over Medraut. What am I to do then?'

I did not know. I could only hold his hand and press it until his dark reverie was troubled and he turned to look at me again. Then I kissed his hand, and kissed the ring on his finger, the signet carved with the imperial dragon.

He gave a deep sigh, and the tense muscles relaxed a little. He reached out and stroked my hair back from my face. 'My white hart,' he said. 'Yes, we may yet survive it. All may yet be well.' He rose, kissed me, and added, 'But now there is that feast for the emissaries. We must prepare for it.'

I nodded and went back to combing my hair. I felt as exhausted as though I had spent the entire day journeying, and that on bad roads.

The feast glittered with splendour, and the emissaries of the kings of Elmet and Powys were entertained as magnificently as befitted an imperial court. Our seven hundred warriors filled only half the Feast Hall, and the rest of the places were taken by the wives of the married men – we relaxed the custom which bars women from the Hall, on some occasions – by the entourage of the emissaries, and by priests and potentates and petitioners from all of Britain. Torches in brackets down the walls lit the Hall, and the two great firepits, one at either end, cast light and heat up to the high roof. The whitewashed shields along the wall shone, and the tables were full of the glitter of jewellery and arms and embroidered cloaks, while the collars of sleek warhounds here and there caught the light even under the tables. There were beef and venison, pork and lamb and wild birds to eat, and mead and wine imported from Less Britain to drink till the Hall seemed to whirl in circles. And there was music, songs by Arthur's chief bard Taliesin, who was called the finest poet in Britain, and by other singers as well, till the tables seemed to float in the strains of the harp.

Cei and Rhuawn made their reconciliation at the feast, quietly but publicly. Arthur granted three petitions, one for mercy by a criminal, one for a just settlement of a feud, and one that of the boy Gwyn, who had his place at Camlann confirmed. I had him called in, and he stood before the high table looking very thin and afraid. Arthur smiled at him gently.

'My lord,' Cei said, remembering his irritation from the afternoon, and on edge from the forced reconciliation, 'why not send this boy home and find the Empress a proper clerk instead? He is only a bastard from a monastery, and likely to be no use with either pen or sword.'

Arthur looked at Cei sharply, and the corner of his mouth twitched. The black mood of the afternoon might never have existed. 'Cei,' he said in an even tone, '*I* am a bastard from a monastery.'

'You are an emperor, and were never anything else,' Cei replied without so much as blinking. 'I knew you to be capable of Empire from the time you first came to Camlann, long before you claimed the purple.'

Arthur smiled. 'Spoken with uncustomary gallantry, old friend, but nonetheless a lie. Who was it that called me "the monk" when I first took service with Uther? Yes, and knocked me down when I took exception to the name! And yet, I thank the heart that can so overlook the past. Boy, you are welcome here. You are to help the Empress Gwynhwyfar as she sees fit, and may spend the rest of your time training with the other boys of the fortress. Take note, Lord Gereint, you will have to train him! They use the yard behind the stables in the morning; go and join them tomorrow, if the Empress has nothing for you to do.'

Gwyn flushed with pleasure and bowed very low, his eyes shining. He was a sweet boy, I decided, and I wished him all good fortune. Likely he would need it, for the other boys would hardly welcome a foreign intruder to their well-established circles.

I rose and poured more wine for the high table, as I did at every feast, even the ones most women were barred from – it confers honour, and the men love it. The emissaries smiled and bowed their heads when I poured for them. I knew what they saw – the purple-bordered gown of white silk I was wearing, the gold and the pearls, the confident smile, the lady of the glorious fortress that was the Empire's heart. A lie, and the glory of the feast also a lie, which we told them without speaking a word. The brittle splendour of ice, soon broken; frost on the grass that melts with the morning sun. And yet, the bitter truth of division, of foreign hostility and inner weakness, might fade away, and the glory would remain alone, and who could say then that it was a lie?

Yet that night when I returned to my own house and saw the ashes of Menw's letter in the firepit I grew sickened at myself. I wished desperately to be honest, to weep when I was grieved, to return openly love and hatred, to escape from riches, honour and the sword-edge of power. But Arthur was already in bed, asleep in the sleep of exhaustion. He bore a heavier burden than I, and needed his rest, so I crept into bed quietly so as not to wake him.

Two

I visited the lord Gwalchmai ap Lot the next day, before he
set off for Gaul. He had a house to the east of the Hall, on
the steep side of the hill but with a fine view towards Ynys
Witrin and the marshes. When he was in Camlann – which
because of his value as an emissary was seldom – Gwalchmai shared the house with Cei. When Gwalchmai was not
there, Cei brought his mistress and her children into the
house to live with him, as he disliked being alone. Warriors
are used to close quarters, in the Hall or on campaigns, and
never like solitude. Cei probably would have preferred to
stay in the Hall most nights, but his rank and importance
forbade it, just as it forbade his marrying his mistress. She
was a fat, good-natured washerwoman named Maire and
had been Cei's mistress for some years now. She was a
widow with four children, the last two of whom were
Cei's. She was at the house when I arrived, helping
Gwalchmai's servant Rhys pack while Gwalchmai sat on
the threshold sharpening a spear. Her third child, Cei's
chubby two-year-old son, sat on the other side of the
threshold sucking his thumb and staring at the whetstone as
it glided rhythmically along the bright metal of the spear
head.

Intent on his work, Gwalchmai did not notice me until I
was almost at the door, but when the morning sun cast my
shadow before him he looked up, then set down the whetstone and rose.

'My lady,' he said, 'a hundred welcomes to you.'

Cei's son grabbed the whetstone and began to pound it
hopefully against the threshold. 'No!' Gwalchmai said,
looking for a place to lean the spear. I knelt and took the
whetstone away from the child.

'You mustn't do that,' I told him. 'It will break.'

The child gave a howl of outrage and tried to grab the
stone back.

'Cilydd!' said his mother, emerging indignant from the
house, 'you are a bad boy! Ach, many greetings to you,
most noble lady – Cilydd, be quiet, do not disturb the

lady.'

'Cilydd is like his father: he speaks his mind,' said Gwalchmai, smiling. 'Here.' He picked up another stone, a piece of ordinary flint, and tapped it against the threshold. Cilydd stopped howling and squinted at it. Gwalchmai offered him the stone, and the boy took it and began pounding the doorpost. The warrior straightened and dusted off his hands. 'Again, my lady, welcome,' he said, raising his voice to be heard over the pounding. 'But I am afraid my house is not fit to welcome you, at the minute.'

'Ach, great lord, we can leave,' said Maire cheerfully.

'It would not matter much if you did,' said Gwalchmai's servant Rhys, also emerging from the house, 'for the place would still be inside-out. You have moved in and out often enough, Maire. One would think you could do it better by now.' Maire grinned and bobbed her head, and Rhys, having dealt with her, bowed to me. 'Greetings, most noble lady.'

'I am sorry to have no better hospitality to offer you, my lady,' Gwalchmai said, 'but if you care to come in, there is probably some wine.'

'I thank you, no. Lord Gwalchmai, I wish to speak with you. Perhaps we could walk down to the walls – unless you need to prepare for your journey now, of course.'

'I am the last one needed to prepare for my journey; indeed, I am in the way – am I not, Rhys? It is a sweet morning, my lady. Let us walk.' He leaned the spear against the doorpost, then, looking at Cei's son and his flint hammer, handed the weapon to Rhys instead. I handed Rhys the whetstone, which I was still holding, and Gwalchmai and I set off down the hill. It was indeed a sweet morning. The previous day's clear weather continued, and the sun was bright in a soft sky, the air warm enough to make my spring cloak too heavy. Gwalchmai wore no cloak, and for once was without his mail shirt as well, and he walked lightly. His red tunic was loose, and I could see the end of a scar running up onto his collar bone. He had plenty of scars.

'You seem pleased today,' I said, to start the conversation, and because he did appear happy – a rare thing recently. 'And Rhys did as well. Are you glad to be leaving Camlann?'

'To be leaving Camlann – I am neither pleased nor displeased at that, lady. But I am glad, for Rhys's wife had her child last night, and she and the baby are both well.'

'Ach, good! I must visit them. Is it a girl or a boy?'

'A girl. And Rhys is pleased with that, as well, for now he has both a son and a daughter.'

'I am very glad of it. So, will Rhys be coming with you to Gaul now?'

He shook his head. 'I have told him to stay. He was meaning to stay until his wife was delivered, and there is no need to change the plans. He now says that he will go, because she is safe, but it is plain that his heart stays with her, and I would not wish to drag the rest of him away.'

I was a trifle disappointed. Rhys was a plain, honest, down-to-earth farmer's son, and in his way as great an idealist as Arthur. When he had become Gwalchmai's servant he had eased one trouble from my mind. Gwalchmai was otherworldly enough to forget to eat, and honourable enough that he thought it preferable to be cheated than to stand up for his rights against someone weaker. Without Rhys he would undoubtedly overwork himself. I wanted to order him to be gentle with himself, wanted to mother him, as I had ever since I first met him. Then he had been flat on his back and delirious among the other wounded whom Arthur had left in my father's cow-byre, the first time he came to my home. Gwalchmai had watched me then with the dark eyes of an injured animal, and flinched when I came near him. Most wounded men like having a woman to tend them. They are reminded of their mothers, and feel safer. Perhaps I had reminded Gwalchmai of his mother, and the thought of Morgawse had frightened him. At any rate, I had noticed him, shown him special warmth, until the wariness dissolved suddenly and absolutely into gratitude and friendship. But he was too proud to receive much from another. He would give his heart's blood, for me, or for any of his friends, but I could not tell him not to work too hard. So I said only, 'I hope your journey will not be too long.'

'It is not likely to be long.' His smile faded. He knew as well as I that Macsen would raise new questions for every one that we solved, and that he would have to return to Camlann for more consultations.

'That is what I wished to speak to you about,' I told him. 'You will probably be back in another month.'

He nodded, frowning a little, his eyes fixed on my face.

'Although officially you have heard nothing, you know of this new rumour. If the negotiations are protracted, it will grow. And as it grows it will turn into an attack on Arthur as well as on you. They have begun to move against him, these rumours: they hint more and more that he is a fool, that he listens to flattery, and is partial and unjust. Listen, I want you to bring up the subject of the negotiations tonight and in the hearing of those who believe the rumour. If one of them challenges you on it, appeal to Arthur and have it dismissed. I talked to him about it this morning, and we agreed that this might kill it.'

The frown grew deeper. 'I could speak of it tonight in the Hall. But I do not think I would be challenged. And if I were challenged – my lady, I do not wish to fight anyone. If I were challenged it might well be in such a way that it would be impossible to settle the matter by appeal, and I would have to fight.'

'You could always appeal. No one would suspect *you* of being afraid.'

'They will say that I am afraid to kill; or, more likely, that our lord Arthur prevented me from fighting so that I would not kill, because he did not trust what I would do in combat. And there would be some truth to that. I do not know what I might do, either.'

Gwalchmai was subject to a kind of madness in battle, which took his actions beyond his or anyone's control. He considered it a gift from Heaven. Medraut had made much of it, saying that his brother's mind was disturbed and that he was likely to go berserk at any time. I had never seen this famous madness, and certainly never seen any trace of insanity in Gwalchmai, but most of the Family had fought beside him and were more willing to listen to Medraut's stories.

'Are you really afraid of that?' I asked Gwalchmai. "Have you ever killed against your will – for instance, in a mock combat?'

He hesitated. 'No. No, I do not think I would kill ... but even without killing, I do not wish to fight anyone of the Family.'

'Nor do I want you to fight anyone. But I want the matter brought into the open.'

'If it is, and if I can appeal, and Arthur then decrees for me, it will merely transfer the blame to him.'

'And that will help to bring the matter to a head. Gwalchmai, time is against us. Medraut has worked slowly. First he exclaimed against Agravain as a matricide, and then you. He found a faction of his own. Now there is a continual questioning of Arthur's judgement, and a mask of wronged innocence when it becomes apparent that Arthur suspects and disbelieves him. But if we push the pace, make him accuse Arthur now, before his followers have had their minds quite poisoned, we may force him further than his friends wish to go. We may even catch him in treason, and be able to exile him somewhere and reunite the Family. But if we let him take his own time, he will destroy us. Isn't that his goal?'

'It is. But you have omitted one of the things he has done, my lady. He knows that you are his enemy. He says that you are in league with me; perhaps he even says we are lovers – forgive me! I think he may have hinted that. If Arthur supports me, it will be said that it is your doing, that he is weak, a deceived husband ruled by his wife. It would be very ugly.'

'It will be ugly, and painful. But it will be worse if we delay. We must get it over with.'

'There is another thing Medraut may do,' Gwalchmai said, very quietly. He glanced about to see that no one was near enough to hear us. But we had reached the walls and were walking along them, with open space on one hand and only the rough mass of stone on the other. 'He may accuse my lord Arthur with the truth.'

'It will still take time for him to have the truth accepted,' I replied, after a pause. 'And he will not have the time if we succeed.'

Gwalchmai was quiet for a while, walking with his head down, staring at the grasses. Finally he nodded. 'Very well,' he said heavily. 'Since you think it likely to do good – and very probably, after all this, no one will challenge me.' He smiled apologetically.

'Thank you.' I caught his hand and pressed it. 'And you need not try to fight anyone. I agree that your killing a

571

member of Medraut's faction would be the worst thing possible.'

He smiled again and bowed his head. I had known that he would do as I requested, and had known also that he would be reluctant. I had been the one to speak to him, rather than Arthur, because Arthur he would have obeyed at once, while he allowed me to argue him into it. It was easier for him so. But it was a hard thing to ask of him. He knew that, despite my reassurances, he might be required to fight a duel, and could only hope that he would not be forced to kill. I knew how bitter the thought of drawing his sword against a member of the Family must be to him. I looked at his worn face and wished I had not had to ask it of him. But that is another of the bitter facts of power: those who give freely must be asked to give again and again, till they have nothing left to give, while those misers who hoard every drop of their wealth and strength can escape rich and easy to the grave. Perhaps God will give fair justice to all, but they find none on Earth.

We came to one of the stairways built along the inner face of the wall, and climbed it to the ramparts. The walls were not guarded in time of peace, and the battlements stretched empty to either side, curving about the hill. We turned, and looked back at Camlann, rising lively and strong from the smoke of the morning fires.

I looked sideways at my companion. It was hard that Cei must be restrained from quarrels, when he took them lightly, and that Gwalchmai must be encouraged to court them. But it would do no good to have Cei quarrelling, while Gwalchmai might manage to resolve something ... he looked like his brother Medraut, the cause of his grief. He was said to look even more like his mother Morgawse, the reputed witch. Blood is a strange thing, that can be so at odds with itself ... I thought of my cousin Menw, and turned the thought quickly. 'Gwalchmai,' I said, because it was a bright morning and I could speak of such things, 'your mother – was she beautiful?'

He did not seem surprised at the question, but his hand slid to the hilt of his sword and his eyes widened a trifle, as they did whenever she was mentioned. At times like this he looked as though he had stepped from the hollow hills, and most people seeing him in such a mood crossed themselves.

'She was very dreadful,' he said, softly but quickly.

'But was she beautiful?'

He paused, his thumb idly rubbing the gold crosspiece of his sword's hilt. 'I do not know,' he said finally. "I always said, "She is beautiful", to explain what happened to those who beheld her. Yet when I confronted her – twice I confronted her, once when I left the Islands, and once before she died – then she did not seem beautiful. No. If the sea and the earth are beautiful, she could not have been. But to look at her troubled the soul, and no one who once saw her could forget her.'

'But why? Even now, even dead, she influences us. Arthur and Medraut both fear her still. And Agravian...' I stopped myself; it was not kind to remind Gwalchmai of his brother.

'It was the force of her hatred and the force of her will,' he said, slowly now, but still softly. 'Her sorcery. That was real, as I have cause to know. In her ... it was as though this world and the Otherworld met.'

'You speak as though she were a kind of demon.'

He looked away. 'Perhaps she was.'

I put out my hand to touch his, to call him back to the real world – then, again, stopped myself. Instead, I turned and looked out over the fields outside the wall, beyond the ring and bank defences of the fortress. The nearest field was brown and raw, newly furrowed by the plough; beyond it sheep grazed in a pasture and the new lambs were dancing in the sun. Far off rose the hill of Ynys Witrin, blue-green and mysterious above the deeper green of the marshes. It seemed to float above the cultivated land. I could see why it had its name, 'Isle of Glass'. But now that name made me think of the castles in the tales, the towers of glass which are said to revolve between this world and the next, surrounded by mist, torchlight and sea: gateways to either Yffern or the Kingdom of Summer, to Heaven or to Hell. The tales say that this world and the next penetrate each other. You can walk into a familiar field, they say, and suddenly find that it has grown strange; and turning, discover that all familiar things are gone. And they say that what the world is depends on the heart's intention, that reality is fluid as water, that one can put one's hand through its cool surface and touch some deeper reality, like a rock beneath the surface of a stream. And had Morgawse found some such reality, to trouble the current of the world by the power of her will and the power of her hatred?

I took a deep breath, feeling the wooden upper rampart of the wall warm and real beneath my hand. Too much poetry, too much listening to tales, I told myself. And yet, I was answered. Even dead, Morgawse's influence surrounded us; and perhaps I understood something of the reason. Perhaps I had known it for a long time.

'We must get Medraut away from Camlann,' I said, aloud, and Gwalchmai, turning to meet my eyes, nodded.

The immediate attempt to push the pace, however, failed. Gwalchmai brought up the subject of the negotiations in the Hall that night, and did all he could to rub it in the faces of Rhuawn and the rest of Medraut's faction, but they said nothing whatever to him in reply, merely whispered among themselves afterwards. And the next day Gwalchmai left for Gaul. He was the centre of the dispute, and we did not dare use anyone else to push the pace.

That same day I visited the wife of Gwalchmai's servant Rhys, bringing a gold charm for her new baby. I found Eivlin already on her feet again, with the ever-present Maire attending her. Maire had her own baby with her, but the rest of her children were not there, and had presumably been left in the care of her eldest, a girl of ten. Both women made me welcome, and showed me the new baby with great pride, as well they might, for she was a fine, healthy little girl.

'We named her Teleri, after a nun who was kind to us,' Eivlin explained, while I offered the baby my finger to clutch. 'Though, indeed, I hope this one will not be a nun, nor so strong-willed as her namesake – or as you, you good-for-nothing little fox!' – this to her son, her first child, who stuck his fingers in his mouth complacently, and smiled at her through them. 'Och, look at him! As though he had not drunk all the cream from the milk this morning, and then refused his dinner! Well, Sion, Mama is too tired to thrash you for it, but do you know what your father will say when he comes home?'

'He'll give me some nuts,' predicted the boy through his fingers. 'He promised.'

'Indeed he will, for he's a fool and spoils the boy,' said

Eivlin sorrowfully, 'as I do as well, more's the pity.'

Maire laughed. 'Ach, he's not spoiled; are you spoiled, Sion?'

Sion shook his head.

'You must be a good boy, and look after your little sister.'

Sion beamed at her, and nodded.

'He has been longing for a sister,' Eivlin explained. 'He would have preferred a brother, but now he only wants to play with Teleri. Indeed, it will be a task and a labour and a hard trouble to stop him strangling her with embraces.'

'Who did you name Sion after?' I asked, feeling clumsy and uncertain with these women. Most of my work had to do with administering Camlann, and with affairs of state, and hence with men; Eivlin and Maire inhabited a different world. I often found I had little to say to other women.

'Sion? He is named for Rhys's father, of course. Rhys is a Rhys ap Sion, and his father is a Sion ap Rhys, and *his* father was Rhys ap Sion.'

'Who was *his* father, then?'

'A Sion ap Huw,' she said regretfully. 'Still, *that* Huw's brother was called Rhys, so the name is old enough, and a good name, too. Hush, my love,' to the baby. 'See the pretty thing the gracious lady has brought you?' The baby's blank, unfocused gaze took no notice of the golden charm Eivlin suspended above her head. Eivlin set it in her hand, and the small red fingers half-folded around it, feebly, the way they clutched any object that touched them; then the blurred eyes closed and the child went back to sleep.

'You must be tired,' I said to Eivlin. 'I will go, and let you rest.'

'You are most gracious, most noble lady; indeed, it is fine, to receive visits from an empress! I thank you.'

I made myself smile and excused myself, declining Maire's offers of wine-cakes and new cheese, just made, which she would be delighted to present to the Empress. I walked back up the hill struggling with my soul. I did not want to be an empress, gracious and strong for her husband's subjects. I wanted at that moment, desperately, to be a plain man's wife and to have children of my own.

As I walked past the stables I saw Bedwyr training a horse, a two-year-old brown gelding he had been working on the lead rein. When he saw me he lopped the rein around one of the fence-posts and came towards me. I forced myself to smile.

'My lady! A fine day,' he called, coming up, the warmth of a smile in his eyes.

'A beautiful day,' I returned. I smiled again and began to walk off. I did not want to talk to anyone.

'What is the matter?' he asked, the warmth disappearing from his look and concern taking its place.

'Nothing, Lord Bedwyr; I am in a hurry, that is all. Will I see you in the Hall tonight?'

But he had reached me and caught my arm, looking at my face carefully. 'You are nearly in tears, my lady,' he observed, in the same tone he would have used to say, 'Your gown has a thread loose on the sleeve.' 'Lady Gwynhwyfar, can I be of any help?'

I shook my head, pulled my arm free and began to walk up the hill again. He came after me. 'If I can be of aid to you, do not hesitate to ask it,' he told me. 'If it is your cousin, if you should want help ... my lady, I could beg my lord Arthur's leave, ride north, and speak to him for you. I promise you, if it came to fighting in your name, I would not kill him.'

I stopped, astonished. 'Merciful Heaven, no! Lord Bedwyr, you are most generous, but ... indeed, I thank you, it is kind, it is more than kind! But do not bring up this matter of my cousin, I beg you, before Arthur and the world! And for you to speak for me ... it is noble, but not wise, for how could I speak to my kin after? I ...' I paused, overcome. 'I thank you. But it was not my cousin's letter that troubled me, lord. It was ... something else.'

'Come and have some wine,' he offered. 'You are weary, and it will be better if you rest a moment.'

I went with him to his house, and he poured me a cup of wine, adding an equal measure of water. His house was on the west side of the Feast Hall, near mine. Because he was warleader he had all three rooms to himself. It was much like my house, but plainer, suiting his taste. The only decoration was a rack of books on the desk, at which I sat while I drank the wine. He sat by the fireplace and looked at me.

'Thank you,' I said, managing to keep my voice even again. 'It was a foolish matter. I should never have allowed it to distress me.' I intended to say nothing more, to turn the conversation to the books or to politics, but under his calm, concerned eyes I suddenly found myself saying, 'Oh, Bedwyr, I wish to God I could have children!'

He jumped up, started towards me, then stopped, looking at me. I pressed my hands against my face, drew them down under my eyes to ease the pressure there. 'It is only that I am tired,' I said. 'One feels it, sometimes: all the wars and consultations and factions. And sometimes I wish I could be an ordinary woman – ach, I know, no doubt I would hate it if I were. Only . . . if I had a child, if Arthur had a son . . . he would never have trusted Medraut, if he had a son by me, and we would have a future, someone to inherit the Empire when we are gone . . . and I would so love to have a baby, my own child . . .'

'Hush,' he said, and then did cross the room to me and stooped clumsily over me, patting me awkwardly on the back with the stump of his shield arm. I burst into tears, and he put his arms around me while I leaned against his shoulder and sobbed, bitterly ashamed of myself all the time.

After a while I pulled away from Bedwyr and dried my eyes. He leaned back against the desk, his arm still around my shoulder, still watching me with concern. I fumbled for the wine glass, took another sip of wine, and managed to smile. 'Forgive me,' I said. 'It is very weak and foolish of me.'

'My lady!' he protested. 'God knows, you bear the weight of Camlann: is it strange that you grow weary now and then? I am honoured that you should choose me to speak to.' I laughed a little, wiping my eyes again. 'Truly, I am honoured!' he said, with some vehemence. 'Do not blame yourself, noble lady. There is not one of us who is not borne down by cares sometimes, and few who have as many cares as you.'

'But not all of us imitate a fountain because of it,' I replied.

'True. Most warriors asked to endure what you do would take a sword to one of their comrades over a trivial word or a joke. Fountains are safer.'

I laughed, wiped my face once more, and rubbed my hands dry on my gown. 'But not for your cloak, noble lord;

I can see that I have drenched it as well as any rainstorm.'

He glanced at the damp patch on his shoulder, then smiled, the smile that lit his face from the inside. I returned the smile, then rose shakily to my feet.

'I must be going, lord,' I told him. 'I am supposed to discuss next year's tribute with the emissary from Elmet this afternoon, and I have some petitioners to hear before then. So we must weep a while and part, like lovers in a ballad. I thank you for the wine and for the use of your shoulder.'

'I am your servant, my lady,' he returned seriously. He opened the door for me. As I paused outside it to take my leave he added, 'my lady, you should demand less of yourself, and work less hard.'

'More easily advised than done, Lord Bedwyr. Strange that that saying should apply to so much of your good advice! But I thank you. Truly.'

I felt his concerned gaze follow me all the way to the Hall. I was ashamed that I had broken before him. And yet, I felt better for it. It is useful to weep, sometimes: it frees one to concentrate on other things afterwards. And, as they say, a grief shared is a burden halved. But I wished I could have spoken to Arthur about it. Yet he had burdens enough and more than enough of his own; and I could never quite mention my childlessness to him. That, while it must be his grief as well as mine, was plainly my failure. In that at least Medraut gave true evidence.

The next day there was another almost-duel, but after that Camlann became comparatively quiet. This was not because anything was resolved, however, but because Arthur managed to send some of the most quarrelsome warriors off in opposite directions: one party escorting a supply train to the work on the dyke repairs in the Saxon kingdom of the East Angles, and the other to Dyfed, to enforce a settlement of some debated lands. Medraut himself was kept at Camlann. We could not trust him to leave it, either with his friends or with his enemies.

Gwalchmai returned from Less Britain in the second week of May, looking ill and worn to the bone. The negotiations with Macsen had gone exactly as I had expected: one or two claims were resolved, but five more had been raised in their place. Moreover, Gwalchmai had had to use all of his skill to prevent himself from becoming entangled in a duel with some of Macsen's warband, who had been deliberately provocative. If he had fought them, and won – and he would not have lost – Macsen would have had a legal charge against him, and through him, against us, which he could have used to block future negotiations. Arthur was angered by this, and, instead of sending Gwalchmai back, wrote Macsen a courteous letter requesting that he send an emissary of his own to negotiate the points which remained to be settled. He also commanded Gwalchmai to remain in Camlann and avoided giving him any work. He wanted to give the warrior a rest, but he wanted even more to bring out the smouldering tension in Camlann and resolve it. The plan worked, too, after a fashion, for the conflict burst into open fire soon after the quarrelsome parties returned from Dyfed and East Anglia: and yet still little was resolved.

I was taking an inventory of wool in the storerooms when Medraut came in to find me.

I had been walking along the stacked bales of different weights and dyes, checking them, while my clerk Gwyn trailed along behind me and noted down the amount of each kind on a wax tablet. The sheep of the region had been recently shorn, and I needed to know how much more wool I should buy for the fortress, and so needed to update my inventory. The storeroom was a long, narrow building, windowless, with the wool bales stacked up to the roof, and the sunlight coming through the eaves in dusty streaks. Many of the older bales had been sitting in storage for a long while, and were close-packed, compressed and thick with dust; I had to stoop over and prod them to find out what they were, and they covered my hands with their grease and filled my lungs with the dust. Then the door at the far end of the storeroom opened, letting in a flood of blinding sunlight, and Medraut paused in it like a statue of a Roman god. I stopped counting the bales and straightened.

'Noble lord?' I said, trying not to cough.

He strolled leisurely through the door, out of the sunlight, down the narrow building, and stopped before me. He gave a slight bow, then stood looking at me with Arthur's grey stare and the hint of a smile at the corners of his mouth. He was, as always, impeccably dressed, his short beard neatly trimmed, graceful, controlled, invulnerable. 'My lady,' he said, a dutiful concern in his soft, pleasant voice. 'The lord Goronwy has been hurt in a duel, and the Emperor wishes you to join him in attendence on him at once.'

'Oh God,' I said. I rubbed my filthy hands on the apron I was wearing, then pulled the thing off and tossed it onto one of the bales. Medraut glanced down, not quite quickly enough for me to miss the look of satisfaction in his eyes. 'How badly hurt? Who was he fighting?'

'Most noble lady, how would I know how badly he is hurt? I was not there. I was told he has been taken to the house of Gruffydd the surgeon; I pray he is not much hurt, for he is my friend.' He paused another moment, then added, 'The warleader, Lord Bedwyr, was the one that hurt him.'

'Bedwyr?' I asked, staring at him. I could not imagine Bedwyr embroiled in a duel. Yet Medraut would not fabricate such a thing. He nodded now, still with that faint hint of a smile. Goronwy was one of his followers, his supposed friends; but he was pleased that there was bloodshed, if I judged him right, and did not mind whose the blood – though no doubt he would have preferred Bedwyr's to Goronwy's. 'Where is Arthur?' I asked, suppressing my sudden loathing of him.

'With Goronwy, at Gruffydd the surgeon's house, noble queen. May I have the honour of attending you there?'

'I thank you, no. Undoubtedly the lord Goronwy should not be disturbed by many visitors. Gwyn, leave that now. Lord Medraut, your pardon.' I gave him a slight curtsy, the politest way I knew of saying, 'I want no more of your company', and hurried from the room. Gwyn gave one frightened look at Medraut and ran after me.

'You don't have to come,' I told the boy as we hurried through the hot, sullen afternoon sun. 'I won't need you again this afternoon. You can go to weapons practice – or is it riding this afternoon?'

'Riding, noble lady,' he said. He sounded utterly wretched.

'Why, what's the matter?' I asked him, registering his distress for the first time.

He stopped, fixing me with his oddly dark eyes. I had grown very fond of him in the short time he had been at

Camlann. He was a sweet-tempered boy, with a great deal of courage. He suffered the dislike or cruelty of the other boys at Camlann with patient persistence, and worked at his weapons with unflagging determination. I had once found him weeping in a corner of the stables, but he had at once dried his eyes and denied that he had cause to weep.

'Noble lady . . .' he said, then, in a rush, 'I know I am no one, no one at all, but you should not trust Lord Medraut. It is his fault that Bedwyr fought Goronwy.'

I looked at him in surprise. 'You seem very certain of that.'

'Everyone knows it,' he replied. 'Goronwy is the lord Medraut's friend, and the lord Bedwyr is the lord Gwalch-mai's friend: why else would they fight?'

I put my hand on his shoulder, feeling the bones through the plain tunic. He had learned very quickly. But he was an intelligent boy. 'Why do you hate Medraut so?' I asked gently.

'He . . . once he hit my mother.'

'What? How could he? Was he on some expedition?'

'It was at the convent, in Gwynedd. I had nightmares about it for years.'

'But you said that your mother was at a convent in Elmet.'

He blushed. 'Oh.' He looked at his feet. 'I didn't want to say it was in Gwynedd because the monasteries there are so full of sedition. I was afraid you would not accept me here if I said I came from Gwynedd. Please, noble lady, don't tell anyone that it is really Gwynedd. The others will say . . . you won't tell them?'

'Of course not. But what happened?'

'He came to the convent, with some of his followers to . . . to take something which he had no right to. My mother tried to shame him out of it, but he hit her with the side of his sword and rode off without looking back. He hit her, and knocked her down, and she was bleeding. I saw that he had no honour and no shame, and I swore that one day I would become a warrior and challenge him. But when I came here, I found him, proud and powerful, and many of the warriors following after him like . . . like dogs looking for titbits. And he does nothing but engender quarrels and slander his brother Gwalchmai. I have heard people talking ... my lady, people talk in front of me because they think, "He is just a servant; he must be a fool". I know what Medraut says to his followers, and it is all lies. The lord Gwalchmai,' with a plain and desperate intensity, 'the lord Gwalchmai is a great and good warrior. He is the best, the very greatest warrior in Camlann. If I could be like any of them I would like to be like him. You must not believe what the lord Medraut says of him. I know that I am only a nun's bastard, as the lord Cei says, but please, please believe me, my lady. You must not trust Medraut.'

I thought over what Gwyn had said, and regretfully decided that there was nothing that would be useful. 'Hush,' I told him. 'We do not believe what Medraut says of Gwalchmai.' I turned and began to walk up the hill again.

'Then why do you let him stay here?' Gwyn cried out, running after me. '*He* says that you would send him away if what he says was false, and many people believe him. And he says that the Emperor is set about with flatterers, and does not know whom to trust, and he says that you, most noble lady, are the worst of the flatterers – oh, forgive me! I did not mean ...'

'I know what Medraut says, Gwyn,' I told him, without looking at him. 'But you see, we cannot send him away. Rulers cannot send people away without charging them with some crime, and we have nothing to charge him with. And he has fought for Arthur for some years now. We must pretend to overlook him, and hope that we can weather whatever storm he manages to raise. But do not be afraid to tell me what Medraut says. If there is something important, I want you to tell me immediately. It would help me, and the Emperor as well. And we can hope that Medraut will find nothing to confirm his accusations, and they will eventually fail for lack of evidence, so that men will see him for what he is. But do not tell anyone what I have just told you, Gwyn. Officially, Medraut is one of us and trusted, and I cannot be reported to have said differently or many people will think Medraut is right and that I am his cunning enemy.'

'Yes, my lady,' he whispered. 'But the lord Gwalchmai ...'

'No one who knows Gwalchmai at all well will believe

Medraut's accusations. But come, why do you so admire him, Gwyn? You can scarcely have met him.' I looked back at the boy, managing to smile.

The distraction worked He flushed a little. 'I always admired him – from the songs, you know. And I saw him once in Gwynedd. I thought he looked like an angel of God. He rode by on his horse, looking like the Word of God in the Apocalypse ... there was a picture of that in a gospel I copied, my lady. But he is courteous, even to people like me, and he notices. The other day,' – the flush grew deeper – 'he told me how to use a spear from horse-back, and he showed me himself what I had been doing wrong, and was so kind! And he said I ride well.'

I smiled again, this time a real smile. I could imagine Gwyn seeing Gwalchmai, in Gwynedd: a small boy raised on songs and illuminated gospels transforming the great white stallion, the gold, crimson and glitter of arms into wings of light, something as much greater than the world as his own hopes. Well, he could have chosen worse men for his hero-worship. It said much for Gwyn that he admired gentleness and courtesy as well as strength of arms. 'Gereint the riding-master says you ride well, also,' I told him. 'And he thinks, as I do, that you will make an excellent warrior, if you continue to learn as quickly as you have done.'

'I ... I thank you, most noble lady,' he stammered, his eyes shining. He was as transparent as spring water, that boy, and could not more hide his feelings than he could fly.

'Then go and practise riding, most noble warrior, and we will finish with the wool inventory tomorrow morning. Is it well?'

'Very well, my lady!' he replied and, seizing my hand, pressed it to his forehead before running off. I was able to smile again, really smile, as I hurried on to Gruffydd's house.

The surgeon lived on the north-west side of the Hall, half-way down the hill. He was by birth a townsman from Caer Ebrauc, and had received some education there, and some training in surgery from those in that city who remembered the skills of the long-vanished Roman legions. On coming of age he had joined a monastery and learned some physic to supplement his knowledge of surgery, but had quarrelled with his abbot and been forced to leave. He joined Arthur shortly after the death of the Emperor Uther, before Arthur himself claimed the purple. He was a sensible, hard-headed man who never had a good word or an unkind deed for anyone. When I entered his house he was pouring some sticky syrup into a cup of wine, scowling. Goronwy, the injured man, lay on a bed. His sword arm was bound across his bare chest and his side and shoulder were bandaged. His face above his black beard was pale and he was sweating.

Gruffydd nodded and grunted when he saw me, but did not greet me. He set the cup in Goronwy's left, uninjured hand: the wine wavered as his hand shook. He swallowed some of the potion and made a face.

'Drink it all,' Gruffydd advised him. 'It will dull the pain – no, here.'

'I can drink it by myself; I left my mother years ago. Why didn't you give it me before, if it dulls pain?'

'I did give you some before; I'm giving you more now. I wanted you to have some of your wits about you while I worked. It would be easy enough to cut through a nerve, cleaning a wound like that, and under a broken collar bone. *Gloria Deo!* Are you eager to lose the use of your arm? As if you hadn't already given enough proof of your foolishness by duelling!'

'My lady,' said Arthur, emerging from the shadows beside the bed. I had not noticed him till that moment, and my heart leapt suddenly. He took my hands a moment and pressed them. The lines about his mouth and eyes were very pronounced.

'Medraut told me you were here, and wanted me,' I said.

He nodded, letting go of my hands. 'I saw him on my way here, and sent him.'

'Medraut!' said Goronwy, trying to sit up. 'He knows of this, then? Already?'

'I imagine half the fortress knows that you and the lord Bedwyr fought, Lord Goronwy,' I replied, keeping my voice even.

'Ah.' Goronwy fell back on the bed again. 'Well. If you see him, tell him that I would welcome his company. It was for his sake that I fought, and, had he been present, he would himself have fought, so this matter concerns him.'

584

Gruffydd grunted. 'It is for me to say whether or not you are well enough to see visitors. And I say that you will see none, not until tomorrow.'

Goronwy tried to sit up again, groaned and fell back. Gruffydd took the cup from him, poured some more wine, and added some more syrup. 'Take it,' he ordered. 'It will put you to sleep.' Goronwy took it without argument.

'Why did you fight the lord Bedwyr?' Arthur asked, as soon as the cup was empty. His voice was quiet, calm. Only I, who knew him so well, could hear the tension in it.

Goronwy blinked at him. 'My lord, he . . . damn his spear! He said I was a liar!'

'Did he so? Why?'

Goronwy blinked again. The drug was having its effect, as Arthur no doubt had calculated. 'He said I . . . no, first we were talking about the lord Gwalchmai, my lord. Morfran ap Tegid, and Constans, and I. We were in the Hall. And I said that you did not send Gwalchmai back to Gaul because you suspected him of negotiating with King Macsen in bad faith. But Morfran said . . . he said, "By Heaven, it was false," and that you did not send Gwalchmai because he was ill. And Constans said that he could well believe that, and that Gwalchmai was indeed ill – in his wits, from killing his mother. He has a quick tongue, Constans! And Morfran went very quiet and shifty-eyed, and asked whether it was Medraut who said this; and Constans asked why he wished to know – and it was then that the lord Bedwyr came up – he had been sitting down the Hall from us – and said that Gwalchmai was not ill, but that you, my lord, wished him to rest, and that no one doubted his loyalty. And I said that that was false, for there are plenty that doubt it, and with reason; and he called me a liar. How can an honourable man endure it? I challenged him to fight me then and there. He said nothing, merely nodded, and we went out to the stable yards and saddled our horses and set to it. But damn his spear! On the very first attack, before I can get in one good blow, he jabs me under the arm and pushes me off my horse, so I am unfit to fight anyone for months. And, my lord, it is true that you distrust Gwalchmai, is it not?'

'I trust Gwalchmai above my own shield-hand,' Arthur replied evenly. 'And Bedwyr I trust above my sword-hand. You have given too much belief to idle rumours, Goronwy.' He took the cup away from the warrior, gently. 'Listen, cousin. This quarrel within my Family grieves me as deeply as your wound does you. I wish you to end it.'

Goronwy looked up at him, still blinking sleepily, his lower lip caught between his teeth. 'But you would trust Gwalchmai, after all? To such a degree as that? He is a matricide!'

'Cousin, that too is false. Think a moment, of the form in which you first heard the tale of the death of Queen Morgawse of the Islands. At first, were not all agreed that she died at the hand of Lord Agravain? And you have heard why. Think also of Gwalchmai. You have known him as many years as I have, and fought beside him from here to Caledon. Think how often he has saved us in battle, and how well he has served us on embassies, and how slow he is to quarrel with anyone, even the lowest servant. Can you truly believe that he is mad, and worse, treacherous? And can you believe that I would not know or act if it were so? Am I a fool, Goronwy?'

Goronwy looked at me, suddenly, uneasily; then returned his eyes to Arthur with a look of bewilderment. Arthur leaned forward and caught his hand, clasping it. 'Cousin,' he said, 'again, you think of wild rumours. But think of what you yourself have done and seen, what you know. You know who and what I am, and you know Gwalchmai, and Bedwyr.'

Goronwy continued to look at him in bewilderment.

'Will you be reconciled with Lord Bedwyr?' Arthur asked, after a silence.

'With Bedwyr? Yes, damn his spear. If he takes back the name of liar.'

'He will do so. But you must not stir up your friends against him.'

'If you desire it so, my lord, I will keep silent about this quarrel.'

'I do so desire it. Excellent, my cousin. Sleep now.' Arthur set Goronwy's hand down on the bed, where it clenched slowly and relaxed. My husband watched his warrior a moment, his face grim, then turned and left the room.

The neighbouring room was Gruffydd's kitchen, also

where he prepared his drugs. Arthur leaned wearily against the heavy table while Gruffydd closed the adjoining door, then asked, 'And Bedwyr is unharmed?'

'Entirely. It was he who brought Goronwy here. Nor is Goronwy hurt badly, besides the broken bone. He should mend quickly.'

Arthur nodded, then, in a low voice, said, 'He is not to see the lord Medraut. Prevent him any way that you can: tell Medraut that he is asleep, or is then too weak to see visitors. But allow Bedwyr to visit him.'

'I will do that, lord. And I will keep Rhuawn away as well, and all the rest of Medraut's faction, to give Goronwy a chance to regain his wits.' He met Arthur's steady eyes for a long moment, then added, 'It is what you wish, isn't it, my lord?'

Arthur nodded. 'It is. But do not be obvious in the doing of it.'

'Never fear. But I will work on him myself, and see if I can talk him out of his slanders.' As Arthur continued to fix him with his eyes, Gruffydd added defensively, 'Gwalchmai is my friend, and it sits ill with me to hear him called a traitor by some golden weasel such as Medraut.'

'The whole business is very ill, but Goronwy is a good man despite it. Whatever you say, do not begin any more quarrels! We can only hope that this will wear itself out with time, and that someone will challenge Gwalchmai directly.' After another moment, Gruffydd nodded, and Arthur sighed, rubbing his mouth. 'Good. If you need anything for Goronwy, or want him moved, the servants will have orders to help you. Gwynhwyfar, Bedwyr will be waiting at our house.'

Bedwyr was sitting on the edge of the desk, reading a book. He set it down quickly when we entered and stood still, waiting. There was blood on his tunic and cloak, Goronwy's blood, and his face was hard and bitter.

Arthur crosssed the room quickly and caught Bedwyr by the shoulders. 'It was well done,' he said, the grimness falling away from him suddenly. 'It was very well done, my brother. But do not risk yourself: I could afford to lose both Goronwy and Morfran more easily than I could afford to lose you.'

Bedwyr's expression relaxed, and he clasped Arthur's

arm. 'There was no other way to stop it,' he said. 'If I had not intervened, Morfran would have fought Goronwy, and one of them would have been killed.'

Arthur nodded, shook him very slightly, then let him go and sat at the desk. 'I have just told Goronwy that I trusted Gwalchmai above my left hand and you above my right, and I pray God that word of it gets around. And since it was you who fought Goronwy, perhaps that faction will begin to believe that their leader is attacking me, not Gwalchmai. But, God of Heaven! I trust nothing now. There is nothing that is beyond his powers to twist into something sinister.'

No one needed to ask who 'he' was.

'It would have been just as bad if you had sent Gwalchmai back to Gaul,' I said. 'He may not be the issue, but I think that Medraut hates him.'

Arthur nodded, heavily. 'And no one has challenged Gwalchmai directly. He has been back for two weeks and courting trouble, and still no one has challenged him.'

Bedwyr shook his head. He pulled out a chair by the fire for me, then reseated himself on the edge of the desk.

'Rhuawn said some violent things to Gwalchmai two days ago,' I said. 'But there was nothing that Gwalchmai could have appealed to us to refute. He would not say what they were, merely that he would have had to fight Rhuawn if he had taken note of them. So he twisted their meaning into a joke and excused himself.'

'This is still the old trouble, only more blatant, more immediate.' Arthur stood, walked over to the hearth and leaned against the wall, staring back into the dead ashes of the firepit. 'Yet there must be something more to it, or someone would have challenged Gwalchmai.'

'It will be easier for a few days now,' Bedwyr said.

Arthur did not stir. His wide grey stare fixed itself on nothing, and I knew, with a sudden rush of grief, what he was considering now.

'Perhaps you should send Gwalchmai somewhere,' I suggested, to distract him from the nightmare. 'You could send him on an embassy, to Ebrauc – or, better still, to the Islands, with an escort of some of Medraut's followers and some of his own friends. He might be able to resolve something then.'

Arthur shook his head, without looking at me. 'No. If

anyone did challenge him on the journey, he would be unble to appeal to us for judgement: he would have to fight. And if there were killing the rest of Medraut's faction would be out for his blood – God forbid it, but there might even be full combat on the road. No. I do not like this reluctance to challenge Gwalchmai in anything that I might be judge of. It suggests that already they distrust my judgement. Perhaps ... perhaps already they believe other rumours. It is working quickly now, this sickness. More quickly than I had believed. I must send Medraut away ... in God's name, where? I dare not send him on an embassy.'

'Send him to Gwynedd, to discuss the latest tribute problems with Maelgwn,' suggested Bedwyr. 'He will not dare to deceive us in something we can check, like tribute, and he can hardly make Maelgwn more our enemy than he is already. Indeed, if he presses Maelgwn too hard, the king may begin to distrust him, and he will have one ally the less.'

Arthur's hand, resting against the wall, clenched slowly. 'If I send him to Maelgwn ... He is ready to tell the secret. he will tell Maelgwn.' His stare went far beyond the grey heap of ashes, off into a deep darkness, and his face was lined, old. His voice had sunk to a whisper.

'My lord?' asked Bedwyr, also in a whisper, looking at Arthur intently. He did not know 'the secret', but he had known Arthur for many years, too long not to be aware of that shadow on him, or fail to recognize that stare into the blind dark.

Arthur looked up at him abruptly, bitterly. 'My wife knows.'

I looked down at my hands, folded in my lap; at the purple glint in the amethyst of the signet ring I wore, the carving of the imperial dragon. I would not meet Bedwyr's dark, questioning eyes. But I could feel it when he turned them back to Arthur.

'Now?' Arthur said, very softly, to himself, then, 'You should know. You are my warleader.'

'I am your friend,' replied Bedwyr, very quietly. 'And your servant.'

The two pairs of eyes met, held: Bedwyr's solemn in a straightforward humility, contented with whatever Arthur might say to him; Arthur's hard and cold, as he himself was cold, twisted with the pain of a memory.

Then Arthur sighed, opening his hands in a gesture of surrender. 'You are my friend and brother. And I know that, even knowing this, you will follow me. But I tell you now that I do not think it just that you should. I will accept it because I must, but it is not justice, and it was not just of me to l.ave so long concealed this. Medraut...' he stopped, caught a deep, sobbing breath, 'Medraut is my son.'

Bedwyr stared at him. I watched the realization of what it meant creep over him slowly, first darkening his eyes with shock, then gradually draining the blood from his face. He rose, tried to speak; stopped, the fingertips of his one hand resting against the surface of the desk. 'Your sister?' he asked, at last.

'Yes.' Arthur stood perfectly still, almost calm, only his eyes alive, brilliant and terrible. 'Did you never notice that he resembles me?'

'I . . . he is your nephew. I thought that accounted for it.'

'He is my nephew, and my son. He is born of the incest I committed with my sister Morgawse. By all the traditions of the Church I am eternally damned.'

'He didn't know' I burst out, unable to be quiet longer. 'He did not know who his father was. She planned this to destroy us.'

'Silence, silence,' Arthur said, half closing his eyes in pain, and then, turning on me with sudden ferocity, cried, 'Do you think that makes a difference?'

The colour returned to Bedwyr's face all at once. 'My lord, there is no reason to shout at the Lady Gwynhwyfar.'

Arthur nodded, then sat down abruptly by the fire, as though his strength had at last given out. He covered his face with his hands. I jumped up and went over to him, knelt beside him, held him, but he was motionless in my arms. Morgawse had wounded him more deeply than I could heal. Bedwyr stood by the desk, watching us, saying nothing.

After a long minute, Arthur lowered his hands and again met the eyes of his warleader. 'So,' he said, his voice flat with exhaustion, 'now I have told you. But the tale will be current soon. You ought to know that it is true. Ach, if you like, add to that knowledge this, which Gwynhwyfar told you: I did not know. It was . . . a long time ago.'

Bedwyr bowed his head in assent, a movement which began a deeper bow, for he sank to his knees, drawing his sword. He offered it, hilt first, to Arthur. 'My lord,' he said, his tone as quiet and expressionless as Arthur's, 'I gave you this many years ago. Had I known then what you have told me, I would have done no differently.'

Arthur stared at him, then rose, pulling away from me, and touched the hilt of the sword. I thought he would help Bedwyr to his feet and embrace him, but he did not, only stood, looking at the warrior. 'I thank you,' he said at last. 'Sit down.'

He returned to his place beside me, and Bedwyr rose shakily, sheathed his sword, and sat down. Arthur took another deep breath and renewed the conference in a calm voice. 'So you see: I fear that Medraut will begin to spread the story soon. Therefore I will not send him to Gwynedd, or to any king who, like Maelgwn, would be able to use such a tale as a weapon against us.'

'Medraut could tell Maelgwn himself, without leaving Camlann,' I said, into the silence. 'By letter.'

Arthur turned his head and looked at me. His face was scarcely a foot from mine, but his eyes seemed to regard me from a great distance.

'Send him to Gwynedd,' I said. 'My dear lord, some of the men will doubt him now. If he is absent, no matter where, his spell will wane. And if he tells the tale to Maelgwn it will do less damage than told to some king who is our friend.'

'But he will wish to go to Gwynedd. He has spoken with Maelgwn before; we know that. He would not trust a tale like that to a letter. He will want to tell it in his own fashion, preparing his way with hints and rumours, and ending with a pretence of injury to the king himself. Dear God, I can almost hear him.'

'My dearest . . .' I began again, reaching out to touch him.

But he jumped up, strode to the door, turned and looked back at me. 'The best thing would be for me to abdicate. No, be silent. If there were another man in my place, someone untainted by any of this, all would be well. And why should Camlann, and you, and all Britain, pay for my sin? Why should anyone suffer for it but me? It is because I am Emperor, because I seized the purple, usurped it. If I could abdicate—'

'My lord!' exclaimed Bedwyr and I together.

He shook his head, angrily. 'It would be best. But there is no one I could appoint to succeed me who would be accepted by all, and the end would be war, another war, and things would end as they were when I seized power, and no doubt I should seize power again.' He struck his hand against the wall, hard, then stopped, cradling it in the other hand. 'There is nothing to do but go on.'

'Arthur!' I cried, rising from my stiff knees, pained to the heart because he would receive no comfort and no hope, and yet had set himself to struggle on.

'No! Gwynhwyfar, your pity is a reproach to me; can't you see that? Must I speak so plainly? This is my fault, mine! Leave me be for a while. I will go riding – indeed, I will take Medraut and Rhuawn with me as escort, and try to see if I can gather anything of their plans. Bedwyr, you will have to visit Goronwy. Take back the name of liar which you gave him and he will be reconciled and keep silence about the quarrel. Should anything else come up, I will be back by dusk.' He opened the house door, then stopped, looking back once more. 'Forgive me,' he said, very quietly, and was gone. Bedwyr and I looked at each other in the deep silence, and saw the desolation in each other's eyes.

'You have known – how long?' Bedwyr asked at last.

'Just four years,' I replied.

'And no one else knows?'

I shook my head, looked about, and sat in the chair by the fire which Arthur had just left. It still held the warmth of his body, and I wanted him, suddenly and terribly. 'Only Gwalchmai,' I said to Bedwyr. 'Arthur told him before Gwalchmai swore him fealty. Arthur thought he knew already, and had treated him badly because of it.'

'So that was the reason.' Bedwyr traced the line of his sword's hilt, then picked up a fold of his cloak, staring at the bloodstain on it. 'If I had known . . .'

'What?'

He dropped the stained material. 'Nothing. What could I have done? My lady, I would not fight for any man living but Arthur; I would have hung up my sword years ago, if I were called to serve any lord but him. What he has done is nothing less than a miracle. He has fought for the Light, when every other man fought for himself alone. No god would punish him for this thing he committed in ignorance; it is some work of Hell to weaken us all.'

'Gwalchmai,' I said tiredly, 'thinks the Queen Morgawse was a kind of demon.'

'By Heaven, her heart must have been blacker than any mortal's, to have done this thing. Does he really imagine that anyone could rule better than he does? Even now, even with him as Emperor, we are scarcely able to hold to what the old Empire was; what would we do without him?'

I shook my head, my hand clenching, feeling the line of the signet ring against my palm. 'I think that all we have done to this day has been to build a thornbrake against the wind,' I said, 'and since the peace we have been trying to light a fire behind it. But I thought we had the substance of a fire to light the world, here in Camlann, given time. Only Medraut will tear our thornbrake down, if we let him. Arthur knows, and he thinks it his fault. By you are right, without him we have nothing but the darkness and the winds, the kings of Britain fighting among themselve over a purple cloak. He will not let that happen.'

'I pray God it does not.' Bedwyr looked at me again, then crossed to me, knelt before me and took my hands clumsily. He kissed them. 'Most noble lady . . . you do not need me to tell you that he loves you beyond any other. If anyone can comfort him, it is you.'

'I have tried. But he does not want comfort. He will hold the fortress, but he will punish himself for this, and I cannot stop him.'

'Try again, my lady.' His expression was earnest and tender. 'You are no coward; I know you would fight on even if the fight were hopeless, and it is far from hopeless now.'

My longing, his kindness, Arthur's pain: I was stunned with too much feeling, and could not feel. 'I am . . . justly rebuked, lord,' I managed to say. 'Very well. And for yourself, you deserve the trust he gives you, and deserve it as much from myself as from my lord. If I were to thank you as your kindness merits, I would never have done with thanking you.'

He looked at me earnestly a moment longer, then again, hurriedly, kissed my hands. He stood, looking at me, then bowed. 'I must go and find Gwalchmai, and tell him what has happened. God keep you, my lady.'

And you, noble lord.'

When he was gone, and I had the house to myself, I put my face in my hands and strove to calm myself. Be still, still . . . I could hear the breeze in the thatch and the hollow sound it made under the eaves; distant, indistinguishable voices shouting far off down the hill. There. My skin felt hot, and I stood up and went into the next room and found a pitcher of water. I splashed it against my forehead and cheeks. But calm eluded me. I felt as though a fire had begun below my heart in that web of grief and helplessness, and I could not extinguish it so easily. Though I was glad of Bedwyr; he had been kind . . .

I stopped, staring into the water pitcher. Bedwyr. What had I felt when he kissed my hands? What shape was it that he had made on the air before me, to draw my heart out after him, as Arthur did?

'Oh God,' I whispered, and the lips of my reflection moved in the water, horrified. Not this, not now, not when I had so much else to do! How had this danger crept up on me, that I had not even noticed it until now? I had been secure in my love for Arthur. Oh, to be sure, some men are attractive and the body finds them so, but that is a thing easily laughed away and not to be taken seriously. I had never loved any man but Arthur, never thought I could. There were many I counted as close friends, and Bedwyr had been among them, but now I was surprised, trapped into another feeling, one that bit more deeply into the heart.

I thought again of how he had looked at me, so tenderly and earnestly; of the hurried touch of his lips against my fingers . . . I could feel it still, like a ring of invisible gold. I clenched my hands to fists, pressed them against my eyes. The thought of that look in his eyes, of his rare, warm smile, melted my soul away within me. And it had struck him, it had trapped him as well, of that I was certain.

'Oh God,' I said again. My voice sounded strange to me. I wiped my dripping hands on my gown and went back to the conference room. The book Bedwyr had been reading when I came into the house was still on the desk: I picked it up to put it away – anything, to distract myself from the turmoil within me. It was the *Aeneid,* and when I lifted it it fell open at the beginning of book four:

At regina gravi iamdudum saucia cura
vulnus alit venis et caeco carpitur igni . . .

But meanwhile the queen, wounded with a heavy grief
Feeds the wound with her blood and is seized by a blind fire . . .

I threw the book down on the floor and stared at it. Unhappy Dido, in love with Aeneas, who was bound for Rome. In love, in love, in love. I had not noticed it coming, and now that I saw and understood it was too late: love seized me savagely, bitter-sweet, irresistible. And adulterous, treacherous, ruinous.

With trembling hands I picked the book up again. I smoothed the bent pages and set it back in its place in the bookcase, then stood a moment, my palms flat against the cool, scarred wood of the desk. 'Very well,' I said, aloud, feeling the beat of blood in my ears. It had happened; I loved Bedwyr. But still, Arthur ... I closed my eyes, thinking of my husband: the eyes that could enforce silence with a glance or glow with pure delight; the confident step, the strength of his hands; the passionate force of his vision. My husband, my own, and if sometimes, burdened with Empire, he would not hear me – well, I had always expected that. But Bedwyr – no, I would not feed this wound with my blood. Nor would I even speak to the warleader, unless circumstances demanded it.

I turned and staggered from the room, stopped in the doorway. The day had grown dark, and clouds spat a few small drops of rain. I must ... I must speak to the servants, and see that a few of them knew what Arthur had said regarding Gwalchmai, so that the rumour of his words would spread quietly, naturally, together with the tale of the quarrel. Yes. And as for Bedwyr...

Best not to think of him at all.

Three

I was finishing the inventory of wools with Gwyn the next morning when Gwalchmai came into the storeroom looking for me. He smiled when he saw us, nodded to Gwyn, and gave me a slight bow. 'My lady, I would like to speak with you, if you are free.'

'Is it urgent?' I asked, with wearied anxiety.

'Indeed not. I can wait – when will you be done here?'

'We're almost finished now. If you wish me to come to the Hall when I'm done, or to your house . . .'

'Do not trouble yourself. I will wait here, if I am not in the way. Can I be of any assistance?'

'None whatsoever.'

'A pity. I feel like a horse let out to pasture, with nothing to do but graze and watch his fellows working. I had not thought thirty so old as all that . . . Hai, Gwyn! How goes the riding?'

Gwyn, who had been watching Gwalchmai with shining eyes, stammered his reply eagerly. 'I c-can hit the target from a gallop now, since you showed me, noble lord. But I can't pick up the ring, and the others told me I should be able to. I tried it yesterday, and fell off, and the horse didn't like it.'

Gwalchmai laughed. 'You were riding that chestnut three-year-old again? The beast's half pony and has no more withers than a mule, and less training. One cannot throw all one's weight onto one side of a horse unless he is used to it. What did that one do when you leaned over his neck? Stop suddenly and look surprised?'

Gwyn laughed back. 'Like a hen with her tail-feathers plucked. He stopped as soon as I had my left leg round the cantle, and then I fell off. He sniffed at me when I was on the ground, and looked very puzzled. But the others had all told me I should try it.'

'They probably wanted to see you fall off – and with that beast, there's nothing to hold to if you do begin to fall. But if you could accustom him to the action, and train him to keep running while you do it, you might repeat the move and surprise them.'

'That would be splendid! How do you ... oh. I am sorry, my lady. It was three bales of green, wasn't it?'

'Three green single-weight, two double-weight. Perhaps the lord Gwalchmai could teach you how to pick a ring up from the ground from horseback this afternoon. Whyever do you want to do such a thing anyway?'

'If one can do that, one can deal with an adversary who has fallen, or pick up a dropped sword,' Gwalchmai answered at once.

'And if you can ride entirely on one side of the horse,' Gwyn supplemented eagerly, 'you can use the horse to shield you during a charge. The enemy may not even see you, or might not cast anyway, if he wants your horse.' He looked at Gwalchmai earnestly, received a nod of assent, then sobered and said, 'But I could not trouble the lord Gwalchmai. Truly, noble lord, I know you have much greater matters of concern than that.'

'I have just told the Empress that I have no matters of concern, great or small. And I have a new roan mare that I wish to train for battle. I will take her onto the field behind the stables. Come, if you wish to – that is, if the lady Gwynhwyfar has nothing else for you to do.'

'Nothing this afternoon,' I replied at once, pleased that Gwyn should learn riding from his hero. 'I need that list of women who will be doing the weaving for us, and the quantities of each colour that they want, but you can write that out for me tonight. Very well, Gwyn, three green single-weight, two double; and...' I counted quickly, 'five black, natural, single-weight...'

Gwyn hastily scratched down the amounts with his stylus, self-consciously competent, carefully not looking at Gwalchmai. We finished the inventory, checked through the result, and I told Gwyn to make a fair copy of it and sent him off to do so. Gwalchmai watched him go, smiling.

'That is a clever boy,' he told me, 'and a daring one.'

'He thinks very highly of you.'

That drew a quick glance. 'Does he? He is in love with songs, I suppose. It was a brave deed to come here, and braver still to stay. Most of the other lads in the fortress are cruel to him, though I suppose it is only to be expected.'

'He bears up to it very well. They will tire of teasing him

soon, and he will be able to make friends. But I am glad you
will spend some time teaching him.'

'Och, that. That is a pleasure. I remember still what it is
like to be despised by other children, and it atones for something,
teaching him. Though Gwyn is a quicker learner
than ever I was – but this is not what I wished to speak to
you about.'

I gestured towards the door, and he opened it for me, following
me out into the sunny morning air. 'Cei is in my
house, in a black temper,' Gwalchmai told me. 'Shall we
walk down to the walls again?'

We did so. It was a lovely day, the perfection of early
June. The larks were singing above Camlann, and children
played about the houses where women were hanging their
washing on the thatch and discussing their neighbours'
affairs. We walked down the hill without speaking, for the
day was too fine to burden it with cares so soon. When we
climbed the wall and looked out over the fields, the land
that had before been raw mud was green – silver with
wheat, shimmering with the wind. Gwalchmai stopped,
leaning on the battlements, and I stopped beside him. It
seemed to me that the breeze must draw away the cramped
and manifold care from my mind and scatter it over the rich
land. It would not be so dreadful: the worst would not
happen. Camlann had survived civil war and Saxon wars;
endured poverty and enmity and envy, and it was strong.
Its life continued, steady as a pulse-beat, through all the
doubts and turmoils of its rulers. Whomever I loved or
hated, it would always provide me with work to be done,
and new, small cares to destroy the great ones. Perhaps –
no, certainly – in the end it would save us.

'Yesterday I spoke with my brother Medraut,' Gwalchmai
said without preamble.

My instant of peace vanished as suddenly as a trout does,
glimpsed in the shadows of a calm pond. 'You talked with
him about Goronwy's duel? You were alone with him?'

'We were alone, yes. And we talked about the duel and
. . . other things. You, and me, and my lord the High
King.' Gwalchmai always said 'High King' for 'Emperor':
it was his Irish upbringing.

'Did he tell you much?'

'Very little. He reviled us.'

'Oh, indeed! Did you expect more?' I turned from him bitterly and leaned over the battlements.

'I suppose not. But I had to speak with him. I have long known what he meant to do, but it is truly beginning now; he has achieved bloodshed. So, I went to his and Rhuawn's house, and when they returned from riding with my lord Arthur I greeted him and asked him what he intended to do next.' Gwalchmai shrugged. 'Rhuawn protested and said certain angry words, but Medraut sent him away. Then he himself spoke to me, very bitterly.' He looked down at the bank and ditch below the battlements, the green grasses bent in the wind. The feyness came over him, and I could tell that he did not see what was before his eyes, but looked into something deeper and stranger. 'He has no joy of the Darkness he serves. He walks in a blind horror, like a man in a dark sea where there is neither foothold nor breathing space, but he does not care. He cares only to destroy what he hates, and he lives by hatred, alone.' He paused, then said, 'He was different once. When we were both children – But this is no matter to concern you, my lady. When he had done cursing me and cursing the Family, he told me that he wishes to spread the story of his birth. He did not say as much, but I think he plans to whisper hints of it to emissaries of the kings of Britain, and, when the rumour is well established outside Camlann, answer the questions of his friends and followers with more hints. Moreover he is now devising slanders against Bedwyr as well, since it was Bedwyr who fought Goronwy. My lady, he must be stopped.'

'He told you all of this?'

He looked up at me, human again, and smiled apologetically. 'He makes no pretence with me, my lady. We know each other too well, and have too much in common. And he hates me very badly, because he thinks that I betrayed him and our mother. He wished to taunt me with the names he has been trying to give me, the names of traitor and madman and matricide, and when he saw that these had no effect, he fell to boasting of what he meant to destroy. My lady, I have urged this before, and now urge it again: he mut be sent away.'

'Where would you have him sent? He can write letters wherever he is.'

'They will have less effect if he is far away. Send him back to the Islands.'

I stared down at the wall. 'Arthur also wished to have him gone from Camlann. But he will not send him anywhere. He suspects that Medraut is ready to tell that story.'

'He suspects? How can he?'

I shook my head. 'His feelings for that tale are more sensitive than the horns of a snail, or the tentacles of the sea anemone. And the time is ripe. Medraut could easily lose ground after this duel, for Arthur has refuted the grounds which Goronwy was defending. Medraut needs something new. But he does not dare tell his tale openly, in the Family, or he will be disbelieved. Hence he will tell it first outside Camlann. How could we send him back to the Islands? To sentence him to exile when he is charged with no crime, and without warning, would open a rift in the Family which we might well be unable ever to close again.'

'I don't know,' said Gwalchmai, wearily. 'I have no answers. I merely know that I am afraid for us all if Medraut continues as he has begun. Let him go back to Dun Fionn and see what has become of Agravain. Perhaps it will trouble him: it troubles me.'

Gwalchmai had sailed to the Orcades after completing an embassy in the North the summer before, and had returned to Camlann still brooding over his elder brother's fate. It seemed that Agravain was drunk most of the time, had fearful nightmares if he went to bed sober, and had aged rapidly in the few years since Morgawse's death. He was becoming a figure of derision to the northern kings, and bitter with the knowledge of it. Now Gwalchmai looked up again, saw the expression on my face, and shook his head.

'Do not mind it,' he told me. 'There is nothing anyone can do. I knew when he killed her that it would happen.' Again he looked out over the fields, speaking in a low voice. 'As I knew that Medraut would be driven by her to destroy those who had been her enemies. Strange how her shadow endures among us. Agravain and Medraut, both devoured by it ... and Arthur. And now it lives in the midst of Camlann and feeds on us all. How I wish...' his words trailed off, and he continued to brood over the field like the hawk of his name.

I put my hand on his shoulder. 'Wish what?' I asked softly.

He smiled ruefully, breaking from his abstraction. 'I wish that I had married my lady Elidan, and that there was something more to my life than battles and embassies. I wish I had even a little of ordinary life to turn to, to rest in. I swear the oath of my people, I envy Rhys and Cei their children.'

'And I,' I replied in a low tone. He looked at me sharply, then took my hand from his shoulder and kissed it.

'Forgive me, my lady. I know that you endure more than I, and I intended no complaint.'

'My brother,' I said, 'you complain less than a saint, and certainly less than I do.'

In fact, he suddenly made me feel ashamed. His relationship to his clan had long been as tense as mine, first because he served their traditional enemy Arthur, and secondly because four years before he had been forced to kill one of his cousins who had fought for Queen Morgawse. That was a crime for which he could be disowned by his clan, kin-wrecked, but since his brother Agravain was king the matter had been passed over with a few expiatory rites. But he was never welcome in the Islands. For the rest – I had Arthur, at least. Gwalchmai had had one passionate love affair with the sister of a northern king: the girl's brother rebelled against Arthur and Gwalchmai killed him. The lady Elidan, daughter of Caw, was of royal birth: she would never forgive her brother's murderer, and told him so. Even years after her brother's death, when Gwalchmai had sought her out at the convent in Gwynedd which she had joined, she had held resolutely to her word and refused either to pardon Gwalchmai or to have anything more to do with him. He blamed himself bitterly for what had happened, and in fact he had been to blame: he had lain with her while he was her brother's guest and Arthur's emissary, and he had sworn her an oath not to hurt her brother and broken it. But he had been very young, and quite desperately in love; her brother had been killed in battle; and he loved her still: I think most women would have pardoned him. Unforgiven, he paid little attention to other women's attempts to attract him. It was not only that he still loved Elidan, but that he had hurt her, and was afraid of hurting someone else. So he was left with nothing: no parents, no clan, no wife, no children, and even his comrades in the Family quarrelling about whether he was mad and treacherous. In comparison, I was lucky, very lucky.

'It would be better if you complained more,' I told him, still ashamed of my own weakness. 'We have worked you too hard, my friend: you have more than deserved this rest we are giving you.'

He smiled, gently and ironically. 'So then, I am a worn-out charger, put out to pasture before my time. Well, I cannot say that it is not sweet to have little to do now, even with the fortress on a sword-edge, and half of those who were my friends...' he checked himself from another 'complaint' about the effects of Medraut's slanders, and instead concluded, 'Enough of that. I wished to tell Arthur what Medraut had said, but I found him sitting in one of the gate-towers, staring into the west, and I thought it better not to disturb him. And if he suspects already what Medraut will do, it is not surprising that he is lost in thought. But you can tell my lord Arthur what I have told you, and tell him that I am willing to serve him in any way, if he should wish to send me to watch Medraut, either in the Islands or anywhere else. And I am sorry to have spoken so grimly on so sweet a morning.'

'Gwalchmai my friend, you know that it was necessary, so do not trouble to apologize for it. I will tell Arthur when he is free. And now, lord, weren't you going to train a horse?'

There was nothing much for me to do that afternoon: the spring planting and trading was largely done with, and the summer's business had not yet properly begun. Gwalchmai walked me back up the hill to the Hall, trying to discuss neutral matters, then left to find something to eat before working with his horse. I was not hungry. I wandered restlessly about the fortress, giving unnecessary advice to the servants, then visited a friend. This was one of my few women friends, Enid, Gereint ab Erbin's wife. There were so few women I could talk to that I usually enjoyed our conversations. But now she was in one of her duller moods, able to do nothing but gossip, and I was tense and sharp-tongued. we were both relieved when I excused myself.

I went back to my own house, into the bedroom to be

private, and sat on the bed. Camlann is strong, I had thought that morning, before Gwalchmai had given me his news. But the day before I had told Bedwyr that it was only a thornbrake against the wind, a fragile protection for the weak little fire we had set alight: and that image held the greater truth. Twenty years before, what had Camlann been? The fortress of the Emperor of Britain, a man emperor in name only, with only a shadow more authority than any petty king. And a hundred years before?

A hill overgrown with the grasses, inhabited by foxes and the bright-eyed rabbits and hares. The great cities of the area then were Baddon and Searisbyrig-Aquae Sulis and Sorviodunum. Young men and women still would have been able to remember the Roman legions departing finally from the south, and perhaps they had believed that Rome was still strong. It had still stood, then: Rome, 'the eternal city', as its lovers had called it, not knowing how close they were to the dark. I thought of the ruined Wall in the North, and bare hills behind it. That wall had been the reality: Camlann was only its shadow, attempting to protect the few small fragments that remained. It was not strong. Medraut was raising a storm that would tear it to fragments.

We were trapped. Medraut had set snares for us on every side, and Time pressed close behind us like a huntsman with his dogs. I could see no way out, any more than could Arthur, with his wide stare into the unyielding future, or Bedwyr with his call for courage and another blind battle. No way but one – and that one was not something I could admit. I had thought of it several times over the four years since Medraut had come to Camlann, and always I had thrust the thought from me in disgust, knowing that it was wrong.

And yet, I thought, *this cannot go on*. Medraut would destroy us with these quarrels. He had brought about bloodshed within the Family, and only Bedwyr's quick action prevented killing. What he planned was more: strife between my husband and his realm. Dishonour for Arthur, disaffection in the Family, and rebellion and civil war throughout Britain. The bloodiest kind of war, and the cruellest. Perhaps we could live down the slanders; perhaps we could force Medraut into some mistake – but that possibility grew more remote with every day that passed. Medraut had facts, and knew how to persuade, and to win followers. I was afraid, as I had been since first he came to Camlann. All of us, we were all worn out by the strife, the tension, the constant plotting to protect our future. And it could all end so simply, so easily, if Medraut should quietly die.

I remembered with uncomfortable vividness an incident years before, when I had been helping Gruffydd the surgeon tend a man with a fever. Gruffydd had been keeping that man in his own house, as he kept Goronwy now. I remembered him stooping over the man, taking his pulse and muttering in discontent. He went to his medicine cabinet and took down from the shelf one jar, a blue-glazed earthenware jar with a ragged 'H' scratched onto it. He poured some of the dark liquid it contained into a cup of water and gave it to the patient, explaining meanwhile to me that it would slow the heart and lower the fever.

'What is it, then?' I had asked.

'Hemlock,' he replied shortly.

'But that is a poison!'

He nodded, snorting. 'So are many things: so is mead, in large quantities. But this much,' he laid one finger sideways against the jar, 'this much is a fit dose for a large man stricken with fever, like our friend here, and can save lives. Half of that amount for a small man or a woman. This much, now,' and he laid a second finger beside the first, 'brings sleep, and even death, to some. More than that,' he picked up the jar and set it back on the shelf, 'four or more measures, at any rate, will kill anyone, and many have died by it. But those that have used it subtly have to smother it in mead or strong wine, for it has a bitter taste.'

'How cheerful,' I said. 'What about toad's blood, then, if one wishes to poison someone subtly?'

He snorted again, smothering a laugh, and replied, 'An old wives' tale. Toad's blood will poison no one, and I think it must have spoiled the taste of many a dinner.'

I would have to visit Goronwy soon, to see how well he was recovering, and to show a just concern for him. I could be as free of Gruffydd's house as of my own. It would be easy, so easy, to slip that jar from the shelf, and pour out four finger-measures into a flask – a flask like the empty scent jar of Italian glass I kept under the bed. Then, the next time I poured for the high table at a feast, I could mix it with a skin of mead and give it to Medraut. No, not a skin of mead. I would have to throw the rest out, and that would be dangerously obvious. Better to wait until there was only enough mead left in the pitcher for one person, and then add the drug and pour for Medraut. When it was late in the evening, and he had drunk well enough not to notice the taste. When the fires were low, and the torches flickering, and the others also had drunk well and would not notice if I had to pour in the wrong order. No one would suspect poisoning, if everyone had drunk mead at the feast. And Medraut would go home as though he had drunk too much, staggering a little, and next morning would be found to have died – in his sleep, painlessly. And no one would be able to say whether he had simply drunk too much mead for a hot night, or died from a sudden failure of the heart (as can happen, even to young men), or from some rapid disease. He would have a magnificent funeral, with all the fortress in mourning, and never trouble anyone again. His tale would rest forever untold, and his faction and his slanders at last would be stilled. We could heal the breach in the Family; we could restore the Empire. It would be the pitch of foolish absurdity to let all that we had suffered and bled for, the one last light of the dark West, won with toil and anguish from the collapse of our civilization, to allow all this to slip bloodily away into nothingness because of one sole man.

I jumped up, pressing my hands to my mouth. 'That is damnation,' I whispered through them, hearing the distorted sound of the words in the still air of the empty room. Damned. It was evil. 'You shall not commit murder. No murderer has eternal life,' proclaimed the scriptures.

Arthur called murder 'the tyrants' trick'. Bedwyr said that no expediency, or even necessity, could justify the commission of a mortal sin. Both of them, and Gwalchmai as well, sometimes doubted whether it was justified to kill even in battle. Yet they had all killed ... but no, none of them would ever poison a man at a feast. Such an action would not only carry eternal damnation, but temporal condemnation from all those whom I loved most, whose opinions I most valued. And they were right. How could anyone – how could *I* – poison a man under the cloak of hospitality, charging him with no crime, giving him no warning, no chance for self-defence or for repentance? It was base, cruel, dishonourable, treacherous, abominable: how could I?

And yet . . . what other course was there?

It was the vulnerability of what I loved that tortured me. My husband, my friends were suffering now, and it was only beginning. And that was not the worst; it was not only that we would suffer, but that the future would suffer as well. Or did my fears exaggerate the danger? What did Medraut want? Power for himself? Probably. He had wanted to be king of the Orcades, and resented his brother's election. No doubt he would like to be emperor instead. That bleak stare I had noticed in him when he thought no one was watching sometimes fixed itself on the gold dragon standard in the Hall. But no, that was not what I feared. There were many others in Britain who would like to be emperor. What I feared from Medraut was something more, something that I had at first been unable to name, even to myself. It was the wind out of the darkness, the pure power of destruction undertaken for destruction's sake. I had never seen Queen Morgawse of Orcade, but I knew what she had done to the lives of those she touched. And I was certain that Medraut was still devoted to her, and loyal to her hatred. One understands who and what a man is in many ways, and few of them have to do with what he says. There are actions – small actions of little consequence, often, as trivial as a harsh word to a servant; there are friendships and ways of pursuing friendships; and choices of words, gestures, looks: all things unimportant in themselves but which taken together create suspicion and eventually certainty. I was certain that Medraut meant to break us, to destroy us, in vengeance for his mother. And I knew that his hold on us was strong, and we could not render him either friendly or harmless.

I was sick of carefully weighed reasons and precise justice. Our position was not reasonable, nor was Medraut's. And the need I had to protect was not reasonable, but I knew that my horror of murder would not stand against its force. Whether or not it was right, whether or not I would suffer for it, I knew with cold certainty that I would do it: I would try to destroy Medraut.

How I managed to continue to work, continue to smile during the next three weeks I do not know. Only the force of long habit kept me upright: my heart cowered within me, like a hare when the hounds are searching for it. My intention to murder was a cold, black weight within me. I stole the poison, but then tried to pretend to myself that I would not use it – yet I could not throw it away. As for Bedwyr, it hurt me to look at him, and I avoided him as much as I could. After the first few days, his look of puzzlement vanished and he began to avoid me as well. He understood. How long, I wondered, had he known what he felt? I suspected that it was longer than I had known. I wanted him to talk to, many times; kept thinking of things to say to him, and then remembering that I must say nothing, so that my thoughts were tormented. Arthur would have noticed, but had other concerns. Goronwy, recovering from the duel, wavered in his allegiance, and some other warriors with him. Arthur saw much of them, hoping to restore their loyalty, and for a time thought he had won Goronwy at least. Then we were unable to keep Medraut from seeing him, and found him once again uneasy, once again listening to the rumours. And there were more rumours than ever, now linking Gwalchmai, Bedwyr and me in a conspiracy against Medraut, slandering him to Arthur and trying to murder Goronwy. Arthur decided to send Medraut to Less Britain as part of an escort for Macsen's emissary when he returned to his lord.

This emissary arrived in Camlann in the third week of June. He was a low-ranking, ignobly born warrior of the king's warband, whose status was almost as direct an insult to Arthur as his words and manner. Nonetheless, we played our part correctly and feasted this emissary with the usual magnificence. It was to that feast that I carried my flask of stolen hemlock.

Macsen's emissary, such as he was, had the place on Arthur's left (it would have been an excess of courtesy to put him on Arthur's right; he was embarrassed enough as it was) and Medraut sat beside him. The emissary called for wine during the second course. It was a formal feast, and there were no women present in the Hall, so I entered only then, and poured wine for the high table. I sat down next to Arthur, on his right. I had bound the glass phial of hemlock under my belt, which was a wide, high one, and stitched with gold: the poison was quite invisible. But I could feel it against my side like a piece of ice, slowly chilling me through. I had a savage headache.

'You are pale, my lady,' Bedwyr said, moving over to let me sit down.

'It is my head,' I told him. 'It feels near to splitting.'

'What?' asked Arthur, breaking off a conversation with the emissary. The emissary looked confused, pugnaciously embarrassed, so I left off rubbing my temples, smiled, and raised my glass to the man.

'You are indeed pale,' Arthur said to me in a low voice. 'You have been overstrained lately, my heart. Go to bed now, if you wish; I will make your excuses.'

'No, no,' I protested. 'It will probably go away after a glass of wine, and we should do things twice as graciously if Macsen is ungracious.'

He looked at me steadily a moment, then took my hand under the table, pressed it, and turned back to the emissary. I glanced at Bedwyr, who was still watching me with grave concern, then hastily and resolutely turned to the emissary as well.

The Family was on edge from all the rumours, and many of the men were drinking too heavily while some remained sullen and sober. Medraut did not drink much: when I came to refill his glass the third time, I saw that he had barely touched the second cup I had poured for him. He smiled at me when I stared at it, a very knowing, bitter smile. the pupils of his eyes were contracted into points of hard, cold blackness. It frightened me, though I pretended to smile and passed on. His eyes followed me, still with that cold and knowing look.

It was impossible, I told myself as I sat down again. he could not possibly know. Somehow I must rein in my leaping imagination. Somehow ... I endeavoured to laugh, felt as though for a very little I might begin to scream. If only the night would pass! Here I sat, waiting to murder a man who sat three places from me at the table, feeling the phial of hemlock burn icily into my ribs, while from time to time my intended victim gave me a cold and knowing smile. I could give up the intention . . . the wave of relief that swept me at the thought was greater than I had supposed possible. But no, no, I could not go back now. It was my imagination, I told myself again. And it was imagination that made the torches burn so redly, and made the half glass of wine I had drunk seem more intoxicating than the strongest mead, so that the room swam about my pounding head and I had to gasp for breath. I redoubled my efforts at witty gaiety, felt some of the edginess around me dissolve as I laughed and again poured the wine, but all the while I felt Medraut's eyes watching me until I wished to fling myself from the Hall.

At last the meal was finished and the singing began. Our chief poet, Taliesin, began by singing of some ancient battle, the conquests of the emperor Constantine, and the Hall fell silent, drinking its mead and listening. He paused when he had told how Constantine won the purple and was acclaimed emperor in Rome, and asked for wine. The emissary called for more mead at the high table. I rose and had another cask brought to the back of the Hall; when I filled my pitcher Taliesin was singing again, this time of a battle in our Saxon wars, a lament for Owein ab Urien, son of an allied king. It was one of Taliesin's own songs and the Hall was silent as the snow, with everyone wrapped in it, the fast uneasy circles of melody, violent grief chained in words. The torches were low, as I had foreseen they would be. Medraut still was not drinking heavily, but I judged he had drunk enough. It was time.

Beginning at the far end of the table I poured out the pungent yellow mead until there was only a cupful left in the pitcher, and then, standing out of the torchlight, I fumbled under my belt.

'His spears were swifter than the wings of dawn . . .' sang Taliesin.

The flask which had seemed so cold was warm under my fingers. I fumbled the stopper out and quickly poured the hemlock into the pitcher, then stopped the phial again and put it back in its place. I came forward with the music around me, smiling, and found that Medraut's glass was empty.

Taliesin was singing:

'For Owein to kill Fflamddwyn,
Was easy as to sleep:
Sleeps now the host of Lloegyr
With the red dawn on their eyes
And those who would not flee
Were bolder than was wise...'

I filled Medraut's cup, draining the last drop from the pitcher, then, as though in a dream, went back to the servants for more mead. I poured for the rest of the table quite carefully, not spilling a drop, but when I sat down again I found that I was trembling, and feared to pick up my cup lest it show how my hand shook. But Bedwyr was arguing philosophy with Gwalchmai, and Arthur was discussing politics with the emissary, and no one noticed. It remained only to wait. I felt as though I would burst into tears at any moment, and wished desperately that it was over, that it were already the morning, and that they were coming to tell us that Medraut was...

'My lord,' said Medraut, standing and smiling at Arthur, the poisoned cup in his hand.

Arthur looked up from his conversation with the emissary, then nodded to Taliesin. The music stopped, and the Hall, suddenly bereft of it, was very silent. I could hear the fires burning, the crackle of torches, and the dull pounding of the blood in my ears. I held the edge of the table, staring at Medraut, unable to feel much. Medraut stood straight and slender, the light glinting off his fair hair and beard, shadows caught in the folds of his purple-edged cloak. The cup he held was of bronze, inlaid with silver, and it seemed to burn in his hand, like the sun at noon.

'My lord,' he repeated, still in the same easy tone, his clear voice carrying through the stillness of the Hall.

'Lord Medraut,' responded Arthur, in the same tone, his voice deeper and rougher from the use it had had. 'What do you wish to say?'

Medraut smiled again. 'Many things, in the course of my life, if it is allowed me. Ah, but surely, my lord, one of the best things would be to toast you, for your health, long life and long reign. But I would be reluctant to do so with this cup.' He raised it slightly. 'Though I agree that to wish health and long life to the Emperor is a fitting use for one's last breath, it would not be fitting to drink to them in poison.'

A gasp, a murmur ran around the Hall, stopped. I closed my eyes, aware how beside me Arthur went tense, feeling his grey stare fixing on Medraut, knowing the uncertainty and doubt leaping in his mind. *Dear God,* I thought, *let me die now, here; do not let me see my disgrace* . . .

'I do not see the point of your joke,' Arthur said, his voice quiet but carrying. 'The mead is not so bad as all that.'

This brought a titter of nervous laughter, and abrupt silence again. My eyes opened of themselves, and I saw Medraut still standing, the cup still raised, and the bitterness growing in his face.

'The mead, my lord, is excellent, but the hemlock has a bitter taste. It is hemlock, is it not, Lady Gwynhwyfar?'

Arthur leapt to his feet, his hands braced against the table. 'You are serious! What are you saying, man, to accuse the Empress in this way?'

'She is trying to poison me!' Medraut shouted it. 'She is a jealous, a scheming, faithless woman!' Slamming the cup down on the table, 'A woman whose hand has been against me since first I came here, who has plotted against me with my mad brother. Look to yourself, Lord Pendragon, or she will plot with him against you as well! This cup is black with poison, which she with her own hand just now poured into it.'

'By the King of Heaven, you lie,' Arthur said, not raising his voice, but using it like the edge of a sword. 'I do not know whether what you say is slander or some madman's joke, Medraut ap Lot, but I will have you know that it is treasonous, and I will hear none of it, nor will any here who know the kindness of the Empress.' There was a ragged cheer, my friends leaping to their feet; and in response shouts of anger. Arthur lifted his hand, standing above me, tall and coldly furious, and silence, imposed by the long habit of obedience, ebbed back. 'You joke is in bad taste, Medraut: sit down and be silent.'

'It is not a joke, my lord, it is a matter of murder. Look at the Empress, the most noble lady, the most kind and excellent Gwynhwyfar: look at her, if you doubt me! *She* knows that I speak the truth!'

'Be silent!' shouted Arthur, and even Medraut flinched. 'The Lady Gwynhwyfar has been ill all the evening, and what woman would not be shocked to hear herself slandered thus? Do you say that that cup is poisoned? Give it to me.'

'My lord!' I croaked, finding no air, reaching up to catch at him.

'It is no matter, my heart, I do not believe him,' he said, pushing me aside. 'That is the cup, Medraut, "black with poison"?'

'My lord,' said Medraut, now disconcerted and off balance, 'do you mean to risk...'

'I am taking no risk. Give it to me. As I am your lord and emperor, give it here.'

Slowly, staring at him in amazement, Medraut gave him the cup. Arthur stood a moment holding it, his eyes terrifying, the amethyst on his finger burning deep purple against the bronze.

'My lord,' I said again, trying to stop him. But his foot moved under the table and stepped on mine, hard, though he did not look at me.

'Your cup of poison, Medraut,' he said, 'is nothing but a cup of lies and cheap gossip. And I put no more credence in it than I do in any of the tales told here in Camlann, by which your brother is made to be a traitor, and I a weak fool led about by my scheming wife. So!' He set the cup to his lips. I tried to scream, found all sound frozen in my throat. Arthur drank slowly, his hand completely enveloping the bronze; he raised his other hand to the cup as well, as though he found it heavy, but he drained it and set it empty down on the table. I clutched the table's edge until my fingers ached.

'There is nothing whatever wrong, Medraut,' Arthur said in a level voice, smiling into Medraut's fury and confusion, 'neither with the mead nor with my wife's honour. Your joke was savage and not at all amusing. You have my leave to go. Taliesin!' The chief poet bowed. 'Some music. I do not care what, anything to keep these drunken fools quiet.'

Taliesin struck his harp and Arthur resumed his seat, still watching Medraut with a cold smile. Medraut continued to stare back, pale with shock, for a moment – then began to laugh, loudly, over the music. Still laughing, he bowed low and left the Hall. Arthur snapped his fingers and handed the empty cup to a servant. 'Some more mead,' he ordered, and the servant bowed and hurried off.

'My lord,' I whispered.

'Silence!' he hissed, under his breath.

'Arthur, it was poisoned. I poisoned it. Get Gruffydd, quickly, and some emetics. It's not too late . . .'

'I didn't drink it. Do you understand? I only swallowed a mouthful or so; the rest I poured up my sleeve. Look!' He turned his right arm over, under the table, and I saw that the inner sleeve of his tunic was soaked with the sweet mead. Then I remembered a trick he had showed me once, a way to avoid drunkeness at some other ruler's feast: a trick of holding the cup high along the rim and pouring most of its contents over the palm and up one's sleeve.

I could feel the tears beginning, and I coughed to control them and the choking in my throat. 'But . . .'

'For God's sake, smile, pretend it was only a vicious joke. Eternal God, you don't want them to suspect, do you? Come, now pretend that you are giggling against my shoulder with relief . . . there.'

I pressed against him. The mead on his tunic sleeve was soaking into my gown, and I made a mental note to check that it did not show before I stood. I knew that Arthur was smiling, but as I pressed by head against his shoulder I could feel the bitter rage in him, the anger at betrayal, and I had to fight even harder to control the waves of hysterical relief and of grief.

I saw that the remains of the feast were disposed of before I went back to our house that evening. The feast went on till late, so it was very late when I returned to the house. Clouds skidded over the stars, and the fortress was very silent, except for the rustling of the wind in the thatch. The house was an oasis of lamplight: gold spilled over the swept hearth with its bright tiles, the smoke-stained wall; the inner door, then the bed with its yellow and white woollen coverlet, and the worn hanging oil lamp of red clay. Arthur was waiting, standing by the book rack, still wearing his purple cloak. The dragons worked onto its collar gleamed. His face was closed to me as it had never been closed before, and his eyes were bitterly cold.

'Sit down,' he commanded, indicating the bed. I sat, too tired and grieved to speak. 'You tried to murder my son.'

I swallowed, swallowed again. I could not reply.

'Was it hemlock?' he asked. 'Where did you get it? Purchased from some townsman? Or did you brew it yourself?'

'Gruffydd the surgeon keeps it to treat fevers,' I told him, finding my voice low and unexcited. 'I stole some from him.'

'Then he knows nothing of it? Good. Did you tell anyone else?'

'No one.'

Arthur sat down on the other end of the bed. I saw that he was shivering. I longed desperately to go to him and hold him, but I could not. Again, it was a question of sitting and waiting. 'Good,' he repeated. 'How he knew the cup was poisoned must be a mystery, then, for I would never have noticed the taste. At least he cannot produce anyone to confirm his story. We will not be publicly disgraced, and he has been made ridiculous. I can even send him away now. I could charge him with treason – but that would cause more problems that it would solve.' He stopped, stared at me again, and then the coldness broke and his face twisted with pain. 'In God's name, Gwynhwyfar, why?'

'You know why!' I cried back, as though I were pleading with him. But I would not plead, I would not say, 'I did it for you and for Camlann' – that would make it no less evil, and be shameless begging.

'But it is infamous, it is tyrannical! It is the act of a coward, a sorcerer, a scheming woman; it dishonours all of us.'

'It only dishonours me. And I am a woman, Arthur. I knew what I was doing, and what you would think of it. Perhaps I believe the same myself: nonetheless I thought it worth it, and still I wish I had succeeded.'

Just for an instant something leapt behind his eyes, and I saw that I had misjudged his anger. It was not that he was angry that such a thing had been attempted in his Hall, but that he also wished it had succeeded, and the recognition of that wish in himself was a bitter shame to him. He saw that I saw, and we stared at each other for a long moment in complete, tortured understanding. Then Arthur stood again and drew his cloak more closely around him, still shivering. 'You,'he said slowly, 'you, a would-be murderess. A wicked stepmother. Oh, they will tell tales of this, to be sure.' His teeth began to chatter, and he struck the wall with his fist, then knocked over the pot of wild roses on the bedside table, spilling water and flowers onto the polished wood. He struck them, again and again, crushing the roses and driving their thorns into his hand. I watched, horrified, unable to speak. He stopped and looked back at me, his fingers tightening and loosening in the water on the desk top. 'I almost drank it. I could not believe such a thing of you. Of anyone else, yes, but not of you. Oh, the devil take this chill!'

I realized what the chill was and jumped up abruptly. 'Arthur, it is the hemlock. How much did you drink?'

'I told you. No more than one or two mouthfuls. Enough to feel the cold, but not enough to do harm ... stay away.' I stopped in the middle of the floor. 'I have had enough of your tender care for tonight, my lady.'

'Arthur,' I said. The tears I had checked earlier leapt into my eyes; I could not stop them. 'Arthur, forgive ... I can't ask that. I am sorry, I wish I had drunk that cup. You are cold; please let me help. Oh, it was evil, I know it was, only, please ... you know I love you.'

He did not answer. He turned away, cradling his bruised hand and still shivering. 'Go to sleep,' he commanded in a harsh voice. 'We must not give them one shred of confirmation of their tale. Medraut may hint that I did not drink it, but we will not give him any evidence. Go to bed. I wish to God I had drunk that cup. It would make the world very much easier to endure. Got to sleep! And for God's sake, stop crying.'

I undressed silently, swallowing the tears. Only when I had climbed into the bed did he turn back, put out the lamp, take off his boots and climb in beside me, still fully clothed. He lay with his back to me, shivering, and I lay looking up at the thatch, trying not to cry. The night hours crept by more slowly than sails creep along the far horizon of the world; more slowly than a slug crawling across the petals of a rose.

After an eternity of misery I judged by Arthur's breathing that he was asleep, and slid close to him, putting my arms about him to warm him. In sleep he did not pull away, but moved his head against my shoulder. But when the grey dawn came in under the eaves, and I was at last beginning to drowse, Arthur woke, threw off my arms, and stamped off into the outer day. Then I curled up in the empty bed, with my head against my knees, and wept, wept bitterly because I had hurt Arthur where no one else could comfort him, forfeited my title to his love and my soul's salvation, and had, after all of it, gained nothing at all.

Four

I was determined to act just as usual the day after the feast, since to do anything else would give an occasion for more rumours; I therefore kept to the schedule I had set, leaving the house at midmorning to speak with some freeholders of the fortress about the crops they were growing in the surrounding fields. I had Gwyn called to make notes of the amounts of grain the farmers expected. The boy was anxious, inattentive and distressed throughout the interview, and I was probably not much better. I had a bitter headache all that day – it comes of too much weeping. But I had long years of experience behind me which Gwyn lacked: I did not have to think hard to ask all the appropriate questions and give all the appropriate congratulations and condolences. I may even have smiled at the farmers, though my heart was far away from any such mask-like smile.

I finished the business with the freeholders and dismissed them and Gwyn as well, telling the boy to make a fair copy of the amount of grain expected that harvest and to put it in one of my account books. The farmers bowed and filed off, but Gwyn hesitated. He began to walk away, then turned and ran back. He dropped to his knees beside my chair and clasped my hand.

'It was a foul lie, noble lady, and no one of any sense believed it,' he told me fiercely. 'And everyone expects that Medraut will be charged with defaming the imperial majesty and exiled. Is he going to be exiled?'

'The Emperor will probably dismiss him from Camlann,' I said stolidly, then, forcing a rather wan smile, 'thank you, Gwyn.'

He pressed my hand to his forehead, then again walked off, swinging his wax tablet and scowling savagely. I felt worse than ever at his misplaced trust. It deepened the shame. And yet the words of false comfort were echoed by others. Goronwy, now recovered from the duel, came up to me at the midday meal on some pretext and explained in a loud voice how nasty the joke was and how he hoped that Medraut would be charged with treason. I was glad that he seemed finally to have broken from Medraut and his faction, but I wished he'd had better cause.

But in the afternoon I saw Gwalchmai, and the conversation was a rather different one.

I wished to check the amounts of grain which Gwyn had noted down that morning against some other accounts, and discovered that the boy had not finished his fair copy. I went in search of him to get from him the original wax tablets, and found him in the yard behind the stables. He and Gwalchmai were teaching Gwalchmai's roan mare how to behave in battle and Gwalchmai was teaching Gwyn the same. This had somehow become a regular pattern of affairs, and seemed to give a great deal of pleasure to both Gwalchmai and Gwyn, though some of the other boys in the fortress objected to Gwyn all the more strongly for having a friend among the great warriors. Nonetheless Gereint as a riding-master and the mule-like chestnut gelding as mount had gradually been superseded for Gwyn by Gwalchmai and the roan mare. When I came up, Gwyn was standing in the middle of the yard holding a whip, while Gwalchmai rode the mare around him in a wide circle. They had finally arrived at the stage of picking up the ring.

'Now,' Gwalchmai was saying, 'this time I will keep her at the canter. If she falters while I'm out of the saddle, don't use .the whip unless you have to. Shout at her first: she knows now what that means.'

Gwyn nodded gravely, and Gwalchmai touched the horse to a canter. She was a beautiful animal, the offspring of one of Gereint's horses by Gwalchmai's war stallion Ceincaled, and she could run as lightly as a deer. Gwalchmai rode her about the circle once, Gwyn turning on his heel to follow them, then dropped his head down beside the mare's neck, his weight shifting to his right side, one hand clasping at once the reins and her mane. Her ears flicked back as he whispered something to her, but she did not break her pace. Gwalchmai drew his left leg up, hooking his knee around the cantle of the saddle, and seemed abruptly to fall. The mare faltered; Gwyn shouted and she recovered. Gwalchmai, suspended upside-down, snatched at the ground with his right arm, his fingers trailing a moment in the grass, then, somehow, miraculously, he was upright in the saddle again, laughing and holding between thumb and middle finger a gold ring. He tossed it in the air, checked the mare and rode over to Gwyn at a trot.

"So much for what my brother Agravain used to call a trick fit only for tumblers at a fair.'

'My lord, it is beautiful!' Gwyn said warmly. 'Gereint has to try two or three times at the least, and he can't do it so . . . so . . .'

'Can't he? He must be growing old. He used to do better than that. Here, you try it now.' He jumped from the saddle, taking the bridle and handing Gwyn the ring. Gwyn took it, stood a moment patting the mare's shoulder and whispering to her, then vaulted into the saddle. He gathered the reins and looked about, and only then saw me. His face fell.

'Noble lady,' he called. 'Do you want me now?'

I hesitated. I did not want to stand about telling lies to Gwalchmai, but I could not find it in myself to drag Gwyn away at that moment. 'You can come when you've finished with the ring,' I returned. 'It's only the list of crops.'

Gwyn nodded, happy again, but Gwalchmai looked at me seriously. 'My lady,' he said, 'perhaps you would care to stay a moment and watch?'

Again I hesitated, then, because the uncertainty looked ill, came across the yard and joined them, though I wished I could put off the lying until tomorrow or the next day or week. 'Will I be in your way here?' I asked.

'Indeed not,' replied Gwalchmai, 'but stand on my left, for I may need to use the whip if Seagull here forgets to keep her pace steady.' He clucked his tongue to the horse, who pricked her ears forward, then flicked them back again to listen to Gwyn. The boy smiled proudly and turned the horse, walking her to the circle already worn into the grass of the yard.

'Shall I put the ring down here?' he called to us.

'Even so. But take your time, and be certain that it is the most comfortable distance.'

Gwyn nodded, and, after a moment's solemn concentration, turned the mare and walked her around the circle to see if the distance was indeed agreeable.

'My lady,' said Gwalchmai in a low voice, 'Last

night . . .' he hesitated, looking at me, his dark eyes unreadable.

'It was a vicious joke,' I said, steeling myself.

He looked away again quickly. 'So Medraut himself now says, and so the fortress repeats, if uncertainly. Medraut hints at deeper things even while he denies them. And yet Arthur drank the cup and is unharmed, though some claim it for a miracle that he is so.'

'Medraut among them?'

'No, my lady.' Gwalchmai looked back to me. 'I heard that from Gruffydd the surgeon. He said it in secrecy, to me only.'

'Gruffydd? But he . . . I thought him Medraut's enemy.' I stopped myself, turning away and struggling for composure. Gwyn had completed the circle, and now was hooking his knee about the cantle and carefully practising the first stages of the drop, the ring clasped in his hand.

'He is Medraut's enemy. He thinks that to poison my brother would be an honourable, even a heroic action. He told me that if such had indeed been your plan, it was a sensible and a courageous one, and he wished it had succeeded. And he told me that he'd noticed some hemlock missing from his stores. All this was in strict privacy, of course. Gruffydd knows how to hold his tongue.

Gwyn made the drop from the saddle, set the ring down on the grass, then rose again in a movement already filed smooth by practice. He turned to Gwalchmai, beaming, and Gwalchmai nodded. Gwyn touched the mare to a trot.

"Take your time," Gwalchmai shouted to him. 'If you hurry or hesitate from uncertainty the move is ruined.' Gwyn nodded.

'Why are you telling me this?' I asked in a whisper.

'My lady . . . my lady, I pity my brother Medraut. Once . . . once he was something like Gwyn. It has cut deep to see him so twisted, and living in such hatred. If I knew that one of my friends had felt compelled to poison him, I would . . . it would grieve me. And yet, I can understand it. Perhaps it is even what Gruffydd said, sensible and courageous. I am not a ruler: I cannot say.'

'Gwalchmai . . .' I began, and could think of nothing to add. He looked at me, waiting, the same grave look in his eyes, and finally I recognized the expression as compassion.

'My lady, I know that you would not resolve on such a thing lightly, or without anguish, or desire it from any but the purest motives. Now that it has failed ... Hai! Back, there!' – for Gwyn had tried the move, and the mare had slowed to a trot when he dropped from the saddle. She broke into a canter again, and the boy struggled upright, looking glum.

'I didn't get the ring,' he told Gwalchmai.

'On the first try. You yourself, cousin, said that Gereint must try two and three times at the least, and would you, scarcely more than a puppy, be a finer rider than he? Come, try again ... my lady,' lowering his voice again, 'whatever has happened, I am your friend and servant, as ever.'

'My brother and lord,' I replied, 'Gwalchmai, that I am not Medraut's murderess is due only to your brother's fore-knowledge and Arthur's quick thinking, for the one refused the cup and the other poured it down his sleeve. But at heart I am as guilty as I would be if I had succeeded in killing your brother, and still, I wish I had. I am sorry. I deserve nothing from you, not your friendship or your service, and certainly not this kindness.'

'You have deserved my love and obedience for many years and many things done. And I said that I understood why you should wish it. I do not bear the responsibility of Empire, so it is not mine to judge whether the plan was just. I would have opposed it if I had known of it, even to warning Medraut – though probably he has inherited sorcery enough to have foreseen it on his own. And he is well acquainted with poisons, able to protect himself from them. As it is, the attempt failed, and you do not bear the guilt of it.' He stopped, watching, as Gwyn again dropped for the ring, got his timing wrong and snatched at it too late, almost fell as he twisted around reaching for it, and rose unsteadily back into the saddle empty-handed. 'No matter, cousin,' Gwalchmai called. 'She is running better now. Try again!' – then, in the low voice, 'My lady, do not feed on the darkness and grief. Your strength is needed now. The very greatest of rulers have planned worse things, and carried them out as well. Think of the Roman High Kings our lord Arthur so admires ... what does Arthur say of this?'

'He knew nothing of it,' I said quietly. 'I never dared to

tell him. I knew he would oppose it.'

He looked at me evenly for a moment, and I had to continue, 'I have hurt him. Perhaps he will never love me again.'

He still looked at me, in open disbelief.

'He has reason! I plotted murder behind his back. I betrayed him – I betrayed his trust in my honour. And I have dishonoured him in his own eyes, forcing him into lies and empty gestures, trying to carry out something he half wished done but would never have attempted.'

'I cannot believe he hates you. His first thought was to protect your name.'

'No,' I replied, wearily, my dry eyes aching again at the thought. 'He wished to refute Medraut and to preserve *us* – Camlann, the Empire. Not me. And that is as it should be.'

'I do not think . . . och, well done, *mo chara*!' for Gwyn had dropped triumphantly upon the ring, and now turned the mare back holding it glowing and victorious in his hand. He slid from the sweating horse and gave it to Gwalchmai with a bow.

'Did you see me, noble lady?' Gwyn asked hopefully.

'Indeed I did. It was beautifully done, Gwyn.'

He smiled with delight, stood for a moment as though bursting with something to say or shout, then restrained himself and asked, 'Shall I fetch the lists now, noble lady, and the account books?'

He had his eyes fastened on me, and Gwalchmai gave me the same questioning look, one hand on the mare's bridle; the two sets of eyes equally dark.

'You can stable the horse first,' I told Gwyn, knowing that this was what they wanted. 'Even I know that is a rider's first concern. When you're finished, bring the list and the books to my room.'

Gwalchmai smiled very gently, then took my hand and touched it to his forehead, the same gesture that Gwyn had used, but used far differently, filling me with a terror of it: knowing what he knew, and still subjecting himself to me. That he knew set me free, that he remained my friend . . . but I had never had any right to friendship, his or anyone else's; no one can have. That was freedom too, if a bitter freedom where I ceased to matter and existed only in another's nobility. I was grateful, more than I could say.

'Many thanks for your kindness, lady,' said Gwalchmai. 'If you wish to speak further, I am your servant, as ever.'

I nodded and left the two of them to discuss the mare and Gwyn's riding, the fair head and the dark bent over the horse's sleek back.

Arthur that day gave Medraut the command to leave Camlann. He did not charge him with anything, but simply wrote out a letter to the effect that Medraut was relegated to the Orcades, and that all persons reading this letter were to offer him assistance to his journey. Arthur then took Bedwyr and Cei to Medraut at his house and presented him with this document. Medraut greeted them with smiling courtesy, unrolled and read the letter, and pretended astonishment. Cei told me of it afterwards. 'He said, "For what crime am I being exiled?" as though he'd never heard of such a sentence and couldn't think of anything he might have done, except perhaps it was throwing stones at cattle. But our lord would have none of it. "Because of your royal blood and your position," he says, "you have not been charged with any crime, although you have read enough history to remember that defaming the majesty of the emperor is a capital charge, and that offering deliberate insult to the emperor's wife is defaming the imperial majesty. However, I am bringing no charges. Moreover, you are not being exiled, but relegated: your property and your rank in Britain are secure, together with all your rights and privileges except that of staying here. You may leave tomorrow. Take as many horses as you want, and if you need fresh mounts, you can request them from the kings of Britain." Medraut began to protest his shining innocence, but our lord Arthur went on and said, "Cei will go with you," and I grinned at him, and he went quiet. My lord Arthur had just told me the same, my lady, and much as I dislike that eel Medraut, I'll be glad enough to be able to keep my eye on him. And it will be good to see Agravain again, however much he has changed these last years. But, my lady, you should see to it that Medraut cannot take all that Arthur has offered him for travelling expenses. He has poured out the gold as though Medraut were an allied king, and not the next thing to a criminal.'

'Of course,' I replied, 'Medraut's friends are angry enough that their leader is sent away without a trial. If he has been obviously well treated, he can claim less indignation from them and from the kings of Britain. And with you beside him, he cannot use the journey to further his intrigues.'

Cei grunted.

The two did indeed leave the next morning, with an escort of three others who would accompany them as far as Ebrauc, where Medraut and Cei would take ship for the Islands. I worried continuously until we heard that they had actually arrived: worried whether Medraut would start some trouble along the way; whether he would goad Cei into a fighting a duel; whether Cei would start a duel on his own – he was a lover of fighting – and, killing some northern nobleman, be killed by some northern king. But the journey passed apparently without incident, and a short note in Cei's own laborious lettering informed us that the pair had reached Dun Fionn in the Islands. By then, though, I had other things to worry about.

The first few weeks after the attempted murder were even worse than the weeks before it. Arthur, though in public as attentive to me as ever, in private could not bring himself even to speak with me. Silence grew between us; at night in bed we lay side by side as though we had the full half of the world parting us. In the morning I would wake and find Arthur watching me with a set, haggard face, and when I sat down at my mirror I would find the answering expression of guilt and misery still fixed on me. I had to smooth it away carefully before I could face the world. I hated the pretence of innocence, hated it more and more as the days went by and the wild speculations of the fortress gradually gave way to fresh affairs and new gossip. At first, of course, every possible explanation was put forward by someone or other: I had poisoned the cup, but Arthur was miraculously preserved; Medraut had poisoned the cup, to incriminate me, but Arthur either cunningly disposed of the poison or was miraculously ... or the cup was unpoisoned, but I, or Medraut, had been deceived into thinking otherwise by Arthur, or Medraut, or some other party. Some people even believed our official explanation, that it was a joke with treasonous overtones. Some friends of Medraut's even guessed the truth. And all the interpretations of what had happened were endlessly discussed and argued, while I went about my business, trying to appear unconscious of it all, as though nothing whatever had happened. At times I wanted to stand up in the Hall and shout the truth at them, simply to be free of the endless, unspoken questions. But eventually all possible explanations had been searched out and found, and the frenzied questioning calmed. Medraut's departure had lessened much of the tension. Without his presence there to inspire them, many of his former followers began to think for themselves, and to decide that he had gone beyond the limit. This became apparent when, despite all the initial questioning and arguing, there were no more duels, and fewer quarrels. I worked very hard at convincing some of Medraut's waverers to distrust their exiled leader, and the more successful I was, the more I hated myself afterwards. My life was a lie, like my smiles, and I wished heartily that I had never come to Camlann, but married instead some fat farmer in the North and died bearing him fat babies. The heroines of songs are fortunate, able to die from grief or shame. In reality one is able to bear much more misery and suffering than would seem even likely. When one cares nothing for life, when all the world seems one great, corrupting falsehood, and even love seems shallow and pointless – still the hours grind steadily on and one continues to arrange their details. The most I could manage was a fever.

We had heavy rains in July, but at the end of the month a period of hot, sunny weather, which filled the air with fevers. I came down with one, lay in bed for a day or so, then, feeling better, got up and tried to begin the preparations for the harvest. This, of course, brought the fever on again, and more fiercely, and I was forced to go back to bed. As soon as I was able I had Gwyn called and dictated letters and accounts to him – the harvest season takes no account of human infirmity. Near the end of the second week of August Bedwyr came, asking what supplies of grain would be available for feeding the cavalry horses that winter.

I had not spoken to him since that feast. I had learned from Gwalchmai that Bedwyr knew the true story. He had been close enough to notice Arthur's trick with the cup, and had afterwards spoken to Arthur about it. What Arthur had said to him and he to Arthur was something I did not like to think about: it made me ashamed before both of them. I wished, more than ever, to avoid Bedwyr, but as warleader his responsibilities overlapped with mine in many areas, and I could not avoid him for ever.

At that time I was able to sit up in bed, and in fact felt recovered, though I did not dare go out for fear of bringing the fever on again. But I had dressed, and even had the bed moved so as to get the best light for reading. I was checking through some accounts Gwyn had left for me when I heard the muffled sound of a knock at the outer door. I called 'Come in,' and, after the inevitable pause, 'in here!' But I was surprised when it was Bedwyr who opened the inner door and stood in the threshold, pausing to allow his eyes to adjust to the light.

'Noble lord,' I said in greeting. Despite my desire to avoid him I was glad to see him standing there, looking as he always did, plain and sombre. He looked away from my gaze, however, and at this I became embarrassed as well, tense, uncertain how to receive him.

He turned the sideways look to a bow an instant too late for it to be convincing, and closed the door behind him. 'My lady. I am sorry to trouble you while you are ill, but no one else seems able to tell me how much grain we are likely to have this winter, or how many horses we can feed on it.'

'Oh,' I said. 'Oh yes.' I fumbled through the accounts, hoping to find the answer and be rid of him, then realized that I did not have any of the necessary lists by me, and struggled to remember what they said.

Bedwyr noticed my confusion and added quickly, 'It is not urgent. I need to know soon, for next week I wish to send the horses we will not keep here up to the winter pasturage. But I do not have to know today.'

'I think we will have enough for two thousand horses,' I told him. 'Or a little more: say, three horses for each member of the warband. But I cannot be more specific than that just now. I can probably send you some slightly better estimate by tomorrow afternoon.'

He nodded, but, instead of taking his leave, stood looking at me. 'God speed your recovery, my lady,' he said after a moment. 'You are much missed.'

'I am nearly recovered now,' I said, trying to smile. But the smile was a failure. Bedwyr was not a stranger, not someone to be easily fooled by tensing a few muscles in the face. Indeed, it was easier to conceal a grief from Arthur than from his steady eyes. I felt worn and wretched, and I could see that he knew it, and felt my face growing hot for shame at my lies, my many lies. But I could not bear speaking with him honestly, tasting his anger and bitterness as well as Arthur's. 'I may be up and about tomorrow,' I finished hurriedly.

'Do not press yourself too hard, my lady. Much depends on you.'

There was another minute of silence while we looked at each other and I wished desperately that he would go and leave me to my misery. Then he added, deliberately, 'Our lord Arthur misses your help.'

I looked away hastily. This gentleness where I had expected scorn confused me. 'Does he?' I asked, trying for a tone of uninterested inquiry but sounding merely flat and bitter. This additional piece of stupidity, my lack of self-control, disgusted me. I bit my lip, having to blink at tears: they come far too easily after a sickness.

At this Bedwyr took two rapid strides towards me and caught my hand. 'Lady Gwynhwyfar.' He dropped to his knees so as not to stoop over me, 'Forgive my presumption in speaking thus to you, but I must speak. Your husband loves you deeply, even if now he is bitter against you. We have spoken together since Medraut's exile, and it is as plain to see as the wide heavens. He longs for some words which would reconcile him to you again, but he does not know what to say. I beg you, my lady, do not grieve yourself so. Speak to him, make the reconciliation. You have more skill at such things then he does, and it will console you both.'

I pulled my hand away, biting my lip until I tasted blood. 'Why are you saying this to me? I have broken all the laws that you and Arthur live by in the name of your own goal, and thus betrayed you. And I can repent neither to Arthur nor even to God, because I still wish I had succeeded and that Medraut were safe in Hell. So how can I make a reconciliation with Arthur? And you, you must despise me as well. Do not lie to me, Bedwyr. I am sick of lies; I would prefer your hatred to more of them.'

He met my eyes a moment with an expression of shock,

then bowed his head almost to the bed. 'My lady,' he whispered, 'how could I hate or despise you? If what you had done had been a hundred times worse, still your grace and goodness would force me to love you, even against my will, and . . .' he broke off abruptly, staring at the coverlet, his hand clenching among its folds. I touched his shoulder in wonder and he looked up, and my heart came into my throat at that look.

'Do not,' he resumed after a pause, 'do not believe that your lord despises you. He is the more troubled because he so loves and honours you – and because he fears Medraut, and is himself ashamed because he begot Medraut and now wishes him dead. He is as bitter with himself as with you. Believe me, for I would not lie about this even to please you.'

I began to cry in earnest at this, and then sneezed and had a coughing fit, for my fever had left me with a cold. Bedwyr handed me one of the cloths by the bedside, sitting down on the bed as he did so. I wiped my face and blew my nose, managed to check the tears.

'I am sorry, Bedwyr. I always seem to cry when you are kind to me. If Arthur feels as you say he does, why doesn't he tell me so himself? No, you said that he hopes for some miracle to reconcile us. To console us both. And I am to produce this reconciliation? Lord God of Heaven, must I really lie to him, and say that I repent when I have not, and tell him I am glad that Medraut lives?' I called on God, but I was looking at Bedwyr, at his dark, compassionate eyes.

'You need only say that it would have been wrong, my lady. That I know you do believe. He cares more to have you back than to prove the rights and wrongs of the case.'

I laughed bitterly, coughed, found another cloth. 'Ah, is that all? And do you think it will be that simple, that I can simply say a few words and make all well again? No, I am sorry. Your advice is, as always, good, true, and difficult to follow. My friend, my heart, I thank you. But can you justify even to yourself this crime I have attempted – although you treat me with such kindness?'

His face was tense and strained, but his eyes were alight, intense, very warming to me after so much cold misery. 'I do not much care for such justifications. You acted from excess of love, to protect the realm at all costs. How can I say you were wrong? To be sure, I know it is evil to poison a man. But to justify or to condemn you – that is beyond me. And the thing was not done. Moreover, it has been bitter to me to watch you, seeing you conceal your grief and knowing that it devours you within.' He reached out for my hand again, touched it to his lips. 'Gwynhwyfar, I know that you have condemned yourself, but no one has the right to condemn but God, who alone can weigh the heart. Sweet lady, be merciful to yourself also.'

'Go on as though I had done nothing, as though it were unimportant, complacently awaiting the Last Judgement?'

'What else is there to do, except die? We must live with our sins. One chooses between evils and endures that choice. I . . . I once decided that it was evil to kill, even in battle. Arthur showed me that it can be evil not to act, when action might save something of value, even if the action includes killing. I agreed. But they are still there, all those deaths; I can clean the blood from my sword, but from my heart, never. All those men I have killed for the sake of the Empire, for the sake of the Light, are as dead as if I had killed only for hatred or to prove myself a better warrior than them. But you have never killed anyone.'

I shook my head, staring at him. His soberness was gone. For once the passion was on the surface, and with it the pain. He leaned forward, clutching my hand hard, leaning upon the stump of his shield-hand. 'It is easier than you would expect. It makes little impression, at the time. Afterwards, afterwards, one remembers it and feels differently about it. But the only alternative we have had is to allow others to be killed, and if that leaves no blood on a sword, it must leave more on the soul before God. What you have done – what you meant to do – must count for less in Heaven than the crimes I know I have committed, the deaths and the maimings and pain, the widows and children starving after their men's deaths, the burned fields and plundered towns – all done with this hand.' He pulled it from my fingers and held it before me: his sword hand, calloused from the sword, the spear and the reins, scarred on the back from practice matches and the hazards of war. He regarded it with a degree of pain and horror that tore my heart. I caught the hand and kissed it. He looked at me as though he had forgotten I was there, as though he had never seen me before. He drew his fingers along my lips, touched the tears that were still on my cheek, smoothed back my hair; caught hold of my shoulder. He leaned forward and kissed me.

I meant, at every moment of the next hour, to stop it: to say, 'No more.' But I did not. It was sweet, so very sweet that I wished always just one more minute of it, before returning to the cold and the loneliness and the futile longing for Arthur, the shame and tension and approaching dark. No doubt Bedwyr meant to stop it, also, but he too said nothing. Neither of us said anything until it was over and we lay side by side, knowing we had betrayed Arthur and everything we lived for. Then I turned towards the wall and began to weep again.

Bedwyr raised himself on his elbow and stroked my hair and shoulder, whispering, 'Hush. It is my fault, all my fault. Hush.'

'No, no. Mine. Oh, why did we?'

'My lady, my most sweet lady, I love you. I have always loved you. I told myself otherwise when I saw that my lord also loved you, but I could not believe that for ever. I have wanted this for such a long time ... I should never have come here. You were sick and grieving and could not help it. It is my fault.' The gentle hand slipped lower and I shivered. I sat up abruptly and looked at him.

'It does not matter whose fault it was. Arthur must not know. It would hurt him too much. And we must never do this again.'

He stared at me for a moment, then turned away. He sat up and swung his legs over the side of the bed. 'You are right. Oh, Heavenly God!' He bent over with pain, clasping the stump of his shield arm. 'What have I done? My lord's wife, in his own bed – '

'We must not do it again!' I said, more urgently. 'You must go somewhere far away, until we have forgotten this a little, and until I am reconciled with Arthur.'

He nodded, keeping his back to me, still bent over double. The grey light through the eaves fell along his back, picking out a long scar which ran up from his right side. Arthur had similar scars. All cavalry fighters have them ; they cannot fight and defend themselves at the same time.

'It is my fault, too,' I told Bedwyr.

He shook his head, still without looking round.

'I love you,' I said. The words seemed meaningless. 'I love Arthur, but you, as well.'

He reached down, fumbled about for the breeches thrown aside not long before. He pulled them on, then, standing again, turned and looked at me. He had to hold them up because he could not fasten his belt with one hand; in a tale it would have made me laugh. But his eyes were very dark with the pain, and the skin drawn tight around his mouth.

'You must go to Arthur,' I said, thinking desperately. 'Ask him to send you to Less Britain, to talk to King Macsen. He needs to send someone, and he is determined not to send Gwalchmai again.'

Some of the pain ebbed. 'Yes,' he said, after a minute. 'I knew Macsen when I served his brother Bran; I could talk to him. Though my lord might be reluctant to allow me to leave for any length of time . ... but I could urge business, a desire to see my family and look to the estates. He will certainly give me leave to spend time on that.' He looked around for his tunic, picked it up, pulled it over his head with his shield arm. I got up and fastened his belt for him, then tied the fastenings of his tunic, carefully repeating the knots his servant customarily used. He let me finish, then caught my wrist.

'Gwynhwyfar.' His voice was resuming its usual quiet tone, but shock and confusion gave it still an edge of harshness. 'My lady, you know now that I love you, and am ruined. I have betrayed my lord. I do not even know that I can repent, for I still desire you – but enough of that. If ever this should be discovered, let me suffer for it. It would be a plain case of treason, but my lord would probably commute the sentence from death to exile. I could endure that. I could not endure it if you were made to suffer for my crime, for it is my fault – no, it is true! I swear I would feel your disgrace more than my own. I know that if this is ever discovered you will not escape punishment altogether, but you might escape lightly, if you did not try to intercede for me or shift the blame onto yourself. We would both suffer more if you did. And do not grieve yourself for it; it is my fault.' His struggle for calm failed for an instant and he kissed me once more, hard.

When he released me I said nothing, merely found his sword for him and buckled it on, and helped him on with his boots. Only when he stood in the doorway did I whisper, 'God keep you.' He bowed his head and was gone. I looked at the door for a long minute, then collapsed back onto the bed. I crawled under the blanket and lay there, trembling, remembering, until evening when I fell asleep.

Bedwyr spoke with Arthur that same evening, and set out for Less Britain within the week, despite the fact that he had, by then, come down with my cold. I stayed in the house until he had gone, and by then was recovered enough to get back to work on the harvest.

I worked also on reconciling myself with Arthur. Despite what had happened afterwards, I decided, Bedwyr had been right. I was punishing my husband as well as myself by continuing to wallow in guilt and grief. And it did no one any good at all. A few days after Bedwyr left, I came back from supervising the disposal of a feast's remnants, resolved to speak.

The house was dark when I entered it, carrying the dim rushlight that had shown me the path round the Hall. When I entered the bedroom I saw that Arthur was already in bed, but he flinched as the light fell across him and I knew he was still awake, though he lay with his back to me and did not otherwise move. I knew that he was trying to avoid the pain of the silence between us, and was afraid. I set the light in its holder beside the bed and undressed in silence, wondering what to say, wishing to put it off. Almost, I extinguished the light without speaking. But I sat on the bed a moment, looking at Arthur, and touched his shoulder. 'I am sorry,' I managed to say, hearing how rough and uncertain my voice was. 'It was an evil intention. I am very sorry.' And suddenly I was not thinking of Medraut, but of Bedwyr, lying where Arthur lay now: of the betrayal that was greater than Arthur knew.

He turned, looking up at me strangely – not coldly, but in puzzlement. He caught my hand from his shoulder and looked at it, studying the carving on the signet ring, then looked back at my face. The room was dark, for the rushlight was flickering, almost out. Arthur sighed.

'I am sorry,' I whispered again.

'I know,' he replied. 'But don't you see that it needs more than that? This thing . . . Medraut has crippled us.'

'I wanted us to escape from him.'

He touched my hand to his lips, his eyes seeking mine. 'Oh, my white hart, if only we could! But that, that degrades you. I know you would accept that, for the Empire, but I cannot. And he is mine, my son, my fault.'

'Please,' I said. I could not reason with him; reason meant nothing to what was between us.

He touched my face and stroked back my hair. 'You are cold,' he said, after a moment. 'Here, get into bed and go to sleep.'

He put his arms round me when I was under the coverlet, and I lay very still, not daring to move. My heart was crying for him, but it was a beginning.

The silence vanished slowly. But the harvest is a busy season, and, with Bedwyr away, Arthur and I had to consult each other more than usual. We had first learned to trust each other from the affairs of the Empire: from tribute received and dispatched, from the supplying of a warband, from the plans of kings. These restored our trust. Eventually, even in private, we could speak to each other freely, and even laugh. The last barrier dropped early in December, when Cei returned from the Orcades with the news of Agravain's death.

Perhaps we should have expected it. We had long known that Agravain was unwell, and in my heart I had always been afraid of what Medraut might do in the Islands. Nonetheless, the news came as a shock. Cei brought it fresh: he had sailed from the Islands with the first tide the day Agravain died, and posted from Ebrauc at a pace that must have left a trail of foundered horses behind him. The winds were from the north, very good for the voyage, and so he had made the whole journey in a week and six days. He arrived about midnight on a cold December Saturday and burst into our house at once, shouting that it was urgent. It was snowing a little outside, wet flakes mixed with rain. Cei had ridden from Caer Ceri that morning, changing horses at Baddon, and he was grey-faced with exhaustion and shivering with cold. As soon as Arthur had thrown his over-tunic and cloak on he began building up the fire in the conference room, while I poured Cei some wine and put more on to heat. Cei, however, did not wait to take off his wet cloak or take more than one swallow from the cup before he burst out, 'Agravain is dead. *He* murdered him. That honey-mouthed bastard murdered his brother.'

I almost dropped the pitcher of wine. Arthur froze for a moment, kneeling by the hearth, a piece of firewood in his hand. I know that the fire must have been roaring, the water dripping from the thatch: there must have been sound, but I can remember none, only a great stillness. Then Arthur set the piece of wood on the fire, stood, and pulled a chair closer to it, gesturing for Cei to sit down. Cei did so, unfastening his cloak and hanging it over the back of the chair to dry.

'Now, what happened?' Arthur asked quietly. 'Agravain ap Lot is dead?'

'Near two weeks ago. He was found cold in his bed one morning, with no mark on him. But Medraut had been drinking with him the night before, and Medraut is a devil and a follower of devils, and knows ways of killing men which leave no mark. I'm not the only one that thinks so, my lord: the royal warband of the Islands has always thought as much. They're dogs, those Irish warriors, a pack of curs that will lick the hand of any man that can beat them. They began cringing up to Medraut the moment he arrived, though when Agravain was present they pretended differently.'

'Then the warband supports Medraut, now?'

'Yes, the dogs! Medraut used to lead them, and might have been made king before, had his mother lived, for they were all in terror of their very souls from that witch. They loved Argravain better, for he was his father's son and a man who had fought beside them, but Agravain . . . was no longer his old self.' The furious indignation dropped for a moment, and Cei went on in a strange, hurt voice, unlike his own. 'And what was the worst of it, my lord. It was wormwood to the heart to look at him. He was not himself. I extended my stay to help him – you had that second letter – I tried to warn him against what was happening. He was too drunk, most of the time, to take any notice, and when he was sober he never really cared. That a warrior, a king and a king's son, should be so broken, so terrified and unsure! And he was my friend, a man who was a shield to me in battle, and like a brother to me. Poisoned, in his own home, by a smooth-speaking witch's bastard! God in Heaven! We must have justice for him; we must...'

'Hush,' I said.' Tell the full tale, and then rest, for you are overtired. Here, the wine is hot now.'

He set his cup down and I filled it with steaming honeyed wine. He sipped a little, cautious because of the heat, and curled his cold-reddened hands about the sides. 'There is not much more to the tale,' he said, wearily now. 'Agravain was found dead, as I said, the morning after he had been drinking late with Medraut. I woke up to hear them keening and wailing. Some of the royal clan, who hate Medraut though they do not dare say so openly, came to me and told me the news before Medraut did, and helped me to the port and a ship before the day was old. They wished to know what you would do; I said that I was certain that this murder would anger you. They say that they cannot oppose the election of Medraut to the kingship, but that if you wish to contact them you must send a message to Eoghan the shipwright in northern Pictland – I think he is one of their spies. I was glad of their help, my lord, for I had no wish to be on that island when Medraut was king.'

'Is it certain that he will be made king?' asked Arthur.

'No one dares to oppose him. He can have the kingship if he wants it, and it is certain that he does want it. My lord, Emperor of Britain, do we declare war?'

'No.'

When Cei leapt from his chair in anger, Arthur lifted his hand, looking at him. It was the calm look I knew so well, the look with which he commanded something that he hated but considered essential – an execution, a task which would cost the lives of those who did it. Cei also recognized the look and, though he loomed above Arthur, he seemed to shrink before it. Slowly he sat down.

'On what grounds can we declare war?' Arthur asked him. 'Medraut will doubtless give his brother a splendid funeral and mourn extravagantly, then hasten south to swear an alliance with me. We can prove nothing. And if I contact these enemies of Medraut, who neither dare to oppose him openly nor even to be known to have received messages from me, what am I to say? "Murder him, and I will reward you"? That is more shameful than poison, and far less likely to succeed. No. We must prepare, and be ready for whatever Medraut plans next.' He paused, then added in a gentler voice, 'Go to bed, Cei. I will need your strength.'

Cei nodded. He set down his empty cup, stood slowly. Then he stopped, remembering something, and his remembering touched mine.

'He shares a house with Gwalchmai,' I said. 'He should not have to tell this tale to Agravain's brother tonight.'

Cei nodded. 'You have it, my lady; it is bitter news to bring. I sent for Gwalchmai when I arrived, so as to speak only once. I do not know where . . .'

The door opened suddenly and Gwalchmai came in. His face was very calm, but for a moment I could not recognize him, he looked so unearthly and remote. He had plainly been outside for some time, for the snow was melting in his hair and had soaked the shoulders of his cloak. 'Your pardon,' he said, in a voice only slightly roughened, bowing to me and Arthur. 'I have been outside. I was listening. But I guessed what had happened when your messenger woke me, Cei, and I feared to come in. Cousin, it is a long way to the islands, and you had better sleep. No more words. My lord and lady, good night.' He held the door for Cei. Cei, after staring at him for a minute, crossed himself, picked up his own cloak and pulled it over his shoulders, walked out. Gwalchmai gave one more slight bow and slipped back out into the night; there was the faint clunk of the bolt of the door falling back into its place, then silence.

Arthur tore his eyes from the door, then sat heavily in Cei's empty chair and stared at the fire for a long time. I came and sat on the floor beside him. After a while he put his arm around me, and I leaned my head against his thigh. The fire crackled, and the smoke which the snow trapped in the room stung our eyes. 'My heart,' Arthur said at last, 'perhaps you were right, even then.'

'It is evil to poison.'

'But now Medraut has poisoned his brother, my warrior.'

'Perhaps it was not so. Agravain had long been ill.'

'And do you believe it was a natural death?'

'No.'

Arthur ran his hand through my hair, then turned my face towards him. 'I am sorry,' he said, in a very low voice. 'And yet, still, it must have been evil; we are no better than our enemies if we do such things. Only I am bitterly grieved for Agravain, and for Gwalchmai, and for us all. Gwynhwyfar, my white hart, it would have been better for you if you had never met me. Then the way of virtue would have been a Roman road, while now ... now we draw furrows on the pathless waves. My joy, I am sorry.'

After that we had to hold each other, for around us was only the silence, the darkness and the wind.

Five

Gwalchmai had loved his brother Agravain. He would have been much afflicted by his death in any circumstances, and that the death was probably caused by his other brother made it worse. I remembered Agravain and Gwalchmai sitting together at table in Camlann, years ago, talking rapidly in Irish: Agravain gold-haired with hot blue eyes, angry, excited over something someone had said to him; Gwalchmai calmer, regarding his brother with patient affection and a touch of amusement. Agravain had always taken a kind of proprietary pleasure in his brother's achievements, and was enormously proud of him; Gwalchmai treated Agravain almost as he might a sensitive child, protectively, defending the occasional outbursts of bad temper and violence — for Agravain always had been quickly moved to anger, overly-sensitive to insult. Yet I had gathered from a few things each had said that once the closeness had been between Gwalchmai and Medraut, with Agravain an outsider, a potential enemy. What Gwalchmai thought now was anyone's guess: he behaved as he always did when troubled, politely refusing to speak of it to anyone and spending most of his time riding his horse or playing the harp and brooding. But when Medraut sent a letter from the Orcades, lamenting Agravain's death and promising to pledge his new kingship to an alliance with Arthur, Gwalchmai asked to be sent to the Islands as an emissary. Arthur sensibly refused. There was no need of it, and Gwalchmai was the last person we could trust to Medraut's good faith. Instead, Arthur replied by letter that the King of the Orcades was welcome to visit Camlann peacefully.

Even before he could have received this letter, Medraut sent another letter saying that he hoped to come to Camlann in the spring or early summer, when he had established his realm in greater security and when it would be easier to travel. Arthur was content to wait until then. He sent a message to Eoghan the shipwright in northern Pictland, to be sent to those of Medraut's cousins who were dis-

pleased with their new king. In this he said that he grieved
for Agravain, but that Medraut was his nephew and would
be received as such. This letter was so worded that it would
cause no difficulty if it fell into Medraut's hands, but
equally made it plain that, if Medraut were overthrown,
there would be no reprisals.

The sentence of relegation which Arthur had passed on
Medraut was allowed to sink into oblivion. It had been
passed against a private individual, and could not be
allowed to obstruct relations with an important allied
kingdom. So we waited, knowing that in the spring or
early summer the contest would begin again.

It was a strange, bitter-sweet winter. The year was a wet
one, with much snow and more rain: the thatching of the
Hall and houses grew dark and heavy, and the rooms filled
with smoke even with a hot dry fire. But a kind of truce
was established in the Family. Medraut as an allied king far
away in Dun Fionn was a different man from Medraut a
warrior in Camlann, even to his friends. Foreign kings
were no concern of the Family, unless they were inclined
towards war with us; Medraut had no further claim on
anyone's loyalty. Oh, things were not as they had been
once, not as they were back in the days of the war, or the
first years of the peace, when Camlann had seemed almost a
new Rome. Then we knew that we had set ourselves a
battle that all the world had lost, and which we were
winning. We had fought as no one else had fought, not for
power, gold or glory, but to preserve the Light, the
Empire: knowledge and justice, law and peace. It had given
a kind of exaltation to our lives, even amid hardship, violence and grief. Now the peace was old, familiar, taken for
granted, and the battles were all fought; and now hatred
and distrust had crept in among us. Yet there were times
when it seemed we were still innocent, and all things were
possible to us. We held festivals in the Hall, celebrating
Christmas and the New Year for days on end. The splendour was greater than it had been during or soon after the
war: everything glowed and glittered, and it seemed that
the benches even of the lower Hall were afire with jewels.
Taliesin sang of great things accomplished, by us and by
others, until the men were as dizzy with music as with
mead, stunned by the glory of the past and eager to emulate

And there were times, too, apart from the great festivals, when Camlann seemed apart from the rest of world, half-way to Heaven: clear winter days when the snow lay thick on the ground, and from my doorway I could see the fields stretching out and away, further even than Ynys Witrin, shining like glass and silver in the light. The children of the fortress would run about shouting and throwing snow-balls, and sometimes the warriors would ride their horses about the hill at full gallop for the sheer joy of running, a splendour of plunging hooves, white breath and back-flung snow, the jingle of harness and the flash of the rider's smile in passing. Indoors by the smoky fires women sang at the loom, craftsmen at their workbench – or else, gathered together, friends and families laughed and argued. There was not much for me to do; I could join any party gathered for talk or music. Winter is a quiet season: the harvest is gathered and stored, everything checked and inventoried; the tribute all delivered. It is difficult to travel, so there are few petitioners for justice, and any emissaries sent out generally wait until the spring thaws the roads and calms the seas before returning. So I had time, time to spend with Arthur, to listen to songs, to read books purchased from travelling merchants the summer before and lying on the shelf since, waiting my attention. I felt even in the midst of it that this quiet winter was the calm before the storm – but I was resolved nonetheless to make the best of it. And, I told myself, we can very likely weather the storm when it does come. We have some strength here yet.

One of the things that continued to grieve me was Gwalchmai. The festivals of December and January passed, and he remained courteous and remote, brooding over his brother's death. He only seemed to cheer up when he gave lessons to Gwyn.

The boy was now doing very well at Camlann. He had caught up with the other boys of the fortress in knowledge of weapons, and he was beginning to be accepted by them. He was now growing rapidly and always seemed too large for his clothes, but did not, like many boys, lose his sweet temper together with his treble voice.

However, one day in early February, when Gwyn and I were going over the preceding month's accounts in the

Hall, a monk came into the building and looked about as though searching for someone. Gwyn recognized the man at once.

'It's Father Gilla, from Opergelei monastery, near my mother's abbey!' he told me in great excitement, as I eyed the monk dubiously – monastics tended to disapprove of Arthur quite strongly, and it was rare to see one in Camlann on any errand but complaint. 'He must be bringing me some news. Hai! Father Gilla, here I am!'

Gwyn wrote to his mother whenever he could find some trader or traveller who would be going to Gwynedd and could carry the letter. Most travellers were willing to do so, as such a letter would assure them of a night's lodging and provision from the grateful mother. Gwyn had once had a letter back, but that had also been carried by some casual traveller. I had gathered that the boy's mother was angry with her son for running off to learn war against her wishes, and it was because of this that she had not written more often. Never had a messenger been especially sent, and I was suddenly afraid for the boy, the more so when the monk came nearer and I saw his face. Good news goes on two feet, they say, but bad news has wings – and, moreover, good news does not wear an expression like Gilla's.

Gwyn also realized this as the monk came up to us, and his first excitement was replaced by apprehension. 'Why . . . what is the matter?' he asked.

The man looked at me nervously, then let his eyes slide over Gwyn and away. He was a small, fair, wispy man whose plain black robe was worn through at the elbows and patched. He seemed unwilling to speak.

'Has something happened?' Gwyn demanded. 'Is Mama sick? Father, tell me. What is wrong?'

The little man finally looked at the boy directly, then embraced him. 'My child,' he stammered, then, proceeding in a rush, as though to get it over with, 'Gwyn my boy, I have bad news, bad indeed. Your mother . . . she wished me to come, she said, if she . . . she grew sick, three weeks ago, with a fever, and at first she wished you were with her – but you know how it grieved her, that you ran off here, when she meant you for the priesthood – but she said she forgave you, and that it was better, indeed, those were her words, that it was good that you were here . . .'

'Father, what has happened?' Gwyn interrupted. 'She had a fever – is she better?' Gilla blinked at him miserably. 'She . . . she didn't . . . she's not . . .'

'She is dead, child,' the monk said. 'She died a week and five days ago, on a Friday. She gives you her blessing.'

'Oh no,' Gwyn said. He turned from the monk, ignored my outstretched hand, and sat down on one of the benches, leaning his head against his hands.

'It was a rapid fever,' the monk went on, after a moment. 'She stayed up, the first few days, and then she fell down, at dinner, on Epiphany, and took to her bed, and died a few days later. She died very peacefully, after she had written the letter. She was willing to leave this world, and hurry to the next. She blessed you, and wished you all joy . . .' he trailed off again, uncertainly, staring miserably at Gwyn.

'Where is the letter?' Gwyn asked.

'What?'

The boy raised his head. His eyes were too bright, but there were no tears on his face. 'The letter. You said she wrote me a letter.'

Father Gilla flushed. 'No, no, she didn't. That is, she wrote a letter, but not to you. She wrote a letter to the lord Gwalchmai ap Lot, that you said had been kind to you. She sealed it and gave it to me. Perhaps there is another letter with it, inside the seal. We can give it to him now, and see.'

'Oh,' said Gwyn. 'To the lord Gwalchmai. So that he will protect me. No. I . . . I don't want to see anyone now. My lady . . .'

'Gwyn.' I started towards him, longing to put my arms about him, but he threw his hands up between us.

'My lady,' he repeated, 'please look after Father Gilla, and see that he receives hospitality: he is a good man, and not seditious, and notable in his own monastery, and he was always kind to me. Father, please, I will talk with you later, only now . . .' He turned suddenly and ran from the building.

Gilla looked after him, still blinking. 'Poor boy,' he said, 'poor orphaned child. And I cannot go after him, he would never let me, even when he was little.'

'He will want to talk to you later,' I said. 'Father, let me find you a place to rest, and see that you have food and drink. You must be tired after your journey.'

'Indeed, though my poor horse is in greater need of care. Lady, I thank you for your kindness – I do not know your name . . .'

'Gwynhwyfar, daughter of Ogyrfan,' I said and, when he stared, I smiled and went on, 'so you see, I have authority to see that you receive hospitality here, and that your horse is well treated.'

He bowed very low. 'I had not thought it was you, noble queen. I thought queens wore purple and gold; though Gwyn spoke of you often in his letters. I thank your grace. But first I must see the lord Gwalchmai ap Lot, to give him the letter of the lady abbess.'

'Gwyn's mother was an abbess?' I asked, surprised, 'He never mentioned that.'

'But she was a very great abbess! A noblewoman, wise and courageous. She came first to St Elena's fourteen years ago, near her time of bearing Gwyn, and stayed, and took her vows there. She has been abbess four years now, and never was there a finer one.' He paused, recollected himself, and added, 'I must give her letter to the lord Gwalchmai ap Lot. Could you graciously tell me, most noble lady, whether that lord is here now, and where he might be?'

I had happened to notice Gwalchmai practising spear-casting in the yard behind the stables, and I told Gilla as much. I escorted him – and his horse, which he had left tied to a post outside the Hall – to the stables, where I saw that the horse would be cared for; and then to the yard, where I pointed Gwalchmai out to him. Though, indeed, Gwalchmai needed little pointing out. He was casting his spears from horseback, and his white war stallion, famous from a hundred songs, stood out among the other horses like a swan among a flock of geese. Gilla walked out into the yard, waving and calling faintly, then stopped and waited while Gwalchmai threw a few more spears at the target. I began talking with one of the other warriors who happened to be there, telling him about Gwyn, and watching idly while Gwalchmai threw his last spear, turned his horse, cantered over to Gilla and reined in. They talked, I saw from the corner of my eye. I knew that Gwyn's mother had chosen well in deciding to write to Gwalchmai. The warrior would have done much for Gwyn in any circumstances, and the letter would incline him to do more. Still, it hurt me to think of the boy, suffering so, when grief is still new and one is unused to the thought of death. And he was like Gwalchmai in his refusal to accept comfort ... Gilla had given Gwalchmai the letter, and he was reading it.

Suddenly, the distinct figure on the white horse whirled about and galloped off, leaving Gilla gesticulating wildly. I stared, surprised, for such discourtesy was unlike Gwalchmai. I had not have much time to stare, for the warrior galloped over, the snow flying in great wet lumps from the shining hooves of his stallion. He reined in sharply, and the horse danced, arching its neck and tugging at the bit.

"My lady,' said Gwalchmai, shouting to be heard over the horse's impatience, 'where is Gwyn?'

'Let him be for now,' I returned, 'He has just had the news of his mother's death, and he will no more wish to speak of it than you would.'

'Och, Ard Rígh Mor, I know, I know, but where is he?'

'What is the matter?' I demanded, for Gwalchmai was as agitated as I had ever seen him.

He flourished a roll of parchment. 'This letter ... for the love of God, my lady, if you know where he is, tell me!'

This frightened me. I don't know what I thought – perhaps that the letter being sent to someone else was a sign to Gwyn that his mother had not, after all, forgiven him for leaving her, and that he might do something dreadful in his despair, and that his mother knew it – I do not know. 'He ... he sometimes goes to a place in the stables ... here, I will show you.'

Gwalchmai at once leapt off his horse, helped me up, and jumped up behind me. He touched his heels to the beast and we went flying up the hill, leaving the other warriors, and Father Gilla, gaping after us.

We slid off the horse in the middle of the stables, and Gwalchmai caught the stallion's bridle, then paused and unrolled the letter again. He stared at it, reading a few lines under his breath, then lowered it and looked up at nothing. His horse snorted and nuzzled his hair, and he patted the sleek neck absently.

'What is the matter?' I asked again, less frightened now that I had time to think.

He shook his head. 'This letter . . . my lady, I am glad of your company.' His agitation was less, but he seemed almost afraid. 'For he might hate me, and it might not be true, after all, and almost I fear to ask the question. Where do you think Gwyn is?'

I took the other side of the stallion's bridle and led the horse towards its own stall. Gwalchmai released his hold and followed, clutching the letter. The horse had a box by the west wall of the stables, by one of the ladders that led up into the hay loft, and I opened the door of the stall and let the horse go in and investigate its manger. Gwalchmai closed the door and leaned over the top of it, looking at me expectantly.

'Gwyn comes here, sometimes,' I said in an undertone. 'I've had him summoned from the hayloft, once or twice. Gwyn! Gwyn, are you here?'

There was a rustling noise above us.

'I must speak with you,' Gwalchmai said loudly.

Another rustling, and then Gwyn climbed down the ladder from the loft and stood at its foot. His eyes were red and swollen, and he looked at us with a wordless resentment. I was very glad to see him.

'Please, noble lady, noble lord,' he said, 'I would rather be alone now. It is very kind of you, but I would.'

Gwalchmai stared at him as though fascinated. 'Gwyn,' he said, in a hurried, breathless fashion, 'This letter . . .' he took a few steps towards the boy and stopped, extending the roll of parchment.

'Does she ask you to protect me?' asked Gwyn. 'I am sorry, lord, I know it is presumptuous, and I know I am only a bastard, but I wrote to her about how kind you have been to me, and she must have thought . . . do you mind, then? It is only that she wants someone powerful to protect me. Mothers want that.'

Gwalchmai flushed. 'Yes. Of course. She . . . Gwyn, what was your mother's name?'

'Elidan. Doesn't she sign the letter? She is – was – abbess of St Elena's.'

I heard my own breath catch with a gasp as I at last understood what was happening.

Gwalchmai's hand closed on the parchment, crushed it. He closed his eyes a moment; opened them, looked at the letter. He smoothed it again carefully, as though afraid the parchment would dissolve into the air. "And she came from the North,' he whispered.

'Yes. Does she say that?'

'Not here. She was the daughter of Caw, sister of King Bran of Ebrauc. I knew that she had settled in an abbey in Gwynedd. I saw her there, once, and begged her forgiveness, which she refused me. I saw you as well, I think, but I did not realize that you were her son. Why did you tell me that your mother lived in Elmet?'

Gwyn stared back, thoroughly startled now. 'Because the monasteries in Gwynedd are so seditious, and I didn't want people to know. But my mother wasn't a king's sister.'

'She was. I . . . knew her, then. She has written to me. She wrote this, when she was dying. She forgives me. She says she regrets any pain she gave me – me! who lied to her, and murdered her brother! – and she commends . . . her son to me.' He stopped, his voice breaking on the last phrase. 'She never told me she had a son. I never knew that. Gwyn. You must know, I . . . loved your mother once. It was dishonourably, shamefully: I was sent on an embassy and seduced the sister of my host. Afterwards, when her brother rebelled against my lord, I swore to her that I would not harm him, and then killed him. And I asked her to marry me, but after that she could not. But she never told me that she . . . that we had a son. I am your father. Can you forgive me?'

Gwyn went as pale as the crumpled parchment. He stared at Gwalchmai. Gwalchmai returned the stare for a long moment, then dropped to one knee and lifted his hands in a slight, helpless gesture.

'Most noble lord! Don't!' Gwyn cried. He ran to Gwalchmai, and tried to pull him to his feet. 'Not to me, noble lord!'

Gwalchmai shook his head and stayed as he was. 'You have the right to forgive or condemn me.'

Gwyn fell back a pace, blinking, then said, in a newly calm voice, 'Let me see the letter.'

Gwalchmai handed it to him. The boy stood very straight in the grey light of the stable, reading the letter in a low, clear voice:

'"Elidan, daughter of Caw and Abbess of St Elena's, to Gwalchmai son of Lot. I am dying, it seems, and things which once seemed great to me seem less now. It will not matter to God that I am a noblewoman or that I was strong enough to be unforgiving. I forgive you now for the way in which you wronged me; forgive me also for the pain I have caused you. It would have been better if I had yielded before, and married you – but it is an ill world, and what might have been is only a torment. I commend to you now the child I bore, your son. He was christened after you Gwalchaved, but has all his life been called Gwyn. I wished him to be a priest, but Fate is stronger than I, and it is a year since he went to Camlann, and, so I know from his letters, met you and grows already to love you ..."' Gwyn faltered, flushing, then struggled on, '"Care for him and protect him with a peaceful heart, for I swear before the God I must soon meet that he is your own son and mine, and no one's else. And at last I can be glad that he went to you, for it is right that he know his father, and that you should know him. God's blessing be with you both. Believe that I loved you. Farewell."'

The boy lowered the letter and looked back at Gwalchmai. 'You?' he cried, the forced calm gone, passionate and disbelieving.

Gwalchmai nodded.

'But ... *you*! Anyone else ... did you love her?'

For the first time that I could remember, Gwalchmai's face was open and totally unguarded, vulnerable: drawn with pain and fear, with the bruised look about the eyes that comes from sudden grief. 'I loved her,' he said. 'When I loved her, I did not know how much I loved her. But it was shameful for all that.'

Gwyn looked again at the letter. He bit his lip and began to roll it up. It took a long time; his hands were shaking. 'You,' he said as he did so. 'I never dared even to dream that it might be you. I knew – well, for a long time, I guessed – that she loved ... my father. I remember her saying dreadful things about him when I was little, but she cried sometimes at night, and the other sisters used to whisper about it and say she was still in love. But she would never tell me anything about my father, even when I was older and asked her. I never understood why anyone would leave her. And yet, you didn't marry her.'

'She couldn't marry her brother's murderer. When it was too late I wished to marry her, and she said she would kill herself if I came near her again. And I never knew she had a son.' Silence. 'By the High King of Heaven, can you forgive me?'

Gwyn looked back at him furiously. 'Of *course*. I could forgive *you* anything; I would still forgive you if you hadn't really loved her, if you had done it all on purpose. I've thought you were like St Michael in the missals, treading down the dragons; don't you know that? Only this . . . and she is dead, my mother is dead, and I was not there. I abandoned her to be a warrior, and now she blesses and forgives me, but doesn't write to me. To you, she wrote to you, because . . . because it was you . . .' he broke off, panting for breath and trying to choke off the sobs. Gwalchmai jumped up and caught the boy, and Gwyn began to weep, leaning against his father. Gwalchmai also was in tears. I finally remembered myself, turned, and ran out. The grey outside blurred around me and I raised my hand to find my own face wet. It was wonderful, it was terrible, and still (selfish misery!) Gwalchmai had a son, and I was barren.

Gwalchmai quickly took steps to have Gwyn legitimatized. Unfortunately, his position in his own clan was more precarious than ever. The old charge of kin-murder, which had lain dormant while Agravain was king and chieftain of the royal clan of the Islands, might now at any moment be revived by Medraut. There had been no mention of it in the brief months since Medraut became king, but Gwalchmai could not try to have his son given royal status without risking, and probably losing, his own. However, since he was unmarried, he could declare Gwyn to be his legitimate heir under the laws of the Empire, and thus give him the legal position of his son and Arthur's grand-nephew. Accordingly, a few days after receiving the letter, Gwalchmai formally presented Gwyn to Arthur at a feast, swearing that this was his son, christened Gwalchaved by the mother, Elidan daughter of Caw, and petitioning Arthur to acknowledge him as Gwalchmai's legal son and heir. Arthur asked if any gainsaid this and, when no one did, called the Family to witness that Gwalchaved ap Gwalchmai was henceforward to be considered a nobleman and his own kinsman. In token of this last he cut some of Gwyn's hair, as a godfather would, then told the boy to sit beside his father at the high table. Father and son took their places amid cheers from Gwalchmai's friends, and I poured wine for all the high table. Arthur smiled during this ceremony, as I did, but Gwyn looked very grave. Gwalchmai appeared calm, but watched Gwyn as though afraid that the boy were one of the People of the Hills, and would vanish at cock-crow. Gwyn took a swallow of wine, which he was not used to, and began coughing. He set the glass down, going red, but when he saw how we smiled at him, suddenly smiled back, his whole face flooding with pure joy. He lifted his glass to Arthur and to me.

'He is the sort of son any man would want,' Arthur said that night when we were alone together in our house. 'Gwalchmai is fortunate.'

'Indeed,' I said, sitting by the fire and letting down my hair. 'I shall miss Gwyn's help.'

Arthur smiled, watching me. 'You mean you will miss his company. It will be easy enough to find you another clerk. Children are less easily come by.'

I stopped combing and twisted a lock of my hair about my fingers as though I had found a tangle in it. There were still not many strands of grey there, but a few. Children were certainly less easy to come by. And I suppose to a man a child lost in the sixth month is not really a child. I once felt my son move under my heart, before I lost him, and I knew it was real. But Arthur had been away on campaign then; he had come back as soon as he could afterwards, when I was still very sick, and had tried to comfort me, but even then I could see that he had not understood. Only now, did he understand now?

'Arthur,' I said, 'have you thought of taking another wife?'

He smiled at me. 'Have you died, my white hart? I thought even I would be likely to notice such an event as that.'

'I am not joking. There are other separations than death, and if the Church does not approve of them, still they are well known in custom and law. Many nobles divorce each other. And you are not too old to have a child.'

The smile had vanished altogether. He jumped up, came over and caught my shoulders, crouching so as to look into my face. 'Do not be foolish,' he said harshly. 'Do you want to divorce me?'

I knew his face better than my own: the wide-set grey eyes, the beak of a nose, thin lips in the grey-streaked short beard, the strong lines of it, the rapid changes of expression. I could not meet his eyes as honestly as he met mine, and I lowered my gaze, touching his hands with my own. The depth of thirteen years was between us, the weight of habit, of long trust, fulfilled and betrayed and forgiven; a thousand thousand tiny things, unimportant memories, the customary expectation of what the other would think, say, do, dream. 'No,' I said at last. 'No, of course not. But if there was any hope that I should bear you a son, after the war, there is none left, and has been none for a long while. And you need an heir. Another woman might give you one.'

'And what would you do? For that matter, what would I do? Do you think another woman could take your place? I am not lord of this fortress: it is you who rule it. I swear by the God of Heaven, that if any man had served me as you have done, and I set him aside as you would have me do to you, I would straightaway be called the most ungrateful king in all of Britain, and my men would all leave me to seek some other lord who would reward them better.'

'They would not say that, or do that, if you divorced me.'

'They would not, for a woman. But I would. And for that matter, what ... Gwynhwyfar, I do not want any other woman. I have not since I first came to love you. Would you have me marry some empty-headed king's daughter of seventeen, and be content with her, while you did ... what? Joined a convent? Married one of my warriors? I would kill any warrior who offered himself!' He was beginning to smile again, again beginning to treat the subject as a joke. I abruptly thought of Bedwyr and shivered.

'You need an heir. It is all very well to speak of you and of me, but you need an heir for the sake of the kingdom.'

'No. I do not need an heir. Ach, my white hart, you are right, I wish we had children, your children; but it is better without them. Now my usurpation will die with me.' I began to protest, but he silenced me with a hard, deliberate kiss. 'When I die,' he said 'The *imperium* will return to my father's clan; and any successor from that clan will have a legal right to his power. And I can designate anyone within four generations of an emperor as my successor, and, if I conduct the affair correctly, have him recognized as such. I could choose Gereint ab Erbin or Constans, in the Family – and Maelgwn Gwynedd has a claim . . .'

'Maelgwn!' I exclaimed angrily.

He laughed, 'Not Maelgwn, I agree. He rules Gwynedd badly enough. I would not give him my Empire. And the others are not suited to holding great authority. Only now, now – who knows? Since Gwalchmai has declared Gwyn legitimate, Gwyn can be considered a member of the royal clan. He is descended from the eldest legitimate child of my father Uther. True, Morgawse married into another clan – but if Gwyn is not a member of the royal clan of the Orcades . . .' He let go of my shoulders and stood, his eyes brightening with excitement. 'My mother was not noble, but Gwyn's was a daughter of Caw, of the royal clan of Ebrauc. That could be very useful; it might finally settle their hostility.' He began pacing the room. 'True, he is a bastard from a monastery, just as I am, but my father had legitimate children, and could not legitimitize me. People will soon forget that the grandson of Caw, the great-grandson of Uther Pendragon, ever had anything irregular about his birth. If we did have him accepted, legally, by the royal clan of Britain, he would have a very good claim. Not many people would contest it. Did you know,' turning on me and asking a question apparently unconnected with what he had just been saying, 'the Emperor Augustus was the grand-nephew of Julius Caesar? The same relation as Gwyn is to me . . . but this is all dreams and wild conjecture.' He came back to me, pulled me to my feet and held me against him. I was smiling, because he was glad, more hopeful than I had seen him for a long, long time, and I felt hope rising in my own heart like a bluebell pushing aside the dull earth in the spring.

'Let the future wait until tomorrow,' Arthur said, smiling at me the old smile of delight. 'And do not say any more about this foolish business of other wives.'

Gwyn was fourteen in March that year, and was accordingly given arms – the finest Gwalchmai could find – and swore the Threefold Oath of Allegiance to Arthur. He moved into the house which Gwalchmai shared with Cei, where there was plenty of space. Cei, who had originally given the boy the sharp edge of his tongue, told me that he now 'got on well with the lad', though Gwyn had been cold at first. The tension which Medraut had created in the Family had continued to ebb throughout the winter, and everyone was much more relaxed. The whispers against Gwalchmai were no longer heard, both because of the lack of evidence and because it is difficult to hate someone who is truly happy. For Gwalchmai was intensely happy, so much so that one had only to watch him ride his horse across a practice field to know it. He had a son, the child of his old and dear love Elidan; he had her forgiveness for the affair that had long tormented him; he had something more than 'battles and embassies' to live for. Gwyn, in turn, after he had with difficulty managed to accept that his hero was his father, became enormously proud of his father. And the two did in fact have a great deal in common, so there was no hindrance to the love and admiration. While it was not true that they were never apart, they were certainly often together. They would take out their horses for exercise, Gwalchmai on his white stallion, Gwyn on the roan mare which Gwalchmai had now officially bestowed upon him ('Though I was intending to give her to you,' Gwalchmai stated as he handed his son the bridle, 'even before the letter'). Riding about the hills the two would talk of books and battles, foreign lands and old or new songs. Once taught, Gwyn proved to have inherited his father's skill at harping, and had been attempting to learn Irish 'even before the letter'. But he was not only eager to learn Irish songs, but hoped, like his father, to visit many strange kingdoms. 'The next time I am sent somewhere, you must come as well,' Gwalchmai told him. 'Perhaps it will be to Gaul. Bedwyr has been there all winter, but I doubt that all the problems there are settled even now.'

They were not. We did not hear from Bedwyr from December until April, because of the harsh winter and the unwillingness of the traders to risk their ships on the rough seas. We had received one letter from him late in September, written in the first week of that month upon his arrival at Macsen's fortress; and another early in December which had reported that some of Macsen's claims were settled, but that others had been raised. When the spring brought calm seas we had another letter, which had in fact been written shortly after the second one we had received, but which had spent the winter with one of our agents in a Breton port, awaiting a ship. This contained bad news: Macsen remained obdurate on all the points under discussion, and had insistently pressed Bedwyr to forswear his allegiance to Arthur and remain instead in Less Britain as Macsen's warleader.

'When I refused the place he offered,' Bedwyr wrote, 'the king grew angry, and called me a traitor to my homeland. He would hear no arguments for the unity of the Empire; he said that the Empire was dead and ought to remain so. And he has grown very insistent on this, until I thought it better to leave him and spend the winter on my family's estates in the south-east, whither I will go tomorrow. I will return to Britain in the spring, as soon as the roads and the winds permit – unless you wish otherwise, my lord. But I see no point to remaining, for I cannot negotiate with Macsen.'

Arthur agreed that it would be best if Bedwyr did not encounter Macsen again, and wrote commanding his return. So Bedwyr came back to Camlann in May, and as soon as he arrived I realized that what had happened in that grey afternoon in August was not over, as I had believed.

It was a lovely spring afternoon; I came into the Hall on some other errand to find a knot of men standing about and welcoming our warleader in loud voices, and Arthur among them, clasping Bedwyr's hand. Bedwyr stood among them looking travel-worn, plain, and unhappy. I had missed him sometimes in the months he had been away, but I thought that the ruinous love had died, and I missed him only as one misses a sympathetic friend. But somehow he sensed my presence beyond the others, and looked up, searching for me with his eyes. He did not smile when he saw me, but something leapt between us, an idle string on a harp suddenly drawn tight, plucked and drowning out other tones in its sound. I realized from the leap my heart gave that I was still bound to him, and I knew with sudden horror that it was worse for him, that he had not forgotten me for an instant of his absence; knew it without any need for more communication than a look. So I began again to avoid him.

In early June we sent Gwalchmai and Gwyn to Less Britain in Bedwyr's place. We were forced to, for the unresolved claims were beginning to cause problems. Macsen had imposed a tariff on the wine his people exported which was high, the rate traditionally charged on trade with barbarian nations, not even that charged for another province of the Empire. This had drawn loud complaints from the various traders, as well as from the noblemen they supplied, and had encouraged smugglers. Some of these smugglers had been caught and executed by Macsen, and now their clans were besieging us with petitions for vengeance, justice and the blood-price. Several fugitives from justice in Britain had settled comfortably in Less Britain, in defiance of all previous treaties. This outraged the clans they had injured, who joined the smugglers' clans in their petitioning. So Gwalchmai and Gwyn departed with announcements of harsh counter-measures: a trade embargo and an offer of asylum to any and all Breton fugitives.

Gwalchmai's servant Rhys went as well, reluctantly parting from his wife and children. 'After all,' he told me as we arranged supplies for the journey, 'Gwalchmai doesn't need me now. He won't overwork himself this time, not with his son along.'

'You think not?' I asked dubiously. 'He might work twice as hard, to make Gwyn proud of him.'

Rhys snorted. 'He might – but he would never let Gwyn work so, and I don't see Gwyn leaving his father to work alone. And he will see to it that he is well-treated, so that Gwyn will be as well. An excellent thing, fatherhood, for making a man take notice of what he does.' Rhys grinned, and added wistfully, 'I wish I had seen his face when he found out' – for Rhys, strangely, had known about Gwyn for years. He had learned of the boy from the lady Elidan herself, but had been sworn by her to silence on the matter. 'Though I would have spoken out,' he told me, on the occasion that he informed me of his foreknowledge and asked for an account of what had happened, 'if I had thought that those two wouldn't find out on their own.'

'I think you will find that you are still needed,' I told Rhys. 'Macsen will not make things any easier for Gwalchmai than he did for Bedwyr, and he will need a servant he can trust.'

Rhys sighed, ran a hand through his hair. 'True enough. And it's not that I grudge going – only that Eivlin is due to have the baby in October, and I would like to be on hand. My lord would be certain to send me back before then, if the negotiations drag on as they did last time, but I would rather be here all the while. We've been lucky in two healthy children, and Eivlin is fine now, but still, there might be danger. Still, I always knew I would have to do a lot of travelling if I served Gwalchmai, and it's late to complain of it now – and maybe the matter will be settled soon.'

It was not. Faced with the trade embargo, Macsen rescinded the tariff, but would not agree on a blood-price for the smugglers he had had executed, and denied that the fugitives existed. Letters flowed back and forth across the ocean; our emissaries returned late in July to confer, then sailed back again, and still the negotiations dragged on, with Macsen giving way on one point and suddenly discovering five others to stick on. In September a rough and unsatisfactory settlement was achieved, and the party returned. We might well have sent them out again, but by then we had other things to think of.

That same spring Medraut wrote and postponed his proposed visit to Camlann, explaining that he had some domestic difficulties which could not endure his absence. At about the same time we learned from the disaffected members of his clan that Medraut suspected some of their number, and that they were afraid: they asked if Arthur would grant them asylum, and judge between themselves and their cousin Medraut. Arthur wrote to say that he was willing to judge their cause, but could not promise unconditional asylum. But before they could have received this letter, we had news that five members of the royal clan and some twenty others of different, noble clans of the Islands were accused of plotting against their king. The five were kin-wrecked and exiled, the twenty executed. The five exiles, with their servants, set off from the Orcades in a twenty-oar curragh laden with goods, but were scarcely out of sight of land when a violent storm arose, and the ship was wrecked on the cliffs of northern Pictland, and all but one of the passengers drowned. This man was one of the five. His name was Diuran Mac Brenainn, and he had been warleader for King Lot. Gwalchmai remembered him as a sensible and a just man, passionately loyal to the clan's welfare. He managed to cling to the keel of the ship and was eventually washed ashore. He made his way to the shipyard of Eoghan, where previously he had sent messages to be relayed to Arthur. Here he stayed with the clerk at the yard, and sent a message to Arthur: a miserable, semi-literate letter obviously dictated in haste. It accused Medraut of murdering Agravain and of killing the others in the ship, by sorcery, and it begged Arthur, 'by the faeth of the God yow worshippest', to send him aid, and to lend support to an army of Islanders who would 'redeem the Ercendy Islands from the son of Iffernus'.

Arthur despatched a courier northward with some gold to support the man in his destitution, and with it a cautiously worded letter, inviting Diuran to Camlann, and asking him to represent his cause to the other kings of Britain. But the courier returned with the gold, surprisingly untouched, and with it our letter, enclosed in a letter from the clerk of the shipyard. He was evidently the scribe of the first letter, for his style of bad Latin was the same, and he announced in it that Diuran had died of a fever the week before our letter arrived.

'I offered him the gold,' our messenger said, 'for he was a poor man, and had paid for the other's burial out of his own money. But he refused it. He was a strange little man.'

Despite this, Medraut's 'domestic difficulties' apparently continued, for he again postponed his visit, and put another group of noblemen to death. He then declared war on some of the Western Islands which had been part of King Lot's domain, but which had seceded under Agravain and claimed the protection of the King of Dalriada. Medraut sailed to them with a great army, fought several short, sharp encounters, and defeated them. Their ally, Aengus of Dalriada, made no move to help them. Medraut was allied to Arthur and related also to Aengus's foremost enemy, Urien of Rheged, and no doubt Aengus thought the

Western Islands not worth the risk of a war with the greatest powers of Britain. At any rate, Medraut had a free hand with the Islanders, and showed no mercy. He deposed their ruling clans, executing the men and giving most of the women to the new clans he raised in their place. The old ruling clans were, he said, guilty of treason to himself and to Agravain.

This successful campaign won Medraut more support within the Orcades, for his people admired his military prowess, and were pleased to have reclaimed the Western Islands and the fear of their neighbours. In August he wrote to us again, saying that he was now free to make his deferred visit, and that he would set out in September, after he had returned to his fortress of Dun Fionn and set it in order. But he sent this letter from the shipyard of Eoghan in northern Pictland, and added a note which disturbed us.

'The troubles engendered by the laxity of poor Agravain's reign are widely spread,' he wrote. 'In this very shipyard I found a clerk, one Padraig Mac Febail, probably the only lettered man in Pictland, who had used this very skill in aid of treachery. I had the man brought to me and, on questioning him, found that besides aiding my enemies he had left his monastery in Erin, doubtless for some crime. I therefore had him put to death, seeing that his viciousness was of long standing. Why do I recount this to your grace? Merely as an example of how I am placed: I am certain that you will understand my position, and forgive my long delay in coming to swear my oath to you.'

It troubled me to think of this clerk, who had carefully copied out the messages which the noblemen of the Orcades must have sent him by word of mouth, and put them into his clumsy Latin. He himself was an exile, yet had somehow managed to support Diuran after the shipwreck, and had sent back the gold without even using any to pay for the burial. I could imagine him discovered, dragged before Medraut by the king's warriors, questioned under that cool contemptuous smile, and finally put to death with a casual command intended not so much to punish him as to display to Arthur the extent of Medraut's knowledge.

'My mother ruled in this fashion,' Gwalchmai said, when he returned from Gaul and Arthur gave him this letter to read. 'The Islands were afraid when my father went away on campaigns, for her rule was heavy on them then. But she was more skilled. She had a sense of what could and could not be done, and the people were more afraid of her than they will ever be of Medraut.' He looked again at the letter from his brother, and lifted his eyes to us, frowning. 'This will not be the end of Medraut's troubles.'

Nor, I thought, of ours.

Six

At the beginning of October Medraut sailed into Caer Gwent with two ships and fifty men. Because he came peacefully and in the Emperor's name, he was offered hospitality by Cynyr, Lord of Caer Gwent, while he sent Arthur notice that he had arrived and requested an escort so as not to alarm the countryside by the size of his bodyguard. Arthur himself rode west to meet him and escort him to Camlann, also taking fifty men. He left me and Bedwyr together to keep the fortress.

It had grown difficult for me to avoid Bedwyr even before Arthur left. When the warleader first returned from Gaul he had tried as hard to avoid me as I him, but this effort had lapsed. By September he was actually looking for opportunities to see me. I reproached him for it, once; he looked away from me and whispered, 'I do not mean to,' then, slowly his eyes moved back to meet mine and he added, 'I cannot help it.' It made me ashamed. Bedwyr was serious by nature, not easily moved to love but faithful and constant after he had committed himself, and because of this he was suffering. Men suffer so in the songs all the time, but in reality most of them forget love more easily. But Bedwyr was really almost sick from it. He had returned from Less Britain looking thin and exhausted, and thin and exhausted he remained. He no longer spoke freely with Arthur, which puzzled my husband. 'I do not know what is the matter with Bedwyr,' he confided to me one night. 'Ever since he returned from Gaul he has been as grim and silent as a memorial column. Does he think I am angry because he failed, or because Macsen tried to persuade him to desert me? He ought to know better.'

I said nothing. I knew well enough that Bedwyr was tortured with guilt before Arthur, and perhaps by jealousy as well. But I could say nothing, even when Arthur grew angry. Every time I saw Bedwyr I remembered that sweet and terrible afternoon, and sometimes I lay awake at night, listening to Arthur's quiet breath beside me, aching and ashamed. Sometimes at a feast my eyes would meet Bedwyr's, and we would understand without a word spoken where our thoughts had turned, and I would feel my face grow hot, and would turn and pretend to talk to someone else, but feel his presence like a bright light which cast shadows all about me. So I tried to meet the warleader only in public. I was afraid when Arthur announced that he would meet Medraut at Caer Gwent, and urged him to send Bedwyr instead.

'You rush off to meet him as though you were champions out to fight single combat,' I said. 'But you are Emperor, and he is only ruler of a few islands on the edge of the world. Moreover, he is officially your subject ally. You have the position of greater strength. Let him feel that, and the rest of the world see it; let him come to you.'

But Arthur only stood in the doorway of the conference room, keeping his back to me, gazing into the west and fingering the hilt of his sword. 'Why should I allow Medraut to act the part of subject and ally when we both know that he is my competitor in Empire?' he demanded bitterly. 'Let him, and let the Family and all the rest of Britain, see that I am matching myself against him, and let them realize that it is a question of choosing. Besides, I wish to see for myself how he conducts himself with my subject lords. Perhaps he has told his tale to Cynyr of Caer Gwent now. I can see what Cynyr makes of it, and of me.'

'My dear lord, if he has told Cynyr we will know soon enough from our other sources. In seeing for yourself you will only hurt yourself.'

'I wish to know! In God's name, am I remain here like a statue in a niche, smiling at all comers while they whisper, "Ah, he looks fine, but really is a bastard, a begetter of bastards on his own sister, and a usurper"? No!'

'But Arthur . . .'

He whirled about and looked at me. 'I am leaving tomorrow for Caer Gwent, and that is the end of it.'

I looked away from the cold eyes and nodded.

I could feel the hardness leave the stare, and looked up again when I thought it was gone. He flinched, seemed to begin an apology, then stopped, awkwardly. He shrugged. 'I must arrange it, then. In a few hours . . .' he turned, looked again out over the walls westward, then started down the hill, his purple cloak flapping and his hand on his sword.

He was, in fact, impatient. All the summer he had been bracing himself for Medraut's arrival, for the gradual onset of the rumours that would disgrace and discredit him, and reveal his most painfully held secret to the scorn and hatred of the world. He could bear it, just, and hope to hold onto power long enough to find a suitable successor. But Medraut's constant deferral of his arrival, the postponing from week to week of the anticipated struggle, were wearing him out with expectation and fear. He gave little public sign of it; he could not afford to. But he grew increasingly hard to reach, and irritable. Sometimes he even uncharacteristically lost his temper, usually with me. I was the one who knew him best, the one he could afford to be honest with. But after he had broken and shouted at me, it was always harder still to draw near to him. Ashamed, he recoiled from me. And I wanted him more and more as the autumn continued. The harvest is always exhausting, always demands more than it seems possible to give. I would wake in the morning, feeling that I could scarcely muster enough energy to rise, and my husband would look at me wearily, not daring to apologize for some scene the night before and not touching me. And most of the day would be utter madness, dashing wildly about the fortress checking and making inventories of goods stored for the winter, arranging payments, receiving tribute, hearing petitions, organizing, ordering accounts, paying attention – and feeling Bedwyr's gaze now and then like a searing fire.

> Tell me, oh you learned ones,
> From what is Longing made?
> And what cloth is it woven from
> That with use it never fades?
>
> Gold wears out and silver,
> Silks and velvets tear,
> All adornment ages:
> Longing never wears.
>
> Longing, Longing, back a pace,
> Do not weigh on my breast so heavily,
> But move over from the bedside
> And let a brief sleep come to me.

It's a common song, but it ran through my brain for weeks on end, until I was heartily sick of it.

Oh, after Arthur left it happened in a way that was as obvious as the course of flood waters down a dry stream bed, and as irresistible. For two days Bedwyr and I held stiffly aloof, speaking to each other with stilted formality, hoping, making one last effort against the humiliating treachery we both knew was near. Then, on the third day, we were in the conference room, alone together. We were discussing what to do with the tribute.

'I can send another three hundred head of cattle, under guard, to the holding near Llefelys's Stone,' Bedwyr said, 'but we will be short then, will we not, noble lady? Maelgwyn Gwynedd sent us fifty fewer cows than he gave his word for.'

'I calculated that he would send us seventy fewer cows, noble lord, so we have a good margin of safety.'

He looked at me in surprise.

'Well, what is wonderful in that?' I asked. 'Maelgwn tries to cheat us on the tribute every year; it would be amazing if he did not. During the war, he often succeeded. In the spring we'll send him the usual party to correct his "unfortunate mistake" – and perhaps this time we'll make him pay their travelling expenses.'

'But you can calculate by how much he will cheat us?'

'Of course. We set the tribute by the size of the harvest. Maelgwyn's tribute is the size of the harvest less 15 or 20 per cent, and plus a factor of how difficult he's been that year. If he's guilty of too many other incidents, he grows nervous, and a trifle more honest.'

Bedwyr laughed, and I laughed as well. Then I saw that he was looking at me with that particular light in his eyes and I stopped laughing. He grew very serious, reached out and caught my hand. I turned away.

'But . . . but we must have another two hundred head of cattle nearby . . .' I began uncertainly. His hand against mine was like the warmth of a fire to a blind man, something more real than the vision of the eyes.

'My lady . . .' he whispered.

'You must have the sheep moved from the south pastures, with a guard or two over them to see that they reach . . .'

'Gwynhwyfar.'

I stopped trying, and looked at him. The pulse of my blood dizzied me: I could feel it over every inch of my body. 'We must not,' I said. 'It is treachery, and that is the worst of all sins.'

'Please,' he whispered. 'Just this once more.' He moved closer to me, his hand sliding up my arm.

I closed my eyes, trying to pray. 'But think what would happen if Medraut discovered this. Think how he could use it.'

'Just once more, only once. Please. I cannot live like this. I cannot think for thinking of you; I cannot sleep or rest. My most sweet lady, I cannot bear it.' He was beside me now, his arm around me, touching my breast.'

I meant to stand up. Instead, I only said faintly, 'But you must bear it.'

'Please. Only once more.' He kissed me. I could not think after that; when he pulled away and looked at me, I held to him and nodded, weeping.

When it was over with we again vowed that this was the end, that it must not happen again. But when one has twice been unable to keep a resolve, one begins to expect failure, and that expectation breeds failure. We held our resolve for less than a month, before breaking it in a new crisis and losing ourselves once again. After that we began to hope that desire would be satisfied by much loving, but only succeeded in becoming necessary to each other. And with repeated sins, the conscience, which is at first tender, grows gradually numbed, finds excuses, ceases much to be moved. After a time it was even possible to behave naturally to Arthur. But that came later; at first he might have noticed something, if he had not been himself too tense, too depressed, to speak naturally to his friends.

Arthur returned, with Medraut, on a golden October morning the week after he set out. One of the guards came from the gates an hour or so before noon to tell me that the party had been seen approaching, and I went with him back to the gate, and climbed the gate-tower to watch. Bedwyr was at the gate already, but stayed before them, mounted on his horse and waiting to welcome Arthur and relinquish the military command Arthur had temporarily given him. He nodded to me when I arrived, but no more. We could hold our resolve that long, at least.

The sky was cloudless and had a hard glow like blue enamel, and the trees at the edges of the fields seemed cast in bronze by sunlight. The fields themselves, though, were drab, for the harvest was in and the earth was stubble-marked and grey, or black from the annual burning, and hazed over with smoke from the fires. In the distance, Ynys Witrin rose tall and green over the dark marshes, seeming to float above the main road where a long column of horsemen trotted steadily forward. They were already near enough, when I climbed the tower, for me to pick out a few individual figures, and I saw that Arthur's fifty warriors were interspersed with Medraut's, for greater safety. Two figures rode side by side at the head of the column, one wearing a purple cloak, riding a familiar grey horse, the other in a cloak dyed with saffron and a gold collar, riding a fine bay: Arthur and Medraut. As they came nearer, I waited for the line to increase its speed, to sweep up to the gates at a canter with a jingle of harness and glitter of weapons and jewellery, as Arthur always did in the gladness of coming home. But the column maintained its slow, jolting trot, and, as it drew nearer still. I saw that Arthur's shoulders were hunched as though against the cold, while Medraut rode with his cloak tossed back over one shoulder, sitting his horse with easy grace. Already the shadow had fallen on us; already Medraut had set some chill upon the heart.

I climbed down from the tower and went back up the hill to the Hall. I had no extraordinary power in Arthur's absence, nothing to hand over at the gates, and no one would expect me to welcome Medraut to Camlann, not after the way he had left it. And I wished to postpone, even for a few hours, the inevitable grief.

I saw Medraut in the Hall for the midday meal of course. He bowed stiffly, and I nodded my head, equally stiffly. But I could see that his kingship agreed with him. He looked sleeker than ever, graceful and regal in the saffron cloak, gold about his neck, fastening his cloak, on his arms and fingers. He had the same easy, ingratiating smile as well; the smile I had long before been disturbed by, and which I had grown to hate. But he also looked more like Arthur than he had done, and I realized that he had cut his beard and hair in the same fashion that Arthur customarily used.

After the meal, while ostensibly resting from his journey, Arthur told me what had happened at Caer Gwent. 'Medraut has begun to spread his story, as I thought,' he said, very quietly. He looked older than his forty-three years, and hunched over the fire like an old man whose blood has grown thin. 'Cynyr of Caer Gwent has certainly heard it. No, he said nothing – but he looked at me, and looked at Medraut, and looked at me again, all the time I was there. And he was very quiet. Ordinarily he gossips like a barber, but this time he was quiet. And also – you know I was in Caer Gwent for Sunday? When we went to Mass, Cynyr made some excuse, and would not take communion. He looked at me then, as well. He is afraid of being tainted in God's eyes by taking communion after a man who slept with his sister.' Arthur laughed, very bitter- ly. 'And his men had heard, and my men will have heard it from them. And I could not tell whether Medraut has simply started the rumour there, now, or whether he has been spreading it for months and our spies simply have not heard it. But it is established, now, and he need not say any- thing, not himself, not directly. He can merely wait until someone asks him questions. Did you notice the way he has cut his hair? He is ready to begin the battle in earnest. But still he will not admit as much to me: when I met him he was all smiles and bows and courtesies. There is no winning through to anything real in him. I do not know how to fight him any more than I did before.' Arthur rubbed his hands, held them out to the fire. His signet ring gleamed. 'If the kings of Britain believe this rumour, they will have an excuse for a rebellion. A bastard emperor is bad enough, but an emperor guilty of incest – that will pollute the land, and draw down the wrath of God, or so my enemies and the Church will say. How long can we hold on?'

I shook my head. 'Medraut still cannot prove anything. We can still deny it, perhaps successfully. We might hold power till our lives' end.'

He looked up and smiled, a little half-smile of ironic amusement. 'Might we? Come, my white hart, you are wiser than that. Medraut is no fool, and has no lack of skill.

Perhaps when actually in power he is too heavy-handed, but he can play upon the discontents of Britain as skilfully as his brother does on the harp. And he has strings enough to hand: dissatisfied and revengeful kings, like Maelgwyn Gwynedd; the enmity of the Church; the boredom of my own warriors. Our wars with the invaders are finished, but the Empire is not entirely restored, as we promised, and the frustration of that is burning in Britain, like a stubble fire, waiting for fuel to blaze up. It only needs a skilful leader to direct it. Medraut can break us – or make us pay such a price for power that we would be better off dead. It's not worth ruling if one has to be a tyrant to do so, or if one has to destroy one's own people. No, we must hold on as long as we safely can, and then abdicate. The problem is still to find a man to give the power to, one I could trust to rule justly, who would be strong enough to hold his own against Medraut. And still, there is no one.'

'It would be very dangerous to abdicate,' I pointed out.

He gave the same tired smile. '"For this Empire which we have acquired is a kind of tyranny,"' he quoted – it was one of a collection of sayings of famous men, most of whom I had never heard of, which Arthur had brought from the monastery where he was raised – '"which it may be wrong to have taken up, but which it is certainly hazardous to let go." But what does that have to do with either of us? We did not take it up to be safe, and have risked death for it often enough.'

'I meant it would be dangerous for the Empire. The kings of Britain know you, and if they do not believe in your justice, they at least believe you are a skilled war-leader. They might be willing to fight a successor of yours, especially if he was young, where they would not fight you.'

He sighed and rested his head on his hands. 'You are right, of course. It might come to war before I could afford to abdicate. And if I were to be defeated, and if Medraut seized power – no, I must trust God that that, at least, he will not permit.' He looked into the fire again, and continued in a voice so low I could barely hear it. 'And yet, this darkness was of my getting. I myself am responsible for Medraut. The unrest in the kingdom, too, is my fault, for I got my power by strength of arms and contrary to the law, and it is not surprising that I have enemies. I thought I was doing right at the time, but perhaps, in God's eyes, it was as grave a sin as incest.'

'No,' I said, laying my hand on his.

He shook it off. 'The destruction is coming from within us, and from within me. The Saxons could not defeat us, but we ourselves are destroying the Empire; the faction in the Family, the flaw within. Once I thought that merely the shame and dishonour of being known to have loved my sister would be intolerable. Now that seems unimportant. That only affects me, while this, this is the ruin of the West, the Darkness coming upon us. Why must we love the Light so much when we are bound to work its destruction?' He looked up at me as he asked this, raising his voice, as though I might have the answer. The fire crackled softly on the hearth.

'My dearest, we have not lost yet,' I said at last. 'And you yourself said we must trust God: surely he will not permit the Darkness to conquer. We have too much to fight for to give way to despair.'

He sighed. 'I am tired.' He rubbed his face. 'I have been fighting for the better part of thirty years, and I begin not to believe even in victory. And to be responsible for it . . . but you are right. We have a great deal to fight for. Indeed, we are fortunate to have so much, to be able to love it and fight for it. It would be cowardly and ungracious to surrender before the battle is under way.' He rose and kissed me, then stood, holding me against him. He was still wearing his mail-coat, and I could feel the links under his tunic and feel the strength of his body under that. I thought of Bedwyr, and of my own desire to be weak, and was bitterly ashamed.

'Gwynhwyfar,' said Arthur, 'I do not deserve you. Forgive me that I have been angry with you – and that I undoubtedly will be again, for I am very tired, and most bitterly grieved at heart.'

'Oh, my heart's dearest,' I said, and could not think of anything more. But words were not really necessary.

That night, at the welcoming feast, Medraut swore the Threefold Oath to an alliance with Arthur. He knelt in the centre of the Hall, under the roof-tree with its golden dragon standard, offering his sword hilt-first to Arthur and swearing in a clear voice, with apparent solemnity, to hold his kingdom at peace with Arthur, to make no wars against him or his subjects and allies, to respect the laws of the Empire, and to offer no refuge to enemies of Britain. Arthur took the sword and vowed to keep peace with the kingdom of the Orcades, and so on. The Family cheered as Medraut rose again and, smiling, sheathed his sword, but Medraut's own men, brought from the Orcades, watched Arthur with a grim, unblinking stare.

Neither they nor Medraut ever returned to the Islands. Medraut had stayed at Camlann two weeks, and was preparing to leave again – after engendering the old tension in the Family – when a messenger came from the Orcades to say that the royal clan was deposed, and that the Islands would henceforth be ruled by a branch of that O'Niall family who ruled most of Erin. There had always been hostility between the O'Niall and the royal clan of the Islands: King Lot had originally left Erin when his clan lost its position in Ulaid to the O'Niall. The O'Niall had now been invited to Dun Fionn by one of the noble clans that Medraut had injured: this clan, and its allies, on a day previously arranged, took the port on the largest of the islands. A fleet from Erin put in, and the combined forces marched across the island to Dun Fionn. If Medraut had been present, the fortress would undoubtedly have been able to resist, but, as it was, half the inhabitants mutinied and opened the gates to the invaders. All the male members of the royal clan, with its staunchest allies, were then put to death, and the women distributed among the invaders in marriage or concubinage, usually the latter. All this had happened shortly after Medraut left the Orcades, probably before he even reached Caer Gwent; it had undoubtedly been arranged months before.

We gave this messenger – who was a member of the injured, revenging clan – an audience in the Hall. He had arrived in the middle of the afternoon, and there were not many people about when he took his place under the rooftree and began to speak – we had had to send for Medraut. But more people came hurrying in as the man continued, telling his story with evident pleasure, colouring the details in favour of his new masters, the O'Niall. The Hall began to fill with whispers, explanations to newcomers, exclamations of horrors, demands to know what would be done, but the messenger did not look around, but faced Arthur steadily. When he had finished his narration of the events in the Islands he drew himself up, laid a hand on his sword, and addressed Arthur proudly in conclusion.

'Do not think,' he declared in his excellent British, 'that it will still be possible for you to have an unjustified and ruinous influence on our Islands. We are Irish, not British, and now – rightly! – are bound to Erin. We will swear no further peace with you, High King of Britain. The accursed line of Lot did so, and all our evils sprang from that, from his marriage with a British witch for your thrice-damned alliance, and from his sons – the drunkard and the sorcerous traitor, and the last and worst, the one not of *his* getting, that shamefully begotten bastard, the witch's son and curse of his people. If you, Pendragon, mean to send this tyrant back to rule us, there will be a thousand spears to meet you, and a thousand swords, and not easily will you win through them, nor easily hold the Islands if you do. This we have sworn by the Sun and the Wind, by the oath of our people and by the new God of Erin and the O'Niall, now our God. But if you,' and he spat this at Medraut, who had stood silent and unmoving on Arthur's right, 'presume to return to the Islands, know that you are sentenced to death, and no matter how many guards and warriors you set about yourself, or how many men you sorcerously seek out and kill, still someone, one day, will find a way through to you and make you pay for your tyranny. This also we have sworn.'

Medraut stared at him, his eyes bleak, frozen with hatred, though his face was still, unmoved. 'And perhaps,' he said, in a smooth, conversational tone, 'you also are sentenced to death, overly boastful messenger.'

The messenger laughed. 'You killed my father, though no one could prove it, though he was charged with nothing and no blood-price was paid for his death. My cousin you had publicly butchered in your Hall. I asked for this mission, Medraut son of no one, so that I could see you when you heard this message; and having seen, I am not afraid of death. Lennavair, daughter of Durtacht, whom you had contracted to marry, sleeps with Laeghaire of the O'Niall as his concubine, and is glad to be a true man's woman and not a bastard's wife.'

'Look well to your ship when you sail home,' Medraut said quietly.

'He came as an emissary,' Arthur said in a quiet, but carrying voice. 'And he will be permitted to leave in peace, according to law and custom. I do not know what you mean by telling him to look to his ship, son of Lot. Doubtless he is accustomed to sailing, even in autumn, and needs no such warning.' Medraut turned his cruel stare on Arthur; Arthur met it. After a moment, Arthur added very quietly, 'For if you wish ill to this man, I would have you recollect that sorcery is a capital crime.'

Medraut stared for another long moment, then dropped his eyes stealthily and bowed. 'Why do you mention sorcery, my lord? Do you believe the wild charges of those who have declared themselves your enemies, and who have deposed and murdered a clan allied to you by many oaths and much blood? I do not think you can or do believe such charges. I ask your leave, noble lord, to depart and to inform my kinsmen and followers of this calamity.'

Arthur nodded, and Medraut bowed and started from the dais. He paused by the messenger and gave him another cold, measuring stare, then smiled and walked out slowly down the length of the Hall, with everyone making way for him. Many of his friends trailed out after him.

The messenger, however, looked at Arthur with surprise. 'You preserve the tradition concerning emissaries,' he said, after a moment. 'It is well. What message shall I take from you to the lords O'Niall, the rulers of the Orcades?'

Arthur leaned back in his chair and studied the messenger thoughtfully, until the man, up to then so bold, began to look uncertain and fidget with his sword.

"Tell your masters," Arthur said at last, still not speaking loudly, sounding tired, but causing a silence through the rest of the Hall, 'that I grieve for the Islands. Tell your cousins and their allies that I grieve for the royal clan, most savagely murdered. And tell your people that I grieve for them as well, that they destroyed the line that had always been their kings, and called in foreign masters to rule over them. Say to your masters, moreover, that it is easier to say that the Islands are bound to Erin than it is to rely upon Erin for aid. If the O'Niall trouble my subjects by raiding the coasts they will regret it; and I will follow that custom I have always followed, and put to death any raiders who are captured in Britain, and take no ransom for any of them. But if the O'Niall wish for British goods – and they will want wood, and tin, and iron, for they cannot get those in the Islands – then they will have to come to terms with me and swear oaths to respect my lands and my subjects.'

The emissary looked in the direction in which Medraut had gone. 'But the tyrant?'

'By birth he can be considered one of the royal clan of Britain. He has a place here, if he no longer has one in the Islands.' There was another moment's silence, then Arthur rose from his seat at the high table and walked down the steps from the dais until he was facing the messenger. 'I will not go to war with Erin for the sake of a tyrant, even if he is of the royal clan of Britain,' he said quietly. 'If you wish, you can have peace with me. I will arrange the terms for you to bring to your masters. Meanwhile, Camlann offers you the hospitality due to emissaries.'

The emissary stared at Arthur for another moment, not quite believing him; glanced about the Hall, back to Arthur. Then he bowed deeply. 'Lord High King, I thank you.'

When the messenger departed for the Orcades, Arthur had Medraut watched, gave the messenger a carefully picked escort back to his ship, which had been kept under a reliable guard, and finally sent money to the monastery at Ynys Witrin for a Mass to be said for those voyaging on the sea. Whether because of these precautions or because Medraut had decided to sacrifice his wishes to the need to make a good impression, the ship arrived safely back at Dun Fionn, and we presently heard that our arrangements for peace-oaths from the O'Niall to prevent piracy and raiding in return for some rights to trade in Britain – were acceptable. And Medraut stayed at Camlann.

Although it was plainly something he had not anticipated or desired, Medraut's deposition worked in his favour. The fact that Arthur would not support him in a bid to reclaim his kingship gave him cause for complaint: he was Arthur's nephew, and had sworn the oath of alliance, but Arthur had made a peace with those who had murdered his kin and usurped his kingdom. It did not matter that the alliance had never extended to mutural defence – it was old, established, sealed by marriage in the previous generation, and it had been set aside in an instant. Even in the family there was strong feeling that Arthur should have supported Medraut. Medraut's actions while in power were not taken very seriously: Medraut himself blamed 'poor Agravain's laxness' for the fact that he had put so many noblemen to death, and men are never as concerned about tyranny in a foreign country as about some slight problem in their own. It did not help matters that Arthur arranged to have the sons of Morgawse formally recognized as members of the imperial clan of Britain, now that their father's clan was destroyed: this served only to strengthen Medraut's claim on British help.

The only bright spot for us among these calamities was the fact that, since Gwalchmai was now officially a member of the royal clan of Britain, Gwyn was as well. As Arthur had predicted, most of the warriors were already beginning to forget that Gwyn was not legitimate by birth. The boy had travelled with Gwlchmai to Gaul, and afterwards to the North – King Urien of Rheged had been having some disputes with his Saxon neighbours, and had requested arbitration from Arthur. Urien was a very powerful king, the strongest of all the northern rulers, and he was much impressed by Gwyn. He was apparently reminded of his own son, Owain, who after an unpromising childhood and youth had suddenly emerged glorious in a string of brilliant battles and expired winning victory in the last one. When Urien gave Gwalchmai the usual set of gifts – one for Gwalchmai himself as emissary, one for Arthur, in honour of his position, one for the Saxon King Gwalchmai had concluded the negotiations with – he bestowed one on Gwyn as well, and when the two left, he heartily wished the boy good fortune.

On concluding the negotiations between Urien and his Saxon neighbour, our embassy stopped in Ebrauc to break the journey back. King Ergyriad ap Caw made them welcome to his fortress, and at once claimed Gwyn as his kinsman, the son of his half-sister. This recognition enabled Gwalchmai to resolve some of the enmity between himself and the rest of the sons of Caw, who had hated him since he killed their brother Bran. Gwyn got on surprisingly well with some of them, and they too gave him gifts when he left Caer Ebrauc.

Arthur was very pleased when the two returned. He hoped, still, to have time enough in power to be able to appoint Gwyn as his successor. Urien's support in this would be invaluable, as would that of the sons of Caw. He made a point of talking to Gwyn about the different countries he had visited and came away persuaded that the boy was capable of considerable political insight – as he ought to be, with Gwalchmai to teach him. Gwalchmai himself would never have been acceptable as a successor, despite his political skill, both because of his foreign birth and because he was far too gentle and otherwordly to be suited to power; but Arthur thought that Gwyn might be capable of Empire. Perhaps Arthur was merely fascinated by the parallel between Gwyn's background and his own. But we both had hopes which we did not dare speak of much, and we hoped the more intensely as the situation grew steadily worse.

The fifty warriors that Medraut had brought with him from the islands soon began to cause problems. A few of these were of the royal clan and savagely indignant with Arthur; all were devoted solely to Medraut and completely obedient to him, while extremely hostile to everyone else. They formed a solid, self-contained group within Camlann, isolated from the rest of the warriors by the barriers of culture, language and religion, which they managed to breach enough only to carry out quarrels. After a few duels between them and some of our men, Arthur sent most of them back to Medraut's ships and had them patrol the western coast against raiders. In December it was discovered that one of these ships had engaged in some raiding of its own, and Arthur had the men responsible put to death. Unfortunately, this included two members of the royal clan, and their execution nearly brought on armed conflict with the others. For a long time afterwards the whispers circulated: 'The Pendragon wishes to finish what the O'Niall began.'

At the same time, the rumours Medraut had started about his own parentage were circulating widely, and our spies reported them from every corner of Britain. No king dared to ask Arthur if they were true, but we soon saw who believed them by the uneasiness of some who had to have dealings with us, and the reluctance of others to contact us at all. But the uneasiness the rumours caused was nowhere so marked as in Camlann. Medraut had managed to gather most of his faction under him yet again, and the quarrelling among the Family began anew. But there was a difference. Before, Medraut had attacked principally his brother Gwalchmai, and only questioned Arthur's judgement in his support of Gwalchmai, and hinted that my husband was subject to my partial whims. Now the attack was direct: Arthur had treated Medraut unjustly, because of a dreadful secret, a secret whispered about the fortress, searched out by hundreds of shocked or troubled eyes fastening on Arthur wherever he went.

Some of Medraut's followers grew uneasy as the direction of the attack grew plainer. Some had been lost after the poisoning attempt, and some after Agravain's death. But there was still a sizeable body of men whom Medraut could rely on, a hundred and six of them, with another fifty or so who were unsettled in their loyalties. This last group grew steadily smaller as the men decided gradually whom they chose to believe, and whom they would follow.

That winter was not quiet. Arthur drove himself as he had not done since the height of the war, rising before dawn and working all day, trying to keep the men occupied, to prevent quarrels, setting up half a hundred distractions for them to gain us time. He sent continuously to the kings of Britain on any pretext whatsoever so as to keep his authority before their eyes and maintain the contact so many of them were eager to break. He pretended that he had never heard the rumours, trying to act as though his energy and forcefulness were unimpaired by time, as though he were still moved by the old enthusiasm and delight. But in the evenings he collapsed on the bed in exhaustion, scarcely able to move. In the night he had dreams: he woke often, crying out the name of Morgawse. Then he would go to the desk, light the lamp, and read through our worn books or write furious letters for hours at a time. I would wake, and rise to see him bent over the desk in the adjoining room, the lamplight picking out the bones and hollows of his face until he seemed worn to a death's head. I would go over and try to persuade him to come back and rest, for he desperately needed sleep. For all his forced energy during the day, he could not hide that. The nightmare etched its record in his flesh, more and more deeply, and I could not smooth its carving away.

For my part I grew so exhausted that my main desire was to escape. I had as much to do as Arthur, and I felt that all our labour was to catch our own shadow. No matter how hard we worked, or what we said and did and what advantage we gained from it, still the rumours kept pace with us. Often we felt that we could do no more, only to find that we must do more, and, doing it, discover yet another thing, and another, till the days were whirling by like the blows of a hammer.

I had Bedwyr; I needed Bedwyr. He was my one refuge, a place of springtime in the midst of that dark winter. Though the nightmare surrounded him too, he did not live in the heart of it, and he had time, as Arthur did not, to talk and to breathe. I could rest with him, and find strength; I could, for a little while, lay my cares at his feet and forget them. Of course we were careful and very discreet. We had frequent legitimate causes to see one another, and could easily enough make arrangements for meeting somewhere in Camlann where we would not be disturbed. The sin of treachery became my solace – and still, even in consoling, a torment. Sometimes when Arthur had woken from a black dream and I lay in bed listening to the scratch of his pen I would wish that it was already over with, even if the end were defeat and if I myself should be eternally damned. In death there is at least some finality, and, after the unremitting struggle, rest. And the next day I might weep on Bedwyr's shoulder, because I had not been able to give comfort to Arthur, and ached for comfort myself.

But in fact the end did come soon – far too soon, I thought, when finally it was upon us.

In late March a new rumour began to circulate in Camlann. Arthur came back into our house one evening before a feast, tossed a bundle of dispatches onto the desk, collapsed into his chair and commented, 'My heart, there is a new rumour which you had best know of. You are now supposed to be sleeping with Bedwyr and plotting my downfall.'

'With Bedwyr?' I asked, feeling the coldness come over me, staring at Arthur.

But he merely remained slouched in the chair, his feet up on the grate. 'Indeed. One wonders why Medraut fixed on Bedwyr. One would think Gwalchmai the more likely candidate for such a tale. But he has tried that already. Besides, he has already called Gwalchmai matricide, traitor and madman, and has so far been unable to attach any stain to Bedwyr, so must invent this. Ach, I suppose it is clever enough, in its way. Bedwyr is not British, not of a royal or important clan, and yet he has power and influence. Medraut can use any resentment that causes to fuel belief in this tale, and can further blacken your name at the same time . . . ah, dear God, now Bedwyr as well. Now we have no one left who can mediate in a quarrel, or communicate with any of Medraut's faction. But a tale like this!'

I came over and sat down by his feet. I felt very tired, and rested my head against his knee. What if I should tell him, I thought suddenly, confess it all, escape the burden, take the consequences? But when I looked up into my husband's haggard face I knew that I could not speak, could not add to his pain or abandon him to suffer the ruin of his power alone. 'Do you want me to be cold with Bedwyr?' I asked. 'Avoid him during the next few weeks?'

Arthur laid one arm loosely around my shoulders. 'No. Do not trouble yourself. Medraut would only explain it to his followers as guilt fearing to be discovered. We can only hope that the thing will die out on its own. It must do so. It is too absurd for any thinking person to believe. You, and Bedwyr! My wife and my most loyal friend, the two people who care most for this realm, guilty of treason! No, my heart, leave it. It is sure to die out of itself.'

It did not, however, though it several times seemed likely to do so. Always as it was beginning to be laughed at it would rise again, with some new fabulous instance of proof. We could disprove or explain the instances – one was that I was seen wearing a hawthorn flower in my hair after Bedwyr wore one in his cloak-pin – Bedwyr and some six hundred others! – and yet still the tale persisted, and each time it faded it returned stronger and more pervasive.

Towards the end of April Bedwyr had a dispute with one of Medraut's Irish followers in the stable. This man, one of the royal clan, wanted some provision for a journey to his ship which Bedwyr thought excessive. The argument grew heated, and Bedwyr finally turned and began to walk off saying, 'I will speak to you again when you are cooler, Ruadh.'

'That is right!' the Irishman shouted after him, in the hearing of some dozen people (one of whom later recounted the whole incident to me indignantly). 'Run off to your lord's wife; do his business for him!' – and he made an obscene gesture.

Bedwyr stopped and looked back at the other. The man repeated the gesture, and Bedwyr turned and walked back to him. He looked the other up and down and said very quietly and very coldly. 'What foolishness is this? Are you drunk?'

The Irishman was completely unabashed. 'Must I be drunk to speak the truth? I am tired of your pretended virtue. Brave, loyal Bedwyr, the philosopher, the perfect warleader! All the West knows that you sleep with that whore-queen Gwynhwyfar, your lord's wife – much joy may you have of her!'

Bedwyr looked at him in silence for a moment, then still quietly but with a hard note under the quietness, said, 'You are guilty of defaming the majesty of our lord the Emperor. And you are lying.'

'Prove it,' said the other, eagerly. 'Prove it with your sword.'

"Gladly. Here and now."

The Irishman hesitated, then nodded. 'On horseback or on foot?'

'Whichever you wish.'

That created a stir among the onlookers, whose numbers were growing as the crowd drew together from nowhere, pulled by the expectation of blood. Bedwyr was no more than ordinarily skilled as an infantry fighter, but he was a brilliant horseman. Ruadh, however, was a very fine infantry fighter. Ruadh knew this and stared for a moment in disbelief before rapping out, 'On foot!'

At this one of the other members of the Family decided that Arthur should know of the duel, and ran off to find him. Arthur and I were together in the Hall, hearing petitions, and the warrior ran up and shouted loudly enough for all the world to hear, 'Bedwyr is fighting Ruadh, on foot!'

I did not consciously think of what could have happened;

I knew, at once, and I felt the colour go from the world. I rose without thinking and said to the petitioners, 'The hearing is suspended.' Arthur caught my arm and we started down the Hall.

'Where?' Arthur asked the messenger.

'The stables. They...' and the warrior gabbled out the whole story on the way.

We arrived to find a knot of men standing about and arguing. When they saw us they pulled apart and fell silent. In the centre of the knot was a space of trampled, bloody straw and a body: Ruadh.

'What has happened?' asked Arthur.

The first response was an indistinguishable babble, and Arthur raised his hand for silence, singled one man out of the crowd. 'Goronwy. What happened? Where is Bedwyr?'

Goronwy was very much excited, and ignored the second question. Having himself once fought Bedwyr, he had a great interest in the duel. 'It was a near contest, my lord,' he said, 'that dog Ruadh insulted her excellency the Lady Gwynhwyfar, and Lord Bedwyr fought him, on foot. Ruadh managed to get a thrust under his shield and stab in the thigh, so that he went down. Ach, but he was fast; Ruadh didn't expect that, came in to finish him, and found Bedwyr's sword up under his own shield, and into his stomach, quick as the lightnings of Heaven. Glory to God, it was a pretty stroke, and from his knees, too!'

'Pretty?' cried another warrior, one of Medraut's faction. 'God of Heaven, it is a man dead, a man of the royal clan of Britain!'

'Where is the lord Bedwyr?' Arthur demanded again, raising his voice over the renewed arguments of his warriors. They fell silent.

'We bound his leg up, and had him brought to Gruffydd the surgeon,' replied Goronway. 'Cei is with him now. Many of us would have gone, but he himself commanded us to remain here out of the way.'

I had not realized how my heart had been pressed, until that word freed it. Bedwyr was alive, and in control, commanding himself and the others. I felt Arthur relax beside me, though his face did not change from its set calm. 'Very well,' he said. He lifted his hand to hold the eyes of the crowd, and looked from one to another of them. 'It is enough, my cousins. No more quarrelling. Rhuawn, go and find Lord Medraut ap Lot, and tell him that his kinsman Ruadh is dead, and that he has my leave to do as he will with regard to the burial. The man was a member of the royal clan, and his body will be respected accordingly: four of you stay here to guard it. The rest of you are dismissed to go about your own business. I repeat, there has been blood enough shed for one day, and I wish no more. Gwynhwyfar, come.'

We hurried from the stables to Gruffydd's house, arrived to find the surgeon just wiping the blood off his hands. He nodded to us, then jerked his head towards the bed in the corner. Bedwyr was lying on it while Cei sat on the ground beside him, folding a bloodstained cloth. The warleader was very pale, sweating with pain, but conscious, self-controlled and, most important, alive.

'The worst of it was the loss of blood,' Gruffydd said, answering our unasked question. 'The wound was bound up at once, fortunately: otherwise the fool would now be chasing Ruadh to Hell. He should recover quickly, if there's no fever. Tell him to take the drug I have made him for the pain; he has refused it.'

Arthur went to the bed and grasped Bedwyr's hand. 'You fool,' he said angrily. 'Why, by all the saints, did you offer to fight him on foot?'

Bedwyr shrugged. 'I was angry,' he said, his voice hoarse from the pain, 'and I wished to kill him.'

Cei snorted angrily. 'You could have done that better from horseback.'

Bedwyr looked away. 'This way more of the men will believe his death is a sign of divine justice.'

'It was not worth the risk,' said Arthur. 'My friend, my brother, it was not.' The anger faded from his voice and he looked almost happy; Bedwyr was alive. He continued, with incongruous lightness, 'You have lost your philosophic detachment, old friend. What would your Victorinus say?' He released Bedwyr's hand, looked around, took the cup of drugged wine which Gruffydd was now holding ready for him. 'Here, drink this. There is no reason now for you to keep your head clear.'

Bedwyr did not offer to take it.

'I said the same,' Cei told us, 'but he seems to think he

must stay awake – as though none of us were fit to look after him.'

'Take it,' I said.

Bedwyr looked at me for the first time, and the bitter misery in his eyes shocked me. Then he looked at Arthur, nodded, and held out his hand for the cup.

'I was ashamed,' he told me, afterwards, when he was on his feet again. 'I killed Ruadh for a lie. He spoke the truth, and died for it. I could not have fought him from horseback, and given him so little chance. Yet I did wish to kill him. He had angered me, and I wished to see him dead and bloody before me. But after it, when I had killed him – then I wished to suffer.' He looked at the earth beneath his feet for a minute, then suddenly struck the half-healed wound on his thigh. He went white; I caught his arm, his shoulders, pulled him against me. We were alone for the first time since the duel, and I had thought during the two weeks he had been ill that I could not go on. My friends had all congratulated me, and attributed Ruadh's death to God's justice striking down a liar, and that hurt me even more than the insults of our enemies. And I had been afraid for Bedwyr, miserable at his misery, and still torn for Arthur, with no one to turn to who could make me whole again. I could talk freely only to Bedwyr.

I still thought about ending the relationship, sometimes. Once I meant to. I was in the Hall one morning, hearing complaints from some farmers and tradesmen, and sitting at the high table, when Gwalchmai came in. Since Gwyn was sitting over at one side of the Hall, playing the harp with some friends, I thought that Gwalchmai was looking for his son. I smiled and nodded and continued to listen to one old man's endless account of a strayed cow. I was disconcerted to look up a few minutes later and see the warrior standing in the circle of farmers, evidently waiting for me to finish. 'Is there anything the matter?' I asked.

'I would like to speak with you, my lady, when you are free,' he returned.

'Of course. Is it urgent? Then it may be a while.'

'I will wait.' He looked very serious, and there was no trace of his usual courteous smile. The old man coughed and proceeded with the cow, and I listened, feeling decidedly uneasy. Gwalchmai glanced at the numbers waiting for a hearing, then went over and joined Gwyn. Presently, over further details about cows, I heard him singing: someone must have passed him the harp.

'So-o,' went my old farmer, 'I saw her at the market, I did, at Baddon, last Sunday it was. It was my own cow, Strawberry, but this fellow – the lying dog' – he said it was his cow! But he must have found her on the road and taken her in, indeed he did, and...'

Gwalchmai was singing:

> 'The blackberry's white flower is she,
> The sweet flower of the raspberry,
> She's the best herb in the day's light
> And excellence of the eyes' sight.

'And this man's a fool, most noble lady, for claiming that my cow is his. Am I to blame that he can't keep his cows home? You know me well; I've farmed from Camlann twenty years, and I swear that it is my own cow, raised by me, and my kin and my neighbours can...'

> 'My pulse and my secret is she,
> The scented flower of the apple tree,
> She is summer and the sun's shine
> From Christmas to Easter, in the cold time.'

I pressed my hand to my head, feeling the headache coming. It was good, I reminded myself, that ordinary people such as these trusted us enough to come to us for justice – but I wished they would not do it just then, and not at such length. I recognized the tune of the song, though I had never heard the words. Bedwyr had been humming it for weeks.

Eventually I had the cow, and someone else's grazing rights, and someone else' frightened sheep all resolved, and was able to walk over to where Gwalchmai was sitting with the others. I smiled at them all, and Gwalchmai stood and bowed. Gwyn, who had the harp, just then, smiled and began to set it down to do likewise.

I motioned him to sit. 'Do not trouble yourself, Gwyn – I mean, Lord Gwalchaved. I only need to talk your father, if you can spare his company.'

By then, however, Gwyn was on his feet. He bowed. 'Couldn't you stay and talk here, my lady? If it is business, it would not disturb us, and we would be glad of your company when it is done. It is too long since anyone has heard you sing.'

'A mercy which all must be glad of,' I returned. 'But I believe that the business is confidential – fortunately for you. Otherwise I might accept your noble offer, and spoil your fine harping by trying to croak a melody.'

We walked down the Hall together, Gwalchmai and I; Gwalchmai paused in the doorway, listening as his son began to sing. Gwyn's voice had settled from its adolescent squeaking into a deep tenor. He was fifteen now, no longer a child, already as tall as his father. Gwalchmai smiled, glancing back into the Hall, then walked resolutely out into the sun, and I followed him.

It was one of those spring days which make one feel as though the barriers between worlds have dropped, and that Britain must have become the Kingdom of Summer. The air was soft and sweet, the grass impossibly green, and sky seemed alive with light. The larks were singing, and even the scattering of chickens about the fortress preened themselves and beat their wings as though they too wished to soar. My spirits lifted; perhaps I was wrong about what Gwalchmai meant to say to me. But when I hummed a bar of the song he had just played in the Hall, he looked at me sharply.

'Cei was in the Hall,' he said, 'so my house will be empty, my lady, if you have time for private speech.'

'Thank you, noble lord,' I said, trying to harden myself. 'We will go there.'

He offered me wine when we arrived, and I took some. He poured a cup for himself as well, but set it down untouched on the table by the fire, and sat a moment looking at me with that same dark, serious look.

'So,' I said, feeling entirely empty and almost uninterested in how it would actually happen, now that it came to the direct question from a friend. 'What is the matter?'

He looked away, quickly. 'My lady, last week, when my son and I returned from our embassy to Powys, we found that Camlann still repeated this new rumour. We were surprised to find that it was not yet discredited, especially after Bedwyr had fought for it.' He stopped, looking back to me and waiting. I said nothing, and, after a time, he resumed.

'Medraut came to me and spoke to me about it in private. He is very pleased with it. He says that it is true.'

'Everyone knows that Medraut begins all the rumours,' I said. 'Why should you pay special attention to this one?'

He stood up quickly and walked to the door, which was open for the sake of the light, and leaned against the frame, looking out at the walls and the distant fields. 'My lady,' he said, in a low, pained voice, 'do not play games with me. I know that half the tale is a lie. Medraut admitted as much. But he says that something of it is nothing less than the truth. And I have known Bedwyr many years, and I know ... what might be possible. And Medraut cannot lie to me.'

I had lived through this discovery a thousand times in imagination, and the reality left me feeling merely tired, and, in a curious way, relieved. 'Why did he go to you and tell you all this?' I asked. 'And why should he be unable to lie to you?'

'He does come to speak to me sometimes, very rarely. You know that, my lady. I am the only one that he cannot lie to, and I think that gives him relief, of sorts. And I knew our mother as well as he did. My lady, is the story true?'

I was silent. He turned and looked at me. I felt my face go hot slowly, and stood. 'I will go,' I told him.

'No, I beg of you, wait. My lady, for the sake of any friendship there has been between us, sit down.'

I sat again, and he sat down opposite me. He looked very remote, tense with unhappiness, and I felt something in the emptiness within me: pity. Pity for him, and a deeper, agonizing pity for Arthur. 'It is true,' I told him in a low voice. I took a swallow of the wine. 'I have been sleeping with Bedwyr. The rest – the supposed plotting and treachery – the rest is false. But that much is true.'

He was silent for a long minute, then said, intensely, 'You must end it!'

'Oh God!' I said. 'If we could! But we – I am not strong enough. We have tried, but it is no use. We need each other.'

'But, my lady – my lord Arthur, your husband, do you know what it will mean to him if this is found out? And more, you must know that the Family will never believe that you were guilty in one thing but not in another: they will say, 'The Empress and the foreign warleader were plotting the overthrow of the lawful Emperor!' taking the adultery and treason together. We will lose you, and Bedwyr, and our faith in everyone who remains, all at one stroke. My lady, how can you do this thing? This is the breach in the shield-wall, and Medraut knows it. He will attack here, and our defences will be gone like mist before the wind.'

I looked at the table, hunching my shoulders, feeling hot and cold at the same time. My wine glass was there, the cup bronze, chased with silver in the shape of birds; it had been given to Gwalchmai by some Irish king. I picked it up and drank some of the wine, too disgusted with myself to speak. I should end it. I should tell Gwalchmai that I would do it, tomorrow, and see . . . but I knew it was impossible. I could not do it. I could desire it, for the safety of the realm, for Arthur's happiness – but that was all. 'My friend,' I said 'love once made you an oathbreaker, and it has done nothing less to me. I cannot end it. Please try to understand.'

'My lady.' Gwalchmai reached out, touched my hand, and I looked up: the misery was plain on his face now, the remoteness vanished. 'What is to be done?'

'You must tell Arthur, of course,' I said, then swallowed and cleared my throat, for my voice was rough.

'I could not betray you.'

This surprised me, and I stared at him, saw that he meant it. It hurt. 'You must,' I repeated. 'It is your plain duty to your sworn lord. And it is better that Arthur learns of it from you than from Medraut and his friends, and better that he learns privately, and can take steps to ease the effect the news will have.' He continued to look at me without agreeing. 'Gwalchmai, the thing is certain to come out somehow, eventually, if not by you than by some other. You could not betray us any more than we have already betrayed ourselves.'

He shook his head. 'I have been your friend, I hope, and your friendship has meant much to me. My son adores you above the Blessed Virgin. And Bedwyr has been a brother to me since first I came to Camlann, for all that he has been afraid to speak with me these past months. How can I betray you to disgrace, to exile or death? And how could I tell my lord that his wife and his closest friend are unfaithful to him? If this thing will be discovered anyway, let it be discovered without treachery from me. But I beg you, my lady, as you love your husband, your friends, and the kingdom, end this thing. I would plead with Bedwyr, but when you scarcely hear me, I know that he would not.'

He was so desperate, so caught with love for all of us, that I said, 'I will try,' and half believed I would. I wished that I were dead. In a way, I supposed it would be better if I were; it would certainly be a better end to our problems than discovery. But there were blind hopes and immediate needs to meet me every day, and I did not want to kill myself. Bedwyr and I might yet successfully deceive everyone, or the situation in Camlann might improve and we might end our relationship.

I finished the wine, trying to compose myself, then walked, with Gwalchmai, back to the Hall.

I had arranged a tryst with Bedwyr that afternoon. Camlann was large, and much land was enclosed within its walls. Some of this had not been built on, and a few stray trees, young oak, birch and alder, straggled up the slope on the east. I knew that no one was taking their pigs or cattle there that afternoon, and there was a storage shed built against the wall where I had arranged to meet Bedwyr. He was there before me. I heard him humming the tune Gwalchmai had played as I came down the hill, and my heart leapt.

Bedwyr was sitting on a tree-stump before the shed, holding in his hand the white wing-feather of some bird, turning it this way and that. He heard my feet among the remnant of last year's leaves, and stood, his face lighting with that warm smile. The wind was among the trees, and the sun danced through the branches, and I knew that it was hopeless: that I could not tell him that it was over, and go.

'Gwalchmai knows,' I said, coming up to him. 'But he will tell no one. He is unwilling to betray us. But he begs us to make an end of it.'

Bedwyr's smile vanished, but he had already put his arms around me. I leaned my hand against his shoulder, feeling the sun warm against my back, longing for a moment of light and joy among the shadows. 'We must end it,' I whispered.

'We must,' he returned, but neither of us moved.

Seven

Early in June Arthur left Camlann to visit the king of Elmet, who was quarrelling with the king of the East Angles but did not wish to bring the dispute to us for our official judgement. Bedwyr and I were once again left in charge of the fortress and, more surprisingly, Gwalchmai remained there as well. Arthur wished to give the warrior a rest, and hoped that Gwalchmai could keep an eye on his brother.

The tension in the fortress became very great. Some of Medraut's followers may even have suspected Bedwyr and me of meaning to seize power while Arthur was away. At any rate, there was a duel shortly after he left, and one of our faction was killed. His opponent was badly injured, and when we had him sent to Gruffydd for healing, further violence almost erupted. Gruffydd's sympathies were well known, and many of the men believed he would either poison the wounded man or let him die of neglect. In the end Bedwyr and I managed to settle the matter without more fighting – we announced that Arthur would sentence the man on his return; we forbade Medraut's faction's setting up a guard; and we allowed the man's friends to stay by him unofficially until he was well enough to be moved to a friend's house. At least we did not have to keep him a prisoner: he was far too sick to escape. But still there was muttering in the fortress, and comments of 'cunning whore' and 'upstart foreigner' behind our backs. There were no more duels, but this was largely because the tension had grown so great that the two factions no longer insulted each other by ones and twos. The next quarrel, I felt, would risk not a duel but armed conflict throughout the fortress. But this was something I did not think Medraut was quite ready for, so I waited, as he did, in silence.

Some two weeks after Arthur left, shortly before he was due to return, I ordered a feast. The tension had ebbed a little, and I thought that a feast, full of songs about the old war, might bring back some memory of the old comradeship, and ease things further. Moreover, since it was a private feast, the women could share the tables with their men, and they unquestionably eased the tension.

It went very well, at first. Cei had asked my permission to bring his mistress Maire up to sit beside him, and she duly appeared in her best gown and some borrowed jewellery, as excited as a young child and laughing delightedly at the slightest excuse. Nearly everyone at the high table began laughing as well, and by the time the meal was over and we had heard several old eulogies from Taliesin, it seemed almost as though Medraut had never come to Camlann, even though he was sitting silent in our midst. The lower tables were full of laughter and joking and old battles refought. Taliesin came and sat at the end of the high table and smiling, passed his harp to Gwalchmai, saying that he was tired of singing and that it was someone else's turn. Gwalchmai laughed and played some Irish song about the spring which he had put into British some while before, then offered the harp to Bedwyr. Bedwyr was in an exceptionally good mood: he took it, smiling, and said, 'So I am to play first after you, and look a fool? Why don't you give it to Cei, and make him look a fool? But if I must . . .' and he played a one-handed setting of a a Latin poem I was fond of. He did not have a fine voice, but his harping was excellent: sparse, difficult, powerful. When he finished he offered the harp to me. But harping was one of the things I had neglected in favour of reading when I was young, so I declined to play, and instead offered the harp to Medraut, who sat on my left.

Medraut took it, smiling with all courtesy, and began to play the prelude to the tale of Blodeuwedd – a song about an adulteress. He ostentatiously caught my eye before he actually began to sing, however, looked disconcerted, paused just long enough for it to be noticeable to anyone who was listening – then began to play something else. It was very neatly done, an insinuation made perfectly plain without a word spoken, and all I could do was look calm, smile, and pretend that I was too innocent even to notice it.

But when Medraut finished his song and offered the harp to Gwyn, who sat next to him, Gwyn accepted it with a very grave look. He pulled at a few of the strings hesitantly, as though they were out of tune, then looked up resolutely.

'I do not see why you did not finish the first song you played,' he told Medraut in a clear, carrying voice. 'Was the harp tuned to the wrong mode?'

Medraut's smile was unchanged, but his eyes glittered. He had hated Gwyn passionately from the moment he learned that the youth was his brother's son, and so merited hatred rather than contempt. Dissembler as he was, he had obvious difficulty in disguising that hatred. Gwyn, of course, made no futile attempts to hide his loathing for Medraut, and a peculiar honesty prevailed between them.

'No,' said Medraut. 'But I thought the tale too long, and not suitable for the present company.'

Gwyn smiled, pulling a few more of the strings. 'Indeed, it would have bored us all – it has been sung so often that everyone knows it by heart. Nor is it suitable because of any great truth in it – I was talking to a priest, a learned man, the other week, and he said it is a pagan tale about the old gods, and is altogether false and wicked.' Maire giggled at this, and an instant later there was another ripple of laughter from everyone who had been following the talk. Gwyn looked at me, his smile changing into a look of wonderful and secret delight, sharing his pleasure at Medraut's discomfiture.

I smiled back, loving the boy. 'Play that song you were playing in the Hall the other day,' I suggested. 'It had a lovely tune, but I couldn't hear the words clearly.'

Gwyn flushed slightly. 'Oh, that song. It is of little value – but since it is you who ask for it, my lady, I will sing it.'

From this I gathered that the song was of his own composing, and tried to look serious and attentive again. Gwyn played a short prelude and sang,

'Where are you going? The whitethorn quickens
Up on the hill where the blackbird's singing,
While down the stream beds water wakens
As fresh from the sea the wind comes, bringing
The black-backed swallows from the blue south shaken:
Where are you going?

'I ride to the east where the streams are flowing
White with the snows and the haste of waters
Over the bright rocks and green weeds going

Into the swirl of the swollen river
That over the cloud-shadowed fields goes rolling
Off to the eastward.

'I ride east to war, and no more linger
For life is brief, gone sooner than spring-time,
Sooner than sun-glint goes from the river:
Why, then, delay till the coming of noon-tide
Or complain about death in the face of the winter?
Soon comes the cold, and no spring stays forever.'

It was, indeed, a lovely melody, with a curious lilt that ran through the mind unexpectedly when one thought it forgotten. Cei, however, who was sitting next to Gwyn, took the harp with a snort when the youth finished.

'You are a fine one to be singing about death, puppy,' he said. 'You've never ridden east to face the Saxons, and God send you'll never need to. It would be a cruel shame for a maker of sweet songs to die on a Saxon sword.'

Gwyn smiled. 'I hope that the Saxon would die, not me. Sing a sweet song yourself, most noble Cei.'

Just before Cei could strike up, Medraut leant forward across the table and interposed. 'There would be no fear of your being killed by a Saxon, nephew. I do not think you would see much of a battle.'

Cei responded to this before Gwyn could. 'What do you mean?' he asked, in the tone of polite inquiry which meant he wished a fight.

Medraut smiled contemptuously. 'Even if our young hero went to the battle, or took up some quarrel in a duel, do you think his father would allow him to risk his tender limbs among hostile swords? Oh no! Even in the grip of his famous battle madness, my brother would tremble with paternal fear, and chase glory from the field.'

Gwyn went pale and his eyes glinted, and Gwalchmai interrupted at once: 'You are much mistaken, brother. Neither would I command my son to be a coward, nor would he be so commanded if I did. I have seen my friends killed in battle, and know well enough that some griefs must be borne.' There was a pause, and Medraut and Gwalchmai watched each other in apparent calm but with a dark undercurrent of total understanding and irreconcilable opposition. 'Of course,' Gwalchmai went on in a tone too casual for the tension, 'if my son were forced or tricked into some quarrel, or murdered by treachery, that would be altogether different. Death in an equal contention must be borne as one bears death by flood or fever, but the laws promote justice to those who have been wronged, and to obtain justice in such a cause I would go to the ends of the earth; I would take no blood-price, and spare no life in the world for pleading or claims upon me. And such is only right in cases of deceit or treachery – but in battle one must trust to one's own skill and the mercy of God.'

Medraut dropped his eyes, but Gwalchmai continued to stare unwaveringly. Gwyn also watched, uneasy, his hand looped through his baldric and resting beside the hilt of his sword. 'Of course,' Medraut said in a low voice. 'Everyone knows your passion for justice – even justice for an imagined evil, brother. And, of course, your son is able to defend himself. He takes after you in that – as in other things.' He looked up again, his pale eyes malignant.

'In what other things?' demanded Gwyn.

Medraut smiled cruelly. 'Why, you both abandoned your homes and kin, scorned your mothers as though they were strangers, and left them to die.'

Gwyn's hand closed about his sword, and he began to jump up. Medraut added at once, 'But, of course, I know nothing about that. And the law does not permit me to quarrel with my kinsmen, or fight duels with my own blood. My lords and lady, and I am grown unaccountably weary; I hope you will forgive any rough words that I may have spoken, and excuse me the rest of the feast. Good night.'

He stood and left the Hall. As he did so a number of other warriors rose, looking confused and surprised, and hurried out after him. Cei, still holding the harp, spat at their retreat. 'Lost his temper for once,' he observed of Medraut. 'We're well rid of them.' He struck up a harsh marching-song. Gwyn sat looking after Medraut, clenching and unclenching his grip on the hilt of his sword; then turned his head away. Gwalchmai watched him silently with concern.

When the feast was over, I was not at peace with Cei's conclusion that Medraut had simply lost his temper when he came so near to offering to fight Gwyn. To be sure, he hated the youth, and could not conceal his hatred, but Medraut rarely did or said anything not dictated by policy. I could not quite believe this; I had never seen the face behind that gold mask, and I did not think I had seen it yet. If Arthur had been there we would have discussed what had happened for hours. In a way, I was glad he was absent and I did not have to talk about it, but the sheer habit of conversation kept me up. The house seemed very cold and empty, without my husband sitting at the desk waiting for me to come in. What with the tension and the extra work I had not spent much time in it recently, and the servant who had cleaned it had been the last person there, and had left it wiped clean of all character, like a guest house. I sat on the bed, took down my hair and combed it out, then found that I was too tense, and missed Arthur too much, to be able to lie down and rest. I went into the conference room and looked through some business at the desk, but could not concentrate. I sat and stared at the lamp until everything was black around the blue of its flame, and I thought upon the scene that had just passed, and on other scenes, and came to no conclusions. I put the lamp out, then went to the door. Outside the Hall loomed black and tall beside the house, blotting out the moon. Beyond its shadow the grass, the paths, the hunched shapes of the houses lay clear and plain, bleached colourless by the wan moonlight. But from Bedwyr's house came a warmer glow, the buttercup yellow light of a lamp. Bedwyr's servant would be asleep in his own house, at this hour, and no one else was about. I stood a moment, looking, then went out, closing the door behind me.

Bedwyr was sitting on the threshhold of his house, staring at the moon and singing, very softly,

> 'My pulse and my secret is she
> The scented flower of the apple tree...'

He saw me and stopped singing. He rose, stepped forward from the lamplight into the moonlight, and the moon made him pale as death. 'I wondered whether you would come,' he said. 'Welcome.'

The moon had laid a chill on my heart, and I pulled him

from the cold light into the house. He closed the door. The fire was burning brightly on the hearth, and the lamp cast a warm dim light over the plain room, over the rack of books and the silver wine pitcher with the two cups set on the table. Bedwyr smiled at me and poured some wine, saying, as he handed me the cup. 'I thought you might come, my lady. Your hair is very beautiful like that.'

I smiled back, brushing it away from my face. 'You know me too well, noble lord. What do you think Medraut hoped to gain just now?'

He smiled again, standing the other side of the table with the cup in his hand but only looking at me. 'Well guessed. I did think you would ask that. Ach, Gwynhwyfar, I do not know. I think for once he did simply lose his temper. He has as much cause to be tense as we have. He has failed to gain ground recently, now that the faction has become a plain matter of following him or following our lord the Emperor.'

'But his following is far more dedicated now.'

'True. But it is smaller than he had hoped.'

'Yet he wanted . . . something. I do not trust his loss of temper. He is too skilled to do that.'

'Perhaps. But Gwyn troubles and angers him, more even than Arthur, though he hates our lord more. And Gwalchmai says that he is honest with him. He might well lose his temper.'

I sat down at the desk, sipped the wine. The room was warm, and it was comforting to speak, to be understood, not to be alone. 'He might – yet now I am afraid for Gwyn. Ach, I know: Medraut cannot himself pick a quarrel with him, the law will not permit him to fight his own nephew. But he could persuade one of his followers to it. And Gwyn is hurt, and angry, and has been taunted with hiding behind his father. He could easily be provoked to fight. Does Medraut wish to destroy him? Does he fear the fact that Arthur favours him?'

Bedwyr shook his head. 'The boy is not altogether helpless, my lady. He is already a match for many men, on horseback. Moreover, he is popular. Such a quarrel would do Medraut little good. And Gwalchmai has made it plain how he would view such a quarrel, and I do not think anyone would care to have Gwalchmai as a dedicated enemy. Rest assured: I do not think Gwyn is in danger. And, bird of my heart, if there is more to the matter you will not find it by this scratching in the sand.'

'No,' I said. I found myself studying him in the warm lamplight: the dark brown hair, still untouched by grey; the grave eyes under the level brows; the remnants of a smile snared at the corner of his mouth. Love was a solid thing, hard-edged and painful, cutting into my breast. We had both known that I had not come just to talk about the terrors of the world, and labyrinths of plots and politics. We both wanted to break free of those for a little while, to be in another world private to ourselves; now that other world was flowering around us. Bedwyr set down his untouched cup of wine, came forward and bent over, kissing my eyelids. He twisted my hair around his fingers, kissed me again. I set down my own wine-cup and rose, pressing against him. One can lose oneself in love; forget identity, ties, responsibilities, everything. In love one can deny everything that one is and means, for everything else becomes nothing, another world, a dream. With Bedwyr I was simply Gwynhwyfar, not Lady or Empress, not old and trammelled with cares and bonds, and there was nothing outside the lamplit walls of his house. He loosened the laces of my gown and drew me down onto the bed.

And then our private world was broken into a thousand pieces.

The lamp and fire flared, leaping with a gust of sudden wind, and the cold smell of the night came in. There was a shout, more shouting; Bedwyr rolled off me and stood, seized his sword from beside the bed and crouched between me and the door. I sat up, trying to pull my dress straight, bewildered and hearing Medraut's voice crying triumphantly, 'She is here! Look!'

The light flickered madly. 'What are you doing here?' demanded Bedwyr. 'Get out! Or shall I kill you as I killed Ruadh?'

'Who is your woman?' yelled another voice, 'Why are you hiding her?'

Footsteps surged forward; Bedwyr backed against the bed, shaking the sheath off his sword; the flaring firelight caught the steel and made it blaze like the sun. 'Disharm him!' Medraut was shouting. 'He is guilty of treason!'

'Murderer! Usurper! Traitor!' came other yells. Steel flashed.

I threw off the cover and stood, pushing past Bedwyr. The room suddenly went very silent. I brushed my hair out of my eyes and pulled my gown up.

There were about a dozen men crowding in through the door, with Medraut in front of them, his face flushed with triumph and his sword drawn. I let my eyes run over him to his witnesses, and saw Gwyn in the front rank, white-faced with horror, a horror which abruptly struck me also so that I wished to sink under the earth. When my eyes met Gwyn's, he turned crimson, tried to back out through the press behind him, was unable to. I looked away, saw a few more shocked, agonized faces in the crowd, men who had been my friends, who had honoured me. Medraut had planned carefully. I had betrayed them, and now I could see it, I was so sick with shame that for a moment I could not speak. I looked back at Medraut.

'You challenged them that I would be here,' I said, and was amazed to find that I could hold my voice steady. 'And your faction clamoured of my guilt, and my friends of my innocence, until all agreed to put it to the test. And you proposed the test, as you had meant to, all along. Well, you have won. But,' looking to Gwyn and the others, 'not all of it was true, for all of this, not all of it.'

The flush had begun to fade from Medraut's face. He spat. 'You lying, perjured whore!' he said. 'Do you still pretend to innocence?'

Bedwyr moved beside me – just his sword arm, raising the weapon and angling it before himself, ready to attack. I caught his arm, pressed it. I felt his eyes on me, startled, but would not look at him. 'I am guilty of adultery,' I declared, to all of them. 'But before God, the Lord of Earth and Heaven, we are both innocent of the other treason with which rumour has charged us. We never wished any injury either to our lord Arthur, or to this Empire; and we never planned to gain power for ourselves. Now you may take us and punish us as you wish, for we deserve all that any of you would do to us, and I would not deny it. But, my friends, if ever you listened to me in your lives, listen now: Medraut ap Lot plans ruin for all of us, and if you distrusted him before, distrust him now even more. Now, let me out, to my house to await the judgement of my lord the Emperor.'

Medraut tried to rush forward and strike me, and one of his friends held him back. The grace and contemptuous smile were gone: he was red-faced, angry, excited, and a stranger to me. 'The liar, the adulterous traitress!' he hissed, spitting at us. 'Both of them, caught in the very act, panting in each other's arms and betraying their true lord, and still she reviles me!'

Medraut's friends gave a yell and surged forward. I dropped Bedwyr's arm and walked towards them. I did not dare look at Bedwyr. His passion had betrayed him again, and I knew he was eager to fight them, to die fighting them, no doubt. But that was the last thing we should do: we must stand trial, be convicted of what we had done, and let the fortress know the whole story so that they would know there was nothing more. I was myself again, what I was by nature, and also what chance and time and power had made me: I could think clearly. When I drew even with Medraut, his followers fell back a little, staring at me, hating me, but I knew that I could command and they would obey.

'I must become your prisoner,' I said, 'as must the lord Bedwyr. Where is Cei?'

A murmur. 'We take you prisoner!' insisted Medraut.

'Cei is the infantry commander, he is next in power after Bedwyr and myself, and now he is of necessity commander of this fortress, not you, Medraut ap Lot. Let him see to it that we are guarded – or do you think he is a traitor as well? Tell me, Medraut, am I sleeping with him as well? You have set so many lies around me that I cannot keep track of them.'

'You ... arrogant, brazen ... do you deny, can you deny what we have trapped you in?'

'I am guilty of one thing, one thing only. Or if there is more, that is for my lord to decide, and not for you. Let me go back to my own house, and wait for his return. I am willing to die, if he should desire it. But I swear again before you all that I never wished or hoped that any other should wear the purple in his place. I was weak, and desired comfort, which lord Bedwyr gave, and that was the whole of the matter. For now, you know as well as I that you may not judge us, or sentence us, or do anything but wait for the Emperor's return.' Behind me I heard a soft thud, and my knees almost gave with the relief: Bedwyr had thrown aside his sword. I went on more confidently, 'You, Rhuawn, and you, Goronwy: you can come and guard me, to make certain that I do not hang myself in despair before morning, as Medraut no doubt fears. Will someone fetch Cei?'

'I . . . I will,' Gwyn said. 'And I will fetch my father.' He turned, shoved his way through the rest, and was gone.

Medraut glared at me with passionate hatred. 'Still you give orders? That will change soon enough.'

I said nothing, merely walked towards the line of men, and they gave way before me. 'Gwynhwyfar,' Bedwyr said behind me. I looked back, saw him standing before the dark corner with the crumpled bed, his sword burning before his feet, his hand raised towards me, and a desperate horror in his eyes.

'We knew it would come,' I told him.

He nodded, lowering his hand. 'Remember what I said,' he whispered. 'It is my fault.'

I did not answer, but turned back towards the door. Rhuawn and Goronway separated themselves from the others and followed me out. I had picked them carefully to represent either party, and so content both. But the clarity of mind, the exaltation of finally speaking honestly to Medraut, departed as I passed the door and left Bedwyr to await what guard Cei would set. Then the depth of shame, of humiliation, anguish and terror for the future swallowed me, and I wished that I would die that night, and never see Arthur or the day again.

I did not see Arthur when he first returned to Camlann and heard what had happened. Gwalchmai and Cei met him at the gates and told him the news. At first he refused to believe it. But when he saw that it was plain and certain, and denied by no one, he ordered everyone to leave him. When they reluctantly obeyed, he turned his horse about and rode away from Camlann at a gallop. He did not return until noon the following day. Then he went to Gwalchmai, still covered with the dust of his riding, and consulted him on the situation and how best to contain it. He then, with Gwalchmai, visited Bedwyr, who was being kept under guard at his own house.

It was Gwalchmai who told me of all this. He had come at once when Gwyn informed him of the discovery, and had said no word of reproach, but instead immediately discussed with me how best to combat Medraut's allegations of treachery. He and Gwyn continued to visit me over the next week, informing me of events, helping me to plan for them, and bringing me accounts and papers I asked for – for I was determined to leave the affairs of the fortress in good order.

'Did Arthur speak with Bedwyr long?' I asked Gwalchmai anxiously.

The warrior shook his head. 'No, Indeed, he hardly spoke at all. He came into the house, and Bedwyr fell on his knees before him and bowed his head. Arthur said only, 'Tell me what happened, nothing more,'' and Bedwyr said, "It was my fault, my lord, and I am most bitterly grieved at it." Arthur said, "Only the tale."'

'Was he angry?'

'Not angry. He looked at Bedwyr as though he had never seen him before. I have told you, my lady, how it is: he is like a man coming to himself after a great battle, stunned, knowing neither what he has done or what he will do. Bedwyr knelt before him with his fingers clenching in the dust of the floor, afraid to look up, and my lord Arthur merely watched him as he might watch an animal, trying to understand what it was and what it wished. Then Bedwyr told him that he had seduced you after ... after you had made your attempt on my brother's life, when you were ill and unhappy. He said that he had loved you for a long while before that. And he said that you had often tried to end your relationship, but that he had always pressed you to continue – is it true, my lady?'

'He exaggerates to blame himself. Oh, the time is true, and perhaps the form of things as well, but he twists it to exonerate me.'

Gwalchmai looked at me closely for a minute, then shrugged. 'He told Arthur all of this without looking up. He did not look at him until the end. Then he raised his head, and they looked at each other for a long time. Then Bedwyr said, "But it was you that she loved. Only you asked more from her than anyone can give. No one can be always a ruler only, always strong, not even you or her. I pressed her to lean on me a little. That was my fault. Do not punish her for it. And, my lord, I have always been your servant in everything else, and this betrayal is bitter to me also." But Arthur said nothing, merely gestured to me to follow him, and left Bedwyr kneeling there.'

'Will Arthur come here as well?' I asked very quietly. I was afraid to raise my voice, afraid to find it twisted by hope or fear. I needed to remain calm.

Gwalchmai hesitated, then shook his head. 'I do not know, but I do not think he means to. He is sleeping in my house now, and he wishes you to stay here until the trial. He has told no one what he thinks of this, or what he plans to do. But I do not think that he wishes to see you.'

And he did not see me, not until the trial itself. This was held about a week after the discovery. It took place in the Hall, before all the inhabitants of Camlann and many outsiders.

The morning of the trial I dressed myself more carefully than I would have to attend a great feast, partly from bravado, and partly to make a point to the onlookers. I tore off the purple fringes of my best gown, the white silk kirtle that travelled the long trade road from Rome and beyond; the silk was hard to tear, and left rough trailing threads of purple and gold along the edges. I wore no jewellery, and took the signet ring from my finger, wrapping it up in the strips of gold and purple silk. Then I put up my hair with a chain of Roman glass beads which as a girl I had found beside the Roman Wall, and which I had worn when I rode south to Camlann. I was surprised when my face in the mirror looked much the same as it had ever done. A week before the purple had been almost a part of me, and now I was less than what I had been when first I came to Camlann. I had no hope of power, and no clan to return to; even my clothing belonged to the Empress I would never be again. I had nothing more than the flesh I stood in, and whatever my lord's will would give me for a future.

My guards rapped on the door, and I set the mirror aside and went with them to the Hall.

It was full of men, almost overflowing: no women, for law is the affair of men. When I entered at the great door a murmur went up, and I could see those at the back craning their heads so as to look at me. I had resolved to bear my disgrace humbly, since it was deserved, but nonetheless I found myself proud and indignant now that it had come to the point, and I held myself very straight and walked the long way up towards the high table slowly. They had lit the torches, although it was day, and the beams of sunlight slanting under the eaves were blue in the smoke. It was hot, both from the warmth of the day, and from the tightly pressed bodies in the Hall, and as I walked I felt dizzy. The faces in the crowd were unfeatured, lost: I could see the glitter of armour and weapons, the white of the shields hung along the walls, but I recognized no friends. At the far end of the Hall, seated at the high table, was a figure like a statue, unmoving in the heat and smoky light. Arthur wore the purple and a collar of heavy gold, and his right hand rested on the scroll of evidence set on the table before him, the light burning purple in the jewel of his signet ring. His face was like a carving in stone, and as I approached his eyes looked beyond me, not meeting mine or answering any more than the eyes of an emperor pictured in a mosaic.

Bedwyr was already standing before Arthur, and I glanced at him as my guards helped me a place on his right. He looked exhausted, his face worn out around the hard pain in his eyes, and, in his dark clothing, without any badge of office or any weapon, he looked more like an impoverished monk than a warrior lord. His eyes met mine briefly, and something leapt in them – pity, apology or love, I could not tell, for he looked away again very quickly. Our guards struck the floor with the butts of their spears, and the trial began.

Arthur rose, picking up the scroll of evidence. 'Bedwyr son of Brendan, sometime warleader of this Family, and Gwynhwyfar daughter of Ogyrfan, are charged with defaming the imperial majesty, according to the laws of the Empire of the Romans and of Britain, by committing adultery. The charge is brought by Medraut son of Lot. Lord Medraut, repeat now before these witnesses the charge you have laid against these persons.'

Medraut rose from a place at the side of the dais and walked to stand before Arthur, on his left. He was not wearing his usual saffron cloak, but one bordered with purple, and a collar like Arthur's; he paused before beginning, to be certain that all the Hall could note the resemblance between Arthur and himself before being distracted by his words. Then, without looking at me or Bedwyr, he gave his own account of how he had discovered the adultery, speaking in a clear voice occasionally tinged with sorrow, as though he were grieved at such terrible events. I watched Arthur. My husband looked very tired, and still more haggard and grey, now that I was close enough to see it, but his face was expressionless. I had seen that look of set calm often enough before to understand what it meant, but I suppose most of the others thought him cold and unmoved.

It felt very strange to stand there before Arthur, listening to Medraut accusing me, when not long before I had sat in Arthur's place and given judgement for others. I clung to that sense of strangeness, of shock, because it was better than the hot shame and the unworthy rage against humiliation, the loathing of Medraut's smooth speech, which were the alternatives.

'There was a feast the night before these crimes were discovered,' Medraut said, finally approaching his conclusion, 'which I left early because of my indignation at the corruption of these two, and so as to keep a clear mind should there be any difficulties during my lord's absence...'

'Explain yourself,' said Arthur, for perhaps the twentieth time in that speech. Medraut had constantly tried to insinuate that Bedwyr and I had been plotting Arthur's overthrow, but had been stopped each time when Arthur demanded what he meant and what evidence he could cite for it. Since he had none he had been forced each time to back away from his hints.

'I wished to remain vigilant,' he said now, at once, 'in case some difficulty should arise in my lord's absence, which these criminals, in their preoccupation with a treacherous love, might have neglected.'

'You had reason to suspect these two persons of negligence?'

'No, my lord; but I thought it possible that they might be negligent, given the circumstances.'

'Ah? And perhaps you thought that they were untrustworthy on some point you opposed them on? I believe a friend of yours, Lord Llenleawc ap Creiddawl, was under arrest at the time, accused of defaming the imperial majesty; perhaps you suspected some ill might come to him?'

'My lord, I affirm nothing. And my friend Llenleawc merely said that these two persons were criminals, as the event has proved.'

'Indeed. It was reported to me that he had called me a criminal as well, and killed another member of the Family in a duel for defending my name.'

Medraut smiled, as though apologizing to the Hall for Arthur's bad taste. 'Indeed, my lord, I knew nothing of any accusations he made against you. As for this, let it suffice that I was concerned for the well-being of the fortress in your absence.'

'Your loyalty is welcome, Lord Medraut. You had no evidence of further crimes by the accused, then, or any reason to suspect them?'

Medraut hesitated, his smoothness finally marred by the merest hint of anger, then, apparently realizing that his hints would get him nowhere in court, finally responded, 'No.'

'I see,' said Arthur. 'You left the feast early, then – I believe after a quarrel with Lord Gwalchaved ap Gwalchmai.'

Medraut's irritation grew slightly plainer. 'Yes, my lord.'

'But you approached Lord Gwalchaved after the feast, and told him your suspicions concerning Lord Bedwyr and Lady Gwynhwyfar.'

'Yes, my lord.'

Arthur looked at the scroll in his hand, looked up at Medraut again. 'In your testimony you say merely that you were discussing the situation with a friend, when Lord Gwalchaved came out of the Hall and challenged you upon your statements. But now you agree with Lord Gwalchaved, and say that you approached him deliberately. What did you do, Lord Medraut?'

Medraut looked back at Arthur, hard; Arthur remained calm, mildly inquisitive. Medraut bowed his head. 'I believe I was speaking to a friend first, my lord, and, on seeing Lord Gwalchaved, addressed him as well.'

'Ah. And you suggested to him that the Lady Gwynhwyfar was with Lord Bedwyr?'

'I did, my lord. He denied it roundly, and I suggested that we test the suggestion. We went first to the lady's house, and received no answer when we knocked on the door; and then, on entering Lord Bedwyr's house, we found the two of them...' the anger surfaced suddenly, 'panting in each other's arms upon the bed.'

'So. And you arrested them?'

'Yes. Lord Bedwyr attempted at first to resist, but the lady insisted on his submitting to us.'

'And I believe the lady had you send for Lord Cei, who on her arrest must be head of the fortress.'

'I sent for Lord Cei, my lord, as soon as the crime became known.'

'Indeed? I have it here on the testimony of ... four witnesses, that the lady demanded that Lord Cei be sent for, while you reviled her; and that Lord Cei was eventually brought by Lord Gwalchaved because of the lady's demand. It was, of course, entirely proper that Lord Cei be present, as you did not have the authority to arrest these two, and as your position was already irregular in that you had broken into Lord Bedwyr's house previous to accusing him.'

'My lord,' said Medraut, his eyes very cold, 'perhaps in the heat of the moment, and in my shock at seeing this crime of adultery virtually committed before my eyes, I used intemperate language, and acted in an irregular fashion, if so, set it down to my passion for your honour. I always meant to send for Lord Cei.'

"Indeed. I thank you, Lord Medraut, without you, this crime would never have come to light. Have you anything to add to your testimony?'

Medraut hesitated again, then apparently decided not to. 'No, my lord, expect my regret at this stain upon your name and honour.'

'I thank you. You may be seated. Lord Gwalchaved!'

Gwyn, Cei and several others were called upon to confirm Medraut's account, which they did as gently as they could. No further mention was made of plots and treason.

Finally, Bedwyr was called, and he took one step forward, went down on one knee to Arthur, and rose again. Arthur pushed the scroll aside and looked at him, as Gwalchmai had described, as though he were a strange and mysterious animal he could not understand. 'Do you admit the charge?' he asked Bedwyr.

Bedwyr bowed his head. 'Yes, my lord. I am guilty of adultery with the Lady Gwynhwyfar, and hence of treason against you.' Arthur watched him, waiting, and Bedwyr raised his head again before continuing, 'I loved the lady for a long time, perhaps almost as long as you yourself, though for long after you married her I would not speak with her. On one occasion, however, which I told you of, when you were absent and when she was lonely, over-burdened with care, and suffering a private grief, I persuaded her to confide in me, and seduced her. She tried often to turn from this crime, but I pressed her to continue, and she yielded, out of pity. For my part, my lord, I am certain that what Lord Gwalchaved ap Gwalchmai says of the events of that night is true, and I do not contest it. But I was driven by love, and not by any desire to do injury to the imperial majesty, which it has been my great joy to serve. My lord, in all but this my life has been at your command, and this was a madness that forced me out of myself. Believe that I have never otherwise betrayed you, and I am well content to die for this, as I should. And if you sentence me to exile instead of death, I will seek out some monastery and there undertake the harshest penance I can find, to punish myself for this grievous sin.'

Arthur looked at his hands, twisted the signet ring on his finger. I thought I saw a shadow of anger cross his face, but, if so, it was gone quickly. 'Have you anything to add?' he asked Bedwyr, quietly.

'No, my lord. I am content to await your sentence.'

Arthur nodded, then raised his head. 'Gwynhwyfar daughter of Ogyrfan,' he called, and finally met my eyes.

I stepped forward. I had meant to bow, but I was afraid he would look away if I did. My mouth was dry, and I had to keep swallowing. I forgot all the others packing that Hall, forgot the heat, forgot everything but him.

'You are changed with defaming the imperial majesty by committing adultery with this man. Do you admit the charges?'

'Yes, my lord.' I had to catch my breath, swallow again,

think whether I was going to correct Bedwyr's story or not, wonder how to tell Arthur that I still loved him. But after that sole reply he rose, and looked slowly about the Hall.

'Both the Lady Gwynhwyfar and Lord Bedwyr have admitted the charge of adultery brought by Medraut son of Lot. Is there any that would deny it?'

I stared at him, not believing that he was ending the proceedings without any more words from me than 'Yes, my lord'. But he stood still, holding the scroll of evidence, waiting. No one spoke. The Hall was so silent I could hear the swallows chirping in the thatch, and the children shouting outside, down the hill.

'Then I pronounce both Gwynhwyfar daughter of Ogyrfan and Bedwyr son of Brendan guilty of defaming the imperial majesty, for which the penalty is death. However, since both have given long and faithful service to the Empire, and since there is no evidence of any other treason, committed or intended, I here commute that sentence for both. Bedwyr ap Brendan.'

Bedwyr stepped forward.

'You I strip of all honours, ranks and privileges hitherto conferred on you, and sentence to exile in Less Britain, on pain of death if you are found in any other part of my realm after a week's time. You may take your horses, your arms, and sufficient goods to provide yourself and your servant with passage to Less Britain. You must leave this fortress before dusk this afternoon.' Bedwyr dropped again to his knee, bowing his head, and again rose. 'And you, Gwynhwyfar, daughter of Ogyrfan...'

The steady, ponderous words stopped as Arthur hesitated for the first time, looking at me. I almost cried out to him, begging him to give me a chance to speak; I wanted to rush forward and kneel at his feet, try to explain, let him know that, adultery notwithstanding, I loved him. But was there anything I could say that would alter the course of this irrevocable law? And his eyes were cold, bitterly cold. I could not move. The look was not the one with which he had regarded Bedwyr. I saw that he did not understand what I had done, could not understand, and was cut beyond healing by betrayal where he had most trusted. He did not want to look at me, I could tell. It hurt him, and I knew that he did not wish to hear me speak and to torture him with explanations. I bowed my head, and he looked over me down the Hall, once again as calm and distant as a statue.

'Gwynhwyfar, daughter of Ogyrfan, it is not fitting that a woman who has held the imperial dignity should go into exile, or suffer punishments from those who were her subjects. Considering this, and considering also that you were the less to blame than your seducer, I decree only that you shall be escorted back to your own clan, and returned to the protection of its chieftain, there to live out the rest of your life.

'The sentence is decreed; the trial is ended.'

'My lord!' exclaimed Bedwyr. I looked at him quickly and shook my head, and he fell silent, though he started towards me as though he wished to speak with me, and had to be checked by his guards. I bowed low to Arthur, as Bedwyr had. But I remembered, as Bedwyr evidently did, the letter of my cousin Menw. Exile would have been preferable to his 'protection'. It would mean more than simply hard words: I could expect beatings, and whatever else Menw could think of to humiliate and subdue me. Undoubtedly he would welcome the opportunity.

Arthur rose, and the crowd behind began to ease itself out of the Hall, talking in undertones. The set look was beginning to appear strained, as though his strength were failing and he could not hold it much longer. He did not mean to humiliate me, I knew. He knew very little of Menw, and had probably forgotten what he did know. The sentence – both sentences – were merciful, astonishingly merciful. And I would not plead with him, beg him to change his mind, explain. He wished no explanations, and I would not cling to his clemency and weep. I would not use the ties of love, of the fourteen years between us, to strengthen a plea, like a beggar flaunting a sore. I had wronged him, and he wanted nothing more to do with me. That was enough to keep me silent till death.

As Arthur was about to start down from the dais, Medraut intercepted him. 'My lord,' he said, 'I beg that you will allow me to display my devotion to your honour. Let me escort this woman back to her family.'

Arthur merely looked at him.

'I am most deeply moved, my lord,' Medraut went on,

not meeting the other's eyes, 'by the wrongs you have suffered, and I am eager to prevent more by seeing that this woman is kept securely, and is unable to slip her guards and run shamelessly after her lover.'

Arthur pulled away and began walking out with his long, firm stride. 'You speak very insolently of my wife, son of Lot,' he tossed back at Medraut without looking round, 'but please yourself. Cei, choose five others to accompany him – not Gwalchmai, and not yourself, for I will need you. They are to leave tomorrow morning.'

Cei, who had followed Arthur from the high table, looked after him as he departed through the crowd that melted before him; then himself looked round, scowling fiercely. Gwyn jumped off the dais and came over to him. 'Let me go with Lady Gwynhwyfar's escort,' he asked.

Medraut gave Gwyn a venomous look, but Cei nodded to him, grinned, and slapped him on the back. Gwyn smiled back and came over to me. He was still very confused about what had happened, but more inclined to blame Medraut (irrational, but kind) than me. 'At least I will have the pleasure of your company for another week or two, noble lady,' he said.

I smiled, found that my face was stiff, that it hurt to smile. I suddenly wanted to sit down somewhere, alone: not to cry, but simply to sit still until the pain diminished. 'Thank you, Gwyn,' I croaked. 'My lords, let me go back to my house, to prepare for the journey.'

Cei nodded, and I and my guards moved away.

I did not see Arthur when I left the next morning. It was the last day of June, and the light came early; the sun was high when I joined the rest of the party, my escort, at the stables, though the hour was still early. There were six warriors: Medraut, his friend Rhuawn, and Gwyn with three others of the loyal faction. There were also four servants, and our party had sixteen horses. I had my own horse waiting for me, my splendid, spirited little bay mare, and she whinnied eagerly when she saw me, and nuzzled my hand, looking for apples. Gwyn gave me his hand to help me into the saddle, and we set off under the clear pale sky, I riding in the middle, my escort flanking me, and the servants riding behind with the pack horses. The people of Camlann clustered thickly about the road down to the gate, watching. To my surprise, as soon as we left the stable someone called, 'Farewell, noble lady!' and many others took it up. A woman rushed out of the crowd, forcing the escort to stop, and gave me a bunch of roses and a parcel of sweet wine-cakes. 'Good fortune be with you, my lady,' she said, taking my hand and pressing it to her forehead. I recognized Eivlin, the wife of Gwalchmai's servant. 'Better fortune than you have had till now.'

'Thank you,' I returned. 'Farewell.'

Gwyn, who had let her through to me, smiled, but Medraut scowled and motioned the rest back, and spurred his horse to a canter, and the rest of us were forced to follow him, down along the road, past the houses, the open spaces, down to the gate and through it. I looked back at the fortress, rising behind its sheer wall from the gates to the distant thatch of the Hall; looked back again and again as we trotted on down the road, until I lost sight of it among the other hills. Still I rode looking back over my shoulder, unable to believe that I could no longer make it out, that I could leave so easily what I had loved so long.

Eight

The first night of our journey we stayed in a fortified villa some few miles south of Baddon, the holding of a local nobleman who was eager to offer hospitality to such notable or notorious figures, and who eyed me constantly with undisguised and insolent curiosity, so that I was glad to leave.

The next day we continued as far as Caer Ceri, and stayed with the local lord at the fortress there. This was a man I knew reasonably well, who had been useful during the war. He treated us with far greater courtesy, giving us a feast. From him I learned that Bedwyr had passed through Caer Ceri the day before. This circumstance might have gone unremarked, were it not that some half dozen of Bedwyr's friends, those Bretons who had followed him into Arthur's service, had chosen to follow him out of it, and had accompanied him in his departure from Camlann. Any party of armed men larger than half a dozen will be noted and inquired after in any town.

'But I do not understand,' I told the local lord. 'I did not think he was going to go this way. One would expect him to ride to Caer Uisc, or Caer Gwent, and take ship from there.'

'Like enough he will take ship from Caer Gloeu,' said the nobleman. 'The river port is large enough, and there's much traffic there from the upper Saefern, this time of year; one can find a ship quickly there. Perhaps he wished to avoid notice by avoiding the larger ports. Do not trouble yourself, noble lady. I would not have mentioned it, except that I thought he had been sent that way, and wondered at the reason.'

I agreed not to worry about it, though I was still surprised. But my mind felt numb and lethargic, and I did not think about it again.

The following day we took the north-east road that runs from Caer Ceri to Linnuis, where it joins the main road to Ebrauc. It was yet another fine summer day: the road was hazed with a light mist in the valleys, but the rising sun was dispersing it quickly. The damp woods glistened, the corn in the ploughed lands was beginning to turn silver-gilt, and the cattle in the pastures were sleek and shining with contentment. The bright day made my spirits heavier, and I rode staring at the sun on my horse's mane. Thus I could let my mind sink into the numbness, the fatigue that beset me, where every effort seemed too great; I could rest, and not feel much, instead of feeling all there was to feel for what had happened. I was almost dreaming when someone shouted, and the horse in front of mine stopped. I reined in my mare and looked up to see another party of horsemen approaching us at a trot, coming down the road from the opposite direction. With a shock, I recognized the foremost rider as Bedwyr.

'Lord Bedwyr!' said Gwyn at the same moment, stopping his horse beside mine. His dark eyes widened, as his father's did when he was tense, though Gwalchmai never showed that he was pained and nervous as clearly as Gwyn did. Gwyn was afraid of some scene, of harsh words, enmity between those he loved. 'What does he expect?' he asked me anxiously. 'Does he expect that . . .'

'He has come to steal the lady,' declared Medraut. He unslung his shield and strapped it to his arm. Some of the other warriors began to do the same.

'In the name of Eternal God!' I snapped, angry with them, and more angry with Bedwyr. 'There is no need to prepare to fight. If that is what Bedwyr has come to do, he will go off without having achieved it, for I will not go with him.'

Medraut paid no attention, but pulled his thrusting spear from its sling on his saddle, and started his horse forward. The other group stopped its advance, and Medraut reined in again, touching his horse with his heels to make it dance.

'You scheming traitor!' called Medraut. 'What have you come for?'

Bedwyr started forward again, then, clear of the others, stopped his horse. He too had strapped his shield to his arm, but held it away from his body at an angle, leaving himself unprotected. 'Let the lady Gwynhwyfar come with us,' he called to Medraut. 'I know that her cousin's house will be little to her liking and, as the Emperor said, it is not fitting for such a lady to be treated as a criminal.'

So that was indeed it. I remembered Bedwyr's attempt at

protesting when I was sentenced, and I cried out wordlessly in exasperation and anger. He should realize that I did not want to be rescued, that he could not protect me from the consequences of our crime; that it was not his task to protect me, that, though I had been weak with him, I was strong enough to endure suffering, and deserved it. Oh, he was kind, as always, but this was madness. I spurred my mare forward. 'Medraut!' I began.

He turned, and for just a moment I saw the triumph on his face, and then the butt end of his spear caught me on the side of the head and knocked me from the saddle. I was so astonished and horrified that I did not even cry out, and the ground seemed to leap at me. Above me I heard Medraut shouting, 'She plotted this with him! Guard her!' I tried to get up – I was sprawled in the dust of the road – but the breath had been knocked from me and I could not make my half-stunned limbs obey me. Hooves thundered past me, and ahead I heard shouting, a scream of rage or of pain. I tried again to shout, could not, managed to struggle to my feet, caught my mare's bridle to go after Medraut and stop him, for I saw that he meant there to be blood and I knew that I must stop him. My mare was unused to such commotion and she danced nervously, trying to turn about and go home, and I jumped after her stupidly. More hooves around me, and then Gwyn's horse was forced against mine, and Gwyn leaned from his saddle across mine, stretching out an arm to help me up. 'Stop them!' I shouted at him, not taking his hand, knowing that every second was precious and he could reach the others more quickly. 'Gwyn, Gwyn my heart, this is utter madness. Go tell Bedwyr that I will not go with him, make him leave; stop them! Oh God.'

Gwyn understood at once, and spurred his roan mare to a gallop. She leapt off like the seagull of her name, and I managed to scramble into my saddle, turn my horse about and gallop after her. Ahead of me was a whirling mêlée of men and horses and weapons: swords flashing, clouds of dust, and lime shaken from shields into the clear air, horses backing and turning. One of Bedwyr's men was lying very still in the dust of the road, soaking it with blood. Medraut was fighting another, trying to reach Bedwyr, who had engaged Rhuawn in combat. And Gwyn was galloping up to all of them, his fair hair streaming in the wind of his motion.

'Stop, stop!' Gwyn shouted, his voice breaking again with the urgency, going high like a child's. 'There is no need – the lady won't go; Bedwyr, Rhuawn, the lady will not go! Bedwyr! Listen!' He threw the shield down from his arm into the midst of the struggle, under the feet of Bedwyr's horse, and he flung wide his arms, 'Bedwyr!'

Rhuawn hesitated in the midst of a sword-stroke, and Bedwyr looked up. I was close enough then to see his face. He had a throwing spear in his hand; the light gleamed on that, and on his eyes. His arm was back, ready to hurl the spear, and, even as I watched, that arm came forward too quickly to follow, and something flashed. Gwyn, poised high in the saddle, perfectly balanced for each step of his horse, suddenly fell. Everything seemed to happen very slowly. I saw Gwyn fall onto the road as though he were falling through water, his horse plunging on past him, flicking her ears back, confused, not understanding what he was doing. Gwyn rolled over into the dust onto his side, rocked back; put out one hand and pushed himself up. He brought his knees under him and tried to stand, but fell back onto the road. Bewyr's spear jutted out from under his collarbone, very black except for the bronze sheathing on the butt of it, which stood out like some incongruous jewel. Gwyn opened his mouth, a look of astonishment on his face, but when he gasped only blood came out. One hand felt at the spear, pulled at it, then slid back down into the dust, palm upwards, and he lay relaxed, twisted on his side with the astonished look still printed on his face and the brilliance fading already from the dark eyes.

I was screaming, I realized, a horrifying loud, shrill sound; I dropped my mare's reins as she finally reached the group of men and stopped where the other horses had. I could scarcely hear someone's shriek of 'Murderer!' or the cry of a horse struck by another spear. I tried to stop screaming and could not. All around me now was the shouting and the confusion, and I thought *They will trample Gwyn*, and looked for him among the dust and the hooves, the shaken dust and the lime in the air and the blood on the road. I pushed my hands into my mouth, trying to stop myself from screaming, and some rider, some half-familiar face, dashed over and caught my mare's bridle, then spurred his horse to a gallop, dragging mine after him. I caught my mare's mane, trying to stop her, and she danced wildly and reared. Not sure what to do, and not even remembering which party this warrior fought for, I kicked my mount back into the gallop. The blood and sunlight of the road vanished behind trees; I realized I had been looking back. There was more shouting, and some other riders galloped after us, caught up with us and drew even.

'They are not following us,' Bedwyr's quiet voice said beside me. 'They are seeing to Gwyn, and to the wounded.'

I looked behind me, and already the road was lost in the trees. I did not know even in which direction our wild gallop was taking us. Branches whipped past us, tearing at me. 'Let me go back!' I cried.

Bedwyr nodded to his friend, and the other let go of my bridle. I gathered up the reins and slowed my mare to a walk. The others did the same.

'Do not go back,' Bedwyr said. 'I beg you, my lady, come with me.'

I stopped my horse. She stood still, her sides heaving and her eyes rolling back at me, ears laid flat against her head. Around us was only the sound of the wind in the leaves, the song of birds. I took a deep breath and looked up through the branches at the obscured sky. 'Gwyn,' I said, and my voice was almost gone. 'You killed Gwyn. You killed him.'

Bedwyr said nothing.

'But he was not even fighting; he had thrown away his shield! You *killed* him!'

I pulled my mare's head around, ready to force her back in the direction we had come, and Bedwyr leaned over and caught my hand. I finally looked at him, and saw his face for the first time. I have seen men dying in agony, from sickness or from wounds, and they have the same white, tortured face, and the same puzzled eyes.

'My lady,' he whispered. 'I beg you. Do not go.'

I let out my breath, found that it was in a sob.

'Your head is bleeding,' Bedwyr said, and the mask of pain faded a little, leaving his features more his own. 'Here, bind it up.'

I put my hand to my head, found a spot of pain, took my hand away sticky with blood from Medraut's blow. I shook my head. 'Let us put more distance between us and them first,' I told Bedwyr. 'I will go with you.'

We reached Caer Gloeu that evening by following one of the old roads through the forest, which joined the Roman road a few miles from the port. There was a ship in the harbour, ready to leave for Less Britain, and Bedwyr had already paid passage money for eight persons and their horses. In fact, there were only six of us, for two of his men had died in the fight on the road.

We tried not to attract attention in the town. We had stopped by a stream around noon and washed off the blood that bespattered us. Fortunately I was wearing only a plain green gown and dark travelling cloak, and there was nothing to mark me out from any woman in the port town; Bedwyr and his men might have been any party of noblemen off to buy horses.

All my things had been lost, and now I truly owned nothing but what was on my back. Bedwyr's passage had been all he had been allowed to take into exile, and though his friends were somewhat better off, we would have to travel some distance after we arrived in Less Britain, and we had little money to spare. Because of this, we did not stay in the town, but on the ship. I had a cabin to myself, and the five men shared the one other room the ship offered to passengers.

The captain showed me the room and I thanked him for it, and was glad to sit for a while on the tiny bed. But after a time I rose, found the captain again, and asked for vellum and ink. He grumbled at this, but eventually produced the ink, a pen, and a bill of lading which he told me I could easily write over. I found a pumice stone and rubbed at the parchment, and finally, though I had pressed so hard that it seemed more fit for a sieve than for a letter, I sat down with it. I sharpened the pen, dipped it in the ink – and sat, staring at that sheet full of holes. What could I say? 'My dearest joy, Bedwyr has murdered Gwyn, and therefore I must go with him, for he is grieved to the heart, and because you might have to have him re-tried, for murder; and me re-tried, for seeking to avoid the sentence you passed'? But I had not meant to go with Bedwyr. How could I say that and have it believed? And Gwalchmai would read this letter, and there were no words I could say to him. Indeed, there were no words I could say for myself. I had thought that discovery, disgrace, exile from Camlann and separation from both the men I loved, were catastrophes almost beyond my power to endure. Now I saw that one can never say that one has seen the worst. Even the ability to express grief failed, and words seemed altogether shallow and meaningless in the face of this reality.

The ink in my pen was dry. I cleaned it, re-sharpened it, and dipped it in the ink again. It was of the greatest importance that Arthur should know the true story. This calamity was a thing Medraut had seized on gladly, and I could not doubt that he would use it to create the greatest ruin he could. I was bound to do all I could to prevent further disaster.

There was a hasty knock, the door opened, and Bedwyr came in. I set the pen down.

He stood with his hand on the latch of the door, staring at me, at my sheet of vellum. 'You are writing to Arthur?' he asked, in a hoarse, uncertain voice.

I nodded. 'I thought we could leave the letter with the port officials.'

'Yes.' He came away from the door, stopped, staring at me hungrily. 'Say ... say that I did not mean to kill Gwyn.'

I took up the pen and wrote the superscription: '*Guinivara Artorio Augusto Imperatori domino salutatem vellit.*' I stared at it a moment, then continued, reading out what I wrote. The sharp marks on the Latin writing looked colder and more remote as I went on.

'My dearest lord, I beg you to believe that I knew nothing of the ambush, and neither planned nor desired that rescue. The lord Bedwyr, however, knowing that there was enmity between myself and the cousin to whose protection you committed me, met us on the road and asked Medraut to deliver me up. He himself used no violence until the lord Medraut attacked him. The lord Gwyn,' – I crossed the name out and wrote 'Gwalchaved' – 'endeavoured to make peace, and was killed by a spear cast by Bedwyr...'

'It was an accident,' said Bedwyr, coming nearer.

I looked up, putting the pen aside again. 'You saw him

before you cast the spear. I know that you saw him.'

'No! That is ... my arm moved quicker than my thoughts. Can you understand that? My lady, you must. One must move quickly in battle: if one pauses to consider whether or not to kill a man, one will die in his stead. I looked up, I saw a man who had left himself unprotected, and I threw the spear. Even as I threw I thought, "That is Gwyn; he is trying to make peace", but I could not stop my hand, or deflect the spear which I had already put into motion. I knew what I was doing, but still, my arm did it. I could scarcely believe that it had happened. My lady, I would rather that I had died than he! My worth is nothing, it has been nothing since first I betrayed my lord.' He paused, caught his breath, then insisted, 'You must believe me, my lady. I could not endure it if you also should think me a murderer.'

'I believe you,' I said after a moment. 'But when the escort arrives back in Camlann, they will say that you attacked us on the road, that Gwyn threw away his shield, and that you killed him. It will not sound well.'

'I know.' He sat on the floor at my feet, picked up the letter and looked at it. I touched his shoulder and he turned, caught me, hid his face against my thigh, shaking.

He suffered yes, certainly, but the image of Gwyn's astonished face rose between us, and I sat cold and silent. After a little while I said, 'Arthur had hoped that Gwyn would grow into a man he could appoint as his successor.'

Bedwyr moved his head from side to side in pain.

'And if Gwalchmai believes the story which the escort tells, he will plead for justice against you with any king on earth.'

Bedwyr lifted his head. 'Macsen has still not agreed to return fugitives. We should be safe in Less Britain.'

'Safe! We will be safe! Why did you ever plan such a mad ambush?'

'I did not think it would come to blows. My friends had resolved to follow me, and I thought that your escort would be unwilling to fight its comrades, men accused of no crime. I thought they might be half eager to release you. I could not bear the thought of what you might suffer from your cousin. I thought that even Arthur would not object, once he understood what you faced in Ebrauc. He is never vindictive, even when much injured. And I would not have fought, even with Medraut – only he struck you.'

'A meaningless blow, such as a woman might have given her husband with a broom handle! No, no, I believe you; never fear. And I believe you did not mean to kill Gwyn. Only there was so much that he might have done and been. He might have changed the world. There was no one else like him. And to die, at fifteen, by accident ... by your hand...'

'He is well out of a bitter world.'

'Oh, doubtless he is; but the world now is bitterer yet. Very bitter. And your men fought my escort, and two of them are dead, with who knows how many of the escort. They were friends, comrades of many years, and they had barely a notion of why they were fighting!'

'I know. Once I led all of them. Gwynhwyfar, my life, do not thrust me deeper into my dishonour. I am nearly drowned in it already. I can scarcely endure myself, when I think of what I have meant to be, and have been, and then of what I am now – a traitor, false, perjured and murderous. Dear God, I had rather die than live so disfigured! But I fear damnation. I am afraid, afraid and in confusion. I cannot think. Nothing I have seen, or thought, or read; nothing I have hoped for or believed in; no philosophy or clarity is left to me, to heart or to mind. I am not myself. My lady, as you hope for salvation, be merciful to me! I did it for love of you, and if you turn against me all the world is drowned and empty.'

'Oh, dear heart,' I said, feeling something within me break, something too deep to overflow into tears, 'how can I turn against you? But I would rather we had both died before seeing this day, and what will come of it.'

He said nothing, only rose and put his arms around me, and I could not be cold to him still. For a little while we again inhabited a world confined to the two of us, where there was no past and no future. But afterwards we lay side by side in the dark, listening with open eyes to the creaking of the ship and the lapping of the waves, waiting for a morning endlessly deferred.

The next day I finished the letter to Arthur, sealed it carefully, and Bedwyr gave it to the port official, explaining that it was important information and must be sent directly to the Emperor or given only to one of the Emperor's known messengers. This request was not so unusual, for some of our agents had sent messages through Caer Gloeu before, and Bedwyr and I both knew the proper procedures.

While Bedwyr was off on this errand, the ship was checked over for sailing – the horses of our party tied tightly in their stalls, and the cargo of woollen and iron goods bound down. As soon as Bedwyr returned, the crew cast loose the moorings and the ship slipped out into the wide Saefern, starting down the river under a cloudy sky.

We followed the current of the Saefern through Mor Hafren, then made slow progress along the north coast of Dumnonia, working against unfavourable winds. I had never travelled by ship before, and was sick, which at least meant I was prevented from worrying. But when we reached the end of the Dumnonian peninsula and turned southwards the wind was behind us, and the ship ran smoothly. By the time we arrived at Bresta, in the north-west of Less Britain, I was beginning to believe that sea-travel was a reasonable proposition after all. And in spite of all that had happened, I was still excited when we caught sight of the coast of Gaul before us. In fact, it looked very much like the coast of Dumnonia, and had even been named after that part of Britain. But Bresta itself was a fine Roman town, with its lofty stone fortifications still intact, and a number of other ships moored in its harbour giving it a busy look.

We had intended to set out for Bedwyr's home as soon as we landed in Gaul, taking our horses out onto the south-east road and buying supplies along the way. But when our ship put in, and we disembarked onto the rain-soaked quay, we discovered that King Macsen had appointed harbour commissioners. This gave us a great deal of trouble. Macsen had been forced to rescind the high tax he had imposed on goods shipped to Britain, and was now apparently determined to lose nothing from the ordinary harbour dues – not for the flea on the cow's tail, as they say. Our ship's captain reported that he carried passengers, and accordingly two cold grey townsmen came up to us while our party was unloading the horses onto the dock, and demanded that we all come to the customs house. This was a Roman building, once very fine, but now half-ruined, and half-repaired in the British style. The conflict between the modes of building had made it uncomfortable: originally it must have had a Roman hypocaust for heating, but now had a hearth without the proper ventilation for one. It was filled with thick grey smoke from the damp wood fire, and filled also with confiscated British goods – sacks of tin ore, bundles of hides, wool and woollen cloths – piled nearly to the roof and threatening to collapse if one brushed against them, which it was hard to avoid doing. The two towns-men ushered us over to the fire, where they sat and kept us standing. They stared at us, peering through the smoke. One coughed, and the other asked Bedwyr, 'You are the leader of this party?'

Bedwyr nodded.

'You did not give your name to the captain of the ship you sailed in. You booked eight places; where are the other two?'

'They could not come.'

'What is your purpose in coming here?'

'I do not see,' Bedwyr said in his calm, level voice, 'why the purposes of private citizens coming into another province are of official concern.'

They blinked at him. The one who had spoken coughed and the one who had coughed said, 'We cannot have armed parties roving about wherever they please. We have bandits enough without importing more from Britain.'

'We are not bandits, but nobly-born Bretons.'

'He speaks like a Breton,' one of the officials conceded to the other. 'What is your purpose in coming here?'

We had no particular necessity to conceal our status. Arthur had written to King Macsen, informing him that Bedwyr had been exiled to Less Britain, though it was unlikely that the king had yet received the letter. Nonethe-less, because the fight on the road had probably changed our situation, Bedwyr had thought it best to come unof-ficially and to avoid the king's notice as much as possible. Thus Macsen could truthfully tell Arthur that he did not know our whereabouts, which might ease any tension which might develop if another trial were demanded. Moreover, Bedwyr had not forgotten that Macsen had once attempted to persuade him to join his own warband, and been angry when Bedwyr refused. 'I do not think he would be angry enough to force us to return to Britain,' he had told me, 'but he might put obstacles betweēn us and my home.'

Now Bedwyr tapped his sword's hilt idly, studying the two officials. 'I do not see that you have any right to question us so,' he said, at last, 'but I will tell you that I hope to return to my family's estates, and there settle peacefully. I trust that, if this does not violate any of your laws or your orders, you will permit us to continue our journey?'

One of the officials whispered to the other. I drew Bedwyr aside, and also whispered. 'If they press us, will you tell them who we are?'

He hesitated before answering. 'Macsen will discover soon that I am in Less Britain, and may send to me when he does. If I am found to have lied it will be the worse for us; I must tell the truth. But they have no right to act in this way, as though we were crossing the frontier into some land outside the Empire.'

One of the officials coughed again. 'You may be criminals,' he said. 'Tell us your names and your purpose in coming here.'

The other official pulled out a wax tablet and a stylus and sat, smug and confident, ready to take the information down.

Bedwyr sighed, took the letter Arthur had given him from his belt. It stated simply his name, the sentence, and a request that the reader render any assistance necessary in finding Bedwyr a ship and means of obeying the sentence. He gave the letter to the officials. They stared at the dragon on the seal, started, then broke the seal and unrolled it, holding it near the smoky fire so as to be able to read it in the dim light. Murmurs of astonishment; they glanced up at Bedwyr, at the rest of us, read on. They whispered together, and one rose and rapidly left the customs house.

'Noble lord,' said the other, 'your name is well known here. For what crime did Arthur of Britain exile his warleader?'

'For defaming the imperial majesty. I trust that we may go now?'

'Ah. Ah.' Coughing. 'Noble lord, perhaps you should stay here for the night. I know that Lord Hywel, lord of this city, would welcome a guest as famous as yourself.'

'I thank you, but I wish to comply with the sentence my lord the Emperor has decreed for me, and return to the estates of my family.'

'But you have already complied with that sentence, noble lord. See,' he tapped the letter. 'This says that you are exiled to the province of Less Britain: it does not specify a city.'

'Again, I thank you, but I have no wish to lengthen my journey. I feel my disgrace too keenly to take pleasure in the hospitality even of my countrymen.'

More coughing. 'Noble lord, the King will be offended if you ride south without first visiting his court and explaining yourself to him.'

Bedwyr was silent a moment, then bowed slightly. 'So be it. I would not wish to offend the King.'

Presently the other official returned, bringing with him some nine warriors and a plump middle-aged nobleman in a scarlet cloak covered with gold embroidery, whom the official welcomed, with a bow, as 'Lord Hywel'.

'Most noble lord,' this man said to Bedwyr, 'I am most honoured that you should come here, though, of course, deeely grieved that it should be on such an occasion as exile. Surely, it is an undeserved ruin, a tyrant's caprice. I beg you, accept my hospitality.'

Confronted by Hywel's warriors we were plainly to be either guests or prisoners, so we gave way as graciously as we could, collected our horses and luggage from the quay, and followed Hywel up through the town to the buildings he used to house his warband and himself. Hywel's own house was winged by the others, Roman-built, well-preserved and luxuriously furnished – finer, in fact, than anything at Camlann. Here our horses were taken from us, while servants carried away our luggage, and Hywel directed other servants to prepare the best guest room for Bedwyr. He then asked politely, 'And whose wife is the lady?'

At this there was an awkward silence, and Hywel looked at me sharply. Before I must have impressed him as a lady, and therefore a wife, but now I could see him taking into account my rough travelling gown and reconsidering. I realized that the tale would have to come out. We were plainly to be sent to King Macsen, so there was nothing more to hope for from concealment. Probably some rumour had reached Hywel already, and I could not disguise my northern British accent, which would set me apart from the others. For that matter, I was sure I could not submit to being treated like some sluttish serving maid.

'Lord Hywel,' I began, choosing my words at the cost of some pain to myself, 'I am not the wife of any of these men. Lord Bedwyr has graciously chosen to give me his protection, in consideration that it was through each other that we each lost our position. Since Bedwyr suffers exile because of the just anger of my husband, the Emperor, I thought it unfitting to escape more easily than he, and so have accepted his protection and his exile. If I also am welcome to your hospitality, I thank you. If not, I ask that you give me some trustworthy escort back to Britain.'

Hywel gaped at me, looked quickly at Bedwyr, was satisfied by his expression that I was not joking. He then looked thoughtful. The fact that he was thoughtful rather than shocked and amazed made me guess that I had been right, that he had heard the rumours but perhaps discounted them.

'Most, um, gracious Lady Gwynhwyfar,' he said, 'it is a pleasure, always, to offer hospitality to a beautiful woman: be welcome, lady. Um . . .' He glanced again at Bedwyr.

I quickly forestalled his next question by responding, 'I am grateful for your hospitality, Lord Hywel. And I would also be grateful if you could give me the use of some private room where I could rest. We have travelled very rough these past days, and I am fatigued.' That would ensure that he did not simply send me to Bedwyr's room. Unfaithful I might be, but I would not give the gossipmongers of Less Britain more material to cackle over, nor parade evidence of my shame about a foreign land.

We were kept at Hywel's fortress for two weeks before being given an escort to Macsen's court, and I grew to know Bresta and dislike it. My first impression of it as a rich and busy town proved false. The port was fairly busy, but the town, like most of the towns in Britain, was more than half empty, falling into decay within its splendid ramparts. It was, nonetheless, the chief city of the northwestern part of Less Britain, the region called Dumnonia after the part of Britain which it resembled. Most of the people were Armorican – that is, descended from those who had inhabited Less Britain before it was colonized from Britain. They spoke a peculiar dialect of Latin among themselves which I found totally unintelligible. Hywel and his warband, with most of the merchants and innkeepers, were within one or two generations of being British – Hywel himself had left Cawel in Gueid Guith in southern Britain when he was twelve, as he told me many times. He spent a great deal of time talking to me and to Bedwyr, generally with several of his warriors about him, though he was too polite to tell us in so many words that he was keeping us under surveillance. He always treated me especially with great courtesy, at least to my face. I knew, however, that he and the rest of the fortress all viewed me as Bedwyr's stolen woman, a show thing, a fine horse captured by a daring raider which they were eager to put through its paces and admire. They made jokes at Arthur's expense, some of the warriors actually laughing at these in my presence. There was nothing I could do about it. That was almost worse than the shame: I was useless and helpless. I had been accustomed to responsibility and authority, and I had become a piece of Bedwyr's luggage, the trophy of a battle. Bedwyr, of course, liked this no more than I did, and for him I was willing to endure a great deal. I told myself that things would have been no better in Britain; that with Menw they might have been considerably worse. Nonetheless, I grew to loathe Hywel, his fortress, his city and his kingdom, and I was even glad when he sent us off to Macsen.

We rode first north-east from Bresta: Bedwyr, his four followers, myself, and ten of Hywel's warriors. We followed the Elorn river towards the hills, then crossed it at Llandernoch and turned south towards Macsen's capital Car Aës. The Bretons all say 'Car' for 'Caer': they speak British in the back of their throats, so that it sounds strange, almost another language. Bedwyr's accent had been softened by years in Britain, and Hywel's and his men's were also gentler, but when we came to the older settlements of the interior the speech grew stranger. Less Britain is in fact several lands and several peoples. The earliest British colonies were made near the end of the Empire of the Romans, in the interior, carved out of the great forests

722

which the original inhabitants had shunned. The coasts were only colonized from Britain later: Hywel's province of Dumnonia, and its neighbour Tregor, were comparatively new. Cernw, the central region, where Macsen ruled directly, was the oldest and strangest part. Bedwyr's family – it was not precisely a clan, for clans are less important among the Bretons – lived further east, near the city called Gwened in the province of Broerec. Macsen did not have uncontested authority so far east, for the eastern parts of Less Britain had partially submitted to a Saxon tribe called the Franks. Yet Macsen's authority was felt everywhere. He claimed his descent from the first lord of Less Britain, Conan Meriadec, and could demand obedience from whomever he pleased. We arrived at his court in the last week of July.

Hywel had, of course, informed his overlord of our arrival, and the King had also by then received Arthur's letter regarding Bedwyr's exile. Macsen himself came down to the gates of Car Aës to greet us – like Hywel, and like most of the Breton nobles, he had settled in a Roman town rather than a hill-fort. He treated us with greater courtesy than our present status merited, and rode with us through the town to his house, pointing out the sights to us. He was a man some few years older than Arthur, with a thin, hard face, lined with bitterness. The thing I chiefly noticed about him was his mouth, which had thick wet lips and strong white teeth that glinted through his heavy black beard. Sometimes he used to bite his upper lip and stare at someone or something with his cold black eyes, and I soon learned to recognize this as a sign of danger. But he was evidently doing his best to be charming.

Macsen's houses were in the centre of the town, the old Roman prefecture and public buildings, and they were in very good condition. He had us shown to very fine rooms, much finer than Hywel's, but he had me shown to the same room as Bedwyr, and the servants would not listen to my protests. It was a room very much in the Roman style, with a tiled floor, heavy, crimson-dyed hangings, and deep rugs by the bed, which was the only piece of furniture in the room. I would a thousand times rather have had a plain British room, clean and whitewashed, with a desk and tables and a case for books: this crimson luxury oppressed my spirits.

I argued with the servants, and Bedwyr stood by the wall watching me. He wanted me to stay, I knew, though he did not ask it. He was unhappy alone. I was as well, for that matter, yet still I feared to stay. I felt that I could not allow myself to be reduced to nothing, to an appendage, to a tool to use against Arthur. But the servants were sullen and insistent, and I had no authority.

Another servant arrived when I was beginning to despair, and requested Bedwyr to come immediately to speak with King Macsen. He hesitated, looking at me; then sighed and left. I sat down on the bed, exhausted, and the servants began showing me the things that Macsen had ordered brought there for my use, holding up silks and jewellery as though they expected me to clap my hands and squeal like a girl at the sight of such fine things. The finest piece was a gown they wished me to wear to a feast that night, 'a gift from the King'. It was of purple silk, heavy with gold. I refused to touch it. The servants would not listen to my refusal until I vowed to wear instead my plain green travelling dress, which was in none the better condition for having been worn for days on end along dusty roads. At this they sulkily left the room and went off to consult Macsen's steward, leaving me in a rage. I would not appear at Macsen's feast dressed as an Emperor's lawful wife, not to advertise my husband's disgrace and give Macsen and his followers a chance to gloat over Arthur's pain.

Bedwyr returned exhausted from his interview with the King, and sat down heavily on the bed. He noticed the gown, which the servants had left draped over the bedstead in the hope that I would change my mind, and gave me an inquiring look. I explained, with some vehemence.

'Yes,' he said, frowning. 'He wishes to make a display of us. To use us.'

My useless anger departed. The position was too hopeless and confined for it; it would merely break the heart, and achieve nothing. I came over and sat down beside the bed, near Bedwyr's feet. 'What did he say?' I asked quietly.

Bedwyr shrugged, rubbed his face. 'First ... first he asked for the details of our sentences, and of the fight on the road – he had heard of it. When I hesitated to tell him of the last, he insisted that, if I wished for his protection, I was bound to speak to him plainly. At this I was honest with him. Then he questioned me closely as to whether I had indeed plotted against my lord Arthur, which I denied on oath, and I think this displeased him. Then . . . then he showed me a letter from Arthur, which he had received a few days ago.'

I looked up silently, afraid, and he nodded.

'It demands that he return us both to Britain. I am to be tried for attacking the Emperor's warriors upon the imperial roads, and for murdering one Gwalchaved ap Gwalchmai, of the royal clan. And you are to be tried for conspiracy and evasion of your sentence. The letter used very strong terms, my heart. It insisted that Macsen return us or he would be considered to have broken all his oaths and treaties of allegiance and begun a rebellion.'

'Oh, Heavenly God,' I whispered. It was worse than we had expected.

Bedwyr nodded. 'Yes. It was threat of war. I . . . was deeply troubled by this letter. When Macsen saw that I had finished reading it, he chewed on his lip for a time, and watched me, then said, "You see what your lord commands me to do. Shall I obey him, or not?" And I replied, "You are King; it is your choice." And he smiled and said, "But it is you who will die if I send you back, since by your own account you are guilty: the matter concerns you rather nearly. And the Lady Gwynhwyfar may escape with some lighter penalty, if your tale is true and she is indeed innocent of conspiracy, but even so her punishment will be severe." And he talked of punishments for a time, and of ways in which we might be executed. When I said nothing, he folded the letter and put it away again. Then he took up the same tale I had refused to hear the year before last, when I came here as Arthur's emissary. First he said much concerning Less Britain, how it should be a separate nation, and no part of the Empire; then he said that he owed no obedience to Arthur, but had previously been forced to yield to the threats and demands of a tyrant. Then he said that I, as a Breton, and as a man wronged by the Emperor, ought to agree with him. To this he added much pointed flattery of how my quality as a warleader was well known, and how Arthur owed much to me, and ought to have at least given me wealth and lands when he dismissed me – as if any other king in the West would not have had me killed for such treachery! And then he recalled to me that he had before offered me a position as his warleader, and said that now he renewed the offer, if I would aid him in rebellion against Arthur: if not, he would send us back. "You know the Emperor's methods of fighting, his allies, his numbers and his strategies," he told me, "and my warband and the people know that you know them. They have already begun to make songs about you, how you stole the Emperor's wife, and took her away with you to your own homeland. If you are warleader, the people will follow me readily into war."' Bedwyr reported this speech in a tone of great bitterness, then caught the stump of his shield hand with his good hand and stared fixedly at the purple gown. 'What could I say?' he asked in a very low voice, after a long silence. 'Macsen has been awaiting his chance for rebellion since first he acceded to the kingship, for he has always hated Arthur. And he knows that I would be valuable to him. If I refuse, he is more likely to try us and kill us himself than to send us back to Arthur. Arthur might well spare you, and that would certainly be of less use to Macsen than killing you to impress his own people.'

'You cannot betray Arthur,' I said.

'I have already betrayed him. Betrayed his trust and my position, dishonoured him before his subjects, and murdered his followers. Does it matter if I add armed rebellion to my crimes?'

'Of course! How can you mean to lead an army against the men whom you yourself have led?'

'Less Britain has never been properly a part of the Empire. After a few battles Arthur might well make a new treaty with Macsen and withdraw. And the Family is finer than any force Macsen can raise, without Arthur's drawing on the forces of all the kings of Britain. Perhaps a foreign war would be useful to Arthur. Perhaps it would heal the Family. And if not, what does it matter? We are doomed as it is.'

I jumped up and caught Bedwyr's shoulders, forcing him to look at me directly. 'You did not tell Macsen that you would lead his army?'

Reluctantly, he shook his head. 'I told him that I would

consider it. He gave me until tomorrow morning to decide.'

'Until tomorrow morning.' I let him go and stepped back, thinking hard. 'We might escape tonight.'

Bedwyr shook his head impatiently. 'We could not. We are in the heart of Macsen's fortress, and have only as much liberty as Macsen allows us. And if we could escape, what then? Are we to run off and live among the Franks or the Saxons, or take to herding pigs, like the heroes of old wives' tales?'

'You cannot mean to fight, in cold blood, against Arthur and the Family.'

'I have already fought against Arthur and the Family! My dearest lady, we will both suffer if I refuse.'

'We have suffered already, and we are suffering, and we will suffer much more, whether you accept or whether you refuse; why, how, can you dream of adding yet more guilt to our suffering?'

Bedwyr stood, went to the bedstead and touched the glowing silk of the gown. 'We are damned upon the Earth already,' he said in a low voice. 'Must we hurry to be damned in Hell?'

'God is merciful,' I said, after a moment's silence. 'If we die because we would not break faith or betray our country and our lord, but give up our lives in sincere repentance, perhaps God will pardon us. But we know that traitors are damned to the lowest Hell.'

'If God were merciful,' Bedwyr returned, without looking away from the purple, 'then none of this could have happened. God is just. In justice I at least am damned, for I have betrayed my lord and all that I believed in. I think that in damnation one has destroyed the image of God within one's soul. Perhaps, perhaps if I live I can repair that a little. But in death the desolation would become fixed and everlasting. Perhaps it becomes impossible even to desire what is good, any more – though perhaps that can happen even to those living upon the earth. But eternal damnation... My lady, we are set about with crimes. If I accept Macsen's offer, that is a crime. But if we allow him to return us to Britain Macsen will still rebel, on some other occasion, and perhaps when Arthur is unprepared. And if we are tried again Medraut will have another opportunity to work at dividing the Family. So to return may give opportunity for more crimes than remaining here. And if we remain here and kill ourselves, that is also a crime. There is no escape. God is punishing us, and has given us over to our sins. Why not, then, take the easiest course, and live longer? At least then I can remain true to you, if to no other.'

I would have argued with him. I would have tried to talk him out of that extreme despair and convince him that he must refuse Macsen's offer, but at that moment two more of Macsen's servants entered.

'Lady,' said one, nervously, aware at least that the air was tense and that she interrupted, 'lady, have you decided to accept the King's gift, which he so generously made you?'

I looked at Bedwyr, who still stood fingering the gown, but he did not look back. If we were ruined and damned, I supposed a purple gown would make little difference to it. But I was not able, like Bedwyr, to view all the world as an expression of abstracts, so that one act of treachery must change my nature. I knew myself a criminal and dishonoured, but yet I could not bear to disgrace myself or my husband further, or take on one scruple of an ounce more of dishonour than I must.

'Give the King my apologies,' I said to the servant. 'The imperial purple is too noble a colour for me now, and it would not be fitting for me to wear it. Besides, it clashes with my hair.'

The servant sighed, nodded, picked up the gown, draping it over her arm. 'It is ungracious, lady, to reject a gift so generously given by so great a king. But, so that you will not shame him at the feast, the King has given you another gown.' She beckoned, and the other serving girl came into the room, carrying a blue-green gown and a great rope of gold strung with amber and blue enamel. I thanked them for this with the utmost courtesy, and asked them to convey my thanks to the King. When they were gone I looked again at Bedwyr, and could not endure the thought of being harsh to him in his despair. Since words would be no use I went over and put my arms about him, comforting him, holding him as a mother might hold an injured child.

Nine

Since Macsen had invited both Bedwyr and myself to the feast that night, I had assumed that it was an informal occasion, where men and women might eat together. But when I walked in holding Bedwyr's arm, I discovered that I was the only woman there. I stopped on the threshold, feeling my face grow hot under the stares of all the men. It was not the whole of Macsen's warband, for living in a Roman town he had no proper Feast Hall and could not accommodate them all – but it was enough of the band for their stares to be heavy. For a moment I considered turning around and walking out again. Then I forgot that, and forgot the stares, for sitting next to Macsen on the dais was Cei.

The entrance to the Roman state room which Macsen used as his Hall was behind the dais, so Cei had to twist about to see what everyone else was staring at. When he did turn his face went nearly as red as his beard and he jumped to his feet.

'What is this?' Cei demanded angrily of Macsen. 'You said when I gave you the letter that they were not in your fortress!'

'And they were not. They arrived this afternoon. I had them brought here.' Macsen returned smoothly. 'Sit down, Lord Cei.' And he looked at Cei in a considering fashion, biting his upper lip.

Cei remained standing. 'Do you intend to grant them sanctuary? They should be your prisoners, not your guests!'

'Perhaps they are. You will hear of that tomorrow, Lord Cei.'

'I am bound by my lord's commands,' Cei said sharply, 'and it would not be fitting for me to eat and drink with my lord's enemies.'

'I am lord here, not you,' Macsen said, more sharply now. 'Either remain here as my guest or leave the feast, but, as for these, they will stay.'

I let go of Bedwyr's arm and came over as Cei hesitated,

fuming. 'Cei,' I said, 'I did not know you were here, but it makes my heart sing to see you. If my lord's orders to you permit it, stay, and tell me what has happened at Camlann, for I am almost sick with longing to hear of it. But if you cannot stay ... Lord Macsen, I am willing to leave, and would sooner do so than cause you to take up, from your courtesy, such a dishonour as sending a guest and an emissary away from your feast.'

Macsen bit his lip and glared at me, for, put as I had just put it, to send Cei away would be a serious breach of hospitality. But Cei hunched his shoulders and gazed at me in confusion.

'My lady,' he began, then, in disgust, 'ach, to Yffern with it, I mean Lady Gwynhwyfar!' But he did not continue. I took his hand and clasped it. I was surprised at how glad I was to see his face; I felt as though some clinging layer of dust were washed away, as though I could be myself again. Cei still looked confused, but almost involuntarily caught my hand and clasped it with both of his. 'Well, then, my lady,' he said, more quietly. 'You have been my lady too many years for me to use another style of talking now, I suppose. And despite it all, we have been friends, you and Bedwyr and I. Perhaps I should walk out and let men say what they will of King Macsen's hospitality – but if he keeps faith, we'll travel together tomorrow on our journey back to Camlann.'

'And I would enjoy the journey, in such company,' I returned.

Cei smiled and helped me to a seat on his right – not the seat which Macsen had meant to give me – and Bedwyr sat down beside me at my right. He did not greet Cei, only stared at the table, and Cei said no word to him. But they had known each other better perhaps than I knew either of them; they had fought innumerable battles, saved each other's lives, camped side by side on numberless campaigns. That would make it more difficult to find anything to say now.

Cei looked at me closely as the meal began. 'Well, my lady,' he said, 'when you came in, I thought you looked the fairest queen since Elena the mother of Constantine, but now I see that you are pale. Have you been ill?'

'No, it is only the travelling, and the grief. But tell me,

how are things in Camlann? How is my lord Arthur? And Gwalchmai – I have been sick, thinking of him.'

Cei gave me a very odd look. Beyond him, Macsen glowered. His showpiece was not behaving itself as he would have wished. Probably he had hoped for a quarrel, and hoped that Cei would storm out, leaving Bedwyr and me to impress his men.

'You believe that I conspired with Bedwyr for my escape?' I asked, guessing the reason for the look. 'Cei, I swear to you I did not; I knew nothing about it until Bedwyr's party met us on the road.'

'And she only came with me,' Bedwyr added, in a low, hoarse, voice, 'because she knew that I was desperate with grief through what I had done.'

Cei did look at him, at that, and Bedwyr held his eyes for a moment, then looked away, out over the Hall. He had gone very pale, the skin around his eyes stiff from tension.

Cei's look of anger gave way to one of uncertainty. 'How did you come to kill Gwyn?' he asked Bedwyr, also speaking in an undertone.

Bedwyr shook his head, as though he were insisting on something he had said many times before. 'I killed him as one kills in battle, the hand moving more quickly than the mind that should guide it. I had no time to think.'

Cei gave a little whistle through his teeth. 'That was a black hour, cousin, when you planned to rescue the Empress, and a blacker one when you let fly the spear against your fellows. But I believe you. Indeed, I never thought that you would have killed our Gwyn, had you had murder on your mind. Not when that golden-tongued offspring of a fox and a devil, Medraut, was among your opponents.'

'But didn't you see my letter?' I asked, and, when Cei looked blank, added, 'The one we left at Caer Gloeu.'

Cei shook his head. 'We sent to Caer Gloeu when the news first came, to see whether you were still there and to find what ship you had sailed on, so we could be sure to follow you. But there was no letter there. Perhaps it was lost, or misplaced by the men you left it with.'

'Perhaps,' I said, but I was wondering whom Arthur had sent to Caer Gloeu. If not Medraut himself, then surely one of Medraut's friends, someone who could have taken the letter from the port officials and destroyed it privately.

I quickly told Cei what I had said in the letter, Bedwyr occasionally adding two or three words in a barely audible voice. When I had finished, Cei nodded.

'A grief to hear,' was his comment. 'One of your escort insisted that you had not gone willingly, and that you had offered to tell Bedwyr that you would not go, but we did not know what to believe. Now it seems that it is all Fortune's wheel turning against us, and even innocent intentions are turned towards ruin.'

'I pray that our Empire may yet escape it,' I replied quietly. 'But I beg you, tell me what has happened in Camlann!'

Cei looked at me with an expression I did not recognize at first, I had seen it on his face so rarely: pity. 'Nothing good, my lady. Indeed, there has been little enough that is good at Camlann since that witch's bastard came there.'

I said nothing, and eventually Cei went on, 'Very well then. Medraut and the rest of your escort returned to Camlann six days after they left it, and returned in sad condition, too. They had two men carried in stretchers slung between two horses and three wrapped in blankets and slung over other horses – and one of these horses was that sweet roan mare which Gwalchmai gave Gwyn. They rode up to the Hall without looking either to the right or to the left, and there they stopped. I happened to be sitting outside the Hall, enjoying the sunlight, but when I saw them coming I stood up and stared at them like any peasant staring at a fair. So Medraut dismounted before me and told me, "Bedwyr has stolen Gwynhwyfar. Where is the Emperor?" So I called for servants to come see to the wounded, and fetch Gruffydd the surgeon, and then went into the Hall with Medraut, for I knew that my lord would be there. Sure enough, he and Gwalchmai were sitting at the high table, talking politics, but they stopped and looked troubled when they saw Medraut come in.

'Medraut, with Rhuawn and all the others who could walk, went straight up the Hall, not hurrying at all, and then Medraut took his time in bowing to Arthur. "Why are you here?" Arthur asked him. "One cannot ride to Ebrauc and back within a week." "My lord," says Medraut, very cool and pretending he's trying not to give way to anger,

"Bedwyr ap Brendan and his friends attacked us on the road from Caer Ceri to Linnuis, and they have stolen away the Lady Gwynhwyfar." And Arthur just stared at him, and frowned. After a moment, Gwalchmai says to the Emperor, "My lord, if this is true, unless there has been bloodshed it is not a crime. You told the lady to return to her family but she has chosen exile, a more severe punishment. And Bedwyr has obeyed his sentence. But if there has been bloodshed we can claim the just blood-price and end it there." Arthur looked away and hid his face in his hand a moment. I think he was stunned by it, as I was. And I did not like the sound of it, for I knew that men had been killed, and even if they had not been, an Emperor cannot afford to have his wife living with another man in a foreign land. "She should enter some convent," says the Emperor. "She might prefer that to her family, my lord," Gwalchmai says, and Arthur nods, looking as tired as I've ever seen him, and I've seen him after all his great battles, in the midst of campaigns that last years and near kill a man with weariness. Then Gwalchmai turned and looked at the others and said, "But where is my son?" And Medraut says, "He is outside." And Gwalchmai smiled, God help him, and got up and began to walk out to see his son. I meant to stop him, but I was uncertain myself what Medraut mean, for Gwyn might have been one of the wounded. So Gwalchmai went out, and Arthur also, and Medraut and the rest. When we came out of the Hall we found the servants and Gruffydd looking at the wounded, and Arthur stops, and looks at Medraut, and says, "There was bloodshed, then." And Medraut bows again, to hide the fact that he's smiling (but I saw the smile first) and he says, "One killed and two wounded of our party, and two killed of Bedwyr's." And Gwalchmai looks around, and looks at the bodies wrapped in blankets, and sees his son's horse. And then he looks at that bastard Medraut and says, in a strange voice, "Where is my son?" And Medraut goes to the roan mare and cuts the ropes that tied the body to her back. And then the body falls onto the ground, and part of the blanket falls aside, and there is Gwyn, dead. And Medraut says, "There." And Gwalchmai stares a moment, and then he give this long, dreadful wail, and goes over to the body, and pulls off the rest of the blanket. And he puts one hand over the wound in the boy's chest, and the other under his shoulders, as though he were trying to help him stand up; but he stops like that, and kneels there, looking at him, and makes no further sound. So Medraut says, "He tried to make peace with Bedwyr when we were attacked. He threw aside his shield and called Bedwyr's name, and Bedwyr looked up, saw him, and put a spear through him." And he goes on to say that you, my lady, rode off with the others. Arthur looks at the other men, and they all agree to this, though one insists that you went unwillingly. But they were all angry. So Arthur asks who else is dead, and hears the names of those who rode off with you; and then he asks Gruffydd how the wounded are, and he tells him. Then he tells some of the servants to take away the bodies and wash them and prepare them for burial. And he goes over to Gwalchmai, and puts one hand on his shoulder, and Gwalchmai looks up at him, looking like a creature from the dark Other-world. And Arthur says, "We must make arrangements to bury him," and calls the servants to take the body. And Gwalchmai says nothing, and lets them take it. Then he gets up, pulls his hood over his face and walks away without saying anything or looking at anyone, and no one wished to say anything to him.

'Well, Arthur had the wounded seen to, and they said Mass for the dead the next morning. Gwalchmai stood through the service without saying a word, and watched the burial with a face like a statue in a church. That afternoon he led the roan mare out of the stable, took her to the slaughter house and killed her. Then he went through our house, found all of Gwyn's things, and took them out to burn them. I came in as he was doing this; I had just been told about the mare. "What do you imagine you're doing?" I asked. "I do not want these things to remind me," he said, without looking round, "And I could not endure that another should use them." My lady, I cannot say what it meant to me; I was sickened by looking at him. It was the same for me when I saw poor Agravain before he died. One should not have to see such a thing done to a friend.

'That evening they had the funeral feast in the Hall. Gwalchmai came in late, walked up to the high table but did not sit down. Instead, he draws his sword and sets it down before Arthur, with the hilt towards his hand, and he himself goes down on both knees and bows his head. And Arthur says, "what do you wish?" At once Gwalchmai says, "Justice, my lord." Arthur says, "I will write to Macsen of Less Britain concerning Bedwyr. Will you agree to a blood-price?" But Gwalchmai says, "I once swore, in this very Hall, that I would go to the ends of the earth and spare no life in the world and accept no blood-price, if my son were murdered by treachery. And I will stand by that oath." Then Arthur looks very grim, but says, "I will write to Macsen." "Do, my lord," Gwalchmai says back, "but do not write to him as you have written before, or Macsen will pretend he knows nothing of any criminals, or say that we have not agreed to a repatriation treaty, and he will do nothing."' (And Cei glanced at Macsen who was now listening enthralled, like the rest of the high table.) '"My lord," he says, "you must promise him war, if he does not give justice." Arthur says nothing to this. He was not eager for war, and I think he understood, lady, how it must have come about; he never believed Bedwyr meant to kill Gwyn. And he was never one to desire the blood of any who had ever done him service. But Gwalchmai remained kneeling and said, "My lord, for seventeen years I have fought for you, the full half of my life. In your service I have endured wounds and hardship, I have journeyed from one end of Britain to the other, crossed the seas, exiled myself from my own clan while I still had one. Never have I asked for any greater gift than that service in itself. And now I will not even demand it of you, but I will beg, like any suppliant, that you will give me justice against the murderer of my son." Then Arthur said, "It will probably mean war. I will give you letters and status as an emissary: go to Less Britain yourself, and ask Bedwyr for justice. I do not think he will refuse to fight you, or prevail against you." But Gwalchmai said, "I have not fought for the Empire and yourself all these years to wish for some private vengeance. No, my lord, let all the world see that you give me justice against this criminal, justice and the law." Then Arthur sighed and put out his hand, and took the hilt of Gwalchmai's sword. "You claim no more than is your due. You will have your justice, if we must devastate all Less Britain to obtain it."'

Cei stopped and took a deep drink of Macsen's wine.

'So,' said Macsen. 'It is Gwalchmai ap Lot who has stirred up this anger against me, on this private quarrel of his.'

'The Emperor is asking nothing more than due justice from one of his subject kings, who is bound by oath to render it,' Cei returned at once.

'But this Gwalchmai ap Lot is not even British, not from any part of the Empire. He is an Irish wolf, howling for vengeance.' Macsen spoke loudly, wanting his followers to hear him.

Cei slammed his glass down, glaring. 'Gwalchmai is a member of the royal clan, the Emperor's kinsman, and one of his finest and most loyal warriors! What king could ignore so just a plea, from such a servant? Certainly not my lord Arthur – as you will learn to your cost it you try to withhold what Arthur has demanded.'

'Which amounts to the life of this man, Bedwyr ap Brendan,' Macsen said. He looked at Cei for another long moment, and Cei looked uneasy and embarrassed. Macsen then looked beyond Cei to Bedwyr, but Bedwyr sat staring at his plate and said nothing.

'But what was the state of things when you left?' I asked Cei, to change the subject. I did not want to see the warrior involved in a quarrel here in Less Britain. Cei was an unusual choice for an emissary because he would gladly quarrel with anyone hostile to Arthur or to the Empire. Presumably Arthur had sent him to intimidate Macsen, and to put the ultimatum in the plainest terms.

Cei shrugged. 'Much the same. Arthur deals with the business of the Empire, the Family mutters and sharpens its swords, and Gwalchmai sits in the house and broods, or rides his horse half-way to Baddon for a day's exercise. Our servant Rhys and myself are the only ones who dare to talk to him, but he says little enough to us. He once spoke with Medraut for hours, but what they said no one knows.' Cei paused, glanced at Macsen again, and added, 'Medraut is as he usually is' – an uncustomary and rather late attempt at discretion.

'A very pretty report,' said Macsen sardonically. 'And that is enough of Camlann and intended vengeance for tonight. Come, let us have something more lively!' and he clapped his hands to summon his bards to sing for him.

Presently some of his men began a sword-dance.

Cei left the feast early, and Bedwyr requested leave to go shortly after Cei. I went back with him to our room, but he wished to speak neither of Cei's news nor of Macsen's offer, but only wished to hold me, and after lie still on the bed, awake and motionless, like a man dying of a fever.

The next morning I asked him what answer he would give to Macsen.

'None,' he replied.

'None? But he said that you must reply.'

'My lady, I have been trying to make up my mind to refuse his offer. Life is too dearly bought by treachery, especially after one has so injured one's friends. But I cannot simply refuse, I cannot. To stand trial by those I have injured, to see you punished – perhaps flogged, or even killed – to be so broken before my friends and before men I have commanded – I cannot do it. But how can I accept Macsen's offer, and commit yet further crimes against my comrades and my own lord? No, I will return no answer, and let Macsen choose for himself. In all probability he will choose to send us back with Cei, and that will be the end of it, without my choosing.'

However, that was precisely what Macsen did not do. He summoned Bedwyr that morning and asked him what he had decided, and Bedwyr told him that he could not decide. So, after a time, he sent Bedwyr back, summoned Cei and commanded him to leave Less Britain as soon as possible, and to tell Arthur that he did not acknowledge Arthur's Empire over him, and would not accept Arthur's dictates respecting a man who was born his subject and not Arthur's. I only learned of this afterwards, or I would have written Arthur another letter for Cei to take with him to Camlann.

Macsen said nothing to us that day or the next, and we did not see him during all this time. We were closely kept, not allowed even to leave our room. I bribed one of the serving girls to find us some books, which helped to pass the time, but there is a limit to how much time one can spend reading.

On the third day after Cei left, Macsen again asked us to a feast. He seated Bedwyr on his right and me beside Bedwyr, and spoke graciously and casually about unimportant things, as though nothing had happened. Later in the evening he began to speak of Arthur's prospective invasion, but with his own warleader – a dour, thin man with prematurely grey hair – and not with Bedwyr. It was only when the meal was done and we were sitting drinking Macsen's excellent wine while one of Macsen's bards sang, that Macsen turned to Bedwyr and asked him about the subject he had just discussed with his warleader. 'What do you think?' he asked. 'Should we barricade the harbours?'

'Ach, it's no use barricading the harbours,' the warleader Lenleawc insisted. 'There are beaches enough, if he uses curraghs, and we cannot patrol the whole coast.'

'But if he uses small curraghs and beaches them he will have to make more trips to bring the army over,' replied Macsen, 'And then we would have warning and more time to move.'

'He will not bring a peasant army,' said Bedwyr.

'Why not?'

Bedwyr realized what he was saying, and hesitated.

'Come, this is not secret information! If you are as opposed to our war for independence as that, as disloyal to your own land as to scruple to give information at your host's table – if so, you should ride back to Camlann tomorrow.'

'Arthur will probably attack during the harvest time,' Bedwyr said, after another moment's silence. 'You will have difficulty in raising your own army at that time, and Arthur's advantage in trained warriors will be more effective. He will probably take a force of picked men, not more than a thousand in number, and strike directly at your fortress here, hoping to end the war quickly.

I stared at Bedwyr angrily, and Macsen noticed this, smiling to himself, but ignored me and put another question to Bedwyr. Bedwyr's reluctance to speak faded slowly as he became engrossed in Arthur's strategies, and I sat silent at his side, listening, and grew colder and colder at heart.

Macsen continued to consult Bedwyr in the days that followed, and the amount that Bedwyr yielded to him grew steadily greater. He knew now that his position was false. He had returned Macsen no answer, and Macsen had taken that silence for consent. Bedwyr could not accept the protection which Macsen had provided for us, which was the direct cause of the war, and still refuse to give Macsen any assistance. In a way he did believe that Less Britain was a separate kingdom from Britain, and that Macsen might do as he pleased in it. But the main reason he agreed to help Macsen in rebellion was the numb despair for which he seemed never to be free. He seemed no longer capable of making any moral decision, and Macsen continually pushed his indecision into agreement with himself. So, from giving advice, Bedwyr moved to setting up a system by which the army could be raised quickly, to helping to establish the coastal defences – barricading the harbours and proclaiming a reward to any peasant who reported a landing on the beaches – to helping to train the warband, and then, finally, in September, to officially accepting a military post under Macsen.

I argued with Bedwyr at each step. He would agree with my arguments, then say that he knew that this or that was wrong, but there was no way to be right, and he could not back out now. Eventually, since my arguments only deepened his despair, I gave them up. I tried to cheer Bedwyr, hoping to bring him to his senses that way. But he would not be cheered. His only escape seemed to be to throw himself into his work for Macsen, and I saw less and less of him as the days went by.

The restrictions we lived under were gradually relaxed as Bedwyr became cooperative. Presently even I was allowed to ride about the town when I pleased, though I was constantly watched in case I should attempt to leave the city. If fine gowns and jewellery had been a source of pleasure to me I would have been delighted, for these were showered on me. Macsen wished me to appear beautiful and valuable, so that his followers would be the more impressed by Bedwyr's having stolen me, and cheered by Arthur's disgrace. He also wanted me to keep Bedwyr happy. He soon realized that for my own part I was in complete opposition to him, but he was content that I had no power against him.

Well, I was at least glad to be able to ride my horse again, to go out into the open air, or ride under guard into the countryside and to the edge of the great forest. And I managed to find some books. But still the hours were wearisome and heartbreaking. Things were as they had been in Bresta, but worse. Sometimes when I walked along the walls of Car Aës I wanted to throw myself off. It was not even the desire to die, but only the soul-deep longing for freedom. Sometimes in dreams I could fly from the walls, but always the flight failed, even in sleep, and I would fall from the steep air into the darkness.

It was worse in late August, when Macsen and Bedwyr rode off to inspect the coastal defences. I was not allowed to leave the city, and two warriors followed me whenever I left Macsen's house. Macsen's steward approached me and suggested that he take Bedwyr's place while Bedwyr was gone. I had left my husband and was therefore shameless, he thought, and I must be eager for a man since my lover was absent. I struck the man and he grinned and tried to kiss me. I only shook him off by threatening to tell Bedwyr of his suggestion when the warleader returned. But of course I could not do that, when Bedwyr actually did return. It would simply have made more trouble for him, since he would undoubtedly have challenged the man. And it would have amused Macsen and his warband.

I grew angry and depressed, and could speak to no one without losing my temper. I spent hours on the wall near the town gates, looking out into the west and wondering when Arthur would come from Britain. From the gate-tower one could just see the end of the cultivated lands that surrounded Car Aës, and the edge of the great forest. The Bretons were afraid of the forest. They said that if you became lost in it you might never find your way back to the human earth, but wander in it for ever. All that was wonderful and terrible was said to inhabit the forest, devils and gods, castles of glass and enchanted springs, the finding of which meant the loss of all else. I wanted to visit the forest, but I was never allowed to ride so far.

Arthur came in September. He had known of the coastal defences – we had always had spies in Less Britain, and Bedwyr had not gone so far as to reveal their names to Macsen. Instead of trying to overcome the defences Arthur had chosen to avoid them. Some of his Saxon subjects had treaties of friendship with the Frankish kingdom to the north-east of Less Britain, and Arthur had agreed with the king of this land to pay a certain sum in gold for the right to use one of his ports and to cross his land into Less Britain.

The Frankish king was probably pleased that Less Britain was to be invaded, for the sum was quite moderate and he caused no trouble for Arthur. The Saxons and the Franks had been enemies of the British for so long that not even Bedwyr had expected this, and the invasion took him and Macsen by surprise after all. However, Macsen's warband was in readiness by the coast, and most of Macsen's nobles, with their warriors, had already been persuaded to join the king. With these forces Bedwyr and Macsen hurried from the coast, and managed to reach Car Aës before Arthur had done much more than cross the border. They had, of course, the advantage over Arthur in that they could requisition supplies from the country, while Arthur had to send out foraging parties or drag along baggage trains, which slowed him.

On reaching Car Aës from the coast, Macsen wished to remain in the fortress and allow Arthur to lay siege to it as much as he wished while Macsen called up his army. Bedwyr, however, persuaded him to abandon this plan and instead set out again from Car Aës the day after reaching it. Arthur, he said, would not waste his time in siege works, but instead would turn about and plunder the country, burning the grain which still stood unharvested in the fields. If Macsen sat securely in his fortress while this was being done, much of his army would not respond to his call to arms, and there was danger that he would be cut off from the rest of it. So instead they hurried north, planning to set an ambush for Arthur, then retreat towards the fortress, using delaying tactics to keep Arthur occupied until the harvest was in and the peasant army had joined them.

Arthur had crossed the border into Less Britain in late September. His forces first encountered Macsen's in the first week of October, and arrived before Car Aës by the end of that month. The delaying tactics Bedwyr had recommended had been partially successful: the harvest was in, with sufficient supplies stored in the fortress to last the winter, while the country people had hidden their goods and could feel secure that they would not starve that winter if they answered the King's summons. A part of the army had been raised. But the numbers Macsen had hoped for had never materialized. It seemed that the call to arms had been disrupted in the south-east by false reports (doubtless circulated by Arthur's spies) saying that the war had already ended. In Cernw and the north-west there was considerable reluctance to go to war against Arthur. If Less Britain had never been properly a part of the Empire of Britain, it had always been bound to it by the strongest ties, and many Bretons felt that Macsen's rebellion was undertaken only to gratify his own ambition and to support a notorious criminal. Many of the older warriors had come with Macsen's younger brother Bran, when he led them to Britain to aid Arthur when he first claimed the purple, and these supporters of Bran's had always disliked Macsen.

On the other hand, attempts to foment a counter-rebellion met with little success. The people were proud of Bedwyr, and respected Macsen's name and ancestry. Macsen therefore returned to Car Aës with the forces he had had in September – his own warband of four hundred men and another four hundred warriors from among his nobles – and an additional army of about a thousand ill-armed and ill-disciplined peasants, with vague hopes of a thousand more. Arthur had brought, as Bedwyr had predicted, about a thousand men: most of the Family and men from the warbands of King Constantius of British Dumnonia, of King Urien of Rheged, and of King Ergyriad ap Caw of Ebrauc. Though in numbers less than Macsen's forces, this was in fact a more dangerous power than Macsen's and, as was customary for Arthur, had an overwhelming advantage in cavalry. Macsen would have been soundly defeated within a week if he had not had Bedwyr. Arthur set half a hundred traps which Bedwyr foresaw or recognized and escaped. I think that for both Arthur and Bedwyr the campaign was like fighting with a mirror. Each knew the other's mind nearly as well as he knew his own.

Macsen and his forces rode into Car Aës one night at the end of October, entering the gates by torchlight. Behind them on the plain I could see other flecks of fire which brought my heart into my throat, for I knew the lights to be Arthur's.

Bedwyr saw me standing on the wall and watching when he rode in beside Macsen, and he raised his hand in salute, but was soon busied with seeing to the men – with the army and the warriors together there were more numbers than the town could easily hold. So I went back to Macsen's house alone – or rather, trailing my two guards – and Bedwyr came back to the room late, and lay down exhausted without taking off more than his boots and his mail shirt, only kissing me briefly in greeting. The following day, however, we went together onto the walls. We looked out over the bare fields and saw the Family encamped between us and the forest. My heart rose like an eagle on the wind when I saw the tents there, and caught, distant and heart-piercingly beautiful, the golden gleam of Arthur's standard.

'He cannot devastate the country now,' Bedwyr told me. 'But he can probably forage foodstuffs enough to support himself. Yet he dare not send parties out too widely, for fear that we should make a foray. It is a matter of time now, and he has the most to lose by waiting.'

I looked at Bedwyr as he said this, standing there in the early November sunlight. Something in his face had grown hard, and there were new lines of bitterness about his eyes and at the corners of his mouth. *He is destroying himself,* I thought. I remembered what he had said about damnation and looked away.

'It was bitter fighting,' he told me. 'We have lost many men.'

'And Arthur?'

'I do not know how many he has lost.' Something in the tone made me look at him again, and I saw that the new lines were not just from this new hardness, but from suffering, self-loathing, and despair.

Arthur did send foraging parties out a few days later, and Bedwyr did lead a foray of Macsen's cavalry out against the camp. Again, I watched from the walls.

Arthur's camp had plenty of time to see Bedwyr coming, and long before the force from the city reached them another column of horsemen was leaving the camp at a gallop, spreading out to weave across the plain. I stood straining my eyes. listening to the comments the guards around me made in their alien accents. I felt an agony of division. It was the first time I actually saw the war with my own eyes, actually witnessed my lovers setting out to kill one another, from despair and for justice.

The lines of cavalry met, and at once became indistinguishable from one another. I wondered how anyone could tell their own side from the enemy's in battle. Of course, it would be easier with Saxons, who tended to wear helmets and use a different style of dress; but when one blood makes war with itself, how can the beholder know where to strike? This war was like a madman in convulsions, beating himself and the bystanders without distinction, possessed solely by the violence itself. Madness, this, all madness: the divine madness that is sent on those doomed to destruction.

The line wavered back towards the camp. I thought I saw Gwalchmai, dreamed that I could pick out Arthur, Bedwyr, any of a hundred familiar forms. But the forces were small with distance, nothing but a glitter of arms and galloping of horses to and fro. Even the sounds were drowned by the wind along the plain, until they could not be heard above the comments of the guards around me. I sank to my knees, leaning my head against the wall, and wept bitterly. Then the guards came and took me back to my room.

I had to escape. I realized that as soon as I was alone again. This was my fault, my fault for being unfaithful, for putting my own happiness above the demands of the Empire. Other women might commit adultery and be guilty only of that, but I had committed treason as well, and I had known it. Perhaps others were also guilty, but I knew my own fault, knew it as I would know a rotting sore, which eats upon the whole flesh and consumes it away. I must die of this: only so could my life end free of that spreading corruption. Somehow I must escape, return to Arthur, and accept my sentence – which, after this rebellion, would have to be death.

In that case, it was no use sitting and weeping; I had done more than enough of that already. I must make plans.

I went to the silver mirror Macsen had provided and looked at my face. I had lost weight over the past months, and I looked pale, hollow-cheeked and sunken-eyed, old. Now my eyes were red as well. Abruptly, I felt ashamed at myself, for the long months of passive misery, for indecision, for weeping in front of Macsen's men. Enough, too much of that. Could I disguise myself and give my guards the slip?

I washed my face and went to see if I could find some cosmetics, or a wig.

I had to humiliate myself before the steward to get the
cosmetics. He had resented his rebuff, and took advantage
of my request to sneer at me for 'losing my looks' and to
wonder pointedly if Bedwyr no longer wanted me. My
position had taught me some patience, and I made no reply
to him. Eventually I managed to extract from the stores
some kohl, white lead, and carmine. When I came back to
the room the door was locked. While I was unlocking it I
heard, briefly, a sound of hammering. Bedwyr must be
back.

When I opened the door I found Bedwyr standing near it
with his back to it; he started violently and whirled about
when I came in. He had taken off his mail coat and tunic,
and his eyes as they met mine were guilty and alarmed.
Some flash of insight told me what he had been doing
before I realized it consciously, before I turned my eyes to
the bed and saw his sword there, wedged carefully upright,
ready to fall on.

'Gwynhwyfar,' Bedwyr said, idiotically apologetic, 'I
did not expect...'

I went over to the bed and touched the sword. He had
thrown the mattress off, wedged the weapon into the
frame, and used one of the supporting leather thongs to
bind it down, hammering the strip of leather back to the
frame to secure it: that had been the hammering sound I had
heard. I began to unfasten the piece of leather. My hands
were quite steady; I felt a remote wonder that I felt so little,
but that was all.

'Why did you think to do it this way?' I asked, without
looking at him. 'Arthur might not have believed it when
Macsen told him you fell on your own sword.'

'I did not think of that.' His voice was quiet, ordinary.

I had the sword free. I picked it up, holding the hilt with
both hands. Though it was a cavalry sword, a cutting
rather than a thrusting weapon, it still had a good point on
it; it would have done what Bedwyr had meant it to do. I
looked from it to Bedwyr, who still stood by the door,
bare-chested, silent, ashamed. Out of the calmness, the ordinary words we used, I had suddenly a vision of him lying
across the bed with the sword through him, twisting on it; I

could almost smell the blood on the thick scarlet carpet. My hands did begin to shake. 'Why?' I asked.

Bedwyr began to turn away; saw the door; carefully closed it again and locked it. He came over to the bed and began to pick up the mattress. I set the sword down on the floor and helped him. When it was back in place he picked his tunic up off the floor and pulled it on – he was shivering a little, for the fire had burned low and the room was cold. Then he sat down on the bed and picked up the sword. He held it point upwards, looking at it. 'If I had two hands,' he said in an undertone, 'I could have held it firmly, and would already be dead.' He looked about, and I picked the baldric off the floor and handed it to him. He sheathed the sword.

'Why?' I asked again. 'Why now?'

He looked at me as though behind me he saw the gulf of death, as though that darkness were reflected and founded within him. 'I have killled Gwalchmai,' he whispered, and turned his head away.

For a moment the words meant nothing. I looked at him. Tentatively, I touched his shoulder. Then the meaning of what he had said washed over me. I remembered Gwyn and Gwalchmai bending together over the back of the roan mare, smiling; remembered Gwyn's astonished face, his blood on the road from Caer Ceri. And now? I leaned against Bedwyr, trembling. He put his arms around me.

'He . . . I sought him out,' he said, talking quickly now in a stammering, broken voice. 'I thought that he would kill me, and that would end it. I know I am no match for him on horseback. But when I rode up to him . . . he paid no attention. At first he paid no attention. Then I engaged him, but he held his hand. At the last minute he looked : . . he looked directly at me. He was in the grip of battle madness; probably he did not even recognize me. I was sure he would kill me then; he had his sword ready. I aimed a blow at his head. It would have been deflected, had he used his sword, but he would not, he did not, he only sat there, looking at me. My sword struck him and knocked him from his horse, and the horse reared and lashed out at me with its hooves. I had to turn and lead my men back, for the Family was too strong for us. Why didn't he strike? I meant him to. Oh God, God, I have lived too long!'

'We must go back,' I said.

He seemed to grow calm at once. He put his hand to the side of my face and looked at me, silent.

'We must go back,' I repeated. 'We have both lived too long. But it will do more good to put our lives in Arthur's hand than to take them with our own. If we are killed by the law we will give Gwalchmai what he wanted.'

Still he said nothing. I pulled away from him and stood. 'Listen, my heart. I decided that I would go after seeing you fighting this morning, and I will go. What is the watchword at the gates?'

'You . . . you cannot simply ride out through the gates.'

'You have put double watches on the walls to keep the men occupied and out of trouble at night. We cannot escape except through the gates.' I went to the cupboard, found my dark green dress and cut a wide strip off the hem with my own small knife. '*I* cannot ride out. But two men on horseback who know the watchword could. I know you have been sending men out to raise the army; you have sent messengers to every corner of the kingdom. If we give the watchword at the gates and leave at night there should be no questions asked.'

'No one would question two men, but a man and a woman would be questioned.'

'Look,' I said. I went back to the mirror and twined the strip of cloth over my head, under my chin and around my neck. It made my face look even thinner, and my hair would not stay under it neatly – but I could braid that and fasten it so that it would not be noticeable. 'I will wear this,' I told Bedwyr, 'and a cloak with the hood up. And I will paint my face so that, in the shadow, I will seem to have a beard. It would not do for daylight, I know, but at night it should pass.' In the mirror, I saw that he was looking at me dubiously. 'You have an armoured jerkin as well as your mail shirt, haven't you?' I asked his reflection. 'Well, I will wear that, and boots, and leggings. And I can ride well enough not to give myself away. Ach, I know it is a wild plan, but, if it comes to the worst they will think we are deserters and kill us if we resist arrest at the gates. They would not expect a woman and so would not see one.'

'If they killed us for deserters they would be right. I would be one,' said Bedwyr slowly.

I turned from the mirror, set it down. 'You would be returning to your true lord.'

'I have sworn an oath to Macsen as well.'

I stared at him, and he explained, 'You know he has appointed me cavalry commander; do you think I could escape swearing him an oath after such an appointment? I will not break that oath as well.'

'If you return to Arthur you will cancel out the first treachery.'

'No. Nothing can cancel that out. I have killed my friends.'

'And therefore you should return and suffer justice for them.'

He shook his head. 'Gwynhwyfar, I was born in this land, I was once sworn to serve its king – Macsen's brother. I was released from that oath to serve Arthur. But I have betrayed Arthur and perjured myself. Macsen may take reprisals against my family if I betray him also; and even if he did not, I will not twice perjure myself.'

'Yet you were willing to commit another mortal sin and die on your own sword, rather than continue to fight the Family.'

'That is different.' He looked at the sword he was still holding, put it down and clasped the stump of one hand with the other. 'I will not twice forswear myself. I would prefer to have died before being once a traitor, but I would rather be once a traitor than twice.'

'Oh, very fine! You would rather serve the devil, once fallen, than return to God!'

'Macsen is not the devil.'

I sat down, angrily untied the piece of cloth. I began to put my hair up again, plaiting it.

'But can you not see that it is worse to be a traitor twice than once?' asked Bedwyr, greatly distressed.

'All I see is that we have done evil to our lord, and more evil has come of it. We ought to go back and suffer the penalty for our crime, not skulk about like dogs that expect a whipping and wish to avoid it.'

'Gwynhwyfar, it is not your homeland, and you have not sworn an oath!'

'And I wish you had not, either. And though you have I do not see why you should weigh your oath to Macsen heavier than your oath to Arthur!'

'Because I have already broken my oath to Arthur.'

'Ach, damn your philosophy! Oaths are meaningless; it is the heart that swears, that binds itself to what a man is and what he stands for. You never meant in your heart to serve Macsen.'

'I cannot escape by asking what I meant in my heart. I swore to serve Macsen, and I must take the consequences. I have perjured myself once, and I know what came of that. I will not do so again, even with greater cause. I will die instead, if God, just or merciful, will grant me death.'

We glared at each other for a moment. Then I remembered what Bedwyr had meant to do, and went to him, knelt on the floor beside him, taking his hand. I could not understand why he refused to leave Macsen, but I had to believe that he acted in accordance with his conscience.

'Very well,' I whispered. 'Stay. But I have not sworn, and I will go. What is the watchword?'

He stared at me for a long moment, then dropped to his knees on the floor beside me and put his arms around me crushing me against himself. 'Do not go,' he cried. 'Do not go.'

'What is the watchword?' I demanded, fiercely because his plea tore my heart open.

He loosened his hold and looked at me again. 'You cannot mean to leave me as well.'

'I love you. You know that. And perhaps I only mean to go because I hate this land and this life. But I cannot endure this division any longer. If you will not help me, Bedwyr, I will find some way to escape on my own, I promise you. Though I love you, I will – must – go.'

As he continued to stare at me I wondered if he would kill himself if I left him. The thought made me shrink inside. But I couldn't let him live only for me, if it was for me in the ruin of all. And I thought he had prepared the sword on the impulse of immediate pain, and that his true hope was for death in battle. He knew that a private suicide would embarrass both Arthur and Macsen, and moreover was another mortal sin. And I hoped that he would die in battle. He had nothing to live for, and it was better than pouring out his blood in the smothering red luxury of that horrible room.

'The watchword of the fortress is "Liberty",' Bedwyr said in a low voice. 'But the guards at the gates have a special one. When they ask for the watchword, say "Liberty"; they will then ask, "Whose liberty?", to which you must reply, "The liberty of the will, and of this kingdom."'

'"The liberty of the will, and of this kingdom,"' I repeated, looking at him, feeling impossibly glad that he would understand, agree to at least this much. 'Was that your idea?'

'No, Macsen's. He gives a new watchword every day, but it is usually something to do with liberty. I will give you the clothing and the armour.'

'Not here. I am watched when I leave this room. Could you hide it somewhere – the stables? I think I could elude the guards when I leave the Feast Hall. They do not follow me when I am with you.'

'Very well,' he said, numbly.

I studied his face, wanting to memorize it. 'You can tell them afterwards that I said I wished to go back for something, and so gave you the slip.'

'No. They will know that you must have learned the watchword from me. I will tell them the truth, and I do not think the king will be overly angry. You are of no use to him, and he distrusts you. But he needs me, and will be content enough that I did not go with you. And if he does grow angry, and dismiss me from his service, all the better. He will either have me killed himself, or I will follow you and leave the execution to Arthur.'

Macsen gave a great feast that night, to celebrate the 'victory' of the foray that morning, and the 'success' of the war so far. Many of the men got drunk, and tried to congratulate Bedwyr for killing Gwalchmai. They had to be drunk to do so, for he looked so grim at any mention of it that the densest of warriors would notice it when sober. I said nothing all evening, only sat looking pale and remote, but this was nothing new and attracted no attention. Bedwyr and I left the feast as soon as we could, in courtesy, and went down to the stables.

It was dark, and the grooms were asleep. Bedwyr found a blackened lamp, and by its light we found the clothing he had left under a hay bale by my mare's stall. I dressed, and he saddled the horse. The clothes were too large, of course, but on horseback, at night with a cloak over them, it shouldn't show. I used some of the kohl I had borrowed to darken my cheeks and upper lip, then wrapped the scarf around my head and pulled the hood of my cloak up. Bedwyr lifted the lamp and looked at me critically.

'Your moustache is crooked.'

I put some more kohl on.

'That will do very well – the guards will have to look up to see your face, and that scarf hides a great deal.' He led my mare out of her stall and handed me the reins, then set down the lamp and kissed me, desperately and hard, several times. 'Good luck,' he said hoarsely.

I nodded. My throat was too choked for me to reply. I mounted the horse and took one last look at him standing there in the pool of dim light from the lamp. The kohl from my lip was smeared across his, and his face was almost as calm as it had been when he was Arthur's loyal and philosophic warleader. But it was a different calm, a calm such as comes to the sick when they are at last worn out by anguish, and can resist the pain no longer, but lie still and wait for the end.

'May God keep you, and be merciful,' I said, then, not trusting myself to say anything more touched my heels to my mare's sides and rode out of the stable.

I met the watch in the street, but gave them the watch-word in a voice as deep as I could make it, and was told to pass. I knew a quick way to the city gate, but on that ride it seemed to take a long time. My mare sensed my excitement and was inclined to be restive. She was a high-strung, nervous animal at the best of times, though she could run as lightly as a swallow flies, and had all the spirit in the world. But this unusual night departure from her comfortable stall made her bad-tempered, and I began to worry that she might cause a commotion at the gate, perhaps even rear so that my hood fell back and I was taken.

Reached at last, the gate was a blur of torchlight which I rode into boldly, my hare's hooves clattering on the cob-blestones. Two guards before the massive oak door snapped to attention, and I could vaguely see others in the tower above.

'Watchword?' asked one of the two before me.

'Liberty.'

'Whose liberty?'

'The liberty of the will, and of this kingdom.'

The guard nodded to his fellow, who went to the postern gate beside the main one, and unbarred it. 'Be careful with that cold, friend,' said the first guard. 'And good luck. The enemy are closer than they were last night, for all of that fight this morning.'

I coughed. 'Thank you. Have a quiet watch.' I kicked my mare, took her through the gate at a trot, then spurred her to a canter. To my right Arthur's campfires glowed, but I held diagonally away from the wall until I was certain that I could not be seen by the watchers there. Then I doubled back and sent my mare galloping towards the fires as though I should die of cold for the lack of them.

I was still far from the fires when I heard another horse galloping on my left, still too distant to see in the cloudy night. I kept my mare at her pace, fearing that my escape had been discovered already, and that someone had been sent to find me. My horse was probably the faster one.

My pursuer realized this fairly promptly, as well, for after another minute at the gallop he called out, 'Halt! Halt, in the Emperor's name!' He had a British voice, a Northern voice like my own. I at once slowed my mare to a walk.

The other galloped up, looming out of the darkness, and drew rein near me. 'Watchword?' he asked.

I hesitated, said nothing.

'Whose man are you, and where are you going?' he demanded.

'I am British,' I told him, finding my voice still low, hoarse from tension. 'I am escaping from the city. I wish to see the Emperor.'

The sentry drew nearer, a dark shadow on a dark horse. 'Watchword?'

'Macsen's is "Liberty", but I do not know Arthur's.'

'A Northerner,' muttered the rider, evidently commenting on my voice, 'and only a boy. Eh, lad, it was well done to escape, if indeed you have. I will take you into the camp myself, for the Emperor has standing orders to bring anyone from the city to him. If you're telling the truth you'll find yourself fortunate. Give me your reins.'

I tossed the reins over my mare's neck and handed them to him. He took them with a nod, turned his horse about and rode back to call an explanation to another sentry before starting back toward the campfires.

'Watchword?' someone called as we passed the first picket line.

'*Lex victrix!*' called my captor, 'The law conquers', then added, to me, 'And now, boy, you do know our watchword. But hopefully you'll have no cause to use it tonight.'

A number of men were sitting about the main fire when we came up to it, drinking and passing a harp around. I recognized most of them, and the recognition came as a sharp pain to my heart, though I was glad.

'Halt!' called one of these men, standing lazily and brushing ashes off his leggings. 'Who are you and what do you want?'

'Morgant ap Casnar,' the sentry replied, 'of the warband of Ergyriad ap Caw of Ebrauc. I caught this lad riding out of the city. He is British, by his speech, and he says he's escaping. I have brought him here because I thought that the Emperor might wish to question him.'

'As well he might. Well, lad?'

'I am not a boy, Morfran,' I said, calling him by name. I tossed my hood back and untied the scarf. There was a profound stillness, in which the fire sounded very loud. More of the men rose to their feet. I rubbed at the kohl on my face with the scarf and asked, 'Where is my lord Arthur?'

The flap of the great imperial tent before the main fire was tossed open, and Arthur stood there. Over the fire our eyes met. I slid off my horse. 'Arthur,' I said; then, 'I have come back to accept my sentence.'

He looked at me for a long moment. 'Does Bedwyr know you have come?'

'Yes. He helped me to escape. Macsen had me kept under guard.'

'Come in here. Morfran, see to the lady's horse.'

I walked around the fire, awkward in the heavy boots. I felt keenly ridiculous in the outsized man's clothing, as though there were not more important things I should be feeling. Arthur held the tent flap open for me and I went in.

There were two torches and a lamp burning inside. Cei was sitting by the light table with a pile of maps; he jumped up and stared in astonishment as I entered. Sitting on the bed, leaning against one of the tent posts, was Gwalchmai.

I cried out when I saw him, started forward and tripped over the boots. Arthur helped me back to my feet. 'Gwalchmai!' I exclaimed, feeling my face almost break with a smile such as I had not smiled for many weary months. 'Bedwyr told me he had killed you!'

'He almost did,' Arthur said, behind me. Gwalchmai stared at me as though he did not recognize me. He had aged since I had last seen him, and he was very pale and sick, his head bandaged. 'However,' Arthur continued drily, 'the blow was not a solid one. Gwalchmai, Cei, my wife escaped from the city with Bedwyr's help.'

'It alters nothing,' Gwalchmai said slowly, 'Bedwyr remains guilty.'

'Welcome, my lady,' said Cei, taking my hand and grinning. 'A hundred welcomes.'

'A hundred thousand thanks. Gwalchmai, I am very glad that you are alive. And Bedwyr will be glad, as well.' I glanced round at Arthur, decided to say it plainly, 'He meant to fall on his sword this morning, when he thought you were dead.'

'It alters nothing,' Gwalchmai repeated.

Arthur took my arm and directed me to another chair. I sat down, and he stood a moment looking at me. I could not read his expression, though I knew his face so well. 'What is that on your face?' he asked.

I rubbed at it, then took the scarf and rubbed with that again. 'A beard. I needed one to get through the gate,' I put the scarf down. 'If it is any use to you, Macsen's watchword tonight is "Liberty".'

'Ah!' exclaimed Cei.

'It may be,' said Arthur, still watching me.

'A night assault!' said Cei eagerly. 'Indeed, lady, that is an excellent idea. We might end it quickly. It would be better than more work on those siege engines' (to Arthur) 'which you took out of that book. Those will only waste time and lives.' He looked at Gwalchmai, seeming to challenge disagreement. Obviously I had interrupted some conference on how to take Car Aës, and Cei and Gwalchmai had had differing opinions. 'And I still say that if our night assault fails we should abandon this accursed city, move off south, take all the plunder we can find and go home. We can come back again next summer. Macsen would be bound to tire of playing host to us and come to terms.'

'We will have to determine more about the defences before we can risk a night assault,' said Arthur, wearily and, to me, 'Will Bedwyr come?'

Everyone looked at me, and I looked down at my hands. I rubbed the finger where once I had worn the ring with the imperial seal, shook my head. I looked up at Arthur; he seemed tired, not at all angry. 'He has sworn Macsen an oath. He . . . I think he wishes to come. But he thinks that he is damned, and will not face you, and he says that he will not be twice forsworn.'

'I see. And Macsen, of course, will keep him as long as he can, for his own generalship is nothing in comparison with Bedwyr's. He will not make terms, not for a long while.' Arthur shook his head. 'Cei, you know that we do not dare stay long away from Britain.'

'What Bedwyr's reasons are changes nothing,' Gwalchmai repeated yet again. 'Justice requires that he die. Macsen is only incidental to that.' He took a deep breath. 'Try the night assault. Since we have the watchword it might work. If not, use the siege engines.'

'I still don't see why you didn't kill Bedwyr yourself this morning, since you are so eager for his death,' snapped Cei. 'You could have.'

'I tell you, the madness was on me!' Gwalchmai snapped back, trying to stand – then stopped short, went white with pain and closed his eyes.

Cei jumped up and took his shoulder. 'Lie down,' he urged, pushing the other back gently. 'God in Heaven, you must keep still.'

'The madness was on me,' Gwalchmai insisted. 'It was as though we still fought the Saxons, and he still commanded me. I could not think clearly, or I would have killed him. But it would be best if he died after a trial, by the hand of the law, in Britain, before all the Family.'

Arthur raised his hand, nodding. 'We will try the night assault, tonight. Gwynhwyfar, what are their defences?'

I told him everything I knew, which my hours standing on the walls had made a good amount, though I had to admit that I knew less of what happened in Macsen's court than the servants did. 'I have been kept virtually a prisoner,' I explained, 'I was under guard whenever I left Macsen's house.'

'I know,' Arthur said, 'I had a man inside the fortress. He was killed a few weeks ago.' He was quiet a moment, still watching me. It was very different from our last meeting, when the sight of me had been painful to him. I wondered what it was that he felt now. 'Cei told me that you claimed to have known nothing about the attack on the road until it took place.'

'I knew nothing of it. But, afterwards ... I went ... I left with Bedwyr willingly, my heart. He was in such desperate grief that I could not abandon him.'

Gwalchmai laughed, then shuddered and closed his eyes again. The laughter must have jolted his wounded head.

'And yet, there was no conspiracy?' Arthur demanded, 'You can swear to that?'

'I, Gwynhwyfar daughter of Ogyrfan, swear in the name of the Father, the Son and the Holy Spirit, that I never conspired to escape with Bedwyr, and that I knew nothing of his plans until he encountered us on the road. Moreover, I swear that Bedwyr himself never meant to come to blows with anyone, and only drew his sword after Medraut had prevented me from telling him that I would not go, and incited the others to attack him. If I lie may the earth gape and swallow me, may the sea rise and drown me, may the sky break and fall on me.'

Arthur smiled very slightly and looked at Gwalchmai.

'Still it alters nothing,' Gwalchmai said wearily. 'We had heard that the lady was kept as a prisoner. We knew all along that she had the lesser share of guilt. But there has still been murder, Macsen still stands firm in rebellion, and there must still be justice for it.'

'You will have me tried again,' I told Arthur. 'I know that. And I am willing to accept my sentence. It is what I came for.' His eyes met mine, still without anger. The silence and the torchlight lay between us like a road, and I felt my blood begin to sing in my veins: he was not angry, he had forgiven me. 'I am grieved to the heart over what has happened,' I went on, uncertainly now, all my determination melting in the light of his eyes. 'I have deserved to die. And I would rather die than help to cause this division among us for even one more day. I cannot live with it . . .'

Arthur began to speak, but fell silent again. He looked at Gwalchmai, then back at me. 'The war will still go on, my white hart,' he told me, very quietly. 'But I am glad that you are no longer part of it; I am glad you are back. And if you were stolen away by force, and kept a prisoner, there may be no need for a new sentence. Perhaps the old one could be altered, even suspended.' He was quiet another moment, then said, 'I received a letter from your cousin, the chieftain of your clan. If Bedwyr knew of him I am not surprised that he wished to rescue you. I do not think it would be well that you go there.' He glared around the room, suddenly, coldly angry, not so much with anyone there as with his kingdom and the purple. 'I do not wish her to die!' he cried, loudly. 'Let Bedwyr pay the penalty!'

Gwalchmai looked at me strangely but said nothing. Cei grinned. 'Why, she has paid her penalty already! She has been kept prisoner by a foreign king. Ach, my lord, my lady, it was a bold deed, escaping from Macsen's fortress dressed as a man: the warband will pardon her anything, after that. There will be songs made about it for years.'

I did not know what to say. I had not expected such a welcome. I was being received as though I had returned from an embassy, and not like an escaped criminal. But I was a criminal, and did not want Bedwyr to pay the penalty for my crime as well as his own. Yet my husband stood near me watching me, and I did not know what to say to him.

Arthur saw my confusion and shook his head. 'We must speak of it tomorrow. For now, my lady, rest. You look very tired.' He went to the entrance of his tent and gave orders for some servants to prepare me a tent to myself, then called various men and gave orders for the assault for that night. I leaned back in my place, looking at the familiar things and faces. I closed my eyes and listened to their voices: Cei's rumbling whisper to Gwalchmai; Arthur's strong voice giving orders outside; jokes, laughter, excited discussion from the men. It did not yet seem real. For a moment I was afraid that I would wake, and find myself back in that smothering red room in Car Aës. I opened my eyes again quickly.

Arthur came back in, went to his desk and checked a plan

he had made of Macsen's defences. Then he looked up at me again and smiled. I thought my heart would break to see him smile. He looked older even than before, worn into a greying shadow, but his smile was the same, and the direct honest force of his eyes. 'I cannot believe that you are here,' he told me. 'I wish – but you must rest, and there is work for me. Do you have any other clothing? Then I will have some found for you – though I doubt we have anything finer than some farm woman's festival dress in this whole encampment.' He helped me to my feet, ushered me to the entrance of the tent and snapped his fingers to summon a guard for me, then paused, still holding my arm. 'Wish me luck for tonight, my lady.'

I turned and caught his arms, looked up into his face. I thought of Bedwyr in the dark stable, and of Arthur decreeing my sentence at Camlann, things that had mattered, that still mattered. But beside this return they were unimportant; looking at him, I was home again. 'God defend you,' I said. 'And good luck.'

As I walked off to my own tent, escorted by a warrior I knew, I prayed that I would die there, among friends and not in humiliation among strangers. And I prayed also that Bedwyr would not be captured that night, not brought back and made to pay the penalty which I should have paid, but that somehow, somewhere, living or dying, he should escape.

Ten

The tent Arthur had ordered for me was a small one, but three men had been moved out of it to make room for me. It had a fire, and when I entered with my guard Gwalchmai's servant Rhys was heating water over this. When he saw me his face almost split with an enormous grin, and he bowed very low. 'Lady Gwynhwyfar! Welcome back. The news of your escape has swept the camp already.'

I took his hand, smiling back. 'Thank you, Rhys. I am glad to see you. How are Eivlin and the children?'

'When I left them, well. I am glad you have come back, my lady. It is a dead weight on the heart to make war against friends. Will the Lord Bedwyr come?'

I stopped smiling and shook my head.

Rhys sighed. 'Well.' He ran a hand through his hair. 'It will go on, then. God have mercy on us.' The guard muttered something and withdrew to stand watch outside, and Rhys bowed to him slightly, then checked the wood for the fire. 'Well, noble lady, you must wish to rest, and I must go back to my lord. He is wounded.'

'I know. He is at Arthur's tent, planning an assault.'

'What? Still?' Rhys stared. 'God in Heaven! He had to be carried there – can't walk, insisted on speaking to Arthur as soon as he realized where he was after the wounding. The surgeons didn't like that, only they liked the thought of exciting him even less. He only woke this afternoon, and he has obviously not yet recovered his senses. The stubborn, proud . . .' Rhys realized that this was an improper way to speak of his lord, so, instead of finishing, lifted the kettle of hot water from the fire and checked the bucket of cold water.

I sat down on the sleeping pallet and pulled off those absurd boots. 'Your lord is very bitter,' I said, tentatively. Rhys knew Gwalchmai as well as anyone did, and would know how things stood with him.

'And is it surprising that he should be? Why did Bedwyr kill that poor child? Excuse me, my lady. My tongue is more insolent than my intentions.'

'Do not apologize. You have been a part of this long

enough to have a right to ask such questions. Bedwyr threw a spear without thinking of whom he threw it at.'

'Ah. Almost, my lady, I could believe we were all under a curse. I could not believe that Bedwyr meant to kill my lord Gwyn, any more than the Emperor wants this war, or you ever meant any evil to the Emperor, and yet all goes wrong. My lady, my lord has been like a man in an enchantment, noticing nothing and caring for nothing. I can scarcely persuade him to eat or sleep, and he does not pay much attention even to his horse, and you know how he loves that animal. This war is bad for him. He has been worse since we arrived in this miserable kingdom. My lady, he does not really wish to kill Lord Bedwyr, but he cannot bear to think that Bedwyr can murder his son and escape unscathed. Well enough, but when today he met Bedwyr in the battle, he found for himself that he does not wish to kill him, and was almost killed himself. It is bad, that head wound. He cannot fight now, at least. God knows, he cannot even stand. The surgeons say that he must keep very quiet and avoid all excitement. But that is the one thing he will not possibly do, not while he is here and the war continues. My lady, the Emperor is sending some of the wounded home the day after tomorrow. Persuade him to send my lord with them.'

I looked at Rhys thoughtfully. 'I will tell Arthur what you say when I see him tomorrow. But why do you think I have any influence? I am a criminal awaiting my sentence.'

Rhys grinned again. 'Perhaps, my lady. But ever since we arrived in Less Britain, the rumour has run about that you were held a prisoner, and had been taken to Less Britain by force in the first place, and the Family has been burning to set you free again. It is strange what a war will do towards changing men's minds. They have almost forgotten the trial in all the excitement.' He coughed. 'Of course, things may be different in Britain. Medraut and his faction are all back there.'

'What?' I looked at Rhys sharply, saw that he was serious. 'Medraut and his faction, left back in Britain to keep Camlann safe for us, while Arthur and all our firmest allies are here? This is madness!'

'My lady, the Emperor could scarcely bring men whose loyalty he doubted here to Less Britain with him, not when he is taking such a small force. Any treachery here and Macsen would destroy us at once. But the Emperor is no fool, my lady. He has not taken all our firmest allies, only parts of their warbands. He has left Constantius of Dumnonia in Camlann to keep the fortress warm for him, and no doubt has told the king to keep a close eye on the lord Medraut. And he has left King Urien of Rheged, and Ergyriad of Ebrauc, prepared to warn him of any rebellion in the North. I would not trouble yourself, my lady.'

Rhys was probably right, though I still did not like the sound of it. I might have questioned him further, but another servant came in just then, carrying a plain dress and some blankets. I thanked him, thanked Rhys, and they both smiled, wished me a good night, and left me alone with the guard keeping watch outside.

I could not sleep. I lay awake, listening to the camp preparing its assault on Macsen's stronghold. I prayed for Arthur, for Bedwyr, lay tossing and turning after the last voices had vanished with the jingle of harness into the night. What would they achieve? Success? It would be good to have the nightmare over, but if Bedwyr were captured, brought back in chains, tried not only for his own crimes but for mine – then the nightmare would only have begun. It is hard, being a woman during a war, and worse when one does not even know what to hope for.

I rose, put on the dress, wrapped the blanket around my shoulders, and went out to talk to my guard. He had a leg wound, I had noticed earlier. Arthur would not set a skilled able-bodied man on an unncessary guard duty. But the form of the thing was necessary, and I suppose it gave the warrior something to do. I knew the man from Camlann, and knew that he would be even more impatient than I at waiting for the outcome of an assault he could play no part in. We sat about and discussed the war, my imprisonment, his leg wound, Britain and the Empire until the dawn was grey over the forest at our backs.

The army returned very worn and tired, but in one group. The assault had failed. At first, we learned, the watchword and a diversionary attack had enabled them to take the gates, but afterwards the men had been trapped in the unfamiliar streets and forced to retreat again. Arthur was safe, we were told; Cei, Goronwy, Gereint, yes, safe;

others, safe; one or two dead, wounded. And Bedwyr, I was told, had commanded the defence, had not been fooled by the diversion at the north wall, but come straight to the gates and managed to foil Arthur's plans. Yes, Bedwyr too was still alive and unharmed.

Only after learning this did the sleep I had thrust aside suddenly present itself to me again, and I went back into the tent and was lost in oblivion as the sun rose over the tree-tops.

It was full light when I woke. I was still tired, and re-alized at once that I had woken because someone was watching me. I sat up and saw Arthur.

'Hush,' he said gently. 'It is only mid-morning. The guard told me that you were awake all night, and you must wish to sleep more.'

'So must you,' I pointed out, 'and I would wager that you have not slept at all. How long have you been here, my lord?'

'Not long. Come, if you will not sleep, have breakfast with me.'

We had breakfast in his tent, and it was like old times at Camlann, with people interrupting every five minutes. Arthur told me of the war, and I told him of the preceding months, and of Bedwyr.

When I told him of Bedwyr's suffering, Arthur nodded. 'I saw Bedwyr last night,' he told me.

'In Car Aës?' I asked, my throat constricting.

He nodded. 'He spared my life when he might have taken it. But that did not surprise me.' Someone came in with a question about horse fodder, and Arthur dealt with it, then resumed. 'We were trapped in a sidestreet, I and some others of the Family. I had miscalculated the width of the streets – or rather, I had not realized that horses would be so difficult to manage in such streets. We are too unaccu-stomed to siege warfare to be good at it. An organized body of spearmen has the advantage over cavalry in such a con-fined space, no matter how fine the cavalry. Bedwyr had troops near the gate, and when he appeared himself with additional troops we were forced to retreat. Only I led my men down a street which had no access to the gate, and the spearmen came after us. It was total chaos. We had set fire to the gate-house, and the fire was spreading widely; the horses were frightened, and there was no making oneself heard above the din. Then I saw Bedwyr over the heads of the other spearmen, and he saw me. He ordered his men back, and we advanced down the street and rejoined the others at the gate. We passed by him, very close, as we went to join the others. At one point I was not more than six paces from him. He is suffering.'

I looked at my hands, clenching them at each other.

'He will tell Macsen, of course, that it would have been foolish to kill me, that my men would have become ungovernable, ruthless and cruel were I killed, and so excuse himself for the orders he gave. It is doubtless true. Macsen owed much to Bedwyr. I have owed him much as well.'

'But you will have him put to death.'

He looked at me closely. 'You still love him.'

'Yes, of course. So do you.'

He shrugged, looking away from me, looking into nothing. 'He has been my friend for many years. He has been the half of my own soul. But I would cut off my own right hand, if it were necessary for the Empire, and it is necessary. Gwalchmai is right: Bedwyr must die as a matter of pure justice. Justice, and the continuance of the Empire. Only . . .'

'Only?'

He reached across the table and caught my wrist. 'Only I do not want that justice to extend to you.' After a moment of silence he went on, 'I expected to miss you. But it has been worse than I expected. And it is not because the fortress and the kingdom are almost ungovernable without you, because the affairs of the Empire are in disorder and the servants and farmers sigh whenever you are mentioned. I miss you. I could scarcely bear our house at Camlann, alone; I kept expecting to find you there, forgetting every morning that you were gone and discovering it again, to my sorrow. Shall I speak more plainly? Before the trial Bedwyr told me that I had demanded more from you than anyone can give. It was true, though I would not admit it at the time. I allowed myself to be weak, to lose my temper and make endless demands on you, but never allowed you the same. No, listen to me. I know well enough that the strongest need rest, at times. I have seen it in war: one can push any man so far, farther than he himself thinks he can be pushed, but in the end he will snap and kill a comrade or flee from the enemy, or forsake a trust. I should have realized what I was doing to you. Then I sat in judgement upon you. I myself have committed adultery, without the spur of love or loneliness, but only that of drunkenness and lust for the Queen Morgawse — how could I pass judgement on Bedwyr for loving you, or you for yielding to him? You would never have been unfaithful had it not been for me.'

'My own heart,' I said, 'you blame yourself overmuch. You committed no crime, and I did. And yet I love you, I loved you even when I was unfaithful. If you forgive me that is all I desire, and perhaps more than I deserve.'

He kissed my hand. 'It requires forgiveness on both sides, I think. My white hart, the people might accept you back now, as Empress, if it were proved at another trial that you had been taken from Britain by force and kept as a prisoner.'

'It is not true.'

'So you said. But Bedwyr must die. You see that, don't you? There is no way of avoiding it. Must you die as well? It would do no good, not to the kingdom, the Family, and least of all to me. We would all suffer for it. My heart, tell them that you were taken from Britain by force.'

'On trial? Under oath?'

'It is almost true. You would have prevented Bedwyr's attack if you had known of it, and you never meant to go with him.'

'But it would not do any good to spare me, either. The people will spit on me, and say that I am a whore who ran off with her lover, caused a war, and was reinstated to the purple by a deceived and doting husband. They will say you are weak and corrupt. Medraut will use it.'

He winced. 'We can bear that. But do not use such terms. Your cousin spoke so of you in his letter to me; he said that he accepted the charge of you and would see that you were fittingly punished. Why didn't you tell me of him? I would never have sent you to his house had I known. But I do not see fit to yield to the opinions of such as he, nor to suit all my actions to Medraut's judgement. I need you. Will you ... not so much lie, as distort the truth, when you are retried? Then I could impose nothing more than the penance which the Church proscribes for adultery, and keep you with me.'

'You . . . you risk much.'

'You do not understand. I need you.'

I had gone with Bedwyr against my better judgement because he needed me. Now, although Arthur was calmer than Bedwyr had been, I could tell that he was no less serious. But if I were dead he might find another wife, one that might bear him children, and be a better lady for him than I had been. To lie under oath and make another bear the punishment for my fault seemed to me monstrous . . . though I knew that if Bedwyr had been there he would have advised me as Arthur did.

'Let me think,' I pleaded. 'I was certain that I would die for my treachery if I came back. I never expected to be forgiven, I thought I would die honestly. Let me get used to the idea of living first.' After a moment in turmoil I asked, 'When would you hold this trial?'

A messenger came in with a question of ransoms, interrupting. Arthur dealt with him, turned back to me. 'It would be better if done at Camlann, after Bedwyr is taken or killed. I could send you back with the wounded tomorrow. Once in Britain you could begin the period of fasting and penance set by the Church, and also give me your opinion of the situation at home. This war should not last too much longer. I do not wish to follow Cei's plan and wear Macsen out with extended raids. It would cause too much division in the Empire and I cannot afford to leave Britain that long, or leave Medraut in Camlann, even under surveillance. Perhaps the siege engines will work. Will you do as I ask?'

'I . . . I will think of it. Give me until you are back in Britain.'

'You mean you will, unless Bedwyr is taken prisoner,' he said, smiling slightly.

'I do not know what I mean. I do not want him blamed for my crime. Rhys thinks you should send Gwalchmai away with the other wounded.'

Arthur smiled slightly more. 'I was planning to, if I can persuade him to go without over-exciting him and making him ill. My heart, do think of it. If we can hold our own against Medraut there is no reason why we cannot outface the kings of Britain.'

If stars were silver nails, I thought, *one could use them to shoe horses*. But I loved Arthur. Perhaps I would be willing to do even this to make him happy. But if Bedwyr were before my eyes and suffering for my crime, I did not know that I could.

I left the next day with the wounded. Arthur did not like having men in his camp who could not travel quickly, who might be endangered if Macsen did manage to call up the rest of his forces and Arthur had to retreat hastily. Gwalchmai, however, insisted that he was recovering quickly and that there was no point in sending him back to Britain. I went to talk to him myself the morning I left. Arthur hoped I could persuade the warrior to leave.

He was in a tent of his own, being looked after by Rhys. He was lying very still when I came in, looking at the blank wall of the tent.

'Gwalchmai,' I said, and he looked over at me, then at Rhys who was standing just behind me. He said nothing.

'Does it hurt you very much?' I asked.

'No. Do not trouble yourself. I need nothing.'

Rhys let out his breath between his teeth, irritably. 'My lord, the lady has come at the Emperor's request, to see if you will leave today.'

'I had thought as much. Do not trouble yourself, my lady. I shall be back on my feet in a few days – I would doubtless be able to ride back to the army before the wounded reach the ships, so there is no point in my leaving.'

Rhys snorted. 'My lady, reason with him,' he muttered to me. 'He should respect your opinion even now. I will go and pack.'

Gwalchmai watched Rhys leave, only his eyes moving. It was obviously painful to him to shift his head about.

'Rhys thinks the war is bad for you,' I said.

'Rhys is always meddling in things that are not his concern. He is supposed to be my servant, but he thinks himself my master.'

'I have never heard you tell him that.'

'What would be the point? Rhys means well.'

His dark stare troubled me. It was hard to see what he was looking at. I touched his forehead; it felt hot. 'You have the fever,' I told him. 'You would do better away from the

766

army.'

'Why do you show such concern for me, my lady?'

'I have always felt great concern for you,' I said, after another moment of silence. 'I have loved you as I would have loved a brother of my own blood.'

'All lies,' he muttered, so indistinctly that I barely caught the words.

I had been doubtful when Arthur asked me to talk to Gwalchmai, and I felt more than doubtful now, felt horror-stricken. 'Have some water,' I said at last. 'You will want it, with the fever.'

He laughed a little, bitterly, but took the cup of water I poured for him. 'It is worse in the morning,' he told me. 'But I am recovering . . . that is enough.'

'As you wish.' I looked at him closely, but he had leaned back into the pillow and looked past me at the low roof of the tent. 'Gwalchmai, you do not really believe that I lie when I say that I am concerned for you?'

'You may feel concern. But what do feelings and intentions matter? You and Bedwyr may have intended no evil, but still, between you you killed my son.' His eyes turned from the tent pole and met my gaze. 'Wasn't it enough for you that I held my tongue when I knew of your relationship, that I did all I could to help you, that Gwyn went gallantly to your aid, but still you must kill him?'

'It was an accident,' I said, but the words sounded empty.

'It may have been carelessness, not intent. But what does that matter? It is done.' Gwalchmai sat up straight abruptly, then gasped in pain and slumped over, holding his head in his hands.

'Don't!' I cried, trying to support him. 'You will hurt yourself.'

'What does it matter?' he asked, speaking like a man I had never met, and not like the friend I had loved for many years. 'What do I have to recover for? You and Rhys and the rest, they do not understand that. My lady, my lady, you had so much. You had a clan, and you were the jewel and the treasure of your father's house. He would not marry you to anyone, for long and long, though many desired it, for he could not find anyone good enough until he found the Emperor of all Britain. And then you became the crown of the Empire, the lady whom all the kings and the peoples loved and admired – justly. I will admit that it was justly. Not content with your husband, you found a lover as well, a man worthy to be another Emperor. And you destroyed them, for all that you did not intend to; and, not content with destroying what was yours, you and yours destroyed my son as well – my son, who was all my clan to me, and all that was left to me of my lover or wife. And you still say that you have concern for me. You would have shown it better by killing me and leaving my son alive.'

Perhaps I might have spoken in answer, but the empty words dried in my throat and choked me. 'It grieves me,' I said at last.

He laughed the bitter laugh again. 'It grieves me, as well. Far worse.'

'Would Bedwyr's death, or mine, ease that grief?'

He sat looking at his feet. 'No. But at least it would be justice. There would remain some justice in the world.'

'Tell me, then. Shall I tell the plain truth when I am tried, say that I left Britain willingly, and die, condemned for treason? Would that please you?'

'You would lie if you said that. You did not leave willingly, but against your will, to comfort Bedwyr. Oh no, you are innocent in intention, and no doubt Bedwyr is as well. Only that alters nothing. And I cannot even wish that you or he should die. I have still some . . . concern for you. There is no justice, even in the heart.' He looked up and through me, remote and inhuman. 'Once I sailed to the Kingdom of Summer, the Otherworld. I thought then that the struggle between Light and Darkness is fought upon the earth, and that the intentions of our spirits reflect it, and bind Earth and the Otherworld. But now that world seems unconnected and remote from here, for even the best intentions of those devoted to Light can create Darkness. And so there is no justice, can be no justice. Perhaps we are wrong to act at all. Perhaps we are all damned perpetually to Yffern. Let me alone, my lady. Tell Arthur I will stay, unless he commands me otherwise.'

I nodded, left him and went back to my own tent, shaking and trying not to weep. It was true. All he had said to me was true. Ah God, God, why should the Earth ever have been created?

The carts with the wounded left around noon. There were three of them, long, covered over with a canopy against the rain and the sun, walled and packed with straw for the comfort of the men, of whom there were some dozen in each cart. There was also an escort of twenty men who would go only to the harbour where we were to embark. I had my mare to ride, but spent some time in the carts as well. I had assisted surgeons before, and knew how to care for the sick. There was plenty for me to do.

The carts jolted badly on the road, though we travelled fairly slowly, trying to keep the pace smooth. We drove north-east for some days, then followed the coast road due east into the region dominated by the Franks. We found Arthur's ships still secure in their Frankish harbour, and the harbour officials helped us to load the ship we were to use, trying to talk to us in bad Latin. They were delighted when they discovered that I spoke some Saxon – which differed only slightly from their own tongue – and attempted to inform me of various noxious remedies for wounds. When the ship was ready to sail they insisted upon providing a feast, for us and for the escort, which was to set out the next day on its return to Arthur. When the ship did set sail I wondered what Arthur's united Empire would be like. There was no reason for enmity with the Saxons, if they would keep the law. But I was not certain now that any such Empire would survive.

We had a shorter voyage than the one I had suffered on the way to Less Britain, crossing directly from Gaul to the south coast of Britain, and sailing along that coast to the port of Caer Uisc, where we put in and unloaded the ship again. The journey from Car Aës had taken the better part of three weeks. Three of the wounded men had died on the journey, but the rest were recovering well.

The journey to Camlann took two days. The night we spent in a small hill fort along the road – a mere clan holding, the name of which I forget. The lord of the place treated us very strangely, seeming perpetually about to burst into speech and never doing so. I judged that he was uncertain of my status, and wondered again what I would do.

We arrived at Camlann on the afternoon of the second

day, in the early dusk of winter. The green hill rose quiet from the drab fields and bare trees; smoke from the fortress drifted across the early stars, and we could see the glow of its fires against the dark east. Something within me began to sound 'Home, home!' like a clear-toned bell, but I was too heartsick and weary to give it much notice.

The gates of the fortress were locked when we came up to them, which surprised me, until I thought that our ally Constantius must have seen fit to take precautions. One of the guards called from the tower, asking our names and business.

'We are bringing the wounded home from Gaul,' the surgeon shouted – he was officially in charge of the party. 'You ought to have more torches here if you can't recognize your own comrades!'

The gates were unbarred and the carts rolled through. I was riding my mare, and again noticed that the guards looked at us strangely. I recognized them as some of Medraut's men. Two of them came from the guard tower and accompanied us up the hill.

The carts rumbled up to the Hall and there stopped. The guards who had come from the gate with us disappeared at once into the Hall and more warriors appeared to watch us as the surgeon went round the carts checking on the men, who were all sitting up and looking about, even the very sick ones. They laughed and joked about what they would do now that they were home. Soon a few more warriors came from the Hall, carrying torches.

'The Empress!' one of these men exclaimed, and at once the men at Camlann began babbling to each other, lifting their torches high so as to see me clearly.

'Why is she here? Has Macsen been defeated?' the first speaker asked the surgeon.

'Car Aës was still under siege when we left,' I said, and they all fell silent and stared at me. 'I escaped from his fortress and came to my lord Arthur for my sentence. He has commanded me to come here and here await trial. Where is King Constantius? We have some wounded here who need care.'

Some of the men laughed and the rest were uneasily silent. 'Where is King Constantius?' asked the first speaker. 'The lady wishes to know where King Constantius is.'

'She had better ask the Emperor – or the Church,' said another.

This mockery began to annoy me. 'The Emperor told me that Constantius was left in command here. Is that not so?'

'Constantius commands no one now. No one but worms.'

'No, the worms command him. They could command him to provide them a fine feast.'

'And, most noble lady, we have another Emperor now, a better one.'

The realization of what they meant seemed to turn the world upside-down, and I saw suddenly what our host of the night before had meant to tell us, realized why the gates were locked, why the guards had come up the hill with us from the gate. And even as I realised it Medraut came out of the Hall, wearing a cloak of the imperial purple. He was smiling pleasantly.

'Welcome to Camlann,' Medraut said to our party, which had grown suddenly silent, motionless. 'Your arrival is fortunate, for you now have a chance of joining our cause, a chance the tyrant Arthur the Bastard would have denied you. Those who will pledge themselves to follow me will be made welcome indeed, and can expect tokens of my gratitude. But how many of you are there?'

The surgeon, standing beside the foremost cart, only stared at him in bewilderment. Medraut strolled past the cart, looking at the men appraisingly. 'No able-bodied warriors? A pity. Still, most of you are much recovered, are you not?' He addressed these words to one man in particular, a fine infantry fighter who had lost his right leg at the knee. The man flushed when he heard himself spoken to, slid off the cart, clinging to the rim so as to be able to stand. 'I would never be sick enough to fight for a traitor,' he told Medraut, then, calling out to his fellows, 'see what this foreign bastard has done! He has used our lord's generosity as opportunity to usurp the purple! The perjured, murdering . . .'

Medraut's smile had vanished when the man first spoke, and he nodded now and stepped back. There was a flash, and the warrior suddenly coughed, bowed, and fell on his face, a spear jutting from his back. I cried out, leapt from

771

my horse and ran over to the man, turned him over. He was dead already, his eyes set in his head. I touched the line of blood beside his mouth in horror, then fell back as Medraut kicked my hand aside, kicked the body back onto its face.

'Lady Gwynhwyfar,' Medraut said in a low, cold voice. 'How is it that you come here? I could scarcely believe the report. It is an honour I did not expect.'

I said nothing, only stared at Medraut. The cloak he wore was one of Arthur's, and its rich purple hem trailed on the ground.

'She said she fled Macsen and returned to Arthur for her sentence,' one of Medraut's warriors said.

'And we know what kind of sentence the Emperor would give her,' Medraut returned, his eyes narrowing, beginning to smile again. 'Ten minutes in his bed, and all would be forgiven!' His men laughed. 'Get up, my lady murderess. Justice is in my hands now.' I remained kneeling by the dead warrior, seeing how the torchlight caught in Medraut's hair, and on the gold of collar and cloak. His cold eyes glittered suddenly and he bent over, seized my arm and dragged me to my feet; held my arm, struck me twice across the face, and threw me at a guard. Someone cried out.

'The lady is the Empress, the lord Arthur's wife!' the surgeon cried, running over to Medraut, while I tried to gather my senses.

'I am the Emperor,' Medraut said. 'I may do as I please with this woman or with any of you. Anyone who wishes can pledge me fealty, and be welcome here. The rest are servants of my enemy, the usurping tyrant Arthur ab Uther: they are under arrest. Which of you will swear me the oath?'

Silence. Swearing of another kind of oath from some of the wounded.

'Take them away. Lock them in the storeroom,' Medraut commanded his warriors.

'But they are wounded, unarmed...' protested the surgeon.

'Then go with them and tend to them. No, do not take the Lady Gwynhwyfar with the others. Keep her ... keep her in the warleader Bedwyr's house. Bind her and leave guards at the door. I will see to her later.'

Medraut's men poured in a mob about the carts, shouting and laughing. The wounded tried to struggle or protest, but the carts were quickly driven off. I saw this in a glance over my shoulder as my guards dragged me away, still half-stunned by the shock and by Medraut's blows, and led me stumbling to Bedwyr's house. They bound my hands in front of me with strips of the coverlet from the bed, took my own small knife away from me, then left, locking the door. I collapsed in a heap beside the bed and hid my face in the rough wool of the blanket. Outside, I could hear the guards joking and exclaiming excitedly.

Think, I told myself, trying to bite back the hysterical tears. You must think. You have been afraid of this all along; you need not be so surprised now that it has come about. Medraut has murdered Constantius and claimed the purple for himself. What has become of Constantius's warband?

I had seen none of the Dumnonian king's men, I realized. Medraut must have planned his move carefully: murdered Constantius, then had his followers take Constantius's men unawares, probably at night, when they were sleeping after a feast. Perhaps some of the men had sworn the oath to Medraut, and the rest? Death or imprisonment – unless some had escaped. Would Medraut have any allies?

Undoubtedly he had contacted Maelgwyn king of Gwynedd. Maelgwyn would support him in any move against Arthur. On the other hand, Medraut could not trust Maelgwyn very far. The king of Gwynedd wanted the purple for himself, and would not be eager to see Medraut wear it. Had Maelgwyn sent men to Camlann? No, I thought not. I had seen none. Though undoubtedly Maelgwyn had raised his army, and was probably hurrying even now to join Medraut.

Medraut, though, must have only his own followers in Camlann at the moment. Even if he had managed to enforce oaths from some of Constantius's men, and if he had been joined by some discontented nobles, he could not have much over two hundred warriors; three hundred at the most. Maelgwyn had another three hundred and an army of some two or three thousand peasants. When had Medraut acted, and seized power? Fairly recently – yet he had obviously had some time to organize the fortress to his own liking. A week before, two weeks? Someone must, even now, be travelling to Less Britain to warn Arthur. Arthur had plenty of spies and plenty of loyal followers: Medraut could not murder them all. And when Arthur heard, he would abandon the siege and return to Britain as fast as he could. Would he be able to match Medraut when he arrived?

Medraut, Maelgwn of Gwynedd. Who else? Dyfed, Powys, Elmet would probably remain officially neutral in the struggle. If they believed the rumours Medraut had been spreading and still remembered Arthur's violent seizure of power twenty years before, they might prove hostile and send some men to fight my husband. On the other hand, Medraut was a foreigner by birth and, by the same potent rumour, a child born of incest, accursed. The kings of Britain would not support him against Arthur, whose reign was at least familiar. And the kings would not support Maelgwn, either. They might rebel independently, but they would probably wait to see whether Maelgwn or Medraut or Arthur prevailed before doing that. Ebrauc, Rheged – they would support Arthur, if they heard in time, though half their royal warbands were off in Less Britain even now. The Saxon kingdoms?

They had a healthy respect for Arthur; who had defeated them against heavy odds. But a Britain torn by civil strife was much to their advantage. They might make common cause with Medraut for a time; betray him afterwards, of course, but support him against Arthur. Still, negotiations with the Saxons took time. Medraut could not have been negotiating directly before – Arthur and I would have heard of it. All in all, I decided, my husband and his son would be evenly matched in the war that lay ahead.

I sat up, wiping my face and feeling somewhat better. I had cut the inside of my lip against my teeth from one of Medraut's blows, and my face was smeared with blood. I stood up, looking around. There was no water in the room. The hearth was cold, even the ashes of the fire cleared away. The books were gone, and the lamp. Only the bed and a few musty-smelling blankets remained. No one had lived in the house since Bedwyr left it that summer, and the dust was thick over the desk. It was very cold, I realized. My bound hands had turned red, pale-mottled, and were numb. I flexed them, twisting them from side to side, trying to loosen the bonds. I went over to the coverlet, which the guards had thrown aside after cutting my bonds from it, and clumsily dragged it round me, then spat on a corner and wiped my face. My hair had come down on one side, but I could not fasten it up again. I sat huddled up against the bed, my hands between my knees for warmth. Medraut would doubtless send someone to care for me soon. Whatever he intended for me, he, he did not mean me to die from neglect.

What he intended ... punishment of some kind, no doubt. A public display of strength, a trial for the woman who had tried to murder him, and a public execution. Burning? Stoning? Torture? I began to feel a cold different from that of the chill, empty room. *Dear God*, I thought, *give me strength*. If I could not escape I must at least die bravely, as befitted an Empress of Britain.

Escape. My bonds were very tight. There were two guards outside – why had Medraut not posted one inside with me to watch me? He must be afraid I would try to kill myself, to have me bound. Whatever his reason, it worked to my advantage. If I could somehow escape – through the smoke-hole? – but then there was the rest of the fortress to cross, and after that the walls. It would be madness to try the gate. Here I would be recognized, and I did not know the password. Still, it should be possible to climb the walls on the inside. Medraut did not have enough men to patrol the whole circuit of the fortress very closely.

A servant girl came in, accompanied by a warrior. She looked about, saw me and went pale with fear. The warrior pushed her forward. 'Build up the fire,' he commanded, 'and see to the prisoner.' He leaned against the wall by the door, watching me. I remained sitting where I was. The girl built up and lit a fire, fetched water and swept the room without looking at me, although I had to stand and move when she came over to make the bed. She was plainly terrified. I suddenly thought to wonder about the servants at Camlann. If they were obedient, they should be safe – except for Cei's mistress, Maire, and the wife of Gwalchmai's servant. Medraut bore the latter woman especially an old grudge, for Eivlin had served his mother and betrayed her. He would be entirely capable of putting the woman and her children to death. And he could use Maire and her children against Cei.

'Eivlin, Rhys's wife,' I said to the serving girl, 'and Cei's Maire: are they at Camlann?'

The girl gave me a terrified glance, then shook her head. 'Quiet!' commanded the guard.

My hands were untied and I was allowed to wash, then was bound again, and this time my feet were tied as well. The servant and the guard left and I sat on the bed and stared at the new-made fire. Could I burn through the rag bindings with it?

They had just left. It was likely that I would now be left alone, for a little while at least. I did not know Medraut's plans, but the sooner I escaped the better. Where to go when I had escaped? Best to think of that later.

I rolled off the bed and crawled over to the fire. It was made of apple wood, and burned steadily. I thrust my hands over the flame, and realized as my skin scorched that this was unnecessarily painful. Taking a stick of loose wood I pushed a glowing coal from the fire and pressed my bonds against it. It hurt, and I bit my lip and closed my eyes, thinking of Arthur while the cloth smouldered. But soon I could flex my hands; the cloth loosened, tore – I dragged my hands back, free, clenching and unclenching my numb fingers. Thank God. I sat back and unbound my feet. Now – how to get out of the house? The smoke-hole over the main hearth could be seen by the guards outside. There was another hearth in the kitchen, an oven. If I pulled some of the thatch loose from the vent I might be able to climb out of it. Best to take the blankets from the bed and use them to make a rope to help in climbing the walls of the fortress. I dragged the blankets loose, looked around the room for something to cut them with. Nothing there. I went into the kitchen, came back, took another smoulder-ing branch from the fire and used that and rough jerks to divide each blanket into three strips. They were old blank-ets, and it was easier than I had imagined. I tied the strips together. There. And now . . .

The door flew open and Medraut came in. Half-way into the kitchen, trapped, I saw him pause, smile, and close the door behind him. I dropped my armful of blanket rope.

'Most noble lady,' said Medraut. 'I had thought you

were bound and secure.' He glanced down, saw the fragments of charred coverlet by the hearth, stooped and picked one up. He looked at me and raised an eyebrow. 'Obvious, but quickly thought of and daring.' He came over and caught my hand, looked at the burns on my wrist, shook his head, smiling. 'I should have expected nothing less. And you have made a rope, too, to climb the wall! How fortunate that I came in just now. I think, most noble lady, you have mistaken my intentions towards you.'

'Do not play the fool, Medraut,' I said, keeping my voice level. 'You know that I am your enemy, and we both know that I am at your mercy now. And I expect no mercy, from you.'

Again the smooth smile, the ironically lifted eyebrow. 'You have always judged me hastily, my lady. What do you believe I mean to do with you, that you go to such lengths to escape?'

I stared at him, trying to penetrate the mask. I did not believe for an instant that he meant to be merciful, but I could not see what he wished me to believe, or what game he was playing now. 'You know that I tried to poison you,' I said at last. 'And I think you intend to have me tried for that, and for whatever crimes you can fabricate evidence for.'

'Ah, but the Emperor drank the poisoned cup, and was unharmed. Plainly, I must have been mistaken. What are you guilty of, my lady, but adultery? And that is no crime against me; indeed, if your husband is not Emperor – and I say he is not – it is not a political crime at all, and no concern of mine. Why should I treat you cruelly?'

I raised a hand to my jaw, still tender from the blow he had given me only a few hours before. 'What do you intend for me, Medraut?' I demanded. 'If you are trying to bargain with me, I will tell you plainly that I will not make peace with you on any conditions, nor give my support to you whatever you promise.'

'My intentions for you?' He laughed. 'This.' He seized me by the shoulders and kissed me violently.

For a moment I was so astonished that I could not react, and then I tried to tear away from him. He grabbed one of my wrists, held me, caught the other wrist, his grip agonizing on the burns.

'My father's wife,' he said through his teeth, 'my father's cunning wife, the wise and lovely daughter of Ogyrfan, the Empress Gwynhwyfar. Oh, you are beautiful, you are a queen indeed. This will hurt Arthur more than the loss of his kingdom; the Prince of Hell himself must have sent you here to me.'

'Let me go!' I said. 'You cannot do this!'

He laughed again, tightened his grip, dragging my hands up so that the tears of pain leapt to my eyes. 'I can, as you will see. I am going to have you, just as my father had my mother – by force.' He dragged me over to the bed, kicked my legs from under me, fell on top of me. I screamed as loudly as I could, got one of my hands free, found Medraut's knife in his belt. Medraut swore. I struck out, blindly, found his hand on my wrist again, smelled blood. My hand was forced back, and I could not hold the knife. It fell to the bed, slid onto the floor with a soft clunk. Medraut pressed against me, our breath mingling, trapping my arms with his right hand. His left hand moved slowly down my body, tearing apart the fastenings of my gown. His eyes stared directly into mine, savage, bitter, with a strange, agonized loneliness.

'He did not rape your mother!' I said, using the only weapon left to me – words. 'She seduced him. She did it deliberately, because she wished to bear you for his destruction. You are her tool, no more than a tool! Think of her! Oh God, God, help me!'

Medraut's body went slack against mine. 'Lies!' he screamed – screamed like a hurt child. Beneath the horror and the outrage, a little hope stirred in me. Everything Gwalchmai had ever said about his brother returned to me with burning clarity.

'She never loved you,' I told Medraut. 'She only loved destruction. Gwalchmai loves you, Arthur wanted to love you, but *she* never loved you. She . . . she only wanted to devour you. She has devoured your father, she devoured Lot, and Agravain, she devours everything. She has eaten away your soul, and left you alone in the night.'

'Lies!' he cried. He slid off the bed, kneeling beside it and struck out at me. I tried to cover my head and he struck frantic, hysterical blows at my head and shoulders without aiming them. 'She loved me! I will kill you . . . you witch!

You proud whore! I . . . I will . . .'

He was sobbing. The blows stopped. I shook my head, lowered my hands and looked at him. His chest was labouring with the sobs, and his face was streaked with tears. When our eyes met he fell silent.

'She is dead,' I said. 'And she destroyed you as well.'

He moaned like a man in delirium when his wound is searched. He raised his hands to his face, then brought them down wet with tears. He stared at the tears for a moment uncomprehendingly, then looked up at me, anger growing behind his eyes. He wiped his face, turned, and without another word left the room.

'Tie her so that she cannot reach the fire,' I heard him order the guard as he left, and there was in his voice no trace of smoothness. I collapsed against the wall, trembling and weeping with relief. Thank God.

But would it work again? If he got himself drunk would he care how much I spoke to him of Morgawse? And if he gagged me – I must escape. I must escape from Camlann, if it was by death.

One of the guards came into the house with a strong rope, bound my wrists again, then tied them tightly to the outer post of the bedstead. As he turned to leave he paused, picked something up from the floor, and stood a moment turning it in the firelight. It was Medraut's knife, and it was streaked with blood. He looked directly at me for the first time, then spat on me deliberately. 'Murdering whore,' he said, and strode out.

I lay still, resting my head against my arms. Tied like that I could sit against the bedstead or lie flat with my arms above my head, but could neither stand straight nor move about. I could not have hurt Medraut badly with the knife. My blow had been wild and had not struck anything solid. It must have grazed him somewhere. He would come back and, bound like this, it would be very difficult to work free; difficult even to kill myself.

My thoughts leapt and ran among impossible escapes which grew wilder still as sleep came over me – one can sleep anywhere, if exhausted enough – till I lay moaning in a nightmare. I remember one dream in which I flew from Camlann on the back of the dragon of our standard, while Medraut, transformed to an eagle, flew behind me,

779

drawing nearer and nearer. He reached me and I woke, screaming, feeling the cruel talons on my wrists – but the room was still and empty, and I had only twisted my burned hands against the rope. The grey dawn fell through the smoke-hole, and I lay motionless, staring at it while it brightened slowly into day.

I must have fallen asleep again, for when next I opened my eyes there were people in the room. I tried to sit up, caught my wrists against the rope, struggled about until I could swing my legs to the floor and sit leaning wearily against the bedstead. I could not see clearly. One of Medraut's blows had swollen an eye shut. My bruises ached, my wrists burned again, and my tongue seemed swollen in a scraped, dry mouth. I shook my head, trying to toss my hair out of my eyes, and managed to focus on the others in the room. One was the servant girl who had come the day before, and the other was Medraut's friend Rhuawn. He was staring at me, in horror or loathing, I could not tell which.

'Rhawn,' I said, my voice reduced to a croaking whisper.

He gestured to the girl, and she hurried over and untied my wrists, fumling with the stiff knots. 'Do you want some water, noble lady?' she asked in whisper.

'Thank you,' I replied. She had brought a jug of water, and she held it to my lips – my hands were too numb to grip anything, and there were, anyway, no cups in the room. The water was bitterly cold, and stung the raw places in my mouth, so that I could drink only a little of it. The girl set the jug down and built the fire up, then put the rest of the water on to heat.

'Noble lady . . .' Rhuawn began in a hoarse voice, then trailed off, still staring at me.

'What is it?' I asked coldly.

'I had heard that the lord Medraut meant to . . . marry you.'

I stared blankly for a moment, then shook my head. 'What Medraut told me of his intentions was rather less gentle than matrimony.' Though it might even be true; it would be an impressive public gesture for him to marry the Empress.

'He has beaten you!' Rhuawn's voice was suddenly loud again. The girl glanced up at him, terrified.

'I was fortunate to escape so.' I said evenly, then bit my lip, for the expression on Rhuawn's face was now plainly not loathing, but shock and horror. 'You do not support him in this!'

He looked away from me at once, and one hand fell to his sword, tightened about its hilt until the bones stood out. 'Medraut is my friend and my lord,' he whispered.

'You once swore an oath to Arthur,' I told him, my voice also low. 'You once told him that you would raid Yffern itself if he wished it. Now Medraut is your friend, your lord, and you are willing to make war against your friends and your comrades of many battles, to support a usurper to your sworn lord's kingdom, and stand by while his wife is raped in his own fortress. What real cause did Arthur give you, Rhuawn, for you to betray him? Do not tell me of those rumours and subtly devised slights Medraut has crammed your ears with. Did Arthur ever harm any of your clan or kindred, or stand by and fail to aid you when another injured them? Did he cheat you of your share of plunder? Did he steal your goods, or let them be stolen? Did he ask more of you in battle than he asked of himself?—Rhuawn said nothing. 'What cause has Arthur given you to perjure yourself and forsake him?'

'None,' Rhuawn returned in a whisper. 'My lady, I did not believe them when they said Medraut intended this .. this crime against you. I did not believe it when they said he sought the purple. And now ... now I no longer know what to believe. But Medraut was wronged, and he is my friend.'

I brushed my hair back from my face. The serving girl stared at us in fear, and I struggled to remember her, to try to determine whether she would report this conversation to Medraut. But even if she would repeat every word, I had nothing to lose by speaking.

'Why?' I demanded. 'What good has Medraut ever done for you? So, he told you that he did not desire the purple? Now you have learned that that was a lie.'

'He says that the Emperor would have him killed if he did not seize power to defend himself.'

'Arthur would do that? Arthur, who bore so patiently with the crime Bedwyr and I committed against him, and would still wish to spare us both, if he could? You know

781

Arthur better than that, Rhuawn. Let me speak plainly. I did try to poison your friend and your lord Medraut, because I feared this very thing that has now come to pass, this civil war, and would rather be damned myself than see the Empire broken by Medraut. But I did not tell my husband, and when he discovered it, he was very angry.' Rhuawn watched me, white-faced, shaken. 'Medraut has lied to you all along. He always wanted power – think! Remember him when first he came here! And now that he has power, does he use it justly, mercifully? Does he even tell you his mind? You are afraid of him now, for yourself and for others.'

Rhuawn's face showed me plainly that I was right, and a desperate, almost overpowering hope leapt in me. I had never thought him evil, only greatly deceived. 'Rhuawn,' I whispered. 'Help me to escape.'

Abruptly the door opened, and another warrior stood in it, looking at Rhuawn grimly. Rhuawn's face at once became blank, guarded.

'Lord Rhuawn, you should not be here,' said the other.

'The lord Medraut wished the lady seen to,' Rhuawn stated. 'And Mabon on the earlier shift knew of no objections to my seeing to her.'

'You mean "the Emperor" wished her seen to,' the guard corrected, giving me a brief glare.

'The Emperor Medraut. I am just going to see him, to speak of her to him.' Rhuawn gave me one more unreadable glance, then left, leaving the other warrior to tie me up again.

The day passed with agonizing slowness. I was brought some food at mid-morning, and allowed to stand and wash myself. I welcomed the chance to stand, to tie together as best I might the tears in my gown and wash in the clean water, but had no appetite.

Some while after noon, more food was brought, but this I could not so much as look at, and none was brought that evening. I tried to work my hands free of the ropes, but could not get at the knots, though I twisted my hands about fumbling at them until my wrists bled. The bed frame was all too solidly made, and could not be wrenched apart.

It grew dark. Rhuawn had not returned, and my brief hope seemed senseless. The fear and misery had grown so that I could no longer feel them, but only sit, leaning against the bedstead, forcing a numbed mind to think.

I was sitting like this when I heard voices at the door, and I looked away from the fire to that dark corner of the room which opened on the world.

'I have Medraut's permission to see her,' Rhuawn's voice said, protesting.

'The Emperor has said nothing about allowing you through,' one of the guards replied.

'I don't need permission. I have been his friend from the beginning.'

'An increasingly cold friend, Rhuawn ap Dorath, ever since he took the purple. Go away.'

'Very well.' There was a strange grunt.

'What?' came another voice – the other guard. 'Hueil – ai!' There was a brief clash of metal on metal, and a gasp. The door burst open and Rhuawn came in, his sword bare, but not shining in the firelight. There was blood on it. He hurried over to me and swung the sword hard against the rope around the bedstead, then caught my hands and dragged me to my feet. 'My lady,' he said, 'we must hurry.'

'Cut these,' I told him, for my wrists were still bound. He stared at me, and I put my hands against the sword. He saw what I wanted, jerked the blade down between my wrists. The cords parted. I turned back to the room, found the rope of blankets I had made the day before, then followed Rhuawn from the house.

The guards lay by the door, one sprawled across the threshold, staring upwards, face twisted in a grimace of pain. His open eyes stared into the darkness of the night, the few wet flakes of snow that drifted from the low sky. Rhuawn stared at him and shook his head. I hesitated, then stopped and unfastened the heavy winter cloak of the one who stared and pulled it loose. I would need it, and he would not feel the cold.

'Yes . . . good,' Rhuawn said, shaking himself. 'And the armlets, take those too. Here, take mine as well: you will need money. I must get your horse.'

'I could not ride her out of the gate, and you could not take her from the stables. But will they let you through the gate? Then take a horse – not mine – and say . . . say you have a message to Caer Uisc, and are taking a spare mount. Bring the horses round to Llary's field, on the other side of the wall, to the far end of it. I can climb over the wall there.'

'Yes. I will bring your horse . . . a horse.' Rhuawn drew a deep breath.

'And yours – do you have time, can you ride out through the gates?' I asked, for he seemed in such confusion that I was not sure he understood me.

'They will not stop me,' he replied.

'Then meet me at the far end of Llary's field, as soon as you can. At Llary's field.'

'Yes, yes . . . I will . . . fetch the horses.' He shook his head again, and said nothing as I pulled up the hood of my cloak and ran into the darkness.

The fortress was quiet at that time of night, and the few who were about saw me only as a figure hunched against the wind. The snow was falling thicker when I reached the grove where once I had trysted with Bedwyr. I stopped and watched. After a little while a sentry passed on the wall above, and, as soon as he was gone, I hurried over to the storage hut, clambered from the woodpile beside it onto the roof, and from there scrambled up onto the causeway that ran along the side of the wall. I paused, panting from the effort, then fastened my blanket rope to an embrasure, struggled over the top of the wall, climbed a little way down the rope, then fell – my hands were still too numb to grip properly. I twisted my ankle in the fall and sprawled in the mud of the field, but jumped up again and tried to shake the rope loose. It was no use; it would not come. I would simply have to hope that, in the snow, the sentry would not notice it. I stumbled away from the wall, down the ditch and up the bank, and started for the far end of the field, hoping that Rhuawn would manage to get the horses through the gate. I did not think I could walk very far.

I had not gone far when I saw the sentry outlined against the sky again, and I dropped to my knees in the mud of the ploughed field, huddled in my cloak, praying that he would not see the rope. He passed without giving me a glance: I was simply a dark patch in the black and white of the field and the snow. When I was certain he had gone, I jumped up, fell over again as my ankle gave under me. I sat up, feeling the tears of exhaustion in my eyes and wishing that I had eaten something that day after all. But I had no option but to stumble over to the far end of the field and wait. There I sat leaning against the fence. The wet snow fell from the heavy sky, and everything was very, very quiet.

After a dark age I heard hooves and the jingle of harness, and stood up. The sound became more distinct: two horses. I hobbled forward.

They loomed out of the dark, an indistinct figure on a dark mount, leading another horse. I called Rhuawn's name and they stopped.

'My lady?'

'Here,' I said. He came over, dismounted, and helped me into the saddle. I was ashamed to need his help.

'Yours is Constans's horse, Sword-dancer,' Rhuawn said. 'He is a war horse, and well-trained.' I nodded, gathering up the reins and patting the horse's neck: the animal flicked his ears back restlessly, uncertain about leaving his stall on such a night.

'My lady;' Rhuawn continued, speaking in a low voice. 'You recall Eivlin, the wife of Gwalchmai's servant?' I looked up at him, trying to make out his face in the dark. 'Medraut wished to kill her and her children, but I thought it dishonourable to make war on servants, women and children. I said nothing of it to Medraut, but I warned the woman when Medraut first seized power, and helped her to leave Camlann. Her husband's clan lives near Mor Hafren, and have a holding on a river called the Fromm: it is reached by the second turning east from the main road from Baddon to Caer Ceri. The chieftain of the clan is called . . . is called . . .'

'Sion ap Rhys,' I said, remembering.

'Yes. If you go there, my lady, I am certain that the woman will remember you, and see that you are concealed and kept safe from Medraut.'

Yes. Medraut would never know or remember a servant's clan.

'Good,' I said. 'But you will come with me, I hope.'

He laughed strangely. 'I think I will soon find a hiding place, my lady, if one not altogether to my liking. But perhaps not. My lady, by now they will know that you are gone. We must hurry, and hope that the snow hides our trail.'

He turned his horse, spurring it to a gallop, and I followed. Constans's horse Sword-dancer ran swiftly enough, though I had to set my teeth to stay on against the jolting.

We galloped a long way, until the horses were sweating heavily even in the cold; then trotted; then galloped again. The wind was bitter, and I bent low in the saddle, riding blind, content from the feeling of his gait that my horse kept to the road. The snow froze in my eyelashes.

Rhuawn's horse shied suddenly across my path, and I drew rein, saw, looking up at last, that the saddle was empty. I stared blankly for a moment, then guided my mount over to Rhuawn's, caught its bridle – not difficult to do, for the horses were both tired – and turned back down the road. We were on the main road by then, the north road; it was about midnight, and we might have come sixteen or seventeen miles from Camlann.

I found Rhuawn a few paces down the road, kneeling in the centre of it and vomiting convulsively. I jumped from my saddle. 'Rhuawn!' I said, and he looked up, his face a pale shadow in the dark. 'What has happened?'

Silence. 'I am sorry. It is so hot.'

The wind whipped the wet snow into our faces. The reins over my arm seemed frozen there. I went to Rhuawn, caught his arm, touched his forehead. Though the collar of his cloak was glazed with ice, his skin was burning hot. 'What has happened?' I whispered, suddenly very much afraid.

Rhuawn laughed, a laugh that ended in a sob. 'I went to Medraut this morning and pleaded for you. He asked me to dine with him that night, to discuss the matter. But he said nothing of it at table. Only . . . he looked at me. I remember that he looked at Constantius with those eyes, the last night that he dined with him. They say Constantius died in a burning fever. Medraut said it was a fever.' There was a long silence. The tired horses breathed heavily, champed their bits loudly in the stillness. 'It must have been in the wine,' Rhuawn said. 'I thought it tasted bitter. But Medraut complained of it and said it was because of the war with Less Britain that we had no good wine. So I did not suspect.'

'You should have told me!' I began – but what could I

have done if he had? Perhaps a surgeon might have helped Rhuawn if he acted at once, but no surgeon in Camlann would have been permitted to. And now it might be too late. 'You must have water,' I said, thinking rapidly. 'Eat some snow.'

'I will lose it.'

'That is the point. The poison makes you sick; if you lose enough of it, and if you can wash enough of it from your body, what is left may not be enough to kill you. Here.' I scooped up handfuls of the snow, and he took them, vomited again and again, began shaking. I helped him to his horse, managed somehow to get him into the saddle, and took some leather straps from the harness and tied Rhuawn in. 'We must hurry,' I told him. 'Perhaps we can find a place to stop.'

'No! We cannot risk stopping. Medraut will find us.'

I did not have anything to say to that, so only shook my head and spurred my horse to a gallop. Perhaps the whole flight was pointless. Medraut had many ways of learning things, by spies and by his private sorceries. I could only pray that neither means would serve him this time, and pray that Rhuawn had lost enough of the poison, and would recover.

The journey became a nightmare. The horses were now too tired to gallop, and we trotted and walked and trotted and walked, while the snow fell harder, and the world narrowed to the road directly before us, and to my horse and Rhuawn's. Presently Rhuawn's mount began to wander from side to side of the road and fall behind. I went over to it and took the reins from Rhuawn's hands. He was delirious and did not reply to my questions, merely muttering incoherently. I looked about for lights, for a place to stop, but there was no light. It was too late for that, and the snow swallowed everything into a white darkness.

Perhaps three hours after we stopped the first time, Rhuawn went into convulsions. I turned off the road, dragging the horse – which was terrified, despite its tiredness – and began to cross a field. The wind stopped, and I found that we had reached a patch of woodland. I followed the edge of this until I found a hollow of the ground, sheltered from the wind and clear of snow. Here I dragged Rhuawn from his horse, hobbled the animals, and collected some wood for a fire. Rhuawn had a tinderbox and a blanket in the pack behind his saddle, and by some miracle I managed to kindle some wood that was not too damp. I then moved Rhuawn closer to the fire, wrapping him in the blanket. I tried to feed him more snow, but his teeth were set and his body torn by the convusions, and he could not take it. His face in the firelight was almost unrecognizable: twisted, flecked with foam and vomit. The pupils of his eyes had dilated until it seemed that a living darkness boiled within his skull. I touched his forehead again, and still it was burning and dry. Standing by that fire off a road in Dumnonia, I remembered suddenly, as from another world, a conversation I had had with Gruffydd the surgeon, about, of all things, cosmetics. 'Nightshade,' he had said, 'is a deadly poison, but if you put it in your eyes it will make them bright. Dilates the pupils. Also causes fever, vomiting, delirium and convulsions. My lady, why do women tamper with such things? No sane *man* would employ them.' 'Men like bright eyes,' I had replied, 'but do not complain to me; I do not use nightshade. Can it even kill?' 'In the right dosage,' he said, snorting with disgust. 'Too much and it is lost in the vomiting. Not a poison for amateurs.'

But Medraut was not an amateur.

We could ride no further that night. The horses were nearly spent as it was. But I doubt that anyone could find us in the snow. I built the fire up, unharnessed the horses, and tried to construct some kind of shelter for Rhuawn.

Rhuawn died some two hours before dawn. He said nothing that whole while and did not regain consciousness. I realized, when he no longer breathed, that I had not thanked him for saving me. *Well,* I told myself, *it is an evil world. May God reward him.*

I sat for a long while looking at his body, then, because the night was cold though the snow had now stopped, I pulled the blanket from over him and wrapped it round me.

I had no way to bury him. I had neither the tools nor the strength to dig a grave. Nor could I load his horse with his body and continue down the road. It would attract too much attention. Alone, in my muddied peasant dress, I might pass unremarked as a farmer's wife who happened to have a fine horse, but leading another horse burdened with a warrior's body I would be noticed, remembered, found, and the whole escape would go for nothing. But I could not simply leave the body lying there for the scavengers: besides, Medraut's men, if they followed, might find it or hear of its finding, and know that I had taken this road. Moreover I had neither food for myself nor fodder for the horses, and could not travel another day without them.

I huddled near the fire, and must have drowsed a little, for when I looked up again the sun was above the fields. The snow glittered brightly, and the trees stood above fields slashed with their long blue shadows. Northeastward, and quite near, a plume of smoke rose white and thick into the morning air.

I rose, caught and saddled Rhuawn's horse, and managed to drag the body over and tie it there. Then I saddled my own horse, mounted, and rode towards the smoke, leading the other animal.

It was a small holding: a barn and two houses. When I rode into the yard a woman was crossing from the barn to one of the houses carrying two pails of milk. She looked at me, shrieked, dropped one of the pails, just caught the other one and clutched it to her.

'I mean you no harm,' I told her, as men ran out of the barn and the nearest house. 'Does your holding want a horse?'

It was a risk, but not too great a one. I knew that the countryside of Dumnonia was very hostile to Medraut – he had killed their king and unleased a struggle which would certainly harm their lands. And it was likely that they would be pleased with the gift of a fine horse like Rhuawn's and, if they took it, would fear to lose it by informing.

The men of the holding clustered around the woman, staring at me. I had a sudden vision of what I must look like, my face pinched and red with cold, blotched with bruises, my hair down in matted tangles, covered from head to foot with mud, riding a spent high-bred horse and leading another horse burdened with a corpse.

'Eeeeh,' said one of the men, then, 'You are from Camlann?'

'Yes.'

He came over to Rhuawn's horse, staring at the body. He touched it gingerly and felt that it was cold. He looked back at me. 'Your husband? Did the witch's bastard kill him?'

'Yes,' I replied, feeling too far removed from the world to add to either lie or truth. 'I will give you the horse if you will take care of the body, and give me some grain for my own horse. I still have far to ride.'

The man could, of course, take from me whatever he wished without bothering to pay me. But this was a Dumnonian holding, and near the road. Law ought to rule here if anywhere – and it did. The man nodded. 'It is a fine horse. And probably he was a fine man, as well. I am sorry for you, lady. Here, come inside and rest. I will see that your horse is cared for.'

'I must hurry.'

'Leave whenever you wish. But do not fear that we will betray you. Indeed, I think it would cost us our souls, to betray a lady to a sorcerer born out of incest.'

I stayed at the holding until the evening. I was lucky to have found the place: had I tried to ride on to Mor Hafren without pausing for food or rest, I believe I might have died. It was bitter weather, and I was already much weakened.

The people of the holding were cautiously friendly. They had heard tales of what had happened at Camlann, heard of executions, of their king's death; knew of a few servants who had fled the place. They treated my horse well and, at my request exchanged its silver-adorned, enamelled harness for one of inconspicuous plain leather, and gave me some clothing to make up the difference in value. They gave me hot food, hot water to wash in, exchanged my muddy clothing for clean, and gave me a warm bed to sleep in. They woke me in the late afternoon, saying that they were ready to bury 'my husband'. They laid Rhuawn in a grave behind their barn with a mingling of old superstitions and Christian prayers, and gave me his jewellery and his dagger – I told them to leave him his sword. I was grateful to them. But I knew that they believed me only a warrior's widow. What they might have done if they had known who I really was I did not know and did not wish to discover, so, when the burial was done with, I took my leave.

'But it will be cold tonight,' the head of the holding told me. 'You should not travel. And there have been many bandits about since the news came of the king's death and the Emperor's absence. It is not safe for a woman to travel alone.'

'It has never been safe for a woman to travel alone,' I replied. 'But it is not safe for me here, or for you while I am here, and it will be better if I travel at night. There are fewer bandits and . . . other dangers about.'

At this he nodded.

The previous night's rapid pace had brought me almost as far as Baddon, despite the snow. Now the snow was largely gone again, and I made good time, reaching the city wall of Baddon while it was still dusk. I circled this, not entering the gates, as Medraut had probably sent men there to watch for me. It was fully dark when I rejoined the road, the north road, and spurred my horse to a fast trot.

The second turning east on the road from Baddon to Caer Ceri, Rhuawn had said. I was afraid that either I remembered his directions wrongly or that he had been mistaken in them, and that I would find the wrong holding. And beyond that, I feared Medraut's sorceries, that he would somehow contrive to find me, and that death followed me, ready to strike down all from whom I hoped protection. But I had nowhere else to go.

The night was clear, and there was a bright half moon. The second turning which might be called a road came some seventeen miles from Baddon. My horse was still tired from the exhausting night before, and I let him slow to a walk, following the rutted, muddy path through the pasturelands. There were a number of holdings in the area, for at several points I saw smoke rising in the clear moonlight. But I judged that the holding I looked for, if it lay near the river Fromm, must be further east.

The stars wheeled about towards the dawn, and, half asleep, I came upon a holding very near the road. I hesitated, then turned and rode towards it.

When I drew nearer dogs began barking loudly, so I did not dismount, but rode close to the door of the largest house and there waited. The door opened a crack, and I could see lights being lit within. A man came out, carrying a hunting spear, and several others came out behind him, one hastily pulling on a tunic, the others bare-chested under their cloaks.

'Who are you and what do you want?' the leader demanded sharply.

'Is this the holding of Sion ap Rhys?' I asked.

'It's a woman!' one of the men exclaimed – as I was muffled in my cloak, they had been unable to tell this before. Now they visibly relaxed.

'I am Sion ap Rhys, of the clan of Huy ap Celyn,' said the leader. He was an older man, stocky, with a wide, strong-featured face: looking at him more closely I realized that I knew his son, who bore the same features, and I caught my breath.

'I seek Eivlin, the wife of Rhys ap Sion. I am a friend of hers.'

They looked at me a moment in silence. 'Are there no others with you?'

'I am alone.'

Sion ap Rhys sighed, handed his spear to one of the others, ran a hand through his hair. 'Dafydd, take her horse and look after it. Huw, check down the road that there is really no one else. Will you come in – is it "lady"?'

'Thank you,' I said, dismounting. I staggered and felt dizzy when my weight came onto my feet again, and I had to lean against the horse, but I recovered myself. The clan chieftain offered me his arm for support, I took it, and we went together into the house.

'She is looking for Eivlin,' Sion told the family, which was massed inside the door. There seemed to be a lot of them, and, almost at once, there were more, for Eivlin herself burst into the room.

'Most noble lady!' she cried. 'King of Heaven! What has happened to you?'

I tried to speak and began coughing. I was helped to the hearth and collapsed on a stool there, badly wanting to cry. Eivlin pulled my cloak from my shoulders, then saw the bruises on my face. She exclaimed again. 'What have they done to you, the murdering savages? Morfudd, fetch some water, the poor lady is ill. My lady, what has happened? Is Macsen dead? Is the Emperor back? Is my husband safe?'

'Rhys . . . was safe and well when last I saw him,' I said. 'I do not know the rest. I came to Camlann . . . was it four days ago? I had not heard of what Medraut had done. Rhuawn helped me to escape. He is dead. Medraut poisoned him – it was nightshade, I think. Medraut is seeking me. Rhuawn told me you might hide me.'

'And indeed we will. Och, Sion, my father, this is the Lady Gwynhwyfar, the Emperor's wife. Look how they have treated her! Medraut is a wolf, without shame or pity, and not a man at all!'

I began to laugh, weakly, while Sion and his clan stared at me in shock. Eivlin knew nothing of how bad it had really been.

But at least for the present I was safe.

Eleven

I stayed at Sion's holding for more than two weeks. Whether Medraut's sorceries did not work or whether he had no time or opportunity to employ them, I do not know, but I was not discovered.

From Eivlin I learned that Medraut had seized power a week and four days before I arrived in Camlann. The thing had happened much as I had guessed: there had been a feast, before which Medraut had advised his followers, in hints, to drink sparingly. That night Constantius came down with a 'fever', and Medraut told his followers that he would – most unfairly, of course – be suspected of poisoning. His men, alert and awakened, fell on Constantius's followers before the news reached them, and killed half of them. Some of the rest managed to escape in the confusion, and the remainder were locked into the storerooms. Constantius died the next day. 'Rhuawn came to me before morning, just after they had done murdering the King's followers,' Eivlin told me. 'He said that Medraut was to be Emperor, and that I must flee. And I was bewildered near to madness, for how could I flee, with the baby, and little Teleri not yet three? But Rhuawn said that Medraut had not yet made sure of the gates, and that there was great confusion, and he had seen some carts being harnessed by the stables. So I dragged the children out into the dark, with Sion and Teleri crying, and ran down to the gates, and God be praised, there was a cart there. Rhuawn helped me, carrying some goods to pay for the journey. I had wronged him in my thoughts, my lady, for I hated him as a traitor. Och ai, indeed no, not all Constantius's men were killed. I have heard that those that escaped rode across the country into the Saxon kingdoms, and from there took ship to Less Britain. It will not be long before the High King returns and peace will be restored again.'

I said nothing to that. I doubted, though, that anything could restore what had been broken. One might go some way towards piecing together a broken pot or a broom handle, but an Empire is a living thing, made of the hearts of men, and when it is broken, even if set well it may never grow straight again. The Family was at war with itself, and Britain divided in civil war as it had been twenty years before when Arthur seized power. Medraut apparently had had allies in the north: Ergyriad ap Caw, king of Ebrauc, had been forced by his own clan to abdicate and cede his title to his half-brother Hueil, one or two days before Medraut seized power in the south. Hueil was a trouble-maker, and hated Arthur, whom he blamed for the deaths of his father Caw and his brother Bran, and under his leadership Ebrauc rose in rebellion. Our ally, Urien of Rheged, had called up his army, and, with such of his warband as was left – the rest being in Gaul with Arthur – was trying to quell the rebellion. We could be grateful for that, for the timing clearly showed that Hueil was in league with Medraut, but, on the other hand, Urien had been our greatest hope of support on Arthur's return. Now I was not sure that Arthur could defeat Medraut and Maelgwn with the forces he had available to him.

For Maelgwn was, indeed, fighting beside Medraut. Two days after I arrived at the holding we heard that Maelgwn's army had crossed the Saefern river to our north and was hurrying southward to Camlann, and there was no united opposition to him. The middle kingdoms of Britain would fight for neither Arthur nor Medraut. Old differences and new rumours combined to make them unwilling to support their Emperor, though if Arthur died they would doubtless cry out against Medraut and go to war with him and with each other, trying to gain what advantage they could from anarchy. Only Dumnonia, of all the southern kingdoms, might have helped us, but Dumnonia was leaderless and powerless, her king dead, half the royal warband in Gaul with Arthur and the rest dead or starving slowly in the storerooms at Camlann.

If this were not bad enough, there was another cause of fear. Medraut's forces were growing steadily. Discontented noblemen, warriors tired of peace and hoping for profit and glory, debtors and criminals looking for a solution to their own problems in the collapse of the realm, all flocked to join Medraut. And Medraut was able to prevent a similar rally on Arthur's behalf. Almost every day there came some report of a nobleman of Arthur's party arrested or executed, of hostages taken from others, of goods confiscated and fortresses lost.

Yet the countryside about Mor Hafren, at least, seemed to support Arthur. A member of Sion's clan – usually his second son, Dafydd – went every day to Baddon, to learn the news in the market there. When the market was closed down by Medraut's order, there were gatherings at various places in the countryside where news and rumours circulated. And we had news from Baddon occasionally as well, for it seemed that Cei's mistress Maire had settled with some of her cousins there, escaping like Eivlin in the confusion that followed the taking of Camlann. One of these cousins came to the gathering places and gave mournful recitations of bad news, which Dafydd reported back to us. All the clans seemed to await the news that Arthur was back, that they could raise the peasant army and join him. Hunting spears were sharpened, and old war spears, daggers and swords brought from barns or hollows under the eaves, or even from graves; cleaned and polished and clumsily practised with for hours. Arthur had ruled long enough and well enough that the people trusted him and feared what his defeat might mean. They always had more to lose by civil war and anarchy than did the nobles, safe in their fortresses.

Twelve days after I arrived at the holding, Dafydd returned from news-gathering to say that Medraut and Maelgwn and their forces had left Camlann and were riding east. 'Echel Big-hip of Naf's clan says it is because the Emperor has landed in the east, and they ride to fight him,' he told us. 'But Cas ap Saidi says it is because they have made an alliance with the Saxons, and go to join them.'

Everyone in the clan looked at me, but I could only shake my head. I could not say which account might be the true one. I had not heard that the Saxons had taken sides, and had been uncertain that they would. Some of the Saxon leaders, as I believed, liked and respected Arthur. On the other hand, I knew that they resented their position as tributaries and wanted more land. If Medraut had promised them lands, they might have agreed to support him. But would they be willing to trust Medraut? But, again, could Arthur trust them, trust them well enough to risk landing at one of their ports after they knew that his people had risen in rebellion? He must know that the thing the Saxons were most likely to do under such circumstances was to entrap him by some trick, kill him, and then fight Medraut.

'I do not know,' I told Sion's clan wearily. 'We must wait.'

We waited. I could not sleep at nights, and the days seemed an endless succession of grey minutes, all exactly alike. It was difficult for me to stay in that smoky little holding. It was not fitting, the clan agreed unanimously, for the Empress of Britain to lift a finger towards house-work; and it would have been discourteous of me to engage in the kind of work I was best used to, and run the holding. In the end I could only play with the children and pray for nightfall, and then pray for morning. Sion's clan was very good to me, and I owed them my life, but I longed for nothing more than to ride away from that holding and never see it again.

Three days later we had another piece of news: Sandde, the young lord of the fortress of Ynys Witrin, had risen in rebellion against Medraut, and declared himself for Arthur. I remembered Sandde from my many visits to Ynys Witrin: a tall, thin youth with the face of an angel and the manners of a frightened hare. His father had always fol-lowed the policy of the monastery of Ynys Witrin and been mildly hostile to Arthur; Sandde had become lord of the fortress on his father's death only three months before, and had had no reputation for supporting either side, and so had escaped Medraut's attention. He now sent men out throughout the Dumnonian countryside, a day's hard riding in all directions, announcing his rebellion and claim-ing that the rumour that Arthur had landed in the Saxon lands was true.

'Do we leave for Ynys Witrin tomorrow?' Dafydd asked eagerly, after delivering this news.

'Give it a few more days,' returned his father. 'This may be a trick.'

'Who would trick us into fighting for Arthur?' Dafydd demanded angrily.

'Sandde – or Medraut,' I told him, feeling very tired. 'Sandde may have no news about Arthur, and may be trying to win confidence in his cause by pretending to. But if that's the case, he has no chance of defeating Medraut and

Maelgwn on his own – he has only thirty warriors at Ynys Witrin, only his own cousins. It would be better to wait for Arthur. And it might be Medraut's plan to draw Arthur's followers into the open so that he can deal with them before Arthur arrives. We must wait until we know for certain that Arthur has come.' And, I added to myself, that might take a long time. The good sailing weather was now over. Arthur might have to wait until the spring before he could make the crossing from Gaul.

And yet three days later Dafydd rode back early in the afternoon, his horse foam-flecked and sweating from a hard gallop, and rushed into the house shouting that it was true, Arthur was back, and in league with Cerdic, King of the West Saxons. He had landed at Hamwih a week before, ridden north and met Cerdic who was riding south with his warband and some of his army to encounter him. He had spoken with Cerdic and instead of fighting him the Saxon king had agreed to support him as long as Arthur was in the boundaries of his kingdom. But there was more: Cerdic and Arthur had ridden west, and met Medraut and Maelgwn with their forces just west of the fortress of Sorviodunum, which the Saxons call Searisbyrig. There had been a fight between outriders of the two armies, developing into a cavalry skirmish which Arthur's cavalry, predictably, had won, forcing Medraut's to withdraw. That night, Medraut had sent a messenger to Cerdic. 'They say Medraut offered him half Dumnonia and a third of Elmet, and no tribute ever, if he would betray Arthur,' Dafydd said. 'Some say even more than that. But Cerdic offered a parley the next morning, and when Medraut rode up to it, he said, "Whatever enmity I may have borne the Emperor Arthur, and whatever grievances I may have yet, I will not betray him to a sorcerous, perjured, tyrannous bastard. If you come further east, Medraut son of No one, you will be invading my kingdom and you will suffer for it." And they say that Medraut is withdrawing!'

Sion ap Rhys began nodding, and Dafydd looked at him eagerly. 'Very well,' said Sion slowly. 'The army will be needed. We leave for Ynys Witrin tomorrow – and may God defend us!'

It was then the last week of December, but, after some snows, the weather had turned mild, and the roads were choked with mud. Sion had planned to take an oxcart full of supplies, but decided not to bring this because of the state of the roads, and instead loaded the two horses and the mule owned by the holding. There were nine men going, all the younger men of the clan, led by Sion himself; and there were also myself and Eivlin. Eivlin had been under some pressure to stay with her children, but in the end had decided not to. 'The noble lady will need an attendant,' she told Sion, 'and the Emperor's forces will doubtless be needing servants. And I wish to be with my husband.' So the children stayed with their grandmother and their aunts, and Eivlin walked in the mud beside the mule. Sion insisted that I ride the war horse I had brought from Camlann, as befitted a woman of my rank, but after the first few miles I dismounted and made him and Eivlin take turns with me. Sion was an old man, and Eivlin a young mother who had had no cause to walk far for years.

It was thirty-five miles to Ynys Witrin. We set out in the early morning, before the sun rose, and arrived after dusk. We met others on the road, bound on the same errand as ourselves, some by ones and twos, others in large clan gatherings like Sion's. They were armed with everything from ancient, rust-eaten Roman swords to pitchforks and ox goads. They all welcomed company, and even those who had never met one another on a market day were soon discussing taxes and the prices of cheese and ale since the markets closed. No one said anything about the war, which was strangely comforting. I did not speak much, but walked or rode among the others, listening to the steady voices and so longing for peace, for victory, that at times I thought I could not breathe.

When we arrived at the town of Ynys Witrin, Sion insisted that I remount Sword-dancer, so as to make myself known to the guards as stylishly as was possible for someone with as much mud over her as I had. So we went through the town of Ynys Witrin, in a party that had now grown to over thirty men, and began to climb the hill to the fortress. The night was already heavy over the marshes, and it was the dark of the moon, but even if it had been clear daylight it was, I knew, impossible to pick out Camlann from the hunched hills to the south-west. Impossible, though I looked again and again.

The fortress gates of Ynys Witrin were closed and bolted, but torches were set thickly about them, and our party was hailed long before we reached them.

'We are subjects of the Emperor Arthur,' Sion replied on behalf of the whole party, resting one hand against my horse's shoulder and breathing heavily from the climb. 'We have come to join Sandde, to fight against Medraut.' And the torchlight fractured on the makeshift weapons as the gates were opened.

I did not have even to tell the guards who I was. While I was yet riding through the gates I was recognized, hailed, and taken apart from the others. When I confirmed that I was, indeed, Gwynhwyfar daughter of Ogyrfan, and that I wished to speak with their lord, I was given little time to take leave of Sion before I was escorted to Sandde.

The lord of Ynys Witrin was worrying over accounts with his clerk when I was shown to his room, and when he saw me he leapt up, nearly knocking the inkwell over onto the parchment. 'Lady Gwynhwyfar!' he exclaimed, staring, then flushed, bowed, grabbed my hand and held it awkwardly, smiling. 'Most noble lady, I had heard of what that tyrant meant to do to you, and I had heard that you escaped; I am very glad, my lady, to see you. Cuall, fetch some wine! They say that your husband is near mad with fear for you, lady. But I am very glad to see you, I remember your grace well, even from when I was a boy. Cuall! Ah, here he is again. Have some wine, noble lady.'

Cuall, the clerk, poured me some wine and offered me his seat at the desk. 'There are another thirty-six just arrived with the lady,' he told his lord. 'A quarter of them have no supplies.'

'Oh. How many does that make?' asked Sandde. 'Numbers, I mean, not supplies.'

Cuall whisked the parchment off the desk. 'Three hundred and sixty-four today. Two hundred and twelve yesterday. One hundred and sixteen the day before. In total, including those that came the first days, before we made the proclamations, an army of seven hundred and forty. Your own forces, with the other noblemen who joined us, now amount to sixty-three.'

'Seven hundred and forty!' exclaimed Sandde. 'What shall we do? How many brought their own supplies? I wish

I had told them to bring their own supplies – how can we feed seven hundred and forty, to say nothing of sixty-three noblemen, and all the servants? Most noble lady,' Sandde abruptly fixed on me again, 'it is a miracle, it is the mercy of God that you have come. I have so often heard of your skill at managing fortresses and finding supplies; my father always cursed you for it. And I do not know what to do. Until three months ago I had never run anything, and this rebellion is more complicated than I expected, not at all like running a small fortress. My lady, if you came here to help – you did, didn't you? – please advise me how to feed this army!'

I began to laugh, and choked on the wine. 'I thank you, Lord Sandde,' I told him, when I finished coughing. 'Are you sure you want me to help?'

'Most noble lady, how could you doubt it? Why wouldn't I?'

'This war might be thought my fault,' I told him. 'For running off with the lord Bedwyr.'

He looked away from me, turning crimson. 'What does that matter?' asked Cuall the clerk. 'There is a war now – and from all I have heard, your loyalty to the Empire was never in question.'

'Exactly,' said Sandde, looking back. 'Exactly. And as to how to feed seven hundred and forty – the monks in the village have been helping, not much, but still, a little, which is a mercy, for Cuall here is the only one in the fortress who can read – but what supplies we have, and how to get more... Most noble lady ...' he took the piece of parchment from Cuall and gave it to me, looking at me eagerly. I pressed my hand against my forehead, feeling my skin hot, wondering whether what I felt was shame or fear at taking up authority again. But I looked at the figures on the sheet and tried to make sense of them, and, as I did so, felt a strange fierce gladness. The war had begun and I once more had a place in the struggle.

I stayed up till after midnight that night, trying to sort out Sandde's affairs, and might have stayed up later except that, tired as I was from the day's ride and the long waiting, after a time I began adding fifteen to twelve and getting fifty-two. At last Sandde noticed that I was weary and still mud-bespattered, leapt up with apologies, and had me shown to the house that had been his mother's. There I found Eivlin already installed and asleep, and I was too tired to even wash off more than a little of the mud before I followed her example. The next morning I found it more difficult than I had expected to get up, but it was essential to get back to work. I had learned from Sandde that Medraut's forces had retreated from their position near the Saxon border, though at the moment they did not seem to have gone far, and that they were expected to return to the neighbourhood of Camlann. It also appeared that Cerdic's support of Arthur would not extend beyond the boundaries of his own kingdom. Saxon and Briton had fought each other too often to feel confident about marching in company into British territory, and the Saxon warriors had only the haziest of loyalties to a British Emperor. If my husband wished to pursue Medraut, he would have to do so with nothing more than his forces from Gaul. He badly needed the army Sandde was raising. But by this time, Medraut must have heard of Sandde's rebellion. He would certainly wish to crush it before Arthur could join it. Indeed, I could not see why he was waiting near the border, and expected him at any minute.

Sandde, who had many surprisingly sensible ideas, if little experience, had sent messengers to Arthur as soon as he learned that Arthur was actually in Britain, but he had, as yet, received no reply. It was crucial that Arthur and Sandde should arrange some method of joining their forces, and Sandde was worried whether he should leave Ynys Witrin before Medraut arrived to besiege it. If he did so, however, it would be more difficult for Arthur to contact him, so he contented himself with my suggestion that he designate places for men who wished to join the army to meet, so that if Ynys Witrin were cut off by a siege, Arthur would not be entirely cut off from support. The problem of arranging for a possible siege was in fact more urgent than the problem of food supply for the army. That was quite easy to sort out, at least for the time being. I appointed Sion ap Rhys and some others as supervisors of food distribution, so that those clansmen who had brought supplies for themselves provided equably for those who had not. Appointing men like Sion was one of the better things I did, as the farmers were willing to accept measures from another farmer which they would have rejected from a noble. We had supplies to last for a while at least, and began to send messages to the meeting places which had replaced the markets, requesting more food – but we would not have enough to endure a siege.

As that first day passed, I continually expected to hear that Medraut's army was approaching. But no news arrived, and Sandde's scouts reported only that the countryside was quiet. Another five hundred men arrived to join the army, some coming from as far away as Elmet and Powys across Mor Hafren, and the number of our army was raised above a thousand. All the space within the fortress was filled, and most of those who had arrived the day before were already sleeping on the ground, under carts or shelters of firewood, straw and thatching. I had working parties sent down to the town to repair the old municipal defences as best they could, and billeted men on the town and in the monastery. And I had others cut reeds from the marshes, and others use them in constructing slightly better shelters for the army. And still there was no sign of Medraut.

The following day we heard wild rumours of Arthur: he had gone with Cerdic back to the Saxon royal fortress; he had ridden north of Medraut's army by night, and was hurrying towards Maelgwn's kingdom of Cwynedd; he had passed Medraut's army on the south, and was trying to make his way to Ynys Witrin or to Camlann. The only certain thing seemed to be that he was no longer by the Dumnonian border.

'Should we send men north?' Sandde asked me anxiously.

'He will have to pass through Caer Ceri if he is taking the road to Gwynedd,' I said. 'It is only a town, not a fortress, and there should be no warriors there. It would not take many men to hold it for a few days. Perhaps you should send a force there.'

Sandde agreed to this, and we discussed whether to send another force to Baddon. This city, however, was fortified and guarded, and we decided that we could not spare the men to take it, for if Arthur did come to Ynys Witrin we would need every man we had. This decided, I went down to the town to see if any of the monks were willing to work in the hospital I was establishing in the fortress. The monastery was, of course, a far more obvious place for a hospital, but I had little faith in the town's defences, and would not like to see our wounded come into Medraut's hands if the town fell in a siege.

Another five hundred or so men arrived that day. And still there was no sign of Medraut.

I went to rest late that night. I was very tired: more tired than I ought to be, I thought, as I combed out my hair. But I would be thirty-eight on my next birthday, in a few weeks. I was growing too old to run about like a girl. I remembered the girls I had played with when young, trying to imagine what they might be now. Married to landholders and farmers in the North, keeping a small house in order or a minor holding in peace. They had never walked the sword-edge of power. They would have children – I thought of one or two I knew who had died in childbirth. Perhaps their sons would fight, were fighting, in this war. But how would they have lived over the years? Arguing with a few servants, singing over the loom, spinning, cooking, gossipping with the neighbours – and now the war was howling like a black storm beyond their doors. They would be women grown wide-hipped and long-breasted from childbearing, and their faces would be worn and tightened by the land and its concerns, by time and by peace. I paused, then went over and picked up the mirror which lay on a table in the corner. The room was dim, lit only by one lamp. Eivlin and the two other girls whom the crowding of the fortress had pressed into the house were sleeping in the adjoining room; I could hear their quiet, even breathing. I lifted the mirror to catch the lamplight, and the soft flame hung in the polished silver, casting light back onto my face, making my eyes look very dark. My face was worn, but not by the land and certainly not by peace. My sick weariness seemed stamped upon the bone, and in that light I thought I might already be old.

I set the mirror down. God or Fate had chosen me from among those others to step from beside the loom to the heart of the storm. I had been caught in the lightning flash and the black wind. Once, I remembered, I had spoken to Bedwyr about our Empire being a thornbrake against the wind. And I had been the weak point in the barrier, the place where it had given: now all peace was broken, and the storm had come screaming in.

It was no time to think of such things. If I survived there would be time for repentance, but now . . . now there was much to do. I lay down, listening, before I fell asleep, to the girls' breathing and the wind outside in the eaves.

I was woken from a deep sleep by someone shaking my shoulder and saying softly, 'My lady! My lady!'

I struggled awake and sat up, and Eivlin dropped her hand. 'My lady,' she whispered, 'they say there is news – a messenger. They say to come quickly.'

I shook my hair out of my eyes, jumped up and pulled on my gown without putting on the under-tunic, then slipped on some shoes. 'Come quickly where?' I asked Eivlin.

She handed me my cloak. 'The hospital, my lady. They say that the messenger is dying.'

I had established the hospital in Sandde's guest house, which was large and well heated. At this time it was, of course, partly occupied, but it could be cleared, and it adjoined a storeroom which could be heated if more space became necessary.

'I will go, and stay as long as needs be. No, don't come: go back to sleep. The man who told you this is outside?'

He was, huddled against the door so that he had to stumble back hurriedly when I opened it. There was a fierce wind that left the stars blown brilliant and cold at mid-heaven, though the west was filled with a haze that promised snow. I judged that it was about four hours till dawn, and shivered. We hurried to the guest house, nearly running to keep warm.

Sandde was sitting in the dimly lit room on which the door of the house opened, while a few members of the army lay on pallets by the wall, trying to sleep. The lord of Ynys Witrin looked very glum, but leapt up in his usual fashion when I came in, waved at the door to one of the other rooms, stammered a greeting, then hurried to the indicated door and opened it. I stepped through into a glare of torches and saw Gwalchmai, lying very still on the one bed, his head wrapped in a bandage stained crimson with blood. A surgeon was bent over him.

I stopped, staring, filled with horror. 'What . . .' I began, then saw Rhys kneeling beside the surgeon; he had turned and was looking at me. 'Rhys. What has happened?'

He stood rapidly, looked down at Gwalchmai a moment very grimly. The surgeon nodded to him and he came over, urged me back through the door and into the other room, then closed the door behind him.

'My lady,' said Rhys, then caught my hand and held it very hard. He was pale, and his face and hand were damp with sweat. 'They said that you were here, and they would send for you. I could scarcely believe it. The surgeon here says that my lord is dying. Is he likely to know?'

'He . . . he is a monk from Ynys Witrin. They say he is very skilled. But what has happened? How . . . Arthur sent Gwalchmai here as a messenger?'

Rhys let go of my hand, rubbed his palms over his face and through his hair, stood with his face hidden a moment, then dropped his hands and nodded wearily. 'There was nothing else to be done with him. He would not rest, and he wished to ride into battle as soon as he was well enough recovered to ride at all. It was better while we were journeying back to Britain – he had to keep quiet on the ship. But since we arrived – my lady, the surgeons said that he must not become excited. So the Emperor sent him here with a message, to keep him out of the fighting. But today – yesterday – well, the country northwards is full of armed men, fighting for any lord you care to name, or simply for themselves. We met some who tried to kill us for our horses. Gwalchmai killed some of them, and the rest were frightened enough to let us ride off. But half a mile along the road he fell off his horse and went into a faint, just as he is now, and his head began bleeding. I couldn't wake him, and couldn't stop the bleeding. I tried to cauterize it; that helped a little, and your surgeon here has just done it again. Sometimes on the road he woke up enough to talk, but mostly to people who weren't there. So I brought him on here. But they have told me he will die, and probably in a few hours; that he is dead already from the waist down.'

After a pause Sandde asked, 'What is the message?'

Rhys stared at him. Sandde stared back, chewing his moustache and fidgeting with his baldric. After a moment, Rhys shook his head. 'You never knew him – and it is what we came for, after all.' He fumbled at his belt, drew out a letter. 'Here. I took it from him after he fell.'

Sandde took the letter eagerly, looked at the seal, then handed it to me so that I could read it to him. I stared at it numbly. It was sealed with tallow and lamp black, but Arthur's dragon seal was firmly imprinted on it.

'Please, my lady,' said Sandde. 'We must know what to do.'

I broke the seal, moved closer to the lamp to read. '"To Sandde, Lord of Ynys Witrin, from Arthur Augustus, Emperor of Britain: greetings,"' I read out, then stared at the bold familiar hand and lowered it. 'Sandde, Lord Gwalchmai ap Lot is my friend. Do you know why he is dying? Is there any hope?'

Sandde made an awkward gesture. 'They simply told me he was dying.'

'It is a splinter of bone,' Rhys replied. 'It broke when he was first wounded, but did not come loose; it might have grown together again – so your surgeon says. But now it is cutting the brain apart. The surgeon says it is too deep for him to get out. There is another wound, too, from the fight on the road, but your surgeon says that one does not matter. A few hours, he says. He did not wish even to try to help.' Rhys drew a deep breath and rubbed his face again.

'I see,' I said, then, not knowing what to do, lifted the letter again. '" – from Arthur Augustus, greetings. My friend, I do not know how to thank you. I beg you not to move from Ynys Witrin, but wait there and gather as large a force as you can. Send any messages to the places my emissary will inform you of. He is a man of great skill and experience, and you can trust his words as you would my own. He will inform you of my plans. If you can, send supplies, especially grain, to the places he will tell you of, for we may have to abandon our own supplies to gain speed. When next you hear from me, take all your forces to the place I will tell you of, and there conceal them, for I hope to set a trap for Medraut and Maelgwn. More I cannot trust to ink. God give you aid!"' I hesitated, noticed some additional words smudged across the end of the scroll. '"If . . ."' I began, then stopped.

'What?' demanded Sandde.

'If you have any news of me he wishes to know it. And he says to treat me honourably if I should come here. He says that you can trust me with authority, especially for finding supplies.'

Sandde smiled. 'Unneeded advice. You can write to him yourself, now. But what shall we do? He has trusted too little to ink and too much to his messenger's health.' He fixed his eyes on Rhys again, started, and demanded, 'Do you know what your lord was to have told me?'

Rhys shrugged, ran his hand through his hair again. 'Some of it.' He glanced round, then lowered his voice, 'When we left the Emperor the Family was already riding towards Gwynedd at a good pace. Our lord Arthur judges that Maelgwn will not consider fighting you worth the risk of having his own kingdom plundered, and will set out in hot pursuit. Medraut dare not risk fighting you with only his own followers – most of those who have joined him since the start of the rebellion are sure to stay with Maelgwn, for they wish to fight Arthur, and trust that the kingdom's ruined if they can kill him. But while they are following, the Emperor will send his men away in various groups, with spare horses and most of the supplies, and these will wait at assembly points southwards. Some time before he reaches the Saefern river, he will abandon the rest of his supplies, circle round his pursuers, and come south as fast as he can. He will pick up the rest of his men, and fresh horses, at the assembly points – and he may want supplies then, for, though we had goods from Cerdic, we could not transport enough to last long. Then, I think, he hopes that Maelgwn and Medraut will be following close behind him, and if he has your troops placed in an ambush, he doubtless hopes to lead the rebels directly into it.'

'Ach!' exclaimed Sandde. 'That is an excellent plan, and worthy of the Emperor. But these assembly points, where are they? I must find a place for an ambush, and tell the Emperor where I think would be best. Where shall I send the message?'

'I do not know,' Rhys said. 'Gwalchmai knows – that, and the watchwords, and the timing.'

Sandde exclaimed loudly and wordlessly, fell silent. 'Then what shall we do?' he demanded, after a minute. 'Is your lord likely to wake again?'

Rhys smiled bitterly. 'How should I know? Your surgeon couldn't tell me. He said only that my lord would die in a few hours.'

'Here,' I said. 'Find me some wax tablets and I will wait here and write the information down if Gwalchmai wakes.' I walked over to the door of the other room, and stepped again into the torchlight. After a moment Rhys followed me, then Sandde.

The surgeon was sitting on a sleeping pallet in the corner, taking his shoes off. He looked up at us with an expression of irritation, but stood, and bowed to Sandde.

Sandde walked over to the bed and looked at Gwalchmai, then at the surgeon. 'Is there nothing you can do?' he asked. 'Will he wake, before the end?'

The surgeon shrugged. 'Possibly. It depends how soon that is. Soon indeed, if there is noise and he is disturbed.'

'I will stay here, but be quiet,' I said, looking about for and finding a stool. I moved it to the bedside and sat down.

'As you please, noble lady,' said the surgeon. 'If your benignity does not object, I wish to sleep.' There was a tone of bitter irony in his voice. He must have long shared his monastery's hostility to Arthur, and doubtless found this alliance displeasing.

'Sleep while you can,' I told him. He bowed again, extinguished one of the torches, then lay down on his pallet, covered himself with his blanket, and turned his back on us.

'I will have someone bring you the writing materials,' Sandde whispered to me. 'I thank you, my lady. And I pray God he wakes!' He left, taking another of the torches to light his way back to the Hall.

Rhys sat down on the floor at the foot of the bed, leaned back against the bedpost, then covered his face with his hands.

'I am sorry,' I said, not knowing quite what I meant by it. 'Rhys, you have had a long journey, and must be very tired. Rest, and I will wake you if anything happens.'

Rhys shook his head. 'Thank you, my lady. But I will wait.'

We waited in a silence so deep that we could hear each flicker of the single remaining torch, hear the soft brush of ash falling to the floor, the breathing of each person in the room, and the loud wind outside the house. A servant arrived with the wax tablets, a stylus, and parchment, ink and pens, then left again.

I rested my head on my hands, looking at Gwalchmai. I had noticed first how gaunt his face had grown, eaten away by grief and sickness. But now in the torchlight he looked fearfully young, almost as he had looked when first I saw him, when he lay wounded in my father's house. He had always had a look of being haunted by something greater than the world; now he looked as though he were melting into it, balanced between Earth and the Otherworld. The red torchlight on his sweat-damp skin made it look hot, like metal in a fire, as though the bones beneath were melting into another shape. I touched his forehead lightly, but it was not hot. My hand brushed the bandage and it fell aside, for it had only been drawn across his head, and not fastened. I drew it back hurriedly: his head had been dented by Bedwyr's sword, bone very white in a ruin of red and black cauterized flesh, now crushed and broken by the fall and the surgery even to the shapeless grey of the brain.

I twisted my hands together to make myself keep still, thinking of him in the past, riding his stallion about the practice field at Camlann, dropping in a falcon's swoop upon the ring left on the ground. Then I thought of Gwyn trying the same move; of the way I had seen the boy most recently, crawling on his knees in the road to Caer Ceri, dragging in puzzlement at Bedwyr's spear. And I thought of Bedwyr standing in Macsen's stables, saying farewell to me – his calm face and the total, bleak despair in his eyes. Of such had been our Empire, so much it had meant, and now it was all come to this. I wanted to weep, but there were no tears in me, only a great blank horror of all that was. And around was only silence and, outside, the wind.

About the hour of dawn I glanced up from some momentary abstraction to find that Gwalchmai's eyes were open and he was watching me.

'Gwalchmai,' I said, my breath catching. I put my hand out to touch his, then remembered his last words to me and drew back. Doubtless I was the last person he wished to see – but perhaps not, and there was the message. 'Can you understand me?'

His lips formed the word 'yes', soundlessly. Rhys stood and hurried over. Gwalchmai's eyes focused on him, and he smiled very slightly. 'Rhys,' he said, in the faintest whisper. 'Is it real, then?'

'My lord? Eh, my lord, we are at Ynys Witrin. This is real.'

'And she . . . was she here, before? I talked to her before.'

'Ah, the Empress! Yes, she is really here, now. You were dreaming on the road, my lord, but she is here now.'

He closed his eyes, then opened them again and looked at me. 'My lady,' he said, still in that almost inaudible whisper. 'But, of course you are here. Of course. Medraut did not . . .'

'He did not harm me.'

'Good.' The eyes fixed on Rhys again. 'This time I am dying, cousin.'

The servant said nothing for a moment, then glanced down and muttered, 'They say so.'

Again the slight smile. 'It is true. Have they cut my legs off? No? I cannot feel anything. I had not thought . . . to die this way. Rhys, where is my horse?'

'In Sandde's stables. I told them they were to look after him well or they would need looking after themselves.'

'Good.' The smile, slow and painful. 'Thank you. You must let him go. No one must ride him after I am dead. Let him see . . . that I am dead. Then let him go.'

'Very well, my lord.'

'And my sword . . . fasten that to his saddle. Let them go together. I will give them back.'

Rhys swallowed a few times, nodded.

Gwalchmai looked back at me. 'I . . . am . . . glad you are here, my lady. I should . . . no, I must say that later. Arthur gave me a message for Sandde. It is important.'

I nodded and picked up the writing tablet, and Gwalchmai smiled again.

He had just begun telling of the movements Arthur planned when the surgeon woke and came over. He took the warrior's pulse and shook his head. Gwalchmai politely asked him to leave. 'Though you are a surgeon, I must speak of my lord's secrets, which you should not hear.'

'Very well,' said the surgeon. 'There is at any rate nothing more surgery can do for you. Yet I am also a monk, a man of God. You would do well to make a confession of your sins, and receive the sacrament.'

'Later, if there is time,' said Gwalchmai.

The monk gave us all a look of venomous displeasure.

'You would do better to go before God with a mind hallowed and absolved of sin, not one bound up in worldly concerns and the secret policies of kings.'

'I would not go to my lord God leaving obligations unfulfilled behind me, and that through selfishness,' returned Gwalchmai. 'I beg you, go. If there is time, when I am free of what I am yet bound to, you will be called.'

The monk snorted and stalked out, and Gwalchmai resumed Arthur's message, laboriously, but with careful steadiness.

Presently he stopped for the fourth or fifth time, and closed his eyes. He scarcely seemed to be breathing, and I thought *It is now*, and felt my heart in my throat. But he opened his eyes again and looked at me.

'That is all,' he said. 'The last act I will do in Arthur's service. You must ... you must give him my greetings, and my thanks, and say ... say that I regret nothing in my choice of a lord, except that I did not serve him better. So. My lady, I ... I wish now to send a letter. Will you write it?'

'Of course. Speak. I have parchment.'

He watched while I sharpened the pen and dipped it in the ink, resting the parchment across my knees. Then he closed his eyes.

'Gwalchmai to Bedwyr son of Brendan, greetings,' he said, in a voice louder than any he had used yet. The tip of the pen I was using went through the parchment and broke. Gwalchmai opened his eyes at the sound, and I pulled the pen out and stared at him.

'To Bedwyr?' I asked in despair.

'You agreed. You must write it; I cannot. My lady, there is not much time. This is the greatest debt yet binding me, and I have not much time left to pay it.'

I resharpened the pen hurriedly. 'Speak then. I will write. Only ... remember, I have loved him, and he has been your friend as well.'

'I have remembered it.' Gwalchmai closed his eyes again. 'I wished to ... and now I do not know what to say. I dreamed I was speaking with Bedwyr. It must have been after I fell. "Greetings. My cousin, I am dying. I wished to write, because ... because now ..." – no, don't say "now", say, "Because I so desired your death. And now bitterness seems pointless. I wished for justice with a longing greater than was just, and so . . . so I brought ruin upon our lord, and all we fought for, greater ruin than any you caused. You said . . ." but no, he cannot have said it. That was in the dream. "If the justice I desired were in the world, there would be none left living. How can a man be justly punished for a crime he did not intend? You were right when you said that mercy alone is just. I . . . I forgive you my son's death. Forgive me my vengeance. I . . ."' He stopped abruptly, looked puzzledly over my shoulder for a moment, then, suddenly, his dark eyes flooded with brilliant life and he smiled. 'You?' he asked.

I looked over my shoulder. There was no one there. I turned back, frightened, and caught his arm. Rhys had said that Gwalchmai had raved on the road, and had talked with people who were not there; it seemed now as though he might again. 'Gwalchmai, what is it?' I asked.

He looked back at me, puzzled. 'Can't you see? Och ai, then it is the end. But there is no more to the letter, only that I pray God's mercy for us all. Rhys . . .' The servant caught his hand, 'Rhys, *mo chara*, farewell. My lady, farewell – and if you can, tell my brother I loved him. I am coming.' He looked again into the empty air, smiling like a child. Beneath my hand I felt the muscles of his arm tense, realized that he was trying to sit up, and seized him and leaned against him. I felt his heart beat against me, once, twice, pause . . .

Stillness. I sat up, looking at him desperately for a sign that he lived yet. But the look he had had all his life, the haunted brilliance, had vanished, and the face was almost unknown, my friend's face and a stranger's.

Rhys crossed himself. He was weeping silently. 'Lord God have mercy,' he said, in British, then crossed himself again and added the accustomed form in the Latin of the Church, 'Grant him eternal rest.'

'And let light perpetual shine upon him,' I replied mechanically. But I thought all light in all the world was dead or dying, and my own heart plunged in the darkness.

We pulled the blanket over Gwalchmai's face, and I went over to the last, guttering torch and extinguished it. The day had broken, and the room was already streaked with new sunlight. When I opened the door into the adjoining room I saw that the morning fire had been lit, and a number of people were sitting about it, breakfasting on bread, cheese and warmed ale.

'He is dead,' I told them all.

The monk nodded, took a last bite of bread, and dusted off his fingers. He was beginning to speak when another figure leapt up from beside the fire and shouted, '*Rhys*!'

'Eivlin!' Rhys shouted from behind me, and pushed past roughly. He and his wife locked together like a latch fitting into its place, each holding the other fiercely and painfully. Only when I saw them so did I realize how much each must have feared for the other – and realize how much I myself now longed for Arthur.

'Och, Rhys,' Eivlin said, as I moved from the door, 'Rhys, it is your lord, it is the lord Gwalchmai, that is dead?'

Rhys nodded, tried to speak, and choked on the words.

'Yes,' I answered for him. 'You came here looking only for me, then, Eivlin? Well, see to your husband. Will one of you,' I looked at the men by the fire, the monk and those who had slept in the room over the night, 'tell Lord Sandde of this, and ask him to make arrangements for the burial. Tell him also that I have the message and that I will join him presently.' One of the men nodded, and went with me from the room, outside into the morning.

There was fresh snow upon the ground, and the sky was patched with clouds. While my messenger trudged up the hill I leaned against the outer wall of the house and swallowed the cold air in great gulps, crushing the letter and tablets against me. The pain about my heart seemed almost stifling. But I could not weep, and presently I started back up the hill to my own house, to wash and change before seeing Sandde. There was still much to be done that day.

I wrote letters all that morning to everyone I could think of who might be willing to provide additional supplies on credit – a desperately short list of names, but one very diffi-cult to compile. In the afternoon, when I wrote to Arthur, the bulk of my letter was concerned only with the question of supplies. Only when I was done with it did I realize with a shock that I had not said that Gwalchmai was dead. After only a few hours, with the body yet waiting for burial, it seemed already a thing fixed. *You are tired*, I told myself, to still the wave of sickness that came over me then, and I dipped the pen in the ink and wrote out a full account. At the end, I ran out of space on the sheet of vellum, and had to end abruptly. Almost I added nothing more, but then, turning the page over I saw the amount of space I had left above the superscription, and I added, in my smallest lettering, 'I escaped before Medraut could harm me. I want only to see you again. My soul, my dearest life, tell me to come and join you with Sandde and the army. But in all events, God defend you.' There was no more space, and the cramped letters seemed meaningless, set against the thought of his presence, so I added no more, but folded the letter over, sealed it, and gave it to a messenger. I sat for a moment staring at Sandde's desk, wondering when Arthur would get the letter, of what he would be doing, and when we would see one another again. I wished then, and wished again many times afterwards, that I had demanded another page of parchment and crammed the margins with words. But perhaps I did say what was most important – and perhaps I could not have said more if I had meant to.

We buried Gwalchmai that evening in the grounds of the monastery of Ynys Witrin. While the procession of mourners moved to the grave, Rhys held Gwalchmai's horse, with the jewelled hilt of the sword gleaming beside the empty saddle. The stallion nickered earnestly when the body was brought out, recognizing it, but became increasingly uneasy as the monks prayed and chanted, and when the body was lowered into the ground, neighed loudly and fought to pull away from Rhys. When the burial was finished, Rhys slipped the bridle from the stallion's head, and the horse cantered over to the grave and stamped about over it, looking about and sniffing the air and the ground, and then threw its head back and neighed. The monks crossed themselves and whispered.

'Let him be,' Rhys said and, turning on his heel, started back up the hill. I followed, and the other mourners and the monks dispersed. But when I glanced back, I saw the stallion, very white and splendid in the dusk by the damp grave, tossing its head and neighing again, and again. But in the morning the horse was gone. I feared for a time that someone might have stolen it, it and the sword that was supposed to burn any hand that drew it against its owner's will. But such a horse, let alone such a sword, was too fine to be mistaken for another, or pass unremarked, and they were never heard of again, even in rumour. Gwalchmai had always claimed that the sword, and the horse, had come from the Otherworld. Perhaps the stallion did turn from that dark grave and run off through the night into a day that was now entirely separate from the Earth, to a place where no human grief could reach it, where no further love could hold it back. However that may be, it went, leaving only a few hoof marks around the new grave. And I did not have much time to worry about it.

Twelve

Gwalchmai had told us that Arthur planned to reach the Saefern three days after leaving Searisbyrig – two days after he himself came to Ynys Witrin. Arthur would turn and ride for Camlann very rapidly for the main part of a night, then proceed more slowly through the various assembly points, collecting his men, and arrive near Ynys Witrin about noon on the second day from the Saefern, four days after we received his message. It was on the evening of the day before this that we had our second letter from him. It was very brief, and obviously written in haste. It acknowledged the receipt of my letter, and said that some of the supplies had indeed reached him. It agreed to the place Sandde had recommended for the ambush, and told Sandde to leave Ynys Witrin before dawn the following day, and conceal his forces at that ambush, as Arthur hoped to arrive there about an hour before noon.

'Medraut and Maelgwn are no more than five miles behind me,' he wrote. 'I hope to keep them at that distance tomorrow. May you prosper!' then, written small, 'Gwynhwyfar, my heart, do not go with the army. We will have no camp, and I could not risk you if we should lose the battle. But if all goes well, I will see you tomorrow in the evening. If it goes ill, remember always that I loved you.'

I read all but the last lines to Sandde, then remained seated, staring at the lines I had not read aloud. I thought that the lamp was flickering, but when I looked up I saw that it was only the trembling of my hand.

'Tomorrow,' breathed Sandde. He took the letter from me and stared at it, as though he could wrestle out the meaning by looking at it hard enough. 'Tomorrow, before dawn! And by tomorrow evening, it will all be over.' He jumped up and strode across the room, stood on one foot looking at the fire, twisting his fingers in his baldric. 'How . . . how many men do we have now?' he asked.

'An army of two thousand, one hundred and seventeen,' I told him. I did not need to check the figures: they ran constantly through my mind. 'And ninety-eight warriors, including those we sent with the messages.'

'And Medraut and Maelgwn have how many?'

'Their army probably amounts to three thousand men. Their warbands, combined, and including those who have joined them since the beginning of the rebellion, probably amount to about a thousand trained warriors.'

'And the Emperor has a thousand.'

'Something less than that now. There were men lost in Gaul.'

'But won't some Saxons have joined him?' Sandde turned and studied my face anxiously. I shook my head – the Saxons would not trust the British in a British kingdom.

'We are outnumbered, then,' said Sandde, earnestly, forcing cheerfulness. 'Still, the numbers of trained warriors are evenly balanced, aren't they? And the Emperor, I have heard, is so accustomed to fighting against worse odds than this that this must seem nearly equal to him.'

'Arthur has fought against the Saxons at far worse odds, that is true,' I said, meeting his eyes. 'But Saxons usually rely more heavily on half-trained peasants, and almost never have any cavalry. Part of Medraut's army were members of the Family, and most of the other warriors will have profited by Arthur's example, and have training that nearly equals that of his men. This will not be the same as fighting the Saxons. The enemy's numbers will count.'

'Oh.' Sandde bit his lip, then came over and sat on the desk, still looking at me earnestly, his eyes very blue in the lamplight. 'I have never been in a battle,' he told me. 'I didn't know what I was doing when I raised this rebellion against Medraut. It was simply that ... that Medraut had a friend of mine put to death for treason, and that I admired Arthur, and no one else was doing anything. But now everyone expects me to tell them what to do, and I do not *know* what to do. Most noble lady ...' He clutched my hand suddenly. 'I know it is cowardly to speak this way, but you are like my mother, who understood. Please excuse it.'

I took his other hand. He was too young for it, I thought, far too young. I was indeed old enough to be his mother. 'Don't be afraid,' I told him, as quietly as I dared. 'You have not failed your men once, and you will not fail them tomorrow. Our numbers are nearly even with the enemy, our cause is more just, and, moreover, we will have the advantage of surprise. Trust to God for the victory.'

He kissed my hands and pressed his forehead against them. 'Lady Empress,' he whispered, then broke away, stood suddenly, fingering his sword. He straightened his shoulders and tried to smile. 'It will go well!' he announced.

'It will, as God is just,' I returned. 'And for you, at least, I need not fear, Lord Sandde. Indeed, I think that all in the battle will mistake you for an angel assisting the souls of the dead, and not a spear will be cast at you.' He tried to smile at this, feeble as the joke was. 'Here,' I went on, 'who shall we wake first tomorrow?'

I wondered, watching him as he settled to work at the business of moving the army, whether he would be living when the sun next set, and, if he lived, whether he would be able to stand so straight: whether he would come back blind, missing an arm, a leg, screaming on a stretcher. There would be plenty that would do so, and they would be brought to Ynys Witrin, for it was the nearest town to the battle where we had some control. I thought of my husband, wondering if he would come to me, and how.

Most of the army rose three hours after midnight, and marched out before dawn. Sandde went first, followed by the noble warriors who had joined him – a group which Medraut's oppression had made small – then by the common army, roughly grouped in clans. Eivlin had already said farewell to her husband and his kin, and now stood beside me at the gate, huddled silently in her cloak. When the last pair of feet had tramped past the walls we remained staring after the force a while, watching as they wound down the pale road into the town at the hill's foot, vanishing in the shadows of the dark marshes. Already the stars were pale, and the night air heavy with dew. When a cock crowed in the fortress I turned back and looked at the crowd of women, old men, children, scattered monks and servants, who all waited expectantly for my orders. I wondered briefly why the authority had fallen so plainly to me, and not to Sandde's clerk Cuall, who was waiting with the others. But I knew the reason. Cuall himself was bewildered with events, and no one else was willing and able to exercise the authority. In this crisis, no one cared what I had done, how much I might be to blame for what had happened. All that mattered was that I was the Emperor's wife, and used to riding the storm.

'Nothing will happen until noon,' I told them. 'Go back and rest while you can. When it is time to send out parties to help with the wounded, I will have you called – but you will have to hurry then, and hopefully most of you won't be needed.' And I smiled, trying to look as though I feared only that the victory would be too swift for us to get the carts out in time. It won a few smiles, a ragged cheer; an old man took my hand to his forehead as I walked back through the crowd, and exclaimed that I'd soon be Empress in Camlann again. I laughed, and said that he would soon be back on his farm. When I was back in my own house, and alone again, it was, of course, another matter. I sat on the bed waiting and waiting for the morning, twisting my hands together, rubbing the finger where once I wore the ring carved with the imperial dragon.

That morning seemed to have sprung free from the wheel of time, and hung off apart by itself, unmoving, unending. I had every vessel and water trough in the fortress filled with water, took inventory of our food supplies again and again, arranged again with the surgeons which of them would go to the battlefield and which stay in Ynys Witrin to treat those who were brought back; I went over the places we had cleared for the wounded, I found wood for the fires, and still the sun waited eastward of the zenith. The site of the ambush, I knew, was just by the turning of the main road onto the west road that led to Camlann. Arthur hoped that Medraut would think he was making for the fortress itself, and perhaps expect Sandde to meet him there. He could not help but know that Arthur meant to meet Sandde, and, since he had left Camlann under only a light guard, it might be expected that the Emperor would try to take the fortress itself, and meet his ally there. But still, Medraut might expect and be prepared for an ambush. But even if he did, there was no way of imposing formations on Maelgwn's peasant army, and the precise place and time would be unknown to him. He would have to hurry to catch Arthur before he could reach Camlann, so Arthur's plan should have some effect.

At noon I sent the carts out, with the surgeons and ser-vants who could provide emergency treatment on the battlefield, and with some water, food and fuel. Winter is a bad time for a war. The casualties are higher, for the wounded die quickly unless they can be brought to shelter and kept warm. It would be very difficult for us to care for them properly, ten miles from the site of the battle, short of horses for the carts, and, assuming that Medraut's forces took the main road, with an enemy army between us and the battle. But we hoped that Arthur had brought some extra carts with supplies from the assembly points, and that some of those who were injured could be dragged free and sent off to us.

In the mid-afternoon a cart did arrive, not one of those we had sent out, but one of Arthur's. It was driven by a peasant with a crippling leg wound and filled with men mostly from Sandde's army, one of them dead, the rest needing attention. I saw to it that the cart was unloaded, and questioned the driver.

'Indeed, we reached the place in good time, noble lady,' he told me. He seemed to be in no pain, though his eyes were dark with shock. 'We had time to build the fires and warm ourselves, have a bite to eat and a rest, before the Emperor came and told us to put the fires out. The enemy came up before noon, soon after the Emperor. We ran at them.'

'Did they march into the ambush?' I asked. 'Did Arthur stay with you, or go up the road? Where were the cavalry?'

'I ... I don't know. We ran at them, and when we reached them it was all shoving and shouting. They were Maelgwn's men, farmers like me, not warriors. One of them stabbed me, and I fell down, and my cousin Gwilym jumped over me and went on at them.'

'Where were the warriors, then?'

He waved his right hand vaguely. 'At the side. It was very confusing, noble lady, with the whole air shining with spears, and shouting on all sides, and men killing and screaming. I did not know what was happening. After I was hurt, I crawled away, in case the rest came and trampled me. When I got back to where the fires were, there were other hurt men there, and one or two cowards who had run away and sat crying, and someone told me to drive the cart here. I can drive the cart back, if you wish, my lady. I can't walk, but I can still drive.'

'You have done well,' I told him, despairing of learning more. 'Rest first; we have plenty who can see to the cart, and you must have your leg looked after.' And I doubted that he would be able to drive the cart after his leg was seen to, for he had bound it up so tightly and at such an angle that I suspected it would have to come off.

As he was being helped into the house we had prepared for the wounded, another cart drove up, this time one we had sent out earlier.

I had little time to question the men it carried, for they brought an urgent demand for fuel. It was beginning to snow, and the battle had still been raging when they left, and some of the men needed to rest and were freezing. I ran off to make arrangements to have the returning carts re-loaded with fuel, and when I returned to the sick houses, yet another cart had arrived. This one contained a trained warrior, a member of the Family, who lay quietly among the peasants, looking at them contemptuously if they moaned. When they moved him from the cart he flinched, clenching his teeth together, but made no noise. He was so covered in blood that it was hard to see where he had been hurt.

'Goronwy,' I said, and he looked up at me. His set face relaxed a little.

'They said you were here,' he told me. 'Good. I'll be well treated, then.'

'As well as we can manage. What is happening in the war? No, tell me when you are inside.'

Inside the house, we waited for a surgeon to finish with the others. Goronwy kissed my hand. 'Wise lady, who always knew that Medraut was treacherous,'he muttered. 'The lying dog, the weasel . . . to think that I once trusted him.'

'He was good at lying,' I said. 'But what has happened? Did he enter the ambush?'

'No. We had no such good fortune. No, he stopped at the turning of the road, and began preparing his men in a hurry. He had his – Maelgwn's – army in the fore, to take the first onslaught, and all the trained men behind, and the cavalry behind them. He knew what he was doing. We . . .

have you heard it? No? We'd sent our cavalry back northwards, some distance, so that they were behind Medraut,
and sent our infantry down the road towards Camlann,
round the turn, so that they would not be seen until
Medraut was into the ambush. Sandde's army was in the
hills, just by the turning itself. When Lord Sandde saw that
Medraut had realized we were there, he told his men to
charge at once, and galloped down the hills straight into
Medraut's army. A fine man, Sandde. I hope he lives
through the day.'

'So do I. Did his charge carry, then?'

Goronwy began to shake his head, winced. 'No. They
went deep into Maelgwn's army, with heavy losses on both
sides, and then Medraut sent his infantry in, and Sandde's
peasants were chased up the road, straight into the Family.'
He smiled grimly. 'And that was the last I saw of them, for
Medraut had ordered his cavalry about, suspecting that we
were in the hills somewhere near, and we had to ride
quickly to prevent their encircling our infantry. Oh, we
met them, sure enough, and we were winning. It was a
fierce fight; I'm sorry to be missing it.'

I clasped his hand briefly. 'What more is there? Is Arthur
safe?'

'He was when ... when that traitor Constans put his
sword through me. A man that had been my friend, my
brother ... well, he is paid for it. The Emperor was with
the cavalry. I tried to fight on, after Constans, but ... I am
going to die, my lady.'

'You don't know that. Ah, here is the surgeon.'

I stayed with Goronwy for a little while, as he was
stripped and brought under the knife. But when he fainted I
rushed off with a servant to see that another house was
ready, for another cart had arrived, and there was no more
room in the first house. From that time, for a long time, I
had little opportunity to question or worry.

I was used to wounded men, but not in numbers like this.
Partly this was simply because Arthur's battles had mostly
in the past been fought in distant places: I had not seen such
numbers brought directly from the slaughter before. But
the battle of Camlann was the cruellest battle of the age, and
the casualties were very high. When the two peasant armies
met in that first onslaught, perhaps a thousand men were

killed, and by the later afternoon the road must have been running with blood. The first carts brought only men who could crawl back to safety. By the later afternoon, the battle had moved up the road towards Camlann, and the carts could pick up the casualties of the first meeting, and carried as many new corpses as living men. The reports they also carried varied like the sea: Medraut, Maelgwn, Arthur or Sandde were dead; Maelgwn had fled; Maelgwn was taken prisoner; Medraut had killed Arthur in single combat; Arthur had killed Medraut – uncertain victory hovered over both. I had no time to be afraid for my husband or my friends. I was needed by the surgeons, by the dying, by the servants; needed to find fresh horses for the carts when there were no fresh horses; needed to say where the corpses should be piled, and whom the surgeons should treat first, and what use should be made of fuel, and who should rest. I was Empress, and I could not be a human woman.

Night came, and still there was no official report. The carts that arrived now had left the struggle in the last hour of daylight, and reported that still some fighting was going on, but that the forces had moved back down the road to the turning, and most of the peasants on both sides had fled or stopped fighting. I wished someone could be spared to bring me a message – for a horseman with a fresh horse it would only be an hour, perhaps less. But it seemed that all was complete confusion.

'Maelgwn is retreating,' I was told, again. 'The Emperor has won.' But how could anyone know?

'Where is the Emperor?' I asked at random, as one cart pulled up before the stables, where we were now bringing the wounded. It was a big cart, and full of indistinct forms.

'He is with the cavalry,' came one voice.

'He is dead,' a different one said.

'No, it was his horse; his horse was killed under him, but he got up again.'

'Was that a grey horse?'

'No, he was riding a bay.'

'That was the second horse, after the bay was killed.'

'He was alive . . . before that last cavalry charge,' came a strangely familiar voice from the back of the cart. I peered into it, trying to make out the face, and could not.

Then men unloading the cart dropped someone who

screamed horribly and began to sob. 'Be quiet!' shouted someone else savagely. 'I can't bear it. Do you think you're any worse off than the rest of us?'

'Can your horses make it back to the battlefield?' I asked the driver of the cart.

'No,' he said in a hoarse voice. He loomed over me, only his face visible as a pale shadow in the darkness, with the gleam of his eyes in the distant torchlight. 'The poor brutes could hardly climb this last hill.'

'Wait here, then. Yours is a fine big cart. I will try to find fresh beasts for you.' I summoned another servant over and told him to unharness the sweating team, and give the cart priority if any fresh horses, mules or oxen could be found. Then I went into the stable to check on the wounded. It seemed to me that inventories had become the substance of my life; always I was writing out lists of supplies, of suppliers, and now, of dying and dead. Perhaps I would one day keep inventories of the damned, forever writing out lists of names that my stupidity had helped to kill. But we would have to know who of our followers were yet living, and be able to tell friends and kinsmen what had become of our army.

Names: three peasants who could give them, two who could not, one dead. Gwythyr ap Greidawl, one of the Family. A northerner who had followed Arthur to Gaul. And the voice that had been familiar, but unexpectedly familiar, not associated with these others?

I remembered it, placed it, just before I saw him lying in the far corner of the stable. No one else had recognized him, and he had been brought back in the cart with our own wounded – there had been others from the enemy's forces taken up so already, for friend and enemy lay together on the battlefield with nothing to distinguish between them. But I had never expected to see Medraut so.

I finished with my list and went over to him. He had been watching me from the time I entered, watching with cold contemptuous eyes.

I stared down at him for a long time. He was lying flat on his back and did not move under my stare. Someone must have stolen his purple cloak and golden jewellery, but there seemed to be little wrong with him.

'You need not concern yourself with how to finish me

off, noble lady,' he said at last. 'I will be dead within the hour. But it was not your precious husband and his men that did it; that honour they do not have.' He smiled savagely. 'When my loyal ally Maelgwn saw that my forces were defeated and my father's decimated, he took a dagger I had given him, a pretty thing steeped in poison, and put it in my back while I was trying to see where my men were. Thus, he has inherited my following, and become the strongest contender for the purple. I should have realized that I could never turn my back on him . . . yet at least I am spared having my father gloat over me.'

I went down on my knees beside him and looked at him. 'Are you pleased with what you have done?' I asked, hearing my voice very low and shaking.

He smiled, the grey eyes unfathomable with hatred. 'Yes. I am only sorry not to see it all fulfilled. My mother is revenged. And even if my father survives this ruin, your Empire is broken like glass. Maelgwn is going home to Gwynedd, but he will be back. The North is already tearing itself apart with war. Dumnonia is a wasteland. Whether it is my father or Maelgwn who ends up with a few purple rags, doesn't matter: the end result will be the same. Desolation. Think on it, noble lady. Tell my father to make songs about it at his victory feast, and tell my brother.'

'Your brother is dead,' I said sharply. 'He died here at Ynys Witrin four – no, five days ago.'

Medraut's eyes widened, and the stare changed from one of deep hatred to puzzlement. 'Gwalchmai? Dead?'

'From the wound he got from Bedwyr in Gaul, and from his own neglect of it. He never wanted to live after his son's death . . . I heard that you smiled when you told him of that.' Medraut continued to stare at me, and I wished to strike him as he lay there helpless, wished to give him pain. But I remembered what Gwalchmai had said and clenched my hands behind my back, forcing out the words like brittle ice, 'When Gwalchmai died, almost his last words were, "If you can, tell my brother I loved him."'

Medraut looked away. His right hand clenched into a fist, loosened, clenched and struck the ground violently. 'No,' he said, and gave a sob that seemed wrenched up from the heart. 'Not him, och, *mo brathair* . . .' I had never before heard him cry out in his father's tongue, and I stared at him in amazement. He struck the ground again, shouted aloud, in anger now, and heaved himself up so that he was sitting. His back was soaked with blood. I jumped back as he tried to crawl onto his knees, but he fell over onto his face and began to sob. A servant girl hurried over.

'Is he delirious?' she asked me in a whisper. 'Shall I help tie him down?'

'No,' I replied. I went back and knelt beside Medraut, in great confusion. For all that Gwalchmai had said about his brother, I had never expected that under his hatred and his many masks Medraut might still love anyone. But there could be no mistaking the look with which he had greeted my news.

The pale eyes saw me again as I knelt, fixed on me, and he opened his mouth to speak, but only brought out blood. He had injured himself in that attempt to rise. He shuddered violently, coughed, went very still. After a moment I touched the side of his neck, just under the jaw, and found that the beat of blood had ceased. Arthur's son, his only child, was dead. I took my hand away and looked up at the servant.

'This was the enemy's leader, Medraut ap Lot,' I told her. 'You can put the body outside by the south wall as soon as we need the space in here.' The girl's eyes widened and she bobbed her head, staring at the corpse that lay there quiet and bloody, with the torchlight caught in its hair. I pressed my hands to my face a moment, brought them down, saw that they were stained with blood. Medraut's, or someone else's? I couldn't tell. And I had another list of names to make, and needed to find fresh horses.

About midnight, Cuall, Sandde's clerk, came and found me. By that time we had been worrying for some while where to put the unscathed survivors of the battle, who had been returning in steadily growing numbers for some time, and were badly in need of warm places to rest, warm food and drink. We were also almost entirely without transport. If there were any more wounded on the battlefield they would die of the cold before morning. Oh yes, by that time it was certain that Maelgwn Gwynedd had withdrawn with his warband and the remnants of his army – all that had not scattered on their own account. And still I could get no clear report of Arthur.

'Noble lady,' said Cuall, as I tried to discover what a casualty's name had been, 'Lord Sandde has returned with the army. He begs you to come and speak with him.'

'Sandde?' I asked, straightening and brushing back my hair. 'What of my husband?'

But the clerk shook his head. 'I do not know.'

I closed my inventory book and followed Cuall up the hill from the stables. I was numb and blind with weariness of soul and body. Everything seemed a great distance away, and I little part of it.

We had filled all of Sandde's own rooms with the wounded, and the Lord of Ynys Witrin was sleeping in the Hall with his men. He was inside when I came up, and Cuall with an absurd sense of propriety stopped me from going into the Hall where the men were sleeping, and himself went in and fetched his master.

Sandde had taken off his mail coat and was wearing a torn and bloodstained cloak over his under-tunic. He had taken his boots off, and kept shifting his weight from one foot to the other because of the cold. He had that blank, stunned expression that I had seen repeated endlessly, mindlessly, on every face returning to the fortress; but he tried to smile, and took my hand. It was snowing, thick, wet snow which melted in the thatch and dripped hissing into the torches he had brought out beside the Hall door.

'Lord Sandde,' I said. 'I am very glad you are unharmed.'

He patted my hand stupidly. 'It was as you said, my lady. Not a spear ... oh God of Heaven, I am glad to see you, glad to be back!' He put his arms around me and clung, like a child, hurt, demanding comfort.

'Have you brought many men back?' I said after a few moments. 'How much more space do we need?'

He pulled away, nodded. 'I ... I have been trying to make a list, with Cuall, of those we have. We have most of the Emperor's men ... those that can still fight, that is. Maelgwn has withdrawn northwards. We don't know where Medraut is.'

'He is by the south wall of your stable, dead,' I said levelly. 'They brought him in with our own wounded.'

He stared at me in disbelief, then smiled, hesitantly. 'We have won, then?'

I closed my eyes, wanting to scream, to wail out grief and weep until I was blind and voiceless. 'If anyone has won, we have,' I said. 'But, noble lord...'

'Oh. Yes. The Emperor.'

I opened my eyes again, fixing them on Sandde's face. It was terribly still after the heat and madness of the sick rooms. Sandde's left cheek was smeared with blood. The dripping of the water in the torches behind me was very loud. 'Is my husband dead?' I asked.

Sandde shook his head. 'I don't know.'

I turned away, and he reached out after me, touched my shoulder. 'My lady, he had three horses killed under him today, and yet he lived. I ... I met him, near the end. The enemy were on the road eastwards, and in the hills. The Emperor was trying to gather and rally all the cavalry he had left. He was galloping up and down and shouting. He was so hoarse from shouting that no one could understand what he was saying. But we did rally, and made one last cavalry charge. After that Maelgwn began to retreat. We pursued them northwards for perhaps a mile, and then I called the men back, because it was dark, and snowing, and they were so tired that any bandit or pillager could finish them off, if the cold didn't, should they get lost. And then I realized that no one knew where the Emperor was. I had them all gather at one point, and sound horns to draw in the stragglers. We drew in a lot of men. But there was no more news of the Emperor. I ... I took some men and went about, looking. Many men had seen him at the beginning of the charge, but none afterwards. We ... perhaps he is wounded. Perhaps he took a party of his men after Maelgwn, and will come in later. We can search in the morning.'

'Yes,' I said, after a moment. 'Lord Sandde, do you have any horses that might be useful for drawing carts? There must be many on the battlefield who will die before the morning, and if my husband is there...'

'The horses are foundered,' Cuall told me. 'Not one in fifty could gallop to save its life. But what we have, we will send off.'

'Don't despair, noble lady,' said Sandde. 'He may well be unharmed.'

'He may be,' I agreed stupidly.

After a long silence, Cuall said, 'We do not have enough space for all the men, my lady. Which of the wounded can be moved?'

I bit my lip, trying to think, then realized from the expression of helplessness and confusion on Sandde's face that I must be weeping. I wiped my face, not caring if my hands smeared more blood onto it. 'I will show you who to move,' I said. 'Can you give orders about the horses?'

The labour, and the counting of names, went on all the night. When the sun rose pink and lovely over the snow-covered land next morning, the dead lay in tall stacks by the wall. By then some of the horses were rested enough to be harnessed again to the bloodstained carts and sent back down the road towards Camlann to pick up what remained.

Our scouts reported that Maelgwn had camped a few miles to the northward, and was burying some of his own dead, who were many. We sent him a messenger request-ing an official truce for the burial of the dead, and he at once agreed to this. We also sent a messenger to Camlann, telling the men whom Medraut had left there to guard the fortress that we would permit them to follow Maelgwn home to Gwynedd if they would surrender Camlann without a struggle; they asked to be allowed to send to Maelgwn, which we permitted.

The carts began returning heavy laden with the dead, leading baffled war horses behind them like so many oxen. The horses, like the bodies of their masters, had already been mysteriously stripped of rich harness and ornament, either by pillagers during the night or by the salvage parties themselves. Men and beasts seemed reduced to something unimportant, ordinary, broken and dishonoured. I had the corpses laid out in long lines by the wall for people to claim, and always I looked for one particular body, but never saw it.

'Perhaps he took shelter at some holding for the night,' said Sandde. I nodded wearily and made inventories.

Names. Some of them were Medraut's followers, the traitors from the Family, men I had known, whose loyalty we had struggled to win: Iddawg and Constans and Cadarn and the rest. There were warriors from the North, who once had followed Urien of Rheged or Ergyriad of Ebrauc, and who now would never return to their masters and the other war. There were Constantius's men, who died leaving a kingdom kingless and in ruins. And there were members of the Family, many of them, too many, for they had borne the brunt of the battle. Cilydd and Cynddylig, Gwrhyr and Gwythyr ap Greidawl; Gereint ab Erbin, the skilled horseman with the patient smile. Goronwy, who had been called 'the Strong', had died from his wound in the night, unobserved. And Cei, stubborn, quarrelsone, loyal and courageous, was found lying at the far end of the field, where he had stood firm in resistance when Maelgwn's forces were about to break through. He was enormous in death, his features locked into a snarling mask, and his red hair was thickly caked with blood. Of that Family which six years before had numbered seven hundred of the finest warriors in the West, scarcely fifty were left alive.

There were many peasants dead as well, but their numbers were hard to determine. Many must have returned directly to their clan holdings after the battle, and many more left Ynys Witrin without waiting to be counted, as soon as they had collected their dead. Thus we were not certain who was dead and who was merely missing. Only one name among them, one still form, remained cut into my heart like the shape carved into a seal: Rhys ap Sion, found dead among the others at the road's turning, where he had fallen in the first onslaught, to be heaped anonymously with the other dead in the night following the battle, and only recognized the next morning by his wife. Dead, dead, dead: the whole of Ynys Witrin stank of death, and everything I touched, everything I saw, heard, felt, the air I breathed and the food I ate, seemed heavy with it.

In the afternoon Maelgwn Gwynedd sent us a messenger who bore an offer to extend the truce until the spring, and to return to his own kingdom for the time being. We agreed to this. The enemy garrison at Camlann also sent in a message, in which they agreed to our terms and promised to be gone from the fortress the following day, going north with Maelgwn.

'Good,' said Sandde, relieved. 'There is more space at Camlann. If we had this kind of crowding much longer we would have to fear the fever.'

And still there was no sign of Arthur.

The next day Maelgwn started north again, and Sandde sent men to all the cities of Dumnonia, proclaiming that we had a victory, peace was restored, and the markets were open again. I had wished in my heart to proclaim a reward to anyone with news of Arthur, or of his body, but I knew that it was unwise to tell the whole countryside that we also did not know if he were living or dead. There might be more risings, or Maelgwn might break his word and come back, and so much of our army was gone that we could risk no further struggle.

Sandde sent the men off to Camlann, where there was both space and supplies enough for them. On the first day he sent off all the uninjured men, then all the less severely wounded. I offered to stay at Ynys Witrin with the more severely injured until they could be moved without risk and, after some hesitation, Sandde agreed, and left me in charge of Ynys Witrin while he went to Camlann.

I waited. The peasant army did not trouble itself with moving to the imperial fortress, but went home in the days after the truce – those that had not gone before it. Sion ap Rhys and his kinsmen left five days after the battle. They would have gone sooner, but they had to send one of their number back to the holding to fetch the ox cart, for another of their number was wounded and could neither walk nor ride. They also wished to bury Rhys in the clan's lands. I guiltily gave them a few gifts, small return for their kindness to me, and perhaps shamefully like a payment for their kinsman's life, which was beyond price – yet the things might be useful. And I went down to the gates with them that morning to see them off.

Eivlin went with the others, leaving only one serving girl at my house. She had not said much to me or anyone else since her husband's death, but went about red-eyed, hard-faced, with the kind of callousness that springs from great grief.

'I am sorry,' I said to her, and to all of them.

Sion ap Rhys shrugged, staring at the long bundle in the back of the cart that had been his eldest son. 'We all knew we might die if we went to this war, my lady. We thought it worth the risk.' He picked up the ox goad. 'And Rhys believed in your Empire more than any of us, and set much of his life on it. Perhaps it is for the best that he does not see it now. We must all die some time.'

'It is not for the best!' Eivlin cried out sharply. 'Indeed, how can you say such things, a man to leave his three children fatherless, and they thinking him a finer man than the Emperor of Britain, and waiting yet for him to come home and bring them presents? Best? That such a man as my husband should . . . och, ochone!'

Sion set down the goad and covered his face a moment, then lowered his hands, ran one through his hair with a gesture that had been his son's also. 'The children still have their clan, daughter. And they have a mother. And she has them.'

'Indeed,' said Eivlin, more quietly, but looking at the bundle in the back of the cart. She looked up at me again, and saw something on my face I – I do not know what – that made her jump off the cart suddenly and put her arms around me. Something in my heart gave way and I embraced her, biting my tongue so as not to cry out. For a moment I forgot that I was Empress and ruler of the fortress, and we were only two women who had lost the men they loved. Then Eivlin drew away. 'I must look to my children, my lady,' she whispered, 'or I might stay, for you have not deceived me into thinking you do not feel it and need nothing, whatever the others may believe. God bless you, my lady.'

'And you, my cousin, and your children.'

Eivlin let go of me, nodded, bit her lip, climbed back into the cart and sat beside her father-in-law. Sion goaded the sullen oxen, and the cart lurched slowly out and down the hill, vanishing into the quiet farmland of Dumnonia. I never saw them again.

And still I waited.

About a week and a half later, Sandde sent me a messenger from Camlann, bringing more supplies and some trivial news. The news did not surprise me, but the messenger did, for he was Taliesin, who had been Arthur's chief bard and a sometime cavalry fighter, and of whom I had neither seen nor heard anything during the whole of this last war. When he arrived, and presented me with a list of the supplies he brought, I asked him up to my house and, when he was there, poured him some mead.

'I am glad to see you well,' I told him as he sipped the mead. 'I had assumed that you were dead.'

He made a face and shook his head. 'No. I was merely away from Camlann.'

He offered no further explanation; he never did. He was a mysterious man whom no one knew much about, and he rather enjoyed making himself yet more mysterious. Gwalchmai at least had been firmly convinced that Taliesin was from the Otherworld, and only stayed upon the Earth for some unknown purpose of his own. But many people had thought much the same about Gwalchmai himself.

'Oh?' I asked, impatient with mysteries. 'Where?'

Taliesin smiled, a quick acceptance of my impatience, amusement that became sad. 'Arthur sent me north to Urien King of Rheged when he left for Gaul, first as a messenger, and afterwards to reconcile Urien to the absence of half his warriors. The war between Rheged and Ebrauc broke out while I was there, so I stayed in the North until I heard that Arthur was back. I arrived at Camlann two days ago.'

'So you were in the North – when? Two weeks ago? What is happening there?'

He shrugged. 'Rheged raids Ebrauc, and Ebrauc raids Rheged and shouts forth bold defiance at the idea of being subject to an Emperor. There were no pitched battles and it is unlikely that there will be any, and neither side can take any clear advantage. If Arthur is indeed dead, and there is no Emperor for Ebrauc to rebel against, there may be a truce declared again – for a time.'

'If Arthur is dead,' I said. It was the first time anyone had spoken those words to me. 'What would you do then?'

He looked down at the desk and traced a pattern idly on its polished surface. 'What I have always done, my lady: make songs. I can play in the court of any king in Britain, even that of Maelgwn Gwynedd, and be welcome.'

'Songs about the fall of the Empire?' I asked, before I could stop myself.

He looked up. He had grey eyes, like Arthur or Medraut, but of a lighter shade. In the dim house they looked almost silver. 'Songs about the fall of the Empire, yes, and songs about the Emperor. There will be no more emperors now, not in the West. No one will claim the title, because everyone now is too weak for it, and none has a better claim than another. There will be many eager for songs about the Emperor Arthur and the Family.' He looked down again and hummed a bar of music softly; one of his new tunes, no doubt, for I did not recognize it as an old one. I felt a slow tide of anger and bitterness rising within me. 'The glory will not fade, my lady, because it will have no successors. And my songs will be remembered. The times that come will remember us. Something of you, and something of what we fough' for, will survive.'

'Do you think,' I demanded, 'that we fought for *songs*?' He looked up again, mildly surprised, calm and unmoved, and the anger, the blind wild loss suddenly took possession of me. I jumped up, swept my hand over the desk, and the jug of mead crashed to the floor and broke. The serving girl came rushing in from the next room, but I waved her back. 'Do you think songs feed the hungry, or administer justice, or keep peace between kingdoms, or restore the ruins of the Empire of the Romans? Go and sing your songs to the Saxons; I am sure they will pay great attention to your melodies sung in an unknown tongue. Songs! They are no remedy. Glory is not a consolation. It's lost, don't you understand? It is all lost. The Light has gone, and the Darkness covers Britain as closely as the air, and there is nothing left of what we once dreamed and suffered for.

'And if you sing your songs, and if they are the greatest of songs, and able to move men to believe in an ideal, what sort of ideal will it become in a few years? An Emperor commits incest with his sister, and begets his own ruin in the person of a treacherous, malicious son; and an Empress divides the realm at the critical time by playing whore with the Emperor's best friend! What a beautiful story! What a theme for songs! Not only is it all lost, it was we who lost it, we who by our own stupidity and weakness allowed ourselves to be divided, and break like a pot flawed in the firing, that spills everything put into it. It is gone like smoke into the air, like mist before the wind. There is nothing left of the Empire, and nothing remaining from which we could build again, and nothing to show for our lives' effort but guilt, shame, and a few lying songs!'

My voice had grown shriller and shriller as I spoke, and

at last I screamed at Taliesin, who sat watching me silently. I had begun shaking, and tried to cover my face. The serving maid rushed out of the doorway again and caught my arm. 'My lady, my lady, sit down,' she said, and, to Taliesin, 'she is over-tired, poor lady, she works so hard. Here, noble lady, I will fetch some water and some more mead. Don't you fear, your husband will come back.'

I laughed, but sat down on the bed. 'My husband is dead,' I told the girl.

'Ach, noble lady, they never found his body; he cannot be dead.'

'He was lost in the cavalry charge,' I said, finally admitting what I had known for some time. 'I never recognized the body because the charge went over it, and it was mutilated beyond recognition. Arthur is dead, and even dead I cannot see him again, or bury him. I wish to the God of Heaven that I were dead as well.'

'Do not say such things!' exclaimed the girl. 'Here, here is some water.'

I drank a little, looked at the girl's shocked, miserable face. The anger was leaving me. 'Don't worry,' I told her. 'It is merely weariness.'

The girl smiled hesitantly and left to fetch the mead.

'I am sorry, noble lady,' said Taliesin. 'I did not mean to offend you.'

I pressed the heels of my hands to my eyes, feeling how the sobs were again locked within me. 'No, I am sorry,' I said. 'Forgive me. It is only that there has been too much death and, as the girl said, I am tired. You spoke to comfort me.'

Taliesin stood, took my hand, kissed it and touched it to his forehead. 'You have endured too much, noble lady.'

'Everyone endures too much.' I wiped my eyes, and the serving girl came back with the mead and gave me some. It was fresh from a storeroom, bitterly cold, and hurt in my tight throat. 'Thank you,' I said to the girl, trying to control my shaking. Then I thought of another thing, and added, 'Can you fetch me some fresh ink and some parchment, Olwen? Thank you.' She bobbed her head and left again, and I turned back to Taliesin.

'You say you can go to any king's court and be welcomed,' I said. It was true, of course: no British king will harm a bard. Law and custom do not permit it – and Taliesin was famous. 'Could you journey through Less Britain as well?'

He nodded, warily. 'You wish me to take a letter to the lord Bedwyr.'

'Two letters. One the lord Gwalchmai dictated to me as he was dying, and one I will write myself. It will only tell Bedwyr of the battle, and say that Arthur is dead and I will join a convent. You can read it first, if you like. You will compromise no one's honour by bearing it for me.'

'A convent?'

'What else does a noble widow do? It is that, or remarry, and I will not remarry.'

'Lord Sandde . . .'

'I am old enough to be his mother.'

'He would be willing to be your client king, not a husband. He admired you very greatly. He means to establish you in Camlann as Empress.'

'I would not last a year. We do not have the warband to enforce such a rule, and the kings of Britain would not permit the unfaithful wife of a usurper to claim the purple. You yourself said that there will be no more emperors. There is no longer an empire.' I felt as though I had been saying nothing else for a long time. 'To pretend that there is, when we have no real power, will only create more wars and factions than there are already. Let Sandde be king of Dumnonia – there is little doubt he will be recognized as that. I will go north and join a convent.' I rose and picked up one of the fragments of the broken mead jar. 'As a girl, I knew a girl who is now abbess of a convent near Caer Lugualid. I know I would be welcome there – perhaps I should write to her as well. If there is a truce proclaimed in the North, I will go there in the spring. I am sure that Sandde will give me some kind of escort.'

Taliesin bowed, and when he straightened again I saw to my astonishment that he was weeping. I had never seen him weep. 'Noble lady,' he said in a rough voice, 'I will carry your letters.' He bowed again and started from the room, then paused in the doorway and looked at me again. 'I dreamed, or foresaw in a vision, years and years ago, that this Empire would fall. I expected it, and watched, and waited, setting it out in my heart for a song. I had not thought to find such bitterness in seeing it. Even my songs seem nothing more than the wind in the reeds, hollow and without life. I am paid for . . .' He stopped, staring at me, his face working. 'For trying not to care. Have me called, lady, when you are done with the letters.' He gave one more bow and slipped out.

I picked up a few more pieces of the mead jug and weighed them in my hand. They were sticky, and the room was full of the sweet honey scent of the mead. I had already composed the letter to Bedwyr in thought, and it would not take long to write it. I cared enough still, I supposed, to want to let him know – but my heart was numb, and my only awareness of him was as another responsibility, another thing to mark off on some interminable list.

I set the broken fragments down, wiped my hands, and waited for the servant to come back with the ink.

Epilogue

It has now been some weeks since I finished this account of the past, set down my pen, and wondered what to do next. I began because one day I found that when I thought of the past only three things stood clear in my mind: the hour, with the water dripping from the thatch and sputtering in the torches, when Sandde told me that Arthur was gone; Bedwyr's face, dark-eyed, calm beyond any more anguish, when he said farewell; and Gwalchmai, innocent, dying in my arms in that hideous room at Ynys Witrin. And all these memories were bright and hard with such pain and bitterness that I grew afraid. I am old now. If I see my reflection, in water or a cup of wine – there are no mirrors in the convent – I can scarcely believe that I am that same Gwynhwyfar whom Arthur and Bedwyr loved. The face I see is an old woman's, lined with use. Much use: many tears, hour upon hour of a grief which can never be eradicated, never be forgotten. Lined with laughter, too. I have laughed in my life, thank God. But the laughter does not weigh even in the balance with the grief. My hair is white, and growing thin. My bones are stiff these days, and they ache deep within, the way the heart aches and is stiff after irreparable loss. Only my eyes still look as I remember them from the past: brown and steady. It is a terrible thing to have worked the ruin of all one loved best, but it is worse to survive that ruin, and grow old, forgetting.

I am abbess of this convent in the North, now, responsible for the well-being of nearly a hundred people, and I am – incredible word – respected again. The local people come to me with their problems, the sisters copy books and look after orphaned children, the world goes on. Bedwyr, I have heard, became a monk after hearing of Arthur's death. When Arthur lifted the siege of Car Aës to come to the aid of Britain, Macsen proclaimed it victory, and at the victory feast offered Bedwyr the title of warleader and various lands and powers as well, which Bedwyr refused. Despite the refusal, Macsen's old warleader was not pleased, and partly because of his displeasure Macsen acceded to Bedwyr's demand for release when the warrior received the news I sent him later that year. A few years ago I heard from an itinerant priest that Bedwyr has become famous throughout Less Britain for his asceticism – scourging himself and fasting, kneeling in icy streams before daybreak and reciting the psalms, and so on. The Breton monastics believe him very holy. Myself, I know he believes the opposite. Bedwyr would not believe he could persuade God to forgive him by torturing himself. And I do not think he will succeed in punishing his body enough to win his own forgiveness, either. But perhaps God is more merciful than Bedwyr. Perhaps.

Sandde became king of Dumnonia and ruled from its new capital, Camlann, until a few years after I left the South, when he died in one of the new wars against the Saxons. There are many wars now, small ones, and there is great uncertainty everywhere. The ships that used to come from Less Britain are more infrequent now, and they no longer bring news from the distant parts of the Empire. Rome now seems as distant and mysterious as Constantinople did in my youth. People live in the moment and are afraid for tomorrow, for the world grows steadily more dark.

A bard passed through this abbey not too long ago, and sang a new song about the death of a minor king, and the song has kept running through my head ever since. They say it was made by the dead man's sister.

> Cynddylan's Hall is dark tonight,
> Without a fire or bed for sleep:
> I will be silent after the hour I weep.
>
> Cynddylan's Hall is dark tonight,
> Without a fire or candle's shine:
> But God, what force will hold my mind?
>
> Cynddylan's Hall is dark tonight,
> With him who owned it gone away:
> Cruel death, why do you let me stay?
>
> From Gorwynnion's mound I looked upon
> A land lovely in summer ease.
> The sun's course is very long
> But longer are my memories.

My memories are long, but they will die with me, and soon no one living will remember our Empire. What remains, then, for all that blood and all that sorrow?

Sometimes I think that nothing remains. For a very long time I thought that the end of Camlann was the end of everything, and the bitterness swelled in me until I grew afraid, for it is not good, when one is old and shortly to come before God and answer to him for one's deeds, to be filled with a wordless bitterness. I began to tell myself that I ought to forget.

But I could not wish to forget, and the more I remembered, the less I wished to forget. I could not lose the memory of Camlann in the morning, the sun shining from the snow on the roof of the Feast Hall, the smoke of the morning fires; the feasts in the great dim building, the glitter of much gold, the strains of the harp. Whatever the bitterness that mingles with the memories, what we had in Camlann was the dream that the hearts of all men have ever longed for. '*O Oriens, splendor lucis aeterna*', 'O Dayspring, splendour of eternal Light and Sun of Justice, come, illumine those who sit in darkness and the shadow of Death.' We tasted on Earth the wine of the New Jerusalem that is forever to come. Of course the loss of that is bitter; more bitter than the loss of all the world. But I cannot wish to forget that it was there, for a few years. No, I wish to forget none of it: Arthur's smile and clear eyes, Bedwyr's warm gaze, the friendships and the loves and the astounding beauty of the world we were making anew.

I have digressed, and begun speaking like an abbess. Well, that is what I am, and it will colour my speech. We failed in Camlann; nothing of what we struggled to build remains, except the longing that drove us in the first place. But it was worth it, to have possessed that joy for a few years, and I cannot regret that we tried. And perhaps though we failed, God has not. Perhaps it is not the end.

Last year a new monastery was founded on an island to our north – founded by, of all people, the Irish. There is nothing so remarkable in that. The head of that settlement sent a few monks here, looking for books: that is remarkable. No one travels miles to look for books, in this age; I had begun to fear that the ability to read would die out and the world would truly be confined to the present. But this Irish abbot is wild for books; his reason for coming to Britain is trouble over one he stole. And these monks are setting about converting the Saxons; they have converted a king, and their influence already spreads like fire in the grass. Arthur and I always wanted the Saxons converted, brought into the Empire, but the British Church would neither undertake this task itself nor permit us to subsidize anyone to undertake it.

A handful of monks on a little island called Iona: it is not much. And they are not Roman, have no understanding of what Rome was and meant. Yet they are as set to change the world as I was when I rode south to Camlann many years ago. Perhaps I am mad to hope that they can achieve anything, succeed where Arthur and I failed. And yet everywhere in Britain the longing is there, the soul-deep desire, waiting for someone to touch it and shape it anew. It is as Taliesin predicted: Britain has not forgotten our Empire, and longs to hear more songs about it, because it is gone and its absence leaves a hole in the world which even its former enemies can feel. I have heard tales recently that Arthur did not die, but sleeps under some magic, to one day wake again. When first I heard these, I loathed them for their blind, deluding hope. But the hopes remain in this realm, more powerful than the spring when the sun circles round from the dark winter. Our failure cannot put out the sun. If someone were willing to offer light to those than sit in darkness and the shadow of death . . . if, if, if.

Those monks were very eager to.

Was I wrong to cling so tightly to the memory of Rome? Perhaps the lightning strikes not from the East and the old Empire, but from the West, the limit of the world. Who knows? Do I dare to believe that life indeed goes on, to trust God and human desires, and die in hope?

Today is Easter Sunday. While I write the birds are loud outside my window, and the sun pours clean gold over the margins of the page, like those intricate designs the Irish paint in their gospels. Outside the early apple trees and the hawthorn are in blossom, and the woods are carpeted with primroses and harebells. Strange how the Earth renews herself, like a snake shedding a skin stiff and dusty with age, and polishing its shining new coils over a sun-warmed path.

It is not the end. It never can be. The tree, stripped barren in last autumn's storm, stands green-gold with new leaves, and by some special miracle, some unexpected magic, life returns from the dead.